A y[...]
possi[...]

He couldn't help recalling Edith Keeler's words to him tonight: *Perhaps your friends aren't coming.* To this point, although he had thought about it, he had been unable to truly countenance such a prospect. Now, he had no choice but to take into account that he had been trapped in the past for a whole year.

A year in my *life,* he thought, *but not necessarily a year in Jim's and Spock's lives.* Though it bedeviled him to contemplate the realities and possibilities of time travel, it seemed plausible that he could have one day journeyed from 2267 to 1930, and then one week later in 2267, Jim and Spock could arrive in 1931 to bring him back home. Yet, it also felt unlikely, more like rationalization than reasoning, like a lie he told himself to keep from going mad. For even as he waited to return home, even as he peppered newspapers around the globe with signposts pointing to his location in time and space, even as he held on tightly to his certainty of his eventual rescue, the notion of being trapped here for the rest of his days haunted him.

It took more than an hour for McCoy to fall asleep. When at last he did, he slept fitfully, beset by the same foggy, partially glimpsed images that so often had invaded his slumber ever since his arrival here. Tonight, other faces joined his nightmares, faces he had no trouble distinguishing. All of them belonged to his daughter: as a baby, as a girl, as a young woman.

In the morning, exhausted and on edge, McCoy began his second year living in Earth's past.

Also by David R. George III

Novels

The 34th Rule (with Armin Shimerman)

Twilight (Mission: Gamma, Book One)

Serpents Among the Ruins (The Lost Era, 2311)

Olympus Descending (in Worlds of Deep Space Nine, Volume III)

The Fire and the Rose (Crucible: Spock)
[Coming soon]

The Star to Every Wandering (Crucible: Kirk)
[Coming soon]

Novellas

Iron and Sacrifice (in Tales from the Captain's Table)

STAR TREK®

CRUCIBLE: McCOY
PROVENANCE OF SHADOWS

David R. George III

**Based upon STAR TREK®
created by Gene Roddenberry**

Pocket Books
New York   London   Toronto   Sydney   Starbase 10

An *Original* Publication of POCKET BOOKS

POCKET BOOKS, a division of Simon & Schuster, Inc.
1230 Avenue of the Americas, New York, NY 10020

This book is a work of fiction. Names, characters, places and incidents are products of the author's imagination or are used fictitiously. Any resemblance to actual events or locales or persons, living or dead, is entirely coincidental.

This book is published by Pocket Books, a division of Simon & Schuster, Inc., under exclusive license from CBS Studios Inc.

ISBN-13: 978-0-7434-9168-6
ISBN-10:   0-7434-9168-8

This Pocket Books paperback edition September 2006

10 9 8 7 6 5 4 3 2 1

POCKET and colophon are registered trademarks of Simon & Schuster, Inc.

Cover design by John Vairo, Jr., cover art by John Picacio

Manufactured in the United States of America

For information regarding special discounts for bulk purchases, please contact Simon & Schuster Special Sales at 1-800-456-6798 or business@simonandschuster.com.

To Anita Carr Smith,
a shining light in my life,
whose remarkable spirit
and boundless heart
always lift up those around her

FOREWORD

Provenance of *Crucible*

So while sitting in the lobby of a hotel in Hollywood, working with me on another of my manuscripts, my intrepid editor—the talented Marco Palmieri—says, "You should think about writing an Original Series book. Maybe a trilogy." My outward reaction is low key, but I'm pleased that my writing has warranted his consideration for me to pen other novels. After our meeting, though, I don't think much about it because I need to put the current manuscript to bed, and because my next two projects are already lined up.

But then at some point, Marco calls me and revisits the subject. Not only would this be a TOS book, and not only a trilogy, but it would be published to coincide with the fortieth anniversary of the show. Wow. Now this was something. With *Star Trek* in syndication for more than three decades, I'd grown up watching the episodes over and over again, and I'd seen all of the films as well—not to mention following *The Next Generation*, *Deep Space Nine*, *Voyager*, and *Enterprise*. I loved *Star Trek*'s heroes, its themes, and more than anything its messages of tolerance and inclusion. This would be great. I signed on to do it, then sat down at my desk with a yellow pad and my silver pen and—

Nothing.

I quickly realized my dilemma. What, I asked myself, had not already been said about these characters? In addition to two pilots, three seasons of episodes, an animated series, and seven films, hundreds of novels and short stories had also been published. Not only that, but some unfilmed, unpublished details—such as Dr. McCoy's backstory of a daughter from a failed marriage—had been generally accepted in fan circles for years. How could I find a new story to tell, and how could I do so without gainsaying previously published work, which collectively is self-contradictory?

Marco and I discussed my concerns and agreed that the best strategy would be to write these tales based solely on the original television episodes and the subsequent films. In that way, I wouldn't have to worry about conflicting aspects of the written fiction, nor would I have to read or reread all of that material. It would also provide a clean entry point for fans who hadn't previously read *Trek* novels to hop on board.

So I once more sat down to figure out what to write. After some consideration, I chose to focus each of the three books on one of the main characters of Kirk, Spock, and McCoy. While I have great affection for the secondary characters of Scotty, Sulu, Uhura, and Chekov (and others such as Chapel, Rand, Kyle, Leslie, and M'Benga, to name a few), the series itself focused primarily on the "big three," and so my approach seemed apt. I'd include all of the characters in each story, but essentially write a Kirk novel, a Spock novel, and a McCoy novel.

But the question still remained: What do we not know about these people? I watched every episode and every film again, and I came to notice a certain aspect of Leonard McCoy's personal history. I didn't think it had necessarily been an intention of the show's and films' writers, but a consequence of their combined work. And then I also discovered a part of McCoy's life that, to my knowledge, had never been explored, and I saw a way to tie it together not only with my first observation, but also with what is widely regarded as one of, if not *the,* finest episodes of *Star Trek* in any of its incarnations. This would also allow me to deeply ground the trilogy in the Original Series itself, something I thought appropriate.

As I beat out the story for the McCoy novel, I noted how the events of that one great episode could have affected both

Kirk and Spock as well. In fact, I could see how this one set of circumstances, which had tested each of them in different ways, could have had a significant impact on all of them. With the trilogy, I could chronicle how this single incident, this crucible, had informed the rest of their lives like no other.

And then, finally, with the approval of Marco and CBS Consumer Products' Paula Block, I sat down to write.

Dark house, by which once more I stand
　　Here in the long unlovely street,
　　Doors, where my heart was used to beat
So quickly, waiting for a hand,

A hand that can be clasp'd no more—
　　Behold me, for I cannot sleep,
　　And like a guilty thing I creep
At earliest morning to the door.

He is not here; but far away
　　The noise of life begins again,
　　And ghastly thro' the drizzling rain
On the bald street breaks the blank day.

　　　　　　　　　　—Alfred, Lord Tennyson,
　　　　　　　　　　In Memoriam A.H.H., VII

Natira: You have lived a lonely life?
McCoy: Yes. Very lonely.

　　　　　　　—"For the World Is Hollow and
　　　　　　　　　I Have Touched the Sky"

OVERTURE

CRUCIBLE

In an instant, he saw how she would die.

As soon as Leonard McCoy pulled open one of the double doors at the front of the mission and stepped out into the cool, damp night, his gaze fell upon the figure of Edith Keeler approaching from across the street. A long dark cloak wrapped her slender frame, and a pale blue cloche crowned her short brunette locks. Street lamps painted the scene with a dim glow, their light reflected here and there in the puddles earlier left behind by an evening rain. McCoy smiled at Keeler, but although her gait carried her directly toward him, she seemed to take no notice of his presence. Her static features betrayed a person lost in her own thoughts.

Movement and a rumble off to the left caught McCoy's attention. He saw a large, squarish ground vehicle barreling down the wet macadam. McCoy jerked his head back toward Keeler and spied the portrait of inner focus still drawn on her face. She clearly didn't see the advancing vehicle, didn't hear the throaty plaint of its engine. In just seconds, she would march into its path.

In that moment, a surge of adrenaline overcame McCoy's grogginess, and his surroundings suddenly became real to him. What he had in his cordrazine-induced madness believed some sort of deception or illusion, what he had later attributed to dementia or hallucination brought on by his accidental overdose, he all at once understood to be none of those things. Somehow, as he watched Edith Keeler walking into jeopardy, all of the explanations and rationalizations for his unusual circumstances dissolved like dreams upon waking.

As McCoy started to move, he called to her—"Miss Keeler!"—but even that did not penetrate her concentration. He took one step, then another, but his reactions seemed sluggish, his torpor doubtless a result of the powerful chemical still not entirely purged from his body. Even as he jumped the curb and into the street, his legs felt as though they were pushing through molasses. He knew that he would not reach her in time.

And still he moved.

Three more running strides, and McCoy himself raced into harm's way. He heard the vehicle as it bore down on him, the mechanical growl of its engine now thunderous in his ears. Just before he lunged forward, the sound of brakes keened through the metropolitan night, and he saw Keeler's expression change, the woman at last startled out of her reverie.

McCoy left his feet, his arms outstretched, attempting to reach Keeler even as the vehicle skidded forward, its wheels scraping noisily along the rain-dampened pavement. He struck Keeler solidly at her waist. His momentum stopped her in midstride, and she tumbled backward, her arms flailing as she fell. A yelp emerged from her lips as she crashed down to the middle of the street.

Landing atop her legs, McCoy braced himself for the impact to come, unsure if he'd thrown Keeler and himself completely clear of danger. When after a moment nothing happened, he realized that he no longer heard brakes whining or locked wheels grating along the road surface. Instead, the patter of footfalls rose around him, and he risked a glance over his shoulder. The left front tire of the vehicle, McCoy saw, had come to a stop less than half a meter from his shins. He shuddered once, hard, a reaction driven by the stark reality of the peril he'd only just narrowly escaped.

Gathering himself, McCoy pushed away from Keeler and up onto his knees. He looked at her, and she regarded him in obvious shock, her eyes wide, her mouth agape. Though shaken, she appeared more or less unharmed. Around them, people scampered over from different directions. Several crouched down beside Keeler, while one man clad in a dark gray overcoat and a light brown fedora bent over McCoy.

"You okay, Mister?" the man asked, raising his voice to be heard over the snarl of the ground vehicle's engine. His concern seemed genuine.

"Yeah," McCoy managed to say between deep inhalations of breath. He adjusted the position of his body, moved his arms and legs, examined his hands, attempting to take stock of his physical condition. He felt pains in his knees and elbows, and a patch-work of bloody abrasions covered his palms, but he seemed otherwise uninjured. "A little banged up," he admitted, "but I'm all right."

Behind the man leaning over McCoy, the vehicle quieted, and its near door swung open. Hopping down onto the street, the driver appeared ashen, his wide eyes a mirror of Keeler's own. "She walked right out in front of my truck," he said in a rush. He addressed McCoy, but raised an arm and pointed to where Keeler still sat sprawled on the ground. "Soon as I saw her walkin' across the street and saw she wasn't gonna stop, I hit the brakes." The driver looked to the man in the gray coat as though pleading for corroboration. "There wasn't nothin' else I could've done. I was just—"

"It's all right," McCoy said, his words coming more easily as he regained his breath. He pushed up from the street and rose, the man in the gray overcoat reaching a hand out to help. When McCoy had stood up fully, he fixed the driver of the truck with his gaze. "It wasn't your fault," he told him. "And anyway, we're fine." The driver stared back at McCoy, evidently trying to gauge the veracity of his statements. Finally, the driver exhaled loudly, and his body seemed to uncoil by degrees, like tension gradually being released from a spring.

McCoy turned toward Keeler just as she began climbing to her feet. A man to either side of her reached down and clasped one of her arms, steadying her as she clambered up from the street. All around, other bystanders pressed in, many chattering about what had just happened and offering their observations and concerns. Keeler still looked staggered, appearing unable to focus on anything. McCoy trod over to her. Her hat had fallen from her head, leaving her hair tousled, with several errant strands fluttering down across her forehead. Her high-collared, navy blue cloak had fallen askew, uncovering her right arm and revealing that the sleeve of her white blouse had been torn open in several places. Where her pale flesh showed through the tattered garment, McCoy saw numerous scrapes and lacerations.

"Are you all right, Miss Keeler?" he asked. She slowly raised her head to look up at him—he stood nearly a dozen centimeters taller than she did—but it took a few seconds before her eyes found his. When they did, she nodded slowly, but said nothing. Around them, the small crowd grew quiet, perhaps waiting for her to speak.

McCoy bent and retrieved Keeler's hat before swinging himself around to her side, the two men who'd helped her stand stepping back. He reached up and straightened her cloak about her, then gingerly took hold of her elbow and hand. The gathering of onlookers and samaritans parted before them as McCoy headed Keeler toward the doorway through which he'd exited into the night only a few minutes ago. The memory of that, though fresh, paradoxically seemed to hark back to another lifetime.

"You sure she's gonna be all right, Mister?" the driver asked as they passed him.

"She'll be fine," McCoy replied without interrupting his stride. "I'm a doctor. I'll take care of her."

McCoy walked with Keeler past the front of the truck, its gray metal grillwork like the long fangs of some fearsome beast, the pungent odor of burned rubber and heated oil its foul breath. As they reached the curb, he heard the people congregated behind them begin talking again, their voices agitated as they spoke of the terrible accident that had nearly just occurred. McCoy steered Keeler up onto the sidewalk and then over to the twin doors that led into the 21st Street Mission. He reached to push open one of the doors, but then Keeler turned abruptly toward him, pulling her arm from his grasp. She peered up at him, some low level of awareness seeming to dawn on her face.

"How stupid," she said, her English accent discernible even in just the two words. "I've been back and forth across this street a thousand times. I ought to have been killed." She delivered her statements in a monotone, clearly not yet recovered from her trauma.

"But you weren't killed," McCoy told her, accompanying his words with what he hoped she would perceive as a reassuring smile. "Try not to think about it. It's in the past." He waved the back of his hand toward the street, the gesture intended to dismiss thoughts of how close they'd both just come to being seriously injured, or even to losing their lives. "It's going to be all right," he concluded.

Keeler glanced over at the truck for a second, and then back at McCoy. She offered a half-smile and nodded, as though endeavoring to convince herself of what he'd said.

"Really," McCoy insisted, reaching again for the door. "Everything's going to be all right." But as he ushered Edith Keeler into the mission, he recognized that he stood in a city on Earth, three hundred years before he'd been born—three hundred years before he *would* be born. McCoy did not belong in this place or in this time. He had perhaps just saved a woman's life, and had avoided being killed himself, but he realized now that, at least for him, there were no guarantees that anything would ever be all right again.

I

The Stars, Blindly Run

'The stars,' she whispers, 'blindly run;
   A web is wov'n across the sky;
   From out waste places comes a cry,
And murmurs from the dying sun:

'And all the phantom, Nature, stands—
   With all the music in her tone,
   A hollow echo of my own,—
A hollow form with empty hands.'

And shall I take a thing so blind,
   Embrace her as my natural good;
   Or crush her, like a vice of blood,
Upon the threshold of the mind?

—Alfred, Lord Tennyson,
In Memoriam A.H.H., III

ONE

When the landing party materialized aboard the *Enterprise,* McCoy felt immediately unsettled. As his crewmates started forward and dismounted the transporter platform by twos—Jim and Spock, Scotty and Uhura, and a pair of security guards, Galloway and . . . Davis, was it?—he hung back, attempting to sort through the jumble of thoughts and memories flooding through his mind. Only moments ago, he'd been on Earth in a centuries-old city, with Jim and Spock, watching in dismay as a woman—Edith Keeler, he recalled now—lost her life in a traffic accident. But then without warning, McCoy had found himself standing with a half dozen of his crewmates amid the ruins of a dead planet.

But not entirely dead, he thought now. There had been that strange . . . *what? Machine? Creature?* McCoy had no idea how to properly classify it. Set among sheer rock formations and derelict architectural structures, with fractured pillars littering the landscape about it, the object seemed like a forgotten remnant of a lost civilization. An irregular ring perched on edge, perhaps six or seven meters in diameter, it looked like no living being McCoy had ever seen, and yet its mottled, tawny surface possessed something of an organic appearance. It had also spoken, its asymmetrical, flowing form glowing in rhythm with its words, its voice deep and resonant.

"Time has resumed its shape; all is as it was before," it had said. *"Many such journeys are possible. Let me be your gateway."*

Before McCoy had even been able to consider the meaning of those pronouncements, though, the landing party had beamed back to the *Enterprise,* further compounding his already acute sense of dislocation. He'd stood in an ancient city on Earth one moment, on a desolate alien world the next, and then less than a minute after that, back aboard ship. His mind whirled with the rapid succession of virtually instantaneous travel from one place to another.

Now, McCoy made his way to the front of the transporter platform. Contributing to his discomposure, he still fought the mental and physical effects of the massive amount of cordrazine inadvertently pumped into his body several days ago. Indeed, the chemical cobwebs suffusing his consciousness, which had come in waves during his recovery, had been what had propelled him out of a back room at the 21st Street Mission and into the night; he'd hoped that a walk in the crisp winter air would help revive his flagging faculties and allow him to refocus his thoughts.

The Twenty-first Street Mission, McCoy repeated to himself. Images of the soup kitchen rose vividly in his mind, but the clarity of his memories did not translate to his emotions. His equilibrium threatened to slip again, and so he sought to stabilize his feelings by concentrating on his immediate surroundings.

Across the room, a familiar click signaled the activation of an intercom circuit. McCoy watched Jim lean in over the back of the freestanding console, over the two-way speaker located there. "Kirk to bridge," he said. Spock and the rest of the landing party waited behind him, and Lieutenant Berkeley, the transporter operator, looked on from the far side of the compartment.

"Bridge, DeSalle here," came the disembodied response of the navigator, the man fifth in line in the *Enterprise*'s chain of command. *"Go ahead, Captain."*

"Break orbit at once, Lieutenant," Kirk ordered. "Lay in a course for Starbase Ten, warp factor six." The words drew McCoy's notice, not for their content, but because Jim had delivered them in an oddly lifeless tone. Spock too seemed to take note, peering over as the captain issued his orders.

Jim waited for DeSalle's acknowledgment, then signed off. "Kirk out." He reached across the console and punched the intercom control with the fleshy side of his fist, closing the channel.

"Captain," Spock said, stepping up beside him. McCoy felt the impulse to go to his friend as well, but remained too unsteady to get himself moving. Instead, he simply looked on as Jim turned to the first officer.

"Yes, what is it, Mister Spock?" he said. Again, McCoy detected an unusual flatness in the timbre of the captain's voice, and it occurred to him that it must be because of what had happened, subjectively, just a few minutes earlier: Jim had prevented him from saving Edith Keeler's life. McCoy had even accused him of doing so—*Do you know what you just did?*—and Spock had assured him that he did—*He knows, Doctor; he knows.* McCoy didn't know why the captain had done what he'd done, but clearly he'd had a reason. Nevertheless, Jim displayed signs now of questioning his own actions—presumably actions he'd had to take. McCoy had seen the distant bearing before, the responsibility of commanding the *Enterprise* weighing down on the captain.

Spock met Jim's impassive demeanor with his own. "I am constrained to point out," he began, "the considerable promise for scientific advancement from further study of the Guardian."

The Guardian, McCoy thought, the appellation echoing in his recollection, as though he'd heard it before, perhaps in a dream. Regardless, he knew at once that Spock referred to the unusual toroidal object—or entity—down on the planet's surface.

"At the very least," Spock continued, "detailed observations could yield the procurement of historical information long believed lost to time." He clearly spoke in his role not only as the ship's second-in-command, but as its principal science officer. "Additionally, thorough examination of such data could prove invaluable to numerous disciplines, including anthropology, archeology, genetics, cosmology—"

"Which is why," the captain interrupted, "I will request that Starfleet Command dispatch a dedicated science vessel here as soon as possible." On the face of it, that sounded to McCoy like a reasonable course of action. At the same time, the mandate of the *Enterprise*'s five-year mission—and Jim Kirk's personal predilection—included exploration and analysis of the unknown. It therefore seemed peculiar, and even significant, that the captain did not avail the crew of the opportunity right now.

"Sir," Spock persisted. He bowed his head slightly and lowered his voice, as though seeking to avoid the appearance of challenging his commanding officer. "I must also call attention to the potentially devastating consequences of permitting this planet to fall under the control of any power with interests inim-

ical to the Federation." McCoy recognized the indications of the
Vulcan's discomfort, signs he'd observed only on rare occasion:
a certain tightening of Spock's facial muscles, bringing his hands
together behind his back, casting his words with even greater
formality than usual.

"Begging the captain's pardon," Scotty said, pacing over to
join the two senior officers. "I have to agree with Mister Spock
about this. We're not all that far from Romulan space, and we're
even closer to the Klingon border, and Organian Peace Treaty or
no, if they should—"

"I understand the point," Kirk snapped, cutting off the chief
engineer. The captain stopped and waited a beat, clearly attempting to rein in his emotions. He looked from Scotty to
Spock, then turned back toward the transporter console and
again reached across and brought his closed fist down on the intercom control. "Kirk to DeSalle."

"DeSalle here," the lieutenant responded at once. *"Navigation is plotting a course to Starbase Ten right now, Captain."*

"Belay my previous order," Kirk said. "Maintain standard
orbit until further notice, and begin long-range scans of surrounding space. Specifically, be alert for any vessels approaching this system."

"Aye, sir," DeSalle replied.

The captain signed off, jabbing the intercom channel closed.
Looking across the console, he addressed Lieutenant Berkeley.
"Secure the transporter," he said. "No one is to beam down to the
planet under any circumstances."

"Yes, sir," Berkeley said. He sent his fingers marching me-
thodically across the control panel, obviously complying with
the captain's order.

Kirk spared a quick glance at Spock, then faced the rest of the
landing party. "Lieutenant Uhura, report to the bridge," he said.
"Transmit a coded message to Starfleet Command. Follow up on
the log entries we've already sent them and recap the events
down on the planet. Convey my urgent request for an immediate
and possibly permanent military presence here, as well as my
recommendation for a long-term scientific contingent."

"Right away, sir," Uhura acknowledged, but before she could
move toward the door, Spock spoke up once more.

"Captain," he said, "given the extraordinary nature of what the landing party encountered on the planet, I'm certain that you would want all of us to report to sickbay for medical evaluation." McCoy's eyebrows rose involuntarily as Spock uncharacteristically continued attempting to tell the captain his job. "In particular," he said, peering over to where McCoy stood at the front edge of the transporter platform, "I'm sure that you would want the doctor to be examined, considering the great quantity of cordrazine recently injected into his body."

Jim turned his head sharply, his expression softening as he looked over at McCoy. "Yes, of course," he agreed. He walked over to the platform and gazed upward. "How are you feeling, Bones?"

"To tell you the truth, my head's spinning a little bit right now," McCoy said, throwing a hand up to rub the side of his temple. He padded down the steps to the deck of the transporter room, where he faced the captain. "I've recovered quite a bit from the overdose," he explained, "but I think I still have a ways to go."

"You've . . . been through a lot," Jim said. He lifted his hands and took hold of McCoy's upper arms. "Have Doctor Sanchez check you out."

The left side of McCoy's mouth curled up in a lopsided grin, a reaction to the captain's display of concern. "Yes, sir," he said. Jim applied reassuring pressure to McCoy's arms for a moment, then dropped his hands and turned back to the rest of the landing party.

"All of you, report to sickbay," he ordered the assembled crew, but then he spoke directly to Uhura. "Lieutenant, head to the bridge first and see to it that my message is sent to Starfleet. Then get checked out."

"Yes, sir," she said.

McCoy watched as Jim started for the doors. The light blue panels parted before him, but then Spock spoke up again. "Captain," he said, and Jim stopped and glanced back over his shoulder. "May I ask if you'll be reporting to sickbay as well?"

"I'll be in my quarters," Jim said, his severe mien returned. "And I don't wish to be disturbed." McCoy thought for a moment that Spock might cite regulations in order to compel the captain to submit to a medical exam, but the first officer said nothing more. Jim continued out of the transporter room, the doors sliding shut behind him.

As if on queue, all the members of the landing party looked toward Spock, and McCoy recognized that he hadn't been the only one to observe the captain's detached comportment. Spock ignored the attentions of the crew, though, and instead addressed McCoy. "Do you require assistance, Doctor?" he asked.

"No," McCoy answered. "I can make it on my own."

"Very well," Spock said. "Then let us all comply with the captain's orders."

McCoy fell in with the members of the landing party as they started toward the transporter-room doors, headed for sickbay. He resolved to have a private conversation with Spock. Obviously what affected the captain so much was Edith Keeler's death, but he wondered now if something more than that had happened down on the planet.

TWO

1930

Edith's knees trembled as McCoy escorted her through the front entryway of the mission. Though she had walked here with him from the center of the street, her legs had begun to waver as soon as she'd stood up. The reality that she had almost stridden into the path of an oncoming lorry remained at the forefront of her thoughts, and she guessed that the incident had forced her body to suffer some form of shock.

Inside, the relative darkness of the city night gave way to the amber illumination thrown down by the bare bulbs dangling from the ceiling. Edith squinted and raised a hand to shield her eyes from the increased brightness, and the movement immedi-

ately disrupted her balance. She reflexively extended her arm out
to the wall left of the doors to steady herself. Her splayed fingers
came to rest on the beige plaster, beneath the place where the pay
telephone hung, and next to the writing shelf just beside it.

"Easy now," McCoy said, strengthening his already supportive hold on her other arm. "Why don't we get you off your feet."
Edith heard and understood the words, but they sounded as
though they'd been spoken to her from a distance.

McCoy slowly guided her toward the nearest of the four long
tables that filled the large main room of the mission. Atop the tables sat overturned chairs, which Edith had placed there herself
after the last meal of the day, so that she'd been able to sweep the
floor clean. Now she reached out, and for a moment she watched
her hands quiver uncontrollably, until she pushed them palms
down onto the tabletop. Pitted and scarred from years of use, the
flaxen wood felt rough to her touch.

Concentrating as best she could on that sensation, Edith
leaned heavily on her hands, at least partially relieving her legs
of their burden. Beside her, wood rasped against wood as McCoy
pulled down one of the chairs. He set it on the floor behind her,
then gently grasped her shoulders and eased her onto the seat.
Edith left her hands lying flat in front of her, though, worried that
she would not be able to restrain their shaking if she lifted them.
Only then did she notice that the sleeves of her blouse had been
rent. Dark patches of dirt covered the ragged white fabric; beneath, visible amidst the grime, crimson scratches and contusions scored her flesh, all doubtless the result of her impact with
the street. Most of her wounds appeared superficial, but blood
seeped from a nasty gash that reached from the top of her right
wrist and up across the base of her thumb. Oddly, she felt no
pain—or perhaps not so oddly, since she felt virtually nothing,
her mind and body numbed by the night's events.

"Now let's take a look at you," McCoy said, his voice still
seeming to come to her from far away. He slid her periwinkle
cloche onto the table, then unbuttoned her cloak, removed it, and
set it down beside the hat. After hauling another chair from atop
the table, he sat down next to her and delicately took hold of her
hands, first one, then the other. Even in her haze, Edith could see
that he examined her injuries with great care. She watched him

as he did so, but as she again spied her flawed porcelain skin, pressure suddenly formed behind her eyes. She clenched her jaw in an effort to keep her tears at bay.

"Nothing too bad," McCoy told her, and Edith clung to the statement as she would a life preserver. "I'm going to see what you've got in this place that I can use to treat you," he said, pushing back from the table and standing up. "I'll just be a minute."

"All right," Edith said absently. Even her own words rang strangely in her ears, as though they'd been uttered with her voice, but by some other person. Although aware of her surroundings, she felt disconnected from them, and her mind seemed to hold only the most tenuous link with her body.

Edith struggled to push herself into the moment. She stared ahead at her damaged limbs while McCoy moved around her and toward the small kitchen at the far end of the room. Edith tried to listen to his footfalls as he marched away from her, but instead heard the rhythm of her own steps as she'd only moments ago crossed Twenty-first Street.

After she'd helped clean up after the final meal tonight, Edith had donned her cloak and hat and started for home. For much of the day, she'd entertained the idea of stopping by the cinema and taking in the late feature. She loved the talkies, though she seldom enough found time to indulge herself. As she'd left the mission tonight, Edith had again considered the possibility and had decided to take in a film after all. She'd started for the theater, but then something had occurred to her—some matter she could not now recall—and she'd turned around and headed back to the soup kitchen. Whatever her thoughts had been, she must have been concentrating so intently on them that she'd failed to check for approaching motorcars before crossing the street.

How could I have been so careless? she thought now. Beyond the obvious danger to herself, she'd put the mission—and therefore the well-being of many other people—at risk. The primary responsibility for running the soup kitchen rested with her; should she become incapacitated, she had no idea for how long it would endure. Edith certainly didn't manage the place alone—a number of others worked there, including several men who'd initially arrived at the mission needing assistance themselves—but only she raised and supervised the funds required to keep the doors open. Had McCoy not bravely rescued her from harm, more than a few people would have paid the price for her recklessness.

"Stupid," Edith announced, but already her discontent with her blunder had begun to ebb. Despite the wisps of fog lingering in her mind, she'd contemplated her foolishness enough, and now she simply resolved to pay more attention to her environs. She shook her head vigorously from side to side, not in self-admonishment, but in an attempt to revive her diminished awareness. After a few moments, she detected in the air the dark, persistent aroma of coffee, and beneath it, the reedy hints of chicken broth. Voices reached her, and she peered across the room, past the chair legs that rose up from the tabletops like the winter-bare tree trunks of a diminutive woodland.

Beyond the far wall of the main room sat the undersized kitchen, visible through the wide rectangular opening at which the men who came here were served their meals. To the left, a pair of olive-drab swinging doors, with circular windows at eye level, separated the two rooms. Another wooden door, also painted olive drab, stood on the far right and led to a hallway, Edith's office, a couple of storage closets, and a stairway down to the cellar.

In the kitchen right now, she saw, McCoy spoke with Rik. The former vagrant held a towel and a large pot in his hands, and Edith knew that he'd been busy cleaning up after the night's last meal. No taller than she was, with a mop of long, silvering hair and a shaggy mustache, Rik had been helping out at the mission for several months, ever since he'd developed the conviction and strength to break off with the booze. Prior to that, Edith had turned him out of the soup kitchen several times, though always advising him that he would be welcome if he returned sober. Even during those uncertain times, Rik, like several of the regular visitors here, had occasionally helped out at the mission.

At one time in her life, it had surprised Edith that men who could not secure employment, and who could not keep homes, could still manage to procure alcohol for themselves, particularly in this time of Prohibition. But as a young woman, she had come to the painful understanding that a weakness for liquor—or any vulnerability of the spirit—could impart a drive that overwhelmed not only the best of intentions, but even the instinct for self-preservation.

Edith didn't know with certainty how Rik had finally managed to climb on the water cart and stay there, but she believed that he had at least in part replaced it in his life with music. On a number of evenings during the past months, he had ladled out soup to the men who'd come seeking a meal, and then he'd entertained them. Rik would pluck at his tatty banjo and sing, striving to serve the hungry, the indigent, the homeless, what he called "food for the soul." He even once in a while would coax a tune from the decrepit upright piano that stood on a raised platform along the left-hand wall.

Now, Edith saw Rik turn his head sharply in her direction, and she suspected that McCoy had just described to him what had transpired outside. Rik quickly set down the pot and the towel he'd been holding, then ducked down below the counter and out of sight. He stood up and returned to view a few seconds later, an old red tin in one hand. Edith recognized it as the first-aid kit she kept for emergencies—and which she'd used three days ago to treat McCoy when he'd first arrived at the mission. Among other minor injuries, the backs of his hands had been badly abraded, and she'd washed them out and applied to them a healing salve.

McCoy accepted the first-aid kit from Rik and carried it back out into the main room. Taking a seat beside Edith again, McCoy placed the tin on the table. Covered with more dents and scratches than printing—*Good Samaritan First Aid Kit*, it read in white block letters—the container measured perhaps ten inches square and a third as deep. "Let's see what we've got here," McCoy said, lifting off the lid and placing it to one side. He examined the contents of the kit, then selected cotton wadding, gauze pads, cloth tape, a bottle of hydrogen peroxide, and a jar of the same salve that Edith had employed on him. "These'll do nicely," he said.

Edith looked on in silence as McCoy ministered to her wounds. He spoke to her while cleaning the blood and dirt from her forearms and hands, but said nothing of particular import; she suspected that he offered his words as a means of distracting her from the periodic sting of the antiseptic. He spent the most time and effort working over the gash in her wrist, dressing it with the salve and gauze once he'd rinsed it fully. Although the entire undertaking required only a few minutes and no real medical expertise, Edith observed the practiced confidence with which McCoy appeared to work.

"You're quite good at this, aren't you?" she remarked, finally starting to feel more like herself.

"Well," McCoy said, a broad smile blossoming on his face, "I *am* a doctor."

"Of course," Edith said, hoping that her words and tone masked the doubts she fostered about McCoy's alleged medical training. When he'd first appeared at the mission, he'd hardly cut the figure of a physician. He'd tottered in, exhausted and barely able to stand, supporting himself by holding on to the gunmetal gray railing that led men past the serving area. Scarlet blotches had dappled a pallid, sickly complexion. Edith had witnessed enough men similarly ravaged to know that McCoy looked less like somebody who prescribed drugs and more like somebody addicted to them.

Still, after sleeping on a cot in her office for nearly an entire day, he'd introduced himself as the senior medical officer aboard the *U.S.S. Enterprise.* Circumstances readily seemed to contradict him, and his clothing—boots, black trousers, and a strange sky blue pullover—hardly resembled a navy uniform. But despite the apparent absurdity of McCoy's claim, Edith had chosen to address him as *Doctor.* Until now, though, as he expertly tended to her injuries, she'd given no real credence to the possibility that he might genuinely be a physician.

"That's all right," McCoy said, still smiling. "I know you don't believe that I'm a doctor." He settled the tape, the gauze pads, and the jar of salve back in the first-aid kit, but used the cotton and hydrogen peroxide to begin cleaning out the scrapes on his own hands.

"As I recall," she responded, feeling a grin play across her own lips, "you claimed the other day not to believe at all in me."

"I guess that's true," McCoy admitted with a chuckle. "Perhaps we were both wrong."

"Perhaps." McCoy continued working over the nicks in his hands, and Edith offered to help him.

"Thank you, but I'm just about done," he said. "It looks like I escaped from our little accident in better shape than you did." As if to illustrate his point, he held up one hand, dabbed at it briefly, then replaced the unused cotton and the bottle of antiseptic back in the tin.

" 'Physician, heal thyself'?" she said.

"Not in my case," McCoy said. He retrieved the lid and replaced it on the first-aid kit, metal clinking against metal. "*You* were mostly responsible these past couple of days for helping me heal."

Heat rose in Edith's cheeks, and she knew that her face had flushed. She glanced down at her hands, embarrassed. She didn't feel comfortable accepting gratitude for her good works, believing that as a member of humanity, she had a responsibility to her fellow man to do what she could to help those in need. Earlier this evening, McCoy had told Edith that her decision to look after him when he'd stumbled into the mission might have saved his life. She replied to him now with something she'd told him then. "You just looked like you could use a friend." Before McCoy could respond, she slid her chair away from the table and stood up. "What *I* could use right now," she said, "is a good night's sleep." She reached down and picked up her cloak and hat.

"May I walk you home?" McCoy asked, also getting to his feet.

"Thank you, Doctor," she said, "but that won't be necessary. I promise to look both ways before crossing the street."

"I'm sure you will," McCoy agreed, at the same time reaching forward and taking her cloak from her. "But I was going out for a walk anyway," he said, "so I wouldn't mind the company." He held the cloak open for her.

Edith turned and slipped her arms through the slits in her garment, surprised by the unexpected display of gallantry. Around Twenty-first Street, she rarely encountered such good manners. Coupled with McCoy's claim to be a physician, as well as the ease and care with which he'd treated her wounds, his simple act of helping her on with her cloak now gave Edith pause. Though she remained skeptical of his professed vocation, she wondered now if her initial assessment of the man had been mistaken. Perhaps there was more to McCoy than she'd at first thought.

Deciding that she'd like to learn more about him, Edith accepted his offer to accompany her on her way home. "I presume that you'll still be staying here tonight?" she asked.

"Honestly," McCoy said, "I have no place else to go." Some emotion seemed to flicker across his face, but Edith couldn't quite make out what it had been.

Yes, there is more to this man than I thought, Edith decided. *I just can't tell what it is.*

But she vowed to herself that she would figure it out.

They walked along the avenues, primarily in darkness, but periodically passing through pools of light, the glow spilling down from street lamps that lined the sidewalks like mute sentinels against the night. The mechanical mutter of automobile engines and the metronomic clop of horses' hooves occasionally drifted to them over the tapping of their own footsteps, but for the most part, the urban valleys of brick and window glass nestled them in comparative silence. About them, the air carried the leaden scent of moisture, though if from rains past or rains yet to come, McCoy could not tell.

He and Keeler had scarcely spoken since leaving the mission, maintaining a comfortable quietude between them. Of the crowd that had formed on Twenty-first Street after the near-accident, many had dispersed by the time the pair had gone back outside. Quickly slipping unnoticed past the three or four individuals who'd remained, McCoy and Keeler had then settled into an easy pace, headed for her home. Here and there, they'd spotted other people—some strolling along, others rummaging through the shadows—but few enough disrupted the surrounding stillness.

As McCoy walked beside Keeler, his thoughts strayed from their earlier excitement and turned instead to his own predicament. He readily grasped the seriousness of his situation, despite having only an incomplete notion of how he'd arrived in this place and time. Although he could not be sure just how many days ago it had happened, McCoy did recall being summoned to the bridge of the *Enterprise* so that he could treat Lieutenant Sulu after some mishap had caused the helmsman to lose consciousness and experience heart flutter. Working amid the gray smell of charred circuitry and the unmistakable tang of scorched flesh, McCoy had successfully tended to Hikaru's condition by administering a small dose of cordrazine. Moments later, though, as McCoy had reached to replace the hypospray in his medkit, the ship had lurched unexpectedly, and he'd fallen against the hypo's dispensing tip. The hiss of the medical instrument had sounded chillingly long and loud as a mammoth amount of the powerful drug had been injected into his body.

Beyond that, and until he'd staggered into the 21st Street Mission, McCoy remembered little clearly. He tried now to dredge up that missing time, but those events flickered through his thoughts in a kaleidoscope of distorted, half-seen images. In his mind's eye, he glimpsed the twisted, malevolent faces of his pursuers, unrecognizable assassins bent wholly on his extermination. Racing frantically from them, McCoy had dashed through corridors and quarters, through maintenance tubes and access tunnels. Eventually, he'd made his way to the transporter room, where in fear for his life, he'd fled the ship.

But the killers hadn't relented, chasing him from the *Enterprise* down to the planet it orbited. In snatches of seemingly vicarious sensation, McCoy evoked his attempts to evade the murderers: the icy stabs of pain as he'd tried to conceal himself along jagged, colorless rock faces; the lonely refrain of the wind as it had wailed through wrecked, alien structures; the parched, granular taste of the dirt and dust as he'd gasped for breath. The hunters had tracked him ceaselessly, until at last they'd encircled him. Just one against many, McCoy had fought them as best he could, but had been unable to prevent his capture.

And yet somehow he'd escaped. Though he could not now recollect by what means, he had nevertheless stolen away from his would-be executioners, into the back alleys of an old city and the far reaches of time. *This* city, in *this* time: New York, on Earth, in 1930.

As he followed Keeler around a corner onto a street lined with what appeared to be low-rise, multi-unit dwellings, McCoy felt profoundly lost—not within the ancient city, but within the larger universe. It seemed unthinkable that he might be marooned here permanently, but the possibility occurred to him. However he'd arrived where he had, when he had, he could conceive of no method by which he could reverse that unexplained process.

Unable to make sense of it all, McCoy turned his attention back to his companion. He'd first encountered Edith Keeler when he'd wandered into the 21st Street Mission, drawn by the stiff aroma of brewing coffee and the sight of disheveled, unclean men making their way inside—men among whom he'd hoped to camouflage himself. Aching, starving, and spent, McCoy had still been openly fearful of those searching for him, and Keeler had without hesitation hidden him away in a back room.

Reflections of the intervening days between then and now rose with progressively greater clarity in McCoy's mind. Keeler's smooth, alabaster countenance dominated those scenes, materializing above him again and again as she'd sought to nurse him back to health. Indeed, her kindly ministrations had helped him recover from the cordrazine overdose—even though she'd never before heard of cordrazine, or Starfleet, or Leonard McCoy.

"Miss Keeler," he said now. His voice sounded small in the empty street.

"Doctor McCoy," she said. Even though he could not see her well in the darkness, he could tell that she'd looked over at him as they walked. He also visualized a grin on her face, given the impish tone of her response.

"I'd like to repay the care and compassion you've shown me over the past few days," he told her sincerely.

"Oh, I think that saving my life tonight ought to be considered payment enough," she said. "Don't you?" Her reply came so quickly, and in such an apparently automatic way, that McCoy recognized its source as something other than mere gratitude. He did not doubt that Keeler felt honestly thankful for what he'd done on Twenty-first Street tonight, but he also perceived that she neither needed nor desired recompense of any kind for her own charitable endeavors. McCoy had known numerous such individuals throughout his life; indeed, though people became doctors and nurses and caregivers for myriad reasons, the simple impulse to help others provided for many the most compelling of all motivations. Of course, McCoy's own reasons for going into medicine had been—

—complicated, he finished the thought. Then, with a facility born of long repetition, he pushed the subject away. Instead, he went back to the matter of the care that Edith Keeler had given him.

"I'd still like to show my appreciation," he said. "You mentioned earlier that we could talk about me doing some work around the mission."

"My, you are persistent, Doctor," she said. Their steps took them into the circle of light surrounding a lamppost, and McCoy glanced over to see Keeler's striking hazel eyes regarding him. Her light blue hat covered her hair, but for where a whisk of strands peeked out alongside her cheek. "I could do with some help: washing dishes, sweeping up, that sort of thing," she said. "In fact, the basement hasn't been cleaned in more than a year. I suppose you could start there."

"All right," McCoy said, pleased. "I'll begin first thing in the morning." As their strides carried them beyond the reach of the street lamp, Keeler's face faded back into the night. The transition reminded McCoy how little he knew about this woman. "Speaking of the mission," he said, "you told me that you run it because it's necessary."

"That's right," Keeler confirmed.

"If you don't mind my asking, why?"

"Because sometimes people need a helping hand," she said sincerely. "As you told me yourself, Doctor, you needed one when you first showed up there."

"I certainly did," McCoy agreed. "But I'm not asking why the *mission* is necessary. I'm asking why it's necessary for *you* to run it."

"But it's not just necessary for *me* to do what I do," Keeler asserted. "It's necessary for *everybody* to look after their fellow citizens." She stopped walking, and when he followed suit, she placed a hand on his forearm. They stood near enough to the next lamppost that McCoy could distinguish her features in the spare light, though the dimness robbed her visage of any color. "Have you ever heard this passage by a man called John Donne? 'No man is an island, entire of itself; every man is a piece of the continent, a part of the main.'"

McCoy nodded slowly, conjuring the words from memory.

"'Any man's death diminishes me,'" he quoted from later in the work, "'because I am involved in mankind.'"

Keeler said nothing for a moment, and she remained so still that she might have been holding her breath. Suddenly, it seemed to McCoy as though a great weight had descended upon both of them. The faint light shimmered in her eyes in a way that made him think tears had collected there. Before he could be sure, though, Keeler dropped her hand and began walking again.

"That's very good, Doctor," she said softly as McCoy fell in beside her.

"I'm a bit of a reader myself, and I have a friend with an interest in classic literature," he explained, thinking of Jim Kirk. "That particular composition is one of his favorites." Not for the first time, McCoy considered the captain's contradictory nature; Jim thoroughly appreciated Donne's meditation on the interconnectedness of humanity, and yet he so often isolated himself in his command.

"'I am involved in mankind,'" Keeler repeated after a while, her voice rising back to a conversational level. "We all have a responsibility to each other. I run the mission because I'm able to help, and so I *must* help."

"That's a laudable perspective," McCoy averred.

"It's a *necessary* perspective," Keeler amended. "Poverty was rampant even before the stock market panic and all the bank failures, and conditions have only gotten worse since then."

The stock market panic, McCoy thought, the phrase triggering an old memory, probably from one of the Earth survey courses he'd attended in school. Throughout human history, he knew, there had been numerous economic disruptions in capitalistic nations around the world, at least before the development and implementation of the Rostopovich-Batista safeguards. As he recalled now, the 1930s had been a period of fiscal turmoil in many countries, including the United States of America. This had been one of several eras branded as the Great Depression.

"So many in want of an honest day's work," Keeler lamented. "So many desperate just to be able to provide food for their families and an adequate place for them to stay." Again she stopped walking, but this time she pointed toward the narrow four-story building before which they now stood. "This is where I live," she said.

McCoy gazed up a wide set of concrete stairs that led to the front door. A light shined from within an arch atop the entry and another from within a second-floor window. Even meagerly illuminated, the structure looked old and weathered. At the base of the stairs, refuse flowed from a number of dented metal cans, one of which had toppled onto its side.

"Will you be able to find your way back to the mission?" Keeler asked. Before they'd left the soup kitchen, she'd entrusted him with a set of keys to the place, so that he could let himself back in and spend the night there.

"I will," McCoy said.

"Good night then, Doctor," Keeler said, and she climbed the steps. McCoy watched her go, but felt the need to say something more to her, to ease the burdens she obviously bore as a matter of course. He called after her as she reached the front door.

"Miss Keeler." He started up the stairs, his knees creaking as he did so. A residual effect of his cordrazine overdose had been pain in his joints, which hadn't yet completely diminished.

At the top of the steps, McCoy peered at Keeler. "Things will get better," he tried to assure her. "The world won't always be like this." To his surprise, Keeler smiled widely.

"Oh, I absolutely agree," she said. "The days and years are unquestionably worth living for." Delighted but puzzled by her enthusiastic response, McCoy cocked his head slightly and offered her a quizzical expression. "Someday soon," she said, "man will find a way to harness incredible energies—maybe even the atom—energies that will ultimately hurl us to other worlds." McCoy stared at her, startled by her sophisticated, forward-thinking outlook. "And the men who reach out into space will also find ways to feed the hungry millions of the world, and to cure their diseases. They'll find a way to give each man hope and a common future. And those are the days worth living for."

McCoy returned her smile now, unable to resist either her passion for the future or her keen intuition about it.

"Are you mocking me, Doctor?" she asked.

"No, not at all," McCoy said at once. "I'm just marveling at how right you are."

"Really?" she said, giving him a questioning look. "Do we share a like vision?"

"I think we do," McCoy said. "Humanity will learn to tap into the power of the atom, and eventually use that knowledge and ability to unite all the world in peace and prosperity. Even before that time, we'll send automated spacecraft out into the solar system, and beyond. People will not only travel to the moon, but live there. And on Mars too, and Ganymede and Titan—" McCoy abruptly closed his mouth.

"Ganymede and Titan?" Keeler asked. Her voice held a note of skepticism, as though she believed that he might be ridiculing her after all. But her eyes gleamed with obvious curiosity. "Those aren't planets."

"No," McCoy said. "They're moons orbiting Jupiter and Saturn." It had been his mention of Titan that had caused him to stop speaking. The man to head the first successful Earth-Saturn probe had been—or would be—Colonel Sean Christopher. Several months prior to McCoy's cordrazine overdose, the *Enterprise* had accidentally been thrown into the past, during which time the man who would ultimately be Colonel Christopher's father, United States Air Force Captain John Christopher, had been transported aboard. Although a means had finally been found to safely return Captain Christopher to Earth, Spock had initially cautioned against doing so, concerned that such an action could result in the changing of history. McCoy realized now that he must confront the same possibility: if he altered what happened here in Earth's past, that could change the future. The *Enterprise,* and Starfleet, and even the Federation itself, might never come into existence.

"I've never considered the moons around other worlds," Keeler said, clearly intrigued by a concept new to her. She glanced upward, and McCoy did as well, but heavy cloud cover blanketed the sky, concealing the stars from view. "But I imagine that if we choose to go to our own moon, we would choose to go to others as well."

"It's just a wild thought," McCoy said, trying to undermine the surety with which he'd spoken. Anxious about what he'd said to Keeler, he recast the flavor of his words. "I do agree that humanity will aspire to greater things than it does now, that the people of the world will come together to concentrate on the common good," he said. "I think you're right to believe that the days ahead are worth living for."

Keeler quickly reached down and took hold of one of McCoy's hands. "I knew there must have been a good reason I took to you so quickly," she said. With a chaste squeeze of his hand, she bade him good night once more, then headed inside.

McCoy watched her go, then turned and started down the steps. When he reached the sidewalk, he stopped for a moment and peered up at the sky again. That the overcast hid the stars seemed an apt metaphor for McCoy's own situation. Although he knew that the three centuries between now and his own time existed—or would exist, if he didn't alter the timeline—he could not see those years. But while he possessed no real understanding of temporal mechanics, he felt confident that his conversation with Keeler had done no damage. Still, until he could figure out a way to return to where he belonged, or until Jim and Spock could come retrieve him, he would have to be more careful.

With no where else to go and nothing else to do, he began back to the 21st Street Mission.

THREE

2267

As she stepped into the turbolift, Ensign Tonia Barrows anxiously spun a finger through the wavy tresses of her shoulder-length red hair. The doors closed behind her with a familiar chirp, and she reached with her free hand for one of the lift's activation controls. She wrapped her fingers around the short wand and triggered it with a twist. "Sickbay," she said. The car lurched almost imperceptibly as it eased into a horizontal glide toward the center of the *Enterprise*'s primary hull.

Recognizing her nervous mannerism, Barrows dropped her hand from her hair and stood motionless in the lift, enveloped in the high-pitched hum of its operation. Her heart hammered away in her chest and had since she'd been contacted a few minutes ago by Christine. The nurse had notified Barrows directly from sickbay that the landing party had found Leonard and brought him back to the ship. According to Christine, his condition had improved markedly, and though he felt weary and lightheaded, he displayed none of the frenzied paranoia that the bridge crew had reported after his unintentional injection of cordrazine.

Alone in the lift, Barrows took in a deep breath, held it for a couple of seconds, then exhaled slowly and loudly, allowing her cheeks to swell as she did so. Despite learning that Leonard had returned to the ship, and that he'd more or less recovered from his overdose, the stress of the last few hours had yet to leave her. She'd been on edge even before what had happened to Leonard, ever since the *Enterprise* had begun periodically quaking, the ship wracked intermittently by an unexplained force. Almost a week ago, long-range sensors had detected some unusual readings, and the captain had chosen to seek out their source in an attempt to investigate their nature. The crew had eventually traced the readings to an uncharted planet, class-M but uninhabited. As the *Enterprise* had neared the mysterious world earlier today, the ship had been buffeted sporadically as it navigated through areas of turbulence, which had continued even after they'd assumed orbit. Not long after that, an alert had gone out ship-wide, with an announcement about Leonard's accident on the bridge and orders to security that he should be located, subdued, and taken to sickbay.

The whine accompanying the progress of the turbolift faded as the car slowed, then resumed as the lift accelerated upward. Barrows felt an ache in her hand, and she realized that she'd clenched her fingers around the turbolift's control wand. She relaxed her grip and tried to calm down, tried to reinforce to herself that the danger to Leonard had passed.

She'd been off duty and in her quarters during the security alert. Even though the crew had been told that the drug accidentally administered to Leonard had rendered him manic, wildly suspicious, and unable to recognize acquaintances, she'd thought that he still might come to her, perhaps seeking a safe haven. After all, they'd been seeing each other, albeit casually, for almost five months now.

Casually, Barrows thought, chuckling to herself—chuckling *at* herself. She and Leonard hadn't ever really discussed their relationship, nor had she examined it too closely, but the time they'd so far spent together had been fun and full and ardent. If she hadn't previously admitted to herself just how much she cared for him, the depth and character of her concern during this incident now made her emotions impossible to ignore. On the other hand, Leonard's feelings for her had seemed clear enough all along, which was why she'd believed that, even in his drugged paranoia, he might show up at her quarters, appealing to her for refuge.

But he hadn't come to her. Instead, he'd eluded security and bolted the ship. Knowing that the captain and first officer had immediately taken a landing party after him hadn't eased Barrows's apprehensions much. In addition to the physiological effects Leonard would endure from the cordrazine, it had remained to be seen what dangers he would confront on the unexplored planet below—a planet from which waves of an unidentified force had emanated and shaken a starship at a considerable remove.

But now he's back on the Enterprise, she reminded herself. *Christine said he's doing well.* Still, Barrows knew that until she actually saw Leonard, nothing would calm her distress.

The turbolift slowed again and this time came to a complete stop. Barrows unwound her fingers from around the lift control as the doors swept open, revealing an empty section of corridor. She hesitated for a moment, took in another deep breath, then headed for sickbay.

As soon as Barrows entered the medical center, she saw Christine. The nurse sat at a desk directly ahead, making notes with a stylus on a data slate. To the right, a pair of security guards occupied two biobeds. Low, steady cadences beat softly in the room, the rhythms of the guards' hearts audibly monitored by the medical scanners. Christine had told Barrows that the members of the landing party were being examined by the medical staff as a matter of routine, though none showed any ill effects from having transported down to the planet.

Christine turned from the desk as the doors closed behind Barrows. "Oh good, you're here," the nurse said, setting the slate down and walking over. "I know he'll be so happy to see you." Since Barrows had become involved with the ship's chief medical officer, she'd consequently encountered his head nurse a great deal. After a while, the two women had formed their own friendship, and if Barrows had come to understand anything in that time about Christine Chapel, it was her unrepentant romanticism. Amazingly, discovering less than a year ago that her fiancé had perished during an archeological expedition hadn't dimmed that aspect of her personality.

Christine briefly took hold of Barrows's forearm, giving a quick tug toward the doorway that led into the inner medical compartment. Barrows could hear a male voice within, the accent divulging the identity of the speaker as the *Enterprise*'s chief engineer. "No time at all," said Lieutenant Commander Scott: "'Twas like the three of you went through a door, then just a moment later, came right back through."

"Excuse me," Christine said, stopping just beyond the threshold. "Doctor McCoy, you have a visitor."

Barrows followed the cue and stepped past the nurse. Inside the medical compartment, she saw Lieutenant Uhura perched atop the near biobed, and Engineer Scott sitting on the edge of the one beside it. In a corner along the far bulkhead, on a third diagnostic pallet, lay Leonard. Propped up on his left side and facing the other two officers, he looked as though he'd been in conversation with them. He appeared tired, as Christine had warned, but other than that, he seemed hale.

Tension drained from Barrows as freely as water pouring from a tap. Whatever fears had troubled her, they now vanished as she regarded Leonard. Her heart rate still galloped along, though, no longer from worry, but from elation.

"Why, lassie," Mr. Scott offered affably. "I almost didn't recognize you."

"The blue uniform suits you, Ensign," Lieutenant Uhura added, obviously making reference to Barrows's recent changes in both position and rank. Though she'd been assigned to the *Enterprise* as a yeoman, Barrows had since developed an interest in the physical sciences. She'd requested a transfer of duties, and just two weeks ago, coincident with her promotion to ensign, Captain Kirk and Commander Spock had approved her move from the engineering and services division to sciences—and as a result, from a red uniform to a blue one. Assigned to the physics lab as an assistant to Lieutenant Commander Homeyer, she'd also as a matter of practicality traded in her skirts for pants.

"Thank you," Barrows said, acknowledging both Mr. Scott and Lieutenant Uhura with glances in their directions. Then she looked back at Leonard. She felt the urge to rush forward and take him in her arms, but though they'd made no secret of their relationship, neither had they flaunted their affections in front of the crew. Mindful of the other two officers present, she settled for simply saying his name: "Leonard."

"Hello, Tonia," he said. "I'm all right."

"We'll let Doctor Sanchez determine that when your test results come back from the lab," Christine chided him.

"I think I'm capable of evaluating my own health, Nurse," Leonard said irascibly, but with a glint of mischief in his eye.

"You're not a physician when you're lying in that biobed," Christine retorted. "You're a patient, *Mister* McCoy." The nurse didn't wait for a response, but turned crisply and marched out of the room. Barrows looked over at Mr. Scott and Lieutenant Uhura again and saw both enjoying the playful exchange.

"I don't know where she learned her bedside manner," Leonard grumbled, fulfilling his self-appointed role as ship's curmudgeon, as though nothing at all had happened to him.

"No," Uhura said, with clearly exaggerated sincerity, "I can't imagine where *your* head nurse could've picked up such an approach with patients."

Barrows couldn't help but laugh. It felt eminently satisfying, like closure after all the events and concerns of the day. She walked over to stand beside Leonard's biobed as he dropped down onto his back. "I'm so glad you're all right," she said, beaming down at him. She raised her hand and tenderly rubbed his upper arm.

"Well, I'm pretty tired," he said, "and off and on I feel faint."

Barrows nodded. "Nurse Chapel told me," she said, "but I just wanted to see you." Again, she yearned to wrap her arms around him and hold him close, but instead she leaned down and spoke quietly to him, so that only he would hear. "I couldn't bear it if anything happened to you," she said, her voice trembling with emotion. Other then declaring outright that she loved him, she couldn't have revealed the extent of her feelings any more plainly.

Leonard looked at her for a long moment, his face expressionless. Barrows stood up abruptly, reacting as though she'd been struck. She hadn't planned to proclaim her love for Leonard—she'd only just confessed it to herself—but now that she had, his wooden response stunned her—stunned, and hurt her.

But then Leonard reached across his body and patted her hand where it sat atop his arm. "You don't have to worry anymore, Tonia," he assured her. "I'm all right." He pushed a wan smile onto his face, and even that small gesture helped her sudden heartache to subside.

Barrows took his hand in both of hers. His skin felt icy and dry. "You're cold," she said.

"It was cold down in—" Leonard started, but then he stopped and began again. "It was cold down on the planet." He paused, then added, "Plus I might still be feeling the aftereffects of the cordrazine."

"Should I tell Nurse Chapel?" Barrows asked.

"No, she and Doctor Sanchez have been taking good care of me," Leonard said. "But really, I'm very tired. I should rest now."

"Of course," Barrows said, fighting the impression that Leonard wanted her to leave not because of his fatigue, but because of what she'd revealed about her emotional attachment to him. Trying to shrug it off, she lifted his hand to her lips and kissed it gently. "I'll visit again when you're feeling better."

On her way back across the medical compartment, Barrows nodded to Scott and Uhura. She passed through the entryway, and then without looking around for Christine, stalked through the outer doors and into the corridor. Barrows then headed for her quarters, her concerns for Leonard allayed, replaced by an entirely new set of uncertainties.

* * *

McCoy watched Tonia leave, touched that she'd come to call on him. He didn't feel entirely comfortable with her earnest show of concern for him, but in light of how long they'd been keeping company with each other, he supposed he could understand it. A sweet, caring woman, Tonia must have been worried about him not only after she'd learned of the cordrazine mishap, but also when she'd heard that he'd taken flight from the ship.

"Ach," Scotty said, "she's a fine lass, that one."

"And she certainly has eyes for you, Doctor," Uhura said.

McCoy nodded slowly. "Yes, she's a lovely young woman," he said, his tone noncommittal in spite of his agreement. He felt awkward talking about Tonia and certainly didn't want the subject to turn toward his relationship with her.

Rolling up onto his left side again, McCoy steered the conversation back to where it had been before Chapel had entered the room. "Scotty, you were saying that, on the planet, we were only gone a short time?" They'd interrupted their discussion not only because Tonia had come to visit him, but also because Spock had advised them not to speak with anybody outside the landing party about their experiences with the Guardian of Forever.

"Aye," Scotty attested. "Vanished one moment, then back the next."

"Actually, you were gone a longer time, Doctor," Uhura clarified. "After you leaped through the portal, it quickly became clear that you'd changed the past, and therefore our present. But it took some time to confirm that, and for the captain to decide on a course of action."

"Uhura's right," Scotty said. "Once the captain and Mister Spock jumped through the portal, that was when they came back right away, and you followed immediately after them."

McCoy tried to grasp all that he'd been told since transporting back up to the ship, tried to comprehend the reality of what had happened to him, but even with his memories of Edith Keeler and the 21st Street Mission, he had difficulty doing so. The idea that he'd traveled into the past and changed Earth's history, and thus had rendered the *Enterprise* nonexistent, seemed virtually unimaginable. And yet the members of the landing party had experienced it, and Jim and Spock had gone back in time themselves in order to rescue him and to undo the damage he'd done.

"Doctor, how long did it seem to you that you were in the past?" Uhura asked.

"Days," McCoy said. Pictures of where he'd stayed, in the back room of the soup kitchen, played across his mind: the dull walls, with black-and-white and sepia-toned photographs hanging on them; the single window that fronted on the brick facing of a neighboring building; the sagging, musty cot in which he'd convalesced; the timeworn desk and filing cabinets. Behind those images followed another, hazy and indistinct, more like a half-remembered delusion than a recollection of something real. A dark tunnel, perhaps, or . . . but no, he couldn't make it out.

"You were in the past for days?" Scotty asked, obviously dubious.

"Yes," McCoy said. "Three days, maybe four. I'm not certain because of the cordrazine. I might have been there even longer."

An expression of surprise crossed Uhura's face, and Scotty sputtered out what McCoy assumed to be some sort of Scottish exclamation. "How much of it do you remember?" the engineer wanted to know.

"Some of it," McCoy said. He thought now of the meals that Keeler had brought to him in the back room and of the cycles of diffuse sunlight that had illuminated the brick wall outside the window each day. "Most of it, I think. Only the beginning, when I first arrived there, is a blur."

"What was it like?" Uhura asked, her voice dropping in volume, as though she spoke with a measure of awe. "Being in the past? Being on Earth three hundred years ago?"

"It felt surreal," McCoy said, and then thought better of his response. "No, not surreal. It felt unreal. Not like a strange dream, but like a realistic hallucination or mirage. Everything looked and sounded and smelled and tasted authentic, but I still couldn't believe that I was in that place, in that time. I almost expected somebody to appear from behind a curtain and reveal it all to be an elaborate re-creation."

"And Captain Kirk and Mister Spock?" Scotty asked. "Did you see them while you were in the past?"

"Only at the end of my time there," McCoy said, remembering how thrilled he'd felt when he'd opened the front door of the mission and seen Jim and Spock standing there. "But almost as soon as we found each other, probably not more than a minute later, we were back on the planet with you." McCoy recalled how dizzying the sequence had been, traveling so quickly from 1930 New York, to the Guardian's world, and then back to the *Enterprise.*

"Speaking of the captain, did either of you notice the look on his face when he came back through the portal?" Uhura asked. "Or the way he acted in the transporter room after we beamed up?"

McCoy had noticed. On the way to sickbay, Spock had confirmed what the doctor already knew—that Jim had purposely prevented him from saving Edith Keeler. The captain's action had preserved history, but had obviously affected him deeply.

"Aye, that I did," Scotty said. "He seemed upset to me. In that brief moment after he and Mister Spock reappeared, and before the doctor did, I thought that they must have *failed* to accomplish the mission."

"I thought so too," Uhura said. "I was shocked when you emerged from the portal, Doctor, and even more so when the *Enterprise* contacted me on my communicator."

"Something must've happened in the past," Scotty speculated.

Before McCoy could decide whether to reveal what had taken place on that centuries-old nighttime street, a voice interrupted. "Something *did* happen." McCoy peered over to see Spock standing in the doorway. "The captain and I successfully restored the timeline." He delivered the statement with such authority and finality that it invited no further comment or question. McCoy found the first officer's reticence on the subject noteworthy.

Spock turned to Uhura. "Lieutenant," he said, "Doctor Sanchez will see you now."

"Yes, Mister Spock," Uhura said. She hopped down from the biobed, crossed in front of the first officer, and left the room. Spock turned toward the door, but before he could depart, Scotty asked a question.

"Mister Spock," he said, "what *did* happen down there, in the past?"

Spock did not answer right away, and McCoy thought that he must have been formulating a response. But then he said, "I will be on the bridge," and exited the room.

McCoy looked over at Scotty, and then back to where Spock had been standing. The first officer had seemed even more stoic than usual. The fact that Jim had willfully prevented McCoy from saving Keeler's life in order to maintain the timeline had been shocking, but it had explained realistically and morally the events through which they'd all lived. Clearly Jim would not have taken the actions he had otherwise. And yet it seemed perfectly clear that Spock was, for some reason, protecting the captain.

Is that how they restored the past? McCoy wondered. *By allowing Edith Keeler to die?* McCoy did not want to believe that. And yet it seemed perfectly clear that Spock was, for some reason, protecting the captain.

"I guess Mister Spock put an end to that," Scotty said, shrugging.

"I guess so," McCoy agreed absently, but wondered if, for Jim, this was just the beginning.

FOUR

1930

Her left hand resting on the railing, Edith stood on the bottom flight of the wooden staircase, mesmerized by what she saw. Before her stretched the basement of the 21st Street Mission—a basement now almost unrecognizable to her. Where dirt and disorder had been the norm just yesterday, she now beheld a clean, open space. The empty barrels and crates previously strewn

about had been cleared away, stacked neatly in one corner. The
old furniture that had found its way down here during the past
couple of years had been buffed and, in some cases, repaired. A
pair of tables, one larger, one smaller, had been pushed up
against the wall, with chairs positioned around them in an unlikely sitting area. Two aged chests of drawers sat beside the
steps, tucked neatly into the low space beneath the upper flight
of stairs. The piles of rags, newspapers, and other rubbish that
had once adorned every surface had now vanished, as had the
layers of dust. Gone too were the milky white cobwebs that had
festooned the place, and the floor had been swept spotless. Even
the permanent fixtures—the squat furnace, the coal chute, the
floor-to-ceiling structural columns, the water pipes—appeared as
though they'd been scrubbed and polished.

"Doctor McCoy, your are an uncommon workman," she said,
appreciative of his efforts. Even with the scarcity of jobs these
days, never had any man she'd hired at the mission put forth
such an exemplary effort. "This basement is cleaner now than
it's ever been."

"Then I can continue working here?" McCoy asked. He stood
in the center of his handiwork, gazing up at her.

"Yes, I think you've earned your keep," she allowed, descending the last couple of steps to stand across from him. She'd
come down here to invite him upstairs for the evening meal, but
instead told him, "I think you might even have earned yourself a
change of clothes too." She watched him peer down at himself,
his arms spread wide. Swaths of dirt and dust discolored his attire from head to toe. His hands looked almost as black as the
coal stored next to the furnace, and though he wouldn't be able
to see it, a dark smudge arced across his cheek.

"I suppose I am a little dirty," he observed.

"A little," Edith said dryly. She'd already laundered McCoy's
clothes once, while he'd been recuperating up in her office. She
could do so again, but now that he'd recovered from whatever
binge had deposited him in the mission, she thought that he
should have more than just the shirt and pants in which he'd arrived here. Not only was his outfit filthy, but it also looked very
peculiar, almost like a Hallowe'en costume. "We have some old
clothes in a closet upstairs, if you'd like to see them."

"Thank you," McCoy said, and Edith led the way up to the mission's back hall. Behind a door across from her office, she showed him two crates filled with secondhand garments. "These have all been washed," she said. "You're welcome to anything you like." Edith had culled the articles of clothing from various sources, though most had simply been left here by some of the men who'd passed through the soup kitchen. They'd warmed up with a meal, then stumbled out having forgotten their hat, or gloves, or jacket, or even an entire bindle of their belongings.

McCoy pawed through the clothes, holding some items up to examine them. He eventually selected a pair of tan trousers and a brown tartan shirt. He draped them over one arm and carried them out of the closet. "I guess I'll change in here," he said, pointing toward the office. Edith nodded, but then had another thought.

"You know, Doctor, you don't have to continue staying here," she said. "You'll have a little bit of money in a couple of days, and there's a vacant room where I live for two dollars a week." Edith had occasionally helped dispossessed men find places to bed down, but she had never suggested that any of them take a room in the building where she herself resided. But even though Dr. McCoy had come to the mission as so many others had, in poor shape, clearly suffering from an excess of drink or some other venomous substance, he hadn't behaved as other visitors to the soup kitchen had. Articulate and soft-spoken, he'd worked today without complaint or supervision and had impressed her with the results. He also seemed to look to the future in the same way that she did, and he treated her with a gentle kindness and respect. All of that and more engendered a sense of trust in her. She'd only known him a few days, but already she felt a sisterly affection for him. She'd never had a brother—or much of a family at all, for that matter—and so she welcomed the unfamiliar feelings.

"If you wouldn't mind," McCoy said, "I'd rather remain in the mission for right now."

"It's not that I mind, Doctor," Edith said, "but don't you think you'd be more comfortable in a room of your own?"

"Probably," McCoy said, "but . . ." His words trailed into silence, leaving his thought unfinished and his desire to sleep in the office unexplained.

"But?" Edith said, encouraging him to go on.

McCoy glanced down at the clothes slung across his arm, rearranged them to no apparent purpose, then looked back up at her. "But I don't think I'm going to be here for very much longer," he finally said.

"Oh," Edith said, surprised. "You have a home then, or a place you're going to?"

"Something like that," McCoy said vaguely.

The equivocation immediately troubled Edith. "I see," she said as she considered how best to respond. She'd run the mission long enough, had observed and interacted with enough of the men who'd passed through here, to discern when one of them sought to avoid her scrutiny. She hadn't expected such evasions from McCoy, and she wondered what he intended to hide from her. *Is he trying to keep ahead of the law?* she speculated. *Or just planning to go back to the booze?* She took herself to task for having trusted the doctor so quickly.

"You may stay here until the end of the week," Edith said, feeling foolish for her misplaced faith in McCoy, but unwilling to renege on her word. "But this isn't a hotel. After that, you'll have to find another place to stay." She didn't wait for the doctor's reaction, but turned on her heel and strode down the hall.

McCoy watched Keeler pace away from him and realized that he'd offended her with his obvious secrecy. He clearly couldn't tell her the facts of his circumstances, and not just because he needed to prevent himself from impacting history. As insightful about the years ahead as Keeler might be, she would never believe that he hailed from the future. Beyond the obvious absurdity of the idea to her—in truth, even McCoy could barely warrant it—he had not exactly distinguished himself as a traveler of any kind when he'd arrived here. Even if he explained the details of his overdose aboard the *Enterprise,* she would never be able to credit any of his story. In the end, not only would she distrust him, she would judge him mentally ill and possibly even dangerous.

"Miss Keeler," he called after her, just as she reached the corner of the corridor, where it turned to the right and led the short distance to the mission's main room. She stopped, put a hand up on the beige plaster of the wall, and looked back at him. He could read her suspicion of him on her face and thought he could identify another emotion as well: disappointment. "Miss Keeler, I'm sorry," he said. "You've been so much help to me, I have no reason to hide anything from you." He felt a twinge of regret for the lie, but accepted that he had no real choice.

"No," she agreed. "No, you don't. Not if you want me to continue helping you."

"I do," McCoy said genuinely.

She walked back down the corridor again, until she stood just a meter or so away from him. "Then tell me, are you in trouble?" she asked earnestly. "Did you do something wrong?"

"No, nothing like that," he said.

Keeler didn't reply for a moment, but she held his gaze, as if trying to determine the honesty in his words. At last, in a quiet voice, she said, "When you showed up here the other day, you told me that you had to keep moving, that you couldn't let them find you."

McCoy recalled his hysterical fear, the sweat it had generated in his palms, the shrieks it had provoked from his lips, the flight reflex it had stimulated in his hindbrain. "Yes, I remember," he told Keeler, though even now the faces of those who had hunted him remained hidden behind the recollection of murky perceptions. But of course, that had to have been a product of the cordrazine; McCoy was now convinced that no one had chased him but his crewmates, and only in an attempt to help him. He said none of this to Keeler, but realized that he had an opportunity to recant some of the statements he'd made to her when first he'd arrived here. "I also remember telling you that I was a medical officer aboard a ship," he said.

"*Senior* medical officer," Keeler corrected. "On the *U.S.S. Enterprise.*"

McCoy forced himself to snicker, hoping to imply that he found even the suggestion of him serving aboard a ship ridiculous. "I said those things, but—"

McCoy heard a door open, followed by the clatter accompanying the evening meal: the scrape of chair legs along the floor, the murmurs of voices, the ring of utensils against plates and bowls. Footsteps approached, and McCoy and Keeler both looked toward the far corner, around which Rik appeared. When he saw them, he stopped. "Miss Keeler," he said. "We finished serving, so I wanted to know if you were gonna talk to the men."

Keeler glanced back at McCoy for what seemed like a momentary appraisal, then told Rik, "No, not tonight. Maybe you can play your banjo for them, though."

"Yes, ma'am," Rik said, and he headed back the way he'd come. A moment later, the door closed.

As Keeler turned back toward McCoy, he decided that he'd rather not continue their discussion standing in the hall. "Here, let's go sit," he said, opening the door to Keeler's office. He stepped back to allow her to go by, then trailed her inside. Moving past her to the desk, he reversed the chair there and held it out for her. She sat down, smoothing her gray skirt beneath her as she did so. McCoy closed the door, tossed the contemporary shirt and pants he'd picked out onto the cot, then took a seat beside the clothes.

"Miss Keeler," he began, "when I first came here and told you that I couldn't let them find me, when I told you that I was the senior medical officer aboard a ship, I was delusional." He knew that she would measure every word he said now, and so he determined to adhere as closely as he possibly could to the truth. "I really am a physician, though," he went on. "Before I ended up here, I accidentally injected myself with a powerful drug. You saw how it affected me."

A crease split Keeler's brow as she studied him, her eyes narrowing slightly. "Accidentally?" she asked, her skepticism plain.

"Yes," McCoy said, and recollecting the level of medical technology in this time, added, "I fell on top of a syringe."

"If that's what really happened and you've recovered now," she said, "then why do you want to stay here in the mission? Why don't you simply go home?"

McCoy consciously forced himself not to blink, not to look away, as he asserted what would be the most critical of his lies. Fortunately, even this fabrication did not stray too far from reality. "Because I don't remember how to get home," he said. "I recall the accident, and who I am, but not much more."

"Yet you remembered John Donne," Keeler countered, "and your friend who reads classic literature."

"And how to treat your wounds," McCoy appended to the list, reminding Keeler—perhaps not so subtly—that he might have saved her life last night. He moved on quickly, though, not dwelling on the point. "Amnesia is a problematic thing," he said.

Keeler stood up, and for a second, he thought that she might leave, her willingness to believe him at an end. But she walked not to the door, but over to the filing cabinets beside it. "Then why not go to the police?" she asked. "Let them help you find your way home?"

"Maybe I will," McCoy lied again. He could not imagine a turn of events in this time in which he'd seek out people in positions of authority. "But I think that two of my friends will come looking for me. Since this is the first place I remember being after the accident, I figured that they'd most likely be able to track me down here."

Keeler walked back over to the desk chair, sat down again, and leaned toward McCoy. "I want to believe you," she claimed. "But could it be that you don't want to go to the police because you intentionally injected yourself?" McCoy sensed that their conversation had reached a decisive point, and he thought he saw a means of regaining Keeler's trust.

"No, the injection was accidental," he said unequivocally. "I remember that very clearly. I just can't recall anything that happened between then and when I showed up here." He paused, waiting for Keeler to draw the obvious conclusion.

"But then you don't know whether you've done anything wrong," she said.

"No, I suppose I don't," McCoy admitted. "In normal situations, I'm not the sort of person who would get into trouble, but under the influence of the drug . . . I don't know."

Keeler straightened and leaned back in her chair. "All right, Doctor," she said, with an intonation that conveyed at least a conditional acceptance of what he'd told her. "You may stay here for the time being."

"Thank you," he said.

Keeler stood up and moved to the door. "But if your friends don't find you here before too long," she said, "and if you still can't recall where your home is, then I think you should reconsider going to the police. Even if you have done something wrong, that would be the proper thing to do."

"I will," he said as positively as he could, though he knew he would never take any such action.

Keeler seemed to accept this, then said, "You should come out and get something to eat."

McCoy nodded. "After I change out of these dirty clothes," he said. Keeler left the office, closing the door behind her.

McCoy sat quietly for several minutes, pondering his dilemma. After a while, he got to his feet and removed his Starfleet uniform, dropping the soiled garments onto the floor. Then he pulled on the clothes he'd gotten from Keeler.

As he buttoned the shirt, he wandered over toward the window. He split the pair of plain brown curtains hanging there, sweeping them open, the rings from which they hung rattling along a metal rod. A narrow alley bordered this side of the mission, leaving only the brick wall of the neighboring building visible through the window.

McCoy looked out on the limited vista for a while, then headed out of the office to once more take his place among the homeless.

FIVE

2267

The mist enfolded him, promising concealment and a soft embrace, but delivering neither. Time stopped as tendrils of the living cloud twined through the universe and held it fast. Flowing, gray-white wisps constricted everywhere, everywhen, squeezing and then strangling each glimmer of existence. Irony steeped the crystallized moment: he'd slipped into the fog to escape the raging murderers, only to find death lurking there as well. Helpless, he waited for eternity to collapse and crush him with the weight of centuries.

And then time exploded, spewing days and decades, minutes and millennia, instants and eons. Thrown back into being, he found himself in a netherworld, dark and hard. Sinister shapes moved in the blackness, and though the demon mist had gone for now, the killers had returned to pursue him. Panic filled his soul, providing an adrenaline surge that got his feet moving. He hastened through the night, searching for others in his position, seeking out allies.

And found one: a bald little man, desperation dripping from him like sweat. He grilled the man, demanding to know how they'd been trapped here. They needed to escape before the assassins found them again.

But already it was too late. The murderers had closed in, encircling them. He wouldn't surrender, though, wouldn't let them simply take him down.

He whirled, the sleek, hot steel of a blade suddenly in his hand. The killers dispensed death, and he would bring it back to them. He thrust the knife forward, plunging it into yielding flesh and breaking bone. The mangled body fell, done, its life force pouring onto the pavement in crimson rivulets. He looked at the face of his enemy, at the one he had vanquished, and saw the little bald man, his only ally, now dead. He threw his head back and—

McCoy awoke with a start, the echoes of his own agonized voice still alive in his ears. He lay on his back, in darkness, his muscles taut. Disoriented, he couldn't remember falling asleep or where he had done so. The phantom figures that had haunted the periphery of his dreams, though still unseen, now seemed unsettlingly close, as though pushing in on him through the surrounding black.

In silence, McCoy waited and listened, trying to attune himself to his setting. He detected nothing at first, no sounds, no movement, until at last he became aware of a low vibration—a *familiar* vibration—thrumming beneath his hands. He flexed his fingers and felt fabric clutched in his fists. *I'm in my bed,* he thought. *In my cabin, aboard the* Enterprise.

Leaning on his side, McCoy reached blindly for the lighting

control in the nearby bulkhead. He found it and brought the overhead panels up one-quarter. The illumination, though muted, pushed away the artificial night, and with it, the specters that had accompanied his slumber.

McCoy swung his feet over and onto the deck, sitting up on the edge of his bed. He peered about this half of the cabin and saw nothing out of the ordinary, but only the few items with which he'd adorned his sleeping area. Centered on the shelf above the bed sat eight volumes of ancient medical texts he'd brought with him from Earth, bookended by a pair of even older *rintu* carvings from Capella IV. On the end of the same shelf stood three vintage apothecary bottles—cobalt blue, sky blue, and yellow—that his daughter had given him a few years ago. A Kaferian dieffenbachia, with purple-patterned white leaves, decorated the corner, reaching up more than a meter from the deck.

Everything in its place, McCoy thought, and then archly realized, *Everything but me.* Since returning to the ship after his sojourn into the past, he'd spent most of the succeeding six days here in his quarters, visiting sickbay only so that Dr. Sanchez could monitor his recovery. Ignacio had cleared all the members of the landing party—but for the captain, who'd so far refused to report for examination—of any medical effects of having been down on the planet, or in his and Spock's case, of having traveled through the portal and back in time. But though McCoy had been issued a clean bill of health in that regard, Dr. Sanchez had detected trace amounts of cordrazine still in his body. Ignacio's prognosis had been that it would require a total of seven to ten days for the drug to fully flush from his system, and for its aftereffects to diminish completely.

McCoy glanced at the chronometer atop the half-wall separating the two sections of his cabin. The first shift had just ended, he saw, which meant that he'd fallen asleep for about an hour. He now recalled lying down, though he hadn't initially intended to doze. He'd been resting all week, though, and his long walk in the arboretum this afternoon had been the first significant exercise he'd had in that time; the stroll had tired him out more than he'd expected. Still, he felt good, and—

The door signal buzzed, and McCoy automatically looked again at the chronometer. The time told him who waited in the corridor: Tonia. Since his cordrazine ordeal and her visit to see him in sickbay, she'd stopped by his quarters often. McCoy appreciated her concern, but worried that her feelings for him had deepened so much that she would end up getting hurt. While he cared a great deal for Tonia, he knew that they wouldn't stay together long-term, that they ultimately weren't well matched. Yes, they enjoyed each other's company, shared similar views and a common sense of humor, communicated easily and well with each other, and took pleasure in many of the same pursuits, but . . . well, he simply knew that he wasn't the right man for her. Almost a decade younger, Tonia needed a man closer to her own age, even if she didn't realize that yet. He suspected that she might finally be coming to that awareness, though, since her stops in to see him during the last couple of days had become shorter and less frequent. Still, she hadn't failed to come by his cabin each day immediately after the end of her duty shift, and so she obviously waited outside right now for him to answer the door.

McCoy stood up from the bed, noticing that he still wore the black exercise pants and short-sleeved pullover he'd thrown on before his excursion to the arboretum. He quickly reached for the lighting control and brought the level up fully. "Come in," he called, gazing through the decorative red lattice that reached from the top of the half-wall up to the overhead. The door withdrew into the bulkhead, revealing not Tonia standing beyond it, but Spock. He carried a data slate in one hand.

"Spock," McCoy said as the first officer entered the cabin. The tall, lean Vulcan stopped just inside the door, which eased closed behind him. "I hope you're here to tell me I can finally go back to being a doctor aboard this ship."

"In part, yes, I am," Spock said. "Doctor Sanchez reports that his examination today revealed your body to be completely free of cordrazine. Based on the rest of your readings, he concludes that you have recovered sufficiently to warrant a return to your duties."

"Good," McCoy said, emerging from the sleeping area and into the other section of the cabin. He swung around the half-wall and over to his desk. "I was starting to go a little stir-crazy from spending so much time in here." He raised both hands to indicate the confines of his quarters. Spock said nothing, and

McCoy saw that the reserved expression he normally wore appeared more serious than usual. "Is there something else you wanted to talk to me about?" McCoy asked, suspecting that Spock might want to discuss the captain's seclusion since their time in Earth's past.

"There is, Doctor," Spock said. He walked deeper into the room, until he stood across the desk from McCoy. The first officer peered down at his slate for a moment. "I've been studying the region of space through which our upcoming course will take us." McCoy recalled the vibration he'd felt when he'd woken up a few minutes ago, which he'd recognized as an effect of the *Enterprise*'s warp drive, but only now did he consider that the ship must have departed the Guardian's world. He knew that the *Appomattox* had arrived there earlier today, to provide the military presence Captain Kirk had requested from Starfleet. "While doing so," Spock continued, "I encountered a reference to the Levinius star system."

"I'm not familiar with it," McCoy said.

"Nor was I," Spock said. "Two centuries ago, the civilization on the fifth planet was completely destroyed, with evidence suggesting that the population had been swept by a form of mass insanity. Several decades later, a similar event appears to have occurred on Theta Cygni Twelve, wiping out that society."

"What?" McCoy said. He sat down at his desk, considering the information Spock had brought to him. The destruction of an entire civilization—let alone two—shocked him, despite that he'd never even been aware of their existences until now. Still, the accounts seemed reminiscent of another, more recent incident. "I don't know anything about Theta Cygni Twelve either," he said, "but what you're describing sounds a lot like what Starfleet Medical believes happened not that long ago on . . . was it Ingraham B?"

"Yes," Spock said. He turned the slate around, set it down on the desk in front of McCoy, then sat down opposite him. Paragraphs of text marched down the screen, inset with a picture of a cloud-covered, blue-green world, all beneath the heading REPORT ON LOSS OF INGRAHAM B COLONY. "Two years ago, the settlement there went silent. It was thought that their communications equipment had failed, but when a freighter crew arrived several months later, they found half of the colonists missing and the other half murdered."

"I remember reading a précis of Starfleet Medical's findings," McCoy said. "Necropsies revealed nothing unusual about the dead, but the variety and brutality of the murders, coupled with the physical state of the colony and the number of missing, led to the conclusion of collective psychosis."

"Affirmative," Spock said. "All records at the settlement had been destroyed, so there could be no direct confirmation, but the verdict of mass insanity is supported by the known facts."

McCoy took in this data and tried to process it all into a narrative. "Are you suggesting that the destruction on the three planets is related?" he asked.

"I am," Spock said. "But not only on those three planets." He reached forward and plucked a long metal stylus from where it attached magnetically to the front of the slate. Leaning over the desk, he tapped at a series of menus along the top of the screen, until another page of text appeared. McCoy read the title: ARCHEOLOGICAL FINDINGS IN THE BETA PORTOLAN SYSTEM. "Scientists have recently uncovered the ruins of ancient civilizations on two planets there. Although the archeologists offered no reasons for the losses of those societies, I have reviewed records of the excavations, and they are consistent with those of Levinius Five, Theta Cygni Twelve, and Ingraham B."

"And all in this same region of space?" McCoy asked.

"Yes," Spock said, "but not *just* in this region." Again, Spock touched the stylus to the menus at the top of the slate's screen. This time, an image of a star field appeared. On it, labels identified the four star systems about which Spock had spoken.

"They're virtually in a straight line," McCoy noted, a knot of anxiety forming in his stomach. "Is there another inhabited world along that route?" But he knew that Spock wouldn't have come to him had that not been the case.

"Deneva," Spock said. The name struck a chord with McCoy, though he could not quite place it. "It is an Earth colony, established a century ago, originally as a freighting-line base. It has a population of more than one million."

"My god," McCoy said. "And you think that whatever caused the mass insanity on those other worlds will also strike Deneva."

"It would be imprudent not to consider the possibility," Spock said.

"Have you told Jim about this?" McCoy asked.

"Yes," Spock said. "He immediately attempted to contact the colony, without result. The *Enterprise* is headed there now."

"I see," McCoy said, the terrible details Spock had revealed to him now swirling through his mind, along with the frightening prospect that another civilization might be facing the same danger.

"While we travel to Deneva," Spock said, "the captain wants the medical department to evaluate the data we have, and to determine any possible causes."

McCoy nodded. "Of course," he said. "But the notion of collective psychosis isn't rooted in biology, but in psychosocial forces: the political situation in Germany leading to Earth's second world war, for example, or the suicide attacks on Catulla. For there to be a single cause for something like this, that happened over such a long period of time and to disparate societies, doesn't make sense."

"And so we must work to formulate a scientific theory that does," Spock said.

"Of course," McCoy said. He laid a hand alongside the data slate. "I'll review all of the details and get the medical staff working on it right away."

"I'll inform the captain," Spock said, rising to his feet. "Perhaps our efforts will help prevent a disaster from befalling the inhabitants of Deneva."

After the first officer had gone, McCoy looked down again at the image of the star field. *Deneva,* he thought, the name still seeming familiar to him. And then he thought he remembered: *Isn't Jim's brother stationed on Deneva?*

As he lifted the stylus and began to study the information Spock had collected, a chill shook him.

SIX

1930

"McCoy," she repeated. "Leonard McCoy." Edith leaned forward in the unsteady chair, its uneven legs causing it to teeter slightly as she shifted her weight. She looked at the policeman on the other side of the desk and waited as he shuffled through a sheaf of papers. Around her, a cacophony of voices fell and rose, ebbing and flowing like a tide of sound in this large, desk-filled room at the 13th Precinct.

"No, ma'am," the officer said at last. A tall man, with broad shoulders and a square jaw, he wore not a uniform, but street clothes. He'd introduced himself as Detective Wright when the desk sergeant had brought Edith over from the police office's entrance hall. "There's no report of a 'Leonard McCoy' goin' missin'." His New York City accent dropped the *r*s in the second syllables of *report* and *Leonard*.

Edith leaned back in the chair, and it wobbled in that direction. It had been more than two weeks now since Dr. McCoy had first shown up at the mission, and though Edith had spoken with him often, she still knew virtually nothing about him. He answered almost every question of a personal nature with a claim not to remember the details of his life, although he'd steadfastly maintained his recollection of his accidental drug overdose. Together with McCoy's unwillingness to move out of the mission or to go to the police for help, as well as his conviction that friends would arrive to bring him back home, what little Edith had learned of the doctor did not seem quite right. She did not even know whether to believe his assertion of being a physician, which seemed like such an outrageous contention for a man in his circumstances. And yet his obvious intelligence and knowledge, and his gentle, caring manner, bespoke a man who indeed could have received medical training.

"Are there any doctors who are missing?" Edith asked the detective.

The burly policeman looked at her with undisguised annoyance. "This man's a doctor?" Wright asked.

"Yes, I believe so," Edith said. She could hear the uncertainty in her own voice.

Detective Wright dropped his hands onto his desk, the stack of papers he'd been perusing still held between them. "Ma'am," he said, the single word spoken with exaggerated patience, "if you want me to help you, you need to give me all the information you have about this 'McCoy' fella."

"Yes, of course," Edith said, but even as she agreed with the detective, she debated with herself how much she should say. While she had serious doubts about McCoy's immediate past, she also recognized that, during his time at the mission, he'd acted as a model citizen. In addition to possibly saving her life, he'd worked every day but Sundays since his recovery, either in the soup kitchen or at a couple of other places where Edith had gotten him employment. The efforts he'd put forth, no matter the job, had been exemplary. His overall demeanor had been pleasant and helpful. Still, she remained concerned about his secretiveness, which she was not sure could truly be attributed to the amnesia he purported to be suffering.

"This man," Edith told Wright, "this Leonard McCoy, is staying and working at the mission. He says that he can't remember anything about his life but for his name and that he's a physician." She described McCoy's appearance for Wright, as well as the slight but unmistakable drawl of his speech. She paused and took a breath, again deciding what more to reveal to the detective. She had to admit that, despite what might be McCoy's evasiveness, she genuinely liked him. At the same time, if he'd done something wrong, whether he recalled doing so or not, she knew that she needed to find that out.

Edith leaned forward again, and her chair once more tilted onto its short leg. She looked at Detective Wright with a steady gaze, and told him everything she knew about Leonard McCoy. She also told him of all the concerns she had about the doctor.

"All right, ma'am," the detective said. "Let me see what I can find out." He pushed back in his chair and stood up to an imposing height. "This could take some time," he said. The bundle of papers now in one hand, Wright crossed the busy room, over to a long row of wooden filing cabinets along the right-hand wall. Edith watched him open several drawers, pulling out quite a few files and poring over their contents. When he'd finished, he walked over to another desk and spoke with an officer there, then disappeared through a door in the far wall.

Almost an hour after he'd left her sitting alone, Detective Wright returned to his desk, and told her everything he'd learned about Dr. Leonard McCoy. It took no time at all.

He strode through the night at a brisk pace, despite how long he'd already been out walking. His Starfleet boots—though he now possessed several articles of contemporary clothing, he hadn't yet been able to replace his footwear—his boots clocked noisily along the wooden planks of the Brooklyn Bridge walkway. The venerable structure, nearly fifty years old already in 1930, would survive into McCoy's time, although he knew that a portion of the eastern tower would have to be rebuilt in the twenty-second century after the *Caledonia* disaster.

A breeze had picked up and now blew cold over the East River. McCoy pulled his navy blue pea coat close about him, flipping the collar up around his neck. He had once before in his life walked the Brooklyn Bridge, though in distinctly warmer conditions. He and Jocelyn had spent part of their honeymoon in New York City, during the summer months, and they had decided to watch the sunset from the landmark. McCoy could not now recall whether they'd actually succeeded in doing so, though he dimly remembered that an argument had sent them back to their hotel at some point during the evening. Certainly the seeds of their eventual divorce had already been sown by then—had in fact been present almost from the very beginning of their turbulent relationship.

Tucking the unpleasant memories away, McCoy stopped walking just past the western tower, having no designs on crossing even half of the one-and-three-quarter-kilometer extent. He took hold of the nearby railing with a gloved hand and peered upward. Two paired sets of suspensions cables reached down in spiderweb-like configurations to support the bridge's dual spans. The elevated pedestrian walkway stretched above and between the two automobile roadways and train tracks, with nothing below it but the river.

Although it had flurried earlier today, the sky had partially cleared as night had fallen. Clusters of stars now shined here and there, visible through broken fields of low, knobby clouds. McCoy picked out those systems to which he'd journeyed: Rigel, Altair, Dramia, and others. He'd never really felt a sense of wanderlust, joining Starfleet less as a way of traveling the galaxy, and more as a means of getting away from his life on Earth. Right now, though, he longed to return to the *Enterprise,* and he wondered how long it would be before he once more had the opportunity to roam the stars.

A few days ago, McCoy had begun taking these long night-time walks. His physical condition had steadily improved during his time at the mission, and after about ten days, he'd felt completely recovered from his bout with cordrazine. He'd started his nightly strolls simply to unwind after ten- and twelve-hour days of manual labor, but his thoughts invariably drifted to Jim and Spock.

Where are they? McCoy asked himself now, as he'd done so many times already. He remained convinced that the captain would stop at nothing to rescue him, not only for McCoy's sake, but in order to prevent the alteration of history. To that end, McCoy made sure always to pay close attention to his surroundings, vigilant for the appearance somewhere of his friends. He also puzzled over the possibility of finding on his own a method of getting himself back to his proper time. *If only I knew how I got here.*

McCoy dropped his gaze from the sky and down to the wooden walkway upon which he stood. Between the slats, he could see the whitecaps of the choppy water fifty meters below. The wind carried a susurrant sound that could have been that of the water, or simply that of the wind itself.

The walkway suddenly began to rumble, and McCoy peered toward Brooklyn in time to see a train appear as it arched across the bridge's highest point. The subway lines ran across the river beside the automobile roadways, below and on either side of the pedestrian thoroughfare. As he watched the train pass, he pulled a glove from one hand and reached into his coat pocket. He found a small cache of coins there and thought that he should probably pull out a nickel, walk back to the Manhattan side of the bridge, and take the subway up toward Twenty-first Street. He'd been out walking for hours now, and he felt cold and tired.

McCoy replaced his glove on his hand and started back across the bridge. It surprised him that he'd been in the past now for as long as he had. He didn't pretend to understand anything at all about time travel, but a particular aspect of his situation gnawed at him. He believed that Jim would take whatever action necessary to bring him back to his proper time, presumably utilizing the same method that had brought McCoy here in the first place. If for some reason that proved impossible, though, McCoy knew that there existed other means of traveling into the past. Almost a year ago, the *Enterprise* crew had needed to cold-start the warp engines as the ship had spiraled down to the planet Psi 2000; the experimental process had worked, but had sent them into a time warp, and three days back in time. And just a couple of months ago, pulling away from a high-gravity black star had caused a slingshot effect that had sent the *Enterprise* hurtling three hundred years into the past, where they had encountered Captain Christopher. So several methods of time travel did exist.

But whatever the means the captain employed to journey backward in time in order to retrieve him, wouldn't he go to the earliest point at which he could do so? McCoy had arrived in Earth's past in 1930. In any rescue attempt, wouldn't Jim travel to 1930 as well, and not to 1931 or '35 or '40?

Unless he doesn't know I've gone back in time, McCoy thought. If that was true, then he stood no chance of being recovered. But as McCoy watched the lights of the subway train recede into Manhattan, he realized another possibility: perhaps Jim knew that he'd gone back in time, but didn't know precisely to when or to where. If the captain didn't know whether McCoy had ended up in 1930 or 1066 or 1000 BCE, or in New York City or Hastings or Rome, then how could Jim possibly locate him?

All at once, McCoy understood an even simpler formulation of his predicament. Even if the captain knew to travel to New York in 1930, how would he go about finding McCoy in a city of several million human beings? Landing parties, clad in period clothing, scouring the city? How long would that take, and would there even be a guarantee of success? McCoy had chosen to stay at the 21st Street Mission because he'd assumed that he'd arrived in the past somewhere near there, but he didn't know that with certainty.

McCoy strengthened his pace, feeling renewed vigor. Finally, he'd found a general course of action to take. He didn't yet know how he would do so, but he had to find a way to send up a flare to Jim—a flare that would cross the centuries.

SEVEN

2267

Captain James T. Kirk led the landing party—Spock, Mr. Scott, Yoeman Zahra, and a security guard, Crewman Tiroli—across the pedestrian plaza, traversing the brickwork amid tall buildings and large marble statuary. Several of the abstract sculptures had been damaged, he saw, and one of them had been toppled from its base, crashing to the ground and crumbling into gray-white chunks and shards of polished stone. Spock had reported such indiscriminate destruction throughout the life-sciences building that housed the laboratory of Kirk's brother, Sam, and which the landing party had searched from top to bottom after Kirk had earlier transported back up to the ship. They'd also spied indications that something had penetrated the structure at a number of points, but had yet to locate the "horrible things" of which Aurelan had spoken.

Aurelan, Kirk thought. He saw in his mind the image of his sister-in-law arching her back and crying out in agony, until she suddenly fell in silence onto the biobed, her life stolen from her. When the *Enterprise* had first arrived here at Deneva, sensor scans had revealed the expected number of human inhabitants on the planet, but had showed almost all of them indoors and curiously quiescent, as though in hiding. When Kirk had taken the first landing party down to the surface, he'd guided them immediately to his brother's lab. They'd found Aurelan hysterical, her husband dead, and her son, Peter, unconscious. Kirk had accompanied his sister-in-law and nephew up to the *Enterprise* sickbay so that McCoy and his medical staff could examine and attempt to treat them. Right now, Peter remained unconscious, but still alive; his mother had not been so fortunate.

Before Aurelan had died, though, she'd struggled to speak with Kirk, fighting through terrible, as-yet-unexplained pain to get her words out. She'd talked of "things" brought to Deneva by visitors from Ingraham B, things that had taken control of the Denevan population and forced them to begin building ships. Sensors had so far detected no harmful life-forms on the planet, but Kirk intended to find out what had killed his brother and sister-in-law, and what obviously still threatened Peter and the rest of the colonists.

As he and the other *Enterprise* personnel marched through the plaza, trying to locate the source of a peculiar buzzing sound, Kirk still had trouble accepting that Sam and Aurelan were gone. Before today, he hadn't seen them in almost two years, since they and their three sons had visited him in the days before he'd first taken command of the *Enterprise*. He felt grateful that two of his nephews resided not on Deneva, but on the Canopus planet, but he wondered how he could possibly tell Alexander and Julius that their parents had been killed. And if Peter died as well—

Enough, Kirk rebuked himself. He would have time later to cope with the losses he'd suffered. Right now, he had a duty to make sense of the desperate situation on Deneva, and to resolve it. Though Doctor McCoy could not determine the cause of Aurelan's condition or death, a cause clearly had to exist. If she could expire so quickly, then so too could any or all of the colonists. Already, ship's sensors indicated that several hundred humans on the planet had died since the *Enterprise* had assumed orbit. More than a million lives remained not only at risk, but at *immediate* risk.

Ahead of Kirk and the landing party stood a ten-story edifice of white stone and glass. As the *Enterprise* crew drew nearer, the buzzing they'd been tracking grew louder. Spock and the others had first heard the odd drone only a few minutes ago, when they'd completed their recon of the life-sciences building and had emerged back into the daylight. Just before they'd set out to search for the source of the unfamiliar sound, Kirk had rejoined them from the ship.

Now, they approached what appeared to be a side entrance to an office building. The single door there hung at an angle, the upper two-thirds of the glass in its misshapen frame shattered. Kirk reached for the handle, but as he attempted to pull the door open, it wedged against the jamb. He stepped back and considered the situation, and then in a moment mixed of necessity and grief, he kicked forward, shattering the remaining glass. He waited a few seconds, listening, but perceived no change in the buzzing coming from within.

Kirk glanced back at the crew, making eye contact with each of them, then proceeded forward through the broken door. He held his boxy, type-one phaser at the ready, the weapon set to force three, to kill. He'd already instructed the members of the landing party that they would take no chances in defending themselves; if they encountered any of the things about which Aurelan had warned, they would give it no quarter.

Inside, the bright sunshine gave way to a dim, unlighted interior. Kirk peered upward through the shadows and saw the lighting panels in the ceiling casting no illumination. Ship's sensors had shown sporadic power outages throughout the city, and this building might have been one of those left dark.

Slowly but steadily, Kirk conducted the landing party through several corridors, pursuing the source of the buzzing. Their path took them along the perimeter of the ground floor, and daylight filtered in here and there through the curtained glass partitions of outer offices that they passed. As they progressed through the gauzy atmosphere, the drone they'd followed here clarified into a collection of individual hums, like the noises of single bees in the group voice of a hive. Kirk's skin felt alive with movement, a visceral reaction to the insectlike sounds.

Up ahead, the right-side wall of the corridor ended. Kirk cautiously made his way past that point, and saw a short stairway descending into a common. On the lower level, beside the steps, a square of low, white concrete benches bordered a small reflecting pool. An avant-garde sculpture twisted up out of the water in one corner. Bushes and a few undersized trees ornamented the periphery of the area in green. A pair of corridors, parallel to the first, led out of the common in either direction, and a rectangular arch in the far wall opened onto a small grassy area. The walkway upon which they stood continued forward past the stairway, edged by a railing, and as Kirk headed down the steps, he pointed Crewman Tiroli in that direction.

The buzzing resonated in the enclosed space, echoes making it seem as though the sounds came from everywhere at once, rendering it impossible to ascertain from which direction they truly originated. Kirk padded down into the common, Spock, Scotty, and Zahra following behind him. They spread out in the small space, their eyes searching all about for whatever made the many hums.

Kirk turned around to his left, gazing at the walls of the place, but then he heard behind him a different sound: not a buzz, but a wet squeak, like suction being released. He whirled toward the noise and spotted something clinging to the underside of the archway . . . actually, *three* things. They looked like nothing he'd ever seen: flat, irregular shapes, perhaps a meter around and a few centimeters through, thickest in the center, with no visible organs or structures. The uneven bodies trembled with tiny movements, and their surfaces rose and fell intermittently, as though from erratic respiration.

"Spock," Kirk called. The first officer stepped up beside him at once, and the captain heard Scotty and Zahra join them as well. Kirk studied the creatures, his phaser aimed at the one in the middle.

Without warning, the creature on the left dropped from the arch and swooped toward the landing party. Kirk ducked, and it passed just over his head. "Form a ring," he ordered, wanting the *Enterprise* crew to position themselves with their backs to each other so that they could protect the group from attack. Tiroli remained alone on the upper walkway, but he would have an advantage from the higher position.

As Spock, Scotty, and Zahra maneuvered around, the creature

dived at them again. This time, Kirk heard a rush of air as it darted past. It flew quickly but awkwardly; that it could fly at all seemed a mystery, considering its unwieldy body and that it not only did not have wings, but possessed no appendages of any sort.

The creature swept back around, and another of its kind slipped from the arch and joined it. One arced downward, and then the other. Kirk bent low again and then saw the first creature climb almost to the ceiling, where it alighted at the top of the wall. The second creature plunged by once more and then it too took a position high up on another wall. Amid the constant buzzing, Kirk saw an opportunity in the moment of sudden still-ness.

"Fire," he said, and he took aim on the creature nearest to him, which still clung to the bottom of the archway. He de-pressed the firing pad, and red energy leaped from his weapon. Behind him, the whine of other phasers joined his, the shrill sound momentarily overwhelming the insectile noise all around.

Seconds elapsed, and Kirk continued firing, the intense red beam striking the creature directly at its center. Finally, he eased his thumb from the trigger. The rest of the crew stopped firing as well. The creature fell from the arch onto the grass below it, its formerly hidden side now up, showing smooth and flat.

Kirk peered around for the other creatures that had attacked. Though they no longer perched atop the walls, neither had they fallen onto the floor below. They'd evidently taken cover in the corridors extending away from the common. The buzzing, Kirk noted, had diminished in volume.

Looking back toward the grassy area, Kirk saw several other creatures fly away, having apparently been hidden from view on the other side of the arch. Sensing a lull in the danger, he moved quickly over to the one fallen creature, the rest of the landing party coming with him. Kirk squatted down just before the grass, but kept alert for another assault. Next to him, Spock worked his tricorder.

"Incredible," the first officer declared, and Kirk looked down at the creature. As he watched, its smooth flat surface trans-formed, becoming uneven and bumpy, as though the side upon which it landed had pushed through to become the visible side.

Bits of its glistening body still quivered, and its thickest part gradually rose and fell once. "Not only should it have been destroyed by our phasers, it does not even register on my tricorder." That fact, Kirk understood, explained why neither the ship's sensors not the landing party's tricorders had detected the existence of the creatures.

"Captain," Yeoman Zahra said, "it doesn't even look real." Kirk had to agree. The creature resembled nothing more closely than a melted piece of plastic.

"It is not life as we know or understand it," Spock said. "Yet it is obviously alive, it exists—"

"And it can bear up under full phaser power," Kirk said, realizing that, even if this one creature had been stunned, the landing party's weapons provided little ability for them to protect themselves. The creatures' apparent resistance to phaser fire might also account for why the Deneva colony had been unable to ward off the invasion of their world.

"Captain," Spock said, "I suggest we risk taking it aboard." Kirk did not like that idea, any more than he liked being in an enclosed space and so near to these creatures.

"It's too close in here, it may be a trap," he said, deciding that he needed to protect his crew. They'd come here seeking some notion of what had happened on Deneva, and having found the creatures, Kirk wanted to withdraw to safety and formulate a plan of action. "Let's move out."

The landing party headed back toward the stairs, Tiroli leading them back the way they'd come, his phaser pistol held out before him. The security guard ascended the steps, Scotty and Zahra behind him, Kirk and Spock in the rear. Tiroli quickly peered into the corridor through which they'd entered, then strode into it. As Scotty and Zahra followed, Kirk suddenly heard the squeaking of the creatures again. Before he could react, a loud smack filled the air, like the sound of flesh against flesh, and Spock grunted. Kirk spun around to see him stagger sideways, the first officer brushing the wall as he lurched backward down the stairway. As Spock fell onto his side, Kirk saw the creature on his back.

"Spock," he called. "Spock!" The normally stoic Vulcan groaned again and again, his voice pained as he dropped his tricorder. With unexpected speed, he rolled up onto his hands and knees, reaching behind him in obvious desperation to remove the creature from his back. Kirk reached for it as well, dropping to his own knees and grabbing for the edges of the alien, curling his fingers around the thin fringes of its body. It was slick and gelatinous, and Kirk felt himself recoil at the sensation, but he refused to let go. He pulled at the creature, and met strong resistance. Climbing back to his feet for leverage, he heaved again, and this time the thing came free. He hurled it aside, hoping that his efforts had not been in vain.

"It's gone," he told Spock, grabbing his shoulders, trying to help him up, trying to make sure that he hadn't been harmed. "Can you stand?" he asked. "Spock, are you all right?"

He didn't respond.

Kirk dropped to one knee and reached an arm around his friend's shoulder and chest, hauling him upward. Spock's eyes stared straight ahead, but appeared unseeing. His arms had spread as Kirk had lifted him, and now they hung in that position. All will seemed to have drained out of Spock.

A chirp sounded. Even as Kirk recognized the telltale communicator activation signal, he jerked his head around to search for the creature that had attacked Spock. It lay several meters away on the floor of the common, twitching minutely.

"Scott to *Enterprise*," Kirk heard the chief engineer say.

"*Enterprise, Sulu here*," came the response.

"Mister Sulu, we have a medical emergency," Scotty said. "Notify sickbay, and beam up the landing party immediately."

"*Right away*," Sulu said, his tone reflecting the urgency of the request. In just seconds, the thrum of the transporter escalated around them. The gold motes of dematerialization filled Kirk's eyes, and then he felt the hard, ridged surface of a targeting pad beneath his knee. Gently, he lowered Spock down to a supine position.

"Captain, Doctor McCoy is on his way," said Lieutenant Kyle, the engineering and services officer now manning the transporter.

Around Kirk, the rest of the landing party dismounted the platform. "Your orders, Captain?" Scotty asked.

Kirk rose and stepped down onto the deck, where he faced

Scotty, Zahra, and Tiroli. "Maintain orbit," he said, recalling something that Aurelan had said to him earlier. "My sister-in-law talked about the creatures forcing the colonists to build ships for them. Keep the planet under constant surveillance, and if any ships try to reach space . . ." Kirk paused, uncomfortable with the order he was about to issue, but knowing he had little other choice. "If any ships try to reach orbit, shoot them down. We cannot allow these creatures to move beyond Deneva."

"Aye, Captain," Scotty said gravely, and he turned and headed for the bridge.

"Yeoman Zahra, Mister Tiroli," Kirk said, "report to the exo-biology lab. Give a complete description of what we encountered to Doctor M'Benga. See if he's got any theories about any of this." Zahra and Tiroli acknowledged their orders and left.

Kirk looked over at Lieutenant Kyle, standing behind the transporter console, then back at Spock. He saw no change in the first officer's vacant stare. Every few seconds, Spock's body shuddered and he emitted a tortured groan.

"Where's McCoy?" Kirk said under his breath, deeply concerned for Spock. He squatted down and studied his face. Though he appeared conscious, Kirk could see no hint of his personality there. This, it seemed perfectly clear, must have been what had happened to the colonists . . . to Peter, to Aurelan, to Sam.

Kirk felt numb. Spock lay before him, possibly dying, just as Peter also lay dying in sickbay. Sam and Aurelan had already gone.

And Edith, he added, despite fighting to keep the thought away. All the universe had been put right when he had prevented Bones from saving Edith, but from that moment on, his own life had begun to unravel. How could he—

The doors to the transporter room opened with a swoosh, and Kirk turned to see McCoy entering with Nurse Chapel. Two orderlies, Althouse and Shaw, followed behind with an antigrav gurney. Kirk stood as McCoy walked over to him.

"What happened?" the doctor asked. He handed his medical pouch to the nurse, then unslung the medical tricorder hanging from his shoulder. As Kirk described the events that had just taken place, McCoy retrieved the small, cylindrical scanner from its compartment in the tricorder and examined Spock. "I'm getting many of the same readings I got from your sister-in-law and nephew," he said. "Excessive autonomic activity, severe pain, diminished reflexes, extreme stimulation of the nervous system, beta-band brainwaves even in an unconscious state—"

"Unconscious?" Kirk questioned, looking down at Spock's open eyes. "I know that Vulcans sometimes sleep that way," he said, "but—"

"Jim," McCoy said, "indications are that Spock is in a deep state of unconsciousness, just short of coma."

"What can you do for him, Bones?" Kirk asked.

"I don't know yet," McCoy said, "but there's no risk in moving him, so I want to examine where the alien struck his back." Kirk leaned down to help, but the doctor placed a hand on his arm and eased him out of the way. "Please, Jim," he said quietly, then called to Nurse Chapel for her assistance. Together, they turned Spock over. McCoy then held out his hand, and Chapel deposited a long-handled instrument in it. The doctor activated it, a short, fine red beam appearing between two nodes at its end. With it, McCoy sliced through Spock's uniform shirt.

As McCoy pulled the fabric away, Kirk stepped forward to look at Spock's back. He saw a half-dozen small spots, centered between his shoulder blades and arranged in a roughly hexagonal pattern. Ringed in the coppery green of Vulcan blood, they appeared to be puncture wounds.

McCoy raised his tricorder and its accompanying scanner, once more assessing Spock's physical condition. When he'd finished, he looked over at Kirk. "Jim, I'm going to have to operate."

"What is it?" Kirk asked.

"I don't know," McCoy said. "And I won't know until I can get inside Spock."

"Exploratory surgery," Kirk said, more statement than question.

"Yes," McCoy confirmed. "Spock told you that the aliens don't show up on sensors, and whatever this one's done to him, it doesn't show up on my tricorder either. But it clearly penetrated his skin, and it must have done something to him internally. I need to go in and see if I can find the damage it's done, and hopefully reverse it."

"Are there any other options?" Kirk asked.

"I don't think so, not for Spock," McCoy said. "I also think that this is the best chance we might have to discover just what the aliens have done to the colonists."

"All right, Doctor," Kirk said, feeling that events continued to spin out of control around him. "Do what you can."

McCoy moved out of the way and motioned to the orderlies. The shorter, gray-haired man and the taller, redheaded woman, both clad in blue medical-department jumpsuits, jockeyed the antigrav gurney up onto the transporter platform. They deftly rolled Spock onto his back again, then lifted him onto the gurney. As Chapel followed them toward the doors on the trip to sickbay, McCoy addressed Kirk.

"I'll keep you informed," the doctor told him. Kirk nodded and McCoy followed his staff out.

For a long moment, Kirk remained motionless, stilled by the anguish he felt. At last, he looked over at Lieutenant Kyle. "No one is to transport down to the planet without my authorization," he said. He recalled giving a similar order when the *Enterprise* had been orbiting the world of the Guardian. *Too late then,* he thought angrily, *and maybe too late now.* Without another word, he headed for the bridge, mindful of what he'd already lost, and of what might yet be taken from him.

They'd done it, McCoy told himself for perhaps the hundredth time. He stood in sickbay over the sleeping form of young Peter Kirk, but all indications of the alien life-form within the boy had vanished. The diagnostic readouts above the biobed all read within normal ranges, and the modified medical tricorder he operated showed no trace of the living tissue that one of the neural parasites had deposited inside Peter's body. According to the captain, the medical personnel sent down to Deneva from the ship had reported the same results observed throughout the colony.

Light, of all things, had been the solution. McCoy had operated on Spock and determined that the parasites attacked their humanoid victims by implanting tissue in their spinal columns.

Once present in a host body, the tissue grew very rapidly, twining throughout the nervous system in a manner far too complex for conventional surgery to remove.

Afterward, Spock had learned to manage the pain and had retrieved one of the aliens from the planet's surface. It had resembled nothing so much as an individual brain cell, and they'd concluded that the creatures, together with the tissue they embedded in humanoids, composed a greater organism, a vast hive-being connecting its component parts despite those parts not being in physical contact with each other.

Soon after, they'd discovered the creatures' susceptibility to light. A wavelength too short for the humanoid eye to perceive had proven lethal to the individual aliens, as well as to the tissue inserted into host bodies. But that determination—that imperceptible light destroyed the creatures—had come only after experiments with the visible spectrum.

The doors in the outer sickbay compartment whispered open, and McCoy turned to see Jim enter. The captain quickly made his way over to Peter's bedside. "Bones," he said, looking down at his nephew, "how is he?"

"Recuperating," McCoy said. "All of the alien tissue within him is gone." He raised the modified medical tricorder, intending to indicate the source of his assertion. Once they had established the vulnerability of the parasitic tissue to light, they had required a means of verifying its obliteration within humanoid hosts. Dr. M'Benga had figured out how to do that, and he'd worked with Scotty and the engineering staff to adjust the ship's inventory of medical tricorders accordingly. "He should make a complete physical recovery," McCoy concluded, trying not to linger over the omission of a mental prognosis for the boy.

Jim nodded. "Has he regained consciousness?" he asked.

"Briefly," McCoy reported. "A few hours ago. But his body's been traumatized, and he's physically exhausted. He needs to sleep."

"Of course," Jim said. "Did he ask about his parents?"

"No," McCoy said. "He was only awake for a minute or two. He didn't say much, other than to ask where he was and if he was all right."

Again, Jim nodded. He seemed distracted, and McCoy understood at least some of what must be occupying his mind. In addition to Jim dealing with his own grief, he would have to tell Peter and his two brothers that their parents had been killed.

And then there's Spock, McCoy thought, but immediately let the thought pass, not wanting to dwell on what had happened, not with Jim here. "What's the situation on the planet?" he asked. McCoy knew that specially configured satellites had been seeded in orbit about the Deneva in order to bathe its surface in light deadly to the aliens. Jim had also told him that the efforts had worked as planned, though not to what extent.

"As far as we can tell, all of the creatures are dead," Jim said. "Scotty's got teams modifying the sensors on the ship and down in the colony so we can make sure of that. If we find any creatures still alive, we'll use planetside transporters to beam them into a facility where they can be bombarded with light."

"What about the colonists?" McCoy asked.

"Most of them appear free of the creatures now," Jim said. "We're setting up the hospitals so that they can positively identify every colonist, living or dead, scan them for the parasite, and treat them if necessary. A search will be done for any individuals not accounted for."

"Do we know . . ." McCoy began, and then thought better of his question.

"How many died?" Jim finished for him, correctly inferring what he had been about to ask. "Approximately seventeen thousand so far. Most directly from the parasites, but some due to violence we believe was instigated by the creatures."

"Does Starfleet intend to—" McCoy began, but then Peter stirred on the biobed. McCoy watched as the boy's eyelids fluttered open. He still appeared very tired, but color had returned to his face.

"Peter," Jim said quietly, leaning in toward his nephew. "Peter, it's Jim. Your uncle."

"Jim?" the boy said, and he adjusted his head on the pillow to look in the captain's direction. His eyes took a moment to focus, and then he said, "Jim. What . . . what are you doing here? What happened?"

"It's all right, Peter," Jim said, lifting a hand to place it on his nephew's shoulder, an action clearly meant to reassure the boy. "*You're* all right."

"Okay," Peter said. Slowly, his eyes closed. McCoy thought that he'd fallen back to sleep, but then he dragged his lids open again. "Mom?" he said. "Dad?"

McCoy peered over at Jim, but the captain never took his gaze from his nephew. "They're . . ." he started uncertainly. He cleared his throat, then began again. "They're not here right now," Jim said, obviously wanting to wait until the boy had regained more of his strength before telling him what had happened to his parents.

"Peter," McCoy said. He waited until the boy had shifted his head to look up at him. "I'm Doctor McCoy," he said. "You're all right, but you need to sleep some more."

"Okay," Peter said, and he closed his eyes again. This time, they stayed closed.

Leaving the boy to rest, McCoy and Jim made their way into the outer medical compartment. "Keep me informed of his progress," Jim said as McCoy took a seat at the desk.

"I will, Jim," he said.

As the captain headed for the doors, McCoy turned to the monitor on the desk, grateful that he'd escaped having to answer the one question he dreaded right now. But then Jim stopped and asked it. "Bones," he said, "what about Spock?"

Without looking away from the monitor, McCoy said, "He's in his quarters, Captain. We've confirmed that the alien tissue in his body has been eliminated."

"And . . . his eyesight?" Jim asked.

McCoy felt a tightening in his gut.

Yes, they'd done it, he told himself again, but at what cost? Once they'd confirmed the powerlessness of the creatures against light, they'd needed to ascertain whether or not the same held true of the parasitic tissue within host bodies. Spock had volunteered to be tested, under the same conditions as the colonists would experience down on the planet—which meant that he hadn't worn protective eyewear. In McCoy's haste to find a means of annihilating the parasitic infestations, he'd utilized the whole spectrum of light, just as he had in his successful attempt to destroy the creature. Only later did he learn that he needn't have done so, that only a wavelength of light invisible to humans and Vulcans need have been used. While the alien tissue within Spock had been wiped out, the first officer had also been blinded.

"No change," McCoy said, still staring straight ahead at the monitor on the desk. He waited for Jim to leave, hoped that he would. Instead, he heard the captain's footsteps moving toward him, then felt Jim's hand on his shoulder.

"Bones, you can't blame yourself for what happened," he said. "It was circumstance. A need to save the population of Deneva."

"Jim," McCoy said, twisting the chair around to look up at the captain, but the words he thought to say next died in his throat. *You're wrong,* he wanted to say. *I am to blame for Spock's blindness. No one else.* But the expression on Jim's face, his entire posture, stopped him. On top of being responsible for the well-being of his crew and, right now, the million inhabitants of Deneva, the captain had lost his brother and sister-in-law, had nearly lost his nephew, and in another way would soon lose his best friend; Spock's blindness would doubtless take him away from his service aboard the *Enterprise.* The last thing Jim needed at this point was to have McCoy's guilt heaped upon him. "You're right," the doctor said. "But I feel bad for Spock."

"I know," Jim said. "I know." He patted McCoy's shoulder, and saying nothing more, departed.

The doctor watched him go, then stood up and left sickbay himself. He would not allow his guilt to prevent him from being a good friend, he'd decided. He headed for the turbolift, on his way to visit Spock.

On the bridge's primary communications console, a green rectangle winked to life on the readout, indicating an incoming transmission. Uhura recognized the call sign and frequency at once, which told her that the signal had originated in Deneva's capital city, Verian, from within the government hub. She tapped at her controls, verifying reception and requesting sender identification. She received a voice message in response, which she routed to her earpiece: "Helena Albrecht."

"Captain," Uhura said, turning from her console to face the

command chair, "I have an incoming transmission from Governor Albrecht."

"Put it on the main viewer, Lieutenant," Kirk said.

Uhura marched her fingers across her panel, pressing the appropriate buttons to establish two-way visual communication with the governor's office and to send the incoming visual component to the bridge's central viewscreen. The controls twittered in response beneath her long, slender fingers.

When Uhura had finished, she peered past the captain, past Lieutenant Sulu and Lieutenant Hadley at helm and navigation, and over at the main viewer. She watched the blue-white image of Deneva fade, replaced by the now familiar sight of Ms. Albrecht standing beside her desk. The slight-framed, towheaded woman looked out from a scene marked by apparent disorder: a monitor visible on a credenza behind her displayed only an interference pattern; one of two curtains covering a large window had been pushed untidily aside; and varicolored stacks of data cards sat heaped on seemingly every available surface. Uhura thought that the governor herself looked disheveled and tired, the cerulean, lace-edged sweater she wore a mass of wrinkles, her eyes full of a heavy weariness despite the small smile she managed.

"Governor," Captain Kirk said, "how are the verification efforts proceeding?"

Until almost three weeks ago, just after the *Enterprise* had arrived at Deneva, Albrecht had served as the colony's deputy governor. But once the *Enterprise* crew had begun eradicating the neural parasites, Governor Newton Armitage had been found dead, a victim of the alien invasion. Obviously understanding the peril the settlement faced, he had at the outset led a successful effort to destroy the colony's small collection of ships, as well as the three vessels that had brought the creatures and scores of hosts here from Ingraham B. He had been beaten to death for those actions, actions which had doubtless helped prevent the spread of the parasites beyond Deneva.

"I'm very happy to tell you that we're finished, Captain," Albrecht said, a full smile blooming on her face for a few seconds. The news did not surprise Uhura, who had been charged over the past seventeen days with coordinating the status reports from

Deneva. She'd worked with more than two dozen hospital administrators on the planet, and the *Enterprise*'s primary communications staff—Lieutenants Alden, M'Ress, and Palmer—to track the progress on identifying every single colonist and ensuring that they no longer carried parasitic tissue within them. Fortunately, sensor records had been found detailing the landings of the three vessels from Ingraham B, allowing Deneva officials to also account for and find the hosts that had come from there. "My assistant will be sending along the details shortly," Albrecht continued, "but we've now examined every colonist, as well as the people who came here from Ingraham B. The parasites have been completely eradicated."

"Excellent," the captain said, clearly cheered by the news. "I'll inform Starfleet Command." After the light-generating satellites had been deployed, killing most of the creatures and freeing their hosts, the *Enterprise* crew had acted with local officials to set up examination centers in hospitals throughout the two dozen settlements that made up the colony. At the same time, the crew had undertaken a painstaking sensor sweep of the entire planet, seeking out any aliens that might have escaped. In all, fewer than a hundred surviving creatures had been found, and only a few thousand colonists had required additional treatments of light to kill the parasitic tissue within them.

"Captain, I want to thank you and your crew for everything you've done for us," Albrecht said. "So many more lives would have been lost without your intervention, not just here on Deneva, but wherever the parasites would have spread." Uhura knew that the last counts she'd seen had put the number of dead on the planet at close to twenty-one thousand, quite a number of whom had been infants and children. "I cannot express my appreciation enough," Albrecht concluded.

"I only wish we could've arrived sooner, Governor," Kirk said, "so that more lives could have been saved." The colonists' grief from the terrible loss of life had affected the *Enterprise* crew not only from afar, but also in a very personal way. Just three days ago, the captain had transported down with his nephew to Verian, where the two had attended a memorial service for Sam and Aurelan Kirk. The bodies of the captain's brother and sister-in-law had been processed in a way common to Earth and to many of its colonies: they had been cremated, although owing to the parasitic tissue that had infested them, a decision had been made not to harvest their organs.

"I'm also very sorry for your own loss, Captain Kirk," Albrecht said.

"Thank you," he replied. "And I'm very sorry for yours." Uhura assumed that the captain referred to all of the people who had perished on Deneva. For the third time in as many days, though, Uhura noticed that Captain Kirk's demeanor had changed from what it had been for weeks prior. Even before the *Enterprise* had arrived at Deneva, really ever since the incident with the Guardian of Forever, he had seemed sullen and withdrawn, behaviors only reinforced by the deaths of his brother and sister-in-law, and the blinding of Mr. Spock. But since the memorial service, the captain had seemed more like himself, spending more time on the bridge, and interacting more often and more easily with the crew. She admired his strength.

On the main viewer, Albrecht inclined her head slightly and said, "Safe journeys to you and your crew, Captain." Kirk returned the nod, and the image of the governor faded.

Uhura turned back to her panel and quickly restored the external view of Deneva to the screen. As she did so, she saw several other indicator lights flash in different colors on her panel. She reviewed them, worked her console to handle them as needed, listened briefly to a message on her earpiece, then informed the captain.

"Sir, I've received the final reports from Governor Albrecht's assistant," she said. "Also, Mister Scott confirms that the planet and the colonists are all clear of the parasites, and that, except for himself and Mister DeSalle, all of the crew have transported back aboard."

"Thank you, Lieutenant," the captain said. "Tell Mister Scott that we're preparing to leave orbit as soon as he's aboard. Have him report to the bridge once he's beamed up."

"Yes, sir," Uhura said.

Less than thirty minutes later, the bridge doors opened, and along with Yeoman Zahra, Scotty stepped out of the turbolift. The two officers walked past the primary engineering console and descended down the two steps to the lower deck. Captain

Kirk stood from the command chair, and beside the helm station, faced the chief engineer. Zahra waited behind Scotty.

As Uhura completed a shift communications status on a data slate, she rose from her station to stretch her legs. She heard the captain as he expressed his approbation for the job Scotty had done over the past weeks, leading the *Enterprise* contingent that had assisted the colonists. The engineer thanked him, then returned to his bridge console, currently manned by Crewman Harrison.

"Yeoman," the captain said, stepping over to Zahra, "record this for Starfleet Command."

"Ready, sir," the yeoman responded, activating the tricorder she carried.

"The alien creatures on Deneva have been destroyed—"

At the sound of the turbolift doors opening, Uhura glanced over in that direction. She felt her eyes widen in surprise as Zahra expressed what Uhura herself thought: "Captain, look: Mister Spock."

Uhura's stylus came up off her slate as she stopped writing. The first officer walked past her, toward the primary sciences station, his eyes open and apparently functioning. Dr. McCoy followed along behind him.

"Spock," the captain said, not bothering to hide his shock. He moved over to the rise behind the command chair and peered up at the first officer. "You can see."

Spock stopped and gave a slight nod, then looked from Kirk to McCoy, evidently prompting the doctor to provide the explanation. For her part, Uhura could not tear her gaze away from Spock. The advent of his condition had seemed tragic to her, especially given that it had happened to him in the service of finding a means of saving the people of Deneva and that it hadn't been necessary. Now, his recovery astounded her.

"The blindness was temporary, Jim," McCoy said. "Something about his optical nerves, which aren't the same as a human's." The doctor's tone carried a note of amused exasperation, something that had been lacking in recent days, and a marked return to form that Uhura welcomed.

"An hereditary trait, Captain," Spock elucidated. "The brightness of the Vulcan sun has caused the development of an inner eyelid, which acts as a shield against high-intensity light." Uhura had never heard of such a thing. Spock looked once more at McCoy. "Totally instinctive, Doctor," he said. "We tend to ignore it, as you ignore your own appendix." The first officer offered an expression that Uhura could only describe as self-satisfied—despite his claims to Vulcan dispassion—and then he continued on to the sciences station.

Uhura glanced up at McCoy, as did the captain. The doctor appeared pensive, but even in thought, his features lacked the tension she'd seen in them during their time at Deneva—since the death of Captain Kirk's brother and sister-in-law, since Spock's blindness. Uhura shared a look with the captain, and he too appeared more relaxed. Indeed, she thought she saw in his aspect the threat of mischief. He climbed to the outer, upper level of the bridge and followed Spock over to the sciences console.

"Mister Spock," he said, clasping his hands behind his back, "regaining eyesight would be an emotional experience for most. You, I presume, felt nothing?"

To Uhura's surprise, the Vulcan did not deny the emotion attendant with his restored ability to see. "Quite the contrary, Captain," he said. "I had a very strong reaction: my first sight was the face of Doctor McCoy bending over me."

Uhura looked from Spock to the doctor, whose harrumph and amused annoyance made it difficult for her not to laugh. "'Tis a pity brief blindness did not increase your appreciation for beauty, Mister Spock."

"If you gentlemen are finished," the captain said, descending from the outer portion of the bridge, back to his command chair, "would you mind laying in a course for Starbase Ten, Mister Spock?"

Between the friendly banter and the order that would take the *Enterprise* away from Deneva, Uhura could not help but smile. While Mr. Spock acknowledged the order and Dr. McCoy headed toward the captain, Uhura sat back down at her communications console, setting down her data slate and stylus atop an empty surface. She reached across her console and worked the controls, opening a channel to the main communications center on Deneva. She signaled the *Enterprise*'s departure, waited for acknowledgment, then ended the transmission.

Sitting back in her chair, Uhura felt a wave of relief wash over her, grateful to finally be leaving this place. The weeks dealing with the neural parasites had been intense and arduous, for none more so than Captain Kirk, Mr. Spock, and Dr. McCoy. But at least the destruction of the parasite menace, along with Spock's unexpected recovery and the recuperation of the captain's nephew allowed them to leave this place on a positive note.

Uhura picked up her data slate and stylus, resuming work on her shift status report. She looked forward to reaching Starbase 10, certain that the captain would authorize shore leave there, since the crew had endured so much during the last few months. Prior to the incidents on Deneva and with the Guardian of Forever, the *Enterprise* had been on the front lines of what had nearly become a shooting war with the Klingons, and before that, there had been the deadly search on Janus VI for the creature killing miners. Uhura also recalled the struggle to evacuate colonists from Omicron Ceti III; the attempt by a group of twentieth-century, selectively bred warriors, revived from suspended animation, to commandeer the ship; and the tensions the crew had undergone when the captain, Mr. Spock, and their landing party—as well as the entire ship's complement—had been declared casualties in the computer-controlled war between Eminiar and Vendikar.

It's been a demanding few months, Uhura thought as she locked down her station, routing communications to a secondary console. She made a notation on her slate, then initiated a diagnostic sequence on her panel. Though monotonous, she didn't mind the work, preferring it to the reports from Deneva she'd coordinated, many of which had included updates on the number of dead found in the colony.

As Uhura monitored the diagnostic, she remembered her previous visits to Starbase 10. Designed like a pair of cones joined at their circular ends, the base boasted a large lake at its center. A beautiful esplanade ran beside the unusual feature, with shops and entertainment venues scattered along meandering paths. In particular, she recalled a nightclub, Starlight on the Water, which on some evenings invited amateurs to perform. Uhura thought now that perhaps she might do a little singing while on leave.

An indicator on the communications console flashed from

green to yellow, and an instant later, to red. Uhura glowered at
the light, set down her data slate once more, and began attempting to isolate the fault. Yes, she definitely would welcome a few
days of rest and relaxation on Starbase 10.

McCoy finished running the shaver over his face, then ran a
hand across his cheeks, chin, and neck, checking for any remaining stubble. He hadn't missed any hair with the laser blades,
though, feeling only smooth skin. He returned his shaver to the
cabinet behind the mirror and above the basin, then headed out
of the refresher, the narrow panel sliding closed behind.

Grabbing his boots from beside the bed, he sat down at his
desk. After pulling on his footwear, he looked at the time currently displayed on his desktop monitor. He still had almost
thirty minutes before the start of his duty shift in sickbay, plenty
of time to stop at one of the mess halls for some breakfast.

On the monitor's base, McCoy saw, a red light blinked on and
off. He hadn't heard any communications signals this morning,
and then he realized that he hadn't reviewed his messages when
he'd come back to his cabin last night. Now, he reached forward
and pushed a toggle, activating playback. The log revealed that
he had only one message.

McCoy watched without surprise as Tonia's image appeared
on the screen. "Leonard, I was wondering if you'd like to have
dinner together tonight," she said. McCoy felt a twinge of guilt.
"We haven't seen much of each other lately, so . . . well, I miss
you." She glanced down briefly, as though unsure of herself.
When she looked up again, she quickly finished. "Well, that's it,"
she said. "Let me know." Tonia smiled with an effort that seemed
forced, and then the screen went dark. A moment later, the current time reappeared on the monitor.

Regret swelled in McCoy, both for not responding to Tonia's
message in a timely manner, and for the truth of what she'd said.
They hadn't spent much time together recently; they'd only
shared a couple of meals during the *Enterprise*'s stay at Deneva
and had gotten together only once in the week since the ship had
started for Starbase 10, having a celebratory dinner right after
Spock had regained his eyesight.

McCoy sighed, already feeling weary, even though his day

had just begun. He reached for another toggle on the monitor, knowing that he should contact Tonia right now, perhaps even invite her to join him for breakfast. Even though he didn't—

The door signal sounded. McCoy sat back in his chair, supposing the obvious, that Tonia hadn't waited to hear back from him, had instead decided to pay him a visit. He rubbed at his eyes, again feeling fatigued, and hoping that his failure to contact Tonia last night would not lead to some sort of confrontation right now. Regardless, he could not leave her standing in the corridor. "Come in," he called.

The door panel glided open, and as had happened not too long ago, McCoy saw that he had mistakenly guessed his caller to be Tonia, when it actually turned out to be Spock. The first officer stepped forward into the cabin, and the door closed behind him. "Doctor," he said, "I wish to solicit your personal *and* medical opinions on an issue, but I am not prepared to do so as a matter of record."

"Well, good morning to you too," McCoy said in mock irritation. When Spock did not respond at all, offering no perfectly logical retort, or a remonstrance of any kind, but simply stood there motionless, the doctor saw that he must have something serious on his mind. "What is it, Spock?" he said. "You know you can talk to me."

"Yes, I do know that, Doctor," Spock said. "But it is proper that I inform you of my desire to keep our discussion private, given that it is about the captain that I wish to speak."

"I see," McCoy said, rising to his feet. He wondered just what Spock wanted to talk about, but understood that it must be significant for the first officer to seek his counsel in this way. "Go ahead. What's said here will stay here."

"Thank you, Doctor," Spock said. "What I want to ask you about is the human grieving process."

"Ah, I see," McCoy said. "Well, as I'm sure you know, grief for a human being is a response to loss. On a very basic level, it's generally accepted that there are five stages: denial and isolation, anger, bargaining, depression, and acceptance. In reality, grieving is more complex than that, an ebb and flow of processes that may include the stages in any order, omitting some, repeating others. In many ways, it is an experience unique to an individual, though the broad parameters allow for an understanding of what most humans go through." Weeks ago, after the deaths of Jim's brother and sister-in-law, the doctor might have expected this conversation with Spock. At that time, the captain had withdrawn emotionally, isolating himself as much as he could while maintaining command of a starship, and he'd also displayed periods of depression and anger. In fact, after the first officer himself had been infected by a neural parasite, Jim had heatedly and single-mindedly ordered McCoy to do whatever he had to in order to help his nephew and Spock, and McCoy had needed to remind him of the million Denevan colonists who also required help. But that had been nearly a month ago, and Jim had seemed far more like himself of late, particularly within the last week or so. He said as much to Spock.

"Would you consider the captain's behavior normal then?" the first officer asked.

"Under the circumstances," McCoy said, "I think he's adapting quite well. We're not all Vulcans, Mister Spock; we can't simply turn off our emotions when they become inconvenient to us." He hadn't intended to sound quite so harsh, but sometimes Spock's expectations demanded too much of people and did not adequately take into account human behavior.

"I think you misunderstand me, Doctor," Spock said, walking farther into the room. "I am not concerned that Captain Kirk has taken too long to accept the deaths of his brother and sister-in-law. I am concerned that he has not taken long enough."

McCoy blinked. "What?" he said, sure that he must have heard Spock incorrectly. "What is it you're concerned about?"

"I believe," Spock said, "that Captain Kirk is not coping with the recent losses he has suffered."

That brought McCoy up short. "Forgive me, Spock, but I find it odd to hear you making a judgment about somebody else's feelings."

"And why is that, Doctor?" Spock asked. "I do not need to experience an emotion in order to recognize its detrimental effect on an individual, any more than a physician needs to have a particular disease in order to diagnose it."

"That may be true," McCoy said, walking out from behind his desk, "but I understand disease."

"And I understand emotion," Spock maintained. "Nevertheless, I have come here seeking the benefit of your experience, both as a doctor and as the captain's friend."

"You're right," McCoy said, feeling a bit sheepish. After all, Spock had stated at the outset that he had come here wanting his opinion. The doctor turned and made his way back around his desk, where he dropped into his chair. "So you're worried that Jim hasn't been showing enough emotion?"

"Not that he hasn't been *showing* enough emotion," Spock corrected, "but it is my belief that his behavior demonstrates that he has not adequately dealt with the string of losses he has just endured."

"I don't know, Spock," McCoy said. "He seemed to me to be clearly grieving during the time we spent at Deneva. It's only in the last week, since we left there, that he's begun acting more like himself. He's also been helping his nephew handle the devastating loss of his parents."

Spock paced across the small room, into the far corner. Folding his arms, he looked over at McCoy. "It is your evaluation, then, that the captain has had sufficient time to cope with recent events?" He appeared unconvinced of that conclusion, and in truth, McCoy didn't know either.

"I can't tell you that," he admitted. "But I can point out that Jim has dealt with death a lot in his life. Three dozen of the crew have died since he took command of the *Enterprise*, deaths for which he feels directly responsible. Both of his parents passed away when he was very young, and at the age of thirteen, he witnessed the cold-blooded extermination of four thousand colonists on Tarsus Four." McCoy paused, momentarily staggered by the scope of his claim. "I know Jim loved his brother and sister-in-law, but the unfortunate fact is that he has often had to weather such losses."

Spock nodded, steepling his index fingers together before him. "I submit to you, Doctor, that this situation is different than any of those the captain has otherwise experienced. I believe that he is attempting, on an emotional level, to ignore the deaths of his brother, his sister-in-law, and Edith Keeler."

"Edith Keeler?" McCoy repeated. He knew that Jim felt terrible about having to allow Keeler to die. Still, she'd been killed in a replay of history, and her name seemed out of place on a list that included deceased members of the captain's family.

"Yes," Spock said. He let his hands fall to his sides and walked over to the desk, where he took a seat across from McCoy. "Doctor, do you know how long Captain Kirk and I spent in 1930 prior to finding you at the 21st Street Mission?"

"I thought—" McCoy started, then realized that he didn't know. "I suppose I just assumed you'd gotten there right before we found each other."

"The captain and I lived in the past for forty-seven days," Spock said. "Enough time, I'm afraid, for Jim to fall in love with Edith Keeler."

The information surprised McCoy and better explained Spock's concern. "How close did they become?" McCoy wanted to know.

"I believe that they loved each other deeply," Spock said. "I believe that Jim considered Miss Keeler . . . I think the phrase is, 'the love of his life.'"

McCoy listened as Spock related an account of the time he and the captain had spent in the past, and of Jim's romance with Edith Keeler. The doctor said nothing, but began to understand the gravity of the first officer's concerns about the captain. When Spock had finished, he sat quietly, apparently waiting for a response.

"I can see why you're worried about Jim," McCoy said at last. "I never ended up speaking with him about his time in the past because of everything that's gone on since: first my recuperating from the effects of the cordrazine overdose, then dealing with the neural parasites on Deneva. I wasn't aware of what transpired between Jim and Edith Keeler. But do you really think his refusal to actively deal with his loss is impacting the captain's ability to command?"

"It does not appear so," Spock said. "But I think it is impacting Jim's life."

"All right," McCoy agreed. "What do you think we can do about it though?"

"I believe that you need to assess Jim's emotional state for yourself, Doctor," Spock said. "If you think it is warranted, then you and I must ensure that he receives psychiatric assistance."

"While that might be a good idea, Spock, I'm not sure we can make it happen," McCoy said. "You know Jim. He's not due for his annual physical exam for another ten months." For the first time, McCoy lamented that, not long ago, the requirement for regular crew medical examinations had changed from quarterly to yearly. "Without concrete justification, it'll be impossible to get him to submit to a psychological evaluation."

"Fortunately," Spock said, "we possess such a justification."

"But you just indicated that his emotional state is *not* affecting his captaincy," McCoy said.

"That is correct," Spock said, and then he cited a fact overlooked by McCoy during and subsequent to his cordrazine recovery: Jim had refused a medical exam after returning from the planet of the Guardian, despite regulations that made a physical mandatory after a visit to a newly discovered world.

"I'll pay the captain a visit later," McCoy said. "I'll have him in sickbay for a workup by the end of the day." Although satisfied that he would be able to examine and speak with Jim and make his own determination about him, McCoy also worried about what such a meeting would reveal.

EIGHT

1930

In the first traces of dawn, Edith reached over the rear of the lorry bed, grasped the near corners of the burlap bag, and pulled. Filled with coffee beans, the heavy sack moved perhaps two inches before she lost her grip. She exclaimed quietly to herself—"Blast!"—and although spring had officially begun a few weeks ago, her breath still puffed out before her in petite clouds, the chill, early morning air masquerading convincingly as winter. She shivered inside her cloak, pleased that she'd worn gloves, but wishing that she'd chosen a heavier outer garment.

As Edith leaned in again for the bag of coffee, she heard the hard scrape of shoes on the pavement behind her. Assuming that the lorry driver had returned from hauling a crate of eggs into the mission, she didn't bother to look around. "I think I'm going to need some assistance with this," she said. Rik normally helped unload the weekly delivery of supplies, but his sinuses had been congested last night, his overly deep voice evidence that he'd caught a cold. Edith had told him to stay home and rest today, and she'd come down early herself to open the mission for the driver.

"I'd be happy to take that for you, Miss Keeler," a man said, and Edith looked over to see Dr. McCoy walk up to her.

"My, but you're up early," she said. These days, McCoy frequently joined Edith and Rik in preparing for the morning meal, but that didn't happen until the hour before she opened the doors of the mission at seven o'clock. Knowing Rik would stay home today, she could have asked the doctor last night to let the lorry driver in and help him unload, but McCoy worked hard, and she hadn't wanted to ask him to rise an hour earlier than usual. Right now, glimmers of orange-red had only just appeared in the sky, ushering in the nascent day. The gibbous moon, recently full, hung low and partially visible behind city buildings as it sank toward the horizon.

"Well, I guess I had to wake up early in order to help you, now didn't I?" McCoy said affably. He stretched his upper body across the back of the lorry and took hold of the sack of coffee beans. As he did so, the light shining through the open front doors of the mission caught his features in a way that drew attention to the dark circles below his eyes. The grayish blue commas lent the doctor a tired appearance, and she suspected that he'd been having difficulty sleeping.

"Thank you, Doctor," Edith said. As he hoisted the bag up onto his shoulder, the strong, rich aroma of the beans drifted to her.

"My pleasure, ma'am," McCoy said. He headed across the sidewalk and into the main room of the mission, and Edith followed him inside. While he and the lorry driver continued unloading the rest of the supplies, she began pulling the overturned chairs down from atop the tables.

When McCoy had brought in the last item—a large container of powdered vegetable stock—Edith went back outside and paid the driver out of the mission's coffers. She went back inside, closed and locked the front doors, and headed toward the kitchen. Along the way, she passed the doctor's coat, which he had draped across the back of a chair. Still cold herself, though, she opted to leave her cloak wrapped about her and her gloves on until the place warmed up.

Making her way into the kitchen, she saw the new supplies stacked neatly in place. McCoy, wearing a denim shirt and black trousers, kneeled at the far end of the narrow space. He had prized open one of the crates and now finished loading eggs into the icebox tucked in the corner. He then stood up and retrieved one of the large percolators, which he began setting up.

"It's still early," Edith said. "We don't need to get ready just yet."

McCoy shrugged. "I don't have anything else to do at this time of day," he said.

"Actually, I thought that you might stoke the furnace for me," Edith requested.

"That's already been taken care of," McCoy said. "It should warm up in here in no time."

"How very efficient of you, Doctor," she remarked good-naturedly, though she also recognized the truth of her statement. In the month McCoy had been at the mission, he had never wavered from his exceptional work ethic. Even among men desperate for jobs, his determined efforts continued to cause him to stand out, which lent credence to his claims of being lost and amnesiac, rather than being on the run. More than that, though, since revealing his unwillingness to move out of the mission, he had given her no reason to doubt him.

With a sense of guilt, Edith recalled her visit to the police office a couple of weeks ago. Detective Wright had been unable to locate any report of a missing person who matched the doctor's description, nor had he identified any unsolved crimes for which McCoy could reasonably have been considered a suspect. In fact,

Wright had unearthed no information whatsoever about the doctor, indicating the likelihood that McCoy had never been in trouble with the police, at least not in New York City.

Edith bent down and gathered a wire rack filled with coffee
cups from beneath the long, deep sink. She lifted it onto the
serving counter, placing it beside the early-morning edition of
The Star Dispatch, which she'd brought from home. Before
emptying the rack, she unfolded the newspaper so that she
could look at its front page while she worked. As she unloaded
the coffee cups onto the counter, she skimmed the headlines.
In the bottom right corner, she saw an article titled GANDHI
AIDE STARTS JAIL TERM. Simultaneously interested and appalled,
she read the dateline—the story had been filed in BOMBAY,
INDIA—and the lead sentence: "National Congress President
Jawaharlal Nehru, a chief aide to Mohandas K. Gandhi, began
serving a six-month prison sentence for his violation of the
Salt Law."

"Doctor," Edith said, "have you been reading about Mohandas Gandhi and what's been taking place in India?"

Now loading coffee beans from a sack into a hand-cranked
grinder, McCoy did not look up. "Gandhi?" he said, as though
not quite familiar with the name. "No, I haven't been reading the
newspaper lately."

Edith remembered the doctor declining an opportunity to
read *The Star Dispatch* just after he'd recovered his health, but
she still would have guessed that a man of his obvious intelligence would keep himself informed regarding current events.
Perhaps the uncertainty of his personal circumstances had prevented him from doing so. "It really is an astonishing story," she
told him. "Do you know about the Salt Law?"

"No," McCoy said, slowly shaking his head, as though unsure. "I'm afraid I don't." With the grinder filled, McCoy began
working the device's crank. The beans snapped and popped as
the mill's blades pulverized them.

"It is one of the means that the British Empire employs to
maintain its colonial rule over India," Edith explained. Feeling
warm now, she peeled off her gloves and dropped them on the
counter. "The law forbids the sale and production of salt in India
by anybody but the British government. They also charge a tax

on the purchase of salt, which helps fund their occupying government."

"I imagine that salt is a particularly important commodity there," McCoy said, "considering the heat and humidity in that part of the world."

"That's right," Edith said. She reached up to the front of her neck and began unbuttoning her cloak. "What's more, salt occurs in abundance in India and is easily accessible to people. But the law forbids them from collecting it themselves, which forces them to purchase it. And many of the population are poor."

McCoy stopped cranking the grinder and at last looked up. "That's terrible," he said.

Edith nodded as she removed her cloak and set it down atop her gloves. "A month ago, in protest, Gandhi began walking with about eighty followers toward one of India's coastal cities. It took them more than three weeks, but they traveled almost two hundred and fifty miles. When they arrived, Gandhi boiled a clump of mud in seawater in order to produce a small amount of salt."

"In defiance of the law," McCoy said, the tone of his voice appreciative. "Quite a symbolic act."

"Yes, but not simply symbolic," Edith said, and she picked up the newspaper from beside her cloak. "It's turned out to be motivational as well." She stepped over to the doctor, folded the paper in two, and held it up so that he could see the bottom half of the front page. "Since then, tens of thousands have broken the law, and many have been arrested—" She pointed to the item about Nehru. "—including some Indian leaders."

McCoy scanned the article for a moment and then asked, "What about Gandhi?"

"He hasn't been arrested yet," Edith said, "but people fully expect that he will be before long." Anger flared within her at the injustice of the situation, at the unconscionable treatment of India's citizenry by the British imperialists. Still, her frustrations could not forestall the esteem she felt for the man they reverently called *Mahatma*. Tossing the newspaper back onto the counter, she said, "Gandhi truly is an extraordinary fellow."

"He is," McCoy agreed.

"He's provoked a rebellion without taking up arms," she went on admiringly. "He has dedicated himself to achieving complete independence for his people, but through nonviolent means such as civil disobedience. It is remarkable."

"That's one of the right ways to change the world," McCoy said.

" 'One of the right ways?' " Edith asked.

"This—" The doctor pointed a finger around the kitchen and then toward the main room of the mission. "—is another."

"My father used to believe that," Edith said. She felt immediately wistful about the man who had by himself raised her into a young woman, and whom she had adored. All these years later, his loss still had the power to overwhelm her.

"I believe it too," McCoy said.

Edith turned back toward the counter and resumed unloading the coffee cups from the wire rack, wanting to hide her sudden sorrow and to find her way past it. "It's a nice thought," she said, trying not to think about her father, "but there's quite a difference between what Gandhi does and what I do."

"Maybe," McCoy said. "Maybe not as much as you think. But what really matters is that you *do* change the world, even if it's one person at a time."

"I don't need to change the world, Doctor," she said. "I just want to help people survive it so that when one day it does change, they'll be here to live in it."

McCoy didn't respond, and when Edith set the last cup down on the counter, silence filled the kitchen. She quickly picked up the wire rack and dropped it back below the sink, where it briefly clattered before coming to a rest. Edith wanted the noise, wanted to fill the soundless moment with something, so that the doctor wouldn't offer his thanks to her. *You don't help people to earn their gratitude,* her father had taught her. *You help people because it's the right thing to do.*

Edith pulled out the rack of plates and hefted it up onto the counter. As she did, she spared a glance at McCoy. The doctor looked back at her with a small, closed-mouth smile, but he said nothing and instead turned back to the coffee grinder. Edith began stacking the plates beside the coffee cups.

No, she thought, satisfied. *I don't need to change the world.*

* * *

McCoy stood in the shadows and stared across the street at the three-story brick building. A narrow band of red ran along the base of the rectangular edifice, reaching up about a meter and a quarter from the sidewalk. Above the unpainted brick, the rest of the wall had been whitewashed all the way up to the peaked façade that crowned the roof. Windows lined the upper floors, and dark architectural molding spanned the breadth of the structure below the second story and above the third.

At ground level, arches built into the wall marched across the front of the building, most of them framing windows. In one of the central arches, light fixtures bracketed the main entrance. Gold letters decorated the glass transom, reflecting the bright glow of the lamps and spelling out 13TH PRECINCT.

McCoy hovered in the darkness, cautiously eyeing the police station. For the moment, this short segment of the street, on this one block, belonged to him, and to him alone. Disrupted earlier by pedestrians and automobiles, the night had now drawn still, the sky moonless to this point, and deep.

McCoy had arrived here nearly thirty minutes ago. He'd come with a purpose, but once he'd reached this section of Sheriff Street, he'd begun questioning his choice. Two weeks ago, while walking on the Brooklyn Bridge, he'd decided that he needed to dispatch a message that would somehow reach Jim Kirk in the future. The idea had energized him at the time, providing him an opportunity to do something more than merely wait for rescue. But as he'd had cast about for a means of accomplishing his aim, the problem had proven intractable.

From somewhere in the distance, the rhythmic beat of shoes against pavement reached the doctor, and he shrank back against the wall of the building opposite the precinct house. The steps grew louder, and a few seconds later, McCoy watched as a uniformed patrolman emerged from around the corner. The officer passed beneath a street lamp, his lean, lined face becoming briefly visible. Taking no apparent notice of the doctor, he headed for the main entrance of the police station and disappeared through it, leaving McCoy once more alone on the street.

Alone with my decision, he thought, struggling to determine what he should do, and what he should *not.*

McCoy had initially considered attempting to locate Captain Kirk's ancestors. He thought that he could present them with a sealed letter, and ask them to pass it down through the generations, ultimately delivering it to Jim on a specified date, sometime after the events that had brought the doctor to New York in the twentieth century. The idea even held a note of romance about it, he thought, like some grand and unlikely scheme out of myth.

As he'd contemplated the particulars of his plan, though, he'd quickly found it unworkable. While he recalled where Jim had been born and raised, as well as the names of his parents, he knew few other concrete details about the Kirk family. How then could he hope to conclusively find any of the captain's forebears? How could he possibly trace Jim's lineage back through a dozen or more generations that, in 1930, had not yet come into existence?

The doctor had thought about trying to track down his own relatives, but while he had more information about his kin than about Jim's, he still had no notion who they were or where he could find them three centuries before he'd been born. Even if he could definitively identify members of the McCoy or Kirk clans, and even if he could convince somebody to begin the long chain of delivery, what real chance would there be for success? He also worried that such actions could themselves disrupt the flow of history. McCoy believed that he could prepare an innocuous enough note—"March 1930. 21st Street Mission. New York City. McCoy."—that would be meaningless to anybody besides the captain, but might simply receiving, storing, or transferring such a missive alter a person's life? Could a small, seemingly harmless change in 1930 propagate over time, creating a major disturbance sometime in the future?

After a great deal of thought, McCoy had abandoned any such plans. Instead, he'd focused on the reason he'd conceived them in the first place: namely, the fact of the unbroken link that his and Jim's families provided between today and tomorrow. What other continuous chains, he'd asked himself, connected the present with the future? He'd answered the question readily enough—Earth itself; the human race; natural formations, such as Victoria Falls and the Grand Canyon; manmade structures, like the Eiffel Tower and the Gotthard Base Tunnel—but none of those provided a reliable means of getting a message to the captain. Even if McCoy could figure out how to secrete away a letter somewhere on the Brooklyn Bridge so that it would last into the twenty-third century, how could he ensure that it would get to Jim?

It had occurred to him then that *documents* from this period had survived into his own time. He'd thought at once of even older works, including the Magna Carta and the United States Declaration of Independence, but other, less profound items, such as census files, had also been preserved. And then he'd thought of two even more mundane types of documents: hospital and police records.

If Jim and Spock didn't know that he'd traveled into Earth's past, McCoy had little potential for recovery. If they did, though, then he had no doubt that they would scour every available historical database for any sign of his presence in another time. Computers hadn't been in use in 1930, but as the decades passed after that, not only would they become common and be utilized to store newly created records, but they would also be loaded with older, existing records. McCoy himself had occasionally studied digitized, indexed versions of medical data from this time period and earlier. If he could insinuate himself into such files, then Jim and Spock would have a means of finding him, his message to them, in effect, a simple *Here I am.*

The doctor had contemplated injuring himself in some fashion and then visiting a hospital for treatment. As a physician, he knew that he could wound himself or generate symptoms of some disease safely enough, but the idea confronted his training and mind-set. He'd also thought about going to the police, confessing to the perpetration of some illegal act, or just claiming to be the victim of a crime. The more he'd considered the matter, the more he'd leaned toward the latter course of action.

Now, though, as he lingered across from the 13th Precinct, he reassessed that decision. He didn't feel especially confident that these particular paper files, created and stored in a 1930s police station, would be transferred at some point in the future to computer memory—or if committed to digital storage, that they would necessarily endure. While many older records had been preserved electronically, many had not, and of those that had, not all had survived the many disasters, conflicts, and wars that had riddled the globe in the twentieth and twenty-first centuries. More than the doctor's uncertain expectation, though, the prospect of involving himself with any sorts of authorities concerned him. While he could not concretize his apprehension, he feared that his contact with the medical establishment or law enforcement would pose a significant risk of impacting the timeline.

Across the street, the front door of the police station swung open, and two uniformed officers walked out into the night. Both of them, McCoy saw, carried short but menacing clubs. The sight induced him to move. After watching the patrolmen head off to the left, he thrust his hands into the pockets of his pea coat and started away in the opposite direction.

As the doctor's boots thudded along the sidewalk, joined now and then by the footsteps of others, as well as the sounds of passing automobiles, he attempted to reformulate his dilemma in the most basic terms. He hoped that doing so would lead him to as simple, and therefore as achievable, a plan of action as possible. As the old medical-school saw stated, "When you hear hoofbeats, think horses, not zebras." He began by generalizing his terms: he needed to send a message to friends that would reach them at a certain place and time, and that would provide them his own spatial and temporal location. *Too complicated,* he thought, and tried again.

I need to contact friends to let them know where I am. Simple enough, but that expression of his plight omitted critical details, and so he gave it another attempt. *My friends are looking for me somewhere, and I need to draw their attention to me.*

McCoy thought about that for a moment, and then stopped walking. That statement still left out the explicit mention of his travel through time, but he realized that it might capture enough of his problem to be of use. In this form, he could ask the question, not of himself, but of somebody familiar with life in 1930 New York City.

The doctor peered in both directions, waited for a couple of automobiles to pass, and then trotted across the street, a new destination in mind. He weaved his way through neighborhoods now familiar to him from his nightly strolls, until he arrived at a familiar four-story walk-up. He mounted the front stoop and entered the building, where a handwritten tag on one of the mailboxes told him which apartment he wanted. He climbed the stairs to the third floor, where he knocked on the door marked with the number 33.

"Who is it?" asked a voice from within, clearly surprised, if not suspicious, at having a visitor this late. McCoy didn't have a timepiece, but estimated that it must be between ten and eleven o'clock.

"It's Leonard McCoy, ma'am," he said. He heard the click of a latch, and then the door swung inward.

"Doctor, this is a surprise," she said. "It's late." Despite the hour, though, he noticed that she hadn't yet changed into nightclothes, but stood clad in the same outfit that he'd seen her in at the mission today: a calf-length gray skirt, topped by a short-sleeved brown knit sweater. A golden locket, which McCoy had often seen her wear, hung on a matching chain around her neck. "Is something wrong?" she asked, obviously concerned by the unexpected visit.

"No, no, not at all," he said, wanting to put Keeler's mind at ease. "I was just out for a walk and I guess I didn't realize the time."

"I see," she said, her tone level and unreadable. "Is there something you need?"

"As a matter of fact, I wanted to ask your advice about something," he told her.

Keeler did not respond right away, but finally gave a quick nod. "All right," she said. "Come in." She reached forward and switched on a light hanging on the wall beside the door. Then she stepped aside, opening a path so that McCoy could enter. He walked past her, and she closed the door behind him.

Inside, the doctor unbuttoned his coat, though he left the garment on. He found himself in a one-room apartment not much larger than the space where he stayed in the rear of the mission. It also resembled the backroom office in other ways, he thought, with a narrow bed in place of his cot, and a nightstand beside it instead of the diminutive typing table. A larger table stood in for the office's desk, and a dresser for the filing cabinets. The apartment also sported a single, curtained window, though an open door in one corner revealed a small closet, a feature McCoy's room lacked.

Atop the table and dresser sat a few framed photographs, and he thought he recognized some of the faces from pictures in Keeler's office. He also saw books scattered about the flat surfaces in the room, as well as some magazines. The lamp on the nightstand threw a circle of light across the bed, where a newspaper had been spread. A pair of pillows pushed up against the headboard still retained the rough outline of a person, revealing where Keeler had just been sitting.

"So what can I help you with, Doctor?" she asked behind him.

"As I mentioned, I wanted to get your advice," he said, still looking about the apartment. Though neatly kept, the room appeared rundown. The wallpaper, patterned in boxes and vertical strips of several shades of blue, had browned from age in places and peeled away from the wall in others. The reddish floor covering, some sort of resilient sheet material, looked worn and faded. The furniture too appeared old and dilapidated, covered with nicks and scratches. A number of runs marred the sheer fabric of the tan curtains.

Finally, McCoy turned his full attention back to Keeler. "You know that I'm staying in the mission because I'm waiting for my friends to find me there," he said. Though not a question, he spoke in a manner that invited a response.

"Yes," Keeler said.

"It's taken longer than I expected it to," McCoy said. "I thought they would have come to get me by now."

"I don't mean to be pessimistic," Keeler said, walking across the room, past the foot of the bed, "but perhaps they're not coming."

"Perhaps not," McCoy admitted. "But I really believe that they are. I just think they might be having difficulty finding me."

"Oh," Keeler said. She absently grabbed the finial adorning the top of the footboard's leg nearest her. "But you seemed so sure that they would show up at the mission."

"Maybe I was overly optimistic," he said, facing Edith across the width of the bed. "I know you wanted me to think about going to the police, but—"

"You needn't do that, Doctor," Keeler interrupted. She looked down at where both of her hands now fiddled with the finial. "I already—" She stopped, and with what seemed a conscious effort, she dropped her hands to her sides and lifted her gaze to peer over at McCoy. "I already went to the police about you," she admitted. "Two weeks ago."

With his decision earlier tonight to avoid contact with the police still fresh in his mind, McCoy felt a rush of momentary panic. He realized at once, though, that nothing had come of Keeler's visit to law enforcement. She confirmed that, describing to him her meeting with a detective at the 13th Precinct, who could find no information about the doctor or any indication that he might have perpetrated a crime. Given that he'd traveled here from the future, McCoy would have expected that no data about him could have been found, but since the memory of his arrival in this time remained clouded, it relieved him to hear that the police did not believe that he had committed any offenses.

"I'm sorry, Doctor," Keeler said. "I'm afraid I didn't completely trust you."

"I can't say I blame you," McCoy told her. "I didn't exactly show up at the mission under the best of circumstances or with a very believable story."

"I'm still not sure how *believable* your story is," Keeler said, "but I *do* believe you. Since you first came to the mission, you've shown that I can trust you."

"Thank you, Miss Keeler," McCoy said. "I appreciate that." Then, returning to the reason for his coming here tonight, he went on. "Anyway, it occurred to me that if my friends can't find me, maybe I can somehow send them a message. The problem is that I don't know where they are either, and so I'm not sure how I can do that. I thought you might have some ideas."

"I see," Keeler said, and she seemed to give the matter some thought. Almost at once, she offered a suggestion. "How about the classifieds?"

"'The classifieds,'" McCoy repeated, careful to keep hidden his lack of understanding.

"Yes, of course," Keeler said. She moved to the head of the bed, where she leaned down and searched through the various sections of the newspaper lying there. At last, she stood back up, holding a portion of the paper. "Here," she said, turning it around and holding it out to him.

McCoy took the newspaper section from her and examined the first page. Under the masthead, he saw columns of text, divided into paragraphs separated by small amounts of white space. He read through a few of them, then paged through the paper and read a few more. He saw headings like HELP WANTED and FOR SALE. Each entry, he realized, in some way mimicked his need to get a message to Jim and Spock: employers sought employees, workers sought jobs, sellers sought buyers. He also saw social announcements and personal messages. The common denominator appeared to be one person seeking another, without knowing the location of that other person.

"This is perfect," he said, understanding that if he placed an appropriate classified ad in a newspaper, and that newspaper later got transferred to computer storage, then there would be something pointing to his whereabouts that Jim and Spock could find. Closing the paper and studying the first page of the section again, McCoy saw a table of contents and instructions about purchasing an ad. "May I have this when you're finished with it?" he asked.

"You may take it now," Keeler said.

"Thank you," McCoy said. He folded up the newspaper and moved toward the door. "And again, I apologize for calling on you so late."

"Think nothing of it, Doctor," Keeler said. "I just hope that you're able to get in touch with your friends now."

"I hope so too," he said, and left.

As he descended the stairs, McCoy started planning for the next day. Since he'd been in the past, he'd seen several different newspapers, including *The New York Times, The World,* and the one from which Keeler had just given him the classified section, *The Star Dispatch.* Tomorrow, he would blanket the city and purchase ads in all of them.

When he reached the street outside Keeler's building, he felt confident that his plan would work, and that Jim and Spock would soon be able to bring him back home. "It's just a matter of time," he said to himself.

NINE

2267

Kirk sat back in his chair as he watched Yeoman Rand pull the silver-colored cover from atop her plate. "Egg salad with lettuce and Swiss cheese on wheat bread," she said, confirming his lunch order. "With coleslaw and mixed fruit." She retrieved a fork and linen napkin from the tray she'd carried from the mess and set them at the edge of the gauzy blue place mat she'd already laid out on Kirk's desk. Rand finished by serving the glass of apple juice he'd requested, announcing it as she had the food.

"Thank you, Yeoman," Kirk said.

"You're welcome, sir," Rand said. "Is there anything else I can get for you?"

"No, that'll be all," Kirk said. "Dismissed."

As Rand grabbed the tray and headed for the door, the captain reached over to the far end of the desk, to where he'd pushed the data slate on which he'd been working when the yeoman had brought his lunch. He'd opted to have his midday meal in the quiet of his quarters so that he could work on the upcoming crew changes, which he needed to complete before the ship arrived at Starbase 10. He set the device down beside his lunch and began to review the lists of promotions, reassignments, and transfers when he realized that, while he'd heard his cabin door open, he hadn't heard it close. He looked over in that direction and saw Rand hesitating in the doorway.

"Yeoman?" Kirk said.

Rand turned and reentered the cabin, and the door slid closed behind her. The tray hung down beside her leg, dangling from her fingertips. "Captain, I just wanted to thank you for approving my transfer," she said. She seemed nervous and unsure of herself, an occurrence not entirely uncommon for her.

"You're welcome, Yeoman," Kirk said. Rand had actually put in for a transfer from the ship several months ago, but the captain had only recently had time to review and consider her applica-

tion. Since the yeoman hadn't served aboard the *Enterprise* for
long—less than a year—he'd been disinclined to approve her pe-
tition when he'd first received it. But Rand had chosen to include
with her request a written statement, in which she'd delineated
her reasons with such candor and emotion that Kirk had been
moved to change his mind. "How long will you be at Starbase
Ten?"

"Three days," Rand said. "Then I'll be taking the transport
Reykjavik to Earth." In San Francisco, Kirk knew, Rand would
attend Starfleet Academy, having reenrolled coincident with, and
contingent upon, her application for transfer. The explanation
she'd offered for the sudden change in her career path had included the emotionally unhealthy reason she'd gone to space in
the first place—running away from an abusive and damaging
childhood—and the realization that she wanted to do more than
simply serve as a yeoman. She also intended to seek counseling.
"I just wanted you to know that . . . that I'm not quitting, Captain," she said. "I'm going to find a course of study, finish it, and
return to starship duty."

Kirk nodded, believing her claim. Based upon the serious
self-examination reflected in the addenda to her transfer request,
along with her aim of getting psychiatric help, he thought he understood the high level of her commitment. "Have you any idea
what area you might want to go into?" he asked.

"I haven't completely decided," Rand said, "but I've been
thinking about engineering, or possibly communications."

Kirk nodded again. "Well, Yeoman, perhaps when you've
completed your studies, you'll think about rejoining the *Enterprise* crew."

A shy smile appeared on Rand's face, the yeoman clearly
pleased by the captain's encouragement. "Yes, sir," she said.
"Thank you, sir." Kirk looked back down at his desk, and he
again heard the cabin door whoosh open, This time, Rand departed, and the door closed after her.

The captain returned his attention to the data on his slate and
saw Rand's name listed at the top of the screen under the TRANS-
FERS heading, along with Ensign Barrows, Lieutenant Farrell,
and Crewman Fisher. While green check marks indicated that
Kirk had already approved three of the four transfers, Barrows

had asked just today to be sent to another starship, an appeal that had come as a surprise. As far as the captain knew, she and Bones had been seeing each other regularly for some time now. He wondered if something had happened between them that had prompted Barrows's request, though McCoy had said nothing about any troubles in their relationship.

Then again, Kirk thought, *Bones hasn't said much of anything at all about Barrows, at least not since they became involved.* He would have to review the ensign's transfer application, then decide whether or not he needed to speak to the doctor about the situation.

In the meantime, he examined the rest of the slate's display. A PROMOTIONS section followed the transfers and identified nearly a dozen of the *Enterprise* crew that had been recommended for advancement by their department heads. A final, much longer group of names ran in columns across the bottom of the screen, beneath the banner REASSIGNMENTS.

Kirk lifted the stylus and touched its tip to the first name in the last section: Pavel Chekov. The entry blinked three times and then the display switched to a readout of the crewman's service record. The captain set the stylus aside and picked up half of his sandwich. As he began eating, he studied the evaluations made of Chekov's performance. Following a rotation in engineering, the young man was stationed in one of the ship's science labs and assigned to sensor control and analysis, although he'd actually graduated the Academy with a proficiency in navigation. Spock had been impressed with the young man's intelligence and drive, despite what the first officer described as a "strange sense of humor focused on Russia as the wellspring of virtually every positive aspect of human civilization." Still, Spock believed Chekov deserving of a duty assignment on the bridge.

As Kirk read through the assessment offered by Chekov's immediate superior, Lieutenant Arlene Galway, somebody activated his door signal. The captain put the half-eaten portion of his sandwich back down on the plate. "Come," he said.

The door panel opened and Dr. McCoy entered. "Bones," Kirk said. "I was just having some lunch. Care to join me?"

"No, thanks, I've already eaten," said the doctor. He crossed the room, sat down, and looked across the desk at the captain. "I just wanted to stop by and see how you were doing."

"Me?" Kirk said, and he felt himself stalling for a moment before answering the question. "Buried in the details of crew evaluations, but otherwise I'm all right." He tapped a finger on the slate.

McCoy leaned back in his chair, rested one hand on the desk, and peered at the captain as though performing his own evaluation. For an instant, Kirk felt certain that the doctor would challenge his claim of being all right, but then McCoy instead asked about Peter. "How's your nephew?"

"He seems to be handling the situation about as well as can be expected," Kirk said, grateful for the truth of his reply. "I stopped by to check on him on my way from the bridge." When Peter had been physically well enough to leave sickbay, the captain had moved him into the guest quarters nearest his own cabin, only a few corridors away. "He was on subspace, talking with his brothers."

"Have Alexander and Julius reached Starbase Ten?" McCoy asked.

"Yes, a couple of days ago," Kirk said. At the mention of the names of Sam and Aurelan's two older sons, he felt anew the torment that had infused him when he'd had to tell them of the loss of their parents. The captain had seen death many times throughout his life, had lost crew under his command and been responsible for informing the next of kin: parents, spouses, children. Though he'd never become entirely inured to the shared pain and the private guilt of those moments—and never wanted to—the process had grown at least somewhat easier for him over time. But he'd never before had to tell people he loved about such a loss. Kirk had watched over a subspace connection as Julius had wept uncontrollably, but Alexander, twenty-five and the older of the two by four years, had stayed strong, offering comfort not only to his younger brother, but also to his uncle.

"I think they're all looking forward to being together on Canopus," Kirk said, redirecting his thoughts and pushing away his pain. He focused instead on Alexander, who had decided almost at once to adopt Peter. Nearly a month had passed since then, and the young man had admirably remained steadfast in his desire to care for his brothers on the Canopus planet. Alexander had studied literature there at Tarbolde University, then had settled in the planetary capital of Lejon after graduating. Julius had followed him to school there, though to study law.

"I'm sure it's important for all of them to spend this time with each other, as a family," McCoy said. "They need to be able to share their grief and lean on one another." He paused, and Kirk knew that he would return to his initial question. "But what about you, Jim? Are you really all right?"

Kirk did not want to have this conversation—not with McCoy, not with Spock, not with anybody. Whatever pain he felt, he did not want to *share* it, but to *bury* it. In as level a manner as possible, he said, "Bones, yes, I'm really all right."

McCoy gazed at him across the desk in that same appraising way as when he'd first sat down. Kirk braced for the argument sure to follow, but then the doctor unexpectedly rose to his feet. "Okay," he said. "I guess I should let you get back to your work then." Motioning toward the slate, he added, "Don't forget to put in a good word for your favorite CMO."

"I'll see what I can do," Kirk said with a chuckle.

The doctor started through the door, but as with Yeoman Rand before him, he stopped before the panel could glide shut. "Oh, by the way," he said, his manner casual, "I've been meaning to tell you that I found an irregularity in my medical logs."

"An irregularity?" Kirk repeated.

"Yes," McCoy said. "When I injected myself with cordrazine, a landing party followed me down to that unexplored planet."

"That's right," Kirk said.

"I spent a few days down there and in Earth's past recuperating from the overdose," McCoy continued, "but when we all finally got back to the ship, I was still in no condition to do much doctoring."

"What's your point, Bones?" Kirk asked. "Nobody expected you to return to duty right away."

"No, I know that," McCoy said. "My point is that Doctor Sanchez examined me, and then in accordance with Starfleet medical regulations, he examined the rest of the landing party . . . everybody except for you, Jim."

The statement surprised Kirk. He thought back to that time

and remembered that he hadn't reported to sickbay with McCoy and Spock and the others, nor had he done so in the time since then. "Bones, that was a month and a half ago. I'm obviously healthy."

"I'm sure you are," McCoy said. "I'm sure you're not a victim of some medical affliction that remains dormant in the body for weeks or months or years. But we were on a world that hadn't even been surveyed, much less explored, and we were in close proximity to that alien . . . whatever it was. Plus you and Spock and I spent time on Earth in its disease-infested past."

"Bones—" Kirk started to protest.

"Regulations, Captain," McCoy interrupted.

"Since when are you so interested in regulations?" Kirk asked in mild aggravation.

McCoy jabbed a finger in the direction of the desk. "Since my performance is being measured by my commanding officer," he joked. "And since the annual crew health evaluations will be due at Starfleet Medical while we're at Starbase Ten."

"All right," Kirk relented, raising his hands in a gesture of capitulation. "I'll be there when I get off duty."

"I'll see you then," McCoy said, and he finally continued out into the corridor.

Kirk stared at the closed cabin door for a few seconds, then went back to his lunch and to the crew assessments. He made solid progress on both, but a couple of times, he looked back up at the door and replayed the conversation he'd had with McCoy. Though he had in his time aboard the *Enterprise* trusted his life to the doctor, he couldn't shake the feeling that his friend had just somehow maneuvered him.

McCoy stood in his office and reviewed the details of the medical exam he'd administered yesterday to the captain. "Four-oh," he said. "He's still a noncontagious carrier of Vegan choriomeningitis, but other than that, he's four-oh and four-oh and four-oh." He read through the data arranged in rows and columns on the display of the slate he held, then glanced over the top of the device at Spock.

"The captain's physical health is not at issue, Doctor," said the first officer. He faced McCoy from the center of the room, hands behind his back, imperturbably—and infuriatingly—calm.

"Maybe not," McCoy allowed, "but all we've got concerning Jim's mental health are our opinions. We can't even cite a single example of his grief, or the way he's avoiding it, affecting his ability to command the *Enterprise*."

"You have examined the captain in your usual professional and thorough manner, have you not?" Spock asked. McCoy thought his use of the word *usual* bordered on the facetious, but he chose to let it pass and stay focused on the issue at hand.

"Yes, of course," he said. He swung his arm down and deposited the slate on the surface of his desk.

"Then as this ship's chief medical officer," Spock asserted, "your informed opinion of the captain's mental state will hold sway with Starfleet Command. When coupled with yours, my view, as executive officer, will also be regarded with some note."

McCoy felt frustration rise within him, as sometimes happened in his conversations with Spock. Despite his exacting logic and well-developed intellect, the Vulcan occasionally seemed obtuse, failing to grasp some argument or another that the doctor had put forth. That appeared to be the case right now: McCoy harbored no apprehensions about convincing the admirals of the seriousness of Jim's situation; he worried only about convincing Jim.

"If you're saying that we won't have any problem persuading Starfleet Command to our point of view, you're probably right," he told Spock. "But that's not what—"

The doors leading to the corridor parted, and Captain Kirk entered. "Bones, what is it now? I've—" He stopped speaking when he spotted another person in the office. "Mister Spock," he said. McCoy could tell that Jim hadn't anticipated finding the first officer here, and he wondered if the captain now suspected the reason for his visit.

An instant later, though, Jim addressed McCoy again, essentially ignoring the unexpectedness of Spock's presence. "You wanted to see me, Bones?" he asked, and then grinning, added, "Haven't you poked and prodded me enough with your medieval medical implements?" He reached up and wrapped his hand around his own upper arm, wincing theatrically. Now that Spock had called McCoy's attention to Jim's continual avoidance of the terrible losses he'd so recently suffered, the doctor saw evidence of it at every turn.

"No, you're safe for another year," McCoy joked, "depending on what kinds of landing parties you lead between now and then."

"I'll keep that in mind," Jim said. "So why is it you wanted me down here? Something in my test results?"

"No, no, you're in fine fettle," McCoy said. He sat down at his desk and picked up the slate exhibiting the captain's medical readings. He feigned study of the information there for a moment, while in reality he steeled himself for what lay ahead. Finally, he looked up at the captain and said, "You're fine physically, anyway."

Jim stared back, his features visibly tensing, and then he peered over at Spock. When the first officer said nothing, Jim looked again at McCoy. "If you have something to say, Bones, say it."

"To be honest, I'm not really sure what to say," McCoy admitted. "Except that I'm concerned about you."

"But not about my physical health," Jim said. "About my mental health then?"

McCoy held the captain's gaze for several seconds before responding, wanting to emphasize the importance of his reply: "Yes."

"I see," Jim said, and then he turned toward the center of the room. "And you, Mister Spock? I take it you share this concern?"

"I do," Spock said. He looked as though he would say more, but then an awkward silence seeped into the room, insinuating itself among the three men and keeping them apart. McCoy searched for the right way to continue, for the approach most likely to help Jim understand his own troubled situation. He'd thought about it a great deal since yesterday, since his medical examination of the captain had allowed McCoy to probe Jim's state of mind. Concurring with Spock's conclusion that the captain had not dealt with his grief, he'd tried to figure out how to talk with Jim about it in a way that would not alienate him, or worse, compound the problem. Having settled on no particular method, he now decided simply to speak to the heart of the matter.

"Jim, Spock and I know the terrible losses you've endured recently," McCoy said quietly. "Your brother and his wife, and—"

"I know that Sam and Aurelan are dead," Jim interrupted, though his voice remained calm. "And I know that you know that too, Bones. I would have known it anyway, but your attempts yesterday to . . . to draw me out . . ." He paused and then raised his open hands before him, as though trying to demonstrate that he had nothing to hide. "I appreciate your concern," he said, including Spock with a glance, "but I'm fine, really."

"With all due respect, Captain," Spock said, "we do not believe that you are 'fine.'"

"Yes, I've gathered that, Mister Spock," Jim said, his expression going cold. McCoy had seen such a look on the captain's face often enough, usually as a sign of his steely resolve, but sometimes accompanying a rigid stubbornness. Now, Jim turned his aspect from Spock back to McCoy. Pointing toward the slate McCoy still held, he asked, "Is this a medical opinion, Doctor? Do my test results provide justification for you to consider me unfit or incapacitated?"

"What?" McCoy said. He looked down at the slate in his hands and quickly thrust it back onto the desk. "No. This isn't about your ability to command the *Enterprise*. It's about—"

"In that case, Doctor," Jim said, raising his voice, "I'll return to my duties." He spun on his heel and started for the door, and McCoy understood that he and Spock had not only not helped the captain, they had exacerbated the situation, putting distance between Jim and his two closest friends. He shot up out of his chair.

"Jim," he said, at the same time that Spock took a step forward and also called after him.

"Captain," the first officer said. Jim stopped. "Doctor McCoy and I are not approaching you on an official level. The conversation we wish to have with you is not for the record."

McCoy crossed the room and faced the captain. "Jim," he said, "we're your friends. We only want to help you."

Jim seemed to study McCoy's face, and then he nodded with

slow, small movements. "Maybe I don't want to be helped right now," he said.

"And maybe that's why you need our help," McCoy told him.

Jim laughed quietly. "I'm not entirely sure I understand that logic, Bones," he said. "Do you, Spock?"

The first officer walked over to join McCoy and the captain. "This is not about logic," he said. The doctor felt his eyebrows lift in surprise, but he stifled his urge to comment on Spock's statement. "This is about emotion," he continued. "Your emotion, Captain."

"Spock, what I'm feeling . . . losing my brother and Aurelan . . ." He shrugged. "It's difficult. But considering the circumstances, I really think I'm doing all right."

"That's just it, Jim," McCoy said. "You *shouldn't* be doing all right. You should be in pain and having to cope with this. Instead, we see you ignoring it, not dealing with everything that's happened."

"Bones," Jim said, and then he breathed in deeply. "I *am* in pain, and I *am* dealing with it."

"I'm sorry to disagree with you, Jim," McCoy said, "but I don't think you are. As Spock pointed out to me, you're walking around this ship like nothing at all happened."

"What should I do, Bones?" Jim asked. "I have a job to do, a duty to perform. I'm responsible for the lives of more than four hundred crew, and for a while there, as you mentioned to me at the time, I was also responsible for the lives of more than a million people on Deneva. I didn't have time to lock myself in my quarters and feel sorry for myself."

"Nobody's saying you should have," McCoy said. "But the crisis has passed, and before we find ourselves in the middle of the next one, you need to begin to work through your grief. Not just for the crew's sake, or because failing to do so *could* impact your ability to command, but for your own sake."

Jim shook his head. "I *am* working through my grief."

"I don't think you are, Jim," Spock said. "Since we've been talking, you have twice mentioned the deaths of the people for whom you would now mourn. But you have not mentioned the death of Edith Keeler."

Jim's head snapped up to look directly at Spock. "Miss

Keeler," he said, as though about to pronounce some fact about the woman, but then his voice faded into silence. Jim moved between Spock and McCoy and walked slowly to the far side of the room. "Edith . . ." he said under his breath, still facing away, the name almost impossible to hear.

"Jim," McCoy said gently, "you need to deal with all of this. Your pain may never fully go away, but if you face it, if you understand it, you can learn to live with it."

Without turning around, Jim said, "I already am living with it."

"But not in a healthy way," Spock said, his voice low and, though McCoy knew he would never admit it, filled with compassion.

Now Jim looked around at them from across the room. "There's nothing healthy about loss," he said. He did not speak confrontationally, but as though searching for answers.

"No," McCoy agreed, "but there are healthy ways to cope with the pain it causes. You may never be able to eradicate that pain, but you can lessen it and prevent it from defining your life." In McCoy's mind, he saw the image of his father, lying in bed wasted and in agony, begging for the release of death. And in the next moment, McCoy saw the old photograph of his mother, the posed portrait of a beautiful woman he had never met. His own pain ran at him, but he stepped neatly aside and then quickly spoke again to Jim. "If you don't deal with this now," he said, "your pain will stay strong. You may learn to ignore it, but it will always be there, and someday, it'll devour you."

Again, an uncomfortable stillness arose, surrounding the three men, but holding them away from one another. McCoy looked at Jim and then at Spock, and he suddenly felt helpless. But then Jim said, "What are you suggesting?"

"Temporary relief from your responsibilities," Spock said at once.

"And counseling," McCoy added.

"A medical leave of absence?" Jim said.

"It doesn't have to be a *medical* leave," McCoy said quickly. "It can simply be a *personal* leave."

"Starfleet regulations provide for this remedy in circumstances such as these," Spock said.

Jim appeared to consider the recommendation and then asked, "For how long?"

"A minimum of one month," McCoy said. "And perhaps as long as two. That'll have to be a decision you and your therapist make, depending on your progress."

"A month . . . two months," Jim said. "It makes me sound . . . lost."

"Not lost, Captain," Spock said. "In pain."

"Jim, you need this," McCoy said.

"I've put the crew in for a ten-day shore leave at Starbase Ten," he said. The ship had been scheduled for a shorter layover there prior to the weeks it had spent at Deneva, McCoy knew, and was now overdue for maintenance and crew transfers and replacements. "I suppose I can simply stay on leave for a while after that."

"I know several of the physicians stationed there, including their psychiatrist," McCoy said. "Farraj al-Saliba. He's a fine doctor."

"Well," Jim said, "I suppose I'd better contact Starfleet Command." He crossed the room and again passed between McCoy and Spock. At the door, he stopped and looked back at them. "Thank you," he said, and then he continued into the corridor.

When the doors had closed, McCoy looked up at Spock. "And I want to thank you," McCoy told the first officer.

"For what, Doctor?" he said, once more demonstrating a remarkable lack of perception with respect to social interaction. Several choice rejoinders occurred to McCoy, but he chose to answer seriously instead.

"For coming to me about Jim's situation," he said. "I think we really helped him just now."

Spock replied to McCoy's gratitude and optimism with a simple bow of his head, and then he too left. McCoy returned to his desk and to preparing his report on the health of the crew for submission to Starfleet Medical. He thought about Jim as he did so and had to admit to being surprised that he'd agreed without much argument to the leave of absence. Either he had no intention of taking leave—a possibility McCoy thought very unlikely—or he actually did understand the need for him to confront his grief.

TEN

1930

Petra Zabrzeski looked up from her copy of *Great Expectations* when she heard somebody approaching the request desk. Despite the hour—in the evening, well before closing—the Periodicals Room had largely emptied out. With her shelving and cataloguing chores completed for her shift, Petra had found an opportunity to indulge her joy of reading, selecting one of the hundreds of thousands of volumes in the library. But while she loved to settle in with a fine novel or anthology, doing so at work made the time seem to pass far more slowly. She much preferred the busier days, when she assisted one patron after another, until before she knew it, the time had arrived to go home.

Like last winter, she thought. Petra had only worked at the New York Public Library for four years, but according to people who'd been here much longer—and a few had started back in 1911 when the institution had first opened—the library had experienced no more active time than the past December, January, and February. The Main Reading Room had often filled to capacity during that period, seeing upwards of eight hundred, nine hundred, and even a thousand people, quite a number of them having to stand. On one particular day at the end of 1929, patrons made requests for almost *nine thousand* books.

As the middle-aged gentleman neared the counter, Petra wondered idly whether he'd been in the library on that day at the end of December. She had no notion of whether he had been or not, but she had seen him here, in the Periodicals Room, many times during the summer months. Always he asked for the latest available Sunday editions of various newspapers, both domestic and international. He spent hours combing through papers published in American cities like Baltimore and New Orleans, Boston and San Francisco, Philadelphia and Washington, D.C., as well as through papers printed in other countries like Great Britain and France, Ireland and Argentina, Switzerland and Italy. Petra assumed that he must be doing research of some sort, a view reinforced by the pad of paper and pencil he always carried with him. His obvious erudition—clearly he read several languages—impressed her, though his threadbare appearance seemed to point to the impact on him of the troubled economic times. Tonight, he wore a khaki work shirt and an obviously old pair of dungarees, the latter discolored with brown patches that suggested the man's day had been expended on manual labor, rather than on some intellectual pursuit.

"Good evening," the man said as he reached the requests desk. Set into a rectangular opening in the long inner wall of the Periodicals Room, the counter separated the patrons seating area from the materials-storage section. Petra looked at the man, perhaps two decades her junior, as he reached for a periodicals call form.

"Good evening," she replied with a smile, which the man made only a half-hearted attempt to return. She noticed that he appeared weary and not particularly happy, the expression on his rounded face dulled from perhaps wakefulness or woe. Even his normally bright blue eyes seemed to hide their light behind his flagging lids.

The man used his own pencil to scratch out a list of newspapers he wished to read. Petra slipped a small strip of paper into *Great Expectations* to mark her place in the novel—the two convicts that had so frightened Pip had just been taken into custody—and tucked the book away on a shelf below the counter. She folded her hands together and waited for the man to finish.

When he did, he slid the request card across the counter to her. "Thank you, ma'am," he said and then he reached for another form. From his previous visits, Petra knew that after the man had done reading the first three newspapers she retrieved for him—three being the maximum number of periodicals a patron could check out at one time—he would immediately request three more.

"I'll have these for you in a moment, sir," she said, and she carried the request card back into the stacks. As the man had asked, as usual, for the library's latest Sunday editions, it did not take her long to collect the three papers he wanted to see. In no time at all, she carried to the counter yesterday's *The New York Times* and last weekend's *The Times-Picayune* of New Orleans and *The Philadelphia Enquirer.* He thanked her again and, pencil in hand, gathered the newspapers into his arms along with his pad.

As the man walked away from the counter toward one of the long, narrow tables that lined the reading area, she observed a slight hunch to his shoulders, as well as a slowness to his movements. She thought back on his first visits to the Periodicals Room, at least during her time at the library, and recalled him having a livelier, cheerier manner. Petra supposed that perhaps a long workday—or even, in this climate of increasing unemployment, no workday at all—must have contributed to the man's melancholic aspect this evening. As she recalled the times she'd seen him previously, including his first smiling, energetic visits here, she reckoned that his life had become much more difficult recently. Of course, with more and more workers unable to find jobs, and banks failing one after another, the same could be said of many, many people.

Still, as Petra watched the man move to the far corner of the room, put down his newspapers, and settle in to read them, she thought that he didn't really give the impression of somebody who'd simply suffered a personal setback. Of late, she'd certainly beheld enough men down on their luck to recognize what personal desperation looked like, and this man did not have that air about him. Rather, the guise he wore hinted at something worse: he carried himself as though bearing the weight of the world on his shoulders.

McCoy read through another page of densely packed classified ads, his eyes tiring from the strain. He'd already hunted through five other newspapers tonight, one of them, like this one, published in a language he neither spoke nor read. After a day of strenuous physical labor—working on a road crew installing traffic lights, he'd excavated through concrete and hard earth using a pickax and shovel—he could barely prevent himself from falling asleep. Despite the lasting ache in his muscles, every so often for the past half hour, he'd felt his head nod and his eyelids droop, and he'd had to force himself to stay awake.

Now, feeling fatigue wash over him once more, he set the newspaper down and rose to his feet. He stretched and yawned,

then rubbed at his eyes, as though doing so might somehow rein-
vigorate them and keep them open longer. Stepping over to the
window, he peered out toward Fifth Avenue. Night had draped itself about the city, the daylight growing shorter as autumn approached. But even as September dwindled, the rings of
illumination that bloomed each evening around a vast population
of street lamps still kept the darkness at bay.

Just ahead and to the left, McCoy spied one of the two lion
statues that reposed majestically on either side of the library's
main entrance. The doctor lingered there for several moments, in
the archway that framed the wide, tall window. He stared first at
the great stone beast, and then beyond it, at the automobiles and
horse-drawn carriages and pedestrians flowing left and right
down the boulevard.

When he felt sufficiently roused, McCoy turned back to the
long table at which he'd been sitting and reading. From the corner where he stood, the spacious Periodicals Room extended
away from him. The hardwood floors, the four chandeliers, and
the rich, ornately carved woods that adorned the walls and the
high ceiling, affected an ambiance of warm elegance. Only a
handful of people had come and gone since he'd arrived here
earlier this evening, and he saw now that only three remained,
scattered widely about, well outnumbered by the procession of
reading lamps along the center of each table.

McCoy took a seat once more and leaned over his open copy
of *Corriere della Sera*. The title of the Italian daily translated, he
knew, as *The Evening Courier*. McCoy did not read Italian, but
he had perused a bilingual dictionary and a grammar reference in
order to pick up enough words and phrases for his own purposes.
He found the lines where he'd stopped reading—or more accurately, where he'd stopped *looking*—and continued on from
there through the columns of classified ads. His gaze danced
across entry after entry, searching for text he recognized. Specifically, he sought two names: *McCoy* and *Kirk*. Fifteen minutes
later, he located them both:

> Sto cercando James T. Kirk. Contatto Leonard
> McCoy. Missione della Via 21, New York City. Marzo
> di 1930.

McCoy had cobbled together this entreaty, as well as the brief ad request he'd sent, along with cash payment, to the newspaper's offices in Milano. The editorial staff might have approved the few lines if they'd been written in English, but he hadn't been certain of that, nor had he wanted to draw any more attention to himself or his ad than necessary. As he did with all of the papers in which he'd purchased space, McCoy reviewed *Corriere della Sera* to ensure that his entry had appeared and been printed correctly. He also checked for responses to any of the ads he'd previously had published.

In truth, McCoy expected never to come across any such replies. If through the placement of these public notices he managed to communicate the time and place of his location to Jim, he believed that the captain—or Spock, or some other Starfleet officer—would immediately retrieve him and whisk him back to his life in the twenty-third century. Whether Jim or anybody else searched for him from the future, or had already journeyed back in time and searched for him contemporaneously, McCoy doubted that they would attempt to communicate with him through periodicals, rather than simply traveling to New York and finding him at the 21st Street Mission.

Still, he checked anyway.

McCoy had begun these efforts five months ago, after the advice he'd received from Keeler. He'd initially procured ad space exclusively in New York City papers, but as time had passed without result, he'd expanded the placement of his announcements into the rest of New York State, and then into other domestic localities, and finally to international cities. If Jim or somebody else had already traveled back to this time and now searched for him, they might think to look for such public communications. If they conducted their quest of him from the future, then perhaps some of those newspapers in which he'd placed ads would eventually be digitized and stored on computer memory for them to find. McCoy did not know which such databases had endured into his own time, but by increasing the scope of his endeavors across the globe, he hoped that some—or at least one—of his classified ads ultimately would find its way into a long-lasting electronic archive.

But in nearly half a year, he'd met with no success. He'd

worked with relative regularity during that time, thanks to Keeler, and he'd spent much of his compensation on posting newspaper notices. He had virtually no other expenses, save for one. Because he continued residing in the backroom at the mission and still took many meals there, he had convinced Keeler to allow him to contribute money to its cause; he donated two dollars per week.

For that reason and others—such as that he often helped out at the mission, that the police had found no indication that he'd committed any crime, and that he consistently demonstrated his trustworthiness—Keeler seemed to have grown comfortable in her interactions with him. Likewise, he found his relationship with her an easy one. He remained wary of getting too close to her, though, or to anybody. While he'd conceded his need to interact with people in this time, he did so as cautiously as possible. He supposed that he could make his way out of the city and into a wilderness somewhere, and live off the land in isolation. But such a course did not appeal to him, for more than the simple inconvenience of it: he had studied survivalist training at Starfleet, and even ignoring the fact that he'd barely made a passing grade, he doubted that he could live in such a manner for a prolonged period.

A door opened near the corner opposite McCoy, beside the request desk. The woman working here tonight emerged into the Periodicals Room, and he watched as she approached the reader nearest the counter. Her shoes beat conspicuously along the intricately designed wooden floor.

Closing time, McCoy thought, and a glance at the clock hanging beside the desk confirmed the hour. He quickly checked his copy of *Corriere della Sera* and saw that he only had a page and a half more of ads to inspect, a task he could complete in the twenty minutes before the library's doors shut for the night. Turning his attention back to the newspaper, McCoy peered again at the concise Italian entries. He'd nearly reached the bottom of the page by the time the librarian drew near.

"Pardon me," the woman said, and McCoy looked up at her. Older, perhaps in her sixties, she was short of stature, but possessed an aquiline nose that suggested a commanding presence. Her nametag, pinned to the white collar of her conservative, otherwise-blue dress, read *Miss Zabrzeski.* "I'm afraid you only have fifteen more minutes before you'll have to leave," she said.

"Quite all right, ma'am," McCoy said. "I'll be done by then."

The librarian favored him with a smile and said, "I'm glad to hear that."

McCoy finished with the paper, returned it and the two others he'd withdrawn, and bade Miss Zabrzeski good night. A few moments later, he exited the front of the grand beaux arts building through one of its bronze doors and continued through the central of three enormous arches composing the massive entry façade. Passing towering Corinthian columns, he descended the block-wide marble staircase to the street. He walked up Fifth Avenue to Forty-second Street, where he turned right, toward Grand Central Terminal. There, he would catch the IRT down to Twenty-third. From there, he would walk back to the mission—or maybe because he felt so tired tonight, he would hail a Checker cab.

You know this city too well, McCoy told himself, suddenly wistful for a life now six months removed. Certainly his familiarity with Manhattan provided ample evidence of the significant length of time he'd been marooned here. He'd seen a great deal of the city, particularly the areas in the neighborhood of the mission, but also many places beyond that. The subway system, with which he'd become well acquainted, afforded convenient, inexpensive transportation throughout New York City, and he used it often.

In the distance, McCoy spied the impressive sculpture that topped the main entrance to the neoclassical train station. Illuminated from below, three mythic figures crowned a large clock. The timepiece somehow underscored his melancholy, offering a reminder of his displacement in time, and of the days passing—and that had already passed—with him so far from his real life.

He thought of Jim and Spock, not with respect to his attempts to contact them across the hundreds of years that now separated them, but about how he missed their friendship. The faces of the other *Enterprise* doctors—M'Benga and Sanchez and Harrison—rose in his mind, along with those of Chapel and the rest of the medical staff. He thought briefly of Tonia, and then of Jocelyn, and finally, most painfully, of Joanna.

As McCoy crossed Forty-second Street, headed toward a corner entrance to Grand Central, he thought about the fact that he not only hadn't seen his daughter in the months he'd been stranded in Earth's past, but that he hadn't seen her in more than two years, since before he'd been assigned to the *Enterprise*. McCoy's service in Starfleet, combined with the volatile, at best strained relationship with his former wife, had over the years impacted his ability to spend time with Joanna.

Now, pensive and unsure of his fate, he wondered if he would ever see his only child ever again.

ELEVEN

2267

Barrows stood in her quarters and held the stuffed animal up before her face. She found the little white bear adorable, with its tiny black beads for eyes, and the delicate black thread sewn into its downy fabric to form a nose and mouth. Leonard had given the trinket to her—had effectively thought it into existence for her—back on a world in the Omicron Delta region that Mr. Spock had termed an "amusement park." There, an advanced race had implemented a remarkable system designed to read visitors' thoughts and in short order produce substantive recreations of those thoughts, for no other reason than the enjoyment of those who came calling. The *Enterprise* crew hadn't known that, though, had actually believed the planet uninhabited. Scouting parties—which had included Barrows and Leonard—had transported down to evaluate the suitability of the place for shore leave. Unexpected events had begun happening almost at once, which the ship's personnel at first had regarded as bizarre, and later as frightening.

Alone in her cabin, Barrows squeezed her eyes shut as the memories of those initial hours on the strange planet assaulted her. In the beginning, their experiences had seemed harmless—Leonard seeing apparent replicas of the white rabbit and golden-haired Alice from Lewis Carroll's children's stories, Sulu finding an antique firearm he'd long been seeking for his collection—but then the situation had turned decidedly more serious. Barrows had been accosted by a man in the guise of Don Juan, and then—

And then, she thought, not wanting to picture the armor-clad knight charging on horseback across the glade, thundering down upon them, until he drove his lance into Leonard's chest. But the recollection came anyway, and even though the caretaker of that unique, wondrous world had seen to Leonard's "repair"—a return to full health—that didn't entirely alter the reality that she'd watched him die, a weapon run through his heart, his blood jetting from his torso in a horrible torrent of red. She remembered screaming, and running to his fallen form. She'd kneeled beside his body, along with Captain Kirk and Mr. Spock, and cried at the realization that Leonard had been killed. She'd grown almost hysterical, blaming herself for the turn of events, until the captain had sternly compelled her back into her role as a member of the crew, needed during the crisis in which they found themselves.

In the quiet of her cabin, Barrows opened her eyes, still holding the stuffed animal up before her. She tried to focus on the small bear, not much larger than her hand, as a touchstone for her experiences back on that incredible world. Certainly the circumstances had improved dramatically after the caretaker had appeared and explained what had been happening to the *Enterprise* crew, and after Leonard had shown up alive and well. The captain had subsequently authorized two full days of shore leave on the planet, and Barrows had spent all of those off-duty hours with Leonard, at the end of which he'd given her the stuffed bear.

With their leave nearly finished, the two of them had chosen to enjoy high tea in a reproduction of a place called The Gilded Rose. As a girl, Barrows had often visited the cozy establishment, where her mother would take her so that they could spend time alone together, away from her father and brother and the everyday bustle of their home life. Out in the English countryside, the Victorian structure had boasted a warm, ornately decorated parlor where guests would be served, mostly at tables intended to accommodate only small numbers of people. Near the end of their shore leave, Barrows had described the tea house to Leonard, and not long afterward, they had stumbled upon it, nestled in a grove beside a narrow road that meandered through verdant, rolling hills. They'd spent the afternoon sipping an herbal blend of apricot and orange flavors, and snacking on scones, Devonshire cream, and fruit preserves.

Their time there had felt sweet and romantic, and it had ended with a stop in the small backroom gift shop. Leonard had taken the shopkeeper aside and described the present he sought, and moments later, it had appeared on a shelf, tucked into a collection of larger stuffed animals. Leonard had given her the little bear—which he had dubbed "Teabag"—as a token of his affection for her, and as a memento of their visit to the faux Gilded Rose.

Back then, the gift had delighted and touched Barrows, but as she looked at it now, it served only to wound her, a bittersweet reminder of what she had lost. *Or maybe I never had it in the first place,* she thought. Maybe her relationship with Leonard had never held the potential for more than merely a casual affair. In truth, she'd treated it that way for a long time, although she'd realized later that her feelings had actually reached far deeper. Had the intensity of those early experiences—watching Leonard die, and then seeing him alive once more—had those unusual experiences contributed to the seriousness of her emotions in a way that Leonard couldn't possibly have shared?

Maybe, she thought, but Leonard had also demonstrated his love for her many times, in many ways. Only recently had he begun backing away from that, seeing her less and less frequently, for shorter periods, and in less romantic contexts. He'd hurt her, not only because he'd put distance between them, but because he'd done so without explanation.

Feeling her jaw set, Barrows tossed the bear underhanded onto the bed. It bounced to a stop next to a pillow. She looked at the stuffed animal lying on its side, as though wounded itself, and thought that, yes, she'd made the right decision. Of course, at this point, the time had passed for any misgivings she might have had about her transfer. Though she'd made her request to leave the ship only a few days ago, Captain Kirk had been gracious enough to approve it already. When she'd completed her application for transfer, she'd hoped that her honesty would sway the captain, and now she thought that it probably had. She'd written candidly about all of her reasons for seeking a different environment in which to work, including her own failings in choosing a suitable career path for herself. But she also hadn't shied away from explaining the difficulties she'd been having because of her troubles in her relationship with Leonard, though she hadn't referred to him directly. The captain and crew knew that they'd been seeing each other, of course—though she and Leonard had practiced discretion, they hadn't hidden their romance—but she thought that such details didn't belong in official records.

None of that mattered now. Whatever the length or depth of her relationship with Leonard, all of that had passed, and now she had to move on. With an effort of will, Barrows beat back the miasma of emotion surrounding her. As she pulled her gaze away from Teabag, turning from the bed and checking her dresser for any overlooked personal belongings, it occurred to her that she'd left a couple of items in Leonard's quarters. She had no interest at all in addressing that, though; she'd rather just leave.

Barrows glanced around her cabin, at the walls, the desk, the shelves, all now empty. She'd packed up most of her possessions late last night, and just a few minutes ago, Crewman Bates had arrived with an antigrav cart to take her things to the transporter room. Now she had to go too.

Reaching down to where her duffel leaned against the bulkhead, Barrows cinched the drawstring tight. She threw her arm through its strap and hoisted it up onto her shoulder. At last ready to leave, she took one more look at the bed, at where Teabag lay beside one of the pillows. Indecision suddenly preyed on her mind, and it required almost a full minute for her to decided whether or not to leave Teabag behind, as she'd intended to do. Finally, she made a decision, then exited her quarters for the last time.

Barrows started for the transporter room, but would stop along the way at Leonard's cabin, for what she wanted to be a brief farewell. She actually dreaded even the few moments it would take for her to tell Leonard of her transfer, but she could not leave without seeking some measure of closure, both for herself and for him. He might have neglected her recently, but she would not do the same to him.

Barrows moved quickly through the *Enterprise,* its silent, empty corridors seeming larger and brighter than usual. The ship had arrived at Starbase 10 a couple of hours ago, and much of the crew had already transported down to the planet for leave. A part of her hoped that Leonard had left the *Enterprise* as well, obviating the need for her to say good-bye in person. He didn't respond to the door signal when she called at his cabin, and so she headed to sickbay. If she did not find him there, she decided, she would quickly record a message for him and then be on her way.

When Barrows entered Leonard's office, though, she saw him immediately. He sat at his desk, his face bathed in the glow of the monitor there. Turned away from the text and pictures displayed on the screen, he hunched over a data slate beside it. As Barrows approached, he looked up from scribbling notes on the device.

"Tonia," he said. The smile that lightened his weathered good looks appeared genuine, and tore at her heart.

"Hello, Leonard," she said, pleased, at least, that she'd found him alone. She'd intended to speak flatly, conveying as little as possible other than through the meaning of her words, but she could hear the disappointment in her voice. Leonard must have recognized it as well, because even as his gaze moved to the duffel slung across her shoulder, he seemed to understand why she had come.

"Going on leave already?" he said, but his smile now looked forced, and his tone revealed the answer he expected from her.

"I'm leaving the ship," she said. "For good." She felt like setting her bag down on the deck, but didn't want to signal even the possibility of this exchange lasting more than another few moments. Instead, she hiked the duffel back up, resetting its carry strap on her shoulder.

Leonard slowly and deliberately reached up to his desk and, beside the slate, set down the stylus he'd been using. When he peered back up at her, his smile had completely gone. "May I ask why?" he said. It didn't sound to Barrows as though he really needed an explanation, and she didn't offer him one.

"I think you know why," she told him. "I just thought I should tell you in person that I was transferring off the *Enterprise*."

"I see," he said. He looked away, down into his lap, where he clasped his hands together. Then with what seemed like an effort, he peered up at her again. "Tonia," he said, "I care about you—"

"You 'care' about me?" she snapped back at him before she could stop herself.

"Yes," he said, improbably showing annoyance. "I *do* care about you." Despite his protestation, his words could not have cut her any more deeply.

Not wanting this to end with any more bitterness than she already felt, Barrows tried to calm herself with a deep breath. "I believe that you do care about me, Leonard," she said. "And I care about you. But somehow it's not working out between us, and I think we both know that it's not going to work out." She could have laid the blame for this at his feet, but she elected not to do so. She really did believe that he *cared* for her, but she *loved* him, and that made all the difference. She couldn't be angry at him for not feeling for her what she felt for him, only that he'd pretended to those feelings, and that rather than be honest with her, he'd ultimately begun to put distance between them.

Now, he slowly rose from his chair. "I'm sorry, Tonia, I—" he started, but she interrupted him before he could continue.

"Don't," she said, raising her hand to him, palm out. "Please don't."

They stood like that for long seconds, neither of them moving or talking. She felt the tension between them, and worse, the emotional gulf that separated them. She dropped her hand, realizing that the time had come for her to go. But then Leonard spoke again, asking a question she hadn't anticipated.

"Where are you transferring to?" he said.

Does it matter to you? Barrows thought. Would Leonard contact her aboard the ship to which she'd newly been assigned? Would he strive to maintain a friendship with her? Did she want that? Could she *handle* that? Her instincts told her not to answer his question, not to raise her own hopes that she might hear from him sometime, that the possibility might even exist of a reconciliation at some point in the future. But she told him anyway. "The *Gödel*."

"That's a science vessel," Leonard said. "I'm familiar with it." Barrows nodded, unable to say anything more until Leonard began to step out from behind his desk. She raised her hand again.

"No," she said. "Good-bye, Leonard." She moved quickly to the door, which glided open before her. She waited for him to call after her, to stop her from leaving, and she felt foolish and vulnerable for it.

Even as she strode down the corridor, headed for the transporter room, Barrows wondered if she would hear from Leonard. In the days that followed, first at Starbase 10 and then aboard her new posting, the same thought occurred to her again and again, despite her opposing desire to put this episode of her life behind her. Over time, her pain eased, and her months with Leonard faded into oft-forgotten memories. But she still occasionally thought of him, and sometimes when she found a message waiting for her in her cabin, she wondered if it might be from him.

Barrows served aboard the *U.S.S. Gödel* for almost three years, and in all that time, she never heard from Leonard again.

McCoy watched Tonia go, his office door sliding neatly shut behind her, like a scalpel slicing away a wounded portion of his life. He felt bad in a vague, unsettled way, but knew one truth with specificity: he had hurt the woman who'd just walked out of here. Worse than that, he'd done so intentionally. He hadn't *wanted* to hurt her, hadn't *tried* to hurt her, but he'd known how she felt about him, so how could he have expected his behavior to do anything *but* hurt her?

"You're a fool," he muttered in the silence of his office. He believed that he'd done the right thing—*for* both *of us,* he told himself—but that he'd gone about it in the wrong way. He'd been a coward, running away from Tonia when he simply should have been candid with her. He should have—

His office door opened again, and McCoy reacted with a jolt, thinking that Tonia had returned. Instead, he saw Chapel enter, an empty Erlenmeyer flask in her hand. "Oh, Doctor McCoy," she said. "You're still here."

"Where else would I be?" he said irritably. He stepped back behind his desk and took his seat.

"Well, I thought you'd be on leave with just about everybody else," Chapel said. She leaned in beside McCoy and set the flask down on one of the shelves behind his desk. "Didn't you tell me that one of the tavern keepers on Starbase Ten made the best mint julep this side of Atlanta?"

McCoy picked up the stylus with which he'd been working a few minutes ago. "I never said that," McCoy claimed, fully aware that he'd told Chapel that very thing not more than a week ago. "Besides, it's a little early in the day for alcohol, wouldn't you say, Nurse?"

Chapel moved out from behind the desk and toward the door. "Didn't you also tell me that it's always happy hour somewhere?"

"No, I never said that either," McCoy maintained, despite the truth to the contrary.

"All right," Chapel allowed. "Well, I'm headed over to Starbse Ten now, and you should too. After the last few months, we could all use some leave."

"Believe me, as soon as I can, I will," he said. "I just have to finish the annual crew evaluations for Starfleet Medical." He held up the stylus to illustrate his point.

"You're not done with those yet?" Chapel asked reprovingly.

"No," McCoy admitted. "With my cordrazine overdose and then the crisis on Deneva, I just haven't had time. But I should finish today. I've only got a few more to do."

"Good," Chapel said. "Then maybe tomorrow you can get me one of those mint juleps."

McCoy smiled as the nurse left. Chapel had given up a career in biological research in order to sign aboard a starship, with the hope of one day traveling to the far-flung planet Exo III. There, her fiancé, a brilliant expert in archeological medicine, had set up a dig, but he hadn't been heard from in years. Months ago, the *Enterprise* had visited Exo III, only to discover that Dr. Korby and the rest of his research team had been killed. Afterward, Chapel had opted to remain aboard ship, which had pleased

McCoy. She'd proven to be a solid head nurse, with whom he found it very easy to work. He also empathized with her: he could think of no better motivation for retreat to life aboard a starship than the bitter end of a serious romantic relationship.

McCoy leaned in over his desk and set his elbows down on either side of the data slate on which he'd been working. An image from the *Enterprise*'s identification files showed in the top left corner of the display, along with the name of the officer it showed: David L. Galloway, one of the ship's security contingent. Below that, McCoy's own physician's scrawl crept down the screen, offering his appraisal of the lieutenant's medical status.

McCoy quickly reread what he'd written, then glanced up at the monitor on his desk, which still exhibited the results of Galloway's most recent physical examination. Dr. Sanchez had performed the exam immediately after the landing party had returned from the world on which they'd found the Guardian of Forever. The readings confirmed the health of the lieutenant, as well as the constancy of his physical condition; his numbers remained virtually unchanged from those of his previous medical assessment.

It took twenty minutes for McCoy to finish his write-up on Galloway. He then tapped an option on the slate display, and his script transformed into digital characters. He read over his report, corrected a couple of errors, then signed it. With a few more touches of the stylus, he filed away the Galloway evaluation, then brought up a blank form for the next member of the crew: James T. Kirk.

McCoy looked at the picture of the captain, at his serious and determined mien that also managed to convey a sense of easy confidence. It contrasted with Jim's bearing this morning, when he'd stopped by sickbay before reporting to Starbase 10 and Dr. al-Saliba. McCoy couldn't recall a time when he'd seen the captain appear quite so vulnerable. Oh, he'd been privy to Jim's self-examinations, his penchant for questioning his own reasoning and decision making, but in those moments, the captain had always maintained his air of authority, had always somehow projected the certainty to come, the certainty with which he would ultimately issue his orders. Earlier today, though, when he'd shown up here simply to say good-bye, Jim had seemed like a different man: smaller, unsure, in pain.

Although McCoy felt terrible for his friend, for all that the captain had so recently lost, he hadn't been displeased with what he'd seen this morning. If Jim was to deal successfully with all that he'd been through, he would have to admit to his grief and face it. From the way he'd looked on his way to the transporter room, it seemed to McCoy that he'd already begun that process.

With practiced ease, the doctor ordered the computer to present the captain's medical records, including the results of his last two exams. McCoy had performed the most recent of those physicals just a couple of days ago, and the previous one—Jim's annual examination—more than three months prior to that. Carefully, he started studying the newest readings, both scrutinizing them on their own merits and comparing them with the captain's historical numbers.

Laborious but straightforward and well defined, the process had lasted almost an hour and was approaching completion when McCoy noticed the anomaly. So infinitesimal were the measurements involved, and so slight the difference between them, he'd almost overlooked the divergence. And had it not been for the crisis on Deneva, he *would* have missed it. Back at the colony, when normal scans hadn't been able to detect the alien parasites within the bodies of their hosts, Dr. M'Benga had devised a means of doing so. He'd generated an algorithm that, utilizing readings already collected by standard medical tricorders, would calculate the expected energy of a subject's nervous system and compare it to the actual energy. Inelegant and often only grossly accurate, the procedure had nevertheless worked well in identifying victims of the parasites, given the dramatic rate of growth of the alien organisms along their hosts' nervous systems.

Included now in the *Enterprise*'s medical database, M'Benga's algorithm gathered the raw input of diagnostic scans and deposited its results alongside other refined data. The captain's numbers, while not so dissimilar as to suggest the presence of a Denevan parasite, still showed a discrepancy. *Or is this even really a discrepancy?* McCoy asked himself. The difference between the numbers from Jim's last physical, and those from the physical he'd taken several months ago, fell well within the standard deviation of M'Benga's process, and so it hadn't even been flagged as an issue. Still, McCoy had noted the figure because it reached a higher level than any of those he'd yet seen—not just for Jim, but for anybody.

He set down the stylus, reached forward, and pressed the audio-interface toggle set below the monitor. "Computer," he said.

"Working," came the mechanical reply.

"Display the raw sensor readings taken during Captain Kirk's last physical examination," he ordered.

"Working," the computer said again, and then a different set of data began to fill the monitor.

McCoy studied the information, wanting not only to verify the source scans that had led to the unexpectedly high reading, but to reconfirm that the other scans fell within expected norms. He saw nothing out of the ordinary, including nothing he thought would have led to the discrepancy. "Computer," he said, and waited for it to signal its readiness before continuing. "Transfer all source scans from Captain Kirk's last physical examination to diagnostic pallet number two."

Once the computer acknowledged the order, McCoy stood up and made his way to the open entryway that separated his office from the outer sickbay compartment. Striding over to the pallet, he reached up and activated the scanner in the bulkhead above it, setting it to process the computer's automated feed. The monitor came immediately to life, white triangular arrows climbing up the vertical biofunction scales, red circular indicators blinking out pulse and respiration rates. McCoy studied each of the readings, then cycled through the rest of the available measurements, covering the breadth of quantifiable biological processes and states.

Then he did it again.

"He's in perfect health," McCoy concluded. All of the captain's readings fell within established human norms for his age and gender, many of them within narrower ranges considered optimal. The doctor could identify only two blemishes on Jim's otherwise-spotless bill of health: in his blood, he still harmlessly carried the microorganisms of Vegan choriomeningitis, and ac-

cording to Dr. M'Benga's algorithm, his nervous system produced a higher amount of energy than expected. McCoy could
see no cause of the latter condition and no consequence. He had
confirmed the numbers, but now supposed that the discrepancy
might simply be an artifact of the methodology employed to de-
rive those numbers.

McCoy switched off the diagnostic monitor and returned to
his office, where he ended the automatic feed of the captain's
medical data. Sitting back down at his desk, he completed his report on Jim's health. He noted the one anomalous reading, along
with his judgment that the reading did not indicate any actual
medical problem. Once he'd rechecked what he'd written, he
signed it, filed it away for Starfleet Medical, and moved on to the
next member of the crew.

McCoy had studied the results of Uhura's last physical for ten
minutes when he stopped and returned to the captain's records.
He reviewed his findings yet again and yet again he remained
convinced of their veracity. Still, he couldn't shake the most
basic question he had about Jim's abnormal reading: *What the
devil is causing that?*

At the moment, McCoy didn't have the slightest idea.

TWELVE

1931

Edith watched as Schoolboy Joe crouched low before the icebox,
his knees producing loud popping noises as he eased his bulk
down toward the floor. "Oh, Joe, I can get it," she said, feeling
sheepish for having asked the large, lumbering man to carry out
a task better suited to herself. She'd spoken quickly, though, requesting as soon as McCoy had left for his backroom that Joe re-

trieve the packet. She knew that the doctor had endured a long and tiring workday, spending most of it over in the speakeasy belt, toiling in construction on the Rockefeller endeavor. Tonight, he'd partaken of the late meal at the mission, then helped to clean up afterward. Now, she wanted to get to his room before he retired for the night.

"'T ain't no nevermind, Sister Edith," Joe said in his slow, southern drawl. Edith didn't particularly like being addressed as *Sister*—she didn't belong to any religious groups—but she understood the sentiment. Joe leaned into the icebox and a moment later pulled out the small white carton she'd asked him to get for her. He stood back up, his knees crackling again, and turned toward her. The white cardboard container looked insubstantial in the fleshy stubs of his fingers. A large, ungainly man, Schoolboy Joe had worked uninterrupted with Edith for a longer span than anybody else. Rik might have put in more days at the mission, but across several periods, and in any event, he'd left for parts unknown last autumn; fortunately, at least as far as Edith knew, it had been Rik's wanderlust, and not his drinking, that had impelled him to move on from Twenty-first Street.

"Thank you, Joe," Edith said, taking the box from him. She set it down on the counter, opened it, and removed the small chocolate cake. Then she found the small candle she'd brought from home and set it into the middle of the deep-brown icing. "Are you ready?" she asked Joe.

"Yessum," he said, and he picked up the plates and silverware she'd earlier set aside.

"What about you, Deke?" she asked, louder, calling from the kitchen out into the main room. There, Deke looked up from settling the chairs upside down onto the tables. An older, red-haired man, he'd begun working regularly at the mission several months ago, after relying on it for food and clothing in the few months prior to that. "Are you ready?"

"Yes, ma'am," Deke said.

Edith found the box of kitchen matches, struck one against the counter, and lighted the candle. The she picked up the cake and carried it out of the kitchen, headed for the hallway and the back room. Joe and Deke followed behind her.

At McCoy's door, she knocked and heard a muffled response

from within. "Just a minute." She peered around at Joe and Deke, the former wearing a sweet, wide-eyed smile. He looked as excited as when she'd performed the same ritual for him a year and a half ago.

After a few seconds, the knob turned and the door opened partway. Holding his red and black plaid shirt in one hand, clad now in his black undershirt, he'd clearly begun preparing for bed. He gazed out at Edith, then at Joe and Deke in turn, and finally down at the single candle flickering atop the cake. "What is this?" he asked, obviously perplexed.

"This is for you, Doctor," Edith said. "May we come in? I know you must be tired, so we won't stay long."

"All right," McCoy said, and he backed up into the room, opening the door fully. Edith entered and placed the cake on the desk. Again, McCoy peered over at Joe and Deke—who now stood just inside the doorway—before addressing Edith. "What's going on?" he asked with a smile. "I know it's not my birthday."

"Not your birthday, Doctor," she said. "Your anniversary."

"My anniversary?" he echoed, seemingly bemused.

"Yes," Edith said. "It was one year ago today that you first arrived at the mission." Although McCoy's smile faltered only for an instant, the light vanished from his eyes like a lamp being extinguished. Despite that she hadn't expected such a reaction, Edith thought she understood it. However much the doctor had settled in here—and his days had certainly become a matter of routine at this point—he still didn't actually *want* to be here. Edith recognized that, while he gave readily of his time and effort—voluntarily serving meals, cleaning up, even providing first aid to some of the impoverished men who visited the mission—he gave sparingly of himself. He often spoke of the work he'd undertaken and of things he'd done and seen in New York City, but he revealed little else. More than anything, Edith saw a man attempting to keep distance between himself and everyone he encountered, including her. Even after all this time, she felt that she barely knew him.

"Make a wish, Doc," Schoolboy Joe said. "Blow out the candle." Edith and Deke offered their own encouragements.

McCoy nodded and said, "Of course," though Edith perceived his discomfort with the entire proceeding. Still, he crossed over to the desk and bent toward the cake, evidently ready to participate in their little celebration. As Joe continued to urge the doctor to make a wish, McCoy closed his eyes and took a deep breath, and Edith wondered exactly what thoughts rose in his mind. Did he actually take this time to make a wish? Did he simply long to return home, wherever that might be, or did he contrive something more specific than that?

What is it you want right now, Doctor McCoy? she thought. Edith believed that if she knew just what he hoped for at this moment, she would likely understand him a great deal more than she had up to now.

A year, McCoy thought as he leaned forward. *How can I possibly have been here for that long?*

Aware of the attention directed his way and reflexively wanting to avoid any discussion of his personal circumstances, he pursed his lips and blew out the already sputtering flame of the single candle atop the cake. Images played through his mind in a montage of memories. He saw places—the country house in Georgia that he'd last called home before deciding on a life in space; the cozy campus on Cerberus where Joanna had attended middle school; his sickbay office aboard the *Enterprise*—and he saw people—Jim, Spock, Tonia Barrows, his daughter. Every locale and every person seemed impossibly distant to him.

"Whatcha wish for, Doc?" Schoolboy Joe asked eagerly. Though a rotund figure, probably in his late thirties or early forties, Joe possessed a youthful face that had doubtless inspired his moniker.

"If he tells you what he wished for," Deke observed, "then it won't come true."

"That's right," Keeler told Schoolboy Joe. "But I think I know what *you* wish for." Joe's expression drew into a question mark, until Keeler said, "A piece of cake," and then his face brightened. He rambled over with some plates and flatware, and Keeler quickly served everybody a slice of the dessert.

As they all stood about the room eating, Joe offered that he hadn't tasted anything better since "Sister Edith" had presented him with a cake on his birthday. McCoy used the comment as an opportunity to ask Joe about what he did outside the mission, and thereby to prevent the conversation from turning back to his own life. Once everybody had finished eating, he made a show of raising a hand to stifle a yawn, and Keeler reacted immediately to the less-than-subtle hint.

"Well, we just wanted to recognize your time at the mission, Doctor, and to express our gratitude for all you've done here," she said, moving about the room to collect the plates and forks from McCoy and Deke. "But I know you've had a tiring day, so we'll leave you to your sleep." She crossed back over to Joe, adding his plate to the bottom of the stack and his fork to the top, then handed it all to him. "Would you put these in the kitchen sink for me, please?" she said. "I'll be there in a minute to clean them."

"Yessum, Sister Edith," Joe said. He wished McCoy a happy anniversary and left the room.

Keeler picked up the remains of the cake, along with the knife she'd used to cut it, and then passed them over to Deke. "And would you put this back in the carton and back in the icebox for me?" she said.

"Yes, ma'am," Deke said, and he too exited.

McCoy waited for Keeler to turn back toward him before speaking. "Thank you," he said, grateful for the swift end of the unexpected gathering. "I really am very tired," he explained. "But thank you for the cake. It was a nice surprise."

Keeler angled her head to one side and seemed to evaluate McCoy in some way with which he did not feel comfortable. "Was it, Doctor?" she asked.

"Yes, it was," McCoy said, a bit taken aback by the question. Much as he despised the reality that he'd been stranded in Earth's past for an entire year, that did not detract from the kindness inherent in Keeler's gesture, nor from his appreciation of it. "It was very sweet of you," he concluded.

Her head still aslant, Keeler nodded her acknowledgment of his compliment, but then quickly moved past it. "I think our little celebration might have been a surprise for you, but I'm not convinced you found it a nice one." Before he could protest, she clarified her statement: "It seems clear to me that you're not happy here."

McCoy felt stung, not by her frankness, but by the truth of her words. While he didn't want to confirm her assessment, though, neither did he want to insult her intelligence by contradicting her all-too-accurate observation. "I . . . I don't know what to tell you," he admitted.

Keeler glanced over her shoulder at the open door to the hall, then reached out and pushed it closed. Folding her arms across her chest, she paced into the far corner of the room before going on. "Tell me why you're still here," she said.

"I'm . . . I'm waiting for my friends," McCoy said, feeling foolish for reiterating the claim he'd already made so many times over the past months. He thought that, like a sound repeated over and over again until it had lost all meaning, his words surely must ring hollow to Keeler by now. But rather than debate his assertion, she accepted it. Instead, she questioned the outcome he sought.

"I mentioned this possibility to you once before," she said, "and you really need to think about it: perhaps your friends aren't coming." Again, Keeler's observations, perceptive despite being uninformed, wounded McCoy. He had many times wondered not only when he would be rescued, but *if* he would be. Always, though, he had settled confidently on the expectation that he would return home. He could not imagine Jim and Spock relenting in their search for him.

Unless they believe I'm dead, McCoy suddenly thought, and then even more darkly, *Or unless they're dead.* The idea, however irrational, saddened him.

When McCoy didn't respond to Keeler, or maybe *because* he didn't respond, she continued in a softer tone. "I don't mean to be negative, Doctor," she said, "but you've been here for a full year. I've taken you at your word that you're not on the run or hiding out, that you've had a loss of your memory, and that you truly expect your friends to come find you and bring you home." She took a few steps toward him, which had the effect of emphasizing what she said next. "I believe all of that because I believe in *you.* You've worked hard, you've caused no trouble, and you've lent your time and effort to this place." Keeler unfolded her arms and spread her hands, clearly indicating that she spoke of his contributions to the mission. "But you're unhappy here."

"But not ungrateful," McCoy said. "I genuinely value all that you've done for me."

"I know that," Keeler said, "but please don't misunderstand me. I'm not offended that you're not happy. Why *would* you be? This place is for men down on their luck, men who need some assistance, men often incapable of helping themselves." She folded her arms and moved forward again, until she looked up at him from barely half a meter away. "I don't think you fit into any of those categories, Doctor McCoy."

"I did at one time," he said.

"On the day that you first showed up here, and over the days that followed, yes," she said. "You needed help then. But not anymore. At least, not the type of help that I or the mission can give you."

"Just what sort of help do you think I need?"

Keeler didn't reply right away, instead peering into his eyes as though searching for an answer there. Time seemed to elongate in the near-silence, and McCoy became acutely aware of the faint ticking of the clock on the desk. Finally, Keeler dropped her hands to her sides and paced away from him, retreating once more to the far side of the room. When she turned back to look at him again, she exuded an air of thoughtful concentration. "I don't know," she said. "But I do know that whatever help you need, you won't find it here."

"No," McCoy said. "I guess not." He remained unconvinced that Jim and Spock wouldn't eventually find him here, but how long could he realistically expect to live here in Keeler's back-room office? He'd initially decided to stay at the mission because of its proximity to the location of his arrival here in the past, but over time, he'd also come to view this small, out-of-the-way room as a sanctuary of sorts, a place where he could sequester himself away as much as possible and in that way better avoid altering history.

He'd also realized, though, that Keeler likely would not have allowed him to remain indefinitely at the mission had he not found work and fed himself. And so he'd done that, but had still attempted to limit his interactions with people, including with Keeler herself. He'd willfully made no friends during the past year, although he had out of necessity developed genial relationships with Keeler and a number of the men who helped out at the mission. Of course, how could he possibly know what small action might ripple down through the centuries and change the timeline? Maybe Jim and Spock hadn't come back for him yet because, despite his efforts to the contrary, he'd done something that had made it more difficult for them to find him.

Or maybe I've already irrevocably modified the past and they can't come back for me, he thought.

Gazing around the room, McCoy said, "I suppose it's time for me to move out of here."

"I'm not asking you to leave," Keeler said.

"No, I know that," McCoy said. "But you've been more than generous with me. I should find a place of my own and let you have your office back."

"I can't argue that it would be nice to have my privacy again," she said, though rarely had Keeler needed to use the office during the scant time McCoy spent there. On most days, and for most of the daylight hours, he worked at whatever jobs he could find around the city. Since he'd arrived in the past, the economic crisis plaguing the nation and the world had deepened, but New York City appeared less affected than most other places he read about in the newspapers. Sizable capital projects, both public and private, had continued to arise throughout the metropolis. He currently worked in midtown on a project of considerable scope, in which a dozen or more buildings would ultimately be built around large open space. And not long after he'd arrived in 1930, he'd labored for a few weeks on the nascent Empire State Building, which would open in a couple of months as the tallest manmade structure in the world.

Some things never change, McCoy thought wryly, picturing the vast Erickson Transporter Complex stretching along the coast of Manhattan just above the mouth of the Hudson River. Even in the twenty-third century, New Yorkers thought big.

"If you're interested," Keeler said, "there are vacant rooms available where I live for two dollars and two bits per week."

McCoy considered saying no, thinking that maybe he should search for a place on his own, find a different apartment building where there would be no possibility of interacting with Keeler. *Does it really matter?* he wondered. He would still see her at the mission, where he intended to continue volunteering his assistance. He could stop doing that too, but . . . no. It had been difficult enough during the past year not practicing medicine, other than to administer first aid to the men who occasionally arrived at the mission with minor injuries. McCoy needed to contribute; as a medical man, he had that inclination, and it hadn't disappeared just because he hadn't been able to work as a doctor. He knew that he could find another establishment to which he could donate his time and services, but he would still face the issue of mixing with people. No, better to limit his intermingling with the people of the past to as few individuals as possible, rather than to concern himself with how well those he'd already met knew him.

"All right," he told Keeler. "I'll go by your building tomorrow evening after work."

"That's very good," Keeler said, evidently pleased. "I'll let the landlord know to expect you." She started for the door.

"Good night, Miss Keeler," he said.

As she swung open the door, she stopped and looked over at him again. "Edith," she said.

"Pardon me?"

"My name is Edith," she said. "We've already known each other for a year, and if we're now to be neighbors as well, I think you should call me Edith."

McCoy smiled, warmed by her suggestion. He thought a great deal of Edith Keeler, not only for the work she did and for her charitable nature, but also for the person he'd observed her to be. He respected her, and he also liked her. "Leonard," he said now, reciprocating.

Keeler—*Edith,* he corrected himself—smiled back at him. "Well, then," she said, "good night, Leonard."

"Good night, Edith," he said.

After she'd gone, McCoy finished changing into his nightclothes, turned out the light, and then crawled beneath the blankets on his cot. As sleep—and the often troubled dreams that came with it—loomed in the darkness, he realized that, strangely enough, he actually felt good about leaving the mission and living in an apartment of his own. He resisted thinking of it as a new start of some kind, still clinging to the belief that he would return to his life in the twenty-third century.

Still, he couldn't help recalling Keeler's words to him tonight: *perhaps your friends aren't coming.* To this point, although he had thought about it, he had been unable to truly countenance such a prospect. Now, he had no choice but to take into account that he had been trapped in the past for a whole year.

A year in my life, he thought, *but not necessarily a year in Jim and Spock's lives.* Though it bedeviled him to contemplate the realities and possibilities of time travel, it seemed plausible that he could have one day journeyed from 2267 to 1930, and then one week later in 2267, Jim and Spock could arrive in 1931 to bring him back home. Yet, it also felt unlikely, more like rationalization than reasoning, like a lie he told himself to keep from going mad. For even as he waited to return home, even as he peppered newspapers around the globe with signposts pointing to his location in time and space, even as he held on tightly to his certainty of his eventual rescue, the notion of being trapped here for the rest of his days haunted him.

It took more than an hour for McCoy to fall asleep. When at last he did, he slept fitfully, beset by the same foggy, partially glimpsed images that so often had invaded his slumber ever since his arrival here. Tonight, other faces joined his nightmares, faces he had no trouble distinguishing. All of them belonged to his daughter: as a baby, as a girl, as a young woman.

In the morning, exhausted and on edge, McCoy began his second year living in Earth's past.

II

Clouds of Nameless Trouble

O heart, how fares it with thee now,
    That thou should'st fail from thy desire,
    Who scarcely darest to inquire,
'What is it makes me beat so low?'

Something it is which thou hast lost,
    Some pleasure from thine early years.
    Break, thou deep vase of chilling tears,
That grief hath shaken into frost!

Such clouds of nameless trouble cross
    All night below the darken'd eyes;
    With morning wakes the will, and cries,
'Thou shalt not be the fool of loss.'

—Alfred, Lord Tennyson,
In Memoriam A.H.H., IV

THIRTEEN

1931/1932

Edith gazed around the sodden expanse, looking for Leonard, the vapor of her breath floating before her like an estival ghost in the crisp winter air. Pieces of wood and glass and other wreckage lay strewn about the great, muddy tract, the urban flotsam the only remnants she could see of the ramshackle brownstones that until recently had stood here. Over the past months, she knew, Leonard had helped pull down those buildings, the demolition bit by bit driving away the seedy squatters and delinquents that had once overrun these grounds. In their place, Leonard and the other workmen had left behind a blighted landscape, a long block of pockmarked earth scarred by destruction and softened by wet weather. In recent days, the temperature had dipped, but not low enough to freeze the saturated soil. Littered with debris, the large patch of empty ground sat separated from the surrounding neighborhood not only by the plank fence enclosing the space, but seemingly by the advent of civilization visible all around and yet absent from this bleak lot. The grand, gothic structure of St. Patrick's Cathedral looked down from across Fifth Avenue as though mocking the vacant land.

Edith felt a cold lick of wind at her throat, and she reached up to refasten the topmost button of her heavy winter coat. The small, brown paper bag she carried flopped against her as she did so. This morning, before going off to work, Leonard had helped with the early meal at the mission, as he often did. Today, like most days, he'd prepared a small lunch for himself, but after he'd gone, she'd found it still sitting in the icebox. As the noon hour had approached, she'd decided to make the trek uptown to bring his midday meal to him.

Now, she stood at a lorry entrance to the work site and peered around the large, open space, searching for Leonard. To her right, numerous vehicles—including a large diesel-powered shovel—sat parked along the inside of the fence. Several other flatbed lorries had been scattered throughout the area, and as she watched, workmen loaded them with the rubble they'd collected, obviously preparing the spread of land for construction. She'd read in the paper that two new low-rise edifices—the British Empire Building and La Maison Française—would be built here on either side of a public plaza.

After a few minutes, Edith spotted Leonard a good distance away, recognizing his long, gray winter coat and weather-beaten black fedora. She watched him briefly, confirming his identity by his familiar movements. Carefully, she began toward him, making her way along the fence in order to avoid intruding upon the workmen. As she trudged through the mud, she congratulated herself on her foresight in donning an old pair of men's shoes she'd pulled out of the boxes of clothing she kept at the mission.

When Edith had gotten as close to Leonard as she could without moving away from the fence, she called his name, then did so a second time. He looked up from where he crouched, an armload of broken wood and building materials clutched across his chest. A couple of other men looked up as well, and one standing near Leonard reached over and gave his shoulder a quick push. Edith recognized the action as the teasing of one man to another about a woman.

She smiled to herself, pleased at the show of camaraderie. Nearly two years since his arrival at the mission, Leonard remained something of an enigma to her, continuing to reveal little about himself, past or present. But however much or however little she truly knew Leonard, she nevertheless considered him a friend. For that reason, she felt grateful to see his apparent acceptance by at least one of the men with whom he worked on this massive construction project.

Leonard nodded his head at Edith, letting her know that he saw her. Then he turned and made his way over the moist, uneven ground to the lorry nearest him, upon which he deposited the debris he'd gathered. Once unencumbered, he tramped through the mud until he reached her.

"What brings you here?" he asked.

She held out the small paper sack she carried. "Your lunch," she said, and then, lifting one muck-covered foot, she added, "and one very old pair of shoes."

Leonard smiled and took the bag from her. "Thanks," he said. "I realized when I was halfway here this morning that I'd forgotten it, but I didn't have time to go back to the mission."

"It's my pleasure, Leonard," she said. She looked past him, out over the wide sprawl of sludge. "You've done a lot of work here," she said. "This place looks a lot different than the last time I was up this way."

"Yeah," Leonard said, peering around. "I'm sure whatever they build here now will be an improvement."

"I should hope so," Edith said. "I read in the paper that—"

To Edith's left, she heard the rumble of an approaching vehicle, the sound bitingly loud in the raw air. Both she and Leonard glanced over at the entrance to the site, through which she'd passed just a few minutes ago. She expected to see a work vehicle of some sort, perhaps an unladen lorry returning from discharging its load of scrap. Instead, to her surprise, she saw one of the long flatbeds, not empty, but carrying a large balsam fir. She had little doubt of the use to which the triangular, twenty-foot-long evergreen would be put.

"A Christmas tree," she said, delighted at the idea of somebody bringing holiday cheer to this dreary place. Despite her own agnosticism, Edith enjoyed this time of year, as it often seemed to bring out the best in people.

As she and Leonard watched the lorry stop near the fence that ran along East Fiftieth Street, many of the workmen started toward it. Edith heard several voices rise excitedly even before the vehicle's engine sputtered to a halt. The driver and another man emerged from the cab of the lorry, and Leonard identified the latter as the assistant foreman. The man, tall and thin, with a dark mustache, stood on the passenger-side running board and called to the workers advancing toward him. "We might be poor and hungry," he yelled, his words carrying through the late-morning chill, "we might be cold and overworked, but we can still celebrate Christmas."

The workers surrounded the flatbed as the assistant foreman climbed down from the running board and then up beside the tree. Edith didn't see him pick up a knife, but the ropes holding

the evergreen down along its length slackened as he moved from
one to another. "C'mon, men," the assistant foreman called, waving his hand toward the tree, but he needn't have; already several
men had begun crawling up onto the rear of the lorry, clearly intending to help unload its yuletide cargo.

"I'd better go help out," Leonard said, his voice matter-of-
fact, filled with neither satisfaction nor displeasure. Edith recalled making similar observations during the previous winter's
holiday season. While Leonard had helped with the mission's
meager decorations and taken part in Christmas Eve and Christmas Day observances there, he'd seemed to do so in a distant
manner, different from his everyday reserve. Edith had wondered about his beliefs and on a couple of occasions had attempted to broach the subject, only to find her questions
ultimately left unanswered.

"Thank you for this," Leonard said, holding up his lunch, and
after Edith acknowledged his gratitude, he hurried to join his fellow workmen as they dragged the evergreen from the lorry. Edith
walked back along the fence toward the entrance, watching as
Leonard found a place among the men and helped carry the tree.
The assistant foreman jumped to the ground and hustled ahead of
the workers. By the time Edith reached the street, the tree had
been upended and its trunk pushed down into the mud. Despite
the foul condition of the ground, several men crawled beneath the
fir's lowest branches, and Edith assumed that they were attempting to steady and secure this addition to their work site.

Even unadorned, the Christmas tree brought a wisp of joy to
this desolate place, a welcome dash of color. Still, Edith thought
that it could use something more. She wouldn't want to remove
any of the scant decorations at the mission, but she could part
with the few shiny garlands bedecking her apartment. She resolved to take down her festoons tonight and to send them down
here tomorrow with Leonard. Surely the men here would appreciate even that small embellishment of Christmas cheer.

With a spring in her step, Edith turned and headed back
downtown to the mission.

McCoy wrapped his arms about his chest, tucked his hands
beneath his biceps, and huddled against the wall of the building,

trying to insulate himself against the cold. Although the temperature of the night air probably hovered north of freezing, the
wind blustering through New York's concrete canyons made it
feel like ten below. Despite that, throngs of people still crowded
about Times Square. The size of the multitude had surprised him
when he and Edith had first arrived here, as he'd expected the
prevailing climate of want and need to suppress the turnout at an
event still celebrated in his own time. He supposed, though, that
the great numbers of people here made sense: with conditions as
dire as they had become for so many of them, they must all be
looking to the coming year with hope for a better life.

Beside him on the sidewalk, Edith pushed her gloved hands
into the pockets of her long winter coat, but she seemed otherwise unaffected by the weather conditions. She peered with evident anticipation toward the slender Times Tower, atop which a
great lighted ball would soon descend, ushering in the new year.
McCoy hadn't wanted to attend these festivities, rejecting Edith's
invitation several times before ultimately relenting. He suspected
that her goal had been to lift his flagging spirits.

McCoy watched her for a few seconds and felt grateful that
upon arriving in the past, he had stumbled into the 21st Street
Mission, and into Edith's life. From that first day, she had helped
him in so many ways, and he thought now that her friendship
and support had actually allowed him to retain his sanity, even
though she did not fully understand his circumstances. For all of
that, though, McCoy still felt lost and alone. Even standing next
to Edith, even crowded among the thousands upon thousands of
revelers in Times Square, his continued presence in the past left
him isolated. Some days, he found, he could almost forget about
his plight, could almost become so caught up in the minutia of
everyday life, that the dangers of his inadvertent time travel
would slip away from him. He would for a short time shrug off
his solitary existence and his growing sense of abandonment.
But reality would never remain hidden for long. In a sudden
memory of an event that had not yet occurred in this time, in the
mere consideration of a morsel of information not yet known by
the population of Earth, the enormity of McCoy's situation
would come back to him in a rush.

Around him now, the swell of people moved forward and

back, moved side to side, like a living tide. Anticipation seemed to grow as the final minutes of the calendar year, and the first moment of the new year, approached. The wind carried the sounds of voices, but few distinct words. Everywhere, the bright lights of capitalism shined as though desperate to draw attention to themselves. Movie and burlesque houses advertised their wares with gusto, none more so than the marquee across the way that announced the premiere of *Dr. Jekyll and Mr. Hyde.*

McCoy knew the old Scottish tale and found it somehow apropos of his own circumstances. In some regards, his existence seemed dual in nature: future and past, doctor and civilian, extrovert and loner.

I've changed history, McCoy thought. *Or I will.* He must've done, or would do, what Spock had feared Captain Christopher would do: change the past, and thereby alter the future. Did Jim—*would* Jim—even be born in Iowa in 2233? Would he command the *Enterprise*? Would the ship even exist? Would Starfleet?

Whatever I've done, whatever I will do, McCoy forced himself to admit, *it will make my recovery impossible.* And on the heels of that came another unpleasant thought: *I should kill myself.*

Even in the cold weather, a greater chill shook McCoy. During the worst days of his father's terrible illness and the black period after he'd finally succumbed, McCoy had never considered suicide. In the dark hours when he and Jocelyn had torn down whatever love they'd had for each other and had moved inexorably toward separation and divorce, taking his own life had never been an option. But now . . . now . . . might it actually provide a solution?

If, despite his efforts, he'd already modified the past, then he could do nothing now to change that. But if his history-altering transgression still lay before him, then perhaps his death could preserve the future. Would Jim and Spock then be able to retrieve him from an earlier point, *prior* to his suicide?

McCoy shook his head, as though doing so might clarify his thoughts. Time travel, temporal mechanics, causation and paradox, all confounded him. He knew better than to make such an important and irreversible decision when he felt as low as he did right now, but he also realized that he would have to seriously consider his own death as a legitimate option.

"Here it comes," Edith said excitedly, grabbing his arm.

McCoy looked over and saw her pointing upward, and he followed her gaze over to the Times Tower. Atop the narrow front edge of the roughly triangular building, the illuminated ball had begun to descend. Around them, the collective voice of the crowd grew, screams and cheers rising in commingled expectancy. The wind, agonizingly constant all night, now seemed to recede, as though choosing to withdraw in deference to the moment at hand. McCoy watched the lighted sphere as it—

Suddenly, a rapid succession of reports rang out, evoking the recollection of the firearm Sulu had found on a planet in the Omicron Delta region. Reacting instinctively, McCoy turned away from the cruel sounds and spread his arms, shielding Edith's body with his own. Bright flashes threw their shadows against the wall behind her as the blasts continued.

Around them, the noise of the crowd rose louder still, doubtless the knell of 1931. McCoy risked a look over his shoulder and saw people arrayed in a semicircle a few meters away, watching as charges continued to detonate before them. Blue smoke swirled upward from the sidewalk, where bits of paper danced about wildly. McCoy peered at the faces of the people ringing the spectacle and saw light flare across their features. For just an instant, they looked like the victims of phaser fire, targets who had been caught by a weapon set to dematerialize.

Oh no, McCoy thought, even as he realized that the miniature explosions posed no danger. But in his mind, in his memory, he saw the face of another man, a small man, bald and unshaven, with a wide, misshapen nose, and clad in dirty clothing. McCoy knew at once where he'd previously seen the man with the rodent-like appearance: in the tortured dreams that still occasionally plagued his sleep. For the first time, though, McCoy remembered *beyond* that, to the frantic moments following his arrival in the past, the intense, chaotic moments from which those nightmares had been born. And he thought again: *Oh no.*

"Leonard?" Edith said, and then more insistently, "Leonard." She took him by the arms and turned his body around, toward the place where the unexpected blasts now ceased their jarring addition to the clamor of the multitude. Edith stepped up beside him and said, "They're just penny bangers." She hesitated for a second, and then added, "Firecrackers."

"Yes," McCoy said, knowing that he needed to say something. "Yes, of course." He turned away from the scene and moved to lean a hand against the wall. "They just startled me," he explained. His words, surrounded by the uproar of Times Square, sounded to him as though they had been spoken by somebody else, and from a distance. He felt only peripherally aware of his environs, though, his thoughts instead fixed on the man from his dreams, the man from his first minutes in Earth's past. McCoy had . . . what? He'd chased the man, believed him an ally against the assassins hunting them.

"Leonard?" Edith asked, concern coloring her tone. "Are you all right?"

"Yes, I . . . I . . ." he began, struggling to respond at the same time he tried to latch on to his memories. "I was just startled, that's all," he repeated. *Biped . . . small,* he recalled himself saying, describing the phantom figure while standing before him.

"You don't look well," Edith went on. "Do you need to sit down?"

"No, I . . . I just need a minute," he said. He moved forward to lay his forearm against the wall, and then rested his head against his sleeve.

"All right," Edith said, and McCoy felt her hand on his shoulder blade.

He closed his eyes, and the sights and sounds, the scents and textures of Times Square dissolved into nothingness. He saw his own hand clutching the small man's bald pate, measuring, analyzing. *Good cranial development,* he recalled concluding. *Considerable human ancestry.*

McCoy had been in bad shape, paranoid and delusional from the cordrazine still coursing through his body. Had he talked to the little man about medicine in the twentieth century, about the barbaric state of health care and hospitals? He thought now that he had, images of physicians hacking and stitching their patients like garments occurring to him in a vague, slippery way, like a memory of memory or a dream of a dream.

And then you fell, he told himself, still fighting to summon the entire experience to mind. Elusive and paper-thin, the recollections threatened to skitter away like leaves upon the wind. With an effort, he tried to tighten his grip on the memory at hand. He concentrated on the remembered feel of the pavement against his back, the hardness of the surface, its cold dampness in the dark night. He had battled to remain conscious, fearful that if he passed out, the assassins pursuing him would track him down.

It was then, McCoy thought, horrified. As he had resisted the blackness that would have left him vulnerable, he'd heard it: the piercing whine of a phaser set to self-destruct—a phaser he now dimly recalled stealing from the *Enterprise*'s transporter chief. The shrill cry of the weapon had increased in pitch, higher and higher, reaching upward until it had become inaudible—or nonexistent. Did he imagine now the blue-white glare on his closed eyelids, or had the little man accidentally triggered the phaser to destroy itself?

"Leonard, I'm getting worried." It took McCoy a moment to recognize Edith's voice. He felt the pressure of her hand on his back.

"I'm all right," he said without moving, and then he reached desperately for the last part of the memory. He'd regained consciousness in daylight, in an alleyway filled with antiquated machinery. He'd been shaky on his feet, and physically, mentally, and emotionally exhausted. But he'd awoken in that alley, and he'd looked all around there. There had been no dead or wounded bodies, no evidence of an explosion.

Soft self-destruct then, he thought. The small man had activated the phaser's auto-dematerialization cycle, and the weapon had disintegrated itself—and him along with it. Had it not, had the phaser only destroyed itself, McCoy didn't think the light he'd perceived through his closed eyelids would have been nearly as bright as it had been. *Or was that all a dream?* he asked himself. *Am I making all of this up?*

"Leonard?" Edith said.

"I'm all right," he said again, pushing away from the wall and turning to face her. All about them, people continued to celebrate the new year, though the volume had decreased from the height it had reached at the end of ball's drop. "I'm sorry," he said, "but I think I need to go back to my apartment."

Edith nodded, but asked, "Did something happen? I mean, besides the firecrackers? Are you feeling well?"

"It was just that," McCoy maintained. "I'm also pretty tired. I worked very hard today." Though a prevarication intended to avoid telling Edith the truth, he had labored at the Rockefeller site almost twelve hours today. "You don't have to go with me."

"Nonsense," Edith said. "Of course I'll go with you. Besides, we've seen what we came here to see." She gestured in the general direction of the Times Tower.

"I know it's cold," McCoy said, "but do you mind walking for a while?" They'd taken the subway to get here, but McCoy wanted to avoid the crowds right now, wanted a chance to process what had come back to him tonight.

"Not at all," Edith said, and they made their way over to Broadway and followed it south. For a few minutes, Edith spoke about the past year and the year to come, but soon enough, she seemed to understand McCoy's desire for quiet. They walked together in silence after that, and McCoy returned to the matter of his phaser and its destruction.

Did I make all of that up? he asked himself again, realizing how much he wanted to believe that he had. At the same time, he knew that he hadn't invented any of it—that he had purloined a phaser from the *Enterprise,* that it had been taken from him, and that the small man had vaporized himself. And he knew something more. Something worse.

That's how I changed history, he thought. *That's how I changed the future.* Jim wasn't going to come to the twentieth century to find him and bring him back home. For all he knew, Jim would never even be born now. The circumstances that had led to McCoy's travel back in time would never occur and so could never be undone. It seemed like a paradox, defying logic, but McCoy still understood the inevitable conclusion. He was trapped in the past, and there was nothing at all he could ever do about it.

FOURTEEN

2268

"Do I have to do this?" Chekov asked in his thick Russian accent. Changed out of his duty uniform and into a blue patient's coverall, he stood poised to raise himself up onto a diagnostic pallet in the outer sickbay compartment. He'd stopped with his hands palm down on the pad, though, evidently in order to protest his pending examination.

Just like he always does, McCoy thought. Ever since their experience at Gamma Hydra IV, when every member of the landing party but Chekov had suffered a radiation sickness that resembled accelerated aging, the ensign had been reluctant to undergo any physical exams. At the time of that mission, more than six months ago, he'd been required to endure scores of tests, owing to his singular resistance to the affliction. McCoy understood the distaste Chekov had developed for being poked and prodded, injected and inspected, but the doctor had his orders.

"If you ever want to return to duty," McCoy said, "then you'll get up on that pallet and let me do what the captain told me to do."

"But I'm obviously fine," Chekov remonstrated.

"You may think you're fine, Ensign," McCoy said, beginning to lose patience, "but I'll be the judge of that." To emphasize his point, McCoy activated the small portable scanner he held in his hand. The small, cylindrical device hummed quietly, its mesh-enclosed sensor dish spinning as it operated. "For all I know," he added, "you're still dead." Earlier today, the *Enterprise* had ventured into the territory of the Melkotians on a first-contact mission ordered by Starfleet Command. McCoy and Chekov had transported down to the alien world with Jim, Spock, and Scotty—or at least they thought they had. In reality, the five of them hadn't actually left the ship, but the Melkotians, powerful telepaths, had convinced them that they had, generating a collective virtual experience in which they'd all taken part.

The setting had been an oddly incomplete version of a nine-teenth-century town in the American West, a surrealistic re-creation of a place called, of all things, Tombstone, Arizona. McCoy and Chekov and the rest of the sham landing party had been cast in the roles of a group of men known as the Clanton gang, on the day in 1881 when they had fought—and lost—the so-called *Gunfight at the O.K. Corral.* Before they had even faced that deadly confrontation, though, Chekov, as gunslinger Billy Claiborne, had seemingly been shot and killed by a mem-ber of the Clantons' rivals, the Earps. Only later, when Jim and the rest of the landing party had been given the opportunity—even the apparent necessity—to kill and had refused to do so, only then had all five men been released from the communal hal-lucination and found themselves still aboard the *Enterprise,* un-harmed.

Evidently having convincingly demonstrated to the Melko-tians the benevolent nature and motivations of the citizens of the Federation, the crew had then been welcomed to the aliens' world. Jim had actually taken down to the planet a smaller group—just Scotty and xeno-anthropologist Delgado—to make first contact, leaving Spock in command of the ship, and order-ing McCoy to confirm Chekov's health after the ensign's illusory death. The doctor didn't particularly mind not being included in the real landing party—he generally embraced any chance to avoid having his molecules scattered through the universe by that infernal transporter—though if pressed, he'd have to admit to a curiosity about Melkotian physiology. If the being he'd seen during the counterfeit landing party had been an accurate depic-tion of a Melkotian, then they possessed an interesting bodily structure. Through simulated fog, McCoy had made out a thin and extremely long neck, a roughly textured gray-green hide, and a mouthless face with large, glowing eyes. For now, though, he would have to settle for reviewing Lieutenant Delgado's scans and report once the landing party returned. In the meantime, he would follow the captain's orders and examine Chekov.

"I'm not dead," the ensign said, "but one of these days, I think a visit to sickbay might just change that." He smiled, but in a nervous way that betrayed his anxiety.

"Relax," McCoy said, "and that's an order." Chekov looked

momentarily as though he might continue to object, but then he shook his head and hopped up to a sitting position on the edge of the diagnostic pallet. He muttered an acknowledgment while McCoy moved in closer to him. The doctor raised the scanner and waved it slowly in front of the ensign, beginning the physical as he almost always did, by checking his patient's heart rate, blood pressure, and respiration. The readings all appeared well within the normal range for a healthy human male of Chekov's twenty-three years. "According to my instruments," McCoy joked, "you really *are* still alive."

"Then I can go?" Chekov said, his expression brightening for a moment.

"One more comment like that," McCoy replied, "and I'll be examining you in the brig." He switched off the portable scanner and placed a firm hand on Chekov's shoulder. "Now lie back and let me do my job so that you can get back to yours." The ensign resisted the pressure McCoy applied to his upper arm for just a second, but then relented and reclined on the pad. The doctor reached up and activated the diagnostic panel above the head of the pallet. The display came to life, the circular pulse and respiration monitors blinking red in time with Chekov's heart and lungs, corroborating the readings McCoy had already taken. The white triangular indicators rose along the vertical scales as they too measured the ensign's bodily components and processes.

Just as McCoy prepared to call to Nurse Chapel, she entered from his office. She held out a data slate to the doctor. McCoy took it, handing her his portable scanner in exchange for the device. He peered at the display and spied a list of Chekov's previous exams, with a brief summary accompanying each. McCoy quickly scanned the list, recalling the incidents that had necessitated the repeated certification of Chekov's health: his removal from the *Enterprise* by the android Norman, and his subsequent exposure to Harry Mudd; his contact with tribbles, Klingons, and other aliens aboard Space Station K-7; his abduction by the Providers of Triskelion, and his ensuing captivity among members of various alien races; his proximity, along with the rest of the crew, to the vast, enervating, spaceborne protozoan that the ship had encountered; and his transformation by the Kelvans into a compact polyhedron comprising his essence.

Several other entries filled the rest of the screen, and McCoy took note of them before bringing up a record of Chekov's most recent medical evaluation. As he reviewed it, Chapel moved across the room and returned with a small rolling cart of medical equipment. With the nurse's assistance, McCoy began his examination of Chekov.

For some time, the physical proceeded without incident. McCoy ran tests, recorded observations, and discussed the process with Chapel as they worked. Chekov for the most part remained quiet, though he did ask several questions along the way, and at one point, balked at McCoy's assurance that a particular procedure would not hurt.

McCoy had nearly completed the exam when he noticed an aberrant, and yet familiar, reading. Not wanting to alarm Chekov—especially since there appeared to be no real reason for concern—he asked Chapel to assist him with inputting the ensign's medical information. He told Chekov that they'd be back shortly and then walked with the nurse back into his office.

Once they reached his desk, out of earshot of the ensign, McCoy said, "Do you see a discrepancy there?" Standing on the opposite side of his desk from the nurse, he held out the data slate to her, pointing to a set of readings on the far right side of the display. Chapel studied the screen for a few moments.

"I don't see any abnormalities," she finally said.

McCoy walked back out from around his desk and over to the nurse's side. He found the set of readings that had caught his attention and again pointed to them with his forefinger. "There," he said. "The expected and calculated energy output of the central nervous system."

"From Doctor M'Benga's algorithm?" Chapel asked. "I looked at those numbers. They're well within the range he established as normal."

"What concerns me aren't the numbers themselves," McCoy said, "but the fact that one of them has changed."

"What?" Chapel said. "Which one?"

McCoy grabbed the stylus and used it to split the screen in two, keeping Chekov's current readings on the upper half of the display. On the bottom, he called up another set of measurements, recorded the last time that the ensign had been examined. That physical had taken place just a few months ago, during the annual crew evaluations. McCoy found the numbers provided back then by M'Benga's algorithm and circled them. "There," he said. "From Chekov's last exam."

Chapel looked with McCoy at the readings. The first, gauging the expected energy output of Chekov's nervous system, precisely matched the corresponding calculation they'd made today. The second number, though, which quantified the actual energy output of the ensign's nervous system, now showed an increase. McCoy could see that the change hadn't been dramatic, and that the new assessment still fell well within the expected norm, but—

"This change is negligible," Chapel said, echoing his thoughts. "And according to Doctor M'Benga's paradigm, there's nothing unusual about such a value."

"I know, I know," McCoy said. "But in all the other crewmembers we've examined in the year or so since we started using the algorithm to calculate these quantities—"

"Since we visited Deneva," Chapel said.

"Yes," McCoy said. "In all the time since then, only one other member of the crew has ever shown any change at all in their numbers." McCoy thought back to the *Enterprise*'s time at Deneva, and how the value measuring the actual energy output of Jim's nervous system had spiked immediately afterward. The captain's numbers had remained constant since then, and he'd shown no ill effects as a result of the higher reading, but it bothered McCoy that he did not understand the cause of the change.

"Could it be a simple flaw in Doctor M'Benga's formulae?" Chapel asked. She handed the slate back to McCoy.

"Possibly," he said. "But here's what concerns me." He quickly tapped out a series of commands on the slate, then showed its display to the nurse. "Chekov's had a lot of exams in the last year, and here are his M'Benga numbers from each of those evaluations." He ran the stylus down a list of paired numbers, each duo identical to the next, but for the last entry.

"They're all the same," Chapel noted.

"All but the final reading we took today," McCoy said.

"What do you think it means?" Chapel asked.

"I don't know," McCoy said. "Maybe nothing. As you say, it may simply be a flaw in Doctor M'Benga's algorithm. And even if it's not, there's no indication at all that such a small change in the numbers is any reason for concern." Though he did not say it, McCoy thought about Jim's readings, which had shown a far greater increase than Chekov's now did, and yet the captain had been in virtually perfect health in the year since that increase had first been detected.

"What should we do?" Chapel asked.

"Take these readings over to Doctor M'Benga," McCoy decided. "We should find out what he thinks. Ask him to run an analysis on the numbers, and on his algorithm."

"Yes, Doctor," Chapel said, and she accepted the slate back from him. He reached over and settled the stylus back in its place above the screen. The nurse exited into the corridor, and McCoy headed back into the outer sickbay compartment.

"Is there a problem, Doctor?" Chekov asked, raising himself up onto his elbows.

"Not at all," McCoy said, his manner intentionally casual. "Now lie back so I can finish up here and get you back to the bridge." Chekov complied, and McCoy resumed his examination. It didn't take long to complete the ensign's physical, and no other readings appeared out of the ordinary. As best McCoy could tell, young Ensign Chekov seemed to be completely healthy.

And still, even after Chekov had left sickbay, even after M'Benga had reported no problems with either his algorithm or the ensign's readings, McCoy could not shake the feeling that he himself had missed something, that he had overlooked the significance of the discrepant numbers, both for Chekov and for Jim. For two days, McCoy pored over the medical records of both men, enlisting the assistance of the ship's entire medical department, and still he could find nothing. Finally, despite having nothing concrete to report, he decided to take his concern to Spock.

FIFTEEN

1932

Edith set the spoon down in the empty bowl that one of the visitors to the mission had left on the table, then slid the bowl to one side. Using the damp cloth she'd brought with her from the kitchen, she wiped clean the breadcrumbs and spills of soup the man had left behind, then dried the surface with a second cloth. When she'd finished, she tossed the makeshift towels—actually remnants from the mission's boxes of old clothes—over her shoulders, picked up the bowl, and started for the kitchen. As she did, she caught sight of Leonard standing on the other side of the counter, doling out cups of coffee to the men lined up there. On his face, he wore no expression at all, and that troubled her.

Edith continued into the kitchen through the swinging doors, where she put the bowl down in the long sink with the other dirty dishes piled there. Stepping up beside Leonard, she asked, "Do you need a hand?"

"No, that's not necessary," he said as he tilted the large metal coffee pot down, pouring the dark, steaming liquid into a white cup.

Edith didn't move, instead waiting until Leonard looked up at her. "How are you feeling?" she asked.

"I'm fine," he said, and he offered her a smile that fell a long way from touching his eyes. She returned it and went back out into the main room of the mission, but she knew that the time had come. She didn't really understand why, but she could pinpoint *when* it had happened.

In the months since New Year's Eve, when a skein of penny bangers had been set off near them in Times Square, Leonard had shown a marked change in his demeanor. He still worked his construction job, still volunteered his time at the mission, still lived in the same flop in her building, but now the life seemed to have gone out of him. Edith recognized the similarity of the sound of the firecrackers to that of gunfire and feared that the incident had reminded Leonard of some traumatic event from his past. He appeared careless and despondent, and it concerned her.

An hour later, the matter remained at the center of her thoughts. She stood over the basin in the kitchen, washing the night's dishes, as the last of the visitors to the mission left. When she heard the front doors close a few minutes later, she knew that the two other volunteers who'd worked here today had also departed. She peered over her shoulder and into the main room, where she saw Leonard locking up and pulling down the shades. Edith rinsed the bowl she'd just scrubbed, and after setting it in the drying rack, she went out into the main room. "Leonard," she said.

He looked up from the front of the room, where he'd begun overturning chairs and placing them atop the table. "Yes?" he said, and she interpreted his unanimated face as a mask of despair.

"I'd like to talk with you," Edith said. She walked over to the table nearest the kitchen and gazed across the room at Leonard. "I'd like to know what's wrong."

"Wrong?" Leonard said, shrugging and looking down at the upside-down chair in his hands. "Nothing at all." He put the chair down on the table, then moved to the next chair. Edith sensed that even he knew that his words sounded unconvincing.

"If you don't want to say anything to me, that's fine," Edith told him, "but I'd very much appreciate it if you'd listen to me."

Leonard set the next chair down and then moved on to another. "Of course," he said.

"I've known you for a long time now," Edith said, lifting her hand to the top of the table beside which she stood, and nervously tapping on its surface. "Even though I don't know where you came from or what sort of life you lived before we met, even though you refuse to talk about yourself—" Leonard stopped lifting the chair and opened his mouth as though to speak, but she raised the flat of her hand to him. "If you're going to protest that you've no memory of your life before the 21st Street Mission, please don't. I'm not disputing that. What I am saying is that despite all of that, I think I've gotten to know you."

"Probably so," Leonard agreed. He held the chair motionless before him.

"Please believe me then when I tell you that I know there's something wrong," she said. "And that I know that it's something different than your failing memory, or that your friends haven't come here to take you back home. And whatever it is that's wrong, it started on New Year's Eve."

Leonard set the chair back down on the floor and rested his hands atop its back. "You're very perceptive," he said.

Edith bowed her head in acknowledgment of the compliment, but quickly moved on. "I can't imagine that after all this time, you'd want to talk with me about your troubles."

Leonard lifted one hand from the chair and then dropped it back down in a gesture of helplessness. "I really can't," he said.

"Can't?" Edith said. "Or won't?"

"Does it really matter?" Leonard asked.

"I think it does," she said. Suddenly, Edith felt the distance between them in an almost palpable way. She crossed the room until she stood before Leonard, where she pulled out two chairs still on the floor. She took a seat and said, "Would you sit with me?"

Leonard didn't move for several seconds, a long enough time that she thought he might refuse her invitation. Finally, though, he sat down with her. "Edith," he said, "I don't want you to feel insulted, but—"

"I don't," she interjected. "Not at all. I know that whatever's bothering you has nothing to do with me, and I know that I've been a good friend to you."

"You have," Leonard said.

"Well, it's because I'm your friend that I want to talk with you right now," she said. "I don't know what's distressing you, and I'm not even asking you to tell me. Whatever it is, though, let me help."

Leonard smiled then, in a way that he hadn't earlier. His teeth showed, and his skin wrinkled at the edges of his eyes. "I know that you want to help," he said, and at that moment, Edith knew that he would never allow her to do so. She also knew what she would have to do. "If there were any way at all that you could help, I'd tell you," he said.

Edith leaned forward in her chair. "Leonard," she said as gently as she could, "I think it's time for you to leave."

"What?" He seemed genuinely startled by the suggestion.

"You're stagnating here," she explained. "You're not happy here. You never have been."

"I . . . I thought my work here was appreciated," he said, conspicuously not denying her characterizations.

"It is," she said. "It most certainly is. Because of that, I know that wherever you go, you'll help people."

Leonard stood up abruptly and strode away from her. He reached the front corner of the room, away from the doors, and then spun back around. "Are you really asking me to leave?" he asked, apparently incredulous.

"Leonard," she asked him, "where did you come from?"

"I told you that I have amnesia," he said, somewhat belligerently.

"I don't mean where were you before you came to the mission," she clarified. "I mean, where were you born?"

"Oh," he said, and he hesitated, evidently disarmed. Edith wondered if he would keep even this piece of information from her, but then he didn't. "I . . . was born in Atlanta," he said.

"Atlanta," Edith repeated. "Georgia." She couldn't prevent herself from smiling at even this small detail of Leonard's life. He had kept so much hidden away that just the disclosure of his birthplace delighted her. "I suppose I always knew you came from the south."

"Yes, ma'am," Leonard said with an exaggerated drawl. She laughed and then he did too, diffusing the tension that had risen between them. Leonard walked back over to the table, where he stood behind the chair in which he had sat just a few moments ago. "Edith, do you really want me to leave?"

"I don't *want* you to leave," she said. "I like you, Leonard, and I certainly appreciate everything you've done here at the mission. But I think you *need* to leave. This isn't the place for you."

"But it is for you?" he said.

"It is," Edith said. "I decided to start this place, to run it, and I choose to be here every day."

"So do I," Leonard said.

"That's true," she said. "Not because you sought to be here, though, but because circumstances left you here." Edith stood up to face Leonard, his chair still between them. "You've done good work here," she said, "but this isn't what you wanted for your life."

"We don't always get what we want," Leonard said with such a heavy sadness that Edith could not fathom what ills must have taken place in his life. She'd seen so many men beaten down by drink, by poverty, by a federal government concentrated more on the needs of business than of the country's citizens, that on a daily basis, as a matter of her own emotional survival, she had become inured to the pain around her. She still cared as much as ever, of course, but in order to assist the visitors to the mission, she had to divorce herself emotionally from their plight. And yet the sorrow she distinguished in Leonard right now nearly moved her to tears.

"Leonard," she said, and she moved forward and placed her hand on top of his where it rested on the back of the chair between them. "I realize that you are the sort of man who does choose to help people. I have no doubt that, wherever you go from here, you'll be driven to keep doing that. Perhaps you'll even be a doctor again. But I also know it's time for you to move on."

"Move on where?" Leonard asked. "I truly have nowhere to go."

"Why don't you go home?" Edith asked.

"I would love to," he said, "if only I knew how to get there."

"Why not just hop a train and go?" she suggested.

"Go?" Leonard asked. "Go where?"

"Home," Edith said. "To Atlanta."

"Atlanta," he repeated, as though sampling the possibility for the first time.

"It might be just the place to start," Edith said.

Leonard stared at her for a long time, but seemed not to see her. She imagined him picturing the skyline of Atlanta, not nearly as large or impressive as that of New York, but still with its share of tall buildings. Edith had never been to Atlanta, but she had read about it, had seen pictures in newspapers and magazines. Though she could not tell what Leonard visualized right now, she hoped that it included blue skies and peach trees.

"Maybe that would be a good place to start over," he said at last. "I'll think about it." He circled around the chair and moved in close to her, opening his arms. They embraced, and he thanked her for what she'd said just now, and for her friendship.

Edith didn't know whether Leonard would heed her advice and leave the mission, but she thought that he might. Whatever ghosts still haunted him from his past, he needed to put them to rest, and the best way for him to do that began with leaving the place that in one form or another had provided him with a refuge for the past two years. If Leonard did leave, Edith knew that she would miss him. But she also knew that tonight, maybe, just maybe, she had saved his life a second time.

McCoy stood in a line of nondescript men at the 21st Street Mission, waiting his turn to step up to the counter and claim a bowl of soup. He felt out of place and anxious, as though he did not belong there and risked a great deal simply by his presence. He looked around and saw that the tables and chairs in the main room of the mission had gone; so too had the walls, though the floor continued on for as far as he could see. Curious how the story above could remain in place, he lifted his gaze upward and saw not bare bulbs hanging down from a dingy ceiling, but a cold expanse of stars.

I'm dreaming, he thought, and he realized that it didn't matter.

"We're on Earth," said the man directly in front of him. "At least I think the constellations look right."

McCoy peered down from the sky and recognized the figure from the time of his arrival in the past, the shabby little man who'd stolen his phaser and accidentally dematerialized himself. Dematerialized himself, changed history, and destroyed the future. "What are you doing here?" McCoy asked him.

"You're right, fella," the little man said, looking down at his ragged, untidy clothing. The others in line wore well-kept, finely tailored suits, as did McCoy himself. "I don't belong here," the little man said, and he slipped from the line and scuttled away. McCoy turned and watched as he quickly faded into darkness.

"McCoy?" a voice asked, and he looked back to see that he'd advanced to the head of the line. On the other side of the counter, in the mission's kitchen, an older woman McCoy did not recognize peered down at a bundle of papers.

"Yes," he said tentatively. "I'm McCoy."

"Leonard H. McCoy?" the woman asked. She had curly white hair and wore eyeglasses.

"Yes," he said again.

The old woman shuffled through the documents in front of her. "You want to go home, and you want to renew your medical license, is that correct?" she asked.

"It is," McCoy said, his spirit buoyed by the possibility of returning home to practice medicine again.

The woman continued searching through the papers, which multiplied before her, filling the counter. "Do we have your qualifications?" she wanted to know.

"I am chief medical officer aboard the U.S.S. Enterprise," he said. "I have board certification from Starfleet Medical and the United Earth College of Surgeons. I attended medical school at the University of Mississippi—"

"When?" the old woman demanded, glaring up at him. Stacks of papers overflowed the counter and fell onto the floor. "When did all of this happen?"

He had graduated from the School of Medicine at Ole Miss in 2253, had become board certified by the UECS after years of internship and residency, had joined Starfleet still later, but he didn't want to reveal any of that. Not here, not now. "It was a long time ago," he prevaricated, citing his subjective experiences, rather than objective dates.

The old woman continued hunting through the masses of paper all around her, until at last she removed one sheet from the stacks and studied it. "Leonard H. McCoy," she read. "Graduated from the University of Mississippi School of Medicine in—" She abruptly stopped speaking and looked up at him. "This is three hundred years in the future!" she cried, turning the certificate around and displaying it to him.

McCoy could only gape at her in silence, lost for a response. To his dismay, the old woman returned to pawing through the whirlpool of documents now spinning about her. She pulled out another piece of paper and read it. "Leonard H. McCoy, college diploma," she said, again holding it up for him to see. "Three hundred years from now." Then she extracted another, and exclaimed, "Acceptance into Starfleet, three hundred years from now." She found another sheet, and another, and another. "Commendation into the Starfleet Legion of Honor, Award of Valor from Starfleet Surgeons, Citation by Captain James T. Kirk for Distinguished Service." Paper began to rain down on the woman, and she plucked one after another from the air, identifying them: "Birth certificate, marriage license, divorce decree." She looked up at him, her horrified glare an unqualified accusation, which she then once more put into words: "All three centuries in the future!"

"I . . . I'm sorry," McCoy said. "I didn't mean to—"

"To kill us all!" she raved. She suddenly brought her hands together, crushing the document she held into a twisted ball. Then she cocked her arm back and hurled it at him.

McCoy flinched as the balled-up piece of paper struck him in the front of his right shoulder, which flared in pain. He glanced down to see a patch of blood spreading across not his suit jacket, but his blue Starfleet uniform shirt. He gazed at the old woman in shock and saw her compacting another sheet. "Don't," he said. "Please." But she brought her arm back again and fired the misshapen paper sphere at him. It flew toward his face, but he raised his arm and deflected it. His wrist burned with pain, and when he examined it, he saw blood seeping from a newly opened wound.

"Murderer!" the old woman screeched at him. "Assassin!" She pressed more documents into projectiles, casting them all at him. Each struck him with great force, blasting holes in his flesh.

"Stop it!" McCoy yelled, holding his hands and arms up before him in defense.

"Shields up," a voice ordered from somewhere behind him, and McCoy looked around to see Jim standing beside the captain's chair on the Enterprise bridge. "Arm photon torpedoes," he said.

"Photon torpedoes locked on," reported Lieutenant DePaul at the navigator's station.

McCoy whirled around to see the main viewscreen. On it, the old woman stood behind the counter in the mission. She'd stopped heaving paper missiles and now stood there motionless. Tears streamed from beneath her eyeglasses and down her face, leaving behind watery trails. "No, don't," McCoy said. He turned and ran to the front edge of the combined helm and navigation console, leaned on it, and looked over at the captain. "Jim," he told his friend, "they're all innocent down there. They didn't do anything. It was all my fault."

But Captain Kirk didn't even seem to hear him. Instead, Jim addressed the helm officer. "Mister Sulu," he said, "fire photon torpedoes."

"No!" McCoy called out, but too late. Sulu worked the controls on his panel, and the mechanical rush of a torpedo launch filled the bridge. McCoy turned back to the main viewer in time to see the image flare red, the mission rocked by an explosion. Flames erupted all around the old woman, and she screamed in agony.

Behind McCoy, Sulu continued to fire. Again and again, the rush of the torpedo discharge sounded. On the viewscreen, the weapons found their mark, setting the volumes of paper ablaze. The old woman shrieked.

And still Sulu worked his controls. Firing and firing and firing. Again and again and again. The rhythmic sound repeated incessantly, until McCoy thought he could bear it no longer, and finally the terrible cadence drove him to—

Wake up, he thought, and his eyelids opened in murky light. The repetitive beat of the photon torpedoes persisted from his dream, but transformed into something else now, something real, though McCoy could not immediately place the sound or his surroundings. A dusty, earthy smell seeped into his awareness, and his throat felt parched.

He lay on his side, his head atop a soft object, but the rest of his body on an uncompromisingly rigid surface. As he pushed himself up, his aching muscles punished him for the effort. His head, he saw, had been cushioned by a duffel bag—a cylindrical, sea green carryall that Edith had given him for his travels. Beneath his hands, dry wisps bit into his skin.

He gazed around, trying to make sense of the shadows, and saw a corner not far from him, a pair of dark walls meeting the floor. Carefully, he pulled himself across the short distance and leaned up against the closer of the two vertical surfaces. It felt hard against his back, with no give to it at all.

Where am I? he thought, even as the cyclical clack emanating from below brought it all back to him. "The train," he said in a thin, whispery voice still muted from sleep. Disoriented after waking from such a vivid dream, he tilted his head back and waited for the nagging haze to leave him completely.

As he sat there, his body rocked back and forth in time with the movement of the boxcar that carried him. In the dimness, other sounds reached him: the wood-on-wood grind of the doors as they shifted in their tracks; the dull thud of the latches that kept those doors closed; the heavy, metallic ring of the couplers that bound the train cars together. Above it all, though, came the relentless throbbing of the wheels moving along the steel rails—a throbbing which, in the terrible fantasy of his slumber, had morphed into the recurring launch of photon torpedoes.

McCoy attempted to recall his dream—his nightmare—and found that the evanescent images had already begun to fade. He remembered his desire to go back home and be a doctor, and Jim aboard the *Enterprise* ordering the weapons strike, and the old woman . . . but no, her face had gone from his mind. Still, the horror he'd felt remained—though it now mixed with relief that the woman behind the counter had not been Edith.

Despite everything that had happened during the past two years, Edith Keeler had imparted to his time on Earth a warmth, grace, and kindness that had eased his burden beyond measure. It had been difficult last week to say good-bye to her. He'd promised that he would write, that he would let her know where he settled, but he did not intend to honor that pledge. As much as he respected and cared for Edith, he wanted to fade into the past as best he could, unacknowledged and unremembered. Although his desire for anonymity could not prevent the damage he'd already done, he conceived to do no more harm.

Beneath McCoy, the floor of the boxcar inclined upward, while at the same time, he perceived a decrease in the speed of the train. As it obviously climbed a grade, the pounding pulse of its motion slowed as well and quieted. The wheels whined intermittently against the rails, and in the distance, McCoy heard the low moan of the engine's whistle. The car bucked once, then a second time, as the long, heavy train fought against gravity.

Meanwhile, McCoy thought, *I'm bucking as I fight against time.* Except that he'd ceased actively fighting, hadn't he? A couple of months ago, Edith had suggested—more than that, had really *demanded*—that he leave the mission and get on with his life. She hadn't known his true circumstances, of course, and never would, but still she couldn't have been more right. Though he'd continued to spend most of his money on placing classified ads in newspapers throughout the world, by that point he had in his heart given up hope that he would ever be rescued and understood that he would spend the rest of his life in this time.

In some ways, the certainty of that realization had set him free. If, barring illness or injury, he experienced a normal lifespan, he could expect to live another sixty, seventy, eighty years. Despite his guilt for having changed history, he recognized that he had done so not only unintentionally, but unknowingly, his disruption of the timeline the culmination of an improbable sequence of accidents. Now, he had been left with the choice of either *surviving* here in the past for the remainder of his days, or *living* those days.

In the end, thanks to Edith's intuitive suggestion, McCoy had looked southward, to Atlanta. He had been born and raised within the city, and even through his travels on Earth and in space, he'd thought of the place as home. He'd waited until the spring had matured and the weather had grown warmer, and then at Grand Central Terminal he'd purchased a ticket and boarded a passenger train bound for Philadelphia. Edith had accompanied him to the station, telling him that she felt sad to see him go and that she would miss him, but also giving voice to her delight that he had chosen to make the most of his life. She'd exacted a vow from him to keep in touch with her, and another that he would stay safe. He hadn't told her that he had little money to pay for his travel beyond Pennsylvania, though he'd still planned to make his way to Atlanta.

Feeling better now after his dream, his head cleared, McCoy got to his feet, steadying himself against the wall. He stretched and inhaled deeply, then regretted doing so as he began coughing, having breathed in motes of hay. He'd been fortunate to find on this longest leg of his journey a boxcar emptied of cargo, but vestiges of the fodder that must have been loaded aboard at some point still remained. In the scant illumination, McCoy peered down at himself, and saw his clothing littered with the desiccated, yellowish fibers. He patted down his clothing, brushing away as much of the detritus as he could.

Carefully, with one hand tracing along the wall of the car just in case the train made any sudden movements, McCoy ambled over to one of the wide doors on either side of the center of the compartment. Here and there along the way, light peeked in through narrow gaps between the upright slats that formed the walls. Through a wider opening between the wall and the edge of the door, McCoy saw the green of the countryside by which the train passed. Pushing his fingers through the opening, he un-hitched the latch. Then, setting his feet to maintain his balance, he took hold of the crossbar and heaved the door sliding to the right. It scraped open, and he squinted against the brightness of the morning.

When his eyes had adjusted, he beheld a lovely vista. The train clung to the side of a gently rising hill and overlooked a wide, verdant valley. Trees and other foliage filled the slope below, a dawn mist hanging among the leaves like an earthbound cloud. Farther into the dale, rich grasslands ranged left and right, split by a sinuous, glistening stream.

"Hey, buddy, ya mind?" The loud, gruff voice startled McCoy, and he turned swiftly toward its source, toward the far end of the boxcar. The light from outside penetrated only so far in that direction, but he could make out the shape of two legs on the floor, extending out from the darkness. Obviously somebody else had stolen onto the train during the night, after McCoy had.

"Sorry," McCoy said, raising his voice to be heard. "I didn't realize anybody else had gotten on." He reached for the door and pulled it almost all of the way closed, leaving a slender band of light shining across the middle of the compartment. Bedimmed again, the far end of the car became even more difficult to see. McCoy sensed movement, though, and an instant later a large man lurched into view ahead of him. He fought the urge to shy away from the imposing figure.

"Where ya headin?" the man asked. He talked slowly and sloppily, and even several steps away, McCoy could smell the sour tang of alcohol on his breath.

"Atlanta," McCoy said, uncomfortable divulging any information about himself, but not wanting to take too long to answer.

Though barely visible, the man projected an air of menace, and McCoy knew that he would have to take care. In the weeks leading up to his departure from New York, he had spoken with a few of the men who'd passed through the mission from other places, gleaning from them the particulars of how they moved freely about the country. Many had shared with him the practice of "freight hopping," which he'd ultimately decided to employ himself. Among the many hazards they'd cited in surreptitiously riding the rails—including the railroad police, who they called "bulls," and boarding and disembarking moving trains—they had emphasized the dangers posed by some fellow travelers, low, angry men with no regard for any but themselves.

"Where ya comin from?" the large man wanted to know, taking a heavy step forward. McCoy's eyes had readjusted to the faint light, and he saw that the man stood close to two meters tall, with a strapping frame and enormous hands. He wore a faded jacket—either brown or gray, McCoy could not tell which—and frayed dungarees.

"I got on at Richmond," McCoy said, truthfully identifying where he'd climbed into the boxcar. In the days prior to that, he'd ridden an empty gondola car out of Philadelphia with half a dozen other itinerants, then waited in a Baltimore freight yard overnight, until he'd found a suitable southbound train. He'd shared the rear platform of a grainer all the way to Washington with a character who called himself "Tote 'Em Pole" and then had stayed on alone to Richmond. There, it had taken two chilly nights before he'd come across the empty boxcar on a train headed directly for Atlanta. "Where'd you get on?" McCoy asked, stalling for time as he considered his options should the large man become belligerent.

"Charlotte," he said, and he plodded forward another step.

McCoy resisted the impulse to shrink off to the side, not wanting to provoke the man. Instead, he pointed back toward the corner where his duffel bag still lay, though he did not take his gaze from his potential adversary. "I've got some food back here," McCoy said. "Can I get you something to eat?"

"You got food?" the man said, unashamedly interested.

"A little," McCoy said. He had few possessions—the clothes he wore; the clothing, toiletries, and food in his duffel bag; and the few dollars stuffed into his sock—but he had no qualms about sharing—or surrendering—any or all of it. Given the opportunity, though, he would seek to retain the carryall filled with his garments, suspecting that it might soon prove to be of greater use than expected.

McCoy started toward the corner where he'd left the duffel bag, but then another voice stopped him. "What kinda food you got?" a second man asked, from out of the far shadows where the first had emerged. McCoy peered past the large man to see another figure stride forward. Closer to his own height and build, the second man wore a wide-brimmed hat. Unlike his companion, he did not sound inebriated.

"Uh, I've got a few things," McCoy said. Without turning away from the strangers, he continued on toward the corner he'd occupied. "Some dried meats," he said, and then recalling the contemporary term, added, "Jerky." As McCoy's foot struck his duffel, he saw the second man advance to the middle of the car, until he stood beside the first. "I've also got some fruit," he said, quickly bending toward the duffel bag and taking hold of the end with the opening. "Some apples and pears and other things." He dragged the bag upright and then forward, toward the two men.

As McCoy neared the center of the car, he spied something that essentially confirmed his concerns about the intentions of the two drifters: a rod or a bar of some sort, straight and inflexible, half a meter or more long, hanging down from the hand of the second man. McCoy also saw now that heavy growth darkened the smaller man's face, as though he hadn't shaved in a week. Thinking of his own bare face, McCoy suddenly remembered the straight razor in his bag. If necessary, and if he could get to it, he supposed that he could use it as a weapon, though it had been a long time since he'd utilized any of his Starfleet hand-to-hand combat training, and an even longer time since the training itself.

McCoy pulled open the maw of the duffel bag, loosening the drawstring that held it closed. At the top of his belongings sat two wrinkled paper bags, and he lifted one of them out. "Here we go," he said, extracting an apple from within and holding it up for the men to see. He offered it to the larger man, who grabbed it, studied it for a moment, then bit noisily into it. While he ate the piece of fruit, McCoy reached back into the paper bag and withdrew another apple. "For you?" he said to the second man, holding it out to him.

"Sure," the smaller man said, but he made no move to take the red orb. McCoy recognized the tactic, intended to draw him in for an attack. He obliged, but not without his own plan. He stepped forward, and the instant he saw the second man bringing the rod up, he tossed the apple and the bag of fruit toward his face. The smaller man instinctively raised his hands to ward off the improvised projectiles. As he did, McCoy leveled a kick at the knee of the larger man, who cried out in pain as he collapsed to the floor.

As quickly as he could, McCoy bent and reached for his duffel bag, gripping the fabric as tightly as he could in his fingers. He intended to head for the partially open door, but saw the second man recovering and swinging the rod back up. McCoy launched himself at the man, leading high with the duffel. He heard the unnerving whisper of something speed past his ear, then felt the impact of the rod on the bag. McCoy hammered his feet against the floor and drove himself forward, pushing the second man from his feet. The rod flew from the man's hand and clattered into the darkness.

Still moving as swiftly as possible, McCoy scrambled back to his feet, hauling the duffel bag up with him. He ran to the door he'd stood at just a few minutes ago, and with one hand, pushed it back open. Outside, the landscape moved past, the dense undergrowth on the hill below appearing far softer and more inviting than it no doubt would be. McCoy brought the duffel bag up in front of him and, without hesitating, jumped.

He cleared the ends of the railroad ties and the ballast in which they sat, but still landed hard. Though he tried to use the duffel to pad his fall, his legs struck first, coming down on the solid ground just below the tracks. McCoy allowed his legs to give way, and he toppled forward. He managed to get the bag down before him, but then he rolled. His back struck something hard, and something else tore across the back of his hand. The duffel bag flew from his grasp as he continued to spin out of control, side over side. Leaves whipped past his face, twigs and branches snapped beneath him. He slammed his eyes shut as he plunged down the hill, gaining speed. Without thinking, he pulled his arms up before his face, covering his head as best he could.

He fell for what seemed like a long time. Sensation mercifully abandoned him as he waited to reach flat ground. His thoughts tumbled with him, wheeling past images of Edith's face, and Chapel's, and the antiquated facilities of twentieth-century hospitals. In his mind, he screamed, and only a few seconds later did he realize that he'd opened his mouth and actually cried out.

With great force, his thighs slammed into a tree trunk, sending waves of intense pain down his legs. His upper body jackknifed past the tree and then jerked to a stop. With the tumult of his descent finished, an imperfect quiet gathered about him. The sounds of the wood—pops and cracks, the easy sough of leaves—enveloped him, while from a distance, he heard the steady resonance of the train's wheels on its tracks.

McCoy slowly lifted his head and looked back up the hill. At first, he saw only the dense verdure through which he'd plummeted, until he looked higher. Far away, barely visible through the trees and bushes, he saw color and movement. For a second, he thought that the two drifters had followed him from the boxcar and now gave chase, but then he made out the form of the train itself. As he watched, the red structure of the caboose passed. Then the sound of the train faded . . . and with it consciousness.

SIXTEEN

2268

In the ship's gymnasium, Jim Kirk worked the heavy bag. Hanging near a corner in one of the gym's smaller satellite compartments, the fifty-kilo bag showed signs of wear in its durable royal blue casing, and Kirk wondered how many of the crew utilized it in their conditioning routines. Perhaps Lieutenant Leslie, who right now stood in the opposite corner, sending a rhythmic flurry of punches into the speed bag suspended there.

Kirk normally employed pugilistic training only occasionally in his own workouts, though in recent days he'd made it a regular component of his physical regimen. Of late, life aboard the *Enterprise* had been relatively calm, but he still found himself uneasy. The last two assignments—first contact with the Melkotians and ferrying the Elasian Dohlman, Elaan, from her home planet to Troyius—had proven far more arduous than he'd anticipated. While his resulting disquiet had diminished on its own over time, the change to his fitness program seemed to hasten the process.

Bare chested and wearing lightweight training pants, Kirk had begun his exercises only a few minutes ago, but already perspiration coated his skin in a thin sheen. He stood with his shoulders square to the bag, his left side forward, and toiled through an outside drill. He circled in both directions, throwing frequent jabs, interspersing them with left-right combinations. For three minutes, he moved around the bag, focused on delivering well-timed and well-executed punches. Finally, he finished the set by stepping back, spinning, and delivering a roundhouse kick.

Tired, he retreated to the nearby bulkhead to rest a moment before advancing to his next drill. As he retrieved his towel from the hook where he'd placed it, he saw Mr. Leslie exit, obviously having completed his own workout. Kirk patted down his torso and arms, lightly drying himself before continuing. He'd rehung the towel and started back toward the heavy bag when the door to the compartment slid open, and Spock and McCoy entered. Kirk lowered his cocked fist as the two officers approached.

"Gentlemen?" he said.

"Pardon the intrusion, Captain," Spock said, "but we require a moment of your time."

"And this is something that can't wait until I'm through here?" Kirk asked.

"We don't know, Jim," Bones replied. "But we didn't want to take any chances."

"All right," Kirk said, immediately concerned. Though prone

to emotionalism and occasional hyperbole, McCoy did not promote concerns without rational cause. And Spock, level headed and logical, always provided the voice of reason. "What is it?"

"It's Chekov," McCoy said. "You ordered a full workup on him after our experience with the Melkotians."

"That's right," Kirk said, stepping back over to the bulkhead and again collecting his towel. He began wiping down his arms and chest, drying himself more thoroughly this time. "You reported him to be in perfect health and recommended his return to duty."

"And I stand by that," McCoy said. "But I did find an anomalous reading when I examined him. It appears harmless, but it was unexpected. So I spent some time studying it before taking it to Spock."

"To Spock?" Kirk said, looking from the doctor to the first officer. "Not to me?" Kirk hung his towel back up and grabbed his workout tunic from the hook beside it.

"Doctor McCoy believed it appropriate to speak with me first," Spock explained, "because this issue involves you directly, Captain."

"Me?" Kirk asked. "In what way?"

"You remember the algorithm Doctor M'Benga developed at Deneva?" McCoy said.

"In order to determine whether or not a person was infected with one of the neural parasites," Kirk said, recalling all too well the circumstances that had robbed him of his brother and sister-in-law. "You said my reading changed, but not enough to indicate the presence in my body of a parasite."

"That's right," McCoy confirmed. "But you were the only member of the crew who ever showed a change in that reading."

"Until now, I take it," Kirk said.

"That is correct," Spock said. "Ensign Chekov now shows a similar increase, though not nearly as substantial as your own."

"I see," Kirk said. He slipped his hands inside his tunic and pulled it on over his head. "But there's no danger to Chekov," he said, "or to the crew?"

"We don't think so," McCoy said.

"But you're not sure," Kirk surmised, "or you wouldn't be here now."

"Our initial concern developed not because of the reading itself, which despite the change, appears harmless," Spock said, "but because the medical staff has been unable to explain the cause of the change."

"And there's more," McCoy revealed. "After I spoke to Spock this morning, we decided that I should conduct an exam on him, just to be sure that some unidentified disease or condition wasn't spreading throughout the crew."

"As with Mister Chekov, I showed an increase in the energy output of my nervous system," Spock said.

"Is there any chance at all that this *does* indicate infection by the parasites?" Kirk asked. "Could some of them have remained dormant in your body, Mister Spock, or could some other members of the crew have become infected when they worked down on Deneva?"

"We don't think so, Jim," McCoy said. "Chekov wasn't among the crews that transported down to Deneva, but more than that, he shows absolutely no signs at all of the parasites. Neither does Spock."

"Then what is it?" Kirk asked. "A disease of some sort?"

"We think it's nothing," McCoy said. "Either a flaw in M'Benga's algorithm or in our interpretation of the results. Maybe the increase in the reading is simply the result of some normal bodily process. We just don't know."

"In order to exercise prudence, though," Spock said, "we believe that it would be wise to conduct medical examinations of the entire crew."

"Bones, didn't you just complete the annual crew physicals a few months ago?" Kirk asked. He remembered that his own yearly exam had taken place shortly after the crew's visit to Omega IV.

"I did," McCoy said. "I also went back over all the results before I consulted with Spock. I found no changes in the M'Benga numbers of any of the crew. Which is one of the reasons we want to conduct new exams now; we've got two rounds of readings for most of the crew, and for those more recently assigned to the *Enterprise,* we can use the latest results as their baseline."

Kirk considered the information and recommendation he'd been given, as well as the disruption another round of medical exams would cause the crew. He paced slowly past Spock and McCoy, weighing the alternatives and searching for any other possible courses of action. He'd almost reached the speed bag in the far corner when he turned back to his senior officers. "How long will it take to examine the entire crew?" he asked.

"A week, maybe two," McCoy replied. "We don't want to perform complete physicals. We just want to take enough readings to be able to employ Doctor M'Benga's algorithm and determine if there's been any change in those values. Of course, that also depends on what sorts of incidents you get the *Enterprise* involved in."

Kirk appreciated the harmless gibe, taking it as indication that although Bones felt that this situation warranted immediate attention, the CMO did not think that the crew faced any real danger. "All right, Doctor," Kirk said. "Conduct your exams."

"Yes, sir," McCoy said.

"Thank you, Captain," Spock said.

"Then if there's nothing else . . ." Kirk waited for a response, and when the two officers remained silent, he said, "Dismissed."

After Spock and McCoy had left, Kirk walked back over to the heavy bag. He reached out and idly placed a hand on its sturdy blue surface as he went back over all that he'd just been told. Comfortable with the orders he'd given, and confident in the condition of the crew, he chose to resume his exercises. He quickly stripped off his tunic, set himself before the bag, and began the next set of his workout.

McCoy speared the last cube on his plate, a dark green morsel, the color of which at least closely matched the broccoli it approximated. As he ate it, McCoy longed for some "real" food, but knew that the ship's provisions had grown low during the past few months. The *Enterprise* hadn't had its foodstuffs replenished in quite some time. Although the ship had visited a repair base not all that long ago, the station itself had at the time held only synthesized rations in its stores. "What I wouldn't give for a warm slice of peach cobbler right now," McCoy said, holding his empty fork up before him.

"Peach cobbler?" Hadley said from across the table. "How about a cranachan?"

"A what?" Dr. Sanchez asked from beside McCoy. The three men sat together in the crew mess, just finishing their dinners. "I've never heard of that."

"It's probably a dish Scotty would know about if we asked him," McCoy observed. Hadley, he knew, shared a Scottish heritage with the chief engineer. "Am I right, Bill?"

Still in his command-division gold uniform after his shift—none of the three men had changed their clothes prior to their evening meal—the navigator drew himself up in his seat. Tall and thin, with a long neck, Hadley seemed to gain a couple of centimeters in the process. "Being a man of refined breeding and taste," he said, clearly feigning annoyance at the question, "Mister Scott has sampled cranachan on many an occasion, I'm sure." Somehow he kept a smile from his face.

"I'm sure too," McCoy agreed, amused.

"What's in it?" Sanchez asked.

"It's a mixture of toasted oats, raspberries, whipped cream, honey, and whiskey," Hadley said, dropping his look of irritation. "It's quite tasty."

"Whiskey?" Sanchez asked, sounding skeptical.

"For flavor," Hadley replied.

"And to kill the pain," McCoy quipped, and the men chuckled at the echo of the line they'd all heard Scotty utter on numerous occasions.

As they bused their table, Sanchez and Hadley discussed what they wanted to do this evening, mentioning bowling and table tennis as possibilities, before settling on backgammon in a rec room. "Are you going to join us, Doc?" Hadley asked.

"I'd like to," McCoy said, "but I've got to finish the crew evaluations." After discovering the increase in Ensign Chekov's M'Benga numbers, McCoy and the medical staff had reexamined the ship's entire complement. Their initial findings had proven startling: every single member of the crew had shown a similar rise in the energy output of their nervous system. All of the readings had been within the range Doctor M'Benga had defined as normal, and all but two had climbed a similar, negligible amount. Only Jim and Spock had shown larger increases—Jim by the far the largest—but even their measurements had remained within normal limits.

McCoy had gone to the captain as soon the pattern had become clear. The medical conclusion had seemed obvious: either all the crew suffered from some unidentified affliction; the readings did not correspond to any condition beyond the value they measured; or M'Benga's algorithm suffered some sensitive dependence or fault not yet understood. McCoy had recommended that the crew undergo complete physicals. Jim had agreed, and McCoy and the rest of the medical staff had then spent several months conducting full exams of the entire crew. They'd now completed those exams, and once the results of the last few lab tests were completed this evening, McCoy needed to finish preparing his report for the captain.

As Sanchez and Hadley headed off to one of the ship's recreation rooms, McCoy started back to his office. He waited for a moment at a turbolift before its doors slid open. Inside the car stood Dr. M'Benga.

"Jabilo, aren't you on shift now?" McCoy asked as he entered the lift.

M'Benga looked up, his dark eyes widening for a second in apparent surprise. "Len," he said as McCoy entered the car. "Yes, I am on shift." He spoke as he always did, with a slightly formal, almost stilted, inflection. "I was actually just coming to see you."

"Well, I'm heading back to sickbay myself, if that's all right with you," McCoy said. M'Benga nodded, and McCoy ordered the turbolift to their destination. The car began to descend, but then M'Benga took hold of its activation wand.

"Hold," he said, and the lift slowed to a halt. "Len," he said gravely, "I need to speak with you in private."

"Of course," McCoy said. "What is it?" He inferred at once that his colleague had detected a medical problem with one of the crew.

"I just got back the lab results from the final physicals I performed," M'Benga said, essentially confirming McCoy's suspicion. He hesitated and looked away, obviously disturbed by whatever the lab tests had revealed. McCoy couldn't recall ever seeing his fellow physician so flustered.

"You found something in one of the crew," McCoy prompted.

M'Benga looked back over at him. "Yes. Xenopolycythemia," he said. The word shocked McCoy. He knew little beyond the basics of the malady—that it was an acquired, extraterrestrial disorder of the bone marrow that caused erythroid and myeloid hyperplasia—but he did know that, unlike its Earthly counterpart, it was always fatal to humans. "Len," M'Benga intoned, "you've got it."

McCoy felt as though an electric charge passed through his body. The urge to deny the reality welled up within him, the words *There must be a mistake* flashing through his mind, but he knew that Dr. M'Benga wouldn't have come to him without ensuring the validity of the lab results. Unaccountably, he thought of Jocelyn, even though he hadn't seen her or spoken to her in quite some time, and despite that what little contact they had shared since the painful end of their marriage had been tense and uncomfortable.

Then he thought of Joanna, saw the image of her in his mind—her fair, delicate features beneath her long, fiery red hair—and he thought: *I'm sorry.*

McCoy's knees suddenly went weak, and the possibility of his legs collapsing beneath him allowed him to disconnect, at least temporarily, from the anguish he felt for his daughter. He looked over at M'Benga and saw tears pooling in his eyes. "Len," he said again, and moved forward to place a hand on McCoy's shoulder.

"How long?" McCoy asked.

"Not more than a year," M'Benga said with a tremor in his voice.

"It's all right," McCoy said, gratefully reassuming the mantle of his vocation and attempting to comfort his crewmate and friend. "Thank you for telling me yourself, Jabilo."

M'Benga held McCoy's gaze for a moment before nodding and dropping his hand back to his side. "If there's anything I can do," he said.

"Of course," McCoy replied, and reached again for the activation wand. He restated their destination and restarted the lift. "I take it you haven't informed the captain yet," he said.

"No, I haven't," M'Benga said. "Only Nurse Chapel knows. She was in sickbay when I received the lab reports."

"All right," McCoy said. "I'd appreciate it if you kept this to yourself for now." Though he'd had no time yet to think through the situation, it occurred to him that he might prefer people not to know about his condition.

"Len," M'Benga said gently, "Captain Kirk has to be told."

"I know, I know," McCoy said. "I'd like to tell him myself though." M'Benga did not respond immediately, perhaps wondering if McCoy really would inform the captain of his ailment. "Please," McCoy added.

Once more, M'Benga nodded. "Certainly," he said.

The turbolift carried them the rest of the way in silence. They walked together toward sickbay, where McCoy again thanked M'Benga. He then continued on to his office. When he entered, he saw Chapel seated at his desk, a data slate lying before her. She held a hand to her head, as though responding to a headache. She peered over as the door panel closed behind him.

"Doctor McCoy," she said. "Did Doctor M'Benga—"

"Yes, he found me," McCoy interrupted, recognizing that he did not wish to talk about his condition, much less his prognosis.

"I'm so sorry," Chapel said, tension showing in her face. "I just can't believe—"

"No, it's all right," McCoy said, cutting her off as he walked deeper into the room. When he stood on the opposite side of the desk from the nurse, he said, "Please. It's just something I'll have to live with—" He saw Chapel's horrified expression before he even realized what he'd said. "You know what I mean," he said, trying to wave the moment away.

Chapel paused, then turned to the monitor on the desk. She reached up and tapped the screen. "I've been searching through the medical database to find out what's known about the disorder, to see what research is being done—"

For the third time, McCoy talked over her. "That's all right. You don't need to do that right now."

"I just thought . . ." she began, but then didn't finish.

"I know," McCoy told her, although in truth, he hadn't really considered her feelings at all. He hadn't even had time to consider his own. "Actually, though, I think I'd like to be alone right now."

Chapel appeared conflicted for a moment, as though deciding

whether or not she should do as McCoy had asked. Finally, she said, "Of course." She rose, moved out from behind the desk, and walked toward the door.

"Oh," McCoy said just as the door opened, "I'd appreciate it if you'd keep this to yourself for right now."

Again, Chapel hesitated. "All right," she said at last.

"Thank you," McCoy said, and he started around his desk. Before he sat down, though, he looked over to see Chapel stopped in the doorway.

"You are going to tell the captain, aren't you?" she asked.

"To be honest, I don't know," McCoy said. He sat down and then admitted, "I was thinking that I might not tell anybody else, that I might just try to live out the next year as best I can, as though this hadn't even happened."

"Doctor," Chapel said, and she padded back into the office, the door once more enclosing them inside. "Leonard," she continued, obviously attempting to reach him on a personal level, "you have to tell Captain Kirk. Not just because he's your commanding officer, but because he's your closest friend. You have to let him help you."

McCoy gazed at Chapel, at the earnest concern she displayed, and then he looked away. On the desk, to his left, he saw a list on the monitor, and he quickly read the first few entries. *Xenopolycythemia: Diagnosis and Pathology. An Excess of Blood in Humans, From Rigel First Contact Forward. Aspects of Hematological Adaptation and Mutation.* Abstracts followed each title, which clearly composed a list of medical papers relating to McCoy's disorder. He reached forward and pushed the toggle below the monitor, deactivating it. To Chapel, he said, "I know what you're saying, but I don't know that I want any help right now."

"I see," Chapel said in a cool tone that McCoy could not read. As he watched, she moved farther into his office, to the rear bulkhead. Before he knew what she meant to do, she pressed the button beside the intercom on the table there. "Captain Kirk, please report to sickbay at once. We have an emergency that requires your attention."

"Christine!" McCoy said, and he pushed himself up out of his chair.

"This is the captain," came Jim's response. *"What is it?"*

McCoy strode toward Chapel, though he had no notion of just how he would stop her. He couldn't very well argue with her over an open channel.

"Captain, this is Nurse Chapel," she said. "I'd rather speak with you in sickbay, if you don't mind."

McCoy reached Chapel. He considered closing the intercom channel, but thought that an unwise choice. He tried to formulate something he could say to Jim to defuse the situation, but then suddenly felt beset and found himself unable to frame an adequate response.

On the intercom, after a brief pause, Jim said, *"I'll be right there. Out."*

Chapel pushed the intercom button again, and the activation light winked off. "You had no right to do that," McCoy told her, and he could hear the fatigue in his own voice. *Or is that defeat?* he asked himself.

"I not only have the right, I have the responsibility," Chapel said. "You can't expect to go through this alone."

"That's my choice to make," he insisted, "not yours." He walked away from her, back across the room, until he stood in front of his desk again.

"You have to let people help you," Chapel implored him.

"You invaded my privacy," McCoy said. He reached for the data slate on his desk. As he lifted it up, the stylus slid across the display, and he grabbed it before it fell.

"I only want to help you," Chapel said. "Captain Kirk will want to help you."

"But I don't know if I *want* help right now," he said, his voice rising in frustration. "I just found out about this. I don't know what to think about it, or even *how* to think about it."

Chapel didn't respond right away, and when she did, her words carried a note of contrition. "I'm sorry," she said.

McCoy peered at the slate screen and saw his name at the top left, in an entry marked *Patient.* He started to read through the medical information recorded there. He saw the details of his complete blood count and noted the elevated levels of his hematocrit, differential, and platelet count, as well as an increase in his blood volume. He also saw abnormal results for several other tests, including the lactate dehydrogenase test, the B-12 level, and the leukocyte alkaline phosphatase test.

"Leonard," Chapel said, still reaching out to him.

"You're dismissed, Nurse," McCoy said without looking up. He continued reading through the results of his physical for a few moments, until he realized that Chapel hadn't left. He looked toward the rear bulkhead, where she still stood beside the table there. "I said you can go."

"I don't think so, Doctor," she said, and she turned away from him.

He understood that she only wanted to help him through this, but he felt right now as though his head might explode at any second. He marched back over to her. "Crewman, you're dismissed," he said, unable to prevent himself from raising his voice. "That's a direct order from a superior officer."

Chapel leaned forward and set her hands down firmly on the tabletop. "I am a nurse first, Doctor McCoy," she said, her frustration showing, "and a member of the crew of the *Enterprise* second."

"You're excused," McCoy said, his voice still loud. "You may return to your quarters."

"No, I'm sorry, Doctor," she said, pushing up off the table and turning to face him. "I have called the captain, and I'll wait until he comes."

McCoy thought that he should simply leave his office himself, but then the door squeaked open. Both he and Chapel glanced over to see the captain enter. Jim stopped just inside the doorway and asked, "What's the emergency?"

Chapel looked at the captain, and for an uncomfortable instant, McCoy thought that she would tell him about the situation. "I said you were excused, Nurse," McCoy said, trying to preempt her revelation to the captain. She turned away, and though McCoy could see that his harsh words had hurt her, he also saw that, more than anything else affecting her, she remained concerned about him. "Please, Christine," he said, lowering his voice almost to a whisper. "I promise you I'll give the captain a full report." At this point, he had no other choice, and he'd quickly lost the stomach for argument, particularly with somebody who only wanted to help him. He tapped his thumb anxiously against the slate, hoping that Chapel would go.

Finally, she did.

Once the door had closed after Chapel, Jim approached McCoy. "That was quite a scene," he said.

McCoy spun around to face the captain. "I've just completed the standard physical examinations for the entire crew," he said.

"Excellent," Jim replied. "What's the emergency?"

"The crew is fit," McCoy reported. "I found nothing un-usual—with one exception."

"Serious?" Jim asked.

"Terminal."

McCoy saw Jim's entire body tense. "What is it?" he asked.

"Xenopolycythemia," McCoy said. "It has no cure."

"Who?" Jim wanted to know.

"He has one year to live, at the most," McCoy said, not want-ing to tell Jim the truth, though he knew that he would—that he must, for so many reasons.

"Who is it?" the captain asked again.

"The ship's chief medical officer," McCoy said, unable to simply say *me*.

"You," Jim said, the word not much more than a breath. McCoy did not think he could bear the pain he saw in the cap-tain's—in his friend's—eyes.

"I'll be most effective on the job in the time left," McCoy claimed, "if you'll keep this to yourself."

"Bones," Jim said, visibly upset by the news, "is there any chance there's been a false reading, a mistake?"

McCoy glanced down at the slate he still held in his hands. He read again one of the details he'd noticed when he'd first looked at the report, namely that M'Benga had ordered the lab tests performed a second time, on a different set of samples taken from McCoy during his physical. "No, Jim," he said. "There's no mistake. Doctor M'Benga ran the tests twice."

Jim turned and paced away, as though driven by an uncon-trollable impulse. At the far end of the office, he looked back to-ward McCoy. "And there's no hope for a cure? Maybe in the next year?"

"I know there's a lot of research out there," McCoy said, "but

I haven't read anything at all in the medical literature that suggests there's been any significant movement toward any kind of treatment, much less toward a cure."

Jim raised his hands and then dropped them, appearing to search for what next to say. After a few seconds, he asked, "What are you going to do?"

"I don't know," McCoy said. He peered again at the slate, then set it down on the table along the rear bulkhead. "I just found out a short time ago, so I haven't really had time to make any plans, but I think I'd like to stay aboard, at least for a while." He thought about the prospect of continuing to live his life as he had, with no disruptions to it beyond his knowledge of the short time left to him. "I wouldn't want the crew to know," he said. "You'll want to train a new CMO, though. If you can get an immediate replacement for me, they can serve aboard ship as a member of the medical staff while I train them." McCoy considered his current staff.

"All right," Jim said.

"When you talk to Starfleet Command about a replacement for me," McCoy went on, "you can tell them that I think Doctor M'Benga would make an excellent choice." He judged neither Sanchez nor Harrison experienced enough for the job, but he thought Jabilo could settle into the position effectively.

Jim nodded, then walked slowly back across the office, until he stood directly before McCoy. "Is there anything I can do for you?" he asked.

"No," McCoy said. "Thank you, but I don't think there is."

The two men stood there silently for a moment, and then the three tones of the intercom whistle sounded. *"Bridge to Captain Kirk,"* came Spock's voice.

Jim hesitated, then went to the table and pressed the intercom button there. "Kirk here," he said.

"Spock here, Captain," the first officer said. *"We are approaching solar system K-517. Estimated time of arrival at the termination shock: thirty minutes. Survey teams are completing preparations."*

"I'm on my way," Jim said, "but . . . I'll be stopping by my quarters first."

"Acknowledged," Spock said.

"Kirk out." Jim deactivated the intercom with a touch.

"Another new solar system to explore?" McCoy asked. "Just don't get us killed, all right?"

Jim raised his eyebrows, evidently uncomfortable by McCoy's attempt at humor. "Bones," he said.

"Go," McCoy said. "I'll talk with you later."

Jim started to go, then stopped and said, "I'll need your medical records for my report to Starfleet Command."

"I'll send them to your data bank right now," McCoy said.

After Jim left, McCoy picked up the data slate again and took it back over to his desk. There, he downloaded the results of his physical to the ship's medical database, encoding it for availability to the captain's secure library-computer access. When he'd completed that task, he set about finalizing the crew's health evaluations.

When he came to his own name in the crew rolls, he skipped over it.

SEVENTEEN

1932

Lynn Dickinson walked to the beginning of the last unplanted furrow, the canvas sack slung over her shoulder so much lighter now that she'd emptied it of most of its contents. She couldn't believe that today she would finally finish getting the seed into the ground—late, but not *too* late. This year's sowing season had taken longer than usual, even though she and Phil had begun preparing the land on time back in February. But when Mama's health had taken a bad turn—*awful* bad—there'd been no choice for Lynn but to head on up to Pepper's Crossing and see her. She and Phil had worried about the planting and had talked about going up at a later date, but she'd had a feeling that Mama might not make it to the summer. As it turned out, she hadn't even made it to the spring.

Now, only a couple of months after that last visit to Pepper's Crossing, the picture of her dying mother came back easily to Lynn, and she shook her head as though she might be able to joggle it loose and get rid of it that way. The image wouldn't go, though, and so instead she simply tried to forge ahead with what she'd been doing. Reaching into her sack, she scooped her hand through the remaining cottonseed, the fuzzy kernels both soft and prickly against her skin. She bent to drop the seeds into the narrow trench, but then tears blurred her vision, as often happened these days when she thought about either one of her parents.

That's enough, she scolded herself, standing straight again. She tried to remember that she really had no reason to weep. Mama had been sick and in pain for a long time, and truth be told, had been ready to meet her Maker ever since her husband— Lynn's beloved Pa—had drowned in the Saluda River fifteen years ago. Back then, Mama had stayed strong, raising her teenage daughter on her own, but she'd never stopped missing her man.

Lynn had never stopped missing him either. Standing alone in the south field, she suddenly felt lonely for her girlhood, for the days their little family of three had spent in their Pepper's Crossing farmhouse. She reminded herself that, since God had called Mama home, her parents had reunited and now lived happily together again, just not here on Earth. "You cry only for yourself, missy," she said.

Lynn dropped the cottonseed back in the sack and wiped her eyes. Resettling her straw cartwheel hat atop her head, she peered down the length of the final furrow, the slim trough in the raised ridge running out toward the east side of the valley. The sun had burned off the morning haze on its way up the sky, and the temperature had risen into the seventies, maybe even to eighty. The air felt heavy with moisture, and patchy clouds promised thundershowers this afternoon.

That thought got Lynn moving again. She wanted to complete the final planting before the rains came. She reached back into

the sack and pulled out another handful of cottonseed, then
started along the furrow, dropping them into the dirt. When she
at last reached the end of the row, she trudged over to the barn,
where she harnessed up Piedmont and brought her back out to
the south field. There, Lynn walked the mule between the freshly
planted furrows, guiding a flat board over the ridges to push a
light layer of earth over the seeds. Halfway through, darker
clouds appeared off in the distance, throwing down forks of
lighting and pushing low rumbles of thunder across the land.

It took Lynn until the late afternoon to finish, but she managed to lead Piedmont back into the barn before the first rain-
drops fell. As she used a pitchfork to load hay into the mule's
stall, the peals of thunder neared, and soon the skies opened. The
rain beat down loudly on the roof of the barn, the sounds of individual drops lost in the deluge. Lynn used the time to feed the
other animals—the horses, goats, dairy cows, chickens—and
then to brush down Piedmont.

Afterward, she stood inside the barn's large doorway and
gazed outside. The day had turned ruggedly gray, but from her
vantage, she could see brilliant shafts of sunlight breaking
through the clouds on the other side of the valley. The rain had
already tapered down to small, widely spaced drops. Normal for
this time of year, the heavy downpour had lasted only a few minutes, but had still cooled the temperature. The air smelled of
lightning, a scent almost like that of burning metal.

Lynn waited until the rain had stopped, and headed toward
the house. Phil wouldn't be home from the mill for a couple of
hours yet, and so she would actually have some time to herself
before she needed to start cooking supper. She could finally
begin reading the novel that Mrs. Slattery had let her borrow
months ago. According to the schoolteacher, *The Good Earth*
told the story of a farming family, not in America, but in China.
Although Lynn didn't often have much time for books, she liked
to read, particularly about exotic people and places that she knew
she would never get a chance to visit herself.

Nearing the side porch, Lynn stopped to wipe the mud from
her boots onto the grass. As she did, she noticed a figure walking
down the dirt road that passed by the front of the farmhouse. She
watched, trying to make out who it might be. Phil would be

coming home in their truck, but even if it had broken down and he'd had to walk, he'd be coming from town, which sat in the other direction. More than that, Tindal's Lane didn't really go anywhere, leading only to a pair of abandoned farms farther down the valley. Locals sometimes went out that way looking to scrounge something or other from the broken-down houses and barns there, but they most likely wouldn't go there on foot.

Curious, Lynn continued to watch as the man drew closer. At some point, even though she still couldn't make out the details of his face, she realized from his gait that she didn't know him. He moved at a snail's pace and walked with a noticeable limp. As he finally neared the house, she also saw that he carried a small bundle over one shoulder.

A vagabond, she thought, and wondered if he'd hopped a freight and then gotten off somewhere near here. The tracks passed not far from the end of Tindal's Lane, and she'd heard a train whistle today, just after dawn. Over the past couple of years, a number of strangers had appeared in town, mostly looking for work. They never received much of a welcome, since most of the folks in Hayden just got by themselves, and none of them ever stayed for long.

One man *had* left his mark on the town, though, Lynn remembered. After leaving Hayden one afternoon, he'd doubled back that night to try and rob the Seed and Feed. The owner, Gregg Anderson, had caught him and they'd fought. Although Gregg had eventually run off the would-be thief, a lamp had gotten knocked over during their skirmish and the store had caught fire before anybody knew. The men in town had doused it pretty quickly, but not before a dozen sacks of grain and part of one wall had burned. Gregg had rebuilt part of the wall, but part of it still remained blackened.

Recalling that incident, as well as the general misgivings folks around here had about strangers, Lynn briefly thought about running into the house and getting Phil's shotgun. But strangers didn't bother her nearly as much as they bothered others. And assuming the worst about people even before you got to know them didn't seem to her like a particularly Christian way to behave. So when the man had gotten close enough that she could call to him, she waved her arm. "Howdy," she said.

The man stopped in the middle of the road and looked around. He had a head of short, dark hair, she saw. When he spotted her, he called back, "Howdy to you." He didn't raise his free arm to wave back, but he did start walking again. He moseyed over to the side of Tindal's Lane closest to the house, and when he reached the front yard, she saw that his right arm rested in a sling. The man swung the bundle he carried with his other hand down to the ground, then leaned heavily on the post-and-rail fence that ran along the property line. "I don't suppose you could spare some water, ma'am," he said politely.

"Why, yes, of course," Lynn said. "Come on up while I get some for you." She quickly ran up the crooked steps of the side porch and then into the house. In the kitchen, she threw her wide, circular hat onto the table—where Phil's latest jigsaw puzzle still sat on a piece of plywood, half finished—then dipped a tall cup into one of the buckets of water she'd collected from the well this morning. She went back outside, expecting to find the stranger there, but saw that he hadn't moved from the front fence. She strolled across the grass toward him, holding out the cup of water when she reached him, and said, "You could have come on up to the house."

"Thank you, ma'am," he said, "but I'm not sure I could've gone much farther." He reached across the fence to accept the cup from her and then eagerly drank from it.

The man had a nice face, Lynn thought, with bright blue eyes and a nice smile. A series of bright red scratches marred his features, though, and a long gash, encrusted with dried blood, snaked out from beneath the right side of his hairline. He appeared eight or ten years older than Phil, who would turn thirty-one next month, and though the stranger stood a little downhill from her, she guessed his height about the same as Phil's, about five or six inches taller than her own, maybe five-ten or five-eleven.

Sitting on the ground beside him, the man's round bundle looked like nothing more than a torn, dirt-stained green cloth wrapped about a heap of clothing. His sling, she saw, had been tied together out of a grimy shirt. In fact, the clothes he wore— dungarees and a denim shirt—also appeared shabby and soiled, as thought they'd been dragged through the mud.

"Thank you, ma'am," the man said again when he'd finished downing the water. "I surely appreciate it." He handed the cup back to her, and for just a second, her fingers touched his.

"You're cold," Lynn said, and she guessed that he must have been caught out in the rain. She peered more closely at him—at his hair, his clothes, the bundle at his feet—and saw the truth of her realization. "And you're wet," she said. She pointed to the sack of clothing. "Is there anything dry in there?"

"Everything's pretty well soaked through," the man said.

Lynn quickly bent over the fence, grabbed the bundle, and hefted it up over her right shoulder. "Come on up to the house," she said, gesturing toward the opening in the fence. "You can put on some of my husband's things while I hang all of this out on the line to dry." Without waiting for a reply, she strode back across the grass, this time to the front door. On the whitewashed porch that faced the road, she turned to see the stranger following, limping along slowly. "Are you all right?" she asked. "Do you need some help?"

"I can make it," the man said.

Lynn nodded and carried the bundle into the parlor—at least she fancied it a parlor, and had tried to decorate the small room in a way that would be welcoming to guests—and dropped it on the floor just inside the door. She then crossed the hall on the other side of the room and went into the kitchen, where she put the cup down on the table and picked up one of the straight-backed wooden chairs there. By the time she'd carried it out into the front room, the stranger had climbed the steps and come inside. "Here you go," she said, setting the chair down before him. She didn't want him sitting on the davenport or in either of the Victorian tub chairs with his dirty clothes. "I'll be back in just a minute."

As the man fell into the chair, apparently exhausted, she headed into the hall again, this time following it toward the other two rooms of the house. In the bedroom, she searched through the chest of drawers, pulling out some of Phil's older clothes that he seldom wore anymore. She brought them back out into the front room and gave them to the stranger. "The kitchen's through there," she said, pointing. "There's water and soap, so you can wash up if you like. There's also a spare room at the end of the hall, on the left. You can get dressed in there, and then I can clean out that cut on your forehead."

"You're very kind," the man said. "I'm very appreciative, ma'am."

"Lynn," she said. "My name is Lynn Dickinson."

"McCoy," the man said. "Leonard McCoy. I'm pleased to make your acquaintance."

"I'm pleased to make yours," Lynn said, offering a quick curtsy. Mr. McCoy spoke like a southern gentleman, she thought, though he certainly didn't look like one, at least not at the moment.

"May I ask where I am?" he said.

"You're in Hayden," she said.

"Hayden," McCoy repeated, and then asked, "In Georgia?"

"Not quite," Lynn said. "We're in South Carolina."

McCoy nodded, then rose to his feet. "Well, I should take you up on your offer and clean myself up," he said. With Phil's old clothes in hand, he walked toward the hall, but he seemed shakier now, his limp more pronounced. Lynn looked at the leg he favored and saw a long, frayed tear running up from the left cuff of his dungarees. She also thought she saw splashes of red on some of the white threads hanging down.

"Is your leg hurt badly, Mister McCoy?" she asked.

"I . . . had a hard fall today," he said. "I landed on it."

Lynn walked over to him. "May I take a look at it?" she said, concerned.

McCoy gazed at her silently for a few seconds, and then admitted, "It's been cut open."

"May I see?" she asked again.

"All right," McCoy said. Lynn kneeled down and lifted his ragged pant leg. A length of torn fabric, the same dull green color as that holding his bundle of clothing together, had been wrapped and knotted tightly around his calf. A large red stain discolored the crude bandage. Lynn touched it gently, and her fingers came away wet with blood.

She stood up and faced McCoy. "You're bleeding," she said. "Does it hurt?"

"Yes," he said.

"You need a doctor."

"Yes," he agreed again.

"All right," Lynn said. "You get cleaned up and get dressed and then just wait here. I'll go into town and get Doctor Lyles."

To her surprise, McCoy smiled. "You don't even know me," he said.

"I know that you're hurt," Lynn told him. "For right now, that's all I need to know."

"Thank you," McCoy said.

"I'll be back with the doctor as soon as I can," she said. She walked back through the kitchen and out the side door, where she broke into a trot. In the barn, she pulled Belle Reve out of her stall, saddled the horse as quickly as she could, and then climbed up onto her back. Seconds later, Lynn put her head down and raced along Tindal's Lane, headed for town on her errand of mercy.

The sound of an approaching engine woke him.

McCoy looked up at the front door from where he sat on the wood floor, his back against the plush maroon fabric of the large sofa, his leg elevated and resting atop what remained of his duffel bag. He didn't know for how long he'd been asleep after cleaning up and changing into the clothes that Dickinson had provided him, but through the front window, he could see that the afternoon had begun to fade into evening. His body ached in a way it had not when he'd awoken aboard the boxcar this morning, the muscular soreness caused by nights spent sleeping on hard surfaces nothing compared to the many and varied injuries he'd suffered on his plunge down the wooded hillside.

The vehicle stopped outside, and McCoy heard a door open and close. Moments later, footfalls pounded up the front steps, and then Dickinson pushed her way inside. She spied him sitting on the floor, and said, "I've brought Doctor Lyles." Her southern accent stretched the long *i* of the name into a short *a: Lahls.* "He'll be right in." *Raht in.* McCoy found her drawl a welcome sound to his ears. "How are you feeling?" she asked.

"Better now that I've washed and changed," he said. Afterward, he hadn't bothered to use the sling he'd made for himself. He'd have to be careful, but his shoulder felt much better now.

"I'm glad to hear it," Dickinson said. She wore dark blue

denim pants and a green, patterned blouse, which covered a slender, fit figure. She had striking blue eyes and elegant, almost royal features: smooth, creamy skin; high cheekbones; full lips; and a slim, button nose. Auburn hair framed the top half of her face in large curls.

Another door opened and closed outside, and then a second set of footsteps approached. Dickinson moved aside to allow an older man, presumably the doctor, to enter. Very tall but with a stoop to his posture, he had silvery hair and a rugged, lined face. He wore a suit of gray material, a black tie, and eyeglasses with large lenses and heavy, black rims. Had McCoy met him in the twenty-third century, he would have estimated his age at over a hundred; in the rural American south of 1932, he guessed that the old doctor must be in his sixties or seventies. He carried a small black bag in one hand, not unlike the pouch McCoy had used in Starfleet, or before that, in his civilian practice.

"Doctor Lyles, this is Leonard McCoy," Dickinson said, motioning toward where he sat on the floor.

The doctor eyed him, seemingly with unconcealed suspicion. "What's happened here, Mister McCoy?" he said, his words marked by a thick twang.

"He's had a bad fall," Dickinson said, and the doctor glared at her without any apparent attempt to hide his annoyance. He'd evidently wanted to hear McCoy's version of events.

Peering down at his prospective patient, Lyles asked, "Can you get up and sit on the sofa?"

"I can," McCoy said. He gingerly lifted his left leg from where it rested on his erstwhile duffle, then lifted himself up onto the sofa.

Lyles looked around the room, then asked Dickinson to bring over the wooden chair she'd earlier retrieved for McCoy to use. She did so, and the doctor took it from her and set it down opposite the sofa. He removed his suit jacket and draped it over the back of the chair, then dropped onto the seat himself. He placed his black bag beside McCoy before reaching forward and taking hold of his wrist. Lyles consulted a pocket watch, obviously measuring McCoy's pulse rate, then opened his bag and pulled out an old-fashioned stethoscope.

It's not old-fashioned now, McCoy thought. Even after living in the past for two years, he still often thought in terms common to his own time. Of course, stethoscopes still existed in the future, though in a slightly different form. He had trained on them, as well as on other manual medical equipment, both as learning tools and so that he could use them in situations when powered devices might not be available.

Lyles told him to unbutton his shirt, and Dickinson immediately excused herself, saying that she would wait in the kitchen. After she'd left, McCoy removed his shirt, and Lyles donned the earpieces of the stethoscope. He placed a hard, rubber-tipped bell at the appropriate locations on McCoy's chest and back, then switched it out for a cold, metal diaphragm, with which he repeated the process. Once the doctor had finished checking lung and heart function, he retrieved a sphygmomanometer from his bag. Lyles continued to work in silence as he measured McCoy's blood pressure, his demeanor professional but stern. McCoy couldn't tell whether the doctor typically displayed such a bedside manner, or whether he simply distrusted—or even disliked—people he did not know.

"I'm sure my pressure's running on the low side," McCoy said as Lyles returned his equipment to his bag. "I lost some blood today."

The doctor regarded him with what seemed a questioning look, then leaned forward to examine the cut on his forehead. "Lynn says that you've a deep laceration on your leg," he said.

"On my left calf," McCoy specified. "It's probably going to require stitches." He almost couldn't believe his own words. Although in his own medical career he'd been forced to take emergency action under primitive conditions, he'd only twice been called upon to sew through flesh. That he likely needed such a procedure right now seemed to him surreal.

Lyles's bushy gray eyebrows rose on his wrinkled forehead. "Why don't you leave the doctoring to me?" he suggested.

"Sorry," McCoy said. Without being asked, he pulled his shirt back on, then stood up, unbuttoned the corduroy pants Dickinson had given him, and slipped out of the left leg. He then turned and leaned on the arm of the sofa so that the doctor could inspect his wound.

Lyles ran his fingertips over McCoy's bruised thigh, then examined his bandaged calf. "Who wrapped this?" he asked.

"I did," McCoy said. "I tore strips of cloth from my duffel bag." He waved toward the swathed pile of his sullied clothing, which still sat on the floor beside the front door. "While Missus Dickinson went to get you, I cleaned the wound and redressed it." In order to do that, he'd needed to tear off more pieces of his duffel.

Lyles found a pair of scissors in his bag and quickly cut through the cloth encircling McCoy's leg. For a moment, the material directly covering the deep cut stuck to it, and when it pulled free, a spike of pain seared through his calf. He flinched in response, but said nothing.

"You said you cleaned this wound a short time ago?" the doctor asked.

McCoy told him that he had.

"I'm going to have to clean it again," Lyles said. "Blood still seems to be seeping into it. It probably *will* need stitches." He paused and then said, "You've got a lot of lacerations and contusions all over your body, Mister McCoy. Would you care to tell me how you came by them?"

At first, McCoy resented the question. He sensed the doctor's wariness of an outsider and thought his scrutiny the product of an insular perspective. At the same time, he realized that his answer could have medical consequences. If McCoy were performing this examination, he confessed to himself, he'd be obliged to pose the same question. "I jumped from a moving train this morning," he said.

"You jumped?" Lyles asked, clearly skeptical. "Or you were tossed off by the railroad police?"

McCoy turned around toward the doctor. "Actually, I jumped." He sat down and faced Lyles at close range. "I'm sure the railroad police would've thrown me off if they'd found me. I was riding in an empty boxcar on a freight train. I didn't have enough money for a passenger train and I wanted to get home to Atlanta."

"If you were trying to get too Atlanta," Lyles asked, "why did you jump off here?"

"Because two other men hopped into the same freight car as I did, and they wanted to beat me and rob me of my food and clothes," McCoy explained. "Considering the situation, leaping from the train seemed liked the wiser course."

"I see," the doctor said. What seemed like a thoughtful silence fell between the two men, until Lyles called out to Dickinson. She answered at once, from right outside the room, indicating that she'd likely heard the conversation, which pleased McCoy; he thought she deserved to know the circumstances that had led to the need for her acts of charity.

Lyles asked her to bring him soap, water, and some dry cloths, and she said that she would. When she did bring in a basin of water, a bar of soap, and a wad of cloths, she studiously averted her eyes from where McCoy sat. She left the supplies on a small end table, a plain wooden piece that contrasted with the ornate carving on the back, arms, and legs of the sofa.

Once Dickinson had left, the doctor rolled up his sleeves, washed and dried his hands, then suggested that McCoy lie face-down on the floor. He did so, and Lyles began cleaning the wound in his calf. Pain sliced through McCoy's leg as though a blade had been dragged through it. He struggled not to cry out, his hands flexing tightly into fists.

"I know that it hurts," the doctor said, for the first time expressing himself with a sympathetic tone, "but bearing in mind that you jumped from a moving train, you're lucky that you weren't more badly injured."

In actuality, McCoy had been more badly injured this morning. He didn't know how long he'd lain unconscious after hurtling through the trees and brush, but judging from the position of the sun in the sky when he'd revived, it must've been at least a couple of hours. He'd come to feeling pain all over his body, but nowhere more so than in his right shoulder. He'd tried to move his arm and had found his mobility limited. Gently feeling along his upper arm and back, it had taken only a few seconds to discover that he'd suffered a shoulder dislocation.

With few other choices, McCoy had attempted reduction on his own. Maneuvering himself onto his back and starting with his elbows at his sides, he'd slowly raised both hands toward the back of his head. It had taken three agonizing tries, but the head of his humerus had finally snapped back into place. The pain had diminished at once, and a quick neurovascular examination had revealed no nerve damage.

When Lyles had finished washing out the wound and flushing it with an antiseptic, he reached up to the sofa for his bag. From it, he produced a syringe and an ampoule. McCoy asked about it, and the doctor identified the contents of the tiny bottle as a local anesthetic.

"Which anesthetic?" McCoy asked.

"It's procaine," Lyles said, "if it helps you to know that."

"It does," McCoy fired back, driven by the pain in his leg and tired of the doctor's attitude. He searched his memory for whatever he knew about the painkiller. "That's an ester of para-aminobenzoic acid, isn't it?" Lying prone, he could not see the look on the doctor's face, but he could hear the surprise in his voice.

"How would you know that?" Lyles asked.

McCoy immediately regretted feeding the doctor's misgivings about him and thought that perhaps he shouldn't have said anything. Then again, if he truly intended to return to practicing medicine stuck here in the past, then maybe he should stop hiding his knowledge. Back in New York, he'd told only Edith that he was a physician. He didn't feel comfortable making that claim right now, but—

"I have some medical training," he said.

"I see," Lyles said, and this time, McCoy could not read his inflection. "Then I hope this meets with your approval." With no more warning than that, he injected the anesthetic into McCoy's calf. McCoy started, but said nothing.

Fifteen minutes later, Lyles had sewn up the laceration and covered it with a bandage. As he got to his feet, he informed McCoy that he'd finished. McCoy stood up as well, then held his leg out in front of him so that he could see his calf. The rectangular white bandage there looked neat and clean.

"You'll need to keep the area clean and dry for a full day," Lyles said, "and keep the bandage on it for at least two. After that, change it only if the wound continues to seep, or if it gets wet. No bathing for two days either."

"Thank you, Doctor," McCoy said, and he extended his hand. Lyles reached to the back of the chair for his suit jacket, and

McCoy thought that he wouldn't shake his hand. But after the doctor had put his jacket back on, he reached toward McCoy.

"That'll be three dollars," he said flatly as their hands met.

McCoy smiled. He could've been wrong, but he detected a note of humor in the old man's statement. "I had a few bits," he said, shrugging, "but I lost them this morning."

"I figured," Lyles said. It came out *figgered*.

"Doctor Lyles," said Lynn Dickinson, who'd quietly come back into the room. "Phil and I will pay for your visit."

No matter how long McCoy lived in the past, he didn't think he'd ever get used to the notion of individuals having to pay for medical care. Still, he had no intention of allowing this nice woman and her husband to settle his obligation. Before he could protest, though, the doctor did. "Nonsense," he said.

"I insist," Dickinson said. "When Phil gets home—"

"Nonsense," Lyles said again. "I didn't treat you and I'm not taking your money." He reached toward the sofa and grabbed up his black bag, then headed for the front door. Before he left, he pointed back at McCoy's leg. "I don't suppose you'll still be here in ten days," he said, "but if you are, I'll need to remove those stitches." He paused, and then said, "That's included in the three dollars." Then he turned and headed across the porch and down the steps, the front door closing after him.

Dickinson walked over to the door and opened it. "Thank you, Doctor," she called. She stood there, looking out, as McCoy heard the door of the doctor's vehicle open and close, and then its engine start. When that sound had faded into the distance, she closed the door and peered over at McCoy.

"I want to thank you again," he said.

"It wasn't me who just gave you three dollars' worth of free doctoring," she joked.

"Maybe not," McCoy allowed, "but you were the one who brought Doctor Lyles here, and you did more for me than that. Just finding a friendly face when I needed one meant a lot."

"Well, you're welcome," she said, and then peered down at the mound of his clothing still sitting on the floor.

After McCoy had reduced his shoulder dislocation, he'd examined his body for other injuries. He'd found the slice in his calf, and he'd quickly stripped off his shirt and tied it around his thigh as a tourniquet. Then he'd carefully climbed the hill back up to the railroad tracks. There, he'd searched for his duffel bag, finding it in tatters, his clothes scattered. He'd torn pieces from the duffel to bandage his leg, then removed the tourniquet and fashioned it into a sling for his arm. He'd found a shirt to wear, and had collected as much of his clothing as he could locate. He'd found a comb, but not his razor, and none of his food. Somewhere along the way, he'd thought about the small amount of money he'd been carrying in his sock, but that had gone too.

After heaping the clothes he'd found into the remnants of the duffel bag, McCoy had followed the railroad tracks, traveling north instead of south, not wanting to take a chance on meeting the two men on the train at the next stop, where they might well have disembarked, either on their own or courtesy of the railroad police. When he'd seen a road off in the distance, and a farm beyond that, he'd decided to follow it to try and get some help. The first two farms he'd come to had been abandoned, though, but figuring that there would be a town at the end of the road, he'd kept following it. Eventually, Lynn Dickinson had seen him and invited him into her home, where he'd received more help than he'd ever expected.

Now, she gathered up his clothes from the floor and into her arms. "I'll go wash these, like I promised, and hang them out to dry," she said.

"That's not necessary," McCoy said.

"You're wearing my husband's clothes and all of your own are filthy," she said, "so it seems like it is necessary."

"What I meant was, I can wash them myself," he said.

"You were wearing a sling earlier," Dickinson said, "so maybe that's not a good idea."

"Maybe not," McCoy relented. "Tell me, is there a hotel or a place to stay in town?"

"Missus Hartwell runs a boarding house," she said. "At least she says she does. I don't know that she's had but two or three boarders in the last ten years. But since you don't have any money, I guess you won't be going there."

"No," McCoy said. "You've done so much for me already, but I noticed that you have a barn. Would you mind if I—"

"Yes, I would mind," Dickinson said firmly. "If you think

Phil and I would leave a guest out in the barn when we've got a spare room right in back, well, I guess I'd have to take that as an insult."

"I didn't mean—"

"Hush up," she said, and she looked out through the front window. "The sun's fixing to set, so why don't you light the lamps in here. Matches are in that little table over yonder." She pointed across the room, to a small, three-legged stand that sat in the far corner. Without waiting for a response, Dickinson left, headed into the kitchen.

Shaking his head in amusement, McCoy crossed the room and retrieved the matches from the lone drawer in the triangular table. He then walked over to the front window, where a kerosene lamp sat on the sill. He lighted it, and the room brightened with a warm, yellow glow. As he moved around the room to set the other lamps burning, he smiled to himself.

It wasn't 2367, and it wasn't Atlanta, but at this moment, in this place, McCoy felt comfortable for the first time in a very long while.

EIGHTEEN

2268

Joanna McCoy walked along the pedestrian thoroughfares of Pentabo, exhausted from her night's training in the clinic, but unwilling just yet to head for home. On the mornings after she worked a graveyard shift, she normally would take the tube all the way down to Avenue Valent, where the station let out directly across from the high-rise where she lived. She often had only enough energy to cross the way, ride the turbolift up to her twenty-second-floor apartment, and fall into bed.

This morning, though, Joanna had felt the need for some fresh air. No less tired than usual, and perhaps even more so after the night's activity, she'd gazed out of the car when the tube had pulled in to Naker Square—two stops before her own—and had decided that she wanted to walk outside. Though she'd boarded the tube in darkness after her shift, she'd emerged from the underground station into the gleaming sunlight of the new day.

Now, she strolled along a wide promenade that nestled in the heart of the city. At this time of day, most of the population had only just roused, and Joanna enjoyed the relative quiet of a public venue usually teeming with citizens. A few people did move about, alone or in groups of two or three, their hurried pace an indication that most probably headed for their day's work.

For a while, Joanna stayed away from the walking traffic, keeping to the narrow median of the boulevard, between the rows of leafy trees, some purple, some white. The air there smelled clean and slightly sweet, and it revived her flagging senses. She maintained a leisurely pace, with no plan or timetable for how or when she would go home, though she did travel in the general direction of her apartment.

As the sun rose higher over the two- and three-story buildings that helped define this lengthy section of town, Joanna drifted from the median and over to the storefronts. Most still had yet to open, but she had no intention of shopping now anyway. She'd disembarked the tube simply because she'd wanted to get out into the open air.

Wanted to get out? she asked herself. *Or* needed *to get out?*

Did it really matter what level of unease troubled her this morning? Actually, she supposed that it did. If she continued her education and training to become a nurse, she would have to deal with far worse cases than those she'd witnessed last night.

If *I'm going to become a nurse?* Had she actually thought that? More important, had she actually meant it? For half a dozen years now, since at least her early teens—and probably since long before that—Joanna had aspired to the profession of nursing. What would it mean now if, in her second year of study and training, she'd begun wavering in the pursuit of her objective?

She didn't know, but then she hadn't come out here looking

for answers. Really, she'd come out here attempting to avoid questions. Not terribly mature, perhaps, but she'd had a very long night, and she didn't feel like being introspective right now.

Trying to blank her mind and relax, Joanna peered through the windows of the shops she passed. In several, she saw what must have been the newest wave of fashion poised to sweep Verillia: brightly colored saris, worn over black underskirts and cholis. Joanna liked the vibrant hues and the elegantly draped fabrics, but didn't think herself tall enough, at one and six-tenths meters, to achieve such a look. Of course, these days, she rarely concerned herself with sartorial style. Between the hours she spent in class and at the library, for both of which she tended to dress as comfortably as possible, and the shifts at the clinic, for which she wore the required orange scrubs, she had little opportunity to dress up.

Gazing at her reflection in a store window, Joanna chuckled to herself. She saw merely a single adornment, the small black bag she carried over one shoulder, which contained a notepad and her identification. Not only did her plain, single-colored uniform do nothing to embellish her appearance, but it actually detracted from it. The simple, unfitted shirt and pants hung on her body loosely enough to completely conceal her shapely, fit figure. As well, the carroty shade of the garments hardly complemented either her pale complexion or her long, red hair.

Ambling farther on, Joanna peeked at the main display of a bookstore specializing in the most recent Verillian and off-world fiction. She'd grown up an enthusiast of contemporary novels, no doubt inspired by the voracious reading habits of her mother. She perused the titles in the window jealously, looking forward to the end of her schooling so that she would have more free time and could then return to reading for pleasure.

Why not just quit now? she thought, and she realized that her problem would not go away by ignoring it. Joanna wouldn't abandon her undertaking to become a nurse—she couldn't, not and be true to herself—but she would have to deal with what had happened at the clinic last night.

Not just with what happened last night, she thought. She would have to learn how to cope with what *would* happen, again and again, throughout any career in health care.

The rich, piquant scent of brewing *jenli* suddenly wafted through the air. Joanna turned from the bookstore window and looked about the area. A little farther down, she saw, a Verillian street vendor had settled an antigrav cart near the median. A glass pot sat over an open flame, the dark liquid within obviously the source of the sumptuous aroma.

Joanna, a self-described *jenli* devotee, started toward the cart, more out of habit than from a conscious decision. The popular Verillian beverage—much like Earthen coffee, but with the flavor of bittersweet chocolate and a powerful ability to keep both Verillians and humans awake—had seen her through all-night study sessions in the library and through many a graveyard shift. As she approached the vendor, she could almost taste the hot, silken drink flowing across her tongue and down her throat. A cup now would—

Would keep me up for hours, she thought, and in a burst of self-reflection, added, *And it would keep me from dreaming.*

Joanna strode past the *jenli* cart and kept walking. At the next crossroads, she saw that she had come quite a distance from Naker Square, almost all the way to the next tube station. She headed for it, and for home. She would not run from her problems. She had learned many things from her parents, but one of the most important lessons they had taught her—her mother by example, her father by counterexample—had been that fleeing your troubles did not resolve them.

As Joanna rode in the sleek tube car on the way to Avenue Valent, her fatigue renewed itself. She felt tired not just because of her long night at the clinic, and not just because of what had happened there, but because of her attempt this morning to put off dealing with it. She hadn't wanted even to think about the unexpected emergency she'd faced, and she'd feared the dreams—the nightmares—she would experience when eventually she did sleep.

The Andorian whose care she had observed last night had been admitted to the clinic before Joanna had arrived. According to the admittance records, Thraza suffered symptoms typically associated with influenza, including fever, vomiting, and dehydration, and viral infection had been confirmed. A routine examination had also revealed, among other things, a slight, apparently unrelated contusion on her abdomen, which she had sustained during a parrises squares competition. The attending physician had ordered her hydrated intravenously and had dosed her with an antiviral, as well as with medication intended to lower her fever and stem her vomiting.

Early in Joanna's shift, Thraza had begun to complain of stomach pain. The doctor had been informed, but before he'd been able to respond to what he'd believed a reaction to the medication, the patient had thrown off her bedclothes and pulled up the tunic she wore. Where before she'd had a bruise, a hole had now opened in her flesh, about five centimeters in diameter. The wound seeped the indigo of Andorian blood, and its edges had become an intense violet. Within the gruesome cavity, the underlying fat and soft tissue had dissolved, leaving muscle and a section of the woman's ileum visible.

Thraza had screamed and had started to paw at the lesion, perhaps in some mad attempt to mend her injured flesh. Joanna had frozen, horrified both by the grisly sight and by the woman's extreme distress. A nurse had entered the room almost immediately, and had moved to restrain Thraza. He'd had to call more than once to Joanna before she'd come out of her stupor and moved to assist.

The doctor had arrived soon after, immediately identifying the necrotizing fasciitis, a rare Andorian bacterial infection that the scanners had missed. He'd sedated Thraza and had her prepped at once to undergo surgery. A specialist had been contacted, and before Joanna's shift had ended, the infected tissue had been removed from the woman's body, and she'd been treated with antibiotics and immunoglobulin in order to kill the bacteria that had caused the infection. Artificial tissue and a skin graft would later be used to repair the wound. Her prognosis had been for a full recovery.

The nurse had said nothing to the doctor about Joanna's performance, about her initial inability to act during the onset of the event. To Joanna, he had said nothing at first, but before her shift had ended, he'd pulled her aside. "It's all right, it happens," he'd told her, clearly referring to the incident even though he hadn't mentioned it. "You just need to become inured to it all."

The tube arrived at the subterranean Avenue Valent station,

and Joanna climbed the steps to the street. She crossed to the skyscraper she currently called home and entered one of the turbolifts. As the car ascended, she thought about what the nurse had said to her. Afterward, she'd thanked him, grateful that he hadn't said anything about her to the doctor, and also for his advice. On the way home, she'd tried to put all of it out of her mind, but she'd also been unwilling to risk whatever dreams her next sleep might bring. Now, she considered the nurse's counsel that she needed to habituate herself to the suffering of patients, and to their sometimes ghastly illnesses and injuries. As the lift reached the twenty-second floor, Joanna realized that she didn't have to ask herself whether she *could* do that, but whether she *wanted* to do it?

She held her hand flat against the reader beside her door, then recited her entry code. Within the door itself, she heard the familiar snick of the locking bolts disengaging and then the faint hum as they withdrew into the wall. She reached for the doorknob, turned it, and entered her apartment.

Inside, it looked like it always did: as though ten people lived here, rather than only two. Clothes littered the living room as though a laundry had just exploded. Slacks, skirts, blouses, socks, underwear, sweaters, coats, and jackets lay in piles all over the gray carpet and scattered over the few pieces of secondhand furniture that she and Tatiana had acquired before moving in together. Dirty glasses and dishes—most of them empty, fortunately—filled the counters in the small kitchen, as well as the dining table tucked into a corner of the living room. Book data cards, as well as actual books, also contributed to the clutter.

Joanna slipped the strap of her bag from her shoulder and dropped it onto the easy chair sitting near the door, right next to her green blouse, which she couldn't remember wearing any time recently. Embarrassed as always by the mess, she vowed, as she often did, that she would clean later in the day. She knew herself well enough, though, to know that wouldn't happen. The disorder hadn't quite reached that threshold yet at which she and Tatiana would finally do something about it.

She thought about making herself something to eat, but then decided that, dreams or no, she needed to sleep. In her bedroom, she found no reprieve from the disarray. Her bed sat unmade, the sheets, blankets, and pillows rumpled all over the mattress. The clothes, tapes, and books that hadn't made it out into the living room covered many of the flat surfaces, including the floor, and she even saw some tableware here and there. Three of the four drawers in her dresser had been left open, with a pair of stockings hanging from the top one. Even Tatiana's bedroom had never looked quite so bad.

Joanna carefully stepped over and around it all as she headed for the 'fresher. As she passed her computer terminal, she spied a data slate sitting atop it, one of the device's lights blinking red. She picked it up, recognized Tatiana's handwriting on the display, and read it: *Back from class late afternoon. Rory's offered to make us dinner.* Tatiana had signed it with an ornate capital *T.*

Joanna smiled. For all of Rory's faults, Tatiana's boyfriend knew how to prepare a meal. She looked forward to whatever tonight's repast would be.

As she set the slate back down on the terminal, she saw a red button on the panel flashing, indicating that she'd received a message. *Probably Mom,* she thought. With Joanna's birthday less than two months away, her mother probably wanted to talk about coming to Verillia to celebrate. *Great,* she thought. *If Tatiana and I start today, maybe we can finish cleaning the apartment by then.*

Joanna went into the 'fresher, stripped off her scrubs, tossed them on the floor, and slipped into her robe—which, remarkably, she found hanging on the back of the door. She performed her end-of-the-day ablutions, then headed for bed. Before she threw herself down onto the mattress, though, she decided to check the message. She went back over to the computer terminal, activated it, and touched a control. Unexpectedly, her father's face appeared on the display.

"*Hi, Joanna. It's Dad,*" he said. She hadn't seen him in quite some time, as his Starfleet duties kept him occupied and often far from Federation space. "*I wanted to . . .*" he started, and then he glanced away from the monitor before looking back. "*We haven't talked in a while, so I wanted to send you a message and . . .*" Again he hesitated. "*. . . and ask how you're doing.*"

As Joanna listened to her father speak, she began to think that he had something else on his mind, something he wanted to tell her. She pulled out the chair from in front of the computer terminal and sat down, searching his visage for clues as to why he had sent her this message. *"I hope your classes are going well, and your shifts at the clinic,"* he continued. *"You know how proud . . . I hope you know how proud I am of you."*

Joanna closed her eyes and dropped her head. She felt humiliated—not because of what her father had said, but because right now she felt unworthy of his praise. She also recalled something he had said to her when she'd grown serious about entering the health care field. "Care, but not too much," he'd said. "You'll be a better nurse that way." At the time, she'd thought his advice about maintaining emotional distance had been simply a function of his character, not as a physician, but as a man. At least according to Joanna's mother, his detachment had been a major cause of the end of their marriage. Now, though, in light of what had happened last night at the clinic, she wondered if he hadn't been trying to provide her sound guidance after all.

Looking back at the screen, Joanna realized that she'd missed some of her father's message. She quickly touched a control and queued it back to where she'd stopped listening. As she did, she noticed a transparent bottle on a shelf behind her father, in which had been constructed a set of staffs of Aesculapius, an ancient symbol of the medical profession. She had given that to him as a birthday gift years ago.

"Life on board the Enterprise *is, uh, as interesting as ever,"* her father went on. *"I've started making some notes for a reference book I've been considering writing, on comparative alien physiology."* He seemed for a second to hunt for what to say next, but then he smiled. *"You might not believe this, but not that long ago, I actually performed—this sounds ridiculous when I even think about it—I performed a brain transplant."* Joanna felt her eyebrows rise involuntarily on her forehead. *"I'm not kidding. I could never do it again, the circumstances were unique. I still remember standing there and using these amazing tools, executing these impossible surgical techniques . . . I remember doing it, but I can't remember how I did it."* She believed her father, but couldn't imagine the situation that would have allowed him to perform such an opera-

tion. *"It's a long story. I'll tell you about it when . . . when I see you."* His voice seemed to catch.

"Anyway, honey, I wanted to talk to you because . . ." Once more, her father's words trailed into momentary silence. He brought his hands together before him and twisted them together nervously. *". . . because I miss you,"* he said at last. *"Listen, I'd like to come and see you soon."* Again, his words surprised her, though this time on a personal level. As long ago as it had been since they'd last exchanged messages, it had been far longer since they'd actually seen each other. *"I know your birthday isn't all that far off, and that your mother will probably visit you then, but maybe sometime before or after that. I know that you're busy with school and everything, but . . . I won't take up much of your time. Really, I just want to see you, honey."* He touched a hand to his lips, and then to the screen. *"I love you, Joanna."* The display went dark, replaced an instant later by the confused geometric emblem of the Verillian communications network.

Joanna keyed off the terminal, but remained sitting before it for a few minutes, thinking about her father's message. She didn't know quite what to make of it—his continual hesitation seemed strange to her—but it pleased her immensely that he wanted to come see her. She'd have to find out exactly when he wanted to visit, and she'd have to check her class and clinic schedule, but she would make it work out.

Happy that she'd chosen to listen to the message, Joanna got up from the terminal, took off her robe, and crawled into bed. She touched the control to render the windows opaque, and in the darkness, lay on her back with her hands behind her head. Though still very tired, she couldn't help but feel excited that she would soon get to see both of her parents. She'd grown up with her mother, while her father had been an absent stranger for much of her childhood. As she'd become a young woman, though, as she'd begun to understand life more and to view her father from a perspective independent of her mother's, she'd learned to like him and love him very much. She missed him and looked forward to seeing him soon.

When she slept that night, Joanna did not dream of the An-dorian patient and her terrible infection. Instead, she returned to her youth, as a girl of ten, living in the beach house on Cerberus

with both of her parents. That had never really happened—she'd
lived on Cerberus, but with only her mother—but in her dreams,
she lived a joyful life in that imagined time.

McCoy trod out of his office and into Christine Chapel. He
moved backward a step, startled, as did the nurse. The black
medical pouch he carried flew from his grasp, though he managed to hold on to the tricorder, phaser, and belt also in his
hands. "Nurse Chapel," he said, and then, feeling badly about
how their earlier conversation had developed, he added, "Christine."

"Doctor McCoy," she said, "I wanted to apologize about what
happened before."

"There's no need," he told her. "It was my fault. The shock of
the news . . ." He didn't quite know how to finish the thought, but
didn't think it necessary. He still felt numbed by M'Benga's diagnosis of xenopolycythemia, but he really didn't want to discuss the situation with anybody.

"I know. I'm so sorry," said Chapel. "I should have been more
sensitive."

"Not at all," McCoy said, attempting to minimize the nurse's
distress and move past the subject. "You were just being a friend,
watching out for me. I appreciate it. And so you know, I *did* tell
the captain."

"I'm glad," Chapel said.

In his quarters a few minutes ago, McCoy had also tried to
tell his daughter, sending Joanna a subspace communication that
she would receive in he didn't know how many days. He could
never keep track of the *Enterprise*'s location in the galaxy, and
therefore of the distance to Verillia. As McCoy had recorded the
message, though, he'd found himself unable to tell Joanna about
his illness. He had failed her as a father in so many ways
throughout her life, and dying prematurely would be another
one. He couldn't tell her about it from afar; he would have to
take leave and go see her.

Chapel bent and picked up the black medical pouch that he'd
dropped when they'd run into each other. She noticed the tricorder and phaser in his hands and asked, "Where are you
going?"

"An asteroid," he said. "And actually, I'd better get to the transporter room."

"I'll walk with you," Chapel said, and she started down the corridor toward the turbolift. McCoy wanted to tell her not to accompany him, that he'd rather be by himself, but worried that doing so might trigger her to verbalize her obvious concern for him. To avoid that, he walked beside her. "So why an asteroid?" she asked.

"From what I understand," he said, pleased by the change of topic, "it only *looks* like an asteroid, but it's really a spaceship." After McCoy had gone to his quarters and sent his message to Joanna, Uhura had contacted him from the bridge. As part of the *Enterprise*'s standard operating procedures, she'd informed him, as the ship's chief medical officer, that personnel were about to leave the ship. She'd also detailed what had led up to the captain's decision to form a landing party. Half a dozen chemical, sublight missiles had been launched at the *Enterprise,* which Jim had ordered detonated by phaser fire before they could do any damage. Chekov had then tracked the missiles back to their point of origin: the asteroid—or rather, the spaceship—which, traveling just below warp speed, would collide with an inhabited planet in approximately thirteen months. McCoy told Chapel all of this as they boarded a turbolift and rode it toward the transporter room. "Sensors show no life-forms aboard, meaning that it must be automated," he said, "so I assume that the captain and Mister Spock are beaming over to search for a control room in order to alter its course."

Although McCoy didn't much care for traveling by transporter, particularly with no prospect of encountering alien life-forms, he usually accompanied Jim on landing parties, and so he wanted to be a part of this one. Recording his message to Joanna had reconfirmed his initial reaction to the news of his xenopolycythemia, namely that he wanted as much as possible to live out a normal life in the time left to him. For right now, that meant joining Jim and Spock on this landing party.

The turbolift reached its destination and the doors parted. As they made their way to the transporter room, Chapel asked, "Why would somebody build a spaceship to resemble an asteroid?"

"I don't know," said McCoy, having pondered the same thing. "Maybe they intended it as a means of defense, a way of not drawing attention to themselves."

"Except that the ship apparently launched an unprovoked attack on the *Enterprise*," she said. "Maybe they disguised it as an asteroid so that they could get closer to their targets."

"Maybe," McCoy allowed. "Or maybe there's a malfunction. Unless we find some records left by the builders, we may never know."

They arrived at the transporter room and entered. The console had already been activated, McCoy saw, while the operator— Mr. Brent, obviously taking a rotation as a transporter technician—worked at the sensor panel tucked along the inner bulkhead of the compartment. Brent looked up from his station and said, "Doctor. Nurse Chapel."

McCoy acknowledged the officer with a nod as Chapel moved to the transporter console. As she set down the medical pouch, he realized that he still carried his tricorder, phaser, and utility belt in his hands. He quickly hung the strap of the tricorder over his shoulder, then wrapped the wide cloth belt about his waist, to which he attached the phaser.

"Be careful," Chapel said earnestly. She opened the medical pouch and appeared to verify its contents, doubtless a precautionary act motivated by her profession.

"Does it really matter?" McCoy asked, immediately wishing he hadn't, since such a question would inevitably provoke a response.

"Yes, it *does* matter," Chapel said in a serious tone. Behind him, McCoy heard Brent walk over from the sensor station to the transporter console. Chapel closed up the pouch and held it out to him. "A lot can happen in a year," she said as he took the pouch and affixed it to his belt. "Please, give yourself every minute."

McCoy felt terribly uncomfortable that his conversation with the nurse had returned to the issue of his health, even if only obliquely. Brent currently stood close to them and might well have heard just enough to understand that McCoy faced some sort of a problem. Bad enough that Jim and Jabilo and Christine knew; he did not want the rest of the crew to know as well. He did not want people's pity.

Wanting to end the discussion, McCoy responded to Chapel's concern with a look of appreciation, but then quickly walked past her and toward the transporter platform. At the same time, the doors to the corridor slid apart, and Jim and Spock arrived. Before the captain could comment about his presence—he hadn't informed Jim that he'd be joining the landing party—McCoy mounted the platform and took his position on a targeting pad. Once he had, he saw that Jim and Spock had stopped in the middle of the compartment and now regarded him with some degree of surprise. He couldn't tell whether the first officer knew of his illness, but since he'd asked the captain to keep that information to himself, he guessed that Spock's bewilderment had arisen not because of his xenopolycythemia, but because McCoy hadn't been asked to be a member of the landing party.

"Doctor McCoy," Jim said carefully, "Mister Spock and I will handle this."

"Without me, Jim?" McCoy said, choosing to deal with the situation humorously. "You'd never find your way back."

"Well," Jim started, and then he glanced back at Spock, who raised an eyebrow. "I think it would be wiser if—"

"I'd like to go," McCoy interrupted. "I'm fine, Captain." He hoped that Jim would perceive the importance of this to him and not push the issue.

Jim hesitated, and McCoy realized that he wouldn't let this go, and that Spock and the rest of the crew would find out about his condition. But then the captain said, "All right, Doctor. If that's what you want." He climbed up onto the platform, and Spock followed. In his peripheral vision, McCoy could see Jim studying him, but then the captain looked across the compartment to Brent, who set to working his controls. To McCoy's surprise, he saw that Chapel hadn't yet left, but stood behind the transporter console.

For once, the dread of having his atomic structure parsed, encoded, disassembled, transmitted, and reassembled, didn't fill his thoughts, his desire to continue on with his life right now overwhelming all other concerns. For the moment, he wanted only to get out of the transporter room and ignore everything else that had happened today. His vision misted with the golden stardust of dematerialization and then renewed itself as the process reversed.

Before him, the *Enterprise* transporter room had gone, in its place a bleak, rock-infested landscape composed of browns and grays. A quiver of steam emerged from a cluster of boulders, and above, a burnt orange sky hid any trace of the stars. McCoy wondered how an asteroid could possess an atmosphere and then recalled that he actually stood on an object that had been intentionally constructed, not randomly created during the formation of a solar system. Still—

"You'd swear you were on the surface of a planet," he said. Beside him, Spock had already begun taking sensor readings with his tricorder.

"One fails to see the logic in making a ship look like a planet," Spock observed. McCoy tended to agree.

"Wouldn't know this was a spaceship," Jim said, then pulled out his communicator and flipped it open. "Kirk to *Enterprise,*" he said.

"Enterprise, *Scott here,*" came the voice of the chief engineer, obviously left in command of the ship.

"Transported without incident," Jim said. "Kirk out." He closed the communicator and placed it back on his belt.

Jim started forward, toward a break between two rock faces. McCoy and Spock trailed after him, the first officer for the moment putting his tricorder aside. They walked through paths in the rocks that appeared naturally formed, and McCoy had to remind himself again that everything here had been built by someone. Jim and Spock peered all about, and McCoy did too, searching for anything that might indicate controls or an entrance to an operations center. Though he saw nothing, he supposed that they must have beamed down to the area on the asteroid-ship most likely to contain such things.

Jim suddenly stopped, and McCoy at once saw why. Ahead of them stood five cylindrical objects, orange like the sky, two or so meters in diameter and two-thirds again as tall. They all appeared solid, with no obvious breaks in their surfaces or means of entry. One rose from the dirt directly to their left, two a few meters apart a little farther away, and two off in the distance. Spock activated his tricorder and began scanning again.

As the trio cautiously approached the cylinders, McCoy worked his medical tricorder, opting to look for vestigial signs of habitation, or any remnants of biological material that might remain from the time of the ship's construction. Perhaps sensors could provide some clue as to the identity or nature of the builders.

Jim mounted a small rise between the two neighboring cylinders and walked past them, peering at their far sides. "No apparent opening," he reported.

McCoy turned back to the first cylinder and concentrated his scans there. He wondered precisely what the ship's sensors had shown that had compelled Jim and Spock to select this area for the landing party. "You found no intelligent life-forms, Mister Spock," McCoy said, "but surely—"

"The asteroid-ship is over ten thousand years old, Doctor," Spock said, answering a question McCoy had not intended to ask, "but still no sign of life-forms, Captain." They all drifted back to the first cylinder.

For an instant, McCoy saw a spike on his tricorder, a fleeting life sign that had come and gone before he'd gotten a chance to read its particulars. He worked the controls, wanting to play the scan back and freeze it. Something must have caused—

McCoy heard something to his left, and he looked in that direction in time to see a tall figure race past Spock and throw himself at the captain. The doctor had just enough time to note the glint of a bladed weapon before additional movement drew his eye. A second man—they looked like men, in colorful, caftanlike garb—followed behind the first, and McCoy registered that they seemed somehow to be coming from one of the cylinders, which had changed colors from orange to light blue.

Suddenly he saw another man, this one emerging from a different cylinder, but then somebody else sped toward McCoy, a sword held high, ready to strike. The doctor let go of his tricorder and raised his arms in a desperate attempt to ward off the attack. He had no time to reach for his phaser. As the man brought his blade forward and down, McCoy managed to deflect his arm. The man overbalanced as his weapon came swinging down, almost to the ground. McCoy grabbed him with one hand and pushed him past. The man stumbled and dropped his sword, and

McCoy thrust both his hands into the man's side, sending him face first onto the ground.

McCoy breathed deeply, aware of the sounds of struggle all about him. He moved toward the man who'd just attacked him, wanting to subdue him before he regained his footing. But then arms reached around McCoy from behind and held him tight. He battled to break free, then lifted his boot and pounded his heel down onto the man's foot. His assailant cried out in pain, his grip loosening. McCoy spun around, bringing his fist back, but the man recovered, and he grabbed the doctor and threw him from his feet. McCoy rolled, trying to put some distance between him and his attacker, then scrambled up to his knees. He turned back just in time to see the man diving toward him. McCoy brought his left hand back across his body and frantically leveled a backhanded fist into the face of the man, who fell to the ground.

The man wouldn't stay down, though, and as he rushed to stand, so too did McCoy. But as he got to his feet, he saw that another figure had appeared from within one of the cylinders. His arms raised high to continue the fight, he froze, and felt his eyes go wide. Something clicked inside his brain, jolting him in a way he couldn't identify. It felt almost like recognition, almost like friendship, almost like love. . . .

The woman wore a green, patterned dress, which covered a slender, fit figure, leaving her shoulders and midriff bare. She had striking blue eyes and elegant, almost regal features: smooth, ivory skin; high cheekbones; full lips; and a thin, button nose. Her auburn hair encircled the top half of her face in large spirals.

McCoy felt a hard blow to the back of his neck, and his knees buckled at once. He fell forward, toppling to the ground, barely able to get his right arm up in time to break his fall. His mind floated toward unconsciousness, and he fought to remain awake. He could not even brace himself for the next attack, which he knew would come at any second—but then didn't. Woozy, he opted to lie motionless, thinking that might in the short term keep him safe.

Seconds passed, two or twenty, he could not tell, and then voices reached him, though his muddled awareness could not focus enough on the words to make them out. But he heard a woman's voice—*the* woman's voice—and no longer heard the sounds of conflict. Jim spoke, and McCoy tried to listen.

"Let me go to my friend," Jim said, almost pleading. McCoy hoped that Spock had not been hurt, but then somebody's hands closed around his own right biceps and pulled gently upward. McCoy responded without thinking, pushing himself up from the ground with his left hand.

"You all right?" Jim asked him, and McCoy looked at him.

"I think so," he said, still trying to clear the clouds from his head. He attempted to stand, and Jim helped him up. Then the woman whose appearance had stopped him cold spoke.

"I am Natira," she said, "the high priestess of the people." Her words came wrapped in an imperial lilt. "Welcome to the world of Yonada." McCoy couldn't take his gaze from her face, but he did note that she hadn't referred to this place as a *spaceship*.

"I can't say I think much of your welcome," Jim said, and McCoy could easily have seconded that sentiment. The back of his head felt as though it had been hit by a photon torpedo.

The woman—Natira—looked to the men who had attacked, subdued, and now guarded, the three *Enterprise* officers. "Take them," she ordered, her voice commanding without rising in volume, her annoyance with Jim's comment plain.

The guards closed ranks around the landing party, their swords drawn, motioning with the weapons toward one of the cylinders. McCoy saw now that the outer, orange casing had risen to reveal an inner, sky-blue shell, in which there stood an open doorway. Urged on by one of the guards, Jim entered first, at sword point. With a guard on his own heels, McCoy followed.

Inside, a tight spiral staircase wound down into darkness, which suddenly grew more intense, probably because the cylinder had settled back into place above them. The footfalls of the group rang on the metal steps as they descended. McCoy furtively checked his waist, confirming what he'd suspected, namely that he'd been divested of his communicator and phaser. He tried to watch Jim for any move he might make to escape their captivity, though the lack of light made it difficult. McCoy also realized that Jim probably wouldn't take any action right now, not until they had more information about this asteroid-ship and the people who apparently called it home. Their presence here likely would not change the aim of the landing party's mission; if anything, their existence on this ship, headed for a collision with Daran V, made the situation even more grave, the outcome potentially even more disastrous.

As McCoy's eyes adjusted to the darkness, he detected light emanating from below. Finally, the group reached the bottom of the stairway. There, they stood at a corner where the ends of two wide corridors intersected. People had gathered there, McCoy saw, men and women, older and younger, dressed in colorful, loose-fitting clothing of a design similar to the one-piece outfits the guards wore. They peered at Jim and McCoy and Spock in silence, and with expressions that appeared mixed of curiosity and fear. McCoy doubted that this "world" saw many visitors.

Natira came down the stairs last. Without either a word or a glance, she stepped in front of the landing party and started down one of the corridors. McCoy saw now that, on the back of her head, her hair had been arranged into a bun, with longer tresses spilling from its center and down to the middle of her back. A guard pushed at Jim's back, and the captain followed Natira, as did McCoy and Spock. The guards stayed at their backs, occasionally making their presence known with the touch of a hand or the flat of a sword blade. More people lined the corridor.

Not far from the base of the stairway, Natira stopped at an area inset into the wall on the right. She turned to face a trapezoidal set of doors, narrower at the top than at the base. Several large triangles lined the walls on either side of the doors, their raised forms inscribed with complicated symbols McCoy did not recognize.

At the doors, Natira did nothing for a moment, and then she raised her arms in wide circles until her hands nearly came together above her head. She carried a communicator and a phaser in her right hand, and a large, green stone adorned a finger on her left. She waited just a second, then leaned in a graceful movement to her right, where she waved a hand before the symbols there. She then swayed left and performed a similar motion with her other hand.

The doors opened with a whisper, withdrawing into the walls. Natira did not move forward immediately, and McCoy saw past her into some sort of a chamber, only dimly lighted. A raised, five-sided platform of a green, marblelike material sat in the center of the room. Beyond it stood a monolith or monument of the same material, a couple of meters wide and twice as tall. In the upper half of its surface had been inscribed a golden starburst.

Natira entered the chamber, and again the guards encouraged the landing party to follow. When Natira reached the platform, she turned and faced them. McCoy heard the doors close.

"You will kneel," the high priestess said. McCoy felt a hand on his shoulder and the point of a sword in his back. He looked behind him and saw that only the three guards had entered the chamber with them. Jim looked as though he might assault his guard, but then he lowered himself to one knee instead, as did McCoy and Spock.

Natira turned and stepped up onto the platform, then kneeled and bowed her head, her arms at her sides. The lighting in the chamber came up, bathing the surroundings in a soft glow. With an effort, McCoy peeled his attention from Natira and gazed around. Shapes and angles dominated the scene. Polygons decorated the floor around the platform in light shades, and green, marble monuments stood along the perimeter of the chamber. More of the raised triangles adorned the walls, arranged in groups of nine to form larger, inverted triangles. McCoy saw that the wall with the starburst, which stood opposite the door and in front of the platform as the obvious focal point of the room, actually angled downward, held between two uprights. Yet another small, inverted triangle sat below the starburst, and a small chest rested on a step before that. It looked to McCoy like a geometer's paradise.

He regarded Natira again, who remained silent and still as she kneeled on the platform, her head down. To Jim, McCoy quietly said, "She called this 'the world.' These people don't know they're on a spaceship."

"They've been in flight ten thousand years," Jim replied. A guard reached forward and poked the captain in the shoulder with the point of his sword. Lowering his voice to a whisper, Jim concluded, "Maybe they don't realize it."

"O Oracle of the people, most perfect and wise," Natira said, as though reciting the words. McCoy saw that she'd lifted her head and now stared at the starburst on the wall in front of the platform. "Strangers have come to our world." She held up the communicator and phaser still in her hand. "They bear instruments we do not understand."

Seconds passed, and McCoy didn't know whether or not to expect anything to happen. A small circle in the center of the starburst then lighted up. Natira bowed her head as though in response, then stood and turned to face her captives. "Who are you?" she demanded, addressing Jim as the obvious leader of the group.

Jim stood up slowly, and McCoy and Spock then did so as well. "I am Captain Kirk of the *Starship Enterprise*," he said. "This is my medical officer, Doctor McCoy—" Natira looked at him, and he felt powerless to move, still overwhelmed by emotion. And did he see the side of her mouth curl upward ever so slightly when she looked at him? "—my first officer, Mister Spock."

Natira peered at Spock, then back at the captain. "For what reason do you visit this world?" she wanted to know.

"We've come in friendship," Jim said, and a sound like a thunder strike roared through the chamber. McCoy saw Natira flinch almost imperceptibly, and he felt the vibration through his boots. Suddenly, a bass male voice called out, seeming to emanate from all around.

"Then learn what it means to be our enemy," it said, *"before you learn what it means to be our friend."* Again, a great din boomed, but then something like a shock of electricity surged through McCoy's body. It happened with such speed that he could make no attempt to defend himself or flee. His back stiffened at the pain, his head tilted upward, his eyes slammed shut. In his mind, he cried out in agony, though he remained vaguely aware that he could not move, could not even open his mouth to scream. A tremendous buzz, like that of high voltage, filled his ears, and it came to him with great certainty that the year left to him by the alien disease would take too long to kill him; this attack, this pain, would claim him long before the xenopolycythemia did. With the agony permeating his body right now, death would be welcome.

And then, mercifully, McCoy's world went black.

NINETEEN

1932

When the rooster crowed for the first time in the morning, just after daybreak, Phil Dickinson rolled over onto his stomach and went back to sleep, a rare luxury. When Struttin' Henry sent his cry up again an hour later, Phil woke again, this time to the mixed smells of coffee and bacon. He hadn't heard Lynn rise, and so he rolled toward her side of the bed. He reached out to touch her empty pillow, but instead found the tangle of her hair.

"One of these days," she said, "I'm gonna wring that rooster's neck." Lynn said something like that nearly every morning, but sounded particularly serious on days like today—Sundays—when he didn't have to get up and go to the mill, and neither one of them had to get up and work the farm. On more than one occasion, she'd threaten to serve Henry up for supper and might actually have done so by now, had the old bird not helped keep them in eggs.

Phil heard Lynn sniff at the air. "Did you put on coffee?" she asked.

"Yup," he said, sliding over to kiss her cheek. "I'm also standing at the stove cooking up a rasher of bacon right now."

"Wh—?" she started, and then, obviously realizing he'd been joking, said, "Oh." She slapped him lightly on the arm.

"I guess your farm boy's making you breakfast," Phil teased.

"I'm sure he's making *us* breakfast," she said. "And he's not my farm boy." Lynn looked at him for a second, and he saw that slight change of expression on her face that signaled tomfoolery. "He's *our* farm boy," she said, and they both laughed.

"Kind of old for a farm *boy,* don't you think?" Phil said as he threw the covers back and got out of bed. Even this early, he could feel the heaviness of the air, the stillness, and knew that it would be a scorcher. Even though summer had only officially begun a few days ago, it had arrived with midseason intensity.

Fortunately, the afternoon rains had not let up, allowing the land to remain hydrated.

"I don't think he's that much older than you," Lynn said, referring to their unexpected houseguest. Well, Len's stay could be considered unexpected in some ways, Phil thought, but not in others. Since he'd known Lynn, she'd had a hankering for taking in strays. Usually it ran to cats and dogs, sometimes to birds, and once, to an injured polecat, but it hadn't really surprised him when he'd come home from the mill a week and a half ago to find that she'd let a vagabond into the house. That was just her way.

"I don't care how old he is," Phil said, "if he's gonna make us breakfast." He poured water from the pitcher into the metal basin they kept atop the little table in the corner, then used a cloth and bar soap to wash up.

"Leonard's helped me out a lot since he's been here," Lynn said, sounding at least a bit defensive. "And it's not costing us nothing to let him stay in the spare room." With the help of some of the men in town—Gregg Anderson, Ducky Jensen, and the King brothers—Phil had added the second bedroom onto the house seven years ago, when Lynn's mother had first gotten really sick. They'd bought an old mattress from Mr. Duncan up at the mill and put it down on the floor in the new room. Lynn hadn't wanted to put her mother on the floor, though, and so they'd given their bed to the old woman, and they'd used the old mattress themselves.

Mother Myra's health had improved, though, at least enough for her to get around on her own and take care of herself without too much help, and so she'd wanted to go home. Actually, she'd never wanted to leave Pepper's Crossing in the first place, where her beloved husband lay buried in the little cemetery on the outskirts of the town. So they'd bundled her into the wagon and taken her back upcountry.

Since then, they'd used the spare room mostly for storage. They'd kept the mattress, though, and every now and then had even used it for guests. Phil's brother came over from Chattanooga from time to time, and twice, Aunt Lee and Uncle Scott had come out from Nashville to visit. Of course, Phil and Lynn had it in their heads that they would one day use the spare room for a child, but that hadn't happened yet, and at this point, it really didn't seem like it ever would.

"It might not be costing nothing to let him sleep here," Phil said, "but he is eating our food." He didn't bother to tell her that, after what he'd thought about last night, Len would be also taking some of their money.

"Now, Phil," Lynn said, following him up out of bed. "Leonard's been helping with the vegetable patch and with the animals and fetching water—"

"I know, I know," Phil said, picking both his regular clothes and his Sunday go-to-meeting clothes out of the dresser and tossing them on the bed. As he pulled off his undershirt and shorts, Lynn walked around the bed and over to the basin, slipping past him in her white peignoir and playfully pinching his bare hindquarters.

"Hey, we're going to church today," Phil pretended to reprove her. "Don't be sinning."

"Honey," Lynn said in that arch way she had, "it would be a sin *not* to pinch them cheeks."

Phil laughed, something he did often around his wife of nine years. He finished dressing in dungarees and a red, short-sleeved shirt—they wouldn't be going to church for a couple of hours yet—then took something else from a carved wooden box on the dresser and stuffed it into his pocket. He asked Lynn if he should wait for her, and she told him that he shouldn't.

In the kitchen, Len stood at the back window, peering off to the right it seemed, out toward the barn and, beyond it, the fields. He turned when Phil came into the room. "Morning," he said amiably. In his hands, he held a white ceramic mug.

"Morning, Len," Phil said.

"I thought I'd make some breakfast for you," Len said. "I hope you don't mind that I moved your puzzle." Phil looked and saw that Len had moved the piece of plywood with the jigsaw puzzle he'd been working off the table in the middle of the room and over onto the floor by the side door.

"Do I mind having a hot meal waiting for me in the kitchen while I wake up next to my wife?" Phil asked. "I'd say it's a fair bit better than getting poked in the eye with a stick."

"Good," Len said, moving over to the table and setting down

his mug. Phil saw that two places had been set with plates and utensils. "I've got coffee brewed, bacon keeping warm in the oven, and it'll take me just a couple of minutes to fry up some eggs. Is Lynn coming out soon?"

"Yup," Phil said. "She should be out in a minute or two."

"Coming right up then," Len said, and he picked out a pair of mugs from one of the open cupboards. Moving to the cookstove, just to the side of the rear window, he lifted the percolator and poured the coffee. Phil walked over and took them from him, thanking him, then took a seat at the table. He watched as Len took a small tub of butter and a bowl full of eggs from the icebox. He dumped a hunk of the butter into a pan and heated it on the cookstove beside the coffee. Once the butter had begun to sizzle, he cracked the eggs and dropped their contents into the pan.

"Len," Phil said, "I want to talk to you about Doctor Lyles."

"Oh?" Len said, his attention clearly more on the eggs than on Phil.

"Lynn told me that the doc's fee for sewing up your leg was three dollars," he said.

"Yeah," Len said. "Uh huh." He reached up above the oven, which rose up from the range to the right of the cooktop, and grabbed a spatula lying there.

"I think you should pay it," Phil said. He'd been thinking about it all week, and even though he knew that Doc Lyles often didn't take money for his services these days—since so few people had any cash to spare—he still felt that restitution needed to be made.

Len didn't respond, and Phil chose not to push the issue, not until they could speak face to face. When Len finished cooking, he retrieved the plates from the table and slid the eggs onto them, then added the bacon that had been warming in the oven. When he brought the breakfasts over to the table and set them down, he spoke before Phil did.

"I intend to pay the doctor," he said, "just as soon as I have the money."

"I'm glad to hear that," Phil said. "Because that means you can give him something today." He dug into his pants pocket and pulled out the four half-dollar coins he'd taken from the carved box in the bedroom. He jangled them in his cupped hand for a moment, then reached forward and dropped them on the table. One of the coins rolled partway across the table before spiraling down onto its side.

"Phil, I appreciate the offer," Len said, "but I can't accept it."

"You can accept it," Phil said. "You *will* accept it." Although he and Lynn hadn't known anything of Len McCoy before he'd limped past their house almost two weeks ago, it had been Lynn who'd called on the doctor, and the two of them who now provided the stranger with a place to stay. To Phil's way of thinking, that made them responsible. He hadn't yet said that to Lynn, but he knew her well enough to know that she would feel the same way.

"Now, look here," Len said, anger seeming to creep into his voice, "this is a debt I incurred, not you—"

"Len, Len," Phil said, holding his hands up, palms out. "I didn't mean this as an insult."

"Didn't mean what as an insult?" Lynn asked, and Phil turned in his chair to see her standing in the doorway. She hadn't yet dressed for church either, he saw, and he guessed that she'd be working out in the barn after breakfast.

"I wanted to give Len two dollars so that he could pay most of what he owes Doc Lyles," Phil explained. Lynn's mouth blossomed into a smile, slowly, as though she could not contain it. Phil had seen that expression before and understood that the gesture he'd made to Len pleased her.

"I don't see how anyone could find that insulting," she said, crossing the room to the table. "Is this for me?" she asked, referring to the meal across from Phil's.

"It is," Len said. Lynn sat, and without another word, began eating. Len looked as though he didn't quite know how to respond, a reaction Phil had seen her inspire in many a man. Len walked away from the table, over to the rear window.

Nobody said anything for a few moments, and then Lynn asked, "Aren't you going to have breakfast, Leonard?"

"I already had a little something to eat, thank you," he said without turning. Then he seemed to gather himself, pacing back to the table. "It's not that I'm ungrateful," he said. "Quite the opposite: I am *very* grateful. But you two have already taken me into your home, gotten me medical treatment, given me food . . . I don't want to take your money too."

"It's a good thing this isn't about what you want then," Lynn said. "It's about what's right for us, and Doctor Lyles, and the whole town, really."

"How's that?" Len asked, and he looked as unconvinced by Lynn's claim as Phil himself felt.

"The doctor is a good man," Lynn said. "A good Christian. He doesn't take money for his services from people who can't afford it. But if nobody ever pays him, them maybe he won't be able to stay in Hayden. And the town needs to have a doctor." Phil couldn't imagine Doc Lyles moving away—he'd lived here for a long time, had even delivered quite a number of babies in Hayden who had already grown into adults—but he thought that Lynn's argument sounded good.

"Well . . ." Len said.

"Please, take the money," Lynn said. She set her fork down on the edge of her plate, reached forward, and pushed the four coins toward Len. Phil hadn't even realized that she'd seen them there. "If it's that important to you," she added, "then you can just work the money off around the farm."

"You've already given me room and board for eleven days," Len said, "and I've hardly done enough work to repay even that."

"Well, then," Lynn said, "I guess we'll just have to work you harder." She didn't look up from her breakfast, but shoveled a bit of egg into her mouth. Phil could tell from her manner that she knew she had won the argument.

"All right," Len said, giving in to her. He leaned forward and swept the coins off of the table with one hand, depositing them in the other. "Thank you."

"You're welcome," Lynn said, at last peering up from her plate.

Len looked at Lynn for a moment, and then over at Phil. Finally, he turned and pointed to a pair of large buckets sitting over in the corner. "I guess I'd best start working harder right now." He went over and collected the buckets, then headed out the side door, obviously heading toward the well out back.

When the door thumped closed behind him, Lynn peered over

at Phil. "I'm proud of you, Philip Wayne Dickinson," she said.

Phil felt his own mouth widen into a smile. Nothing made him happier than the love and respect of his wife.

Even with the sound of church bells filling the air, McCoy heard the door whine open, as though it remained attached to the body of the truck by rust alone. He stepped out of the cab, then turned to help Lynn out, but saw that she'd sidled over in the opposite direction. On the driver's side of the vehicle, Phil took her hand and helped her down into the parking lot. McCoy pushed the door closed—it creaked loudly again—then walked around the truck to Lynn and Phil. Though he could barely hear it because of the chimes, he still felt the gravel crunch beneath his feet.

"Are you sure you don't want to come in with us?" Lynn asked him, leaning in close. She wore a floral-print dress that reached to her calves, while Phil had donned gray trousers, a white shirt, and a dark jacket and tie.

"No, thank you," McCoy said. He thought to make the excuse that he hadn't dressed well enough to attend church, nor could he, given the currently limited nature of his wardrobe. He decided against it, though, concerned that his new friends might then give him some clothes so that he could accompany them next week. "I'd really just like to see Hayden," he said.

"All right," said Phil, who'd also moved in close, to hear and be heard over the bells. "We'll see you back here in about an hour then."

"Actually, I don't know how long I'll be wandering around," McCoy said. "I thought I might just walk back to the house this afternoon, if that's all right with the two of you." The ride into town hadn't taken more than ten minutes, and so the Dickinson's farm couldn't be more than six or seven kilometers away, at the most.

"Are you sure your leg will be all right?" Lynn asked.

"Oh, it's fine," McCoy said. "Doctor Lyles did a fine job." To emphasize his words, he lifted his leg and flexed it. Though it still seemed surreal to him that a physician had sewn catgut into his body, he had checked the results daily, and his wound had healed quite well.

"All right," Phil said. "We'll see you later then." He and Lynn crossed the lot, weaving through several scores of vehicles parked there. They greeted other churchgoers along the way, and McCoy supposed that such a small town allowed for few, if any, strangers.

Feeling conspicuous, he eased toward the far front corner of the parking lot, moving out of the bright sunlight and into the shade provided by a cluster of tall trees. From there, he turned and peered out at the town of Hayden. The church sat at the end of a long, grassy square, separated from it by a hard-packed dirt thoroughfare named, practically but not inventively, Church Street. He gazed in both directions and saw more motorized vehicles—automobiles and trucks—parked along the sides of the road, as well as quite a few horses and carriages. From the various conveyances, numerous people made their way toward church, some clad in nicer outfits, like Lynn and Phil, and others in everyday farm clothing. Most walked in couples and groups, and none seemed to notice him.

McCoy waited there for about ten minutes, until people stopped arriving, the bells stopped ringing, and the doors of the church swung closed. Then he walked across to the square. Bounded on all four sides by dirt streets, the green of the commons stood out dramatically. Footpaths wound among leafy trees and colorful flowers, with benches scattered off to the side here and there. At the far end of the little park, a gazebo rose like a monument to small-town life.

Meandering along the gravel-covered paths, McCoy looked around at this main section of Hayden. A few people roamed about, and he seemed to draw the attention of some of them, though they did nothing but look his way. A row of one-story buildings lined the streets—Mill Road on the north and Carolina Street on the south—on either long side of the commons, most of the façades attached one to the next, while a larger, official-looking structure sat on the other short side, opposite the church. Raised wooden sidewalks marched up and down before the long frontages, between the row buildings and the streets.

McCoy read signs as he walked, some of them large and plastered above the storefronts, others smaller and hanging at right angles to them: ANDERSON'S SEED AND FEED, JACKSON'S GROCERY,

HAYDEN POST OFFICE, SHERIFF'S OFFICE, PALMETTO MUTUAL BANK AND TRUST, WESTERN UNION TELEGRAPH CO., SEAMSTRESS AND MILLINER, DONNER BLACKSMITH, ROBINSON'S GENERAL STORE. Nothing looked open. At the end of the square, on Main Street, the tall, columned edifice there proclaimed itself TOWN HALL. To the left, across the intersection of Mill and Main, sat a gas station, COLTON'S SHELL. And to the right, across the intersection of Carolina and Main, McCoy spotted a sign identifying one of the places for which he'd been looking.

A low picket fence surrounded the house, and two doors led inside, one in each of the sides facing the street. McCoy traversed the intersection and walked up a stone path to one of the doors, past a simple, neatly carved sign he'd seen sitting atop a post in the front yard. Unsure if he'd find anybody home—much of the town appeared to have turned out for church services—he reached up to knock, but then heard the strains of a piano coming from inside. He waited a few minutes until the music stopped, then rapped on the door.

McCoy heard footsteps within before he saw movement through the gauzy curtain covering the window in the top half of the door. The knob turned, and Dr. Lyles appeared. Wearing a short-sleeved shirt and no jacket or tie, he looked far less formal and much more relaxed than when he'd worked over McCoy's injury a week and a half ago. "Well, Mister McCoy," he said, pushing his black-rimmed eyeglasses back up the bridge of his nose. "I was wondering if I'd see you again. I heard you were still staying with the Dickinsons."

"I am," McCoy said. "I'm helping them around the farm right now, and they've offered to let me stay awhile."

"That's mighty neighborly of them," Lyles noted. "Well, come on in." He shuffled away down a short hall, turning and going through the first doorway to which he came. McCoy followed, closing the outside door behind him.

Inside the house, he detected scents not unfamiliar to him: antiseptics, linen, steel. He followed Lyles through the doorway and found himself in an examination room. Cabinets and shelves lined the walls, filled with supplies and equipment, some of which McCoy recognized, some of which he did not. A tall exam table stood near the center of the room, topped by thick, articulated green cushions. A band of paper covered the length of the table.

"Remove your pants and hop on up," Lyles told him as he closed the door.

"Pardon me?" McCoy said. He'd come here to speak with the doctor, not for any sort of medical attention.

"Hop up, I said." Lyles thumped the top of the examination table with the flat of his hand, crackling the paper. "You need to lie facedown while I take out your stitches."

"Oh," McCoy said. He'd checked the laceration in his calf this morning, and had seen that it had healed quite well. He hadn't thought about his injury since, other than when Lynn had asked about it a little while ago. He hadn't intended to visit Dr. Lyles again to have him remove the stitches, vaguely thinking that he'd simply do so himself.

" 'Oh?' " Lyles echoed. "Did you come here for some other reason, Mister McCoy?"

"Um, yes, actually I did," McCoy said. As he thought about it now, though, it only made sense that Lyles take out his stitches. Although McCoy remembered it being a relatively uninvolved and benign procedure, the doctor would have the tools and materials to do the job properly. "But you can take them out," he said.

"I can?" Lyles asked, his southern accent heavy with sarcasm. "Why thank you. I always enjoy spending my Sundays working over unannounced patients."

"I'm sorry, Doctor," McCoy said, trying to keep his own annoyance out of his voice. "I didn't mean to trouble you. If you'd prefer, I can make an appointment and come back some other time."

Lyles looked at him for a long moment, and McCoy had trouble reading his silence. When the doctor did reply, he did so without contrition for his impatience, but also without further irritation. "Hop on up," he said, "and let's get this taken care of."

McCoy unbuttoned his pants and removed them, dropping them on a chair. He then climbed up onto the examination table, pillowing his head on his hands. He felt the doctor's touch as he studied the wound and its repair. "Do you feel any pain in the leg?" Lyles asked.

"No," McCoy said. The injury had stopped bothering him days ago.

"Any discomfort whatsoever?"

"None," McCoy said, resisting the urge to mention the discomfort he felt with the entire notion of suturing people up.

"It looks like it's healed nicely and the stitches *can* come out," the doctor said. He padded away from the table, and McCoy turned his head to watch the doctor wash his hands in a basin in the corner. Afterward, he retrieved a set of forceps, a pair of surgical scissors, and several towels from a closed cabinet. From a shelf, he removed a glass bottle three-quarters filled with a clear liquid.

McCoy could smell the pungent scent of the antiseptic as the doctor cleaned his leg. Neither man said anything as Lyles grasped one suture at a time with the forceps, cut through each with the scissors, and finally used the forceps again to remove them. McCoy felt a slight tug as each stitch pulled free of his flesh. The entire process took less than five minutes.

When McCoy had gotten down from the examination table and pulled his pants back on, Lyles asked, "So why *did* you pay a call on me today if not to have your stitches removed?"

"For this reason," McCoy said, and he dug into his pants pocket. He pulled out the coins Lynn and Phil had given him and placed them on the exam table. When he saw that he'd retrieved only three of the half-dollar coins, he reached back into his pocket until he found the fourth. "It's not everything I owe you, but it's a good portion of it."

Lyles looked startled, his thick gray eyebrows lifting above the rim of his eyeglasses. He reached over and spread the coins out, until they each lay flat, none of them overlapping. When he peered up at McCoy, though, his surprise seemed to have given way to suspicion. "Where did you get this?" he asked.

"You're welcome, Doctor," McCoy said, weary of Lyles's cynical and disrespectful attitude. He started across the room, ready to leave.

"Did you steal this from the Dickinsons?" the doctor asked. McCoy stopped with his hand on the doorknob and turned back to address Lyles.

"Is this what you call 'southern hospitality?'" McCoy asked.

"Because I'm from Georgia myself and I'm not familiar with this approach of yours."

"I'm just watching out for the people of Hayden," Lyles said.

"I'm sure you think you are," McCoy said. "I'm just not sure how you think insulting me or insulting Lynn and Phil is going to accomplish that."

"I didn't insult Lynn and Phil," Lyles said, clearly outraged by the idea.

"You didn't?" McCoy asked, moving back toward the center of the room. "They've taken me into their home, gotten me a doctor's care, given me clothes and food, and allowed me to help out by working around the farm for them, and you're suggesting that they've done all of that for a thief."

"They might not know . . ." Lyles began, though he did not finish the thought.

"They might not know," McCoy agreed. "But I've spent almost two weeks at their house now. Don't you think they're in a better position than you are to see what kind of a person I am?"

The doctor's jaw set, and McCoy couldn't tell whether he'd grown furious at the challenge to his authority, or mortified by the ring of truth.

"And what kind of a person are you?" Lyles asked in a measured tone.

"Not perfect," McCoy conceded, "but honest." He started once more to go, but then decided to say more. "Look, I can understand being leery of people you don't know, especially in a small town where you probably *do* know everybody. But I've done nothing to you, and nothing to Lynn and Phil, or to anybody else in Hayden, so why don't you consider giving me the benefit of the doubt?" He crossed back to the door and opened it. Before leaving, he looked back at Lyles a final time. "I didn't steal any money from Lynn and Phil," he said, and then he left.

Outside, McCoy walked back down the stone path to the picket fence, and then out to the street. He hoped that his confrontation with the old doctor wouldn't cause any problems for Lynn and Phil. Maybe he should tell them what had happened.

Or maybe I should just move on, McCoy thought. He certainly hadn't intended to stop in Hayden, South Carolina, on his way to Atlanta; hell, he'd never even heard of the place until he'd been sitting in Lynn and Phil's parlor. But circumstances had brought him here, and the Dickinsons had treated him with great kindness. For now, he felt an obligation to repay that—as well as their two dollars—as best he could, by working on their farm and helping them however else they needed.

It's more than that though, McCoy thought. He genuinely liked Lynn and Phil. And although he'd cared a great deal for Edith, he'd never felt completely comfortable at the 21st Street Mission or in New York City. Much of that had been caused by the situation, of course, and his desire to return to the twenty-third century. But although he'd only been in Hayden for less than two weeks and had just come into the town proper for the first time today, this seemed like something of a new beginning for him. He hadn't placed an ad in a newspaper since he'd left New York and hadn't even thought much about being stranded in the past. Instead, he'd begun thinking about finding a place, here and now, that he could call home.

McCoy crossed Carolina Street and walked along Main, passing in front of Town Hall. He walked up the steps and tried to open the large front doors, but found them locked. Holding his hands up around his eyes to shield them from the sun, he peered through the windows in the doors. Inside, a low wooden wall separated a small lobby from an area with some rows of chairs and, beyond those, several desks or tables. He saw no people.

Continuing along Main Street to Mill Road, McCoy looked down both streets as they led away from the commons. Tree lined and heavily shaded, Main Street ran past a number of houses, while Mill passed between the gas station and the town hall, then disappeared as it curved to the left. He also saw another sign that interested him: HAYDEN MILL 2.

If I do stay here, he thought, *I'm going to have to find a job.* According to Phil, the mill didn't operate on Sundays—it didn't seem to McCoy like much of anything did—so there didn't seem to be any point in going out there today. But maybe he would make the trip tomorrow.

McCoy turned back toward the commons and crossed to the plank sidewalk that ran along Mill Road. With everything apparently closed, he decided to walk back down to the church, where he could meet Lynn and Phil when the services ended.

Maybe he could also meet some of their friends and neighbors. If Dr. Lyles's suspicions and attitudes typified those of the people of Hayden, it might take quite an effort for McCoy ever to become accepted here. But he had to start somewhere.

His boots clacking along the sidewalk, he headed back down Mill Road.

TWENTY

2268

Natira gazed at the images of her parents, gone for so long now. She still thought of them often, and though the pain did not come with the same frequency now as it once had, it did come with the same intensity. She would miss them always.

And yet as she reclined into the soft, overstuffed pillows at the head of her bed, her collection of remembrances held in her hands, she smiled. Even after all this time without them, her mother and father gave her gifts still. Natira touched a button on the edge of the shallow octagonal prism, and the three-dimensional projection above it changed, to a moment captured shortly after her parents had wed, when the two had peered lovingly into each other's eyes. Natira looked at their shining faces, at the love they had taught her, that had brought her to this time in her life, and she marveled at the wonder of this day.

"McCoy," she said aloud, and she delighted in the sound of his name. He had come to her unexpectedly, as though from nowhere, but thanks to her mother and father, she had been prepared in both mind and heart. As high priestess herself, Shalira had been permitted to choose her mate, and she had taken a long time in so doing. Given such a privilege, she had told Natira, she had not wished to squander it in haste. She had gladly brooked

loneliness in the hope of finding, not the learned love wrought by
the prescribed couplings of the people, but existent love, real
love, *true* love.

And one day, Natira recalled her mother saying, true love
found her. Zhontu had come into her life later than others would
have, had she selected another, but from the moment he'd arrived, nothing could be measured against his presence in her life.
Others wed as dictated by the Oracle, and then grew into their
love, but Shalira had eschewed such a joining. She had believed
that she would find her true love if she waited, and that she
would know him without doubt as soon as she laid eyes upon
him.

So it had been. When Shalira and Zhontu had looked into
each other's eyes for the first time, they had both known, at that
moment and with full certainty. They had wed at once, and had
lived the remainder of their lives together in bliss.

Natira had been born of that bliss, had grown into woman-
hood hearing the tale and believing in its power. Today, finally,
that power had visited her. As she had watched the guards battle
the three outworlders, she had not at first really seen McCoy. But
then he had stood up, facing her, and their eyes had met, like that
long-ago moment between Shalira and Zhontu, and fulfilling the
promise that their love had given Natira. McCoy had stopped as
though unable to move, and her heart had bloomed.

Touching a second control on the remembrance prism, Natira
watched as the device cycled through a series of images of her
parents together through their lives, each simulacra fading after a
few moments to be replaced by another. She reveled in their special and abiding love, always evident, always present. Today, at
last, such love had arrived for her.

A chime rang through Natira's chambers, and it seemed to re-
verberate through the core of her being. The time had come. The
outworlders would have regained consciousness by now. McCoy
would be awake. It had pained her to see him feel the warning of
the Oracle, but she'd understood the necessity of it: he would
better understand life on Yonada now, would be closer to becoming one of the people, and therefore closer to his life with
her.

Natira looked forward to what would be with anticipation she could barely contain. After deactivating the prism, she set it down on her bed and marched across and out of her chambers, ready to meet her destiny. By the time she had made her way through the labyrinth of passages to the quarters where the outworlders had been carried, Jonsa and Lai had already arrived there, the two older women carrying food and drink as earlier commanded. The Oracle, after meting out its cautionary sentence, had decreed that the strangers subsequently be welcomed as honored guests. Now, as high priestess, Natira would so greet them.

She pushed open the door and entered the strangers' chambers, Jonsa and Lai following behind her. Padding through the vestibule, she saw two of the men standing in the middle of the main room, and the third—McCoy—crouching before them. She saw too that McCoy tended to a gray-haired figure lying unmoving on the floor.

"What happened?" she asked, halting in her tracks.

"We don't know," said the leader of the strangers, Kirk, as McCoy stood up beside him. "He just suddenly screamed in pain and died."

Died, she thought, and she immediately felt anguish at losing one of the people. Suspicion of Kirk rose in her mind, but then she recognized the old man: Jorromlen. She'd seen him earlier, she realized, in his red and pink patterned tunic, observing as she and the guards had first brought the strangers to see the Oracle. That he now lay dead before her, before the strangers, suddenly came as no surprise. Jorromlen had a long history of heretical beliefs and of relating those beliefs to others. He had been punished by the Oracle on numerous occasions, and she could easily surmise that he had attempted one time too many to spread his sacrilege, this time to the outworlders.

Natira looked to Jonsa, who had stopped beside her, and who now peered at the body of Jorromlen with sorrow. "Fetch the guard," Natira told her. Jonsa nodded and moved to do so.

Though she did not wish to carry out before the strangers the rite required upon the death of one of the people, she knew that she must offer up some of it right now, at least in abbreviated form. She stepped forward and kneeled down before Jorromlen, placing the fingers of her left hand in those of her right. Closing her eyes and envisioning the starburst that represented the Oracle, she recited a small portion of the appropriate litany. "Forgive him, for he was an old man," she said, "and old men are sometimes foolish. But it is written that those of the people who sin or speak evil shall be punished." She bowed her head, sad that Jorromlen's life had ended this way.

Looking up at the strangers, at McCoy, she wondered what they thought—what *he* thought. They had been here only a short time and had witnessed only the harsh authority of the Oracle, and not the loving wisdom it mostly bestowed upon the people. Concerned, she stood up and approached the three men. "He served well for many years," she told them, and then she saw that Jonsa had returned with two guards. "Take him away, gently," she ordered.

She watched as they carried him from the room, but noted with some concern that McCoy walked away from her. After she motioned for Jonsa and Lai to prepare the refreshments for the strangers, she followed him across the room to where he'd sat down on a purple-cushioned bed, his head down, a hand rubbing at the bridge of his nose. "You do not seem well," Natira said to McCoy. "It is distressing to me."

He looked up at her, and her heart felt touched anew at the sight of his brilliant blue eyes. "Oh, no," he said, "I'm quite all right, thank you." They gave each other little smiles, and she became acutely aware of the other two strangers watching them.

"It is the will of the Oracle," she said to them, "that you now be treated as honored guests." She turned and moved back across the room to where Jonsa and Lai worked over the food and drink. Jonsa had begun pouring the *alacoya,* she saw, and Natira waited until the four stemmed silver cups had been filled. Then she passed her hand from one to the other, silently invoking the blessing of the Oracle to the visitors.

When Natira had finished, she returned to the strangers. "It is time to refresh yourselves," she announced. Jonsa and Lai each carried a tray over to the group, Jonsa's with the cups of *alacoya,* Lai's with several different varieties of sliced fruit. The stranger with the pointed ears, Spock, picked up a cup and handed it to Kirk, who thanked him, while McCoy selected a cup and offered it to Natira. She leaned forward and took it from him, her hand brushing his and causing a surge of emotion to rush through her. Her gaze met his with no thought to hiding what she felt, and he did not look away.

"To our good friends of Yonada," Kirk said, and Natira bowed her head toward him in acknowledgment. He and McCoy sipped from their cups, though she noted that Spock had left his own sitting on Jonsa's tray.

"We are very interested in your world," Spock said, and Natira thought that perhaps she could find a way to be alone with McCoy sooner rather than later.

"That pleases us," she said to Spock.

"Good," Kirk said, "then you wouldn't mind if we looked around."

"Not at all," Natira said. "The people know of you now." When the strangers had first arrived on the surface of Yonada, they had come without warning, and the Oracle had commanded that they be captured and brought before Him, to ensure that they not surprise or harm the people. Though some had seen the strangers being brought into Yonada, now all the people knew of their arrival, and also that the might of the Oracle had been demonstrated to the three men.

Natira wanted to invite McCoy to remain with her as his friends explored Yonada, but before she could, he began to cough. "Are you well enough to go about?" she asked, concerned, but also seeing a less obvious means of seeking his company.

He looked up at her, his blue eyes arresting. "Perhaps not," he said, and she thought that maybe he had actually tried to find a way of staying with her right now.

"Then why not remain here?" she asked, her smile surely giving away her joy at the prospect. "Rest," she said. "We will talk."

"You are very kind," McCoy said. Natira exulted inside that it had been that easy, and she hoped with all of her being that it signaled McCoy's desire for her.

"You are free to go about and meet our people," she said to Kirk and Spock.

"Thank you," Kirk said, setting his cup back down on Jonsa's tray. "And thank you for taking care of Doctor McCoy." The slight grin on Kirk's face told Natira that her attraction to McCoy had not gone unnoticed.

"Not at all," she said, grinning herself. Peering at McCoy again, she added, "We shall make him well." They looked into each other's eyes again, and she found that, even with the strangers and Jonsa and Lai in the room, she could not look away.

"Mister Spock," Kirk finally said, and the two men departed. McCoy raised his cup to Natira, as though in tribute, and then drank. She did the same.

Lai moved forward and presented her tray of fruit to McCoy. "No, thank you," he said, and then reached to deposit his cup back on Jonsa's tray. Natira did so as well, and then told the two women, "Leave us."

As Jonsa and Lai set their trays down atop a nearby table, McCoy said, "I'm curious. How did the Oracle punish the old man?" The question did not please her, as she wished to talk of far more personal things with McCoy, and also because the Oracle forbade answering such a question from a person not yet part of their people.

Yet, she thought. Did she dare desire that McCoy would soon become one of the people of Yonada? "I . . . cannot tell you now," she said, slowly walking past him and farther into the room. Behind her, she heard Jonsa and Lai leave.

"There is some way the Oracle knows what you say, isn't there?" McCoy asked.

She turned to face him. "What we say, what we think," she replied. Surely the Oracle would not take issue with her sharing the details of life on Yonada with the man to whom she would give herself. "The Oracle knows the minds and the hearts of all the people."

McCoy listened, and then as he had earlier, dropped his head and rubbed at the bridge of his nose, in obvious discomfort. The sight pained Natira. She sat down beside him on the bed, taking the train at the side of her dress and draping it on the mattress. "I did not know you would be hurt so badly," she said.

"It's all right," McCoy said, taking his hand from his face and then looking up at her. "I suppose we had to learn the power of the Oracle." It pleased her to hear his understanding of what had happened.

"McCoy, there is something I must say," she told him. "Since the moment I . . ." All at once, words failed her. The possibility that McCoy might not reciprocate her feelings occurred to her. She believed completely that he was the man for her, but . . . what if he did not believe that she was the woman for him? Suddenly embarrassed by the possibility, she peered down. "It is not in the manner of the people—" she began haltingly, and then realizing what she would say next, looked back up at McCoy. "—to hide their feelings."

McCoy seemed to consider this. "Honesty is usually wise," he concluded.

"Is there a woman for you?" she asked.

McCoy appeared startled by her question, though she could not tell whether because of its content or her directness. Then a slight smile tugged at one corner of his mouth, and he shook his head. "No, there isn't."

"Does McCoy . . . find me attractive?" Natira asked.

This time, he did not hesitate with his response. "Oh, yes," he said with a warm grin. "Yes, I do."

Natira felt weak at the contemplation of his desire for her and then abashed at the raw nature of her thoughts. "I . . . hope you men of space, of . . . of other worlds," she said, "hold truth as dear as we do."

"We do," he said with a crooked smile. She smiled back, then placed her hand atop his.

"I wish you to stay here," she said, unable to contain the extent of her longing. "On Yonada. As my mate."

McCoy felt the smile fade from his face and an eyebrow rise on his forehead. He almost couldn't believe what he'd just heard. Had Natira, a woman he'd met for the first time only earlier today, had she actually proposed marriage to him? He had noticed her fascination with him—he'd had to have been blind not to; even Jim and Spock had noticed. McCoy also understood that she lived in a culture alien to his own, but still . . .

He slid his hand from beneath the warm touch of Natira's fingers and stood from the bed upon which they'd been sitting. He faced away from her and thought of Nancy, all those years ago. By the time he'd met her, McCoy had long before sworn off relationships, a consequence of his ruinous marriage to Jocelyn.

And yet Nancy had fallen for him almost at once and then had fervently pursued him. They'd settled into a long-distance romance, necessitated by his starship duty and her travels in the name of scientific research. In the end, she'd wanted more and he'd given her less.

McCoy knew that he had failed at relationships again and again. He thought back before Nancy to Jocelyn, and afterward, to Tonia. He had known those women and yet not known them—not well enough, anyway, to know how to love them. Yes, he'd been strangely and powerfully drawn to Natira from the moment he'd first seen her, but how could he possibly marry her?

McCoy turned back toward her. She gazed up at him from where she still sat on the bed, love and fear together tellingly on her face. Her honesty and her openness moved him, *she* moved him, but—

"But we're strangers to each other," he said.

Natira shrugged and smiled, as though he had delivered the most trifling and unconvincing of arguments. "But is that not the nature of men and women?" she asked. "That the pleasure is in the learning of each other?" Her head tilted and her chin dipped toward her shoulder in an enticing expression of delight.

He nodded. "Yes," he said. How could he tell her otherwise? He had never had problems courting women, only in establishing lasting relationships with them. Oddly, he thought of his days at Ole Miss, and his mind wandered back to that summer before he'd begun regular classes, to his encounter with the beautiful, mature Emony.

All of the women in my life coming to mind, he thought. *All of the relationships.* He understood why, and that it had to do with far more than Natira's proposal.

"Let the thought rest in your heart, McCoy," she said to him.

"I will," McCoy said automatically, choosing the lie because it was easy to do. But then he realized that maybe it needn't be a lie . . . maybe it *shouldn't* be a lie. Why not think about staying with Natira? What else would he do with his life in the year left to him? He had considered visiting Joanna, but he hadn't even been able to tell her of his illness when he'd recorded and sent a message to her for that very purpose. Would seeing her in person make that any easier, for either of them? Would it improve their strained relationship?

"Are you sure you wouldn't like something to eat?" Natira asked him, motioning toward the trays of food and drink that the two servers had left. McCoy walked over to the table and looked at the colorful fruitlike foods arrayed on one of the trays there. Though it all appeared succulent, he did not have much of an appetite.

"No, I'm not really very hungry," he told Natira. "Would you like something?"

"No, thank you," she said.

McCoy walked back over toward the foot of the bed, contemplating what it might be like, what it would mean to him, to stay here. "Do you enjoy your life here on Yonada?" he asked.

"It rises and falls, as with all things," Natira said. "It is not without complications to lead one's people. But it is a responsibility I conduct very seriously."

"I'm sure that it is," McCoy said. "How long have you been high priestess?"

"I have served the people for half of my life," Natira said. "When Shalira, my mother, died, the title and duties of high priestess passed to me."

"I'm sorry," McCoy said genuinely. For the first time in a very long time, he thought of his own mother—not the woman who his father had stayed with for a while, and whom McCoy had for a time called "mother," but the woman who had given birth to him, and whom he'd only known, more or less, through the lens of his father's memory.

"It is yet difficult, even after all this time," Natira said. "But it is the nature of things, and memories of my parents, and the gifts of life and of love that they gave me, are with me still."

"I'm very glad to hear that," McCoy said, moved and impressed by the obvious peace Natira had made with the loss of her mother and father.

"And you, McCoy?" she said. "Do you enjoy your life on your ship?"

"I do," he answered immediately, but then thought, *Do I?* "For a time, space travel was something of a refuge for me," he said, giving voice to the source of his doubts. "But now I have good friends on the *Enterprise*—"

"Kirk and Spock?" Natira asked.

"Yes, especially them," McCoy said. "But others too. And I'm able to practice medicine and learn about new species and cultures and worlds . . . I do enjoy my life."

"That is good," Natira said. She leaned slightly forward, bringing her hands down flat on the mattress. "But is it a happy life?"

The question—the *logic* of the question—surprised him. How could he enjoy his life and yet not be happy? Except he quickly discovered that he could not formulate a simple response. "Well . . ." he said, but then he could find no words to continue.

"Then come with me, McCoy," Natira said. "Come with me to a new world."

"You're going to a new world?" he asked.

"It is foreordained," Natira said, lifting her hands and gesturing as she spoke. "The people, in the fullness of time, will reach a new world: rich, green, lovely to the eyes, and of a goodness that will fill the hearts of the people with tears of joy." She seemed stirred by the vision she described. "You can share that world with me," she told him, "rule it by my side."

The prospect she articulated thrilled him, as did Natira herself: strong, confident, intelligent, beautiful. But even if he wanted to, did he have enough time to get there with her? "How long will it take you to reach this new world?" he asked.

"Soon," Natira said, though she appeared less than pleased with that answer. "The Oracle will only say 'soon.'"

Soon, McCoy thought, realizing that such words now took on new significance in his life. "Oh, if you only knew how I needed some kind of future, Natira."

"You have lived a lonely life?" she asked him.

"Yes," he admitted. "Very lonely."

Natira looked up at him with sadness and sympathy, but only for a moment. Then her lips curled and parted, slowly, almost slyly. "No more, McCoy," she said. She stood up and walked over to stand before him. "There will be no more loneliness for you," she asserted, and he wanted to believe her.

"There's something I need to tell you," he said.

"There is nothing you need to say."

"But there is," he insisted.

"Then tell me," she said, "if the telling is such a need." He found her smile infectious, her grace alluring, and he suddenly wanted so much to take this woman he hardly knew, this *extraordinary* woman, into his arms.

"I have an illness for which there is no cure," he said. The joy in Natira's expression vanished, as though a cloud had passed over her. "I have one year to live."

In an instant, he saw tears in her eyes, but then she seemed to fight them back. "Until I saw you," she said, "there was nothing in my heart. It sustained my life, but nothing more." She paused and then actually smiled once more. "Now it . . . sings. I could be happy to have that feeling for a day . . . a week, a month . . . a *year* . . . whatever the creators hold in store for us."

McCoy stood there and stared at Natira. He felt weighed down by the knowledge that his life would soon end and yet lifted up by the love that she wanted to give him, wanted to share with him. Had he ever really known such love, he asked himself, and knew that he didn't need to answer the question.

He moved forward, and Natira did too. He tipped his head to one side, and she matched his movements as they came together. He saw her eyes flutter closed a second before his own. Gently, their lips met, and he felt the warmth of her flesh, the soft, supple pressure of her mouth on his. She had not said that she loved him, not in those words, but he sensed her express it now, even without words. This felt right, *she* felt right. Bliss enveloped him, and he thought that he could stay with her forever—

And then recalled again that he had so very little time left. Their kiss ended as McCoy disconnected from the moment, his death sentence looming not so far into the future. The bitter fact of his imminent mortality would end his life before a year passed, but it had already begun to prevent him from living.

But then Natira reached an arm up around his neck, lightly kissed at the corner of his mouth, and nestled her face into the crook of his shoulder. Her heart beat against his chest, her breath warmed his skin. She whispered his name as her other arm came up around his back and pulled him tightly to her. She lifted her head, and once more her lips found his. He gave in to her as his body responded to hers, to her curves, to her heat. His hands wrapped around her waist, and he and Natira moved together, her form fitting sinuously into his.

The kiss lasted, and McCoy immersed himself in the fire of her passion. A low moan escaped her throat as their bodies melted into each other. His hands traveled upward, across her bare back, the touch of her smooth skin beneath his fingertips electric. He felt the single thin strap that crossed her shoulder blades, and followed it to the top of her arm, where it attached to her dress. He nimbly unfastened the connection, and the strap fell away.

Natira stepped back from him, one hand coming up to the front of her dress to hold it in place. He thought for an instant that he had overstepped, but her eyes revealed her ardor. She moved around him, though, and disappeared for a moment into the vestibule. When she returned, she said quietly, "I have barred the door." She lowered her hand, and her dress unraveled around her.

"Natira," he whispered.

She stepped out of her dress and went to him.

Kirk paced anxiously across his cabin, from beside his desk into the sleeping area and then back again. He didn't want to leave Yonada. For now, he'd ordered the *Enterprise* onto a parallel course with the asteroid-ship, although what more he and the crew could do here, he didn't know. "There has to be some other action we can take," he told Spock, frustrated.

"Wherever the control room is," the first officer said, "it is clearly shielded from our sensors, and therefore from the transporter as well." He stood beside the door to the corridor, his arms folded across his chest. "Any further search would therefore have to take place as our earlier efforts did, within Yonada itself. Since our presence there is explicitly unwanted, such an action would be considered, at best, trespass."

"And at worst?" Kirk asked, though he supposed he already knew the answer.

"Invasion," Spock said.

The assessment sounded like an overstatement, but Kirk understood the truth of Spock's words. The two of them had already been caught searching the Oracle room on Yonada. While the high priestess had stayed with Bones, Kirk and Spock had roamed about the asteroid-ship, hunting for its controls. Once discovered in the locked Oracle room, they'd been sentenced to death, although Natira had relented, allowing them to return to the *Enterprise* with a vow that they never set foot on Yonada again.

"Can't we just—" Kirk started, but then didn't finish the question. He'd been about to ask about using the *Enterprise*'s deflectors to alter the course of the asteroid-ship, but they'd already investigated the possibility. In addition to such a process being unable to make more than gross adjustments to the flight path of Yonada, which might then send it into other dangers, the effect of a tightly focused, high-powered deflector beam on the asteroid-ship remained unclear. Power systems and life support might be disrupted, its engines impacted. "Can't we just tell them?" Kirk finally said, though he already knew the answer to that question too: no. Since the people of Yonada didn't know that they lived on a ship, informing them of a need for a course correction would be a violation of the Prime Directive.

Spock didn't respond to the obviously rhetorical question. If no way could be found to safely alter the path of the asteroid-ship, then Starfleet would doubtless order the people of Yonada told the facts and transplanted to another world. Though technically a violation of the noninterference principles, it would provide a justifiable and acceptable alternative to allowing Yonada to collide with Daran V and its nearly four billion inhabitants. Just before leaving Yonada with Spock, Kirk had told McCoy that if necessary, Starfleet would blast Yonada out of the sky, a valid claim, though one he'd exaggerated for effect in order to convince the doctor to return to the *Enterprise*.

Bones, Kirk thought. He still couldn't believe that his friend had chosen to remain on Yonada with its high priestess, let alone that he had only a year left to live. He supposed it made sense that McCoy wanted to spend that time in an atmosphere of romantic love, but the speed with which he and Natira had married—

The up-and-down communications whistle sounded. *"Bridge to Captain Kirk,"* came Uhura's voice.

Kirk moved to his desk and activated the intercom there. "Kirk here," he said.

"Captain, I have Admiral Komack on a boosted signal from Starbase Thirteen," Uhura said. Though far from any command bases, Kirk had decided to take the unusual step of trying to contact the flag officer in charge of this sector.

"Pipe it down here, Lieutenant," Kirk said. As he took a seat at his desk and activated the monitor, Spock walked over to stand behind him. The white-haired image of Admiral Westervliet Komack appeared on the screen, the silver-starburst insignia of his command adorning his gold uniform shirt.

"Captain Kirk," Komack said.

"Admiral," Kirk acknowledged the greeting.

"Captain, I received your report about the medical condition of Doctor McCoy," the admiral said. *"I'm terribly sorry about the prognosis."*

"Thank you, Admiral," Kirk said. He hadn't yet informed Starfleet of McCoy's resignation from the service. "I'm contacting you because my orders have the *Enterprise* scheduled for a patrol along the Klingon border less than a week from now. Because of the situation here, I'm requesting that our itinerary be changed."

"I have your reports on the asteroid-ship, captain," the admiral said. *"It's unclear to me what more you think you can do there right now."*

Kirk glanced over his shoulder at Spock, but the first officer evidently had nothing to add. Peering again at the monitor, Kirk said, "I'm not sure either, but Yonada is still on a collision course with Daran Five."

"I understand that, of course," Komack said. *"I've already taken steps to form a task force to study and resolve the situation. We have a year, and we'll make sure we safeguard the people of Daran Five and the people of Yonada."*

"I appreciate that, sir," Kirk said, "but since both populations are still at risk, and since the *Enterprise* is here now . . ."

"Captain Kirk, I sympathize with your wish to stay," the admiral said. *"But I hope you recognize the necessity that you continue your mission at once."*

"That is the problem, sir," Kirk said.

"Perhaps I haven't made myself clear," Komack said, his voice lowering in volume, and at the same time becoming more commanding. *"Let me restate it: you have been relieved of all responsibility for the asteroid-ship Yonada. Starfleet Command will take care of the situation."* Without another word, Komack reached forward, obviously to an unseen control, and the image on the screen winked off.

Kirk deactivated the monitor on his own desk, then turned in his chair and looked up at Spock. The captain hadn't wanted to hear what he had from the admiral, and now his mind raced to find a way around the unambiguous orders. He didn't want to leave Yonada with the matter of its impending collision with Daran V unsettled.

Is it Yonada? Kirk asked himself, *or is it Bones?*

"I believe it is time to move on," Spock said quietly, understanding in his voice, as well as a gentleness he no doubt would deny if pressed.

"Yes, those are the orders," Kirk agreed, unable to find any justification not to order the *Enterprise* to the Klingon border. As he started to rise, though, intending to head with Spock to the bridge, the communications signal called out once again.

"Captain Kirk," Uhura said. *"Bridge to Captain Kirk."* An undercurrent of exigency now colored her tone.

Kirk opened the intercom channel. "Kirk here."

"An urgent call from Doctor McCoy, sir," Uhura said.

McCoy, Kirk thought. Had he changed his mind about staying on Yonada? Did he want to return to the *Enterprise* before it departed? "Put him on," Kirk said.

"Jim," McCoy said excitedly.

"Yes, Bones?" Kirk said. Whatever the reason Bones had contacted the ship, it didn't sound like he'd regretted his decision and now wanted to come back to the *Enterprise*.

"We may be able to get these people back on course," McCoy said.

"You've located the controls?" Kirk asked.

"No, but I've seen the book that contains all the knowledge of the 'creators,' " McCoy said, referring to those that the people of Yonada thought of as gods, and who had unquestionably built the asteroid-ship. Spock had recognized carvings on Yonada as

the language of the Fabrini, a race whose sun had long ago gone nova. *"And if you—"* McCoy stopped, and for a moment Kirk thought that the transmission had been severed. But then McCoy continued, though his words seemed strained. *"If you can get to it . . . Spock can . . ."* McCoy groaned. *". . . take out the information . . ."*

"Where is it?" the captain asked, but then McCoy yelled in pain. Kirk stood up abruptly at his desk. "Bones, are you all right? Bones, answer me." Kirk listened and heard nothing but labored breathing. "Bones, what is it? Bones, what is it?" He peered at Spock, who despite his stoic demeanor, appeared concerned. "McCoy, what's happening?" Kirk tried again. "What's happening, McCoy?"

But he knew what was happening. When McCoy had decided to stay on Yonada, he'd also agreed to abide by the laws of its people, which included the implantation of a subcutaneous device called the instrument of obedience. Through it, the Oracle could monitor words and possibly even thoughts, and it could administer punishment for anything it considered sacrilege. During their time on Yonada, Kirk and Spock had seen the device kill an old man who had dared to talk to them about his people's hollow world.

Kirk reached over to the monitor and activated it. "Kirk to bridge," he said, and then without waiting for a response said, "Uhura, is the channel to McCoy still open?"

"Aye, sir," she reported.

"Lock on to his communicator signal and feed the coordinates to the transporter room," Kirk said. "Mister Spock and I are beaming back over."

"Aye, aye, captain," Uhura said.

"Kirk out." He deactivated the monitor, crossed his quarters, and headed out into the corridor. Spock followed. As they walked, Kirk said, "The control room may be shielded from our sensors, but if McCoy could get a communicator signal through, we should be able to lock in on it and beam directly to him."

"Logical," Spock said. "Captain, if Doctor McCoy has been equipped with an instrument of obedience and subsequently injured by it, it might be beneficial for him if we remove it."

"Can you do that safely?" Kirk asked.

"I believe so," Spock said. "There is a medical apparatus in sickbay called a subdermal extractor, typically employed to remove items embedded within or under the skin, such as splinters, warts, melanoma."

Kirk stopped at the next intercom he saw and contacted sickbay to have the handheld device brought to the transporter room. There, he and Spock armed themselves, while the first officer also outfitted himself with a tricorder. When they beamed over to Yonada, they found themselves in quarters similar to those they'd been provided when they'd first been there. McCoy lay on the floor, on his back, his eyes closed. Natira sat beside him, her hands holding one of his.

As Kirk and Spock rushed to the unconscious McCoy, the high priestess accused them. "You are killers of your friend," she said. "I will have you put to death."

Kirk quickly dropped to his knees and leaned over McCoy, examining his features, his complexion, the rise and fall of his chest. Almost beneath his breath, he said, "We're here to help him."

Natira reached over McCoy with one hand and then the other, trying to push Kirk away from him. "Until you are dead, he will think of you and disobey," she cried. "I will see you die!"

Realizing that she would not allow them to treat McCoy, Kirk stood back up and reached for Natira. "Spock, take care of McCoy," he said as he pulled her away. He held her tightly by the shoulders, the trails of her tears shining in narrow streaks down her face. She watched with evident sadness as Spock operated the subdermal extractor on the right side of McCoy's head. In just ten seconds, the first officer held up the appliance and peered at its tip, the removal of the instrument of obedience obviously complete.

Natira seemed to deflate, moaning in obvious despair. Spock secured the extractor in a compartment in his tricorder, retrieved McCoy's communicator, and then examined the doctor, using the tricorder to scan him. "He is not part of our people," Natira lamented. "You have released him from his vow of obedience."

Pained at the sight of his injured friend, and despite the high priestess's tears, Kirk could not tolerate her acceptance of the implantation of such a device in McCoy. "We have freed him," he pronounced, "from the cruelty of your Oracle."

McCoy suddenly groaned, and Natira gasped and hurried to him. "Bones," Kirk said as she cradled McCoy's head in her hands. Kirk lowered himself to his knees and once again leaned over his friend. Right now, he wanted nothing more than to correct the course of Yonada and leave this place . . . preferably with McCoy. Kirk would not stand in his way if he still chose to remain here, but he would make sure as best he could that Bones's health would not again be put at risk.

And then Kirk thought of the diagnosis of xenopolycythemia. He pushed it out of his head. "Bones, you said something about a book," he said. "Where is it?"

"They must not know," Natira said quietly as McCoy lifted his head from the floor.

"The . . . Oracle room," McCoy said, his voice rasping, his words low.

"You will never see the book," Natira said angrily. "It is sacrilege." She stood and sped toward the door, and Kirk raced after her, his adrenaline flowing, his own anger rising. "Guard! Guard! Guard!"

He caught her just before she could leave the room, grabbing her by the arm and covering her mouth. "Now listen to me," he told her. "You must listen to what I have to say." He walked her back into the room, to an area separated from Spock and McCoy's location by a latticework divider. "Give me one moment to speak to you."

She glared at him with searing animus, and Kirk's rage seemed to melt away. Natira could not help the perspective she held. By all appearances, her culture maintained a single worldview, living in an illusion created for their benefit, with no dissent permitted. How could she possibly know anything beyond that? And perhaps of more value, the silvery tracks of her tears demonstrated her love for Bones. Kirk could not be angry with that.

"One moment," Kirk pleaded, taking his hand from her mouth, but still holding her arm. "Natira, if you don't believe what I'm about to tell you, you can call the guards. We'll accept any punishment you decree." He released her arm and waited to see whether or not she would run.

She didn't. Breathing heavily from her sprint to the door and her struggles to free herself from his grasp, she said, "What do you wish to say?"

And Kirk told her the truth of her world that was not a world.

Natira shifted on the floor, shaking her head as though trying to clear it, and then turned toward him. Seated on the pentagonal platform in the center of the chamber, McCoy saw her look past him, to where Jim and Spock had found access behind the Oracle to Yonada's control room. She gave him a quick smile, and that quickly, he knew that it would soon be over. All of it.

He cursed himself.

"The Oracle can no longer punish us," he said. After Jim had revealed Yonada as a ship to Natira, a ship that had gone off course, she'd fled, apparently to confront the Oracle. McCoy and Jim and Spock had found her passed out before it, and McCoy had used Spock's subdermal extractor to remove the instrument of obedience from beneath her skin. Jim and Spock had then retrieved the *Book of the People* and consulted it to locate Yonada's control room. Now they worked to bring the asteroid-ship back on course.

"Your friends have prevented it?" Natira asked, referring to the Oracle's power over her.

"Yes," McCoy told her, and he felt a sinking sensation in his gut. The Oracle could no longer hurt Natira, but McCoy himself still could. And as much as he tried to tell himself that he wouldn't do that to this very special woman, he knew that he would.

"And will they send this . . . this ship," Natira asked, still clearly attempting to become accustomed to the idea, "again to the land the creators intended?"

"Yes," McCoy told her, grateful for whatever positive news he could provide her.

"That is good," she said, and he could see that she already sensed what would come next. He'd known her such a short time, and yet he really did find her exceptional in so many ways.

"Natira, your world, your people, are safe now," he said, playing his role, knowing how the conversation would develop, and hating himself for it. "But I'm not."

"I know, McCoy," she said, her eyes downcast. "It grieves me each moment, bearable only because of the love I feel for you."

And I love you, Natira, he thought, but he did not give voice to the emotion. "I thought I could accept my fate," he said. "I thought I could live out my last year without raging against what lay before me, without fighting to preserve my life in the face of my disease."

"Is there . . . is there some way McCoy can fight what is to come?" Natira asked. She seemed suddenly expectant.

"I don't know if I can win, Natira," said McCoy, all too aware of the improbability of battling a disease categorized for more than a century as incurable. "But I'm a physician, and a researcher, and an explorer, and because of all that, yes, I *can* fight." The argument and offer he would make to Natira had already formed in his mind, and he came to them now. "Yonada has one destination, which it will reach a year from now. In that time—in the time I have left—the *Enterprise* will travel to many, many more places. There, at least, I'll have the opportunity to look for a cure, or even short of that, a treatment that will prolong my life." McCoy resisted his next statement, shamed by the calculation in it, and by the lie. "I want you to come with me."

"You want me to leave Yonada?" Natira asked, her eyes widening in surprise.

"Yes," McCoy said, smiling at her through the contempt he felt for himself. He loved Natira, but he had only just learned of his illness and only just met her. How could he have decided so quickly how and where to spend the last, too-short time remaining in his life? He asked her to come with him, knowing that she would not, but believing he would hurt her less by doing so. "Come with me aboard the *Enterprise.*"

"It would be . . . interesting . . . to see and live beyond Yonada," she said, though the level tone of her voice indicated that she felt less then certain of the sentiment. "And I would stay with McCoy."

"Then come," he said, forcing a smile onto his face. He stood up from the Oracle platform and helped Natira get to her feet.

"No," she said, facing him.

"Don't be afraid," he said, though he felt sure that few things could scare this woman.

"I do not fear the punishment of disobedience," she said.

"Well, then come," he said, pushing her in one direction so that she would go in the other. "We must hurry to join my—"

"No," Natira said definitively. "I cannot go with you. It is not fear. I understand the great purpose of the creators. I shall honor it."

"You intend to stay here," McCoy asked, "on Yonada?"

"I shall stay willingly," she said. "And because that is what I must do." She had led the people of Yonada for fifteen years, McCoy knew, since the death of her mother, who had led them before her. How could Natira do anything but continue as high priestess?

"Well then I won't leave you," McCoy said, his voice so flat, his words so unconvincing, that he thought she must surely strike him for his misguided attempt to spare her feelings. Instead, she trusted in what he said and displayed the unconditional love she had professed for him.

"Will McCoy stay here to die?" she asked, sadness imbuing her features as she looked down. When she peered back up at him, though, she managed to smile. "No," she said. "McCoy will not let go of life in the fullness of years."

"Now more than ever," he told her, taking hold of her upper arms, "I wish to search through the universe, to find a cure for myself and all others like me." He hesitated, not wanting to over-sell his lie. "And I want you to be with me."

Maybe it's not a lie, he thought. *If I love Natira . . . but no—*

"This," Natira said, "is my universe. You came here with a great mission: to save my people. Shall I abandon them?"

McCoy lowered his head as she made the argument he knew she would, as she cited her responsibility to her people even as he ran from his responsibility to her. Did she see this? Did she perceive his dishonesty?

She lifted his chin with her hand. "Perhaps one day," she said, "if it is permitted, you will find Yonada again." They looked into each other's eyes, and he hoped desperately that she did not see through him.

After a few seconds, Natira moved forward and leaned her

head against his shoulder. He held her and felt her sobs as she cried. They stood like that for what seemed like a long time, until at last Jim and Spock emerged from Yonada's control room, and the three men returned to the *Enterprise*.

The engines throbbed in the great expanse below, and Spock felt their power as he peered through the observation port at them. The baffling impressed him, keeping as it did the pulse of the drive from making itself known in the populated sections of Yonada. The octet of cylindrical conduits rose up in a line out of the decking, each metal tube half a dozen meters in diameter and running exposed along the deck for perhaps fifty meters before connecting with the far bulkhead.

Spock examined the control panel located beneath the observation port. For a sublight propulsion system, it appeared simple and elegant, an obvious necessity on an automated voyage of such extended duration. Tapping a control, Spock brought up a readout of the one tube in which he'd detected a weakness. The symbols of the ancient Fabrini marched across the display, and he quickly spotted the partial failure of a check valve. Fortunately, he saw, each of the tubes possessed multiple redundancies, some of which had already been triggered during Yonada's long journey through space.

"A very simple problem," Spock said, knowing that the captain would hear him in the control room below. "Easy to correct." He activated a secondary check valve for the faulty engine, then shut down the primary. At once, the readings of the weakened tube changed, and he waited to see if they would rise to the necessary levels.

As Spock watched the display, he returned his mind to an earlier event. As he'd read through the table of contents in the book that had detailed the location of Yonada's control room, he'd seen references to "intelligence files" and "the total knowledge of the Fabrini." Now, he visualized the control room below, and realized that he'd seen something there similar to an illustration beside those terms in the book. He searched his memory for what more he knew of the conclusions that historians and archeologists had drawn about the Fabrini and recalled the accepted judgment that the ancient race had made significant medical advancements. Though it seemed illogical to do so, he thought of the illness infecting Dr. McCoy and wondered if the Fabrini files might provide him a cure.

On the panel before him, Spock watched as the readings of the previously weakened tube attained the optimal performance of the other such drive components. He quickly verified the numbers with his tricorder, then turned and headed for the stairs at the rear of the compartment. He descended to the control room below, where Captain Kirk still stood at the guidance panel. "I believe we can attempt a course correction, Captain," Spock said, walking back over to the controls.

"Good," the captain said, and he switched off the tube monitor, which had superimposed readings atop the guidance display. The numbers vanished from the screen, leaving only a map of Yonada's plotted and actual courses through space. Spock worked the controls to bring the latter back in line with the former. Captain Kirk turned from the console and stepped over to a secondary monitoring panel, where he threw a couple of toggles. "Going back to marked headings," the captain reported.

As the captain returned to Spock's side, the first officer watched the readouts of Yonada's directional equipment. "Guidance controls taking over," he said, satisfied with what he saw. "I believe we can allow this ship to go back to its automatic control."

"Steadying in course marked in red," the captain confirmed. He tapped the console with one hand, obviously pleased with the work they'd done. He started around Spock and toward the access hatch that led back into the Oracle room.

"Captain," Spock said, stopping him. Spock approached the bulkhead beside the hatchway, drawing Captain Kirk's attention in that direction. "Intelligence files," he said. As he raised and operated his tricorder, he said, "Their banks contain the total knowledge of the Fabrini, ready for the people to consult when they arrive at their destination." The people had been left with a book pointing the way into the control room, and consequently to the files, and so it only made sense that the Fabrini had left their knowledge for them. Spock executed a rapid scan of the files, randomly searching for sequences of easily recognizable chemical and biological data. The tricorder identified a considerable volume of such information. "And they seem to have amassed a great deal of medical knowledge."

Captain Kirk looked at him. "Bones?" he said, his hope plain. "The disease?"

"I cannot tell yet," Spock said, still consulting the tricorder screen, "but the amount of technical medical data appears vast." He stopped the scan and moved to the hatchway leading into the Oracle room. There he executed another sensor sweep, this time attempting to confirm information they'd to this point only been able to assume. "I am scanning Natira," he said, "and I read extensive similarities between her biological makeup and that of humans." Spock deactivated the tricorder and looked at the captain. "If the Fabrini did provide a cure for xenopolycythemia," he said, "it stands a significant chance of being applicable to Doctor McCoy."

"Spock," the captain said, "that's wonderful."

"It would appear so," Spock said. "It would be gratifying indeed if the *Enterprise* did not lose a chief medical officer of Doctor McCoy's abilities." But despite his efforts to suppress anything beyond satisfaction, Spock actually felt something more: hope.

"Nurse Chapel tells me that you're now officially cured," Jim said. McCoy peered up at him from where he sat behind the desk in his sickbay office and pretended indignation.

"Chapel?" he protested. "Since when have you been talking directly to my nurses? She reports to me." Though playing his customary character of disagreeable doctor, McCoy didn't have to feign exuberance. Both Chapel and M'Benga had come to announce the news to him this morning, and he couldn't help but feel that he had dodged a photon torpedo. Though his initial treatments had begun five days ago, when the ship had left Yonada, the final confirmation of his restoration to full health had come only today.

"Rank hath its privileges, Doctor," Jim said, delivering with a grin what had to be one of the captain's favorite old saws.

"How well we both know that," McCoy returned, his usual response to Jim's use of the maxim.

"Speaking of privileges, Doctor," the captain said, touching a finger to the top of McCoy's desk, "we're not all that far from the Klingon border."

McCoy's brow creased. He understood neither what Jim seemed to be hinting at, nor his obvious reluctance to speak plainly. "The Klingon border?" he said. "I don't follow."

"The Klingon border," Kirk repeated. "Very shortly we'll be required to maintain subspace silence . . ." He let his words trail off, as though he'd said enough for McCoy to glean whatever he meant to communicate.

"If you're talking about me contacting Joanna," he said, "I sent her a message last week." He paused, then clarified: "Before I'd been diagnosed." Not quite true, of course—he'd recorded a communication to his daughter *after* he'd learned of his xenopolycythemia, but he hadn't been able to tell her about it. Still, he'd made the point to Jim that he didn't need to contact her right now.

"Not Joanna," Jim said. "Natira."

Natira, McCoy thought. He should have realized to whom Jim had been referring. At the time the *Enterprise* had departed Yonada, after the high priestess had made a gift to McCoy of the accumulated medical knowledge of the Fabrini, the prospect of finding even a mitigating treatment for xenopolycythemia, much less of finding a cure for it, remained a possibility only. It had taken hours of translation and study by the linguistics and medical staffs to identify the Fabrini remedy for the disease, and hours more to produce and administer the necessary sera.

"I, uh, I hadn't planned on contacting Natira," McCoy said.

"Oh, I see," Jim said, though McCoy could tell that he clearly didn't see. Jim walked away from the desk and toward the door, and McCoy thought for a moment that he might escape having to discuss what happened, but then the captain said, "Bones, this may be none of my business, but . . . she wants to hear from you."

"I know, I know," McCoy said, raising his hands in capitulation, but he did not elaborate. He hoped that Jim would simply leave, but he didn't.

"She cares for you, Bones," he said, "and when we left Yonada, your prognosis was still for only one more year of life. I'm sure she's terribly worried about you."

"Jim, you're right," McCoy said, searching for some way to avoid talking about all that had taken place on the Fabrini asteroid-ship. "I know that. But everything that happened between us . . . it was so fast, and with my illness and all . . ." He knew that his words said nothing, carrying more implication than actual meaning. He hoped that Jim would see and accept his reticence on this subject.

Jim paced back over to the desk. "Whatever happened, Bones, Natira cares for you, and she was the one who authorized the transfer of the Fabrini medical database to our library-computer," he said. "Whatever you're feeling now, whatever she's feeling, Natira deserves to know that you're going to be all right."

McCoy felt a mix of emotions, chief among them embarrassment. "You're right," he said again. "I will send her a message."

Jim looked at him and slowly nodded his head. McCoy had seen the expression on his face before and knew that the captain didn't fully believe him. Still, thankfully, he didn't press the issue. Instead, he simply said, "We begin subspace silence at seventeen hundred hours."

"Thank you," McCoy said and meant it. "For everything."

Jim appeared uncomfortable himself for a moment, and then he turned and left the office. McCoy watched him go, then activated the monitor on his desk, knowing that he must do this. But instead of recording a message, he wrote one out instead, using a data slate.

> Dear Natira,
>
> I wanted you to know that the Fabrini medical database did hold a cure for my illness. After receiving treatment, I have now made a full recovery. For this incredible gift, I will never be able to thank you enough.
>
> I know that you are busy preparing your people for the days ahead. I wish you good luck in this, and I wish you peace and happiness.

McCoy paused, holding the stylus in the air above the slate, deciding what more he should say. Finally, he finished by adding:

I will never forget you.

After signing his name, he transferred the note to a data card, then inserted it into the slot below the monitor. He ordered the computer to translate what he'd set down into the written language of the Fabrini. Then he contacted the bridge and asked Uhura to send it on its way.

McCoy deactivated the monitor and sat quietly at his desk for a few minutes. He didn't feel numb, exactly, nor did he feel relieved. He only knew that, after meeting, falling in love with, and then marrying a complete stranger, in virtually no time at all, he never expected to see Natira again.

TWENTY-ONE

1932

Phil had already climbed into bed by the time Lynn returned from the privy out back. She slipped quietly into the bedroom without looking at him, closed the door, then moved to the dresser and pulled out her nightgown from the top drawer. As she changed out of her clothes silently, Phil could tell that something troubled her.

"That was a pleasant evening," Phil said, hoping to distract her. After supper, he and Lynn had spent the evening in the parlor with Len, just chatting about the day and the town and each other. As far as he could tell, they'd all enjoyed it.

"It was," Lynn said. She pulled the white peignoir on over her head and let the loose-fitting white fabric fall down the length of her body. Then she crawled into bed beside him, keeping her back to him.

Phil slid across the mattress and reached a hand to her hip, then leaned in and kissed the graceful curve of her neck. Lynn moved her shoulder, shrugging off his attentions. "Would you put out the light?" she said. On the little table next to his side of the bed, the oil lamp still burned.

Though it had gotten late and they both would be up early to-morrow morning, Phil didn't want to go to sleep without finding out what bothered Lynn. He knew that she would resist, but he hated for her to be upset. "What's the matter, sugar?" he asked, moving his hand from her hip up to her shoulder, bare but for the wide strap of nightgown.

"Nothing," she said with no conviction whatsoever. "Go to sleep."

"I'm not gonna go to sleep until you tell me what's bothering you," Phil said. Earlier in the day, when they'd been driving back from church, he'd thought he detected a problem. Lynn had been particularly quiet, with Phil and Len doing most of the talking. But she'd seemed more herself as the day had worn on, chatter-ing away as she'd fixed supper, and later, telling Len about the people of Hayden. At one point, Len had asked about Lynn's family, and though she'd changed the subject before too long, she had answered, talking lovingly about both of her parents. Phil thought that perhaps her grief had revisited her now. Though her mother had been ill for a long time, she'd still only been gone for a few months, and he knew that haunted Lynn every day. He knew that he could do nothing to ease that burden directly, but he could simply be a reminder that life and love had not abandoned her.

But Lynn would have none of it. "Everything's fine," she said, anger now tainting her words. "Go to sleep."

"Lynn—"

"I don't want to talk about it," she snapped. "I don't want to argue on the Sabbath."

Suddenly Phil realized that it wasn't the loss of her mother that troubled Lynn right now, but something that he had done. Squeezing her shoulder lightly, he said, "We don't have to argue, but you can still tell me what's wrong." Lynn said nothing. "You might as well tell me," Phil persisted, "otherwise neither one of us are gonna get any sleep."

Finally Lynn reacted, spinning onto her other side to face

him. "I'll tell you what's wrong," she said. "I don't cotton to lying, that's what's wrong."

"Lying?" Phil said, confused. "You mean me? When did I lie?"

"And I specially don't appreciate it on the Sabbath," she went on. "Or on church grounds."

Phil felt completely befuddled, and he thought back to when they'd gone into town today. They'd taken the truck and had arrived a few minutes before services had begun. They'd sat next to Daisy and Woodward Palmer and their two boys, but they really hadn't said much. Afterward, they'd thanked Pastor Gallagher, then had chatted with a few folks on the way out of the church. To their surprise, Len had been waiting for them by the truck; he'd earlier told them that he would walk home, but then had changed his mind. Phil had been happy about that, as he and Lynn had then been able to introduce him around. Though Len had arrived in Hayden under strange circumstances, and though he hadn't even been staying with them for two weeks yet, Phil felt a kinship with him.

"Sugar," he told Lynn, "I'm really not sure what you're talking about."

"I'm talking about Leonard," she said. She pushed her pillow up against the wall and propped herself up in bed, folding her arms together across her chest. "You know," she said, "your 'cousin.'"

"Oh," Phil said, raising a hand to his forehead as understanding finally dawned on him. "That."

"Yes, that," Lynn said, determinedly looking forward and not at him.

"Sugar," he said, reaching up and rubbing her bare arm. "I did that for Len." When Phil and Lynn had been introducing their houseguest around after church, Becky Jensen had asked how they knew him. Becky had asked the question innocently enough, but Phil knew that, like a number of the townsfolk around here, she didn't really trust—or even like—outsiders. "He's my second cousin," Phil had said, "from down Atlanta way." He'd then repeated the fib to anybody else who'd asked a similar question.

"I don't care why you did it," Lynn said. "It's still a lie."

"Sugar," Phil said, but Lynn continued looking away from him. "You like Len, don't you?"

"You know I do," she said. "But that doesn't mean I'd lie for him."

"What was I supposed to say?" Phil asked, beginning to grow angry himself. Yes, he'd told a lie, but he'd done so for a good reason, and it hadn't hurt anybody.

Lynn turned to face him. "You didn't have to say anything," she said.

"I didn't?" Phil asked. "So when Becky Jensen asked how we knew Len, I was just supposed to ignore her, like she hadn't said anything?"

"Well, no," Lynn conceded, "but—"

"Was I supposed to tell her the truth then?" Phil asked. "Was I supposed to say that Len's a vagabond, and he jumped off a train near here, and now we're putting him up? What do you think she would've thought of that?" Lynn unfolded her arms and started fiddling with her fingers in her lap. When she didn't answer, Phil said, "I'm really asking you, what do you think Becky Jensen would've thought?"

"Well, she might've been okay," Lynn suggested, but Phil could tell that even she didn't believe that.

"She might've been okay?" Phil said. "She still won't talk to Mister Henderson over at the bank, and he's been in town ten years."

Lynn grunted her agreement. "You're right," she said, and then she quoted the ninth commandment to him. "But, thou shalt not bear false witness."

"I know, I know," Phil said. "But I didn't say that Len was my cousin to hurt anybody, or for personal gain. I don't know how long Len's gonna stay in Hayden, but it seems like he might stay for a while. I said what I said to make his life easier around here, and also to make it easier for the folks in town. Is there really anything wrong with that?"

"No, I guess not," Lynn admitted grudgingly.

"Besides," he said, "you just lied too."

"What?" she said, raising her hand and slapping lightly at his arm. "I did not."

"You did," Phil said. "I asked you what was wrong, and you said nothing. But really you were upset."

"I just didn't want to argue on a Sunday night," she said.

"I know," Phil said. "It's all right. I'm just saying that sometimes we say things to make life a little easier. I don't really think it's bearing false witness."

"Maybe not," Lynn said.

"Besides, if all men are brothers," he said, mentioning a message that Pastor Gallagher often preached, "then Len and I must be related some way."

"Oh," Lynn said, and she playfully pushed him. He quickly rolled over to her side and planted a kiss on the front of her shoulder. "You better stop that," she said, swatting lightly at his back. "If we're all the family of God, then you and I must be brother and sister," she joked.

Phil trailed kisses up her neck, interspersing them with single words: "I . . . don't . . . think . . . so." His mouth reached hers, and he kissed her in a way he doubted anybody would ever consider brotherly.

"Probably not," Lynn said when their lips parted. Phil peered into her beautiful blue eyes, the feature that had first drawn him to her. "Put out the light," she said.

Phil did.

The Model A—that's what Phil had called it—raced down Tindal's Lane quite a bit faster than it had yesterday, when McCoy had ridden with Lynn and Phil into town. McCoy clutched the top of the door with one hand and the edge of the bench seat with the other as the truck bounded over the ruts and depressions in the road. His hair whipped about his head, blown by the cool dawn air coming in through the open windows. The front right tire dipped into a particularly deep hole, and McCoy thought for a second that the top of his head might hit the roof.

"Sorry about that," Phil called over the rush of the wind passing through the cab. His feet danced on the pedals, and he moved the metal rod that rose up out of the floor. The truck slowed with a bit of a jerk, but then the ride settled down.

"That's all right," McCoy said. "As long as you don't bounce me out the window, I'll be okay."

"I like going fast," Phil said, a fact McCoy had already guessed. "Lynn doesn't like it much, so I usually rev it up when she's not in the truck."

"I just hope you don't run anybody over," McCoy said.

"I only go fast out here on Tindal's Lane," Phil explained, "'cause with the other farms down there closed up—" He hiked a thumb up over his shoulder, toward the small glass window in the rear wall of the cab. "—almost nobody comes out this way anymore."

The road curved slightly to the right, and up ahead, McCoy saw where it ended, at an intersection with Church Street. Phil braked even more, almost to a stop, then accelerated again after he'd turned right onto the wider road, though at a much slower speed than before. In the distance, McCoy spotted somebody walking along the left side of the road, carrying a basket in each hand. As the truck drew closer, he recognized the woman as one of the many people Lynn and Phil had introduced him to yesterday outside the church. He could not recall her name.

When they'd nearly reached the woman, Phil touched a button near the hub of the four-spoke steering wheel and a horn tooted. Phil waved out the window as they passed her, and she lifted one of the baskets and moved it back and forth in response. She appeared to be in her late thirties, but McCoy suspected that she might be younger than that, and that days she'd spent in the sun had taken their toll on her skin. "I met that woman yesterday, didn't I?" he asked.

"Yup," Phil said. "That's Daisy Palmer. You met her and her husband Woodward and their boys, Justin and Henry. They got twenty acres down-valley. Cotton farmers mostly, but they also keep a passel of chickens. Probably Daisy had a mess of eggs to sell down at Jackson's this morning and she wanted to beat the heat." Although the chill of the dawn hadn't yet lifted, McCoy knew from the rising temperatures of the last few days that today would likely be hotter still.

"I'm going to need to start writing some of these names down," McCoy said, "otherwise I'm won't remember who anybody is." After they'd come out of church yesterday, Lynn and Phil had been gracious enough to introduce him to quite a few people. Some had greeted him warmly, but most, at least at first, had seemed to regard him with some dubiety—at least until Phil had begun presenting McCoy as a member of his family. After that, virtually everybody had seemed more friendly.

As the truck reached the southwest corner of the town commons, McCoy saw a great deal more activity than he had when he'd walked around here yesterday. A few vehicles, mostly trucks and horse-drawn carriages, rolled along the streets, and a number of people, both men and women, made their way along on foot, many toward the far corner. Phil passed Carolina Street on the right and the church—HAYDEN FIRST BAPTIST CHURCH, a sign proclaimed out front—on the left, then turned right onto Mill Road. As they drove along the length of the commons, Phil called out by name to some of the pedestrians they passed. Some just waved, but more than half a dozen men climbed aboard the truck's flat, rear platform.

"All these people work out at the mill?" McCoy asked, motioning toward all of those walking in that direction.

"Yessir," Phil said. "We got 'tween three and four hundred there most days." He paused and then added, "That might seem like a lot, but they're pushing it with that many. Specially these days."

"I understand," McCoy said as they crossed over Main Street and passed between Colton's Shell and Town Hall. "I don't expect anybody to hire me today, but it's worth taking a look." After supper last night, McCoy had sat with Lynn and Phil in their parlor and talked. As they spoke of themselves and the place they'd chosen to live—Phil had actually grown up here, a little farther south down the valley—McCoy had discovered himself taken with the town. The easy comfort he'd felt while walking through Hayden yesterday—his tense visit with Dr. Lyles notwithstanding—had matured today from a *willingness* to stay here to a *desire* to stay. Although he'd lived for a year at the mission, and then for more than a year in his own apartment, he'd never stopped feeling on the run, looking for an escape. Even if he'd only been here for a couple of weeks, he liked being back in the American south.

The road began to veer left, descending on a slight decline before flattening out. Trees speckled the countryside, and broad, deep fields stretched away on both sides of the road, most of them appearing planted. "Keetoowah's down that way," Phil said, pointing out his side of the truck. He'd mentioned the river a couple of times to McCoy, telling him how they'd had to dredge the mill race this past year. They'd had to dam the channel, drain it, and then clear out the sediment that had settled along its length so that the swift current of the river could better drive the mill wheel. McCoy listened at his window for the sound of rushing water, but could hear nothing over the combined racket of the truck engine and the men talking loudly in the back.

They climbed a short hill, and as they crested it, McCoy saw the mill. Built of stone and with a peaked roof, it consisted of three stories, with rows of windows lining each. Another large building, of one story and with almost no windows, stood beyond it, and appeared connected to the mill by a long pipe. A number of smaller outbuildings sat scattered about. Several projections looked as though they had been added onto the mill building itself after its original construction. At the far end, rising from where the land sloped away from the foundation and up almost to the third story, a tall, narrow structure must have housed the mill wheel. Sunlight glinted off the canal that led away from there, and not too far beyond that, McCoy could see the river itself.

Phil pulled off the dusty road about thirty meters from the mill, parking his vehicle at the end of a line of thirty or forty others. Even before he'd come to a complete stop, the men who'd been riding on the back hopped off. Most started for the mill, but one walked up to the driver's side of the truck and peered inside. "Morning, Phil," the young man said with a nasal twang. Lanky and with a face that had gone unshaven for at least a few days, he looked undernourished and as though he hadn't yet reached his eighteenth birthday.

"Morning, Billy," Phil said. "How's by you?"

"Doing fine, doing fine," Billy said as Phil and McCoy both opened their doors. "So who's this?" he asked, looking across the roof of the truck at McCoy.

"Cousin," Phil said, reaching back into the cab and grabbing his lunch pail. "Len McCoy, this is Billy Fuster. He cleans up and runs the cotton out of the storehouse for us. Works half days." Phil waved McCoy around the truck, and they started down the road toward the mill.

"I been opening the bales some lately too," Billy said, following behind. "And Mister Duncan says he might put me on full-time soon."

"That's good, Billy," Phil said, but McCoy got the feeling that the gangly young man didn't impress him much.

"After that," Billy went on, "I might start feeding the blending machines, maybe then move on up to picking or carding." As they approached the mill, he kept talking, mostly about what he would be doing at different points in the future. It didn't take them long to reach the building, but McCoy supposed if the walk had been much longer, Billy would've revealed his plan for running the mill.

At the near end of the building, a small annex jutted out from the end of the long wall. Phil headed for it, giving a wave to Billy and saying that maybe he'd see him later.

"Where ya going?" Billy asked, but Phil kept walking, as though he hadn't heard.

At the annex, Phil knocked on a worn door, slightly ajar, which might once have been painted green but now looked more like the color of a dying plant. McCoy heard something vaguely like a grunt of assent, and Phil pushed open the door and entered. McCoy followed.

Inside, shadows vied with the bright morning sun shining in through two east-facing windows. Gazing around, McCoy saw that the single room appeared to have two distinct personalities. Near the annex's two doors—the one they'd just passed through and the one in the wall adjacent, which led into the mill itself—tools and parts hung seemingly at random on the walls and lay on tables, chairs, and even the floor. On the other end of the room, though, organization prevailed. A pair of tall wooden filing cabinets had been pushed up against the far wall, and a large desk sat beneath one of the windows. Seated at the desk, a large bull of a man leaned over some paperwork, a thick cigar sticking from the corner of his mouth like a mouse peeking out of its hole. He had short graying hair that had receded to the top of his head, and he looked as though he must be in his fifties.

"Mister Duncan," Phil said.

"Yeah," the man growled without looking up from the desk. Phil had identified Duncan earlier as the mill superintendent.

"I just wanted to introduce you to my cousin," Phil said.

Duncan glanced up, still leaning over his papers. In the bright rays of the sun streaming in through the window above the superintendent, McCoy saw a haze of thin fibers floating through the air. He looked around and noted tufts of gray-white lint spread throughout the room, and realized that it all must be residue from the cotton processing.

"Morning, Mister Dickinson," Duncan said around his cigar. McCoy questioned the wisdom of smoking in a place where flammable material filled the air and probably coated just about every available surface. Duncan pushed his chair back from the desk and lumbered to his feet. "Your cousin, huh?" Though only slightly taller than McCoy, he took up a considerably greater amount of room. Duncan had a bit of a gut, but mostly he was simply larger: broad shoulders, barrel chest, thick arms and legs, huge hands. He crossed toward McCoy, surprisingly spry for such a large man. "Macnair Duncan," he said, extending his hand. "Pleased to meet ya."

"Leonard McCoy," he said. He shook Duncan's hand, which nearly engulfed his own. "I'm pleased to meet you."

"So how this cur related to ya?" Duncan asked. McCoy thought he detected a brogue mixed in with his southern inflections.

"Second cousin," McCoy said, remembering how Phil had introduced him to people yesterday.

"He's the grandson of my ma's uncle," Phil further explained.

"Uh huh," Duncan said, eying McCoy up and down. He gnawed on his cigar, and McCoy saw that it wasn't lighted. "Looking for work, I suppose."

"I know you don't have anything right now, Mister Duncan," Phil said.

"No, we're full up," the superintendent confirmed.

"I figured, but Len wanted to come out anyway, meet you, see the place," Phil said. "He might be staying with us for a while, so if anything does open up, I'd be obliged if you'd let me know."

"Be happy to," Duncan said. Behind him, near his desk, a clock began to chime the hour. "That's you, Phil," Duncan said, and then he excused himself as he stepped past them and through the outside door. McCoy saw him reach up, and then a loud whistle rang out. Every morning at this time, miles away at Lynn and Phil's house, McCoy had heard that whistle.

"I have to go," Phil said. "You sure you don't want to take the truck back home?"

"No, I could use the exercise," McCoy said. In truth, McCoy had never driven an automobile—he'd never needed to in New York City, with its abundant public transportation—and so didn't know how.

"All right," Phil said. "I'll see you later then."

"See you," McCoy said. Phil pulled open the inner door to the mill, and the noise level jumped dramatically for a moment before he pulled it closed. Duncan loped back into the annex.

"Ya ever work in a cotton mill?" he asked McCoy. Despite his imposing frame, the big man presented himself with an affable bearing.

"No, I haven't," McCoy said.

"Any kind of a millwork at all?" Duncan asked.

"No, I can't say that I have," McCoy said.

Duncan harrumphed and headed back toward his desk, though he didn't sit down. "A lot of skilled jobs here, working on the machines," he said.

"I'm a quick study," McCoy said.

"Maybe so," Duncan said, "but if something does open up for ya, it's gonna have to be an unskilled job. I got too many men who know already what they're doing."

"I'll take whatever you can offer," McCoy said.

"Right," Duncan said with a firm nod. "It's good to know ya, Mister McCoy."

"Good to know you," McCoy echoed. As Duncan returned to the chair at his desk, McCoy left the way he'd entered. Outside, the road had cleared of people, all of them evidently getting to their jobs before the whistle sounded.

McCoy started up the road, passing the line of parked vehicles, including Phil's truck. Dust kicked up off the dirt road as he walked, and so he padded over to the patchy grass that bordered it. He hadn't expected to land a job at the mill today, but he felt glad that he'd come out with Phil anyway. As the single largest employer in town, by quite a sizeable margin, he felt sure that if he stayed in Hayden long enough, something would open up there. In the meantime, he would look for whatever else he could find. Thanks to Lynn and Phil, he didn't really have any expenses right now, but he wanted to start earning his own money so that he could repay what they'd already given him. He also wanted to finish paying the doctor.

Determined to find whatever employment he could, McCoy walked into town.

TWENTY-TWO

2813 BCE/2269 CE

Spock felt rage and hopelessness, love and despair. He had but little notion of how to manage any of these emotions, or any of the myriad other shades of feeling demanding expression. Control seemingly impossible, his focus gone, he attempted to concentrate on sensation, tried to distance himself through distraction.

The wind blustered across the boreal landscape, slicing without cease through the crags of rock and ice. Despite the animal hide he'd hastily wrapped about his torso, the fleet air currents bled his body of heat. The touch of the icy cliff face beneath his hand threatened to freeze his flesh, and yet . . . the surface should have been colder still.

Colder still, Spock repeated to himself. *Yes.* The portal had to be here. He and McCoy could push forward into the seemingly impenetrable stone and emerge on the other side, five thousand years into the future of this doomed world and back into their own present. And yet . . . and yet . . .

He turned and looked at Zarabeth, the hood of her fur pulled down around her neck, exposing her lovely face, her long red hair flowing out behind her in the wind. *She's so beautiful,* he thought, and felt shame. He glanced at McCoy, pointlessly wishing the doctor elsewhere, wanting this moment to himself.

To himself . . . and Zarabeth.

Spock went to her anyway. He took her face in his hands, his fingers cupping her rosy cheeks. She looked back at him with her expressive green eyes, and he saw his own emotions reflected there.

"Come on, Spock!" McCoy called, echoing the urgency in Captain Kirk's voice when he had called to them moments ago through the portal.

"You start ahead, Doctor," Spock called back over his shoulder. Despite the illogic of it, he reached for these last seconds with Zarabeth and wanted to hold them with her in private. Time passed relentlessly, though, now and in the future. From the captain's insistence that they hurry through the portal, Spock gathered that, five thousand years ahead, only minutes remained before Beta Niobe would reach the point in its nova cycle when it would destroy the lone planet in its system—this planet, Sarpeidon. Once that happened, he and the doctor would be marooned here permanently.

And would that be so bad? Spock asked himself. The smooth feel of Zarabeth's skin beneath his hands, the ache of love in her eyes, his own reluctance to leave her—all of it told him that he should stay.

"I do not wish to part from you," he said.

"I cannot come," Zarabeth said, shaking her head. "If I go back, I will die." Spock knew that. She had told him already. While most of the inhabitants of Sarpeidon had used their time portal to escape the coming nova by traveling into their world's past, Zarabeth had been stranded here by a tyrant. Serving a life sentence for the sins of two family members, she had been prepared and sent here in a way that would not permit her to survive another trip through the portal.

"What are you waiting for? Hurry!" said the captain, his voice reverberating as he called back to Spock and McCoy from their own time.

"How much time do we have?" Spock asked, raising his voice to be heard over the wind. He heard the activation sound of a communicator, and then the captain and Mr. Scott talking. He heard the word *now.*

Dr. McCoy strode up beside Spock and Zarabeth. "Come on, Spock," he pressed. "Now!"

Spock brushed the hair from Zarabeth's face, then looked to the doctor. He and McCoy shared a strong bond. Spock had known the truth of that for a long time, but he had never felt it in the way that he did right now. But something in his passage through the time portal had affected him, reverted him to the state of his Vulcan ancestors in this period: uncivilized, uncontrolled, *emotional.* And now he made an emotional decision.

He turned from Zarabeth, spun McCoy around, and pushed him into the portal. Spock would remain here, spend his life with the woman he loved—

Except that McCoy struck the ice face and stopped. The doctor staggered backward. "Something's wrong," he called.

Confusion washed over Spock, followed by a sense of elation, his choice reinforced by events. "It appears that we cannot go back," he told McCoy.

The doctor peered at him with shock, and then mistrust, as though Spock himself had somehow rendered the portal unusable. Spock ignored McCoy's suspicions, which he believed would fade over the course of the weeks and months and years that they would spend here. Instead, he went back to Zarabeth, taking her hand in his. "We are staying," he said, and her entire aspect changed, her face brightening like the sky at dawn. Spock smiled back at her.

"Spock, McCoy," the captain called, *"you can't get through unless you both come back at the same time."*

Zarabeth's face fell, and the joy Spock had experienced a moment ago vanished. Not only *could* he go back to the future, he *must* go back to the future. If not, he would have earned McCoy's mistrust, immorally elevating his own desires over the doctor's fundamental need to return home.

Zarabeth understood. Even as Spock found himself unable to move, she stepped back from him. Her courage only deepened his love for her.

"Spock, McCoy, hurry through the portal!" came the captain's voice. *"Time is running out!"*

Zarabeth let go of his hand, turned, and walked away. Spock knew that he must go now, or he would never go. He moved toward the ice face, toward the unseen portal, toward the future and his life aboard the *Enterprise*—and away from Zarabeth. McCoy went with him. They shared a look and then pushed forward.

The sensation felt to Spock like passing through a wall of sand. His vision clouded in a way reminiscent of travel by transporter, then flashed several times and cleared. He peered down at himself and noted that the pelt he had been wearing had not journeyed forward in time with him.

He looked over at McCoy, but then saw movement to his right. Before Spock could react, the keeper of the time portal pushed between him and the doctor and threw himself into his world's past. Spock watched him disappear in a flicker of light and then felt suddenly benumbed by all that had transpired.

Captain Kirk walked up behind him and put a hand on his shoulder. Spock did not—could not yet—look away from the portal. Through it, he imagined that he could see Zarabeth and knew that he could not. He felt powerless to do anything, and he strived to regain his composure.

With a sigh, the captain said, "He had his escape planned," obviously referring to the keeper of the portal. "I'm glad he made it." Then the captain activated his communicator and moved a few paces away. "Kirk to *Enterprise*," he said.

Spock stared at the portal and then noted Doctor McCoy's presence beside him. He looked over and saw the doctor watching him closely. Spock shook his head, unwilling to allow the scrutiny. "There's no further need to observe me, Doctor," he said, clasping his hands behind his back as he tried to hold on to the here and now. "As you can see, I've returned to the present in every sense."

"But it did happen, Spock," McCoy said. He spoke softly, with enough tenderness, enough caring, to convey his intention to speak only of Zarabeth and not of the conflicts the two men had engaged in during their time in the past.

"Yes, it happened," Spock said, grasping onto the facts that would underscore the futility of whatever emotion still lingered.

"But that was five thousand years ago . . . and she is dead now . . . dead and buried . . . long ago."

Behind the doctor, the captain spoke into his communicator. "Scotty, are you there?"

"It's now or never, Captain," said the chief engineer.

"Beam us aboard," the captain said, "and go to maximum warp as soon as we're there. Kirk out."

Spock walked past Dr. McCoy and over to the captain, positioning himself for transport. Seconds later, he stood with his colleagues aboard the *Enterprise.* At the transporter console, Lieutenant Bates pressed the intercom button.

"Bates to bridge," he said. "Mister Scott, they're all aboard."

"Acknowledged," Scott said. *"Bridge out."*

As Spock descended from the platform to the deck along with Captain Kirk and Dr. McCoy, he detected the vibration of the ship's drive as it took the *Enterprise* to warp. "Thank you, Mister Bates," the captain said, and then he turned to face Spock and McCoy. "Are you two all right?" he asked.

Spock bowed his head in response, while the doctor said, "Yeah, Jim, we're fine." He flexed his fingers and added, "Maybe a little frostnip, but otherwise okay."

"Good," the captain said, starting toward the door, and McCoy went with him. "So what was it like where you were? It looked like an artic waste on the discs."

"Captain," Spock said as the transporter room doors slid open. "With your permission, I would like to go to my quarters. I am . . . fatigued."

The captain took a step back into the room. "Yes, of course." He regarded Spock for a second and then asked, "Are you sure you're all right?"

"I simply require rest," Spock said, wanting to make no claims of which he could not be completely certain.

"Very well," Captain Kirk said. "I'll look forward to your report on what happened."

"Thank you, Captain," Spock said, and he walked past Kirk and McCoy and out into the corridor.

When he reached his quarters, Spock set the lighting to a subdued shade of green, then lighted a combination of incense candles. When he'd completed his preparations for meditation, he lay down on his bed, his fingers held tip to tip above him. He closed his eyes and sought to center himself in his logic. In his mind he pictured the *Kir'Shara*, the ancient Vulcan artifact that held the writings of Surak. Spock directed himself to visualize the surfaces of the triangular pyramid, to see the old Vulcan characters adorning them.

But he could not prevent himself from envisioning Zarabeth's face instead: her round cheekbones, green eyes, soft lips, her long, sinuous red hair. "That was five thousand years ago," he said aloud, opening his eyes. "She is dead, and buried." Except that, out in space, the nova of Beta Niobe had by now lain waste to Sarpeidon. The bones of Zarabeth no longer rested beneath the strata under which time and tide had buried her. "Now she is stardust," Spock said.

He closed his eyes, but it was a very long time before he felt centered again.

"Spock, I think I've got it," McCoy said as he looked up to see the first officer enter sickbay. The doctor stood beside diagnostic pallet number two, atop which he had spread several data slates.

"I trust that whatever 'it' is, Doctor," Spock said dryly, "that it is not communicable."

McCoy chuckled to himself. Since the ship's visit to Beta Niobe a couple of months ago, he had been concerned about his shipmate and friend. Despite Spock's assurances to the contrary, the first officer had not returned unaffected from their shared time in Sarpeidon's past. Although McCoy often bantered with Spock about his stoic demeanor and dedication to logic, he also recognized that over the years the Vulcan had actually integrated well into the *Enterprise*'s mostly human crew. While Spock rarely showed emotion himself and seemed discomfited by the strongly expressive displays of others, he mingled freely in his off-duty hours. He frequently played music on his lyre in the rec room, took part in three-dimensional chess and other games, and often demonstrated a sly wit, sometimes even to the point of playfulness.

After Spock's doomed love affair with Zarabeth in Sarpeidon's ice age, though, all of that had changed. Other than in the

performance of his duties, the first officer had become uncom-
municative, and for weeks he hadn't ventured out of his quarters
except to take his shift on the bridge. Jim had certainly noticed
the differences in Spock's behavior, mentioning it to McCoy on
three occasions. McCoy had suggested to the captain that he
needed to give their friend time to recover from the events on
Sarpeidon. The doctor had written nothing in his report about the
nature of Spock's relationship with Zarabeth, nor had he spoken
of it to Jim, believing that aspect of the incident should remain
private. But he had detailed Spock's reversion to the barbarity
and emotionalism of ancient Vulcans, and he had cited that when
recommending to the captain that he allow the first officer a period sufficiently long for him to readjust. Over the past week or
ten days, McCoy had noted such a readjustment, and Spock's
quip just now about communicable diseases appeared to support
that view.

"If I had anything contagious," McCoy retorted, "I'm sure it
wouldn't like that green syrup in your veins that you call blood."

"I do not *call* it blood, Doctor," Spock said, walking over to
McCoy. "It *is* blood."

"Well, whatever it is, your heart should get it pumping when
you see this," McCoy said, waving his hand over the five slates
he'd placed on the pallet. He could have placed all of his research on one slate, of course, but he'd wanted to see all of the
data, all at once. He picked up the one on the far right. "You're
aware that we completed the annual crew evaluations not that
long ago."

"Your uncomfortable invasion of my body with your vast
array of medieval medical instruments remains fresh in my
mind," Spock gibed. "I take it that the evaluations have revealed
something of interest."

"They have," McCoy said. "We've discovered more increases
in the M'Benga numbers of some of the crew."

"That is hardly without precedent," Spock said. "Nor, as those
precedents indicate, are such increases of any apparent concern."

"Maybe not," McCoy allowed, "but this time, I may finally
have found the cause."

"Indeed," Spock said, arching an eyebrow.

"Here are the four crewmembers whose numbers have

changed," McCoy said, handing the slate over to Spock. The first
officer took it and examined its display.

"Captain Kirk," Spock read.

"As usual, the captain's numbers showed the greatest increase, by a wide margin," McCoy said. "Yours showed the second greatest."

"Yes, I see," Spock said, and then he read: "Doctor McCoy
and Lieutenant Bates." He peered up from the slate, obviously
intrigued by that final entry. "Lieutenant Bates," he repeated.

"That's whose readings sent me in the right direction,"
McCoy said. Paul Bates had served aboard the *Enterprise* for
several years, moving up from crewman to ensign, and recently
to lieutenant. A member of the engineering and services division,
he'd functioned in a variety of roles during his tenure, including
security guard and transporter operator. Not long ago, he'd accompanied the captain and Spock on an uncommon mission. To
assist annalists in the investigation of Federation history, the
three men had traveled back in time to the dawn of Orion civilization via the Guardian of Forever. Although they had acted as
observers only, and had done nothing to alter the past, Federation
historians monitoring the Guardian had accidentally changed the
timeline. According to the captain, Spock had subsequently set
things right.

McCoy had no recollection himself of the disruption of time,
but Jim had recounted the story for him. Consequences of the incident had included the banning of all travel through the
Guardian, as well the elimination of direct studies of the enigmatic portal. Starfleet still maintained a security presence on and
about the planet, but personnel were no longer permitted anywhere near the Guardian.

The medical report in Spock's hands described another consequence of the incident, McCoy believed. "Bates serves primarily aboard ship," he explained. "Because he almost never
joins landing parties, he's rarely exposed to anything that the rest
of the crew are not."

"Yes," Spock agreed, nodding. "His presence on the research
mission through the Guardian of Forever was a notable exception."

"Precisely," McCoy said. He retrieved a second data slate and scrutinized it for a moment before continuing. "Bates's latest physical took place after that mission, and it showed an increase in his M'Benga numbers. His previous physical took place less than a year before that, when we rechecked the entire crew and found that everybody on board had suffered an increase." McCoy recalled finishing those exams just prior to his being diagnosed with xenopolycythemia. "But we already knew about that increase, so I decided to go back even further, to all of Bates's previous exams."

"But the so-called M'Benga numbers were not collected prior to our mission to Deneva," Spock said.

"Right," McCoy said. "Doctor M'Benga developed his algorithm as a means of testing for the presence of the neural parasites, but his formulae utilized data already commonly collected. So I went back and applied the algorithm to readings from all of Bates's physicals. I found one more instance of an increase for him." McCoy held the slate out to Spock, who exchanged it for the one in his hands. He read through it, and then looked up.

"Lieutenant Bates shows an increase after his second year aboard, after his third, and now after his fourth," Spock said. "Are you suggesting that this is occurring cyclically?"

"No," McCoy said. "But the physicals are administered at regular intervals for most of the crew, with the exception of those who participate in hazardous landing parties and therefore require additional checkups."

"Such as you, the captain, and myself," Spock said.

McCoy nodded. "That's right," he said. "So I assembled the results of every physical the three of us have taken since we've been aboard the *Enterprise,* and I applied Doctor M'Benga's algorithm to them." McCoy picked up a third slate and offered it to Spock. "I found four increases for each of us, all at the same times."

Spock set down his slate on the diagnostic pallet and took the next one from McCoy. He studied it for a while. "I see no common indicator or event that correlates with each of these times," he concluded.

"It's not obvious," McCoy said, "and I might not even be right. But to double check, I programmed the computer to apply

M'Benga's algorithm to the readings from every exam administered since the *Enterprise* began its current tour of duty under the captain. There appears to be a total of five periods when the numbers increase in clusters, either for the entire crew or for just a few of us." McCoy tapped at the fourth slate on the pallet. Spock picked it up, putting the other one down.

"I am unable to discern any pattern," he said.

"Neither did I," McCoy admitted, "but I had a hunch because of Bates." He grabbed the final slate and handed it to Spock. "This is a list of the events I think have caused the increases."

Once more, Spock peered at the display. "The controlled implosion of the warp engines at Psi 2000," he read. That event had unexpectedly sent the ship backward in time seventy-one hours. "The full-warp breakaway from the black star en route to Starbase Nine." An accident that had propelled the *Enterprise* back in time to the year 1969, when they'd had to bring U.S. Air Force Captain Christopher aboard. "Kirk, Spock, and McCoy traveling through the Guardian of Forever." The three had ended up on Earth, in 1930, where they'd met Edith Keeler. "The *Enterprise*'s mission of historical research, to Earth, in 1968." Utilizing the warp breakaway maneuver, the crew had taken the ship back in time to study events on mid-twentieth-century Earth, where they'd encountered the enigmatic Gary Seven. "Kirk, Spock, and Bates traveling through the Guardian to the dawn of Orion civilization. Kirk, Spock, and McCoy traveling through the portal on Sarpeidon to the planet's ice age." Spock looked up and stated the obvious: "Time travel."

"I think so," McCoy said. "That wouldn't explain why Jim's readings are so much higher than anybody else's, but there could be other factors involved. Or it could be something entirely different, because we don't have direct proof. For that, we'd need these readings made right before and right after somebody travels in time."

"Agreed," Spock said. "But this evidence, though circumstantial, is compelling."

"I'm glad you think so," McCoy said. "Now I just need to figure out why time travel would do this to somebody."

Spock handed the slate he held back over to McCoy. "I can think of no one better suited to the task."

TWENTY-THREE

1932

Gregg Anderson ran the broom over the plank floor, pushing the accumulated dirt toward the open front door. When he got there, he leaned out and peered both ways, making sure that nobody walked this way at the moment. Then he reached the broom back and brought it forward with long movements, sweeping the dust and debris out of the store. He followed it out, pushing it off the sidewalk and out into the street.

Outside, the day had grown hot. An hour past noon, the air had become thick and sticky, headed for hotter temperatures still an hour or two from now. Anderson looked up at the bright sky, hoping to see clouds rolling in, but saw only high, wispy gray smudges that promised no rain whatsoever. It didn't really matter, of course; as August marched toward September, the afternoon storms that often blew in and out so quickly did little to cool off the days.

Standing at the edge of the sidewalk, Anderson looked out across the commons. The heavy air carried the stray scents of the colorful flowers scattered about the square. He saw Mrs. Hartwell sitting on a bench out toward the church, and he waved to her. He saw other folks out and about too: Sheriff Gladdy stood by the Brink's truck parked in front of the bank; a couple of ladies—he couldn't tell who with their backs to him—made their way into Mrs. Denton's seamstress shop; old Doc Lyles shuffled up his walk from the street; and still others too. Among all of them, though, he didn't see Billy Fuster. "Good for nothing," he muttered, and not for the first time. He gazed down the street for a few minutes, out to where Mill Road disappeared from view past the town hall. He saw Phil Dickinson's cousin Lenny walking up from there, but nobody else.

Anderson turned back toward the store and regarded the stacks of feed piled high on either side of the door. He grumbled a curse under his breath. Billy should've been here an hour ago. He got off at the mill at half past eleven, and usually got here—when he got here—a few minutes later. This summer, though, Billy had been late a lot, and on three occasions, hadn't shown up at all. Anderson had done everything he could think of to get the oldest Fuster boy to take his job at the Seed and Feed more seriously. He'd talked to Billy man to man, and when that hadn't worked, Anderson had resorted to lecturing him man to boy. He'd asked him nicely, he'd pleaded with him, he'd threatened to fire him. Nothing had worked. Anderson had thought about talking to Billy's father, but Jack Fuster had never impressed anybody as anything more than a loud drunkard, who'd had four children just so he'd have somebody he wouldn't have to pay to work his farm and tend his still. Betsy had left him—and the town—long ago, the miracle being that she'd stayed with him long enough to give him those four kids. The townsfolk also agreed that Jack had been more than lucky that he hadn't run his farm into the ground before Billy and his two brothers and one sister had gotten old enough to tend it.

God watches over fools and children, Anderson thought, and he supposed that included children who grew up to be fools too. He ducked inside the door and leaned the broom against the wall, then bent to pick up the top bag of feed. He exhaled, then strained to hoist the hundred-pound sack onto his shoulder. Back in the day, Anderson could carry two at a time, one on each shoulder. Now though, pushing sixty, he struggled under the weight of just one sack.

Inside the store, Anderson moved over to the left wall, to where a dozen or so boards still carried the dark shadow of the fire that had broken out inside a few years ago. He lowered the sack to the floor, then returned outside for the next one. On his fourth trip inside, he flipped the feed from his shoulder a little too casually; it canted to one side and missed landing on the other three sacks, instead crashing to the floor and splitting open. Mash and pellets spilled through the torn burlap.

"Son of a mother," Anderson griped. "I'm getting too old for this."

"I don't know," a voice said behind him. "I hope I'm in as good a shape as you when I'm your age."

Anderson turned to see Phil Dickinson's cousin standing in the doorway. "Hey, Lenny," he said. "How're ya'll?"

"I'm fine, thanks," Lenny said. "How 'bout you?"

Anderson glanced down at the heap of grain now on the floor. "Oh, I've had better days," he said.

"Sorry to hear it," Lenny said. "Anything I can do to help?"

"Still looking for a job, huh?" Anderson said. Lenny had been in town for a couple of months now, staying with Phil and Lynn. He'd come in pretty often to the Seed and Feed—and all over town, really—trying to find work. Anderson knew that a few folks had given him some odd jobs here and there, but last he knew, Lenny hadn't found anything regular yet.

"Well, yeah, I'm always looking," Lenny said, "but I was just coming across the commons and saw you hauling these sacks." He pointed over to the three bags stacked against the wall and the one that had come apart on the floor. "I just figured you could probably use a neighborly hand."

"What I could use," Anderson said, "is a hand who comes in when he's supposed to." He gestured over at the broom leaning next to the doorway. "Get me that broom, would you, while I go find another bag." Anderson walked deeper into the store, over to where he kept a pile of empty burlap sacks.

"The Fuster boy not show up today?" Lenny asked.

"Nope, and he's starting to make a habit out of it," Anderson said. He grabbed a sack and headed back toward the mess he'd made. "You seen him today?"

"Yeah, this morning," Lenny said, handing over the broom. "I was out to the mill first thing—"

"Like you always do," Anderson said as he spread the empty sack on the floor and began to sweep the spilled feed into it.

"Yup," Lenny said. "Like you said, I'm always looking for a job. Anyway, I saw Billy running in right at the morning whistle."

Anderson grunted derisively. "I'm amazed Macnair hasn't fired him yet," he said.

"Probably just a matter of time," Lenny said, and Anderson agreed with that. He finished sweeping up the loose feed, then dragged the half-filled new bag and the ripped, half-filled old bag up against the wall. He would finish loading the new sack after he got the others inside.

Anderson walked back outside, where he reached for another of the feed sacks. "Let me give you a hand with those," Lenny said, following him outside.

"You sure you don't mind?" Anderson asked, grateful for the offer.

"Not at all," Lenny said, and he moved to pick up one end of the top sack. Together, it took them less than twenty minutes to carry the seventeen remaining bags of feed into the store.

"Thank you, Lenny," Anderson said. "I appreciate it."

"Happy to do it," Lenny said. Anderson offered him a glass of lemonade, and he accepted. They walked back to the counter at the rear of the store, and Anderson poured out two glasses.

As they drank, Anderson said, "I wish I could get Billy to work like that, even once."

"You going to stick with him?" Lenny asked.

"Naw," Anderson said. "I've had enough. I believe in giving the kid a break, but I've given him too many already."

"You got somebody in mind to do the job for you?" Lenny asked.

"Hadn't really thought about it," Anderson said. "If you were twenty years younger, Lenny, I'd hire you."

"You're not gonna hire me because I'm too old?" Lenny said with a smile.

"Not 'cause you're too old like that," Anderson said, "but this ain't no job for a man: sweeping floors, hauling sacks, cleaning up. I only do it when Billy don't show up and 'cause I own the place. Heck, I'm only paying him five cents an hour, and he only works half days for me."

"Gregg," Lenny said, setting his nearly empty glass down on the counter, "it's honest work, and a man can't ask for more than that. In a lot of places in this country right now, people are struggling to find any kinda job at all."

Anderson looked over his glass at Lenny. "You really want this?" he asked, considering it.

"Well, I wouldn't want you to get rid of Billy Fuster to hire me," Lenny said, "but if you do let him go, I'm certainly available."

Anderson thought about it and decided that it would be nice for a change to have somebody working for him who actually showed up when he was supposed to, who did a good job, and who didn't give him any lip. "All right," he said. He put his glass of lemonade down, wiped his hand dry on his dungarees, and reached out across the counter. "You're hired."

"Thank you, Gregg," Lenny said.

"As a good friend of mine used to say, 'Ain't nothing but a thing,'" Anderson said. Lenny grasped his hand with a firm, confident grip, and the two shook. Already, Anderson knew that he'd made the right choice.

McCoy slipped the three stuffed pillowcases off his shoulder and swung them down onto the bed. He'd had so few clothes left after he'd tumbled from the train back in June that it came as a surprise that he had as many as he did now, just two months later. Lynn and Phil had been very generous, to be sure. Phil had parted with so many of his supposedly old clothes, giving numerous items to McCoy even though they still had plenty of wear in them. And Lynn, despite the long days she put in on the farm, had somehow found the time to make two new shirts for him.

Turning and sitting down on the bed, which creaked beneath him, McCoy suddenly thought about his Starfleet uniform. Back in New York, once Edith had provided him clothing to wear, he'd held on for a while to his old service attire, keeping it stuffed under the cot in the back room of the mission. Eventually, he'd realized the foolishness of hanging on to it—he would never wear it in this time period, and having it in his possession only threatened to bring attention to himself. When cleaning the basement of the mission one day, he'd brought the uniform with him and had burned it in the furnace.

Lately, McCoy hadn't thought much about what he now referred to in his head as his "old life." At this point, two and a half years after he'd arrived in Earth's past, he'd just about given up any hope of returning to the twenty-third century. The time he'd spent in Hayden had seemed strangely comfortable—so much so that his southern accent had thickened considerably. Though a number of townspeople still regarded him with obvious suspicion, most had more or less accepted him. That, he knew, had happened primarily as a result of the Dickinsons' claim that he

was Phil's second cousin. Though McCoy had done all he could
to help them on their farm, and though his hours at the Seed and
Feed and at the other odd jobs he'd worked had allowed him to
reimburse Lynn and Phil the two dollars they'd given him for the
doctor, he would never be able to adequately repay their kindness and generosity.

Leaning back on the thin, quilt-covered mattress, McCoy
looked about the room. Smaller than the room he'd been staying
in at Lynn and Phil's, it held almost nothing in the way of ameni-
ties. A narrow, three-drawer dresser stood against the wall beside
the door, and a wooden chair had been placed beside the head of
the bed. An oval blue-and-red scatter rug lay in the middle of the
wood floor and clashed dramatically with the yellow wallpaper
sporting bright green flowers. Plain brown curtains framed the
one window. The room did not even have a closet.

McCoy stood up and dumped out the three pillowcases filled
with his clothes. One by one, he folded his shirts and pants, his
underwear and socks, and loaded them into the dresser drawers.
As he folded one of his last few shirts, he heard a light knock at
the door, and he looked over to see Mrs. Hartwell peeking her
head inside.

"Mister McCoy," the old woman said in her high voice. Over-
weight and slow on her feet, she had a mass of white curls on her
head.

"Yes, Missus Hartwell, come in," McCoy said. "I'm just unpacking my things and putting them away."

"Well, I hate to disturb you," she said, "but you have a visitor."

"A visitor?" McCoy said, surprised. He'd only just moved
into Mrs. Hartwell's boarding house a few minutes ago. How
could anybody possibly be coming to see him right now?

Mrs. Hartwell's head disappeared, and then the door opened
the rest of the way. Lynn Dickinson stepped partway into the
doorway. "Welcome home," she said.

"Lynn," McCoy said. "What're you doing here?" McCoy had
come to Mrs. Hartwell's directly from the Dickinsons'. He'd
said good-bye to Lynn less than half an hour ago.

"I needed some things in town," she said. "I had to go to
Robinson's and the bank, and Phil and I decided that I should
stop in."

"After I just saw you a few minutes ago?" McCoy said, confused.

"We actually decided that yesterday," she said, and then she stepped the rest of the way into the room. In her right hand, which she'd left hidden behind the jamb, she held a potted plant. Several thin stems rose up to support a half dozen golden orange sword-shaped petals, maybe five centimeters long, with bright red speckles on them. "We wanted to give you a housewarming gift."

"Thank you," McCoy said, warmed by the gesture. He took the pot from Lynn and looked around the room for a place to put it. With few options, he reached over and set it down atop the dresser. "And thank Phil for me. That's very sweet."

"It's a blackberry lily," Lynn said. Peering around the room, she asked, "So how's your new home?"

"New," McCoy said.

Lynn leaned in and, sotto voce, said, "It's pretty small."

McCoy smiled. "That's okay," he said. "I don't take up a whole lot of room."

"Are you really sure this is what you want to do?" she asked, repeating a refrain he'd heard several times this week. When he'd announced to Lynn and Phil that he'd spoken with Mrs. Hartwell about taking a room in her boarding house, they'd both invited him to stay longer with them. But as friendly as they'd been to him during his time with them, he could see that he'd impacted their lives, in particular robbing them of their privacy. Even if that hadn't been the case, though, McCoy felt that he'd imposed upon them long enough.

"Lynn, we've talked about this," McCoy said. "I really liked staying with you and Phil, but I've been intruding on your lives."

"You really haven't been," Lynn maintained.

"I appreciate your saying that," McCoy told her, "but look, you're going to need that room for a baby one of these days."

Lynn smiled. "From your mouth to God's ear," she said, peering briefly upward.

"Soon, I'm sure," McCoy said. "Anyway, I'm going to be seeing you two as much as ever, if not more, with picking season coming up." In September and October, Lynn and Phil would need to harvest the cotton they'd planted, a task for which they usually hired a few locals and migrant workers, depending on who in town needed the work and how many itinerants passed through town. Though he needed to work his half-days at the Seed and Feed, he'd accepted their offer to work for them during the rest of the time.

"You may not want to see us after picking starts," Lynn said.

The work would be backbreaking, McCoy knew. He remembered very well the two summers he'd been forced to pick cotton out in his Uncle George's fields. Despite the availability of modern harvesting equipment, McCoy's father had wanted to teach his son the values of hard labor and self-reliance. The first year, when he'd been fourteen, had been difficult enough—the long hours in the unforgiving sun, stooped over to get at the bolls, the hard, sharp husks cutting into his hands, the elongated sack slung over his shoulder growing heavier and heavier as he dragged it down each row—but the next year had been even worse, knowing the tedium, strain, and pain his mind and body would face. Although he didn't look forward now to returning to the cotton fields, he did want to help his friends.

"We'll get through it," McCoy told Lynn.

"'Course we will," Lynn said.

"And when we're done," McCoy said, "you can make me some of that peach cobbler you promised."

"Spoken like a true Georgia boy," Lynn said.

"That's me," McCoy said. "Anyway, I've got to get going. I'm due over to the Seed and Feed."

"I've got Belle Reve with me," Lynn said, referring to her horse. "If you wanna hop on, I can take you into town."

"No, thanks," McCoy said. "It's not that far, and I really enjoy walking." Mrs. Hartwell's boarding house—not much more than a house really, except that it had five bedrooms and Mrs. Hartwell lived alone—was located on Main Street, about a kilometer and a quarter past Mill Road.

Lynn shrugged, then leaned in and gave him a quick peck on the cheek. "See y'all later then," she said.

"Oh, hey, why don't you take your pillowcases," McCoy said. He quickly collected them from the bed, folded them up, and handed them to her. "Thanks for these," he said, "and thanks again for the plant. Thank Phil for me too."

"I will," Lynn told him, and she left. McCoy watched her go, then went back to the bed and finished putting away the last of his clothes. Once he had, he made his way out to Main Street, where he headed for his job at the Seed and Feed.

TWENTY-FOUR

2270

The incessant call to battle stations blared through the *Enterprise* bridge as the ship approached the planet. Between the helm and navigation consoles, the proximity alert light steadily beat out its warning in red, an automated understatement. Peering into his hooded sensor monitor, Lieutenant Hikaru Sulu saw too much movement about the orbiting Federation research station, Einstein: three Klingon D7-class heavies moving in formation, in pursuit of a Paladin-class destroyer that Starfleet records identified as the *U.S.S. Clemson*. The remains of two other ships floated nearby, too mangled for helm scans to distinguish anything beyond their origins: one Klingon Imperial Fleet, one Starfleet.

"Uhura," Sulu heard the captain say from the command chair, and a second later, the red-alert klaxon quieted. Then Kirk said, "Hail the lead Klingon vessel."

"Sensors identify the lead ship as the *I.K.S. Vintahg,*" Spock announced at the sciences station. "The trailing ships are the *Gr'oth* and the *Goren.*"

"The *Gr'oth*?" Kirk said, and then he echoed Sulu's own thought: "That's Koloth's vessel."

"Intelligence reports that Koloth is now fleet commander, and that Korax commands the *Gr'oth,*" Spock said. "All three Klingon ships show significant damage and evidence of attack by phasers and photon torpedoes. The *Clemson* is heading away from the planet, outrunning them for the moment, but it too has taken major damage."

"There's no response from the *Vintahg,*" Uhura said.

"Try the *Clemson,*" Kirk said.

With the clangor of the red alert silenced, Sulu could hear the snap of buttons as Uhura worked her panel. "Nothing, sir," she said. "The Klingons may be jamming transmissions locally."

"Can you raise the station?" the captain asked. Sulu had been present on the bridge when the *Enterprise* had received the distress signal broadcast by the Einstein facility.

A beat, and then Uhura said, "Negative, but it's not the Klingons. There's too much interference from the drifting Starfleet vessel."

"Sulu," Kirk said, "let's see that ship. Full magnification."

"Aye, sir," Sulu said. He referred to his readout, then quickly targeted visual sensors. He looked up as the picture on the main viewer shifted, a gray-white shape appearing in the center of the starscape, a sliver of the iron-red planet cutting across the lower right corner of the screen. The image of the vessel grew in size as the *Enterprise* drew nearer, but even at this distance, Sulu could see the devastation.

Built for speed and maneuverability, primarily for defensive duty, the Paladin-class destroyers each had a single crew hull, long and elliptical, with two of the new, sleek warp nacelles situated aft, one above, one below. At maximum magnification, Sulu could see that one of the nacelles had been torn from the ship, the strut upon which it had been mounted now twisted and blackened from battle. Worse, at least a third of the hull had been sliced away, from forward port to aft starboard, the ship opened to space on every deck. In front of the bridge superstructure, amid the scarring of what must have been caused by Klingon disruptor blasts, Sulu could read what remained of the vessel's designation—*S. Miner*—and he filled in the rest from his own knowledge of the fleet: *U.S.S. Minerva.*

"Life signs?" the captain asked. Tension gripped Sulu in a stranglehold as he awaited the verdict, fearing the worst, but hoping against hope that at least some of the *Minerva*'s crew—

"Negative," Spock reported. Sulu glanced over at the sciences station and saw the first officer peering into his monitor. "Sensor contact is sporadic, but . . . scans do not show any escape pods in the vicinity. However, I do read several dozen life signs aboard the wounded Klingon vessel, though they are weak. The ship's drive systems are unstable and are venting hard radiation at a high level." Spock raised his head and looked toward the main viewer. "Putting it on screen," he said.

Sulu followed Spock's gaze and saw the image of the *Minerva* replaced with that of a badly damaged top-of-the-line Klingon warship. A bulbous control section projected from the end of a slender neck, which itself emerged from an angular structure that spread like the wings of a bird, its lowered talons a pair of S-2 *graf* units, equivalent in function to the *Enterprise*'s warp nacelles. Clearly undirected, the ship pinwheeled through space, its steely gray surface pitted with seared wounds obviously inflicted by Starfleet weaponry. As one wing swept into the direct light of the system's star, Sulu translated the alien characters on its base that spelled out the name of the vessel: *Rikkon*.

"Sulu, how long until we're in transporter range?" Kirk asked.

Sulu checked their course, velocity and distance from the planet and the field of battle above it. "Just under two minutes," he said.

"Bridge to transporter room," the captain said.

"Transporter room." Sulu recognized the British-accented voice of Lieutenant Kyle. *"Go ahead, Captain."*

Before Kirk could order preparations for the Klingon survivors to be beamed aboard—Sulu assumed that had been his intention—the bridge brightened considerably. Sulu squinted at the main viewer in time to see the vestiges of an explosion fade into the darkness of space. Chunks of wreckage intermittently caught the light of the sun as they whirled away through the void.

"Their drive overloaded," Spock said.

"Mister Kyle, stand by," the captain said. "Sulu, show us the research station."

Once more, the helmsman worked his controls, until the Einstein facility appeared on the viewscreen. To Sulu, it looked like a great crystal ornament hanging in orbit above the planet. Tapering spires reached out into space from both poles of its main

body, an oblate spheroid. With a shimmering blue surface, it
seemed glasslike and incredibly fragile.

"Sensor readings are becoming more discontinuous, but I
read no indications that the station has come under direct attack
yet," Spock said.

"Let's try to keep it that way," Kirk said. "Chekov, target the
Vintahg. Sulu, I want a cross-path attack run." Both men acknowledged their orders. While Chekov worked his controls,
Sulu retargeted the visual scanners, then plotted the *Enterprise*'s
offensive, bringing the ship onto a new heading. On his sensor
monitor, he saw the three Klingon ships arrayed in a *V* formation, the lead ship closing in on the *Clemson*.

How could this have happened? Sulu wondered, still half a
minute away from engaging the Klingons. This star, this barren
planetary system, should not have drawn the Empire's notice.
They didn't explore, they conquered, and without directly in-
vestigating the planet up ahead, they shouldn't have had any reason to come here. Sulu couldn't believe that anybody in Starfleet
with knowledge of the classified Einstein installation and its top-
secret purpose would have informed the Klingons.

Maybe, Sulu speculated, the object of the Einstein team's research had made itself known over a larger area. Three years
ago, as the *Enterprise* crew had explored and mapped this system, sensors had detected the anomaly from millions of kilometers away. Sulu had never visited the source of the unusual
readings, but Captain Kirk had briefed his senior officers about
the object, now long since classified by Starfleet Command. The
helmsman could only imagine how disastrous it would be if the
Klingon Empire commandeered the Guardian of Forever.

He checked the *Enterprise*'s distance from the *Vintahg*. "Ten
seconds," he said.

"Captain," Spock said, "the rear ships are breaking off their
pursuit of the *Clemson* and are veering in our direction."

"Ignore them, Helm," Kirk said, rising out of his chair and
stepping forward. Sulu could feel his presence at his side. "Make
your attack run. Chekov, target the *Vintahg*'s weapons systems,
hit them with everything we've got, phasers *and* photon torpedoes, all banks, all tubes."

"Aye, Captain," Chekov said.

"We need to protect the research station," Kirk explained, "and in order to do that, we need to make this an even fight." For his part, Sulu couldn't have agreed more. Starfleet Command had assigned two destroyers, the *Minerva* and the *Clemson*, to safeguard Station Einstein, but they obviously hadn't anticipated an incursion by four Klingon D7 battle cruisers.

"Here they come," Chekov said. On the viewscreen, the two Klingon ships—the *Gr'oth* and the *Goren*, Spock had said—roared toward the *Enterprise*, one to port, one to starboard. Past them, the *Vintahg* still pursued the *Clemson*.

"The Klingons are charging weapons," Spock said, an instant before bright green disruptor bolts fired in unison from the tips of their wings.

"Steady, Sulu," Kirk said quietly, and the helmsman felt the captain's hand grip the back of his chair.

Sulu felt the urge to send the *Enterprise* into evasive maneuvers, but understood the captain's plan. He held the ship on course as the Klingon weapons landed. The bridge shook hard once, then not as badly a second time. Sparks and smoke—but no fire—erupted from an unmanned panel beside the main viewscreen.

"Three hits," Spock said. "Forward shields down to seventy-eight percent, starboard shields down to eighty-nine percent."

On the viewer, the *Gr'oth* and the *Goren* had disappeared, having flown past, and now the *Vintahg* grew larger, its battered profile an inviting target. Sulu worked his controls, bringing the *Enterprise* in above the stern section of the Klingon ship. The approach would allow the clearest path to their disruptor generators, which sat topside aft, Sulu knew.

"Firing all weapons," Chekov said as the *Vintahg* vanished from view. The bridge filled with the distinctive sounds of phaser banks discharging and photon torpedoes launching. Sulu visualized the lethal blue beams surging from the bottom of the *Enterprise*'s saucer section and the stern of the secondary hull, saw in his mind the brilliant orbs of light leaping from the torpedo shafts and toward their enemy.

The *Enterprise* shook again, but not nearly as violently as before.

"A glancing strike on the starboard side of our primary hull,"

Spock said. "Direct hit on the *Vintahg* with one set of phasers and two photon torpedoes."

"Good shooting, Chekov," the captain said. "Status of the *Vintahg*?"

"Upper dorsal shields down, aft shields buckling," Spock said. "Weapons systems . . . still functioning."

"Where are the other ships?" Kirk asked.

"The *Vintahg* and the *Gr'oth* are both coming about," Spock said, "as is the *Clemson*."

"What about the third Klingon?" Kirk wanted to know.

"Trying to locate it," Spock said, and then, "The *Goren* is heading for the research station."

Sulu peered into his sensor monitor, waiting for the captain's orders. His hands rested lightly on his panel, ready to take the ship in whatever direction needed. "Sulu, bring us around for another run on the *Vintahg*," Kirk said after a few seconds. "Take evasive action as you need to this time, but give Chekov another shot at their disruptor generators. Then follow the *Goren*."

"Aye, aye, sir," Sulu said. He worked the helm, and the *Enterprise* hove to port, circling back around toward their intended target. On the main screen, the lean Paladin destroyer and two of the Klingon vessels came back into view.

"The *Clemson* is firing on the *Vintahg*," Spock said, even as Sulu saw four deadly shafts of blue light stream from the underside of the Starfleet vessel. The *Clemson*'s crew had obviously monitored the *Enterprise*'s attack, because they now emulated it. Two of the beams found their marks, pounding into the warship's upper aft section. "The *Vintahg*'s aft shields are now down," declared Spock.

Obviously wounded, the *Vintahg* fired its disruptors, but the bolts soared wide of their objective. The *Gr'oth* followed with an attack of its own, though, sending its powerful bolts hammering into the *Clemson*.

Sulu checked his scanners again as Spock detailed the serious but not critical damage to the *Clemson,* and the helmsman saw a reduction in the *Vintahg*'s velocity. He adjusted the *Enterprise*'s course accordingly, but then saw the *Gr'oth* streaking toward them. He held down a button as he swept his other hand across his console, altering the ship's heading again. Then he released the restriction control, and the *Enterprise* lurched into a downward roll to starboard. Sulu swayed in his seat as the inertial dampeners took a miniscule fraction of a second to compensate. He braced himself for the impact of Klingon weapons, but on the main viewer, he saw the phased energy of the disruptor bolts scream silently past.

"Clean miss by the *Gr'oth*," Spock said.

Quickly, Sulu pulled the *Enterprise* into an arc, sweeping back toward the *Vintahg* from below. "We'll pass behind it," he told Chekov.

"Aye," the ensign said, his gaze locked on his station.

Sulu watched the helm sensors as he moved his hands over his controls, tuning the ship's course as it neared its goal. He anticipated an attempt by the *Vintahg* to elude the *Enterprise*, but it never came. The phaser and photon torpedo salvos, combined with the previous attacks obviously made by the *Clemson* and the *Minerva*, must have taken their toll on the Klingon vessel.

As the *Enterprise* shot past the *Vintahg*, Chekov punched the controls on his panel, one after another in rapid succession. Again, the rush of the ship's weaponry lashing out saturated the bridge.

"Two phaser strikes, two torpedo strikes," Spock said. "The *Vintahg*'s shields have completely collapsed and its weapons systems are down. I'm also reading an explosion in their engineering section."

"Well done," Kirk said.

As Sulu aimed the *Enterprise* toward the *Goren* and the research station, Uhura said, "Captain, channels are clearing. We're being hailed by the *Clemson*."

Kirk sat back down and said, "Put it on screen."

Sulu saw the viewer flicker, and then the sight of a bridge in chaos came into focus. A conduit hung down from the overhead behind the captain, and a haze of smoke filled the scene. Voices and alert sounds clotted the air. In the foreground, nobody sat at the navigation console, the front half of which had gone, its now-visible inner components charred and partially covered by flecks of white powder that must have been fire retardant. An orange-skinned Edoan woman sat at the communications station, her three hands deftly operating her controls, and a Tiburonian man worked the helm.

A human woman stood from the command chair. *"Captain,"* she said without introducing herself. She had short blonde hair and, to Sulu's surprise, wore gold-rimmed glasses. A comma of blood stood out on her pale cheek. She appeared to be in her middle thirties, but Captain Chelsea's reputation preceded her, and Sulu knew her age to be fifty. *"The Klingons believe that Starfleet has established a presence in this system to develop a new weapon for use against them."*

A familiar complaint, Sulu thought. It seemed like one Klingon official or another constantly protested Starfleet's imaginary efforts to obliterate the Empire, essentially ascribing their own motives to the Federation.

"That's ridiculous," Kirk replied, though his tone indicated to Sulu that he understood precisely why the Klingons would think what they did in this particular case. Clearly they had detected temporal emissions from the Guardian.

"We tried to tell them as much when they arrived here," the captain of the *Clemson* said, *"but they came with four D7s; they weren't interested in listening."*

From somewhere offscreen, a male voice called, *"The Gr'oth is coming around again."*

"Do you require assistance?" Kirk asked.

"Negative," Chelsea said. *"We're pretty banged up, but with the* Vintahg*'s weapons down, we can handle the* Gr'oth."

"Acknowledged," Kirk said. "We've got the *Goren.*"

She nodded once. *"Chelsea out."* The *Clemson* bridge faded from the viewer, and in its place, the planet appeared. The research station floated in orbit above, and the *Goren* headed directly for it. To one side, the carcass of the *Minerva* continued adrift.

"Spock, how many aboard the station?" Kirk asked. Sulu recalled from the *Enterprise*'s second and only other visit here, which had taken place about a year ago, that the Einstein facility supported only a small population of researchers and security personnel.

"Radiation from the *Minerva* is still interfering with sensors,"

Spock said, "but according to Starfleet records, there are seventeen personnel aboard at the present time."

Flashes lighted up the viewscreen. "Spock?" the captain said, rising out of his chair again.

"The *Goren* is firing continuously on the station," the first officer said. "Because of the emissions of the *Minerva,* I cannot ascertain the status of the station's shields."

"They have multiple deflector generators," the captain said, but he surely knew what Sulu did: that no matter how much shielding they had, they would not be able to bear up for long against an unchecked assault.

Sulu's helm scanners showed that the *Goren* had come to a stop before the research station, but as with Spock's sensors, interference made complete readings problematic. "Coming up on the *Goren,*" Sulu said. "It's stopped dead while it's firing."

"Same tactic, Mister Sulu, Mister Chekov," Kirk said. "Hit them in the aft section, disable their weap—"

An instant before explosions rocked the *Enterprise,* Sulu saw the cluster of torpedoes that had been mined across their path. The ship must have struck several of them. Sulu flew from his chair and across the top of the helm console. He got his hands down just in time to protect his head, and he crashed to the deck in darkness. His elbow hit something hard, and then his arm went numb.

Feeling the urgency of the situation, Sulu pushed himself up and looked around. The lighting, the main viewer, and the overhead displays that ringed the bridge had failed, he saw, but fortunately the illuminated buttons indicated that the control stations had not lost power. As he thought that, the lights came back on.

"Kirk to engineering," he heard the captain say from somewhere in the vicinity of the helm. "Scotty, status report." Sulu climbed to his feet and headed back to his station. Around the bridge, he saw others doing the same.

"Power's out all over the ship," Scotty replied. *"The engine's are still online, but just barely. Shields and weapons are down. We're checking the other systems right now."*

"Get those shields back up," the captain said. "Kirk out." He had his eyes to the helm scanner as Sulu came back around the console. "We're drifting," Kirk said to him, looking up, "but we still have power to the helm." Sulu nodded and took his station as the captain backed away to give him room.

"We ran through a line of torpedoes," Sulu told him. "Sensors must not have picked them up because of the radiation from the *Minerva*." Next to him, Chekov clambered back up into his seat.

Kirk nodded and moved back to the command chair. "Spock," he said. "Where's the *Goren*?"

"Beginning pursuit," Spock said. "We've now flown past both it and the station."

"Sulu, get us underway," Kirk said. "Set a course directly away from the *Goren*, but prepare to loop back around."

"Aye, aye," Sulu said, sending his hands back across his panel. The fingers of one hand still had no feeling, and he had to watch his own movements as he worked. Sulu quickly brought the ship back under control, and he continued away from the Einstein facility and the *Goren*.

"Captain," Uhura called, her tone urgent, "I'm picking up a distress signal from the *Clemson*."

"On screen," the captain ordered. "Maximum magnification." Sulu operated the proper buttons, but when he looked up, the main viewer remained blank. "Sulu?"

"Trying, Captain," he said as he rerouted power to the secondary. "The primary junction is—" Sulu stopped talking as the viewer winked to life, the *Clemson* visible at the center of the screen. A large fissure, its edges scorched black, had been opened in its upper nacelle, allowing plasma to vent into space. To the right, one of the Klingon vessels sped toward the wounded ship.

"That is the *Vintahg*," Spock said, and for just a moment, Sulu felt relieved. The *Enterprise* had disabled the *Vintahg*'s weapons systems, which would prevent the D7 from launching an attack now on the *Clemson*. But then he realized the intentions of the Klingon crew.

"They're going to—" Sulu cried, but too late. The *Vintahg* rammed broadside into the *Clemson*. The Klingon vessel gave way first, its thin neck fracturing as the forward control section plowed into the starboard side of the *Clemson*'s hull. But then the wide stern section of the *Vintahg*, the angular wings that carried its engines and weaponry, rammed itself home. Sulu couldn't tell which ship exploded first, but fiery clouds erupted from the crash, doused at once in the vacuum of space. One of the *Clemson*'s nacelles went spinning away, and the *Vintahg*'s stern fractured into uncounted pieces. Then the *Clemson*'s entire crew hull blew apart.

On the *Enterprise,* the undercurrent of voices calling in systems' statuses only accentuated the silence of the bridge crew. "Oh, no," Chekov finally whispered in obvious horror. Sulu knew that he had meant it for the lost men and women of the *Clemson,* but he might just as well have said it for the crew aboard the *Enterprise.* Four D7 Klingon warships had taken up battle against two Paladin destroyers and a *Constitution*-class starship, and now two of each—*Rikkon* and *Vintahg, Minerva* and *Clemson*—had been destroyed. That left two D7 battle cruisers against an *Enterprise* that no longer had any shields. They might be able to outrun the *Goren* and the *Gr'oth,* but that would mean the deaths of the personnel aboard the research station, and worse, would leave the Guardian of Forever in the hands of the Klingons—a situation that, as Sulu understood it, could result in the complete annihilation of the human race, or even of the entire Federation. Clearly, retreat was not an option.

Sulu heard the captain press a button on the arm of the command chair. "Kirk to engineering," he said. "Scotty, what's happening with the weapons and shields?"

"Captain, I've got one torpedo tube back online, but I don't know for how long. The deflector grid's got so many breaks in it, we can't reenergize," the chief engineer said. *"We're doing the best we can, but we only have so many work crews."*

"Captain," Spock said at once, "I can—"

"Go," Kirk said. "Use security or anybody else you need." Sulu looked over to see the first officer start around the upper, outer arc of the bridge toward the turbolift. At the same time, Lieutenant Haines moved at once from a peripheral console to take over the sciences station. "Scotty, Spock is on the way with some help. Get those shields back up." Without waiting for a response, the captain signed off and closed the channel. "Positions of the Klingons?" he said.

"Checking," Haines said as she settled in at Spock's console.

"The *Goren* is still in pursuit of the *Enterprise*," she said just a few seconds later, "and the *Gr'oth* is now heading toward the station."

"How long until the *Gr'oth* gets there?" Kirk asked.

"Their drive appears to have been damaged," Haines said. "Estimating . . . almost three minutes."

"Uhura," Kirk said, "can you raise the station?"

"No, sir," Uhura said. "Still too much interference."

Kirk stood up again and moved to stand between the helmsman and navigator. "Sulu," he said, "bring us around. Feint toward the station, but take us in past the *Minerva*." Sulu worked his panel at once. He had no idea what the captain had planned, but he had no doubt that the *Enterprise* commander wouldn't go down without giving his crew its best chance for survival.

"Aye, coming around," Sulu said.

"Chekov, prepare to fire photon torpedoes," Kirk said. "I want to talk to the research station, and we need to eliminate the interference.

"Of course," Kirk said. "In a few seconds, it'll be the two of them against the one of us." Sulu heard him step back over to the command chair and press a button on its arm. "Kirk to transporter room."

"Kyle here, sir," came the immediate response. *Go ahead."*

"Mister Kyle, get down to the cargo transporter," Kirk said. "We're going to be making an exchange." He told the transporter chief precisely what he wanted him to do. Sulu looked over at Chekov and saw that the navigator's expression reflected the odd mix of emotions that he himself felt: confusion and hope.

After Kyle had acknowledged the orders and Kirk had closed the channel, the captain told Chekov what he would need to do when the time came. Then he said, "Fire on the *Minerva* wreckage the instant we're safely past it. Uhura, I want somebody from the station on screen as soon as those channels clear. Not the head researcher, but the top security officer. Give me a secure channel." Chekov and Uhura acknowledged their orders, and then Kirk moved over to the helm and leaned in over Sulu's shoulder, examining the panel. "Sulu, can you split the distance between the two Klingon ships, so that after we pass the *Minerva* and change course, they'll be relatively close to each other?"

Sulu considered the proposition. He would need to time the *Enterprise*'s approach to the *Minerva* perfectly, but he thought he should be able to do so in a way that brought the two Klingon vessels together. Their captains would want to close ranks anyway. "Yes, sir," he said.

"Good," Kirk said. "Do it. Once we're by the *Minerva,* bring us in past the station, as close to it as possible, but follow a course that takes at least half a minute to get there from the *Minerva.*"

"Aye, captain," Sulu said, beginning to see the plan the captain had devised.

Seconds passed, and Sulu felt the strain weighing down on the bridge crew. On the helm scanner, he watched as the *Enterprise* approached the Einstein station, and he adjusted the ship's velocity in order to carry out the captain's orders. Finally, he told Chekov, "Five seconds until I veer." Then, as he worked his controls, he said, "Bringing us about." On the main screen, the research station slipped away off to starboard, while the *Minerva* moved to the center of view, the great arc of the planet hanging in the background.

"The *Goren* is closest to us," Haines said, "but the *Gr'oth* is not much farther away."

Sulu watched the image of the *Minerva* grow large on the viewscreen, and then the *Enterprise* raced past it. "Torpedoes away," Chekov said. The captain did not ask to see the Starfleet vessel's destruction, for which Sulu felt grateful.

"Setting course for the Einstein station," the helmsman said. "We'll be there in thirty seconds."

"The *Minerva* has been destroyed," Haines said. "The *Goren* is closing on us, and the *Gr'oth* is falling in line behind it."

"Thank you, Lieutenant," Kirk said. "Uhura?"

"Trying, sir," Uhura said, and then, "I have Commander Vort for you."

"Twenty seconds," Sulu said, checking his scanner for the *Enterprise*'s distance to the station. He looked at the main viewer as a Tellarite in a red Starfleet uniform appeared on it. Several men and women in civilian garb stood together behind him.

"Captain, we've been monitoring—" the security officer began.

"Commander, I have no time to explain," Kirk said. "I need you to lower your shields."

"What?" Vort replied, clearly astonished by the suggestion. "Captain, our shields are our only defense."

"Commander, the *Enterprise* is your only real defense right now," Kirk said. "Without it, you'll never get off your station alive."

"Ten seconds," Sulu said as he waited for the security officer to respond to the captain's exigent request.

Vort stared at the screen, seemingly nonplussed.

"Commander," Kirk said, "this may be our only opportunity to save you and your people. We're out of time." As Sulu watched the distance to the station decrease, he took note of the captain's words, juxtaposed with the existence of the Guardian of Forever on the planet below.

"Lower the shields," Vort called to somebody.

"Five seconds," Sulu said. He heard the captain bring his hand down hard on the intercom switch. "Bridge to cargo transporter. Now, Mister Kyle."

Sulu glanced up from his scanner for a moment and saw Vort and the others dematerialize in a transporter beam. A moment later, several low, cylindrical objects appeared in their place, transported over by Kyle directly from the *Enterprise*'s weapons cache: six photon torpedoes.

"Got them, Captain!" Kyle said excitedly.

"Viewer ahead," the captain said, and Sulu quickly complied with the order. As the starscape reappeared on the screen, one of the station's tapering blue spires loomed directly ahead. An instant later, the *Enterprise* zoomed past it.

"*Goren* is fifteen seconds from the station," Haines said. "*Gr'oth* is a few seconds behind that."

"Viewer astern," the captain said, and Sulu touched a button. The glistening shape of the research station now fell quickly away from the ship, the *Goren* and the *Gr'oth* visible just beyond it.

"Ten seconds," Haines said. When she got to "five," the captain called out.

"Now, Chekov!"

His hands already in position, the ensign pushed the necessary controls. Behind *Enterprise,* Sulu knew, within the Einstein station, where seventeen men and women had stood only seconds before, six photon torpedoes detonated. On the main viewer, the structure flew apart. The *Goren* and the *Gr'oth* disappeared momentarily behind a wall of fire that quickly vanished, and Sulu waited to see if they would emerge from the conflagration unharmed.

They didn't.

The *Goren* came past the demolished station in parts, the bulbous control section severed from the main body of the ship. Both twirled end over end, until a series of explosions erupted from them. In just seconds, virtually nothing remained of the Klingon battle cruiser.

"Got him!" Chekov said, pumping a fist.

"Easy, Mister, we're not out of this yet," the captain said. As though providing support for his statement, the *Gr'oth* appeared on the viewscreen, still chasing the *Enterprise.* As Sulu watched, though, he saw electric-blue surges crackling across the hull of the Klingon vessel, and he saw something protruding from the underside of one wing.

"A piece of the station penetrated the *Gr'oth*'s hull," Haines said. "I'm reading heavy casualties. They've lost most of their systems, including shields and weapons, and their life support is faltering."

Sulu studied his helm scanner. "They're now drifting," he said, and when he peered at the main viewer, saw the attitude of the Klingon vessel beginning to falter.

"Sulu, reverse course. Close to within transporter range," Kirk said. Then, into the intercom, he said, "Mister Kyle, have our guests escorted to quarters, and then have security report to the cargo transporter. We may be taking on some prisoners."

"Aye, sir," Kyle said.

"Kirk out."

"Captain," Uhura said, "we're being hailed."

"Now they want to talk," Kirk said. "Put them on screen, Lieutenant."

"Aye, sir," Uhura said.

On the main viewer, Sulu saw the dark, hard-edged bridge of the *Gr'oth* appear, its dim green lighting tinting clouds of smoke.

At its center stood its commanding officer, a man Sulu had never met, but who he recognized, and who he knew had once picked a fight on Space Station K-7 with Scotty, Chekov, and Ensign Freeman. Goateed and with a mop of unkempt brown hair, he wore the standard black-and-gold uniform of the Klingon military. "Kirk," he roared, staring straight ahead with an expression that seemed equal parts hatred and glee. "You managed to conduct a battle without the help of the Organians." Sulu had wondered about that himself. Three years ago, the powerful energy beings had forcibly prevented a war from breaking out between the Federation and the Klingon Empire, but they'd subsequently absented themselves from relations between the two powers. "Could it be because the Organians don't approve of Starfleet attempting to build a new weapon to use against us?" Sulu found Korax's brashness startling, given the circumstances.

"There is no weapon, Korax," the captain said.

"Then you won't mind me sending a landing party down to the planet to investigate for myself," Korax said.

"Not at all," Kirk responded, in what Sulu recognized as a brazen bluff. Of course, the Klingon crew were in no position to do anything but attempt to survive.

Sulu checked his scanner and saw that the *Enterprise* had come within transporter range of the *Gr'oth*. He worked the helm to bring the ship to a stop as Korax spat out something like a laugh. "Funny," the Klingon commander said. "The captains of the *Minerva* and the *Clemson* didn't seem quite so accommodating as you."

Kirk stood from his chair. "I'm an accommodating fellow," he said evenly. "Let us transport your crew aboard the *Enterprise* before your life support fails."

Korax threw his head back and laughed heartily this time. "You are also an amusing fellow, Kirk. I look forward to bringing your ship back to the Empire. A minor trophy, to be sure, but still a trophy." Sulu couldn't believe that—

"Uhura!" the captain called, and the image of the *Gr'oth* tumbling through space returned to the viewer. "Chekov, fire torpedoes!"

What? Sulu thought. Had the captain perceived something in what Korax had said? Sulu watched Chekov punch at his controls, but nothing happened. "Captain, weapons are all offline."

"Clear the bridge!" the captain ordered, startling Sulu. "Now!" Kirk called, and Sulu bolted from his chair and sprinted for the turbolift. When he got there, Leslie had made it into the car from the engineering station and Uhura from communications, and Haines and Sulu entered at the same time. He turned and looked back into the bridge and saw Chekov and the captain striding toward the lift. Beyond them, in front of the main viewer, flickered the red-and-orange patterns of a Klingon transporter beam.

Chekov entered the car, and then the captain. As Sulu heard somebody order the lift to another deck, he saw at least ten Klingons materialize on the bridge. One of them peered around and made eye contact with Sulu, then leveled a handheld disruptor in his direction. As the turbolift doors closed, a burst of green light pulsed across the bridge.

Sulu felt himself thrown backwards before he realized that he'd been hit. Incredulous, he peered down at his chest, where a large, dark circle had formed in his gold uniform shirt. He saw wisps of smoke rising from the wound, and he smelled the aroma of his own burned flesh.

"Sulu," he heard somebody say from a long distance away. His legs let go beneath him, and he collapsed to the floor of the lift. He couldn't feel the wound or anything else. And then he couldn't hear or see anything.

And then there was nothing at all.

McCoy helped Lieutenant Rahda from the antigrav gurney, supporting her as she hopped forward on one leg. During the *Enterprise*'s battle with the Klingons, she had been thrown against a bulkhead, fracturing her tibia. With the number of other wounded—including Nurses Chapel and Doran—who'd arrived in sickbay at the same time, none of the doctors had yet had a chance to treat her. When the *Enterprise* had responded to a distress signal from the Einstein research post, Uhura had contacted sickbay to inform McCoy of the reason for the red alert, namely that the ship had encountered a squadron of Klingon vessels and would be going into battle. She'd forewarned him of the potential for numerous casualties, and unfortunately, the notice she'd provided had been well founded.

As McCoy walked Rahda though the low, circular hatchway, her leg struck its side and she winced. "Sorry, Sitara," McCoy said.

"It's all right," Rahda said as Lieutenant Palmer reached up from the bench seat to assist her. "I know we need to move quickly." With Palmer's assistance, Rahda sat down, then shifted as far into the module as she could, leaving room for two more.

Behind him, McCoy heard footsteps, and he quickly turned. As far as he knew, there should have been nobody left in sickbay. He saw no patient standing there, nor any of the medical staff, but Spock. "Doctor," he said, "have you finished evacuating sickbay?"

"These are the last two," McCoy said, pointing into the escape pod. "Well, and me." He still had trouble believing that this had happened on the *Enterprise*'s way back to base, its five-year mission concluded. In all that time, they'd never had to abandon ship. "Have you located the captain?" he asked.

Spock looked down for just a second. "The captain remains unaccounted for. He was on the bridge when the Klingons first boarded the ship."

McCoy nodded slowly. It seemed unthinkable. How could Jim have brought the ship and crew this far, for this long, only to die on the way home? "Spock—" McCoy started, but the first officer interrupted him.

"You should go, Doctor," he said.

McCoy hesitated in the hatchway and then asked, "Spock, are you sure this is the right thing to do?"

"Doctor, the Klingons have commandeered the *Enterprise* and taken over the vital functions of the ship," Spock said. "If we do not leave, they will surely kill us."

"And what makes you think the Klingons won't shoot our escape pods out of space?" McCoy asked. He found the notion of flying in a three-hundred-meter-long starship bad enough, but to limp through darkness in a tin can, with an armed enemy watching you do it . . .

"The Klingons have a warrior culture, Doctor," Spock said. "They will stand and fight to the death, but they are less inclined to fire upon an adversary in retreat."

"This seems like an awfully big risk to take on sociological grounds," McCoy said.

"Doctor, we do not have time to stand and argue this point," Spock said. "I'm ordering you into the escape pod."

McCoy nodded, knowing that Spock only did what he thought best and that his judgment could be trusted. He ducked down low and sidled through the hatchway. When he sat down, he turned to give Spock a hand boarding the pod, but he saw the first officer still outside, reaching to close the hatch.

"Spock, aren't you coming?" asked McCoy, rising and moving back toward the door.

"I am in command at the moment," Spock said, "and I therefore bear the responsibility of making sure that all of the crew make their way off the ship."

"Spock," McCoy called, "let me—" The first officer—the acting captain—slammed the hatch closed. "Spock!" McCoy called, but he saw the horizontal meter above the hatch cycle from green, through yellow, to red. Spock had sealed him, Palmer, and Rahda in the escape pod.

McCoy sat down a second before the module shot through its launch tube and out into space. In the transparent canopy above, he saw the form of the *Enterprise* for a moment, and then the pod turned, and he lost sight of the great ship. The rust-colored planet came into view, and McCoy recalled his two other visits here: one, when he had overdosed on cordrazine and Jim and Spock had gone back in time to 1930 to bring him home, and another, when Spock claimed to have restored a timeline that only he and Jim recalled being altered.

Seems like this place wants to get rid of me, he thought. He looked at the control panel set into the bulkhead before him, and asked Palmer and Rahda, "Does anybody know how to operate this thing?" Before they could answer, though, he began to work the console, the crew's periodic escape-pod training quickly coming back to him. He set the controls for a soft landing on the planet below, and then with nothing else to do, sat back and waited.

They've got my ship, Kirk thought as he climbed in the dim glow of emergency lighting.

Worse, they would soon have the Guardian, and with it, all of human history, all of Federation history. How would they destroy the past, and by extension, the present and the future? Allow the Nazis to win the second world war, or the Holy Roman Empire to control the planet from ancient times? Or something far greater, far more permanent, like poisoning the atmosphere of primordial Earth, or simply murdering the first hominids to arise? It would not take much.

Kirk reached the next deck, his destination, and pressed his ear against one of the door panels. As he did so, he looked down. Far below, he saw the turbolift, the hatch in its roof still open. When the car had braked to a halt, doubtless robbed of power by the invading Klingons, he'd ordered the others to various destinations: auxiliary control, the armory, the hangar deck, engineering. They and the rest of the crew would try to take back the *Enterprise,* but they all probably had less time than they thought. If Korax chose to send any of his crew down to the planet and they discovered the Guardian, then it could all be over very quickly.

Hearing nothing at the door, Kirk reached up to the control panel beside it. He touched a button, but received no response. Clearly the Klingons had cut power all over the ship.

Climbing up another few rungs, Kirk searched for the door's manual release. In the shadowy tube, barely illuminated by the muted emergency lights, he reached around until he found the release handle. Before he threw it, he glanced down once more, imagining that he could see a patch of Sulu's gold uniform shirt through the open turbolift hatch.

Hikaru, he thought, and then pushed away the image of the helmsman being shot. He didn't have time for that right now. But time was what he needed more than anything.

Kirk worked the release, and one of the two door panels slid open. He listened again for a moment. When he heard nothing, he stepped from the ladder and onto the deck. In the muted light, he made his way down the corridor and into the next, and then from there to the transporter room. He removed the access panel beside the doors and once more found the manual release. He went inside, then pushed the panel closed behind him.

In the transporter room, Kirk found, as he'd expected, that the power had been cut here too. He moved to the equipment cache in the rear bulkhead, opened it, and pulled out a utility belt, communicator, tricorder, handheld beacon, and four phasers. Setting everything but the beacon down atop the transporter console, he switched it on, dropped to his knees, and rolled over onto his back. On the underside of the console, in the spare light of the beacon, he removed the access plate, then started rerouting both the primary and secondary couplings.

Five minutes later, Kirk had found enough power for a single transport. He stood up and operated the controls, utilizing the targeting sensors to pick out his destination. Once he'd set the automatic function, he wrapped the belt around himself and attached the communicator and phasers to it. Then he gathered up the tricorder and headed for the pad. As the beam took him and the *Enterprise* faded from his view, he wondered if he would ever see the ship again.

Kirk materialized on a vast, broken plain. A grim twilight reigned, and a ceaseless wind moaned across the unwelcoming terrain. Fractured columns and other remnants peppered the landscape, but not as they had before. Since he had discovered this place, it had changed.

Only the Guardian had remained constant: its peculiar, irregular shape; its coarse surface; the power it exuded.

When first Kirk had come here, mounds and vertical walls of rock had surrounded the enigmatic temporal artifact. In the lands beyond that, large architectural ruins had provided mute testament to a civilization that had come and gone a million years in the past. Or at least that's what they'd thought.

In the three years since the *Enterprise* had tracked ripples in time to this planet, Starfleet had attempted to build a research facility on the surface nearby. Every attempt—even those halfway around the world—had been met with violent earthquakes that had altered the landscape, burying ruins, carving through the land, and toppling some columns while leaving still others unaccountably unaffected. Although the Guardian would not confirm their suspicions, the project team who had worked here had concluded that the vortex itself would permit no such endeavors on its soil. As a result, the Einstein research station had been constructed in orbit.

A chill shook Kirk. He hated this place. When he'd initially seen the Guardian of Forever, and when he'd come to understand its significance, it had proven a source of mystery and possibility that had spoken to his imagination. But in chasing McCoy through the Guardian, back through time, it had quickly become a vessel of unbearable anguish. Even the second time Kirk had visited here, the promise of the Guardian's potential had been overshadowed by the ease with which its use could destroy everything, great and small.

And yet now I seek salvation from it, Kirk thought. This place had wounded him so deeply, but now, he sought its relief. "Guardian," he said, stepping up to the great, asymmetrical ring, "do you remember me?"

The Guardian did not respond. Kirk had read the literature of those who had worked here, not out of curiosity—he would as soon forget this place, this thing, as study it—but in support of his mission on his second visit here. The researchers reported that the vortex did not always reply to their questions, while sometimes it offered comment when none had been requested. Beyond that, much of what the Guardian did say came, as Spock had once put it, couched in riddles.

"Guardian," Kirk tried again, "are you machine or being?" This had been one of the first questions he had asked the vortex three years ago. As Kirk recalled, it had told him that it was both machine and being, and neither machine nor being, and that it was its own beginning, its own ending. Now, it said nothing.

"Guardian," he tried again, "I wish to visit yesterday."

"Behold," it said, its voice reverberating even in the thin air. *"A gateway to your own past, if you wish."*

The great, roughly circular opening through the center of the Guardian appeared to mist over from the top, and then images began to form: humans riding on camels in the desert, living in ancient cities, soldiers marching. Earth, thousands of years ago. But Kirk could not select one day out of millions, could not accurately step through the portal to the time he chose, with all of it passing so quickly. That had been a problem in tracking McCoy three years ago back to 1930, but since then, the researchers had learned how to refine their requests.

Kirk activated the tricorder and checked the time. Just before he had spoken with Korax, he had noted the stardate and hour, and now he calculated to what moment he needed to travel. He wanted to change the past, but only in one very specific way; he would risk nothing else. "I wish to visit the Starfleet vessel *Enterprise*," he said, "in orbit of this planet, twenty-three Federation minutes ago. Location: the bridge."

The images within the Guardian faded, the mists within which they hid evaporating into nothingness. A gust carried dust and dirt past Kirk, its low whimper accompanying his rising doubts about his chances of succeeding in his mission. But he remembered what he had seen, and knew that this would happen.

At last, the mists formed once more within the Guardian, and Kirk saw there the bridge of his ship, the half-formed bodies of the Klingon boarding party in the process of materializing. This had been the moment.

"The time and place are ready to receive you," declared the Guardian.

"Thank you," Kirk said. Once, he had let the love of his life die in order to save the Federation. Now, in a fitting bookend to that, he would give up his own.

He deactivated his tricorder and then drew each phaser in turn. He adjusted the setting of each, maximizing its destructive yield. Once enabled, every one of them began to emit a high-pitched whine. Carrying two in one hand and two in the other, Kirk counted out half the time it would take the weapons to overload. Then he took two steps and leaped through the time vortex, the fragile convergence of all possibilities.

He landed on the outer, upper deck of the *Enterprise*'s bridge, near the sciences station. Ahead and to his left, a dozen Klingons materialized, their disruptors drawn. They looked around frantically, and Kirk could tell that some of them, and then all of them, heard the overloading phasers. They turned toward him, obviously trying to evaluate the situation, trying to make sense of what their eyes and ears told them. Kirk raised his arms high, providing a target for them, deciding that death by disruptor would be preferable to the alternative.

That was when the phasers in his hands exploded.

* * *

McCoy sat in a chair in auxiliary control, staring at the viewscreen. He watched the Klingon ship lumbering away and didn't know what to think. He felt exhausted, and in pain, and he knew that he would remember this day for a long time, no matter how hard he tried to forget it.

Earlier, McCoy had treated his share of the wounded—including Nurses Chapel and Doran—who'd arrived in sickbay at the same time. He'd finished up by tending to Lieutenant Rahda, who during the *Enterprise*'s battle with the Klingons had been thrown against a bulkhead, fracturing her tibia. After that, the *Enterprise* had been shaken by a huge explosion, one he later discovered had wiped out the entire bridge. Though nobody seemed quite sure what had happened, it had apparently prevented a Klingon boarding party from taking control of the ship. It had also apparently killed the six crewmembers on the bridge at the time: Jim, Sulu, Uhura, Chekov, and Lieutenants Leslie and Haines.

At the same time, a second group of Klingons had transported from their vessel to the *Enterprise*'s engineering section. But the crew of the *Gr'oth* had been devastated during its battle with the *Enterprise* and the other Starfleet ships, and it had only so many men left capable of mounting an attack. Significantly outnumbered by the *Enterprise* crew, the boarding party in engineering had been defeated—though not before killing eleven Starfleet officers and wounding twenty-seven others.

Now, McCoy sat in auxiliary control, where Spock and the second-shift bridge crew worked to guide repair efforts. Though not laid out precisely like the ship's main bridge—it had a large console arcing across the center of the compartment, as well as a handful of peripheral stations—auxiliary control could be utilized as a centralized command center if necessary. When the *Enterprise*'s bridge had been destroyed, all command and control functions had automatically been routed here—though the engines and many of the ship's systems had gone down, and even now remained offline.

His gaze absently on the viewscreen, McCoy hadn't even noticed the *Gr'oth*'s movement until it had turned almost entirely toward the planet. "Spock," he said, and when the first officer—

now the acting captain—looked over, McCoy pointed to the viewer. "Where are they going?"

Spock looked at the screen and stood from where he sat near the central console. "Mister Hadley," he said, "is the tractor beam operative?

"No, sir," Hadley said from one of the secondary stations. Spock didn't ask—he obviously didn't have to ask—but McCoy knew that neither the transporter nor any of the weapons currently functioned. If Spock wanted to stop the Klingon ship from leaving, he would have to think of something else.

"Mister Immamura, has warp power been restored aboard the *Gr'oth*?" Spock sounded skeptical, and with good reason, McCoy thought. Sensors indicated only a handful of Klingons left alive aboard their ship, with virtually all systems failing, including life support.

"Negative, Mister Spock," Immamura said. "They're moving on thruster control alone."

Hard to get back to the Empire that way, McCoy thought.

"Lieutenant Palmer," Spock said, walking around the central console to stand between it and the main viewer. "Hail the *Gr'oth*."

"Yes, sir," the lieutenant replied.

Static appeared for a moment on the viewscreen, and then a Klingon bridge appeared. Dark and quiet, McCoy thought it looked more like a tomb than a starship command hub. He could see only one panel with illuminated controls on it, located before and to the right of a raised central dais containing what had to be the captain's chair. Several Klingons lay inert around the bridge, on the deck or collapsed atop their stations. Only two appeared alive and conscious, one in the command chair and one at the seemingly working console.

"Kirk," said the Klingon seated atop the dais. It sounded as though he would say more, but then didn't. He had trouble breathing, and his purplish complexion indicated cyanosis. McCoy did not doubt that, before long, he would lose consciousness and eventually asphyxiate.

"Korax," Spock said. "Almost all of your crew are dead, and your ship is crippled. Your transporters are still functioning. If you beam over to the *Enterprise,* our doctors will treat your crew and you will survive." The functioning transporters of the *Gr'oth*, McCoy knew, had been a source of concern for Spock once the Klingon boarding parties had been stopped. Concerned that the remainder of Korax's crew would escape their dying ship by beaming down to the planet, and that they would then discover the Guardian of Forever, Spock had sent two shuttle-craft down to the surface, carrying security teams to prevent Klingon access to the time vortex. But the few surviving crew of the *Gr'oth* had remained aboard their ship. Now, McCoy thought he knew why. With the battle cruiser moving, but with the ability to go virtually nowhere, they could have only one destination.

"Survive," Korax said, echoing Spock's last word. "To see the Federation . . . use their . . . new weapon . . . against the Empire?" It appeared increasingly difficult for the Klingon commander to breath, let alone talk. "No," he said. "You will not . . . succeed."

"Korax," Spock said, "the Federation has created no such weapon, nor do we seek the extermination of the Klingon Empire. We wish only peaceful coexistence."

Even facing death, Korax managed to sneer. "Peaceful . . . no." He hauled himself up out of his chair with obvious effort. "Will destroy . . . your weapon," he said. "And it will be . . . a good day to die." The Klingon bridge faded from the viewscreen, and in its place, the *Gr'oth* reappeared, now farther away from the *Enterprise*.

Spock turned and pressed a button on the central console. "Auxiliary control to engineering," he said.

"Scott here," replied the chief engineer. *"Go ahead, Mister Spock."*

"Mister Scott, how close are you to restoring engine power?" Spock asked.

"Engine power?" Scotty said. *"We're barely able to keep life support intact right now. It'll be at least twenty-four hours before we can move on impulse, and it might be days or even weeks before we can get the warp drive back online."*

McCoy stood up and walked over to Spock. The Vulcan looked haggard, and if the doctor didn't know better, he would have thought him troubled by grief. The crews of two Starfleet vessels, as well as those of three—and maybe four—Klingon ships, had been lost here today, and the *Enterprise* had suffered seventeen of its own casualties: eleven in engineering and six on the bridge. And among the dead had been Jim Kirk, Spock's best friend.

"You know what he's going to do," McCoy said quietly to Spock, referring to Korax.

"Yes," Spock said, "and we appear powerless to stop it."

"What's going to happen?" McCoy asked.

Spock looked at him. "I do not know, Doctor," he said. Then he peered across the compartment to one of the secondary stations. "Lieutenant Palmer," he said, "raise the shuttlecraft."

"Yes, sir," she said.

When the pilots of the two shuttles appeared onscreen, Spock warned them away from the Guardian.

Lieutenant Jimmy Clayton held the shuttlecraft *Kepler* at high altitude, as ordered. He checked the sensor readout on the main panel, verifying the position of the second shuttle, the *Herschel,* which he saw currently kept station at a safe distance. Then he looked to the small viewscreen located in the bulkhead to his left. Behind him, the security contingent Commander Spock had ordered down to the planet surface had already crowded around so that they could see.

The display had been split into two images. On the left, at maximum magnification, sat the peculiar alien artifact, looking to Clayton more than anything else like a large, misshapen doughnut standing on end. He had no doubt of its interest to xeno-archeologists—it even intrigued him—but that seemed right now like a moot point. The right side of the display showed the object's imminent demise.

As the *Gr'oth* streaked through the atmosphere of the planet, its outer hull began to heat, but the duranium-tritanium composite easily withstood the rigors of reentry. As it plunged toward the planet, it became abundantly clear that, as Commander Spock had suspected, it targeted the artifact. The officers aboard the *Kepler* watched in silence.

The body of the Klingon battle cruiser blocked a direct view of the impact, but as best Clayton could tell, the D7 warship slammed into the artifact dead on. The display aboard the shuttle dimmed automatically as the resulting fireball grew more luminescent than the planet's star at midday. Temperatures at the point of impact soared to millions of degrees. Within ten seconds, the hot, luminous cloud had widened to two kilometers, mushrooming into the air at a hundred meters per second.

With the Klingon ship obliterated and the impact confirmed, Clayton reached forward to his flight-control panel. Per Commander Spock's instructions, he headed the shuttle back to the *Enterprise.* On his sensor readout, he saw that the *Herschel* had also set course for the ship.

As he piloted the *Kepler,* Clayton continued to scan the planet surface. Where once there had stretched a flat, barren plain, a crater two hundred meters deep and a kilometer in diameter had now been opened. Nowhere in all of that violent destruction was there any sign whatsoever of either the Klingon battle cruiser or the alien artifact. Both had been vaporized instantly.

"DeSalle to sickbay."

What now? McCoy thought as he finished studying the readings on the diagnostic panel above his patient. After the Klingon ship had destroyed the Guardian, he'd left auxiliary control, worn out and thinking that he should try to get some sleep. Instead, he'd returned to sickbay to check on the wounded.

Now, he made a notation on the data slate he carried, gave Lieutenant Rahda the best smile he could muster, and then crossed the compartment to the intercom. "Sickbay, McCoy here," he said. "What can I do for you, DeSalle?"

"Doc," DeSalle said, the excitement in his voice apparent, *"we need a medical team on deck three immediately. We've found the bridge crew."*

"What?" McCoy said. *The bridge crew? Did he mean Jim and the others?* "Where?"

"They're in a turbolift," DeSalle said. *"They were leaving the bridge when the explosion hit. The concussion damaged the car they were in and wedged it sideways in the tube. They've been unconscious and trapped between decks."*

"Are they all right?" McCoy asked breathlessly, almost not wanting to pose the question for fear of what news the answer might bring.

"They're a little banged up, and the captain and Lieutenant

Sulu are unconscious," DeSalle said, *"but all six of them are alive."*

All six! McCoy thought. "Where are you exactly, DeSalle?" he asked.

"Deck three, central turboshaft," DeSalle said. *"We've turned off the gravity in the tube and we're floating them out right now."*

"All right," McCoy said. "I'll be right there." He closed the intercom channel, then looked over at Lieutenant Rahda, who had a wide smile on her face. So did the other two patients in the compartment. As quickly as he could, McCoy retrieved a tricorder and a medical pouch, then left sickbay.

As fatigued as he was, he found the energy to run.

TWENTY-FIVE

1932

As Phil drove through the November morning chill, he waved to the folks he saw walking along the commons. As usual, half a dozen men climbed onto the rear platform of his truck as he passed them. When he reached Main Street, he saw Len McCoy just heading down from Mrs. Hartwell's. Phil called out to him, and his friend hurried forward and jumped aboard as well.

Len had been living at the boarding house for a few months at this point, though Phil often joshed with him that he and Lynn saw him more often now than ever. In September and October, he'd spent mornings out at their farm picking cotton before trundling off in the afternoons to his job at the Seed and Feed. He'd also started attending church with them from time to time. Though he didn't participate much, he did sit and listen respectfully, and Phil knew that it made Lynn happy to have him there; he figured Len knew that too.

As Phil followed Mill Road along the curve that dipped down to the left, he thought about how he and Lynn had become such good friends with Len in so short a time. Honestly, Phil felt closer to Len than to his own brother—and probably trusted him more too. They spent a great deal of time together, with Len often coming out to the house after work, spending many an evening with them in the parlor spinning stories. Though the conversations frequently turned to Phil or Lynn or the folks in town, they'd also learned a few details about Len. He'd once spoken briefly about his childhood in Atlanta, and he'd revealed that he had no family left—other than his "cousin" Phil, of course. They'd all laughed about that. And late one night, when Lynn had been missing her parents fiercely, Len had shared with them that his ma had passed on while bringing him into the world, and that his pa had gone too after a long and painful illness.

The truck topped the last hill along Mill Road, and Phil pulled off and parked beside the other vehicles already there. After grabbing his lunch pail from the seat, he climbed out of the truck. Len stood near the back, waiting for him, while the other men had already started toward the mill. "Morning, Phil," Len said. His southern drawl had thickened since he'd first arrived in Hayden.

"Morning, Len," Phil said, walking over. "Still begging Mister Duncan for a job, huh?" After months of visiting the superintendent in the hopes of securing work, Len still came out to the mill at least a couple of mornings a week. So far, Mr. Duncan hadn't been able to hire him on—though with all the cotton coming in recently, the mill had taken on a few new men, but those jobs had gone to folks who'd lived in town a far sight longer than Len had. Len understood, though, and he came out anyway.

"Hey, one of these days Mister Duncan's going to get tired of seeing me in his office and he's going to give me some work," Len said.

"Sure, sure," Phil said as they began walking down to the mill. "I know I'd give you a job if it meant not having to see your face first thing in the morning."

"My good man," Len said, "you don't *deserve* to see my face every morning."

"Dang right," Phil said, and he gave Len a playful shove in the shoulder. "You coming out to the house tonight?"

"That depends," Len said. "My pride has been wounded, and there might be just one thing that can help it recover."

"It wouldn't be peach cobbler, now, would it?" Phil asked. "Probably not. Guess I'll just have to eat the pie Lynn's making today by myself."

"If you insist on my presence," Len said, "I suppose I'll just have to be there."

"That's what I thought," Phil said with a laugh.

When they reached the bottom of the hill, Len headed off to Mr. Duncan's office and Phil went inside the mill. Even though the whistle hadn't blown yet, Phil heard some of the machines had already been started up in the back. He crossed the width of the large, open floor, past a row of carders, and then along the back wall toward his own machine. Near the corner, he saw that a number of men had gathered round, and as Phil approached them, Danny Johnson stumbled forward and out of the group. Some of the men laughed, but two or three looked concerned. Danny threw his hands high against the wall and bent forward.

"Danny, y'all okay?" Phil asked as he reached him. Danny shook his head, then slapped at his chest. "What's the matter, you hurt yourself or something?" Phil asked as the other men walked over. Danny still said nothing, but now he reached up and motioned to his throat. His eyes had grown wide. "You choking?" Phil asked. Danny nodded frantically, and Phil quickly reached up and started pounding him on the back, attempting to help him clear whatever had gotten lodged in his windpipe.

It didn't work.

"I'm going to get Doc Lyles," he told Danny. "Somebody keep helping him," he added, addressing the other men and indicating his patting motion on Danny's back. As Rufus Dooley stepped up to take over, Phil raced back across the mill floor, then ran outside and over to Mr. Duncan's office. There, he reached up beside the door and pulled on the whistle, once, twice, three times, the town's signal for a medical emergency at the mill. If Doc Lyles was home—and where else would he be so early in the morning? Phil thought—he would reach the mill in just a few minutes.

The door of the office swung all the way open and Mr. Duncan stepped outside. "What's wrong?" he asked, obviously concerned.

Phil pulled on the whistle three more times, then said, "Danny Johnson's choking."

"Where is he?" Len asked appearing in the doorway.

"Inside," Phil said, pointing toward the mill's main entrance. "In the back."

"Show me," Len said. His voice carried an authority that Phil had never before heard from his friend, and he responded to it. He sprinted back toward the mill entrance and through the wide opening. He felt Len's presence directly behind him the entire way.

On the far side of the mill floor, the men had circled around, some of them talking excitedly. Phil could not see Danny past them. "Where is he?" Len yelled over the combined din of the men and the machines, but he didn't wait for an answer. He hurried by Phil and pushed his way into the group. "Let me through," he said, and the men parted to allow him past.

Phil saw Danny then. He'd collapsed to his hands and knees, and now rocked back and forth. Buddy McPhilamy crouched beside him, slapping him on the back, just as Phil had done. Len reached in and took hold of Buddy's arm. "Stop it," he said, then dropped to his knees next to Danny. "Are you choking?" he asked, but Danny did not respond. "Can you talk?" Still nothing. Looking around at the men, Len said, "Was he eating something?" Buddy said that he had been.

Len moved behind Danny and put his arms around his midsection, just below his ribs. "What're you doing?" Buddy asked. Len didn't reply, but instead pulled his hands in quickly, jerking Danny's torso backward. It looked peculiar, but Phil thought he understood Len's intention; his actions resembled somebody squeezing a hot-water bottle in order to pop out the stopper.

But nothing popped out of Danny's throat.

Len tried again a second time, a third, a fourth. Finally, he stood up and reached down beneath Danny's arms. "Here, help me get him up," he said to no one in particular. Buddy stepped forward on one side and Rufus on the other. They both reached down, took hold of Danny by an arm, and hauled him to his feet.

Again, Len reached around his middle and pulled his hands into Danny's stomach. He did it over and over, and still nothing happened.

And then Danny's body went limp. Buddy and Rufus helped lower him to the floor. "On his back," Len said, and the men did so without question. Phil saw that Danny's eyes had closed. Len leaned over his now-motionless form and put the heel of his hand up by the bottom of Danny's ribs, then placed his other hand over it and pressed down hard half a dozen times.

When nothing happened, Len leaned in over Danny's head, opened his mouth, and reached inside with two fingers. Phil heard one of the men ask what he was doing, but nobody answered. When Len pulled his fingers free, Phil saw that Danny's lips had begun to turn blue.

Len felt along Danny's neck, examining him almost like a doctor would. After a few seconds, he peered up at the men crowding around him. "I need a knife," he said. "A sharp knife." Phil felt his mouth drop open, unsure just what Len planned to do. Did he want to slice open Danny's throat and pull out whatever blocked his airway?

Nobody said anything, and nobody moved. "This man is choking to death," Len cried out, his voice loud and serious. "I can save him but I need your help."

Some of the men stirred then, as though waking up. They reached into their pockets, and then somebody—Phil couldn't see who—held out a red pocketknife. Len took it and unfolded the blade, then looked back up. "All right, listen," he said. "I need these things: matches, some clean rags, and a tube of some sort." He pronounced his words crisply, Phil noticed, his accent diminished. "I need something at least eighty millim—at least this long." Len held his thumb and forefinger three or four inches apart. "About this round," he said, curling his forefinger into a circle maybe half an inch through the center. "And alcohol," he added. "Does anybody have any alcohol around here?"

"I do," Mr. Duncan said. Phil hadn't even realized that he'd come inside the mill. As somebody handed a book of matches to Len, the burly superintendent said, "I'll get it," and he turned to go.

"Let me, I'm faster," Billy Fuster spoke up, and Phil knew

that the lean young man must be right about that. "Where is it?"

"The bottom drawer of my desk," Mr. Duncan said. Billy took off running at once, but Phil saw that nobody else had moved from around Danny.

"I need those other things now!" Len yelled, his tone commanding. Finally, several of the men turned and rushed away.

Len pulled a match from the book he'd been given and struck it. Mr. Duncan started to say something—as he and his ever-present unlighted cigar could attest, even a single small flame could endanger a cotton mill—but then he held his tongue. Len placed the match under the blade of the pocketknife, drawing it slowly back and forth along one side, then the other. When he finished and extinguished the flame with a wave of his hand, Mr. Duncan stepped forward and reached out to take it from him.

Certain now that Len meant to cut into Danny, Phil walked over and leaned down beside him. "Are you sure you know what you're doing?" he asked.

"Danny's choking," Len said. "If he doesn't get air soon, it's going to cripple his brain and then he's going to die." He turned his head and looked Phil directly in the eyes. "Yes, I know what I'm doing." Phil nodded, realizing that he had no other choice but to trust his friend.

Suddenly, rapid footsteps beat through the mill, signaling the return of Billy Fuster. In one hand, he carried an almost-full bottle of whiskey, and in the other a clutch of white rags. He pulled the stopper out of the bottle and handed it to Len, who poured some of the amber liquid onto Danny's neck and then onto his own hands. Then he set the whiskey down on the floor and waited.

A moment later, Jake Dinsmore ran up with a length of pipe in his hands, far thicker and longer than what Len had requested. He waved it away. Ray Peavey rushed over and held out something much closer in size. Made of metal, it looked like something Ray might have pulled out of one of the carding machines. Len took it and said, "All right, this will have to do." But then Al Ward ran up and offered what he'd found. About six inches long and slightly curved, the flexible black tube appeared to be made out of rubber. Len examined it, then handed it up to Buddy and told him to pour some of the whiskey over it, inside and out.

As Len set down the tube Ray had brought and then stripped off his jacket, he gazed over at Phil. "I'm going to need some help," he said. "Can you do it?"

"What?" Phil said. "I . . ." He didn't know what to say.

"Phil, I need your help," Len insisted. "*Danny* needs your help."

"All right," Phil sputtered. "What do you want me to do?"

"Get down here," Len said, pointing to the floor on the other side of Danny. While Len rolled up his jacket and placed it beneath Danny's shoulder blades, Phil went over and dropped to his knees. "Take the rags," he told Phil. "Cover a few of them in alcohol." Buddy handed over the whiskey and Phil picked up some of the cloths to do as Len had asked. "I'm going to make an incision in his neck," Len continued, tilting Danny's head back, exposing his throat. "I'm going to provide him an airway so that he can breathe. What I need you to do is to gently wipe away the blood when I ask you to."

Blood! Phil thought, but he forced himself to keep listening.

"Do it quickly and gently," Len said.

"All right," Phil said, and then he watched in disbelief as Len leaned forward and pressed the pocketknife to the lower part of Danny's neck. The blade penetrated the flesh and blood spilled from the wound and down onto the floor.

"Now," Len said, pulling his hands away. Phil reached in and gingerly dabbed at the blood. "A little faster," Len said, and he guided Phil's hand, obviously demonstrating how he wanted him to do it. Then Len pushed his hand away and brought the knife once more to Danny's throat.

In all, only a minute or two passed before Len asked Buddy for the tube, but it felt like hours to Phil. Len pushed the tube into the hole in Danny's flesh with what seemed like a great deal of skill at something Phil had never even imagined. Len then collected one of the clean rags and used it to clean up around the area where the tube extended out from Danny's neck.

"He's breathing," Mr. Duncan roared, just as Phil saw Danny's chest rise. Len did not react, other than to wipe his hands with the rag. Around him, the men began congratulating him, some of them patting him on the back.

"It's not over," Len told them earnestly. "We need to get Danny to a hospital."

"What—?" a voice said in obvious dismay. Still on his knees, Phil turned to see that Dr. Lyles had arrived. "What's happening here?" the old man asked, eying Danny and no doubt seeing the bloody rag in Len's hands.

"Doctor," Len said, rising to his feet. He walked around Danny and over to Lyles, where he took him by the elbow and guided him away from everybody. Phil watched them as he stood up himself. The two men spoke for a minute or so, and then Lyles looked toward Danny.

"Somebody get the stretcher from the back of my car," he called as he paced over. "We need to get Danny to my office right now." Lyles bent down to examine Danny's neck.

"Is he going to be all right, Doc?" Buddy asked.

"Yeah, I think he is," Lyles said. "But we really need to move him."

The stretcher arrived a few moments later, and the doctor directed the men on how to load Danny onto it. Once they had, they carefully carried him outside. Some of the men followed, while some, including Len and Phil, stayed in the mill.

As Buddy and Jake and the others began asking Len questions—How could he cut somebody open like that? How did he know how to save Danny?—Phil hung back. He watched his friend still wiping his bloody hands with a rag, calmer than anybody else around him, and knew that he would never look at him the same way again.

McCoy left the Seed and Feed just after sunset. The procession of the seasons had grown markedly more noticeable of late, the daylight hours dwindling as autumn advanced toward the winter solstice. As dawn had this morning, the gloaming possessed a briskness, a brittle tightening of the air that foreshadowed the darker, cooler days ahead.

Yet for McCoy, each tomorrow now promised a brightness long missing from his future. As he stepped down from the plank sidewalk to cross Carolina Street, he felt energized. This morning, he'd plied his trade as a doctor, something he hadn't done—hadn't *really* done—in quite some time. He'd provided first aid back at the 21st Street Mission, but had carried out nothing remotely like the procedure he'd performed on Danny Johnson.

McCoy reached the edge of the commons and started across it, toward the intersection of Mill Road and Main Street. The temperature had obviously fallen below the dew point, the grass wet with evening moisture. Finished now with work, he intended to clean himself up at the boarding house, eat the supper Mrs. Hartwell cooked, and then walk out to Lynn and Phil's. He looked forward, as always, to spending time with the couple, although earlier he'd considered canceling his plans to see them. Shortly after Danny Johnson had been toted out of the mill, McCoy had managed to extract himself from the scene without answering the many questions put to him. He'd known, though, that Lynn and Phil would be just as inquisitive when next he saw them, and he had no idea how he would respond.

But he'd found out soon enough. When people in town had heard the emergency whistle this morning, many of them had hurried out to the mill. Word had evidently spread quickly from there. Everybody who'd stopped by the Seed and Feed today had spoken about Danny Johnson choking, and about how McCoy had saved his life; some townspeople had even come by, not to purchase anything, but specifically to talk with McCoy about what had happened. Many had asked the same questions as the men at the mill had: How had he known how to save Danny, and when and where had he learned to actually do it?

Mabel Duncan, the wife of the mill superintendent, had already been at the Seed and Feed, talking with Gregg Anderson, when McCoy had shown up for work. Unlike earlier, immediately after the incident, he'd been unable—or at least unwilling—to evade the direct questions they'd put to him. He wanted neither to walk out of his job nor to be rude to Mrs. Duncan and Mr. Anderson. He'd thought to tell them that inserting a tube into Danny's windpipe to allow him to breathe had simply seemed like the smart thing to do, but such an assertion—and the implication that he had never before done such a thing—would have strained credulity. Not only had he performed a surgical procedure, not only had he saved a man's life, but he'd taken charge of an emergency situation in order to do so. For so long now, McCoy had sought to avoid revealing "too much" about himself so that he would not alter history, but he knew that ship had gone to warp. Convinced that he'd already irrevocably changed the past, he'd left New York to make a new start and a new life for himself. He'd done that here in Hayden, but now the time had come for him to take the next step. And so he'd told Mrs. Duncan and Mr. Anderson the truth about himself: that he was a physician, though he hadn't practiced recently.

Thinking about all that had happened today, McCoy reached the northeast corner of the commons and started across Mill Road. He'd only gotten to the center of the street when he heard a voice call to him from behind. "Mister McCoy." He turned to see the tall but stooped figure of Dr. Lyles walking in his direction down Main Street. McCoy had been anticipating this conversation. He returned to the corner and waited for the doctor to reach him. "Thank you for stopping," Lyles said.

McCoy nodded. "How's Danny?" he asked. During the course of the afternoon, several of the people who'd visited the Seed and Feed had heard that the doctor hadn't needed to send Danny to the hospital—a positive development, considering that would have necessitated a two-hour drive into Greenville, over mostly unpaved roads. Instead, people had told him, Lyles had treated Danny himself, a fact he now confirmed.

"Resting comfortably," the doctor said. "I cleaned up his stoma and re-intubated him. This afternoon, I gave him a muscle relaxant, sedated him, and was able to get the offending bit of food out of his trachea. 'Twas wedged in there pretty good."

"Did you remove the tube after you cleared his airway?" McCoy asked.

"Not yet," Lyles said. "It's been a long day for Danny. I decided to do it in the morning."

"Will somebody watch him tonight?" McCoy asked.

"Doreen's in with him now," Lyles said, mentioning Danny's wife. "And Lorinda was there most of the day." Lorinda was Danny's mother.

"Well, that's fine," McCoy said. "I'm glad everything worked out."

"Thanks to you," Lyles said.

"I was happy to help," McCoy said.

Lyles regarded him silently for a few seconds and then motioned toward a bench in the commons, half a dozen meters away. "Would you care to sit for a minute?" he said. "These old bones get tired of standing after a while."

"Of course," McCoy said, and the two walked over to the bench. When they arrived there, McCoy saw that dew had condensed on the green slats. "Just a second," he told Lyles, then crouched and wiped the arm of his jacket across the seat and back a couple of times, drying it. Lyles thanked him and, taking the arm of the bench, carefully lowered himself onto it. McCoy sat down as well, still waiting for the doctor to broach the subject of his medical training. He did so at once.

"Mister McCoy," he said, "I've been hearing tell from folks today that you say you're a doctor."

"I am a doctor," McCoy said, "and I don't think you needed to hear that from people to know it's true." When Lyles had arrived at the mill this morning, McCoy had taken him aside and explained Danny's choking, and that he'd had no choice but to perform an emergency tracheotomy. He'd tried to recall exactly when Chevalier Jackson had codified the modern surgical method—historical knowledge and use of tracheotomy techniques went back millennia on Earth—but unable to do so, he'd decided to risk speaking in medical detail about the procedure. Since Lyles would subsequently treat Danny, it had been most important that he knew precisely what McCoy had done.

"You certainly have a great deal of medical knowledge," Lyles said. "Where did you study?"

Nobody else in town had asked McCoy this, but he'd expected the question from the doctor. Though McCoy had chosen to reveal to people that he was a physician, there remained the practical problem of proving his credentials. While the University of Mississippi had been founded in 1848, its School of Medicine hadn't existed for at least a century after that. Regardless, McCoy hadn't earned his degrees—*wouldn't* earn his degrees— for another three hundred years. Though he did not wish to lie, he wanted to provide an answer not as readily verifiable as a claim of a medical education at Ole Miss would be. "I studied abroad," he told Lyles.

"I see," the doctor said, sounding dubious. "Have you practiced in the States?"

"No," McCoy said. "No, I haven't."

"Did you serve in the war?" Lyles asked. It seemed to McCoy very much like the doctor wanted to find some source of information that he could check.

"No," McCoy said, opting not to elaborate. Lyles shifted on the bench and then again looked at him for a moment without saying anything. Finally, the doctor spoke his mind.

"Should I believe you, Mister McCoy?" he said.

McCoy fought the impulse to identify himself as *Doctor* McCoy. Instead, he appealed to Lyles as honestly as he could. "Should you believe me?" he repeated. "I can see why you wouldn't, because I've lied to you. Well, I haven't lied to you directly, exactly, but I'm sure you've heard folks saying that I'm Phil Dickinson's cousin."

"Yes," Lyles said. "I've heard that."

"You've heard it," McCoy said, "and you know it's not true."

At that, the doctor actually smiled. "It didn't seem likely," he said. "You told me you hopped a freight to get to Atlanta and then jumped off when two vagabonds attacked you. Seemed like an awful coincidence that you would've jumped off right in your cousin's backyard."

"I'm sure stranger things have happened," McCoy said, "but no, I'm not Phil's cousin. I also didn't ask him to tell people that I was. It was just something he started saying when he introduced me around."

Lyles seemed to consider that. "Maybe Phil did that 'cause folks don't cotton to strangers round these parts," Lyles said with what might have been an arch tone.

"Really?" McCoy said. "I hadn't noticed."

Lyles blustered in a way that might have been amused acceptance or righteous indignation. McCoy heard the mechanical chug of a vehicle, and he peered across the length of the commons to see Woodward Palmer driving along Church Street. "Mister McCoy," Lyles said, and then he corrected himself. "*Doctor* McCoy, what are you doing here?"

"I'm just trying to live my life, Doctor Lyles," McCoy said honestly, and then, not quite as honestly, added, "The crash affected a lot of folks." He hoped to insinuate that the current worldwide economic decline had been responsible for his itinerancy, which had ultimately brought him to Hayden.

"That it did," Lyles said.

"Now I just want to live my life," McCoy said again. "Just like anybody else. I'm not on the run and I haven't done anything wrong. And if you want me to leave, Doctor, well, I don't think I'm going to, but if you push me, I just might. I don't want any trouble. I only want to live a quiet, peaceful life, nothing more."

"It wasn't quiet this morning," Lyles observed.

"No, it sure wasn't," McCoy agreed. "But it does bring a kind of peace when you can help somebody like that."

"Yup, I know that it does," Lyles said. He took a deep, raspy breath, then lifted his hands and dropped them flat on his thighs, as though deciding something. "I don't want you to leave Hayden, Doctor McCoy. I don't dislike you, but I have been suspicious of you. But you also paid me the money I charged you for stitching up your leg. And when you paid that first two dollars, I was rude to you."

"You were just watching out for the folks in town," McCoy said, wanting to put his differences with Lyles to rest.

"Well, I'm sorry anyway," the doctor said. "Like you told me that day, that ain't the way of southern hospitality."

McCoy shrugged. "I accept your apology. Thanks."

"So I've been thinking about you being a doctor and all," Lyles said. "And I was thinking maybe you'd want to help me in my practice."

McCoy's head jerked back in surprise, almost as though he'd been struck. "Pardon me?" he said, thinking that he must have heard Lyles incorrectly.

"I'm getting older, Doctor McCoy, and most of what I do these days isn't all that difficult," Lyles said. "Why, part of the time I end up treating folks' animals instead of folks themselves. But I'm moving slower, and even the simple things are getting harder. I could use an assistant."

"I'm . . . shocked," McCoy said. "And honored."

"Don't be too honored, son," Lyles said, pulling himself up to his feet. "I'm just talking about you *assisting,* and I'd pay you as an assistant. I'd still do the doctoring. We could start out a couple days a week, see how it goes."

McCoy stood up and faced the doctor. "I'd very much like that," he said. "Thank you, Doctor."

"You're welcome, Doctor," Lyles said. "Why don't you stop by my office after church on Sunday and we'll work out the details."

"I will," McCoy said, and he held out his hand. Lyles took it and then pulled him in close. Even with his stoop, he towered over McCoy.

"I saw the work you did on Danny Johnson," Lyles said. "With no medical equipment, and no time to waste, you saved his life. More than that, you kept his brain from getting damaged. That's good work." He let go of McCoy's hand and headed toward Main Street.

"Thank you," McCoy called after him, still stunned by the turn of events. He stood there and watched Lyles make his way slowly back down Main, then diagonally across Carolina Street and into his house. McCoy was still there five minutes later when Sheriff Gladdy came out of his office a little farther down on Mill Road. The slam of the door closing broke McCoy from his reverie. As the sheriff began lighting the gas lamps along the street, McCoy hurried across Mill Road and down Main Street, headed for the boarding house. Now he couldn't wait to see Lynn and Phil, to tell them what had just happened.

Since he'd arrived in the past, this had been the best day of all.

TWENTY-SIX

2270

Kirk stood in the far corner of the nearly empty observation lounge, peering out through the deck-to-overhead viewing ports at the wounded husk of the *Enterprise*. The starship hung lifelessly in space, surrounded by Starbase 10's repair dock, a brace of horseshoe-shaped platforms set at right angles to each other. The flurry of movement and activity about the ship did nothing to ameliorate her moribund appearance, but rather served to re-inforce it. The power tethers stretching at various points from the platforms and into the *Enterprise,* the work bees gliding about, the space-suited engineers teeming around the hull, all served to highlight the essential inertness of the once-vital vessel. Kirk could not bear to look at her, and yet he could not look away.

Gazing at the ship from alongside and above the circular primary hull, he had a select view of what remained of the bridge. The place from which he had commanded the *Enterprise* for the past five years had been reduced to rubble. Only shards of the white dome that had covered the control center now remained, blackened by the heat of the explosion that had destroyed it. The curved bulkheads that had housed the various crew stations had been blown outward, the hull splitting open like the scarred, mis-shapen petals of some great metal flower.

Kirk finally turned away, troubled by the scene. He wondered why the admiral had wanted to meet with him here. Had it simply been a matter of convenience or preference, or had he intended to convey some unspoken message? In Kirk's experience, Heihachiro Nogura took few actions, made few decisions, without due consideration of the smallest details.

Folding his arms across his chest, Kirk looked about the lounge. Describing a long, narrow arc, the compartment traced a section of Starbase 10's biconic hull, at the midpoint between its highest and lowest decks. Small circular tables paraded along the outer perimeter and food synthesizers lined the inner bulkhead. Indirect lighting provided faint illumination, allowing a clear view through the ports. At the moment, only a handful of tables were occupied, all of them by personnel in Starfleet uniforms. Besides the *Enterprise,* several smaller vessels currently visited the station, including the transport *Tucker,* which had just ferried Admiral Nogura here.

As Kirk waited at the far end of the lounge, away from the others present, he couldn't keep himself from staring back out at the *Enterprise.* At numerous places on both the primary and secondary hulls, he could see where the Klingon torpedoes mined across their course had torn through the ship. In his time as the *Enterprise*'s captain, he'd never seen her appear so . . . defeated. More than anything else, the demolished bridge laid bare her ruin.

Did I do that? he asked himself. If he had, he couldn't remember it. The concussion of the blast that had wrecked the bridge had not only sent the turbolift askew and lodged it in its shaft, but had knocked out each of the six members of the bridge crew it had carried. When they'd recovered—Kirk had taken three days to come out of a coma—none of them had been able to recall the minutes leading up to their loss of consciousness, a common consequence of such an injury, according to McCoy.

Regardless of whether or not Kirk had somehow sabotaged the bridge in order to prevent a Klingon boarding party from taking control of the ship, he bore the responsibility of what had happened to the *Enterprise*—and to her crew. *Eleven dead,* he thought grimly. While he had lain insensible in the turbolift, his crew had beaten back a contingent of Klingons down in engineering, but at the cost of nearly a dozen of their own lives.

In the days Kirk had been comatose in sickbay, Scotty and his team had mended the ship enough to get her back to base for more extensive repairs. In the three weeks since they'd arrived at Starbase 10, Kirk had spent sixteen days in recovery and only the last five on his feet, but he'd used all of that time to contact the families of each of the crewmembers who'd been lost. In addition to speaking with them directly over boosted subspace signals, he'd written letters to them, detailing the service records of their loved ones and adding whatever positive personal observations he could. He found it terribly difficult, but felt the obligation deeply.

So deeply that you've become inured to the deaths, he rebuked himself. That wasn't true, of course; the loss of a crewmember still pained Kirk to his core, and he always did his best to balance the ship's mission to explore the unknown and sometimes dangerous corners of space against the safety of the people in his charge. And yet . . . it had gotten easier over time, hadn't it? The last death hadn't been as hard to deal with as the first, had it? Hadn't hurt him quite as much? At the beginning of the five-year mission, when one of the crew had gone down, he'd been unable to sleep soundly for days afterward. By mission's end, though, he'd trained himself to slumber through the night no matter the circumstances. Right now, he loathed himself for that.

In the viewing port, Kirk spied the reflection of the admiral as he approached from the doorway. Just arrived from Earth, Nogura had set up this meeting with the captain only a few minutes ago. Kirk hadn't expected to see the admiral here, but then Starfleet Command wasn't in the habit of informing him of their members' itineraries.

"Captain," Nogura said in his deep, sonorous voice.

"Admiral," Kirk said, turning to face him. Shorter than the captain, Nogura had a sallow complexion and short black hair. He wore his gold uniform shirt, the starburst insignia of Starfleet Command on its left breast. With a lean, toned frame and a relentlessly serious manner, Nogura commanded every room he entered. Even now, Kirk noticed many of the officers in the lounge stiffen in their chairs as they saw the admiral.

Nogura looked past Kirk, in the direction of the *Enterprise,* but he made no comment. Motioning toward a table, he said, "Shall we sit?" In response, Kirk moved around the table and sat down, and the admiral took a seat across from him. "Captain, I'm here at Starbase Ten as part of a tour I'm making of Starfleet facilities and vessels," Nogura said, characteristically eschewing pleasantries. "With you here as well, this affords me an opportunity to discuss your next posting with you."

Kirk had considered that this might be the reason Nogura wanted to meet with him, though he'd also thought the admiral might want a firsthand account of the Klingon attack on the Einstein research station. But Commodore Stocker, the base commander, had already debriefed the captain regarding those events, from the moment Lieutenant Uhura had received the distress signal to Korax's destruction—or had it been murder?—of the Guardian of Forever. Kirk had been unconscious in the turbolift during that last desperate act by the Klingon commander, but Spock and other officers had also been interviewed about it. Nogura would have read all of the reports about the incident, and since high-level talks had begun in the past few days between the

Klingon High Council and the Federation Council, there seemed little need for the him to discuss the incident.

Kirk hesitated, unsure if he should reveal to the admiral the thought that had occurred to him again and again since arriving at Starbase 10. He glanced out at his broken ship and couldn't help envisioning her whole once more. To Nogura, he admitted, "I had hoped to take the *Enterprise* back out. I know she's beaten up pretty badly right now, but she's still a fine ship."

"*Enterprise* will go back out," the admiral said, and Kirk felt a momentary rush of adrenaline. "But not for some time. Reports indicate that it will take upwards of six months to make it spaceworthy again. It's a miracle your chief engineer managed to get the ship back to base."

"He'll be pleased to hear you think so," Kirk said, smiling to cover his disappointment and trying to project a nonchalance that he did not feel. Knowing that he should not pursue the issue, he did anyway. "In six months, though, when the *Enterprise* does go back out—"

"It will likely be longer than that," Nogura said. "Command is strongly considering a redesign of the Constitution class. Once *Enterprise* has been repaired sufficiently to allow it to make the trip back to Earth, chances are that it will undergo a complete refit." The admiral paused, as though intentionally separating out the next words he would say. "But you'll have a say in that."

"I'll have—?" Kirk asked, confusion and hope mixing as he puzzled out the meaning of Nogura's assertion. "Then I'm being left in command of the *Enterprise*?"

"No," Nogura said. "You're being promoted to admiral and reassigned to Starfleet Operations as its chief."

Kirk's eyebrows rose in surprise and his mouth dropped open. During the past few months, he'd heard the occasional rumor that he might be up for promotion, but he'd always assumed that if he did receive a bump up in rank, it would simply be to commodore. He'd also known that Starfleet Command might post him off the *Enterprise,* but he'd figured that it would be to another vessel or to a starbase. "I'm . . ." he started, knowing that he should say something, but not entirely sure how he felt.

"It's an honor," Nogura guided him.

"I'm honored, yes, of course," Kirk said, and he meant it. Responsible for the supervision, monitoring, and coordination of all fleet and base activities, Operations functioned as the backbone of Starfleet. Further, its chief played a significant role in determining the distribution of resources and the manner in which those resources were utilized. As a practical matter, and of considerable interest to Kirk, the Operations chief in large part established the direction and philosophy of Starfleet's exploratory endeavors. "What about Admiral Hahn?" Kirk asked.

"She's stepping down," Nogura said. A former starship captain herself, Hahn had served as CSO for more than two decades now. Under her leadership, Starfleet had conducted longer and longer single-ship missions of general exploration, including the previous *Enterprise* assignments under Captains April and Pike, and culminating—at least to this point—in the five-year voyage under Kirk. He had always held Admiral Hahn in high regard.

"That'll be a great loss for Starfleet," Kirk said, even as his mind began to conjure up the possibilities of what he might do in his new position.

"It will be," Nogura agreed, "but Command is confident that we're replacing her with somebody of at least equal capabilities."

"Thank you, Admiral," Kirk said, bowing his head slightly at the rare compliment from Nogura. "I look forward to this opportunity." Already he saw ideas that he could champion: more and longer extended voyages, support for colonization in the outer reaches, perhaps even generation ships to cross the galaxy. The notion of being able to shape the imperatives of Starfleet—and really of the Federation itself—strongly appealed to him.

Nogura pushed back his chair and stood up. "As I mentioned, I'm making a tour of Starfleet facilities and vessels," he said. "You should accompany me. It'll provide good input and a richer viewpoint for you in your new position."

"I agree," Kirk said. "When—"

"Tomorrow at oh-six-hundred," Nogura said crisply. "We'll be traveling on the transport *Tucker*. I'll have the ship's quartermaster deliver a new uniform to your cabin here on the base." He started toward the door, but Kirk called after him. Everything had just happened so quickly, he had difficulty processing it all. In time, he would learn and acclimate to his new role, he had no doubt, but he still felt the responsibilities of the *Enterprise*'s captain. When Nogura turned back around, Kirk paced over to him.

"My crew, Admiral," he said. He knew that reassignments of the lower echelon had already begun, but the senior staff had not yet been reposted. Kirk had hoped that might've indicated a willingness on Starfleet Command's part to keep the officers together, either on the *Enterprise* once she'd been repaired, or on another vessel. At the same time, he'd recognized that some of the command crew would want to move on in their careers, and they'd certainly earned that chance. He told Nogura that. "Mister Spock, in particular," Kirk said, "merits a command of his own."

"Your senior officers received their reassignments today," Nogura said, "and Commander Spock was offered a captaincy."

Kirk felt both pride and elation for his friend, as well as a sense of relief. Spock had seem preoccupied in the days following the battle with Klingons—and for a longer time than that, according to Bones, who'd been concerned about the first officer since the time the two had spent in Sarpeidon's past. Perhaps his new assignment would redirect his thoughts and provide him some fulfillment. "Do you know what ship he'll be commanding?" Kirk asked.

"Commander Spock was offered a captaincy," Nogura said, "but he turned it down."

For years, Spock had claimed no interest in assuming a position of command, despite that in the normal discharging of his duties as the *Enterprise*'s first officer, he'd often had to do precisely that. "Let me speak with him," he told Nogura. "I think I can—"

"Commander Spock not only turned down the captaincy offered to him," Nogura said, "he resigned his commission."

"What?" Kirk said, stunned.

"We hate to lose an officer of Spock's accomplishments and capabilities, but his decision seemed firm," Nogura said. "Is there anything else?"

Kirk had wanted to ask about Bones and Scotty, Sulu and Uhura and the others, but he would find out on his own later. Right now, he needed to talk with Spock. "No, nothing else, Admiral," he said.

"Good," Nogura said. "Then I'll see you at oh-six-hundred, Admiral." Without waiting for a response, Nogura spun on his heel and left.

Kirk stood there for a moment, feeling more emotions than he could handle all at once: trepidation about leaving the *Enterprise* and her crew, excitement about serving as chief of Starfleet Operations, curiosity and hope about his senior officers, and confusion and concern about Spock. At the moment, the last two overwhelmed the rest.

Kirk looked back at the *Enterprise* one more time, at its battered shell, and then he turned and headed out of the lounge to go find Spock.

As the simulated day aboard Starbase 10 approached midnight, McCoy exited the turbolift amid a group of Starfleet officers returning to their vessel, the light cruiser *U.S.S. Grampus*. They all hurried through the docking port in a ritual McCoy had witnessed—and in which he'd participated—many times: the last-minute sprint back to ship at the end of shore leave. He trailed behind the mostly young officers as they hurried ahead of him and aboard the *Grampus,* apparently scheduled to depart shortly.

Spock had already arrived there, McCoy saw. Standing beside the gangway, he wore not his Starfleet uniform, but traditional Vulcan vestments. The brown, loose-fitting robe reached to the deck, and several scrolling symbols adorned its right side in a thin, vertical line. As McCoy walked up, he saw that Spock held a hardcover book in one hand.

"What's so damned urgent that it couldn't wait until morning?" McCoy asked, although he suspected he already knew.

"The urgency, Doctor, is that I will no longer be aboard Starbase 10 in the morning," Spock said.

McCoy regarded his friend. He'd been concerned about him for some time now, though somewhere along the way he'd allowed Spock to talk him out of his legitimate apprehensions. Ever since those two time-travel incidents, though, the Vulcan had frequently shown an increased stoicism, which McCoy had attributed to the reverse problem: a decrease in his true emotional control. Just because Spock didn't display his feelings didn't necessarily mean that he didn't experience them. Now, McCoy thought, he might just be running away.

"You'll no longer be aboard?" the doctor said. "Did Starfleet Command finally hand down your reassignment?" McCoy had received his orders just today, and he presumed that Spock had as well. He also supposed that Spock's new posting had little to do with his leaving right now.

"I did," Spock said, "but that is not directly responsible for why I will no longer be aboard tomorrow." He paused, gazing down at the book he carried in an atypical moment of hesitation. When he looked back up, he said, "I have resigned my commission, Doctor, and I will be returning to Vulcan."

"Why, Spock?" McCoy asked. In some ways, he simply couldn't believe it. The last few weeks at Starbase 10 had been strange, filled with grief at the recent loss of eleven crewmates, with concern for Jim during his recovery, with uncertainty about the future after the *Enterprise,* and with just a general sense of standing still while the universe whirled about in a frenzy. But of all the events McCoy might have predicted or simply guessed at, Spock's departure had not been one of them.

Maybe it should've been, he thought. In the pit of his stomach, he felt that he had failed his friend.

"My reasons are my own," Spock said. "But I wish to thank you for your . . . fellowship."

McCoy nodded slowly, trying to think of something he could say to convince Spock to reconsider. Instead, he simply said, "You're welcome. And I thank you for yours."

Spock closed his eyes and dipped his head in silent acknowledgment. He then held up the book in his hands. "I would ask a favor of you, Doctor," he said. "Would you inform the captain of my decision and also give this to him?"

"I've got a better idea," McCoy said, despite knowing that Spock would not agree. "Why don't you tell Jim yourself? There'll be another ship going your way before too long."

Spock said nothing, and for just a moment, McCoy thought that he might actually be considering his suggestion. But then an alert sounded in the docking port, and the signal light above the gangway switched from green to yellow. "I must go," Spock said, and McCoy suddenly realized the truth of that necessity.

What troubled Spock would not be resolved in whatever posting to which Starfleet had assigned him, or in any other position for that matter.

He reached up and took the book from Spock's hands. "What should I tell Jim?" he asked.

"Tell him . . . simply tell him what I have told you," Spock said.

"All right," McCoy said.

"Thank you," Spock said, then raised his hand in the traditional Vulcan salutation. "Live long and prosper, Doctor McCoy."

"Thank you, Spock," McCoy said, touched by the emotion he thought he could see in his friend's eyes. McCoy held up his right hand and used his left to coax it into matching Spock's gesture. "Peace and long life," he said.

Spock turned and headed across the gangway and into the *Grampus*. McCoy waited there another ten minutes or so, until the alert sounded again, and the light went from yellow to red. Ahead of him, the hatch in the hull of the *Grampus* slid closed, the sound reverberating as it locked physically into place. Then the hatch in the hull of Starbase 10 glided closed as well. McCoy stepped up and peered through a viewing port as the starship retreated from the space station, then watched until it disappeared into the background of stars.

Finally, he walked slowly away from the docking port, the book in his hand, wondering how he would tell Jim. In addition to the news of Spock's return to Vulcan, he had his own news as well, namely that he'd had enough of Starfleet life himself. He'd run to space after his marriage to Jocelyn had failed so spectacularly, but that had been a long time ago, and lately he'd found himself missing a home of green grass below and blue skies above. He'd been making notes for a while now on alien physiology, with the idea of eventually compiling a medical reference. He'd also had it in mind to return both to private practice and to research—the rise in Jim's and the rest of the crew's M'Benga numbers still intrigued him, and study of the Fabrini medical knowledge still beckoned.

McCoy arrived at the end of the corridor and pushed the call button beside the turbolift doors. While he waited for a car to arrive, he examined the book he'd agreed to give to Jim. An old volume, it remained in good condition, he saw. *"Life Before Man,"* he read the title aloud, and speculated about how he should interpret that. Had Spock intended a message? Curious, McCoy opened the cover—he'd heard of the writer, Margaret Atwood, though he didn't think he'd ever read her work—and thumbed through to the beginning of the novel. He read the first four sentences, then quickly closed the book, realizing that Spock was in even more distress than he'd thought.

He turned and looked back toward the docking port, and beyond it, toward the *Grampus* and Spock. "Peace and long life, my friend," he said, his voice tinny in the empty corridor. "And especially peace."

TWENTY-SEVEN

1932

Lynn slid out of the truck behind Phil, then darted past him and ran through the cold night air. She raced up the front steps two at a time, driven not by the low temperature, but by her own anticipation. Rarely did she sit in church anxious for the service to end, but tonight had been an exception—her annual exception.

At the front door, she looked back, to where her husband still stood beside the Model A, watching Leonard root around in the flatbed. "Come on, y'all," she urged them, then stepped into the parlor and stripped off her gloves, stuffing them into the pockets of her coat. She quickly found the matches and lamp they kept just inside, then used one to light the other. Glad that they'd left the wood stove in the corner burning, she took off her coat in the heated room, draping it across one of the Victorian tub chairs. After adding another log to the round-bellied stove, she took the matches and crossed toward the front window, to where Phil had set the Christmas tree just a few days ago.

Lynn loved the Christmas season. When the nights turned cold and the ground hard here in the upcountry, the twenty-fifth of December and the days around it provided a refuge of sorts, a warm stopover on the journey from autumn to spring. Since she'd been a little girl, when her parents had gathered the extended family together, she looked forward each year to sharing the holiday with loved ones.

Tears formed in her eyes before she knew it. It had been a long time since her aunties and uncles and their families had come to Pepper's Crossing for the winter celebration. Her grandparents had been gone for most of her life, and Pa for fifteen, almost sixteen, years now. Still, she and Mama had continued their traditions with just the two of them, and then with Phil when he'd come along. But now Mama had been called home too, and tonight would be Lynn's first Christmas Eve without her.

As Phil and Leonard pushed their way inside, Lynn reached up and wiped her eyes with the heel of her hand, not wanting to spoil the mood of good cheer. She focused instead on the tree, the first she and Phil had ever had. In the ten years of their marriage, they'd always gone up to Pepper's Crossing in late December. Knowing they would be home for Christmas this year, Phil had gone out earlier in the week and chopped down a Fraser fir for the house. Last night, the two of them had decorated the bushy, triangle-shaped tree using the glittering cotton, paper ornaments, dried pine cones, and candle holders that Mama had left to her. They also had a shiny silver star to top the tree, which Phil had bought down at Robinson's General Store.

"It's about time, you two," Lynn told Phil and Leonard as she started lighting the candles on the tree.

"Len was just helping out Santa Claus," Phil said. Lynn glanced over and saw that Leonard carried two packages in his hands, a smaller one atop a larger. Each had been wrapped in brown paper and adorned with a ribbon tied into a bow, one yellow, one blue.

"Leonard," she said, "you didn't need to do that."

"I know I didn't 'need' to," he said, "but I wanted to." He moved over to the tree, squatted down, and carefully placed his two presents beside the three already there. Standing back up, he said, "The tree looks lovely."

"Why, thank you," Lynn said, pleased by the compliment. As she finished lighting the candles, she spied a flame a little too close to some of the cotton that passed for snow, and she moved the fluffy material to a lower branch. Finally, she stepped back and admired her handiwork. "It does look nice, doesn't it?"

Phil and Leonard agreed enthusiastically, but when she turned to face them, she saw that they both still wore their coats. "Well, come on, come on," she playfully scolded them. "Get those coats off so we can open our presents."

"Presents?" Phil said. "Was I supposed to get you something, sugar?"

"Oh," Lynn said, waving away her husband's teasing. She sat down on the davenport while Phil and Leonard got out of their coats and gloves, dropping them atop her coat on the tub chair. Leonard sat down in the other chair, while Phil crouched down in front of the tree. In the yellow glow of the lamps, Lynn saw that pine needles speckled the floor below it.

"Why don't you give Lynn the one from me?" Leonard said, and a thrill of excitement ran through her. She knew that Jesus had said that it was more blessed to give than to receive, and she believed that too, but she had to admit that she loved getting presents. "It's the one with the yellow bow."

Phil reached down and plucked the package from beneath the tree, handed it to Lynn, and then sat down beside her. Almost a foot long, seven or eight inches wide, and an inch through, it felt stiff in her hands, and she knew at once that her friend had gotten her a book. As she admired the pretty bow, she saw writing on the brown-paper wrapping. "'For Lynn,'" she read aloud, "'with great appreciation and affection, Leonard.'"

"Well, are you going to admire it or open it?" Leonard said.

Lynn slid the yellow ribbon from her present, then carefully pulled out the edges of the paper from where they had been tucked together. Beneath, she did indeed find a book. *The Bridge of San Luis Rey,* she read, the black letters marching across the verdigris top of the jacket, "by Thornton Wilder." Below the title, a colored drawing showed a bridge suspended from a mountaintop, and somebody who resembled a monk looking on. "I think I've heard of this," she said.

"I know you like to read, and that you often borrow books from Missus Slattery," Leonard said, mentioning the town's schoolteacher. "So I spoke with her to see what sorts of things you like and what you've read already. She said you like to read about faraway places, and so I thought you might like this one."

"It looks interesting," Lynn said, intrigued not so much by the cover art as by the title. "Where is San Luis Rey?"

"The story takes place in South America," Leonard said. "In Peru."

"Ooh," she said. "That does sound interesting. Thank you so much, Leonard." She stood up and crossed over to him. She felt touched by his thoughtfulness, not just in giving her a gift, but in taking the time to find something he thought she would enjoy. Bending down, she hugged him and gave him a peck on the cheek. "You're a sweetheart."

"Absolutely my pleasure, Lynn," he said.

"So who's next?" she asked, sitting back down.

"Here, let me give this to Phil," Leonard said, and he went over to the tree and got the other, larger package he'd brought. Lifting it very gently, he handed it to Phil. "Now, be careful with this," he said. "It's fragile."

"All right," Phil said, but as soon as he moved to read what Leonard had written on the paper, the package rattled. Phil looked startled for a moment, as though he might've broken whatever Leonard had given him, but then he seemed to realize something. He shook the package back and forth a few times, and Lynn recognized the sound herself: a jigsaw puzzle.

"Well, I guess there goes the surprise," Leonard said.

"Hey, I'm surprised right now," Phil said. He slipped the blue ribbon off and removed the paper, revealing a box covered with shapes of various colors. More than anything, it looked to Lynn like a stained-glass window, though it contained no picture that she could see.

"It's called *Moonlit Waters*," Leonard said as Phil opened the box. "It's a picture of a windmill on a bay, with a sailboat in the water." Phil picked up a couple of the pieces and spread them out in his hand to look at them. Again, Lynn felt taken by Leonard's wonderful thoughtfulness.

"This is great, Len," Phil said. "Thank you kindly." He replaced the top on the box, placed it on the davenport, and turned to Lynn. "Should we give him our present?" he asked.

"Yes," she said, excited at the prospect. She got the small package from beneath the tree—she'd wrapped a green ribbon and a red ribbon around it, tying them into a two-colored bow—and handed it over to Leonard.

"The wrapping is certainly very pretty," Leonard said. From the paper, he read, " 'To Leonard, Merry Christmas from your friends, Lynn and Phil.' " He found the end of the two ribbons and pulled them, and the bow vanished. Lynn watched excitedly as he pulled the package free of the brown paper. She could feel her heart beating in her chest, and she hoped Leonard liked his gift as much as she and Phil thought he would.

Dropping the ribbons and paper to the floor, Leonard placed the box on his knees. Square, about the size of his hands, the plain box had arrived with a label along one side, identifying the contents, but she'd stripped it off so Leonard wouldn't know what it contained until he opened it. Carefully, he lifted the top off. "Oh my goodness," he said, clearly surprised. "I can't believe you two did this." He reached in and pulled out the stethoscope.

"Do you like it?" Lynn blurted, though she could see that he did.

"Of course I like it," Leonard said. "I'm . . . at a loss for words . . ."

"It's engraved too," she said, getting up and going over to point out where his initials had been etched into the device. "On the . . . oh, what did Doc Lyles call it?" she said, looking to Phil.

"The diaphragm," Phil said.

"Right," she said, as she tapped on the engraved *L.M.* "Now that you're helping out the doctor, we thought you could use some things of your own."

Leonard stared at the instrument, then stood up and embraced her. "Thank you," he said, his arms holding her tightly. "Thank you for everything." He released her and padded over to the davenport, where Phil stood up and offered his hand. Leonard took it, but then pulled Phil in close and embraced him as well. "Thank you, Phil," he said.

Lynn felt tears pooling in her eyes again, but this time for a very different reason. She felt overwhelmed by Leonard's reaction to their gift, moved by how deeply they had apparently touched him. *It is more blessed to give than to receive,* she thought.

After that, she and Phil opened the presents they'd gotten for each other—a beautiful rose-colored hat for her, and a new pair of boots for him—which they both loved. But later, when the house had grown quiet and the two lay nestled together in bed, they both agreed that nothing had been better than Leonard's reaction to the stethoscope. Phil had fibbed when he'd told people that Leonard was his second cousin, but in truth, the man from Atlanta who'd become their friend really did feel like family.

McCoy walked past the Hayden First Baptist Church, his gloved hands buried in the pockets of his coat, the white mist of his breath drifting out before him. At the corner, he turned down Mill Road, heading to the boarding house from Lynn and Phil's. The two had offered to drive him back, but living in New York City for two years, he'd gotten accustomed to walking just about everywhere. He enjoyed it, actually, utilizing his constitutionals not only to keep himself fit, but as a time for reflection. Tonight, on Christmas Eve, he did just that.

McCoy hadn't celebrated Christmas during his two winters in New York, not really. He'd helped Edith decorate the mission— and last year, the tree at the Rockefeller work site—and he'd served the men the 21st Street Mission's version of Christmas supper, but he hadn't participated in any personal way in the rituals associated with the holiday. Edith had inquired a couple of times about his faith, but despite his perception that she did not believe in any god or gods herself, he hadn't wanted to risk alienating her.

Tonight, though, Lynn and Phil had asked McCoy to Christmas services with them, and he'd accepted. Though not religious, he had taken to attending church here in Hayden, for the most part as a means of fitting in to the community, but also because Lynn had asked him to do so on several occasions. He had expected to find the services difficult to sit through, but that hadn't been the case. Pastor Gallagher preached messages of love and inclusion, which had impressed McCoy. In his own experience, he'd seen religion divide people far more often than he'd seen it unite them. Here, though, the almost humanistic sermons appeared to have taken hold among the townspeople. Certainly they had accepted McCoy readily enough into their midst—although Phil's fabrication about being his second cousin obviously hadn't hurt matters either.

Lynn and Phil had also invited McCoy to spend the evening with them after the service. Aware of the tradition of exchanging gifts at Christmas, he suspected that the couple had something for him. For his part, he'd used the holiday as an excuse to get something for each of them, small tokens of his appreciation for everything they'd done for him. He'd brought his gifts with him to church, hiding them in the back of Phil's truck before going inside.

As McCoy reached the end of the commons and turned left onto Main Street, his gloved hand closed around the stethoscope in his right pocket. He still could not believe the incredible thoughtfulness of the gift. It put him in mind of the Aesculapian staffs in a bottle that Joanna had once given him for his birthday, which perhaps had contributed to just how much Lynn and Phil's gift touched him. For them even to have thought of getting a stethoscope for him, let alone going to the effort of speaking with Doctor Lyles about it, ordering it, having it engraved . . . he felt privileged to have found such wonderful friends.

McCoy smiled in the darkness as he approached Mrs. Hartwell's. He looked forward to the first opportunity he would have to use his new stethoscope. For the last month and a half or so, ever since the emergency tracheotomy he'd performed on Danny Johnson, he had been assisting Doctor Lyles. At first, it had been only a couple of days a week, but the doctor had soon begun calling on him to help out more and more often. And while Lyles had initially sworn that he would "still do the doctoring," he'd actually allowed McCoy to do so too.

At the same time, Mr. Duncan down at the mill had finally offered him a job as well—part-time, twenty-five hours per week—but McCoy had been reluctant to accept it given the time he'd been putting in with Dr. Lyles and down at the Seed and Feed. But Gregg Anderson had been happy to see McCoy take a job down at the mill, which paid better wages than he could. So now McCoy worked mornings at the mill and afternoons with Lyles.

Arriving at the boarding house, McCoy bent to unlatch the gate in the picket fence that bordered Mrs. Hartwell's yard. As he walked up the front walk, it occurred to him that, although he could not imagine what had happened to the future he once knew, he no longer felt marooned in the past. He'd accepted that this was his life now, and he had to admit, he liked it. He'd begun practicing medicine again, he had good friends, and he lived in a nice southern town.

He was home.

III

The Far-off Interest of Tears

But who shall so forecast the years
    And find in loss a gain to match?
    Or reach a hand thro' time to catch
The far-off interest of tears?

Let Love clasp Grief lest both be drown'd,
    Let darkness keep her raven gloss:
    Ah, sweeter to be drunk with loss,
To dance with death, to beat the ground,

Than that the victor Hours should scorn
    The long result of love, and boast,
    'Behold the man that loved and lost,
But all he was is overworn.'

               —Alfred, Lord Tennyson,
               In Memoriam A.H.H., I

TWENTY-EIGHT

1934

On his way to the truck, Phil stopped and peered out across its hood at the sun-drenched fields. In the heat of the afternoon, as he had so often this summer, he shook his head at the sight. Even after gazing out at the same barren view for months, he still had trouble accepting what he saw. At this time of year, in September, the cotton should have been ready for harvest. The neatness of the rows of the waist-high green plants, separated by the equally straight lines of soil between, should have been interrupted by scattershot clouds of white bursting forth from the bolls.

Instead, Phil saw only an unbroken, colorless plain of dirt.

Our situation could be worse, he told himself as he climbed into the cab of the Model A. He'd repeated that phrase, that thought, over and over again since February, when he and Lynn had *not* prepared the fields for planting. He also knew the truth of it, though that did not make the circumstances any easier for him.

Phil started the truck and pulled out onto Tindal's Lane, heading for town. Last year at this time, in the afternoon on a Friday, if he hadn't been out in the fields picking cotton, he would've been at the mill, processing it. But life had changed in the last few years, and in this year especially. The stock market crash in 1929 had been the beginning of a different era in the United States, though the worst of its effects had taken some time to reach fully into the rural upcountry of South Carolina. But they had reached it now.

It could be worse, Phil thought again. In Kansas and Oklahoma, in Colorado and New Mexico and Texas, across so many of the plains states, it had become impossible not only to farm, but to live. Phil read the Greenville newspaper delivered out to Hayden each week, and he knew about the dust storms and drought that had plagued the heart of the country since 1931.

Land that had been plowed too much, land that had seen too much grazing, had combined with low rainfall and high temperatures to send black blizzards howling over what had once been fertile farmland.

It would be bad enough to have crops wither and die, Phil thought, *but to choke when you breathe* . . . The "dust bowl," they called it, and with good reason: more than a dozen dust storms two years ago, more than *three* dozen last year, and the worst drought ever in America this year. The winds of the Great Plains, unhindered on the vast, open plateau, would lift the dry soil, no longer held in place by crops or ground cover. Enormous, billowing clouds of dirt would darken the skies for miles and miles, and sometimes for days and days. Phil had seen pictures in the paper of dust heaped in drifts like snow. The news accounts said that no house could keep out the dust, not with wet sheets hung over the windows or towels stuffed beneath the doors. People couldn't eat without the taste and grit of dirt in their mouths, and they sometimes breathed through damp cloths in an attempt to keep their mouths and lungs clear. And still people died of "dust pneumonia," especially the very old and the very young.

Already tens of thousands had fled, with more expected to follow. They went west, most of them, with as much of what they owned as they could carry. They sought only clear skies and a livable wage, a means of providing food for their families. But there were only so many jobs.

"There but for the grace of God go I," some folks around these parts said. Phil understood the sentiment, though he didn't care much to think of God favoring some people over others. But he could not disagree that he and Lynn had been lucky. They had their home, and even though South Carolina's rainfall had dropped considerably this year, he felt sure that they could have produced at least an adequate cotton crop—that is, if they'd actually planted one.

His thoughts aswirl, Phil pulled into town, turning onto Carolina Street and driving along the commons. He saw a lot of people strolling about, including a number of people who, like him, normally would've been at the mill right now. With agricultural prices down across the country, though, mills and farmers had suffered alike. President Roosevelt had tried to keep prices high enough for textile mills to stay in business, and for workers to be able to make a living. That had worked some, but not enough. Here in Hayden, the mill had needed to cut its costs in order to remain open.

Here too, though, things could have been worse. Mr. Duncan could've fired people outright, but instead, he'd cut everybody's work hours and pay. That had made life harder for all the folks in town, including Phil and Lynn, but it had also left everybody in the same situation.

Phil turned onto Main Street and parked in front of Town Hall. As he got out of the truck, he saw Len walking on a path through the commons. Phil waved, and Len waved back. A while ago, Phil had been surprised to find out that his friend didn't know how to drive, and so he'd taught him. The experience still made him laugh when he thought back on it, though he would never want to go through it again. More than anything else, Len's surprisingly colorful language had startled and amused him. He'd eventually learned, but even though Doc Lyles had offered him the use of his car—Lyles rarely drove anymore himself—Len still seemed to want to walk everywhere.

Phil headed up the stairs to Town Hall. The doors had been propped open, probably because of the day's heat. He stepped inside and crossed the small lobby to the short, wooden half-wall that closed in a few rows of wooden chairs and the desks—just tables, really—beyond them. The three members of the town council—Bill Jenkins, Audie Glaston, and Gregg Anderson, who currently served as mayor—worked here when they did town business, though Phil saw none of them right now. He did see Judy Bartell, the town clerk, sitting at her desk just ahead, chatting with Jefferson Donner. Phil had come into town specifically to see Judy.

Reaching down and opening the small door in the half-wall, he started toward her desk. When she saw him, she said, "Hey, Phil," and Jeff Donner looked over and greeted him as well.

"How y'all doing today?" Phil asked as he reached the pair.

"Hot," Judy said. Short, with a doughy, freckled face and curly red hair that was almost orange, the older woman fanned herself with a stack of papers. Phil saw that the tall windows on either side of the room had been opened, but the air just seemed to sit there anyway.

"Hot and then some over to the forge," Jeff said. About Phil's age, the tall blacksmith had a lean muscular body and always seemed to have three days' growth on his face. "When you gonna bring in Piedmont and Belle Reve for shoeing?"

"I'll have to see," Phil said, "but we ain't been working 'em, so . . ." He shrugged.

"I know, I know," Jeff said. "Nobody in town's farming much at all, and so no one needs their animals shoed or their tools fixed." He didn't sound angry, but frustrated.

Phil shrugged again. "Sorry, Jeff."

"Aw, it's not your fault," Jeff said, clapping a hand on Phil's shoulder. "I just wish things could be like they was."

"Ain't that right?" Judy agreed. They all nodded along with her. Though it didn't help matters any, for some reason it made Phil feel better to hear other folks talk about how things had changed.

"Well, I guess I should be getting back," Jeff said. "If someone does come by, I don't wanna miss any business." Phil and Judy said their good-byes, and Jeff Donner headed out.

"I suppose you know why I'm here, Judy," Phil said once the blacksmith had left.

"Yes, indeedy," Judy said, pulling a stack of papers over to her. "You always seem to be the last one in to get their check." She pulled an envelope from the pile and handed it to him.

"I don't know, Judy," Phil said. He took the envelope from her and, without looking at it, folded it in two and stuffed it into the back pocket of his dungarees. "I'm taking the money, and I guess it's the right thing to do, but it just don't *seem* right." As soon as President Roosevelt had taken office in 1933, he'd worked with Congress to pass one law after another aimed at helping people beaten down by the terrible economic times in the country. One of the first ideas he'd proposed had been the AAA: the Agricultural Adjustment Act. In order to keep the prices of certain crops—including cotton—from falling too low, Roosevelt had decided that the government needed to control the supply of those crops. The AAA actually allowed the government to pay farmers *not* to plant their land.

Most still planted some, though with Phil working at the mill, it had worked out best for him and Lynn to leave all their land fallow. Sometimes when he thought about it, Phil guessed it seemed reasonable, but then he'd get to thinking that fewer crops meant less for the mill to process, which meant less income, which meant they had to cut costs, which then affected the workers. It all seemed connected and complicated and impossible to fix all at once.

"Things is tough," Judy said. She pushed the stack of papers to the side and picked up the large ledger sitting on the side of her desk. She opened it to a marked page, then turned it around and set it down before Phil. "You got to take the money," she said. "Now give me your John Hancock." She uncapped a fountain pen and handed it to him, then pointed to an empty line on the page. He leaned down and signed his name.

"I know, you're right," he said. "But I'm like Jeff: I wish things could be like they was."

"I think everybody does," Judy said. "But ain't that the way of life? Everything always changing?"

"Yeah, I suppose so," Phil said. "I suppose so." He set the fountain pen down on the ledger. "Guess I ought to get this in the bank afore Mister Roosevelt changes his mind."

"Say hey to Lynn for me," Judy said.

"I will," Phil said. "Hey to Jimmy and Bo." Jim Bartell, Judy's husband, worked as Sheriff Gladdy's deputy, and her son Bo, who had to be almost twenty-one now, worked down at the mill, out in the storehouse with Billy Fuster.

Phil made his way back outside and down the Town Hall steps. Under the bright sun, and with a pocketful of money he would have traded for a field full of cotton, he started across the commons, headed for the Palmetto Mutual Bank and Trust.

His black doctor's bag in hand, McCoy walked along one of the gravel paths that wound through the commons. He'd just come from the Gladdy house, out on Riverdale Road, down Church Street in the opposite direction from Tindal's Lane. There, he'd diagnosed Dwight, the town's sheriff, with bronchitis. He'd prescribed aspirin, as analgesic and antipyretic, and cough syrup, as antitussive and expectorant. McCoy had carried both medications with him after Beth Gladdy had come by to request a house call and she'd described Dwight's symptoms.

Now, making his way through the commons, he saw Phil Dickinson waving to him from in front of Town Hall. McCoy waved back, then watched Phil pad up the steps and go inside. Other people outside this afternoon greeted him as well, most calling him "Doc" or "Doctor," even those who'd called him by his given name when he'd first come to Hayden. He'd been sharing the duties of town physician for just a few months short of two years now, and he'd been readily accepted in that role.

While that time had been fulfilling for McCoy, it had also proven particularly instructive. Absent the diagnostic tools he'd become accustomed to using in the twenty-third century, he'd been forced to return to the manual procedures he'd studied in medical school, but which he'd rarely employed in the field; in some cases, he'd even had to learn new methods—well, ancient methods, but new to him. He'd also needed to become familiar with the medical instrumentation and pharmacology of this era. Initially, the primitive state of health care on 1930s Earth had frustrated him, but he'd quickly accepted it. He wasn't going to invent the tricorder or the physiostimulator, or develop masiform-D, so he simply needed to identify and understand the tools available to him. He did this by observing Dr. Lyles, by asking questions, and by reading the *Journal of the American Medical Association, Hygeia,* and the other professional publications to which Lyles subscribed.

McCoy reached the southeast corner of the commons, waited for Ducky Jensen to drive by in his pale yellow Studebaker, then headed diagonally across the intersection to Dr. Lyles's house. Since the two men had begun working together, the elder physician had allowed McCoy the use of his office, which had worked out well. He walked past the low picket fence and turned up the stone path. The wooden sign sitting on a post in the front yard still declared "WILLIAM LYLES, M.D."

McCoy opened the door and stepped inside. "Doctor Lyles," he called, "I'm back." Though they had known each other for two and a half years and had worked together for all but the first eight months of that time, they still addressed each other by their titles. It wasn't that they didn't like each other, or that they didn't relate to each other in a personal way—although even when they spoke privately, it tended to involve medicine on one level or another. On the one hand, though, Lyles seemed to want to maintain a professional relationship between them, and on the other, he for the most part kept to himself. According to Phil, the good doctor had essentially withdrawn socially after the death of his wife fifteen years earlier; she and several other people in Hayden had died of "consumption," the old name given to tuberculosis.

"Doctor Lyles?" McCoy called again. He stopped in the hall and listened for any sound, but heard only the loud mechanical beating of the grandfather clock from up ahead in the living room. Lyles might be in the privy out back, he supposed, or perhaps he'd been asked to make a house call.

McCoy walked down the hall and through the first doorway on his right, into the examining room. He set his bag down on the small table just inside and—

For a second, McCoy froze. Lyles lay on the floor beside the examination table, collapsed onto his left side, his head and neck leaning awkwardly against the cabinets lining the far wall. McCoy grabbed his bag back up and dashed across the room, throwing himself onto his knees beside the doctor. He took hold of his shoulders and gently shook him. "Doctor Lyles, can you hear me?" he said.

No response.

McCoy eased Lyles away from the cabinets and flat onto his back. He quickly opened his medical bag and pulled out his stethoscope, even as he noted that the doctor's chest did not rise and fall, indicating that he had stopped breathing. McCoy set the earpieces of the scope in his ears, but before using the device, he reached up to Lyles's neck, just below the angle of his jaw, and felt for a carotid pulse. He found none.

Aware of the seconds ticking away, McCoy pulled the doctor's shirt open with a jerk, causing several buttons to snap off and fall to the floor. Utilizing the bell of the stethoscope, he carried out the standard auscultation sequence, moving the bell to different locations on Lyles's chest: left laternal sternal border, apex, base right, base left. He then repeated the cycle with the diaphragm. Doctor Lyles's heart beat, but very irregularly and with varying intensity, an arrhythmia so severe that it indicated ventricular distress.

"Damn," McCoy muttered. In the *Enterprise*'s sickbay, or in any twenty-third-century hospital on Earth, a portable defibrillator would've provided a strong chance of restoring the doctor's regular, rhythmic heartbeat. Right here, right now, though, McCoy knew that almost no such chance existed.

Unwilling to give up without doing everything he could, he began cardiopulmonary resuscitation. He tilted the doctor's head back, pinched his nostrils closed, leaned in, and covered Lyles's mouth with his own. McCoy exhaled slowly, once, twice, making sure that the doctor's chest rose in response. Then he shifted over, placed the heels of his hands one atop the other in the center of Lyles's chest, locked his elbows, and administered compressions. After he pushed down the third time, the doctor vomited, a direct result of the CPR. McCoy quickly reached down and cleared his mouth, then turned Lyles's head so that he wouldn't aspirate the regurgitated food into his lungs. As the sour whiff of partially digested food reached him, McCoy resumed the chest compressions, completing fifteen in all.

Lyles didn't respond.

McCoy repeated the sequence, from the two breaths of mouth-to-mouth resuscitation to the dozen and a quarter chest compressions. Then he did it a third time, and a fourth. Finally, he rechecked the doctor's vital signs.

Nothing.

McCoy lowered himself from his knees to the floor and leaned back against a cabinet. He pulled off his stethoscope, wiped his mouth, then let out a long, loud sigh. His arms tired from his exertions, he sat that way for a few minutes. He felt sad, not because he'd lost a patient—though he hated that, he had also learned the need to distance himself emotionally from such events—but because he'd lost somebody who had made a tremendous difference in his life. Without Dr. Lyles, McCoy doubted that he would be practicing medicine again.

After a while, McCoy placed his stethoscope back in his bag, then retrieved some towels and cleaned up the doctor's face and the vomitus on the floor. Then he washed his own hands and

face. Finally, he headed out into Hayden and back across the
commons, to the sheriff's office. Dwight Gladdy was home with
bronchitis, but his deputy, Jimmy Bartell, would be on duty.
McCoy would find him and report the death of Dr. Lyles.

TWENTY-NINE

2273

Driven by magnetic levitation, the monorail glided smoothly
along the elevated track, past the main campus of Earth's Centers
for Disease Control and Prevention. Nogura peered through the
window at the interconnecting set of ultramodern towers, illuminated in the night, and wondered if they would still be standing three days from now—or if anything at all would be left on
Earth. The enormous destructive force headed for the planet had
effortlessly fended off an attack by three Klingon K't'inga-class
warships, then had destroyed them with apparent ease. Attempts
both to contact the object and to identify it had met with no success, and the speed with which it traveled and the course it took
left only one Federation starship within interception range. Just
completely redesigned and refitted, *Enterprise* would launch
ahead of schedule, with no shakedown cruise, no adequate trials
of its new warp drive, no opportunity for its crew to acclimatize
to the ship in a deployed setting. All of which had led Nogura to
agree to Admiral Kirk's request—his demand, really—to assume
command of his old vessel.

As the maglev passed a tract of woodland, barely visible in
the scant light of the railway, Nogura turned in his seat and
checked the map displayed on a screen in the bulkhead. He saw
that the monorail had entered the grounds of Emory University
and that his destination would be next. He'd come the width of

the continent at Kirk's request as well, transporting from Starfleet's headquarters in San Francisco to its military operations facility in Atlanta. From there, he'd boarded the maglev and ridden it north to Druid Hills, where he would find the object of his pursuit.

Nogura cursed himself for his shortsightedness. Kirk, the gambling, swashbuckling starship commander, had demonstrated a great deal more prudence in his role as chief of Starfleet Operations than in his previous position. He still took risks, but only under circumstances far more advantageous than when he'd taken them during his time as *Enterprise*'s captain. Kirk had recommended against sending both *Exeter* and *Potemkin* to deal with the Albasynnia affair, thereby leaving this sector essentially unprotected, even if only for a short time. Nogura had overruled him. Considering the power now headed directly for Earth, though, Kirk had clearly been right.

Up ahead, Nogura saw the interior lights of a seven-story building. As the maglev neared, it suddenly darted off the main track and swung onto a station branch. The building loomed above, until the monorail slid beneath an overhang and skimmed to a stop. Past just two people waiting on the platform, signs indicated that Nogura had reached the Bruggeman-Johnson Medical Research Center. As soon as the maglev's doors opened, he exited and crossed to the building's entrance.

Inside, Nogura approached security and identified himself, verifying his claim with hand and retina scans. Though Starfleet did not control or even manage Emory University, he knew that Starfleet Medical often worked closely with its School of Medicine's Research Division. The admiral's rank and position therefore eliminated whatever bureaucratic hurdles might otherwise have slowed or even impeded his access to one of Emory's researchers. After issuing him a visitor's badge, a guard consulted a directory, then escorted him to a third-floor lab.

Nogura entered alone. Within, he found a large, low-ceilinged room, filled with an array of high-tech devices he did not recognize, and an assortment of low-tech equipment he did: test tubes, beakers, burners, and the like. On the far side of the room, a string of windows reached from wall to wall and looked out on the ECDC's brightly lighted towers in the distance. To the left, a wide viewscreen dominated the wall and currently displayed a mix of alien characters and three-dimensional chemical diagrams, neither of which the admiral could read, though he thought he recognized the former. Standing before the screen, on the other side of a long counter from Nogura, stood two figures, one Andorian, one human. Both wore white smocks over their clothes, with what appeared to be identification badges pinned to their breast pockets. They looked in his direction.

"May we help you?" the Andorian asked, a breathy quality to his voice. Heavyset, he had pale blue skin and a bald pate. His white antennae moved in a way that Nogura could not interpret.

"I'm here to see Doctor McCoy," the admiral said. Initially, Nogura had expected to visit the doctor in his home, but a check of his research schedule with an Emory official had shown him working in his lab late tonight. He couldn't recall ever meeting McCoy, but he'd reviewed his personnel file after his conversation with Kirk. Nogura knew him on sight, despite the full beard and mustache he now wore.

"Admiral Nogura," McCoy said, obviously recognizing him as well. The doctor paused, clearly unsure why Nogura had come to see him, and perhaps not wanting to know. "May I introduce my colleague, Chirurgeon Shivol."

Nogura nodded in the Andorian's direction, then peered back at McCoy. "I require a word with you, Doctor," he said, stepping deeper into the lab.

McCoy hesitated, and the chirurgeon looked at him, no doubt sensing the doctor's manifest uneasiness. "Leonard?" he said.

"It's all right, Shiv," McCoy said. "If you wouldn't mind giving us a few minutes . . ."

"Of course," Shivol said. "I'll be in the lounge if you need anything." He set down a small device he'd been holding, then paced past Nogura and out of the room.

Once the admiral had heard the door close behind Shivol, he said, "Doctor McCoy—"

"Admiral," McCoy interrupted, "may I get you something to drink, some tea or coffee perhaps?"

"I have no time for politeness, Doctor," Nogura said, seeking to move past McCoy's obvious reluctance to speak with him. "I've come to see you regarding an urgent matter."

"Right," McCoy said. "How'd I know I wasn't going to like this?" He circled around the counter, but then walked by Nogura and toward the inner corner of the lab. "Excuse me if I make myself some tea."

Nogura followed him over to a small area separated from the main lab and clearly used to store and heat refreshments. "Doctor, what I'm about to tell you is classified, though it won't be for much longer. There's an—"

"*Don't* tell me anything classified," McCoy said, whirling to face Nogura, an empty black mug in his hand. "I'm no longer *in* Starfleet."

"I see," Nogura said. He didn't understand what appeared to be McCoy's antipathy toward Starfleet. Certainly nothing in his service record suggested the existence of such feelings. Perhaps it signaled the doctor's realization that if the commanding admiral showed up to speak with him, it likely meant a request for his assistance. "Doctor," Nogura said, "are you familiar with Starfleet's terms of service?"

"What?" McCoy asked, turning away again. "I don't know. What I do know is that I've done my service, and right now I'm in the middle of several projects, including some very promising research on a cross-species cure for Vegan choriomeningitis." Nogura saw McCoy reach for a carafe of what appeared to be hot water.

"Doctor, in the enlistment agreement that all Starfleet officers sign, including you, there's a clause that most people don't pay much attention to, and that we certainly don't invoke very often," Nogura said. "But during a crisis, Starfleet would be within its rights to recall you to active service."

"What!" McCoy said. He shoved the carafe back onto its heating element—water splashed from the top and sizzled where it landed on the element—and spun around again to face Nogura. "You're threatening to force me back into Starfleet? That doesn't sound legal, and it sure doesn't sound ethical."

"Doctor," Nogura said, raising his hands in a placatory motion. He couldn't believe that the conversation had become so rancorous, so quickly. He'd come here to meet with McCoy in person specifically to convey just why Starfleet needed his assistance. Nogura had thought that appealing to McCoy directly would provide the best chance of procuring his help, but he hadn't even gotten that far yet. "Doctor," he said again, "I have no wish to reactivate you against your will." Something occurred to Nogura, and he gazed back across the lab at the viewscreen. "What language is that?" he asked, pointing.

"You mean the symbols on the display?" McCoy asked, and Nogura nodded. "That's Fabrini. That's one of the projects I'm involved in, trying to apply the vast amount of ancient medical knowledge found on Yonada."

"Interesting," Nogura said, and he allowed the word to linger for a moment. He didn't think he needed to explicitly make the case to McCoy that this work of his had been made possible by Starfleet granting Emory University access to the Fabrini medical database. Looking back at the doctor, Nogura told him, "As I said, I don't want to activate you against your wishes, but because the situation is so dire, I will if I have to. But I ask that you hear me out before we do battle over this."

McCoy peered at him for a few seconds, perhaps trying to gauge his intentions. Finally, he set down his mug and walked away, back toward the viewscreen. "My work is important to me," he said when he got to the counter and looked up at the display. He turned back to face Nogura across the room. "And it's important work, not just to me, but to people all over the Federation." For a moment, Nogura thought he would have to make good on his threat to draft McCoy back into Starfleet, though he also realized that doing so would likely defeat the purpose of returning him to *Enterprise*. But then McCoy said, "But I'll listen to you."

Nogura offered his description of the situation at once. "A huge, powerful object is currently heading through our galaxy at great speed," he said.

"An object," McCoy said dismissively.

"We don't know if it's a ship or a creature or something else entirely," Nogura said. "But it defeated a trio of Klingon warships in just minutes, sustaining no discernible damage itself, and obliterating each ship with just a single shot."

"All right," McCoy acknowledged, and Nogura thought that he might finally have the doctor's attention.

"The object is on a direct heading for Earth," the admiral said.

"It will arrive here in less than three days, and there's only one starship within range to intercept it: *Enterprise*."

"The *Enterprise*," McCoy echoed. "She's a good ship. I'm sure she'll do the job you need her to. But surely there are enough doctors in Starfleet that you don't need me." He seemed to think for a second, and then he added, "As I understand it, the ship's been completely redesigned, so my familiarity with it wouldn't even be a plus."

"Although your record as *Enterprise*'s chief medical officer was exemplary," Nogura said, "you're right: there are numerous other doctors in Starfleet up to the task." He paused, wanting to express the fundamental reason for his request with a sensitivity and a subtlety he did not normally employ. "I'm sending Admiral Kirk out with *Enterprise*, as its captain."

"He's a fine captain," McCoy said. "A fine man."

Nogura knew that, of course, but what he didn't know, what he couldn't be sure of, was Kirk's motivation. He didn't know if Kirk himself could be sure right now. Nogura had listened to his argument that his experience in commanding a starship and in dealing with unknowns trumped Captain Decker's intimate familiarity with *Enterprise*'s redesign. In the end, Nogura had agreed to return Kirk to the command chair—provided that Kirk truly believed himself the best man for this particular situation, and that he wasn't merely using the circumstances to try to maneuver his way back onto the bridge of a starship. As good a job as Kirk had done in the last two and a half years as chief of Starfleet Operations, it had become clear—to Nogura and doubtless to Kirk— that he missed his life in space, and Nogura realized now that it had been a mistake to remove him from starship command.

"Jim Kirk *is* a fine man," he said, agreeing with McCoy. "But he hasn't captained a starship in a long time." He wanted to tell McCoy that Kirk had explicitly asked for the doctor's presence on the mission, but decided that it might be better to keep all of the blame for this on himself. "I have confidence in Admiral Kirk, but I think it would help him for you to be onboard."

"I . . . think I understand," McCoy said. He walked back over to Nogura. "Are you talking about *this* mission?" the doctor asked. "This mission *only?*"

"That is all that I'm asking," Nogura said, hopeful.

"And how soon is the ship leaving?" McCoy asked.

"In eleven hours," Nogura said. "*Enterprise*'s launch is sched-uled for oh-five-hundred, Pacific time."

McCoy seemed to consider this. "All right," he said. "I'll have to take care of some things here at the lab and at home. But I'll be there."

Nogura forced himself not to sigh in relief. "Of course. Thank you, Doctor," he said. "Transport out to Starfleet Headquarters prior to boarding *Enterprise* and report to Admiral Phanomyong. She'll brief you on the information we have about the object, and she'll have somebody there to offer a quick primer on *Enter-prise*'s redesigned medical facilities."

"Fine," McCoy said, "but I'll be taking the tube out to San Francisco."

"Why would you do that, Doctor?" Nogura asked, but then remembered seeing a note in McCoy's records about him being uncomfortable with travel by transporter.

"I haven't beamed anywhere in more than two years," McCoy said, confirming his anxiety. "There's no need to start up again now."

"Very well," Nogura said, unwilling to threaten McCoy's agreement by arguing the point. Though not as fast as the nearly instantaneous travel of a transporter, the tube would still get McCoy to San Francisco quickly enough. And depending when he arrived and how long his briefing took, there might still be time for him to take a shuttle up to *Enterprise.* "Again, thank you, Doctor," Nogura said, and he extended his hand, a gesture he rarely made. McCoy took it.

"You're welcome," the doctor said.

A few minutes later, Nogura made his way out of the research center and back to the maglev platform. As he waited for the monorail that would take him back to Starfleet Military Opera-tions, he hoped that he had just secured the support Admiral Kirk would need to get through the next couple of days. The fate not only of *Enterprise,* but of Earth itself, and possibly even of the Federation, might well hang in the balance.

McCoy looked about his cabin, checking for anything he might have left behind. He actually hadn't brought much with him; after Nogura had convinced him to join Jim aboard the *Enterprise,* McCoy had packed only a few changes of clothing, some toiletries, some handwritten notebooks, and a stack of data cards. But his cabin on this redesigned, refitted the *Enterprise* dwarfed those on the old configuration of the ship and gave him a lot of places to check.

As he peered around the cabin, the events of a month ago— ostensibly the situation for which he'd returned to Starfleet—recurred to him, as did the implications of what had happened. It all had occupied McCoy's mind in the intervening weeks, the issues occurring to him again and again in different forms. In his thoughts, he reshaped the problems in various ways, but always they distilled down to a matter of mechanism: how had V'Ger achieved consciousness? Of course, that formulation carried with it the presupposition that V'Ger *had* achieved consciousness—something that, while not scientifically and rigorously proven, McCoy felt confident in asserting. But that notion begged other questions. Could a machine, something clearly *not* alive, become a living thing? And if not, then could something not alive still become conscious?

McCoy had faced such matters before. There had been the androids that Jim and Christine Chapel—now Dr. Chapel—had encountered on Exo III, and those discovered by Harry Mudd. There had been computers that had demonstrated lifelike behavior: Landru on Beta III, Dr. Daystrom's M-5, the Oracle on Yonada, and the one producing the Losira replicas on the Kalandan outpost. There had been the Nomad-Tan Ru hybrid probe, and perhaps most compelling of all, the Guardian of Forever. But whether or not the Guardian had been a machine or a living being remained an open question; according to Spock's report, it had claimed to be both and neither. With V'Ger, there had been no doubt: it had begun its existence as a machine, as the space probe Voyager 6, created on Earth by humans more than three centuries earlier, and a month ago, it had returned as something much more than that.

Satisfied that he had packed all of his few belongings, McCoy returned to the front section of his quarters and cinched up his duffel. Still, he could not shake his thoughts free of V'Ger and its remarkable story. As best they could tell, the inanimate

Voyager 6 had fallen through a wandering black hole, only to emerge at the far side of the galaxy. There, the probe had been found by a population of machines—"living machines," Spock had called them, but McCoy would need more information before he could agree to that determination. Regardless, the machines had interpreted Voyager's programming—collect all data possible and transmit it back to Earth—literally, and they had modified the probe in a dramatic way, allowing it to deconstruct and store everything it encountered. Once it had learned everything it possibly could, it had returned to Earth.

Jim had postulated that Voyager—calling itself "V'Ger" after three of the letters on its nameplate had been obscured—had amassed so much knowledge that it had become conscious. McCoy found it difficult to credit the idea that there existed some critical mass of information above which the repository of that information achieved consciousness. Still, he could not argue that V'Ger had not come back a living entity; clearly it had, evidenced among other things by the questions it had been asking: Is this all that I am? Is there nothing more? It had taken V'Ger's somehow joining with a human being to give it a greater sense of purpose than mere data collection, and to send it . . . where? They didn't know, but once Will Decker had merged with V'Ger, it had appeared to undergo some sort of massive transformation, and then it had simply vanished.

In the days since then, McCoy had thought about all that had happened. He'd even briefly considered initiating a line of research in which he would investigate the nature of machines and life, knowledge and consciousness. He'd quickly rejected the idea, though, since he'd already done a great deal of work on a number of projects that he hadn't yet completed.

McCoy bent to pick up his duffel, prepared to depart the ship, but then the door signal chimed. "Almost made a clean getaway," he joked to himself. He straightened and called for the visitor to come in. The doors opened and Jim entered.

"Why, Bones, leaving so soon?" he said with a grin, eying the duffel. "We've only been back in Earth orbit for thirty minutes."

"Yeah," McCoy said, "but it took us thirty *days* to get here." After the incident with V'Ger, Jim and Starfleet had wanted to conduct a proper shakedown cruise of the *Enterprise,* and

McCoy had agreed to stay aboard for the month set aside for that. With Captain Decker gone, Jim had remained in command while Starfleet had sought a replacement. During that time, the ship had been put through its paces, and the crew had even conducted a couple of missions. It had been wonderful to spend time with Jim and Spock, Scotty and Christine, Hikaru and Uhura and others. Now, though, the *Enterprise* had traveled back to Earth, presumably in preparation for its next assignment, and McCoy would disembark and return to his research in Georgia. "Anyway, I'm about to catch a shuttle down to Starfleet, and then a tube back to Atlanta."

"A shuttle?" Jim said. "Bones, you're practically a Luddite."

"Oh, no," McCoy protested, rising to his friend's bait. "I don't have a problem with *all* technology. I happily use it all the time. It's just that ridiculous transporter."

"So you say," Jim observed.

"Hey, remember that blasted machine once split you in two," McCoy reminded him, referring to the incident six or seven years ago at Alfa 177, when a flukish combination of circumstances had caused the transporter to create two versions of Jim, one tender and docile, the other aggressive and violent.

"Oh, believe me, I remember," Jim said. "Listen, Bones, I know you're anxious to get home, but do you have a few minutes before you go?"

"Sure, Jim," he said. "Let's go in here." He motioned toward the sitting area of the cabin. Jim took a seat in the corner, and McCoy sat down on the small sofa across from him. "What is it you wanted to talk about?"

"First of all, I wanted to thank you again for coming with us—for coming with *me*—when we went out to intercept V'Ger," Jim said. "We wouldn't have succeeded without you."

"Oh, I don't know about that," McCoy said. "You had a good ship and a good crew, not to mention your own good sense and experience. You didn't need me."

"I really did," Jim said, leaning forward in his chair, his elbows on his knees.. "I hadn't commanded a starship in two and a half years; I was lost. You . . . grounded me. You helped me find my strength."

"Well, you're welcome," McCoy said, very pleased that he'd

been able to help his old friend and touched by the sincerity of Jim's words. "For whatever it's worth, I really think you belong on the bridge of a starship . . . especially one named *Enterprise.*"

Jim sat back in his chair. "Funny you should mention that," he said. "That's the other thing I wanted to talk with you about."

"What's that?" McCoy asked.

Jim stood up. "I've officially resigned as chief of Starfleet Operations."

McCoy blinked in surprise, not because Jim had given up his position, but that a certain admiral had not prevented him from doing so. "Nogura's allowing that?" he asked.

"He doesn't have much choice," Jim said as he began pacing across the sitting area. "Besides, I think he realizes that, like you said, my place really is in command of a starship. I know *I* realize it. Not that I didn't enjoy my time as Operations chief, but this is where I need to be, at least for right now."

"I think that's wonderful news, Jim," McCoy said. "You're staying aboard the *Enterprise* then?"

"I am," Jim said. "And so is Spock and most of the senior officers."

"I'm glad to hear Spock is staying," McCoy said, watching Jim move back and forth across the compartment. "As much as he spouts logic and maintains his Vulcan poise, I think it would've been wrong for him to purge himself of all emotion."

"I agree," Jim said.

"So do you know what the *Enterprise*'s assignment will be?" McCoy asked.

"I do," Jim said with a smile. "Starfleet's detected an unusual arrangement of astronomical objects, with something at their center that nobody's been able to identify. They're calling it the Aquarius Formation. The scientists think it's worthy of investigation."

"Sounds interesting," McCoy said. "Where is this?"

"A good distance from the Federation," Jim said. "We'll take an elliptical course to it, so that we pass through uncharted space on the way there and on the way back. We'll traverse about a thousand light-years, and explore throughout the entire journey."

"A *thousand* light-years?" McCoy asked, stunned. "How long do you expect this mission to last?"

"That depends on what we find along the way, but we estimate between five and eight years." Jim stopped pacing and faced McCoy. "Bones, I want you to go with us."

"Me?" McCoy said. "Jim, I appreciate that you want me to go along, but I've got research I'm conducting."

"You told me what you're working on," Jim said. "The Fabrini medical database, Vegan choriomeningitis, comparative alien physiology, the discrepancies in M'Benga numbers. They're all things you can continue to do on the *Enterprise*."

"I suppose that's true, but . . ." McCoy started. But what? he asked himself. He'd enjoyed the time he'd spent as the *Enterprise*'s chief medical officer, and he *could* still carry on his research onboard. The ship did have state-of-the-art medical labs. Would a shipboard schedule allow him the freedom, though? "I don't know that I'd have the time I needed to continue doing what I'm doing," he said at last.

"I understand," Jim said. "But Chapel's still signed on as the ship's CMO. If she's willing, maybe the two of you could share the position. That might give you the time you want for your research. Plus—" Jim placed his hand flat on his chest. "—you've got a carrier of Vegan choriomeningitis right here, as well as the single largest discrepancy in M'Benga numbers ever recorded."

"Well, that's true," McCoy said. One of the reasons he'd gravitated to finding a possible cure for infection by the arenavirus had been the fact that Jim carried it, and his research into M'Benga numbers had been a direct result of the readings he'd taken of Jim and the rest of the crew. But McCoy had also settled into a life in Atlanta and at the university. Did he really want to go back into space, especially for such a prolonged voyage? "Jim, I don't know," he said. "This isn't something I expected or planned on."

Jim nodded. "I know," he said. "A month ago, it wasn't something I'd expected either. But the opportunity's arisen, and I thought you might want . . . I *hoped* you might want to be a part of it."

"I might," McCoy said. "I don't know. I need time to think about it."

"You can have two weeks," Jim said. "It'll take that long to provision the ship and finalize crew assignments."

"All right," McCoy said, rising up from the sofa.

"Good," Jim said, and he walked over to him. "Whatever you decide, Bones, thank you for what you did." They shook hands, a warm and meaningful gesture between old friends. McCoy nodded, but didn't feel the need to say anything more. Jim let go of his hand, then turned and left.

McCoy watched him go, not moving until the doors had closed behind the captain. *Admiral,* he reminded himself. Except that while Jim might be a Starfleet admiral, he'd also once more regained the position that fit him so well: starship captain.

McCoy crossed back into the sleeping section of his quarters, picked up his duffel, and pulled the carry strap over his shoulder. He would go back to Atlanta and do what he'd told Jim he would: think about this opportunity to rejoin the *Enterprise.* Right now, he had no idea what he would decide.

THIRTY

1934/1936

Gregg Anderson looked up from the piece of paper on his desk when he heard footsteps tapping on the floor of the lobby. In the dying light of the late September evening, he saw Billy Jenkins ambling in with Lenny McCoy. "I got him," Billy said as the two made their way through the small door in the low wall that separated Town Hall's lobby from its main room.

"Yup, we can see that, Billy," Anderson said. "Evening, Doc. Thanks for coming in." Anderson noticed that, as Lenny always did these days, he carried his black doctor's bag with him. "Hope we're not interrupting anything."

"Evening, Gregg," Lenny said. "No, I was just at home reading."

"Just take a seat anywhere," Billy said, then shuffled his old bones over to his desk. At fifty-five, he was only a couple of years younger than Anderson himself, but not nearly as healthy. Pained by arthritis, Billy walked slowly and carefully, as though his legs might collapse beneath him at any moment. When he reached his desk, he lowered himself down awkwardly, leaning heavily on the arms of his chair. Audie Glaston, at forty the youngest member of the town council, already sat at his own desk.

Lenny glanced around, as though trying to decide where to sit. Several rows of wooden chairs sat on this side of the half-wall, lined up on either side of the door, forming an aisle between them. Lenny sat down in the first row, nearest the desks of the three men. "So what can I do for you?" he asked. "Billy said you had some town business you wanted to discuss with me."

"We do," Anderson said. "But first I just wanna say again how much we all appreciated what you said at Doc Lyles's funeral the other day." After Pastor Gallagher had said his piece out at the cemetery last week, Lenny had asked if he could say a few words. "We know y'all didn't know the doctor near as long as we all did, so it was real nice that you wanted to say something. And what you said, well, everybody liked it a whole lot." Billy and Audie nodded and added their agreements.

"Thanks," Lenny said. "I wanted to do it. Doc Lyles didn't really trust me when I first came to Hayden, but he didn't let that stop him from letting me help the folks in town when he found out I was a doctor too."

"Everybody liked and respected him," Billy said. "'Twas a real shame when Leticia passed on. At least they're together again now."

"Folks told me Doc Lyles took it hard when he lost his wife," Lenny said. "They said he didn't talk much to people after that."

"Nope, he sure didn't," Audie said. "He kept pretty much to himself after she died."

"He didn't talk to me all that much either, except about medicine," Lenny said. "But I still considered him a friend."

"Everybody liked him," Billy repeated. Silence drifted over the men, and for a few seconds, nobody spoke.

Finally, Anderson said, "Well, I guess we better get to this." He looked down again at the paper on his desk. "Doc, we asked you to come on in here 'cause of Doctor Lyles." He picked up the paper and held it up for Lenny to see. "This is his last will and testament."

"All right," Lenny said haltingly, obviously still not quite sure why the town council had wanted to see him.

"The doc owned his house and everything in it, the piece of property it sat on, and his car," Anderson said. "He also had a little bit of money in the bank. He left all of it, everything he owned, to Hayden."

"Hayden?" Lenny said. "You mean he left it to the whole town."

"Yup," Billy said. "I guess he was looking out for us."

"We been talking about it," Audie said, pointing in a circle to include all of the town council, "but it seems pretty clear to all of us what he wanted."

"What's that?" Lenny asked.

"He knew that folks here would need a doctor," Anderson said, "so he left a place for him to stay, with all of his equipment and medicine and things. He even left his car so the new doctor would have a way of getting around to make calls on sick folks."

"So," Audie said, "we was hoping you was planning on staying with us here in Hayden, Doc. With Doctor Lyles gone, we need you now more than ever."

"I've been here for over two years," Lenny said. "I got no plans to go anywhere. Hayden's my home now."

"Well, if you want," Anderson said, "you can have another home. We'd like you to move into Doc Lyles's house. The town would still own it, but you could use it for as long as you want. Since it's already got a doctor's office in it, and equipment and medicine and all, we figured it would be perfect for you."

"You can also use Doc Lyles's car too," Billy added.

Lenny didn't say anything right away, and Anderson thought that something might be wrong. "Doc," he said, "you okay?"

"Yeah," Lenny said. "I'm just . . . I'm real pleased that y'all want me to stay and be your town doctor."

"Well, of course," Audie said. "You been doing it now for a while anyway."

"I know, but . . ." Lenny said, but didn't finish the thought. Then he said, "What about the money in the bank?"

"What about it?" Billy asked.

"What're you gonna do with it?" Lenny wanted to know.

"We ain't figured that one out yet," Audie said.

"I was just thinking," Lenny said, standing up from his chair, "if some folks in town get sick and need medicine but can't afford it, maybe you could use the money to buy it for them."

Anderson hadn't thought of that, but once he heard the notion, he liked it. "I think that's a great idea, Lenny," he said.

"Maybe," Billy said. "We should talk about it." They all agreed that they would consider it.

"Well, that's all we needed you for," Anderson said to Lenny. "You can move in whenever you want."

Lenny nodded. "Thanks," he said. "I suppose I'll . . . oh."

"What is it?" Anderson asked.

"I just thought of Missus Hartwell," Lenny said. "She's going to be disappointed about me moving out."

Audie laughed. "Listen," he said, "Mrs. Hartwell calls that place a boarding house, but she's maybe had three folks stay there in the last fifteen years. She'll be fine."

"Yeah, I suppose," Lenny said. "Thanks again."

"We're just happy we still have a town doctor," Anderson said. As he watched Lenny head out of Town Hall, he felt sad that William Lyles had died, but he also felt certain that they had the right man to replace him.

The delivery truck arrived from Greenville later than usual, pulling up to Robinson's General Store in midafternoon. McCoy peered at it from across the commons, which bustled with activity on this unseasonably warm day. With spring still a month in the future and the weeks past brisk at best, it felt good to be outside beneath the energizing rays of the sun. Many of the people in town obviously thought so as well, some strolling about, others sitting on benches or on the grass, a few of them still dressed in their Sunday best after church. The Palmer boys, Justin and Henry, now in their mid-teens, threw a baseball around, and Danny Johnson sat up on the railing of the gazebo, blowing out the occasional tune on his trumpet. Sheriff Gladdy and his wife Beth had spread out a blanket and now shared a picnic lunch with Mabel and Macnair Duncan.

McCoy read the words painted on the side of the box truck in Old English characters: *Greenville Journal Gazette*. A rendering in the lower rear corner showed a man holding the newspaper open and reading it. In a few minutes, McCoy would walk over, as he always did, and pick up a paper.

"Do you know about the REA?" Lynn asked him. She sat next to McCoy on the bench, waiting for Phil to finish purchasing what they needed at the Seed and Feed. This year, they would plant half of their acreage, up from a quarter last year, and from nothing the year before.

"Yup, the REA," McCoy said, attempting to recall the precise words for which the letters stood. Like many of President Roosevelt's New Deal programs—AAA, CCC, PWA, WPA, and the like—its title had been shortened to just its initials. McCoy remembered the REA without too much trouble, as he'd taken note of it last May, when the president had issued an executive order authorizing its creation. At the time, McCoy had thought that the program could have a significant impact on the people of Hayden. "The Rural Electrification Administration," he said.

"Right," Lynn said. "Well, Gregg and Audie and Billy Jenkins drove down to Walter's Bluff last week and talked with the men on their town council about the REA, and those folks in Walter's Bluff already talked to the folks in Weberville and Plattston and Colonee and almost all them towns all the way down to Greenville. They're forming a cooperative so we can work with the REA to bring electricity out to all those places."

"That's great," McCoy said, genuinely enthused. He'd lived for two years in New York City in what he would then have described as primitive conditions, but at least there he'd had power and indoor plumbing. For the last four years, he'd lived without either, and had really come to understand the importance of both. More than just a matter of convenience, it impacted people's health. McCoy could cite the clear and direct case of Dr. Lyles, whom sixty amperes and five thousand volts might've been able to save by allowing the defibrillation of his heart, but he'd also seen less obvious effects of not having electricity. Without deliverable power, there could be no automatic pumps to drive water into homes, and so people bathed by drawing water out of a well and heating it on the stove. As a result of the effort involved, people tended to bathe only once or twice a week, and sometimes in water shared by family members, a practice that facilitated the transmission of disease. The holes dug beneath outhouses also represented a threat, providing a breeding ground for bacteria.

"The cooperative needs every town in it to have at least two families for every mile of power line," Lynn said, her excitement evident. "Walter's Bluff is thirty-five miles away, plus they figure we need maybe twenty-five miles of wires in Hayden itself. That means we have to have at least a hundred and twenty families sign up. So me and Mabel Duncan and Virginia Slattery are gonna talk to folks in town. We're gonna try and sign everybody up, and I just hope we're able to."

"Why wouldn't folks want electricity brought to town?" McCoy asked.

"It's not that they don't want it," Lynn explained. "It's that the cooperative's charging eight dollars to every family to become a member. I think most folks'll be able to join, but that's a lot of money, specially these days."

"It is," McCoy said. After six years living in the twentieth century, he still hadn't become accustomed to how much economic concerns drove everyday life. "Listen, if you find some folks who don't have enough to give to the cooperative, let me know, okay?" McCoy had saved some money over the past few years, and the town also had most of the small inheritance left by Dr. Lyles. McCoy would have to go to Gregg Anderson about using Doc Lyles's money, but between that and his own savings, he thought they should be able to assist everybody in Hayden in signing up with the cooperative.

Lynn reached forward and put her hand on McCoy's knee. "How'd I know I could count on you to help?" she said.

"Just doing my part like everybody else," he said. It felt good to be a part of such a tightly knit community.

"Hey, you two," Phil said, walking up to the bench from behind. McCoy looked up and greeted his friend. "I got everything we need," Phil told Lynn. "You ready to go?"

"You're not still planning on working on the Lord's day, are you?" Lynn asked.

"The Lord's not gonna like it if we get to planting season and we're not ready to plant," Phil said. "I know we're only seeding half a crop, but we're already behind in preparing the land."

"All right," Lynn said. "But only for an hour or two."

"Even that'd help," Phil said. He and Lynn said their good-byes, then headed over to where they'd parked the truck by the Seed and Feed after church. McCoy watched them go, then looked over at Robinson's. When the newspaper truck left a few minutes later, he stood from the bench and walked through the commons, across Mill Road, and into the general store. There, he paid his nickel to the owner, Turner Robinson, picked up a Sunday paper from the pile, and walked back outside. He saw two children, Millicent and Tommy Denton, now climbing over the bench he'd just been sitting on, and so he headed on over to the gazebo. He greeted Danny Johnson with a wave, then sat down on the steps and opened his paper.

As Danny blew out a strangely upbeat version of "Brother, Can You Spare a Dime?" McCoy read through the headlines, skimming most of the articles and looking more closely at those that interested him. When he turned the page, he almost dropped the paper. There, near the top of the middle column, he saw a picture of Edith Keeler. She wore her hair up, as she had when he'd been in New York, and he recognized the blouse she wore and the locket hanging around her neck. A caption beneath the photograph identified her by name, and the article that followed carried the title, FDR MEETS SLUM ANGEL. McCoy read through the two paragraphs.

Feb. 23, 1936—During his visit to New York, President Roosevelt met yesterday afternoon with the city's so-called "slum angel," Edith Keeler. Speaking with her for some time in a back room at the 21st Street Mission, the soup kitchen she runs, he conferred with her about current and new plans to help the needy of this country. A Federal official characterized the meeting as demonstrating before the world the U.S. government's commitment to raising America out of the terrible economic state into which virtually all nations have fallen.

A second topic of discussion involved the new or-

ganization Miss Keeler has founded, the American
Pacifist Movement. Dedicated to preserving the peace
of the world, the APM has in recent months boasted
sizable increases in its membership. With the president,
Miss Keeler spoke at length about maintaining the
country's neutrality and, where necessary, its isola-
tionism. In particular, she warned against committing
any troops to Italy's conflict with Ethiopia, though she
did support economic and moral sanctions against
Rome.

McCoy closed the newspaper and folded it in two. An assortment of emotions rose within him. For one thing, he found that
he missed Edith. Though he had attempted to maintain his distance from her—and everybody else—when he'd been in New
York, he had grown to like her a great deal. In his days at the
21st Street Mission, both in living in its back room and in continuing to volunteer there after he'd moved out, he'd spent quite
a bit of time with her. He'd made new friends in Hayden, but that
hadn't taken away from the affection he still felt for her. He'd
never written to her, as he'd promised to do, and he considered
sending a letter now. But such an idea gave him pause. Although
he'd accepted that he would spend the rest of his life on twentieth-century Earth, and that he'd already irretrievably altered history, New York and Edith seemed somehow tied to the cautious,
solitary way of life he'd adopted when he'd first arrived in the
past. McCoy realized that he might well be compounding the
changes to the timeline with every action he took here in Hayden, but it still seemed more dangerous to him to reconnect with
Edith and his two years in New York. It didn't make much sense,
but it affected him on a visceral level. He would have to think
about it before deciding whether or not to write to his old friend.

Beyond missing Edith, McCoy also felt proud *of* her, and disappointed *for* her. From the moment he'd met her, when she'd
taken him in, hidden him away, and nursed him back to health,
she'd demonstrated her strong humanitarian nature. To see now
that Edith's influence had reached all the way to the halls of the
federal government served only to increase his admiration for
her. At the same time, McCoy saw that she now labored partially

in vain. Though her tireless efforts to improve the lives of the downtrodden would continue to reap benefits for so many people, he knew that her attempts to steer the United States and the world away from war would not succeed. Like so many historic dates—the signing of the Declaration of Independence on 4 July 1776, the storming of the Bastille on 14 July 1789, the first moon landing on 20 July 1969, first contact with Vulcans on 5 April 2063—the day of the United States entry into World War II had been taught in school, and McCoy remembered it: 8 December 1941, a day after Japan had launched a surprise attack on the country. He applauded her efforts, but her vision of peace would not take hold on Earth for another two hundred years.

With a sigh, McCoy opened his newspaper again. Behind him, Danny had stopped playing his trumpet and now chatted with Jordy King, a teenager who'd just started working with his dad, Steve, on the carding machines down at the mill. McCoy read through a couple of articles, but couldn't concentrate. His thoughts kept returning to Edith.

THIRTY-ONE

2276

Chief Engineer Montgomery Scott alternately peered at the monitor and through the viewing port in the front bulkhead of the shuttlecraft. Below, dimly illuminated by starlight, a vast metallic expanse extended in all directions, punctuated here and there by structures and machinery neither he nor any of his engineering team had yet been able to identify. Periodically swinging back and forth in his chair, Scotty moved his feet around the helmet of his environmental suit, which sat on the deck below him. He felt constrained by the suit itself, and a bit warm, but he still looked forward to putting down beside some of the alien equipment, donning his helmet, and heading outside to examine the unfamiliar artifacts.

Earlier today, more than two and a half years into their voyage to the Aquarius Formation, the *Enterprise* crew had encountered what appeared to be an unusual solar system: seven planets orbiting a black hole. As they'd entered the system and approached the outermost world, though, they'd discovered not a planet, but an artificially constructed metallic sphere, four and a half times the size of Earth. Though various structures had been erected on its mostly empty surface, none had been recognizable. The crew had seen nothing resembling propulsion systems nor any obvious means of access or egress. Sensors had failed to penetrate the outside of the sphere, making it impossible to determine the nature of the interior. All attempts at communication had gone unanswered.

The captain had ordered the ship to the sixth world, which had revealed itself to be a synthetic sphere similar to the seventh, though not identical to it. Only sixty percent as large, its surface held some of the same structures, but different ones as well. The fifth sphere measured sixty percent as large as the sixth, and again duplicated some machinery while also introducing new equipment. The fourth sphere, approximately thirteen thousand kilometers in diameter and generating a pull of zero-point-nine-seven gee, continued the pattern.

Given the nearness of the dimensions and gravity of the fourth artificial globe to that of Earth, Captain Kirk had selected it for closer study. In order to observe its surface at close range and to evaluate sites for further investigation, the captain had opted to send down a shuttlecraft. With none of the objects supporting an external atmosphere, the captain, Dr. McCoy, and Scotty had all donned environmental suits and boarded the shuttlecraft *Newton*.

"See anything interesting down there, Scotty?" the captain asked. He sat beside the engineer at the front console, piloting the shuttle.

"Aye, that I do," Scotty said. The structures rising above the great metal plain came in a wide variety of shapes and sizes. None gave any indication of being under power, but most suggested a complexity and configuration beyond that of manual equipment. By all appearances, the sphere—all the spheres they'd observed—seemed abandoned.

"Have you seen anything that might be a way in?" Kirk asked.

"Nothing obvious," Scotty said, "but many of the structures are large enough that they could easily conceal a hatch, either for beings or for small spacecraft."

"I'm still reading no indications of life," Dr. McCoy said from his seat behind the captain. Scotty glanced over and saw the doctor examining a readout on a screen in the port bulkhead.

"Well, Mister Scott, should we find a place to set down?" the captain asked.

"Aye," Scotty said, his attention captured at the moment by a pair of towers up ahead. According to sensors, the two edifices, otherwise alone on this stretch of the sphere, rose from pentagonal bases, one to a height of seven-hundred fifty meters, the other to a thousand. "Do you see the towers up ahead, Captain?"

"Yes," Kirk said.

"Those are the tallest structures we've seen in the system so far," Scotty said. "If the beings who built the spheres left behind a record of their history, or if they left any information at all, perhaps that's where they might have put it."

"A good choice, Mister Scott," the captain said, then pressed a toggle on the console between them. "Kirk to *Enterpr*—"

The shuttle jolted hard, as though struck by something. Scotty flew from his chair into the starboard bulkhead, his feet kicking the helmet of his environmental suit and sending it flying. The cabin shook dramatically as he struggled back into his seat. Next to him, the captain climbed back into his own chair and worked his controls.

"We're yawing to starboard," Kirk called over the suddenly loud, high-pitched whine of the straining engines. "Trying to reestablish attitude control."

Gripping the edge of the console in order to steady his gaze, Scotty called up a sensor display. He expected to read the residual energy of weapons fire or the graviton signature of a tractor beam, but he saw neither. As the captain's hands moved across his own station, Scotty operated the sensors, attempting to determine what had disrupted their flight. He saw no chemical trails of ballistic missiles, no motion of other craft, no ionization—

Then he saw it.

"Captain," he yelled, "we're in some type of warp field. It's causing havoc with the engines."

"I'm bringing the shuttle down," Kirk cried. At once, the *Newton* canted downward, the line of its hull still askew with respect to its forward motion. "Kirk to *Enterprise*," he called. When he received no response, he tried again. "Kirk to—"

The noise in the cabin abruptly quieted, and the shuttle accelerated downward.

"*Enterprise*," the captain finished, the word loud in the suddenly silent compartment. Kirk and Scotty both labored at their stations, their hands speeding from control to control.

"The engines have shut down," Scotty reported. He looked up and saw nothing but the wide plane of the sphere in the forward viewport as the shuttle plummeted. He checked the readouts, then said, "From the looks of this, I doubt the crew will be able to beam us through the warp field or secure the shuttle with a tractor beam."

The captain continued to punch at his controls. "We've still got thrusters," he said. "And antigravs." He peered over at Scotty and then back over his shoulder into the cabin. "Scotty, Bones, into your helmets," he ordered. "I don't know if I'll be able to keep the hull intact."

Scotty reached for his helmet, then remembered that he'd accidentally kicked it across the compartment. He started up out of his chair to retrieve it, but then Dr. McCoy handed it to him. Scotty sat back down and quickly pulled it on over his head, then secured it to the rigid neck of his environmental suit. He raised his left wrist into view before the visor and pressed the activation control mounted there. Immediately, he felt the coolness of air moving across his face as the suit's cycling system engaged.

"Hold on," the captain said, his voice emerging tinnily from a speaker in Scotty's helmet. "Impact in thirty seconds. You two, get to the aft section."

Scotty stood from his chair and stumbled toward the rear of the shuttle along the slanting deck. He saw the captain remain at the forward console and wanted to protest, but knew that to give them the best chance of survival, sómebody would have to stay and operate the thrusters and antigravs. He followed McCoy into the aft compartment, watched as the doctor dropped into crash position, then did so himself, leaning against the rear bulkhead and putting his helmeted head between his knees.

Fifteen seconds later, the shuttlecraft *Newton* pounded onto the unforgiving metal surface of the sphere.

McCoy woke with a start, opening his eyes in dim light and unfamiliar surroundings. The bulk of his helmet surrounded his field of vision, and he could feel the constricting fabric of his environmental suit against his body. He saw a curved overhead a couple of meters above him. In order to look around, he moved to push himself up from the surface upon which he lay.

He felt nothing below him.

McCoy jerked his head around to peer below him . . . except that he could distinguish no "below." When he'd opened his eyes and seen a surface a distance from him, he'd assumed that direction to be "up," but his vestibular system could confirm no orientation with respect to gravity, because he sensed no gravity. Over his shoulder, visible just past an opaque section of his helmet, he saw a figure in midair and discerned it as Scotty. Beyond him floated another person, presumably Jim.

McCoy pondered the circumstances. He remembered leaving the *Enterprise* in a shuttlecraft with the two men for the purpose of surveying and possibly exploring the sphere. They'd approached—

It all came back to him, right up until the *Newton* had slammed into the surface of the synthetic world. He and Scotty had hunkered in the aft compartment, ordered there by the captain as the shuttle had plunged from the sky. McCoy recalled Jim's voice, no doubt at the moment before impact, warning of the crash to come. Then he'd awoken here, floating at the midpoint of this long cylindrical space, about four or five meters in diameter.

"Scotty?" he heard Jim say, his voice emerging from the speaker in McCoy's helmet. *"Bones?"*

McCoy waited for a moment to see if Scotty would respond. He didn't. "Jim, it's McCoy. I'm here."

"Bones, are you all right?" the captain asked.

McCoy flexed his muscles, moved his arms and legs, trying to evaluate his physical condition. "Achy," he concluded, "and a little nauseous, but otherwise I seem to be all right. What about you?"

"About the same," Jim reported. *"Can you get to a bulkhead?"* he asked.

"I don't think so," McCoy said. He flapped his arms, attempting to "swim" through the air, without result. "I seem to be floating in the center of this place."

"So am I," Jim said. *"Listen, I'm going to try to wake Scotty up. You might want to lower the volume on your speaker."*

"Thanks for the warning," McCoy said, and he raised his hand to work the controls mounted on the wrist of his environmental suit. As Jim repeated Scotty's name a dozen times—at different volumes, sometimes including his rank, sometimes his position—McCoy examined the sensor readouts attached to his other wrist. They could breathe the atmosphere here, he saw, though it read somewhat thin. According to his chronometer, they'd been unconscious for almost three hours, though, so they had at least another ninety minutes of their own air remaining.

After a half a minute or so of the captain's exhortations, McCoy heard several low groans. *"Scotty?"* Jim asked, and McCoy returned the speaker in his helmet to its normal setting.

"Aye," Scotty said. *"I'm here, Captain."*

"Are you all right?" Jim asked.

Scotty grunted once or twice, obviously testing his body as McCoy had a few moments ago. *"I think I hurt my shoulder, but otherwise I seem to be all right,"* Scotty said. *"Captain, where are we?"*

"I'm assuming somewhere inside one of the structures we saw on the surface of the sphere, or within the sphere itself," Jim said. McCoy heard the chirp of a communicator channel being opened. *"Kirk to Enterprise,"* the captain said. He waited a few seconds, then repeated himself. He got no response. *"It's no use; they're not receiving us,"* he said, then closed the channel. *"Scotty, can you reach the bulkhead?"*

"I don't know," Scotty said. *"I don't think so, but let me try."*

McCoy looked over and saw the engineer moving his arms and legs about, but he remained suspended in place. *"I can't move, Captain,"* he said.

"Bones," Jim said, *"take a look at the—"*

All at once, lights came up in the cylindrical space. McCoy gazed around and saw a row of illuminated tubes recessed into one section of the rounded bulkhead. Now he could also see drawings on the side of the cylinder, simple linear representations of various shapes. A predominant theme seemed to be a pair of different-sized regular pentagons coupled with two narrow, tower-like figures, one about three-quarters the length of the other.

"Scotty," Jim said, *"is that a hatch near you?"*

"It looks like it might be," Scotty said.

McCoy strained his neck to inspect the bulkhead around the engineer and finally saw to what he thought Jim had referred, a circular metal rim in the side of the cylinder. As he looked at it, it receded half a meter, then rolled to the side. An alien stood there—although "stood" might be the wrong word, since it possessed no legs. More or less cylindrical in shape, its body spread slightly at its bottom and top. Colored a deep forest green, it measured perhaps two meters in length. McCoy saw nothing resembling a face or any sensory organs, but the alien did have two rings of tendrils extending from its body, one about a third of the way up, the other about twice as high. The diameter of each of the lower tendrils appeared about the same as that of human fingers, though they reached about twice the length; the upper tendrils appeared thicker and a good deal longer. Both sets of appendages stayed in constant, sinuous motion, like the fronds of sea plants wavering in a current.

"Jim, do you see that?" McCoy asked.

"I do," the captain said. *"Turn on your external speakers."* McCoy did so, in time to hear Jim address the alien. *"I am Captain James T. Kirk of the Federation starship* Enterprise," he said. *"We are on a mission of exploration and come in peace. We did not know that—"*

A piercing screech filled the air, but contained enough variations in pitch, tone, and volume to cause McCoy to characterize it as speech. Peering at the alien, he saw that a maw had opened

up in its midsection, between the rings of tendrils, and he postulated that the squealing "voice" emerged from there. The alien
paused for a moment, and McCoy watched as another opening
appeared in its flesh. It reached in with one of its upper tendrils
and pulled out a round silver object, which it then placed in its
maw. The second aperture closed, vanishing completely, as
though it had never been. *"I am Lukoze,"* the alien said, its words
now obviously modulated by a translation device. *"We are the
Otevrel. We have been in contact with your ship. We understand
what has happened. You will now come with me as I remove you
from this world."* At first, McCoy liked the sound of that, assuming that it meant they would be permitted to return to the *Enterprise,* but as he thought about it, he hoped it hadn't been
intended as a euphemism for something far more inimical.

The Otevrel, Lukoze, reached a lower tendril up to the side of
the corridor, and McCoy felt gravity slowly reassert itself. He,
Jim, and Scotty immediately drifted downward, until they alit on
the curved surface of the cylinder. McCoy found the footing
awkward, but manageable.

He looked over at Jim and saw him reach to his suit's controls. McCoy understood and quickly shut down the output to his
external speaker. He saw Scotty do the same. *"What do we do?"*
the engineer asked, echoing the question in McCoy's own mind.

"We don't appear to be in any danger," the captain said. *"It
sounded as though they contacted the* Enterprise, *and Spock explained the situation and asked for our release."* Jim took a
breath, then added, *"But stay alert."*

As the captain walked toward Scotty, McCoy did too. When
the three of them had come together, Jim worked his speaker
control again. *"We will follow you,"* he told Lukoze.

At once, the alien's maw and the device it carried disappeared
into its body, swallowed up like an object dropped into a lake.
Lukoze then moved away from the hatch, gliding quickly and
smoothly along another curved deck. Jim followed, and then
Scotty, with McCoy bringing up the rear. When he passed
through the hatchway, McCoy saw that they'd entered another
cylinder, almost identical to the first, but longer. He peered down
and inspected the deck, expecting that he might spy evidence of
a lubricant that the Otevrel had utilized in their locomotion, but

he saw no such thing. *Maybe they move about like snakes,* he thought, picturing the alternate lifting and dropping of scales that the limbless reptiles employed in rectilinear motion, giving the impression of sliding along smoothly in a straight line.

Lukoze proceeded quickly along and the shuttle crew had to hurry to keep up, the Otevrel sometimes stopping and waiting for them to do so. They made several turns into intersecting corridors, all of which bore markings along their circumference. As with the cylinder in which they'd awoken, the dual pentagons and dual towers repeated in many places.

Finally, Lukoze opened another hatch and escorted them into a large chamber, not cylindrical this time, but spherical. Within, numerous metal spheres, about the size of the *Enterprise*'s shuttlecraft, lined the lower half of the bulkhead, sitting atop spoon-shaped shelves. A single sphere rested in the lowest part of the chamber, a circular hatch in its side standing open. Lukoze slid inside, and then its maw and the translation device reappeared. *"You will enter the craft."* It moved away from the door, and Jim, Scotty, and McCoy followed.

Inside, the interior looked very much like that of a spacecraft, though much of the equipment seemed oddly oriented due to the curved bulkheads. Three circular viewing ports looked out of one side of the sphere at its equator, with consoles both above and below it. There were no chairs, but against the bulkhead and in front of the forward stations, columns rose out of the deck, each with a concave side. It seemed clear that Lukoze could rest the length of his body within the hollow of any of the columns.

"You may incline or . . ." Lukoze began, and then hesitated, as though searching for the proper word. *". . . sit,"* the alien said at last. McCoy looked to Jim, who peered around the compartment, then nodded. Carefully, the three humans lowered themselves to the deck and leaned against the bulkhead.

Ahead of them, Lukoze settled the length of his form into the concavity of one of the forward columns, then began to operate the controls. The hatch swung closed, and shortly after, a hum and a vibration began to suffuse the craft. With the translation device once more gone from view, Lukoze began to speak, his native language remaining untranslated, the squalling patterns of its speech sounding almost like the shriek of the insane. McCoy thought he could hear more than one voice and assumed the Otevrel to be in communication with others.

McCoy saw movement through the viewing ports, though he felt nothing but the vibration that had begun earlier. He continued to watch, and before long, the speckled canvas of space appeared. Beside him, Jim reached up to his environmental suit and touched a control, and McCoy heard through his interior speaker the warble of a communicator channel being opened. *"Kirk to Enterprise,"* he said. *"Kirk to—"*

A bolt of light seared into the captain, and he collapsed. McCoy looked back at Lukoze and saw the alien away from his column, holding a device he did not recognize in its tendrils, but that surely must have been an energy weapon of some kind. McCoy had no tricorder or other medical equipment with him, but he saw that Jim continued to breathe, his chest rising and falling with his respiration. He reached over and put a hand above the captain's heart, and even through his gloved hand and Jim's environmental suit, he could feel it beating strongly and regularly.

McCoy peered back at Lukoze. With another tendril, the alien pulled the translation device from within its body and its maw once again formed. *"No communications with your ship are permitted,"* it said. *"You will remain silent as we ford the* incheuto *back to the lower* distaari.*"* The translator apparently failed to interpret two of Lukoze's words.

McCoy looked over at Scotty. They said nothing to each other, but they didn't need to: at least one aspect of the situation seemed clear. Lukoze was not taking them back to the *Enterprise*.

Spock stood over the sciences station on the bridge, hands clasped behind his back, observing as Lieutenant Commander Dennehy cycled through her sensor scans. "Still nothing, sir," reported the ship's second officer. "No indications of an impending jump to warp and no movement within the system."

"Continue scanning, Mister Dennehy," Spock said. The first officer remained convinced that, sooner or later, both events would take place. It had been nearly an hour since their last communication with the Otevrel, the inhabitants of this unique "solar system," whose intent had been plain: They would execute the three *Enterprise* crewmembers who had violated their mores, but they would not do so on their fourth "world," which would also constitute a desecration under their law.

Spock stepped down to the lower, inner portion of the bridge and retrieved the slender data slate he had left on the command chair. He sat down and reviewed its contents. The slate currently showed a representation of the Otevrel's seven-sphere system, along with Spock's attempt to calculate the warp field they had earlier generated about it. At the time, the *Enterprise* had been caught within the field around the fourth sphere and had been dragged through space as the entire system had moved. The ship's engines had been affected and could have become disabled had Sulu and DiFalco not managed to extricate the *Enterprise* as quickly as they had. An inductor manifold had buckled during the incident, but had subsequently been replaced.

Touching a fingertip to the corner of the slate's display, Spock executed a simulation of his latest computations. An electric-blue cocoon flowed around each of the disks that represented the black hole and seven spheres of the Otevrel system. As the simulation progressed, the encircling warp fields elongated, reaching toward each other. Before they merged to become one large field, though, they collapsed in on themselves.

So far, scans had failed to identify the means by which the Otevrel had generated their warp field, or how the field geometry had functioned. Spock hypothesized that individual warp contours had been produced about the black hole and each of the seven orbiting spheres, and then somehow connected one to another, even though his simulations had as yet failed to demonstrate the viability of such an interaction. Regardless of the details of the Otevrel warp field, though, it had impacted not only the *Enterprise*'s drive systems, but those of the shuttlecraft *Newton,* which had also been caught within it. The shuttle had crashed onto the fourth sphere, with the *Enterprise* crew unable to do anything but confirm via sensors that Captain Kirk, Dr. McCoy, and Chief Engineer Scott had survived.

Once Sulu had pulled the *Enterprise* free of the Otevrel warp field and the inductor manifold had been replaced, Spock had pursued the mobile system, which had stopped an eighth of a light-year away. By then, the *Newton*'s crew of three had disappeared from the wreckage of the shuttle. Fortunately, Lieutenant Commander Uhura had managed to establish contact with the Otevrel. It had taken more than an hour, but eventually Uhura and her Otevrel counterpart had been able to program their respective translation devices to permit meaningful communication. At that point, the fate of Captain Kirk and the others had become clear.

The Otevrel, it turned out, held a uniquely parochial and ethnocentric worldview. They believed that the black hole at the heart of their system also marked the precise center of the universe, as well as the location of a physical nirvana. The Otevrel maintained a perspective that, when they erected a warp field about their system, they actually isolated themselves in a way that permitted them to move the entirety of the universe about their stationary worlds. Proximity to the black hole indicated one's spiritual enlightenment and social station, and one had to earn the right to draw nearer. Individual Otevrel, throughout their lifetimes, sought to migrate from the outermost of their worlds to the innermost, and from there into the black hole itself. Each world represented a distinct *distaari*, or caste, with the physical and spiritual gulfs separating them designated as *inchento*.

"Mister Spock," Dennehy said, and the first officer turned in the command chair to face her. "I'm reading an energy surge on the fifth sphere."

"Could it be a part of the Otevrel's warp field generator?" Spock asked.

Dennehy worked her controls as she studied a display. "I don't think so," she said. "I see nothing resembling the energy signature of warp generation. It doesn't appear to be a ship either."

"Could it be a transporter?" Spock asked.

"Negative," Dennehy answered at once. "There's nothing identifiable as a transporter beam, nor are they generating enough energy to accomplish an interplanetary transport."

"Very good, Mister Dennehy," Spock said. "Continue scanning." Based on the Otevrel's stated intentions to execute the *Newton* crew, Dennehy's ability to rule out the cause of energy production on the spheres provided valuable information. According to Korlant, the Otevrel with whom Spock had spoken, Captain Kirk, Dr. McCoy, and Engineer Scott had traveled too close to the black hole, violating the *distaari,* a crime punishable by death. It did not matter that the three men were not Otevrel, nor that they had violated the caste law unknowingly. Korlant claimed sorrow regarding the circumstances, but remained immovable concerning the extreme sentence. But the Otevrel had revealed one piece of information that could be of consequence, though Spock had been unable to tell whether or not Korlant had intended that to be the case. All executions took place on the outermost of the Otevrel spheres, and so the captain and the others would have to be taken there before they were killed. With sensors showing no evidence of transporter technology within the Otevrel system, the *Newton* crew would therefore have to be taken by spacecraft from the fourth sphere to the seventh.

Now, Spock awaited that event. He had ordered Sulu to keep the *Enterprise* away from the plane of the Otevrel ecliptic—about which the vast warp field formed—but within sensor range of the spheres. If the system moved again, the ship would follow. If the Otevrel carried Kirk, McCoy, and Scott out of the fourth world, the *Enterprise* crew would retrieve them. While the surfaces of the spheres prevented penetration by sensors, and therefore by transporters, Spock calculated that the same might not be true of Otevrel spacecraft. If sensors could not pierce the hull of any ships they detected emerging from the fourth sphere, though, then the *Enterprise* crew would simply employ a tractor beam to capture the ship.

Twenty-three minutes later, Spock had his answer.

"Sir, I'm detecting a ship traveling away from the fourth sphere," Dennehy announced. "Heading for the fifth sphere."

"Life signs?" Spock asked.

"Mister Spock," Uhura interjected from her communications station, "I just received a hail from Captain Kirk." She turned to face the first officer. "I think the Otevrel severed the transmission."

"I'm reading three humans on the ship," Dennehy said. "Also another life sign."

"Mister Dennehy, transfer sensor readings to the helm and to the transporter room," Spock said. "Chief DiFalco, set an interception course. Mister Sulu, take the *Enterprise* in at as great a velocity as possible, while still allowing the ship to slow to sublight within transporter range of the craft." Spock activated the intercom. "Spock to transporter room."

"Transporter room, Chandler here," came the response.

"Lieutenant, Mister Dennehy is transferring sensor readings of the three *Newton* crewmembers to your station. Lock on and transport as soon as the *Enterprise* slows to impulse speed. Keep this channel open."

"Aye, sir," Chandler said.

"Chief DiFalco," Spock said, "once the captain and the others are aboard, take the shortest route out of the Otevrel system." He did not want the *Enterprise* caught again within the enormous warp field.

DiFalco operated her controls at the navigation console. "Entry and exit course plotted and laid in, sir," she said.

"Go, Mister Sulu," Spock said.

"Accelerating to warp four-point-five," Sulu said, his fingers jumping expertly across his panel. It would be a risk to move at warp within a planetary system—or the approximation of a planetary system—but a minimal risk, and one that Sulu and DiFalco had demonstrated themselves capable of taking without ill effect. "Warp one," Sulu read from his display as the thrum of the *Enterprise*'s drive rose. "Warp two . . . warp three, sir . . . warp four . . . point five. Now decelerating." Spock detected a distinct change in the tone of the engines. "Warp three . . . warp two . . . the *Enterprise* now traveling at sublight speed."

"Beaming," declared Chandler via the intercom. Spock waited, even as he heard the sound of the transporter accompanying the lieutenant's voice. *"They're aboard,"* Chandler said.

"Acknowledged," Spock said. "Mister Sulu, best speed to depart the system."

"Aye, sir," Sulu said.

Once more, the background pulse of the ship's drive established itself.

McCoy sat in his office aboard the *Enterprise* and reviewed the recording again, stopping it partway through. On the monitor on his desk, he could see all of Korlant, from the slight widening at the base of the Otevrel's body to the slight widening at the top. The doctor found the two rows of tendrils particularly fascinating, but as he looked now at the image of the alien, he focused on a slight stippling of its flesh. The recording had been made during Spock's communication with Korlant, and with the prospect of future contact with the Otevrel questionable, McCoy had wanted to learn whatever he could about their physiology.

After Spock had rescued the *Newton* crew, the captain had contacted the Otevrel. Despite being taken captive, stunned into unconsciousness, and as it had turned out, sentenced to die, Jim had decided to issue a formal apology for having broken their laws. He'd offered an opportunity for another meeting, on their terms, but they had demurred, though they had left open the possibility of establishing relations sometime in the future. Jim had gotten the impression, as had Spock, that Otevrel society might currently be in a state of transition, with some of their citizenry questioning their traditions and their view of their place in the universe.

For his part, McCoy selfishly hoped that the Federation and the Otevrel could come to an understanding. Even from his brief encounter with just one of their species, he'd developed a fascination with their physiology, and he'd love to include information about them in the comparative physiology text he'd finally begun writing. Of course, if he continued adding new species to the list of those he intended to detail, he might never finish his work. Then again, he hadn't actually made much progress so far on any of his research during the *Enterprise*'s voyage to the Aquarius Formation.

McCoy employed an image-enhancement program to attempt to get a better look at the stippling on Korlant's body. He hadn't seen such markings on Lukoze, but then he hadn't really had an opportunity to study the Otevrel, even casually. Now, though, seeing the markings on Korlant, McCoy suspected that they just might form some sort of sensory net.

As he examined the magnified view of the rough, grainy patch of the Otevrel's flesh, the doors to the corridor parted and Spock entered. He carried a slate in one hand and what looked like a slab of metal in the other. "Doctor," Spock said, walking up to his desk, "I would appreciate a few moments of your time."

"Certainly, Spock," McCoy said. He reached forward and deactivated the monitor. "What can I do for you?"

"I would ask you to look at this," Spock said, holding out the piece of metal to him. When McCoy reached for it with one hand, Spock suggested that he use two. McCoy did, and found the slab considerably heavier than he'd anticipated. He set it down atop his desk and examined it. About a quarter of a meter wide and twice as long, it had a silvery sheen and a series of evenly spaced ribs machined into it. On one of the long edges, he spied a hairline crack, four or five centimeters long.

"Well, what is it, Spock?" McCoy asked. "I'm a doctor, not a metallurgist."

"This is a section of an inductor manifold," Spock said. "It is a part of the *Enterprise*'s drive system. During the encounter last week with the Otevrel, when the ship was initially caught within their warp field, the manifold buckled. Engineering personnel replaced it with relative ease and the ship suffered no lasting ill effects. However, I became curious why this particular manifold had failed."

"All right," McCoy said. "But I'm guessing it wasn't caused by synthococcus novae or Rigelian Kassaba fever, so what does this have to do with me?"

"In actuality," Spock said, "the cause might have been simply material fatigue, possibly brought about by a weakening of the manifold during our battle with the Klingons."

"The Klingons?" McCoy said, confused. "Spock, the *Enterprise* hasn't been anywhere near a Klingon in at least five years." McCoy recalled that last meeting, at the Einstein station.

"Precisely," Spock said. "This manifold was a component of the *Enterprise* prior to Captain Kirk initially taking command more than a decade ago. It has not required replacement since then."

"All right," McCoy said, "but I'm still not following you. An old piece of equipment failed under stress. That doesn't seem that unusual to me. What's your point?"

"My point, Doctor, is this," Spock said, holding up the slate in his hand. "In my curiosity to determine why this particular piece of equipment failed, I executed a number of molecular, atomic, and subatomic scans. Among the other data I collected, I found this." He handed the slate to McCoy, who took it and inspected the display. On it, he saw a series of energy readings, along with a graphical representation of some discrepancies discovered in those values. "Does this remind you of anything?"

McCoy saw it at once: the same unexpected divergence, the same pattern of increase, the same energy signature. The nature of the readings in this inanimate chunk of metal mirrored those that the medical staff had found in the M'Benga numbers of the crew during the five-year mission. "Are you sure about this?" he asked Spock.

"I performed my scans a second time," Spock said, "and I also ran diagnostics on my equipment. The results were the same."

McCoy stood up from his desk and paced across his office, still carrying the slate. "I don't see how this can be, unless—" He turned back to face Spock from across the compartment. "—this isn't a medical condition. It must be a physical condition, irrespective of the living or organic character of the subject."

"I concur," Spock said. "Whatever happened to you and me and the captain to cause the increase in our M'Benga numbers, also caused those readings—" Spock pointed at the slate in McCoy's hand. "—in the inductor manifold."

McCoy walked back over to his desk. "Did that cause it to fail?" he asked, concerned that the seemingly innocuous change in readings through the years might actually be a harbinger of deleterious effects to come.

"I don't believe so," Spock said, "though it does bear further investigation."

McCoy nodded. "I agree," he said, thinking that this finding might actually spur their research. During his time away from Starfleet after the five-year mission, McCoy had done some such work, but not much, instead spending a good deal of time on the Fabrini medical database. At the same time, Spock had been on Vulcan, undergoing the *Kolinahr* ritual. In the three years since they'd rejoined the *Enterprise* crew, they had occasionally returned to their research, but the ship's mission of exploration had largely kept them busy with other things. "Spock, have you tested any other old equipment aboard the *Enterprise*?" McCoy asked. "Or any of the new equipment?"

"No," Spock said. "But I agree that we should."

McCoy reached across his desk and picked up a tricorder sitting there. "Let's go," he said.

THIRTY-TWO

1937

Lynn raced Belle Reve along Church Street, knowing that she would be late, but hoping that she wouldn't be *too* late. She and Phil had invited Leonard for a six o'clock supper tonight, and it had to be close to that time right now. She'd taken too long at Jeff Donner's, but she hadn't expected that Pastor Gallagher would be having a wheel repaired on his buggy today, or that, like her, Randy Denton would be having a horse shod. She hadn't wanted to wait, but Belle Reve had needed new shoes for a long time now, and they'd need her when they started preparing the fields for planting in the next couple of days.

Up ahead, near the turnoff to Tindal's Lane, Lynn saw the back of an old red truck. As she galloped closer, she recognized it as belonging to the Bartells, and saw that it had stopped, its right wheels pulled off onto the grass bordering the dirt road, its driver's-side door standing open. Thinking that somebody must've broken down, she slowed Belle Reve to a trot, and then to a walk. Despite running late already, she knew that the Bartells' farm was a few miles farther down Church Street, and if the truck had broken down, then maybe Jimmy or Judy or Bo would need a ride. The sun hung low in the sky and would soon set, bringing darkness within the hour.

As Lynn drew abreast of the truck, she saw Bo standing in

front of it, though with his back to the vehicle and its hood down. The son of the Hayden's deputy sheriff and its town clerk, Bo had grown into a lean, tow-headed figure of a young man, who had to be about twenty-three or twenty-four. He looked back over his left shoulder at her, a smile on his face. "Hey, Missus Dickinson," he said. "Look what we got here."

Lynn didn't understand what Bo meant until she passed the front of the truck. There, on the ground in front of him, a colored man lay on his back, a canvas sack by his head. About thirty or thirty-five, he wore tan pants and a red and blue plaid shirt, dust from the road sticking to his clothes in patches. He had a blue bandana wrapped around his head, covering it, and as she watched, he patted the ground around him as though looking for something. Bo turned back toward him just as the colored man stopped searching around, perched on his knees, and pulled a pair of wire-rimmed spectacles onto his face. He peered up at Bo.

"What're you looking at, boy?" the young Bartell spat. The colored man started to get to his feet, and Bo stepped toward him.

"Bo!" Lynn called, fearful that a fight would break out. "What're you doing?"

"I suppose I'm just keeping our town clean," Bo said. He thrust his hands into the colored man's chest, sending him staggering backward. The colored man spun his arms wildly, trying to keep his balance, and he managed to stay on his feet. Bo moved toward him again.

"Bo!" Lynn called again, imagining the worst. In her head, she saw the colored man punching Bo in the face, beating him, maybe pulling out a knife. "Bo!" she cried again, pulling her foot from its stirrup and swinging her leg over Belle Reve. She jumped to the ground, quickly wrapped her horse's reins around the window frame of the open truck door, and raced over to Bo. The young man had stopped maybe a yard from the colored man, and she grabbed at his arm. "Stop it, Bo," she said, looking up at him. "There ain't no need to fight."

"I weren't fighting, ma'am," Bo said. "Just keeping this here nigger from dirtying our town."

Lynn looked from the Bartell boy to the colored man. Bo

stood a head taller than she did and had a strong build, but she could say the same things for the stranger. "What're you doing here?" she asked him.

For long seconds, the colored man continued looking at Bo— *glaring* at him—but then he turned his attention to Lynn. "I'm just passing through, ma'am," he said, pointing down Church Street toward town. He spoke very precisely, his words clipped like the individual hoofbeats of a horse. "Heading north," he added.

"Not through our town, you ain't," Bo said.

"This is supposed to be a free country," the colored man said.

"Not for you, boy," Bo said. He pulled his arm from Lynn's grasp and started forward again. Lynn followed and took hold of his arm once more, stopping him.

"Maybe you should just go around the town," Lynn suggested to the colored man. "If you go back down that way, you can go right on Merrysville Road, then out to Upper Piedmont Highway. It goes north." She motioned down Church Street past him, and as she did, she saw a cloud of dust farther down, behind a vehicle headed in their direction. She hoped it might be Turner Robinson, who also lived out that way, but he was probably still back in town at his store.

"With all due respect, ma'am," the colored man said, his tone resentful, "I walked up that way. Merrysville Road has got to be seven or eight miles back."

"That too far for you to walk, boy?" Bo taunted him.

"It's farther than I should have to walk," the colored man said. "It's farther than I *want* to walk."

"Like I care what you want," Bo said, and once more, he stepped forward. Lynn jumped in front of him and turned to face him, putting her hands on his chest.

"Stop it, Bo," she said. "There ain't no need to fight here. He's just walking, that's all."

Bo gazed down at her, and she could see the hatred in his eyes—not for her, but for the stranger. "You want *that* walking through Hayden, Missus Dickinson?" he asked. "Through *our* town?"

"I . . . I don't really care, Bo," she said, realizing that it didn't really make any difference to her. The colored man didn't say he wanted to stay in Hayden, just to pass through. She knew what she did want, though: to avoid a fight. "Listen," she said over her shoulder, "maybe you should just go. Maybe that would be for the best." She now heard the engine of the vehicle heading up Church Street as it drew closer.

Lynn peered up at Bo and waited, hoping that the colored man would heed her advice. But then he said, "Thank you, ma'am, but I don't think I want to 'just go.'" She heard the crush of his footsteps on the dirt road as he strode past her, carrying his sack over his shoulder. She watched him go, and so did Bo.

"Well, I'll be a—" Bo said, sounding as surprised at the colored man's actions as Lynn felt. He pulled away from Lynn and started to follow, but then halted as the vehicle coming down the road reached them. It stopped beside Bo's truck, pulling a cloud of dry dust along with it. Lynn squinted her eyes against it and covered her nose and mouth with her hand.

"Hey," somebody called, and she recognized the nasal voice of Billy Fuster. "What're you doing, Bo?" Lynn waved her hand in front of her face, clearing away the dust. Through it, she saw the Fusters' old jalopy, held together with spit and baling wire. Inside, she saw Jordy King in the passenger seat, and the two Palmer boys, Justin and Henry, in the back. At twenty-three, Billy was the oldest of the lot, and at sixteen, Henry was the youngest.

"You won't believe this," Bo said. "We got us a nigger trying to come into our town."

"What?" Billy said. "Where?" Lynn looked past them and, through the settling dust, could just make out the figure of the colored man marching along.

"Right down there," Bo said.

"Come on," Billy said excitedly. Bo climbed onto the car's running board, sticking his hand in through the open window to hang on to the top of the driver's seat. Billy drove off immediately, kicking up another cloud from the dirt road.

Lynn squinted and covered her nose and mouth again and waited a few seconds for the dust to calm down. When it had, she ran to Belle Reve, unwrapped her reins from Bo's truck door, and mounted into her saddle. She sped after Billy Fuster and the others, no longer concerned about Bo getting into a fight, but worried that the peaceful town of Hayden might suddenly have a lynching on its hands.

By the time she caught up to them, all of the boys had gotten out of the Fusters' car. They stood in front of it, spread across the road, facing the colored man. As she watched, Billy and Jordy circled around him, cutting off his means of escape. "What're you boys doing?" she called, but not one of them paid her any attention. Instead, Bo stepped directly up to the colored man, who Lynn noticed no longer wore his spectacles.

He tucked them away so they wouldn't get broken in a fight, she guessed.

"I told you that you can't go through our town, nigger," he said. He rammed the heels of his hands into the colored man's chest again, and the man hurtled backward, his canvas sack falling to the ground. He began to fall himself, but then Billy grabbed him from behind, keeping him on his feet; Lynn saw at once that it was no act of charity.

"Get off me," Billy said, pushing the colored man forward, back toward Bo. Bo reached out and pushed him again, this time in a different direction. The colored man tripped, and tumbled to the road in front of Justin and Henry. As he clambered back to his feet, the two Palmer boys reached for him, but he shook them off and pushed them away.

"I don't want a fight," the colored man said.

"'Course you don't," Bo said. "Not when there's five of us and one of you."

"Is that how it's got to be?" the colored man asked. "Or are you man enough to face me on your own?"

Bo snorted, an ugly sort of a laugh. "Man?" he said. "I'm more of a man now than you'll ever be, boy."

"I don't think you can prove that," the colored man said evenly. "Not by yourself."

"Stop it!" Lynn tried again, but nobody even looked at her. Instead, Bo peered over at Billy, then back at the colored man.

"You *want* to fight me, nigger?" Bo said. "'Cause I'm about ready to lay you out." For a tense moment, the situation seemed to stop cold. Nobody said anything, nobody moved, and Lynn hoped that the colored man would choose discretion. But he spoke up.

"I'm right here," he said. "Either stop me or let me be on my way."

Bo ran at him. The colored man tensed and then moved aside at the last instant, pushing Bo as he went past and turning to face him. Justin and Henry stepped away, but Billy started toward the colored man from behind. Bo righted himself and turned back.

"No," he yelled at Billy, and the Fuster boy stopped. "I'll take him." He ran again at the colored man and this time connected. The two went down hard onto the dirt, and Billy had to jump back out of the way to stop from getting hit.

"Stop it, stop it!" Lynn yelled from atop Belle Reve. She didn't know what to do. She thought about rushing to the house to get Phil and bring him back here, but feared that it would be too late by then.

Bo rolled atop the colored man and pushed himself up, throwing a hand around his throat. He pulled back his other hand, cocking his fist, but almost faster than Lynn could see it happen, the colored man slapped the hand around his neck away, and Bo toppled forward. As he fell, the colored man sent a fist into his face. Lynn thought she heard something crunch, and she couldn't tell if it had been Bo's nose or the colored man's hand. Bo cried out and raised his hands to his face. The colored man pushed him to the side and scrambled back to his feet. Lynn saw blood on his shirt, and then looked to Bo. As the young man pulled his hands away from his bloodied nose, he appeared stunned.

"You son of a bitch," he fumed as he looked at the smears of red on his hands. He staggered to his feet.

"You want some help, Bo?" Billy asked. Bo didn't answer, but yelled angrily and raced toward the colored man again. Just as Bo reached him, though, the colored man hurled another punch at his face, connecting solidly. Bo collapsed to the dirt in a heap.

The boys looked on for a moment in silence—as did Lynn— but then Billy yelled, "Get him." Justin and Henry closed in on the stranger from either side, and the colored man raised a fist and punched Justin in the face. As he reeled backward, his younger brother backed away. Jordy sped forward, though, putting his head down and ramming the colored man in the gut.

The pair crashed onto the dirt, and Jordy began flailing away, looking frantic to fend off the colored man's punches as much as land his own.

Billy ran toward Lynn then, and for an odd moment, she thought that he meant to attack her. But he strode past her and over to his car, where he lifted the trunk, reached in, and pulled out a tire iron. "Oh no, Billy," Lynn cried, flinging herself down from Belle Reve. She stood between the horse and the car directly, in Billy's path as he headed back to the fight. "Billy, you don't want to do this. Somebody's gonna get hurt bad."

"Somebody sure is," Billy snarled, pushing past her and walking around the front of the car. Determined to intercede, Lynn followed. There, she saw Justin still on his knees on the ground, his brother kneeling beside him, obviously trying to help. The colored man now straddled Jordy's waist, holding the boy's hands down on either side of his head. Bo was gone.

Billy walked right up to the colored man and lifted the tire iron up over his head. "No!" Lynn screamed, and the stranger looked up just in time to see Billy bringing the iron bar forward. The colored man raised his arms to try to block the blow, and the hard metal struck his right forearm. He bellowed in pain, but grabbed at the tire iron, trying to wrest it from Billy's grasp. But Billy jerked it back and prepared to swing it again. The colored man jumped from atop Jordy and crawled in the opposite direction. Billy leaped over Jordy and went after him.

Suddenly, another car skidded to a halt on the dirt road, coming from town. As intent as she'd been on what had been happening, Lynn hadn't even heard it approaching. As another cloud of dust rolled through the air, she saw Leonard open his car door and get out. "What . . . what's going on here?" he asked, obviously confused by the scene. Lynn looked over at Billy, and saw him stop and glance up at Leonard.

"This nigger," he yelled, his eyes wide with fury, pointing at the colored man still on the ground, "punched Bo and Justin and Jordy."

Leonard peered at the colored man, and then over at the others. Finally, he looked back at Billy. "And so you're going to hit him with that?" he asked.

"Didn't you hear me, Doc?" Billy said. "Look what he done.

Justin's bleeding and—" He looked around, his brow furrowing. "—wherever Bo's got to, he's bleeding too."

Leonard gazed around again. "All right," he told Billy, and he began walking toward him. "Let me just ask you one thing: Why would this one man want to fight all of you?"

"He didn't," Lynn said from beside Belle Reve. "They all tried to stop him from walking through town, and when he wouldn't go around, they went after him."

Leonard looked over at her, and then back at Billy again. "That right?" he asked, now just a few feet from him.

"Don't matter none," Billy said. "We don't take kindly to his kind in these parts." He gestured in the colored man's direction, as though accusing him of a crime.

"I see," Leonard said. He reached forward then and took hold of the tire iron.

"What're you doing?" Billy asked.

"I'm taking this," Leonard said, pulling the tool free of Billy's grip. "There's no need for it. Now all of you go on home and clean yourselves up, and I'll take care of this man."

Lynn heard the footsteps behind her just before somebody pushed her to the side. When she righted herself, she saw that Bo had returned from wherever he'd gone. He marched toward the colored man, moving to his right. As he did so, Lynn saw the shotgun in his hands, the stock raised to his shoulder, the barrel aiming forward. "I'll take care of him," Bo said.

"No—!" Lynn screamed, even as Leonard pushed past Billy and put himself between Bo and the colored man. Bo lowered his gun a few inches and peered over the hammer at Leonard.

"What're you doing?" Bo said. "Get out of my way, Doc."

Leonard said nothing, instead pacing forward toward Bo. As he got close, he raised the tire iron and swung it. The shotgun flew from Bo's grasp, landing several feet away. Bo cried out in pain and grabbed his hand, and Leonard went over and picked up the weapon.

"You broke my hand," Bo yelled.

"You come by my office tomorrow and I'll mend it for you," Leonard said. "And you can get this from me then too." He held up the shotgun, then went over to the colored man. He bent down and spoke to him quietly, though Lynn couldn't make out his words. Then he helped the colored man to his feet and escorted him over to Doc Lyles's old car, picking up the man's now dusty canvas sack along the way. Leonard opened the trunk and threw the tire iron, shotgun, and sack inside. After slamming it closed, he walked the colored man to the other side of the car and settled him into the passenger seat. As Leonard made his way to the driver's side, he looked over at Lynn. "Are you all right?" he asked her.

"Yeah," she said, though she didn't really feel all right. She didn't know what she felt. "Yeah, I'm all right."

"Tell Phil I'm sorry about tonight," he said, and she realized that he no longer intended to come for supper at their house. "I'll try to come by and see you two tomorrow." He got into the car and started it up.

Lynn watched as Leonard pulled the car off the road and turned it in a wide arc, heading it back toward town. As a new blur of dust rose across the road, she looked at Billy and Bo, at Justin and Henry, at Jordy. They too watched Leonard drive away. Although she felt certain that the boys' anger hadn't entirely dissipated, she saw that their bravado certainly had.

Bo looked at his hand, stained with blood and now visibly swelling. "Come on," he said to the others. "I gotta get home and clean myself up." Slowly, all five of them picked themselves up and headed for the Bartells' truck and the Fusters' car. They mumbled to each other, and the Palmer boys got into the car with Billy, and Bo and Jordy walked back to the truck. Billy turned the car around and followed Bo's truck back down Church Street, away from town and toward their homes.

Nobody said a word to Lynn.

After patching up the rest of the man's scrapes and cuts, McCoy took a second pass over his forearm, bringing the lamp over for a better look. "I just want to check this one more time," he said. "Just to make sure." He felt along his ulna, above, below, and through the area where the tire iron had struck him. McCoy had combated the swelling with ice once they'd gotten back here to the office, but the flesh had still grown a little puffy there. "No, I don't think it's broken," he concluded, partially from what he felt, but also from the man's reaction to the pressure he'd applied to the area. "You can put your shirt back on now."

The man—he'd introduced himself in the car as Benny—hopped down from the examination table and reached for the chair beside it, over the back of which he'd draped his shirt. As he picked it up and started to put it back on, McCoy noticed the dirt and dried blood on it. "Here," he said, reaching for it. "Why don't you let me soak that for a bit and then wash it? I can give you one of my shirts in the meantime."

Benny looked at him through the lenses of his eyeglasses, as though still attempting to gauge the sincerity of McCoy's actions. "All right," he said at last. He slipped his arm from the shirt and handed it to McCoy.

"I'll be back in a minute," he said. McCoy walked out of the examining room, down the hall, and then turned right into the kitchen, which sat at the back of the house. There, under the glow of a lamp, he took a pail and dipped it into a tub of water he'd filled this morning, poured some Oxydol detergent into the pail, then sunk the shirt in after it. He found one of his own shirts—the largest one he owned—in his bedroom and brought it back to Benny. "Here you go," he said. "This might be a little small on you, but it's big on me, so it shouldn't be too bad."

"Thank you," Benny said, taking the denim shirt and putting it on. "For everything."

"I'm just glad I came along when I did," McCoy said. "What happened out there?"

"The same thing that always happens," Benny said, his voice world-weary.

McCoy shook his head, still having a difficult time dealing with what he'd witnessed. "Come on," he said, waving Benny out of the examining room. "Why don't I get us something to eat?" Together, they headed for the kitchen.

When they got there, Benny said, "Maybe just something to drink right now." He'd carried his sack with him, McCoy saw, and he put it down on the floor just inside the door.

"You sure?" McCoy asked. He peered out the back window into the darkness and figured that it had to be past seven o'clock by now. "It's past suppertime already."

"Thanks," Benny said. "But I don't really have much of an

appetite." He spoke in a strangely exact way, with something of a staccato delivery to his words.

"I can understand that," McCoy said. "How about I put on some tea?"

Benny peered at him in a considering way. "Are you sure you want me in your house?" he asked. "What if those boys decide to come over here once they realize that a middle-aged country doctor and a middle-aged colored man are no real match for the five of them?"

McCoy set some wood into the cookstove and lighted it. "Oh, I think we showed 'em we can handle ourselves all right," he said. "And they're not going to hurt the town's only doctor. Who'd fix Bo's broken hand if they did?" Benny chuckled as McCoy picked up the kettle, moved it around to make sure it had water in it, then placed it on the stove. "Have a seat," he said, motioning to the wood table that sat against the wall, a straight-backed chair on each side. McCoy crossed the kitchen and sat down with him. "So tell me, what really did happen out there?"

Benny looked down and shook his head. "Do I need to tell you?" he said. "I think you already know."

"You didn't provoke them in any way?" McCoy asked, genuinely curious.

"Sure I did," the man said. "By being born with this color skin. That often provokes a strong reaction."

Now McCoy shook his head. He'd observed some racism when he'd been in New York, but he hadn't experienced it in the five years he'd been in Hayden. It had never occurred to him before today, though, that only Caucasians lived here. "It's just so ludicrous," he said. He recalled teasing Spock about the differences between humans and Vulcans, and Spock had fired right back, neither of them intending or taking offense. The notion of genuine racism between members of different species seemed foolish enough, but for members of the *same* species to practice such bigotry seemed like the height of idiocy.

"It may be ludicrous," Benny said quietly, "but it's very popular."

"The world won't always be like this," McCoy said confidently, remembering that he'd told Edith Keeler the same thing during his first days at the 21st Street Mission.

"It certainly doesn't have to be," Benny said. "But it's hard to believe things can change with people like those boys out there."

"I know," McCoy said. "And the thing is, I've never seen those boys act that way. As far as I knew, they were decent people. I can't believe what I saw today."

"Believe it," Benny said.

The two sat quietly for a few minutes. When the water in the kettle boiled, McCoy got up to make tea. He brought cups and a jar of honey over to the table and sat back down. "So what do you do?" McCoy asked.

"Recently, I've mostly been wandering," Benny said.

"A lot of people doing that these days," McCoy said. "What kind of work do you usually do?"

"Whatever's honest and puts food in my stomach," the man said.

"A lot of people are doing that too," McCoy said.

"Yeah," Benny agreed. "Let me ask you something: Why'd you do what you did out there?

McCoy shrugged. "It was the right thing to do, that's all."

"But you live here in this town," Benny said. "Those boys aren't going to forget what you did, and I have a feeling that their parents aren't going to be too happy about it either. Doctor or not, you may be in for some trouble."

McCoy shrugged again. "Maybe," he said. "But I have to believe that even if some people in this town are racists, most of them aren't. I guess I'll find out." He thought about it for a second and then added, "Besides, you don't do the right thing because it's easy; you do it because it's right." He looked around the kitchen, and his gaze came to rest on the pail. "Oh, hey, I was gonna wash your shirt for you."

"You really don't need to do that," Benny said.

"No, it's fine," McCoy said, crossing the kitchen and picking up the pail. "I've got a washboard right out here." He pointed to the door that opened into a small yard behind the house. "I'll just be a minute." He took one of the lamps and went outside, where he pulled Benny's shirt from the soapy water and ran it back and forth over the corrugated surface. When he'd finished, he rinsed it at the pump, then wrung it out and carried it back inside, where he hung it on a hook beside the door.

In the kitchen, Benny had opened his sack and pulled out a batch of papers. He sat at the table, writing something on the top sheet with a pencil so short it looked like a toothpick in his hand. "Here, let me get you something better to write with," McCoy said, and quickly found a new pencil in the examining room. He sharpened it and brought it out to Benny.

"Thank you," he said.

Sitting back down, McCoy asked, "Do you mind if I ask what you're writing?"

"I don't mind," Benny said. "I'm just making a note for a story."

"You're a writer?" McCoy asked.

"An amateur," Benny said. "I just started."

"What sort of things do you like to write?" McCoy asked.

"Science fiction, mainly," the man said. "You know, *Amazing Stories* and the *Wonder Stories* magazines. H. G. Wells, Jules Verne, John W. Campbell."

"I haven't read them," McCoy said, "but I do know a little bit about science fiction."

"You sounded like you might," Benny said. "Talking about the world not always being like it is now."

"Is that what you write about?" McCoy asked. "A better future?"

"Sometimes," Benny said. "Like I said, I just really started, but I think about it a lot."

"I'm very curious," McCoy said. "What do you see in Earth's future?"

"Equality," Benny said at once. "Or self-destruction."

"That sounds about right," McCoy agreed. "And if humanity does achieve equality, if humanity does survive, then what?"

Over the next several hours, Benny told him. McCoy eventually made supper for the two of them, but they continued talking long after that, deep into the night. McCoy found the man even more intuitive about the future than he'd found Edith to be. Again and again, he felt compelled to comment, and once or twice, he came perilously close to revealing the truth of his own twenty-third century life.

When finally the two retired—McCoy to the sofa in the living room, giving up his own bedroom to Benny—the time had long passed midnight. He bade his guest good night, inviting him to stay for as long as he needed or wanted. When McCoy woke up early the next morning, Benny had already gone.

THIRTY-THREE

2280

Spock saw the numbers first. The readings measured infinitesimally small—in a sense, *fundamentally* small—and would therefore require a particularly exacting and thorough verification of their equipment's calibrations. Still, after years of research, these figures appeared to provide the first quantifiable evidence of the cause of the changes in M'Benga numbers.

"Doctor McCoy," Spock said, "I believe we may have found an answer." The two men sat at adjoining consoles in what nominally remained the *Enterprise*'s cargo bay number two. Three years into their voyage to the Aquarius Formation, though, Spock and McCoy had approached the captain about allowing them to utilize—and modify—the huge compartment for their own purposes. Because of the apparent correlation of M'Benga-number increases with time-travel events, the two scientists had devised an experiment that would allow them to measure the interaction of energy, matter, and time during nonstandard temporal movement—that is, discontinuous movement along an axis of time. In order to facilitate such movement within a controlled and readily observable environment, they had designed a warp-driven particle accelerator, along with a complex matrix of sensor devices. After assurances that neither the equipment nor the testing itself posed any danger to the ship, the captain had authorized them to proceed.

Now, as the *Enterprise* headed back to Earth near the conclusion of what had turned out to be the crew's seven-and-a-half-year mission, Spock and McCoy sat in a small, shielded booth at one end of cargo bay two's port bulkhead. In the main body of the hold, the helical accelerator reached the entire length and almost the entire breadth of the deck, coiling back on itself both fore and aft. A targeting chamber had been installed at the far end of the arrangement, surrounded by a myriad of sensor packages.

Spock and McCoy had just completed the thirteenth trial of their experiment. The first few runs had demonstrated the need for adjustments to their setup, and the subsequent runs had supplied only inconclusive results. This time, though, Spock spotted a set of readings that, though different than what he'd expected, might give them the information they sought.

"What have you got?" McCoy asked, leaning over to examine the display on Spock's station.

"The K-thirty-one sensor cluster," Spock said, pointing with a stylus to an array of numbers in the middle of the screen. McCoy peered at it, then raised a hand and traced along the column of identifying information beside it. He stopped at a line with one particular value.

"What . . . what is that?" the doctor asked. "One-point-three-five times ten to the negative forty-three . . . seconds? That sounds familiar."

"It should," Spock said. "It is the Planck time, the smallest measurement of time that has any meaning within our universe. It is traditionally defined as the time it would take a photon moving at the speed of light to travel one Planck length, the smallest unit of distance. In this case, we can see from our sensor readings that time within our experiment has incremented and decremented by this value, or by a multiple of this value, at several points. We can also see a corresponding energy emission for each such change." Spock move the stylus over to another set of numbers. "We appear to have observed more than simply the theoretical definition of a quantum of time."

"More than the theoretical definition?" McCoy said. "You're going to have to explain that."

"In the quantum physical interpretation of the universe," Spock said, "energy is absorbed or emitted at the subatomic level in discrete amounts and therefore behaves in some instances like particles of matter. As an example, light absorbed or emitted by an atom can have only certain frequencies, which correspond to the discrete energies of photons, which are the quanta of light."

"And you're saying that our experiment yielded observations of absorptions and emissions of actual time?" McCoy asked.

Spock peered again at the sensor readings, his mind working to interpret what he saw. "It would appear so," he said. "And the absorptions and emissions correspond to movement forward and backward through time."

"And the corresponding energy readings?" McCoy said. "Could they account for the higher M'Benga numbers? An incident of matter traveling through time increasing the release of energy from that matter?"

Spock had already considered the notion, though he presently had no means of knowing its viability even as a working hypothesis. "Possibly," he said.

"That's remarkable," McCoy said. "And not exactly what we expected to find."

"No," Spock said.

McCoy stood from his chair. "All right. So if we have—" He stopped, something seeming to occur to him. "Wait a minute. If we've witnessed the absorption and emission of time quanta, what is it that's doing the absorbing and emitting?"

"That is an excellent question, Doctor," Spock said. "It would seem that there must be a subatomic particle that carries temporal data, in the same way that, for example, an electron carries a negative electrical charge."

McCoy leaned on Spock's panel, staring at the data on the readout. "So we've found the message," he said, "but not the messenger."

"An inexact analogy," Spock said, "but apt."

McCoy pushed back from Spock's station and sat back down at his own. "All right," he said. "Presumably then we can use these quanta of time—" He pointed at Spock's display. "—these . . . chronometric particles . . . to essentially trace our way back to whatever is absorbing and emitting them."

"Possibly," Spock said. "If what we've witnessed just now is accurate, we'll need to analyze the data and perform some new calculations in an attempt to determine at least some broad parameters for that which we seek."

"If this is accurate," McCoy repeated. "With numbers this small, at the limits of existence, it may take some doing to confirm that."

"Indeed," Spock said. "I suggest then that we begin doing so immediately."

"Agreed," McCoy said.

Together, the two men began verifying their equipment, their experiment, and their results.

McCoy lay on his back in the darkness, the beat of the ship's warp drive like an old friend singing him off to sleep. He felt tired, mentally exhausted from the day's activities, but exhilarated at the same time. Today had proven wildly productive, with he and Spock making the most significant strides yet toward identifying the increase in the M'Benga numbers of the crew, and the corresponding readings in the older structures of the ship itself.

Chronometric particles, McCoy thought. *True quanta of time.* If he and Spock had developed an accurate view of these subatomic effects, he wondered what practical uses it might provide. For one thing, even short of the identification of a fundamental particle that emitted or absorbed chronometric data, it would probably be possible to distinguish with a high degree of accuracy whether or not something or someone had traveled discontinuously through time. Except—

Jim's readings continued to puzzle him. He had traveled through time on quite a few occasions now, but not more so than Spock or McCoy. The doctor wondered if the chronometric effects could be combining with something else present in the captain's body but not present within the others. Or perhaps physical events beyond time travel could trigger chronometric effects. Jim had experienced a number of unusual events in his time aboard the *Enterprise,* and while others in the crew had experienced some of those events, no one crewmember—not even Spock or McCoy—had experienced all of them. The captain had encountered the galactic barrier on several occasions, had been pulled into various alternate universes, had been transported through space by unusual and not completely understood means, his mind had been transferred out of his body, just to name a few of the uncommon incidents in his life.

As McCoy pondered the possibilities, he realized that slumber would be a long time in coming tonight. Soon enough, though, his fatigue overtook his excitement and his scientific curiosity, and he drifted off. Eventually, with the onset of the REM stage of sleep, his blood pressure rose, his heart rate increased, his respiration sped up and grew erratic, and his voluntary muscles became paralyzed. Suddenly—

The mist enfolded him, promising concealment and a soft embrace, but delivering neither. The living, pulsating cloud held him fast, held him vulnerable, offering him up to the homicidal madness of his pursuers. He tried to run, but could not, and knew with sickening certainty that they would catch up to him, that they would find him and assassinate him.

"I have a daughter," he said, as though the killers would be moved by his circumstances—and as though he'd ever really lived up to the title of father. He struggled against the shackles keeping him at risk of capture and execution, and against the weight of the years of his failures. How he had failed Joanna . . . how he had hurt Jocelyn and Nancy, Tonia and Natira.

A shape loomed up out of the dark wisps enveloping him, and he shrank back, fearful not of what it was, but of what it could be. The killers had come for him, he knew, and he could not hide. He watched, unable to move, unable to escape, as the shape emerged from the wisps, becoming more tangible, more real. He waited for death to strike him down, and instead found death that he had himself delivered.

"Dad," he said, and he saw his father step forward as a younger man, but still old, still aged past his years. It had always been that way. McCoy had never known a day when his father's heart had not been sick. "Dad," he said again and got no response. He never did, he never had, not until the end, when his father had begged for mercy. In the beginning, he had destroyed his father's spirit, had wounded his heart beyond repair, and in the end, he had simply finished the job.

"I am the executioner," he said. "I am the assassin." And he had never known a day when that had not been true.

"Dad," he told the figure that stepped out of the mists of memory and time. "I'm sorry. I'm so sorry." But his father said nothing, accusing him silently with his solitary existence, his abandoned affections. And then—

"Leonard," his father said, reaching for his hand. "The pain. Stop the pain." But McCoy had done everything he could already. He could do nothing more. "I can't stand the pain," his father said. "Help me."

McCoy felt the burning metal across his palm, gripped in his clenched fingers. Here was release, here was the stoppage of pain. He brought the knife down, plunging it into yielding flesh and breaking bone, finding the defeated heart and shattering it for good.

"This too stops the pain," a voice whispered in McCoy's ear. "This too is a release: a cure."

"No!" McCoy screamed, spinning to face this overdue savior. There, he saw the evil of the murderers that pursued him still. He stumbled backward, falling onto—

Onto dirt. He lifted his hands and saw the dark soil falling from them and back into the field. Above, the sun beat down hard, alive and hot, promising and threatening at the same time.

"Picking season," a woman said, and McCoy looked around. Among the rows of dark green, waist-high plants, he saw the woman, her back to him, a wide, floppy straw hat atop her head. She wore a green-patterned blouse, which covered a slender, fit figure.

McCoy got to his feet. "Can I . . . can I help you?" he said. The killers would never find him here.

The woman turned, the gaze of her striking blue eyes finding him. "The Oracle says that you can help," Natira said. "But very much doubts that you ever will."

"I . . . I don't know how," he admitted.

"You do not promise love and then go," Natira told him.

"No," he said. "I'm sorry." He took a step toward her, but felt his feet sinking into the wet soil. He tried, but could not pull free. "I'm not leaving," he said. "I can't even move."

She walked over to him, stood directly in front of him. "You do not have to leave to abandon me," Lynn told him.

"What?" McCoy asked. "What are you saying?"

"You can promise love without words," Lynn said, "and leave without going."

"I'm sorry," he said again, louder, desperate to be heard, desperate to escape. He felt his feet descending deeper into the earth, trapping him, holding him where he had always been.

Where he had always been. "I'm sorry, mom," he cried, and—

McCoy started awake in the empty darkness of his cabin, opening his eyes without seeing. The *Enterprise* hummed about him, the gray cobwebs of sleep clinging to his murky thoughts. In his dreams, he'd thought of his mother, but he did not want to think of her now. He pushed against his bed and rolled over onto his side, flopping hard back down onto the mattress, as though punctuating an end to the dreams he did not wish to have.

He closed his eyes and waited for sleep to take him once more.

THIRTY-FOUR

1937

As he walked up the stone path, Sheriff Dwight Gladdy hiked up his belt below his ever-expanding stomach. Jimmy Bartell followed angrily behind him, and Gladdy only hoped that he would be able to smooth the situation over. When he got to the house, he rapped his thick knuckles on the front door.

While they waited, Gladdy glanced back at Jimmy. The wiry deputy moved back and forth, anxiously shifting his weight from one foot to the other. "Let me do the talking," Gladdy said, tapping a finger in the middle of his own chest.

"Yeah, well, you better get him to explain hisself, Dwight," Jimmy said, "or I swear I'm gonna—"

"You're gonna do nothing right now," Gladdy insisted. "Just let me handle it."

"But Dwight—" Jimmy stopped when they heard the click of the latch, and they both looked over to see the door open. Beyond it stood Doc McCoy, already dressed for the day, despite the early hour. It had been just after sunup when Jimmy had shown up at Gladdy's house, mad enough to chew nails and spit tacks. Dwight had tried to calm him down some, forcing a cup of coffee on him, but Jimmy had been ready to go before long. It couldn't be much past eight o'clock right now.

"Morning, Sheriff, Deputy," McCoy said. "I can't say I'm surprised to see you. Come on in." The doc stepped back, waving them inside. Jimmy started forward, but Gladdy put a hand up and made sure he walked in first.

As Doc McCoy closed the door, Gladdy peered around the living room. He probably hadn't been inside this house in a few years, since he'd come in for a checkup after he'd had that bout with bronchitis. It didn't look much different now than it had then. To the left, he saw the back of an old, brown sofa, which faced a stone fireplace. A tattered easy chair sat to the right of the sofa, and books lay piled up on shelves all around the room. To the right, a supper table sat in a small room, and Gladdy knew that a doorway there, in the back wall, led across a hall to the room where the doc examined folks.

"Doc, my boy has—" Jimmy said, but Gladdy cut him off.

"Deputy," he said, "I told you I'd handle this." He looked at McCoy, who appeared not only unsurprised, but at ease. "So, Doc," he said, turning and pacing farther into the living room, "you expected us, huh?" Peering over the back of the sofa, Gladdy saw a sheet and blanket spread across it and a pillow at one end, as though somebody had slept there.

"Yup, I did," McCoy said.

Gladdy turned to face him. "You have a guest here last night?" he asked, indicating the sofa.

"Actually, I slept there," McCoy said. "My guest slept in my bed."

"In your bed?" Jimmy said, obviously stunned. "You a nigger lover, Doc?"

"Shut up, Jimmy," Gladdy said. "I told you I'd take care of this."

"But Dwight—" Jimmy protested, but Gladdy threw a look his way, letting him know he meant business.

"So, Doc, what can you tell us about this guest of yours?" Gladdy asked.

McCoy shrugged. "Not much, really," he said. "He seemed like a nice enough fellow."

Gladdy nodded. "Look, Doc, you said you're not surprised we're here, so obviously you know why we come. Why don't you just tell me what I need to know?"

"All right," McCoy said. "Y'all wanna sit down?"

"If it's all the same, Doc," Gladdy said, "I'd prefer to get this done with."

"Well, sure, Sheriff," McCoy said. "I guess what you need to know most about my guest is that when I found him, four boys were beating him."

"Four?" Gladdy said. Jimmy hadn't told him that. Jimmy had said that his son, Bo, had caught a colored man attempting to break into their house, and that he and Billy Fuster had stopped him. "What four?"

"Billy Fuster, Justin and Henry Palmer, and Jordy King," the doc said.

"Wait," Gladdy said. "Not Bo Bartell."

"Not at first," McCoy said. "When I drove up on 'em all, I didn't see Bo."

Gladdy looked to Jimmy, who seemed confused. "So you drove up to the Bartells' house," Gladdy said, "and you saw those four boys beating on a colored man."

"No," McCoy said. "I didn't come anywhere near the Bartells' farm. I was out on Church Street, heading over to Lynn and Phil's to have supper with them. Before I got to Tindal's Lane, I saw Jack Fuster's old heap sitting in the middle of the road, and a truck parked a little farther on. In front of the car, Billy Fuster was going after a man with a tire iron."

"A man?" Gladdy said. "A colored man?"

"A man," McCoy said. "His name was Benny. It shouldn't really matter what color his skin was, now should it?"

Gladdy looked at the doc for a few seconds without saying

anything. He knew what McCoy meant, but he wasn't in the mood for games. "Look, I asked you a question, Doc," he said. "I'd appreciate it if you answered me."

McCoy stood silently for a moment, and Gladdy wondered if he intended to cooperate. Finally, he did. "Yup," the doc said. "His skin was brown. Last I knew, that wasn't a crime."

"You *are* a nigger lover," Jimmy yelped. "I can't believe it."

"I told you to be quiet," Gladdy said, turning on him. "Now, if you're not gonna let me talk to the doc, then you can just go on back to the station." Jimmy clenched his jaw and his hands closed into fists, but he said nothing more. Gladdy looked to McCoy once more. "Go ahead, Doc," he said. "Tell me what you saw."

"I saw Billy Fuster going after an unarmed man with a tire iron," McCoy said. "I asked him what he was doing, and he tried to tell me that Benny had wanted to fight all of them. But Lynn told me that wasn't what happened."

"Lynn?" Gladdy said, again looking over at Jimmy. The deputy just shrugged, and Gladdy realized that Bo hadn't told his father that either. "Lynn Dickinson was with you?"

"Not with me," McCoy said. "She was there already, watching what was going on. She told me that the boys told Benny he couldn't walk through town, and when he tried to, they beat him. He fought back."

"And you stopped 'em?" Gladdy asked.

"I did," McCoy said. "I took the tire iron away from Billy. That was when Bo showed up. He must've gone to his truck to get his shotgun. He was gonna shoot Benny."

"That's a lie," Jimmy said. "We might not love niggers like you do, but we don't go round shooting 'em."

McCoy moved forward, between Gladdy and Jimmy, and over to the front door. There, he picked up a shotgun leaning against the wall beside it. "This yours, Deputy?" McCoy asked, showing it to Jimmy.

Jimmy took the gun. "My boy . . ." he said.

"Your boy is an idiot," Gladdy finished for him. "So what else happened, Doc? Bo claims you broke his hand."

"I might well have," McCoy said. "I hit him with the tire iron to get the gun outta his hand."

Gladdy nodded. "Awright," he said. "I don't think I need to hear any more. How about you, Jimmy?"

"Naw," he said. "I guess I don't."

"You tell your boy to come on in and I'll fix up his hand," McCoy said.

"Yup," Jimmy said.

Gladdy walked to the door and opened it, and Jimmy followed him outside. "If you don't mind, Doc, I'm just gonna confirm all of this with Lynn Dickinson."

"Please do," McCoy said from the doorway.

"Thanks for your time," Gladdy said, and he started back down the stone path toward the street. Before he got there, though, the doc called after him.

"Dwight," he said. "I talked to this man Benny a lot last night. He wasn't just a man. He was a *good* man."

Gladdy nodded. "I gotcha, Doc," he said. Then to Jimmy, he said, "C'mon, let's go." He didn't say what he felt: that he wished all the men in Hayden were good men.

Lynn had already finished making supper by the time McCoy got there that evening, and so they sat down to eat just after he walked in the door. In respect for his friends, McCoy bowed his head as Phil said grace. After the prayer, as they dug into the fried chicken, Lynn asked how McCoy felt, clearly referring to what had happened yesterday out on Church Street.

"I'm fine," he said. "Everything worked out all right, though I did get a visit this morning from Sheriff Gladdy and Deputy Bartell."

"I know," Lynn said. "They came out here this morning too. How was Jimmy when you saw him?"

"When he walked into the house, he was mad at me," McCoy said. "But when he left, after I told him what I saw, I'm not sure who he was mad at."

"Probably Bo," Lynn said around a mouthful of mashed potatoes. "I told Jimmy what I saw too, and how Bo started it all. I was riding home on Belle Reve when I saw it happen."

"I know," McCoy said. "Benny told me the whole story."

"Benny?" Lynn said. "Was that the colored man's name?"

The very question troubled McCoy. Like Dwight Gladdy this

morning, Lynn seemed to employ the term *colored* to differenti-
ate Benny from the others not merely on an individual basis, but
along some imagined qualitative divide. "Yup," he told Lynn.
"The man those boys were beating out there yesterday was
named Benny."

"Well, when Jimmy left here this morning," Lynn said, "I
think he might've been heading home to give Bo a whooping of
his own."

"Maybe that's why Bo still hasn't come by to have me take
care of his hand," McCoy speculated. Of course, the way in
which everything had transpired yesterday might well have provided reason enough for the younger Bartell to stay away. He
might still be angry with McCoy, or embarrassed about what had
happened, or feeling any number of other emotions that might
prevent him from wanting to see the doctor.

"His hand?" Phil asked, looking up from his meal, and
McCoy realized that his friend had been particularly quiet so far
this evening. "What's wrong with Bo's hand?"

"I won't know till I check it out," McCoy said, "but as hard
and as squarely as I hit it, it might well be broken."

"What?" Phil said, evidently surprised. McCoy had simply
assumed that Lynn had told him the entire story of yesterday's
events, but perhaps she'd simply left out that detail. "*You* broke
Bo's hand?"

"As I said, I don't know yet," McCoy said. "Maybe so. I
guess maybe Lynn didn't tell you, but I hit Bo with the tire iron
that I took from Bully Fuster. I didn't mean to hit his hand, but I
did."

"Jesus, Len," Phil said, dropping his chicken leg onto his
plate, which jumped on the table.

"Philip Wayne Dickinson," Lynn said, obviously displeased
with his blasphemous language.

"Len," Phil said, seeming to take no notice of his wife, "how
could you hit Bo Bartell in the hand with a tire iron?"

"I had to do something," McCoy said. "Bo Bartell was aiming a shotgun at Benny and was gonna shoot him for no good
reason."

"What I heard," Phil said, "is that this colored feller was the
one wouldn't listen to reason."

McCoy felt his brow crease. He couldn't believe what he'd just heard from a man who'd become one of his closest friends. "Phil, just because of the color of Benny's skin, Bo and Billy and those other boys wanted to force him to walk all the way back down to Merrysville Road, and then over to Upper Piedmont Highway, only because they didn't want him walking through Hayden."

"And if he'd have just gone ahead and did it . . . " Phil said, and then he pushed his chair back from the table and stood up abruptly. With his napkin in hand, he walked to the other side of the kitchen. "If he'd have just gone ahead and did it, it would've prevented all this trouble."

"You think so?" McCoy said, beginning to grow frustrated, even angry. He put his fork down, too hard, and it skittered along the table. He glanced at Lynn and saw a pained expression on her face, though he couldn't tell its precise cause. "How far south is Merrysville Road?" he asked Phil. "Eight miles? Ten? And then how far to Upper Piedmont Highway? Another five? And then Benny would've had to walk eight miles north just to get back even with where he was. That's more than twenty miles, and it was already six o'clock in the evening. Was Benny supposed to walk through the night? And what do you think was gonna happen when somebody found him sleeping on the side of the road on Church Street or Merrysville Road the next morning? If Bo Bartell found him, he'd might've just shot him dead right there."

"He should've just walked round Hayden in the first place," Phil maintained, refusing to back down.

"Is Benny supposed to walk around every town he comes to?" McCoy asked. "That's where roads go: through towns. And even if they didn't, so what? Benny's a citizen of this country and he wasn't doing anything but walking and minding his own business."

"And he almost got himself killed minding his own business," Phil said. "Would that have been better? He ends up dead and Bo Bartell ends up in jail."

"You're saying Benny almost got himself killed, as though it was his fault that Billy Fuster beat him with a tire iron," McCoy said. "As though it was his fault that Bo Bartell pulled out a shotgun and aimed it at him." McCoy took a breath, tried to calm himself down. Slowly, he got to his feet. Facing his friend across the kitchen, he said, "You weren't there, Phil. I was. Lynn was. And I talked to Benny, I tended to wounds inflicted on him just because he was walking along a road. This wasn't his fault. He suffered a terrible injustice, and yeah, it could've even been worse than that."

Phil said nothing, and in the silence, McCoy realized where he was right now, *when* he was. This ugly attitude he saw in his friend had to be a result of his upbringing. McCoy had always believed that, while bigotry might in some few cases develop naturally, mostly it revealed itself as learned behavior. But even if he could understand the reason for Phil's racism, even if he wanted to avoid arguing with him, he also subscribed to the old saw that the only requirement for the triumph of evil was for good men to do nothing. If McCoy forgave Phil's behavior, or even ignored it, then he tacitly condoned it. He could not do that.

"Let me tell you something," McCoy said. "If you looked at all the folks who live here in Hayden, you'd find a lot more differences among them than you'd find between you and Benny." Phil scoffed. "I'm a doctor," McCoy said. "I know these things." When Phil didn't respond, McCoy went on. "Lynn," he said quietly, hoping that she could help her husband see the inequity of his beliefs. "Tell Phil how it was."

Lynn looked down at her hands, which she twisted together in her lap. McCoy thought she might not say anything, but then she told Phil, "It didn't seem very Christian."

"So now you love coloreds too," Phil replied.

"Phil," Lynn said, and then she stood up and raced out of the room.

Phil glared at McCoy from across the kitchen. Their disconnection seemed to hang in the air between them, keeping them apart, *pushing* them apart. Phil had been such a good friend for years now, and all McCoy wanted was to put this argument, this evening, behind them. "I'd better go," he said. "Tell Lynn I'm sorry for spoiling the supper she made." He moved to the side door and opened it.

"Len," Phil said, but then he could only shake his head.

"Brown men and white men are all the same," McCoy said

gently. "Some are good, some aren't. And if there are blue men somewhere out there in the universe, then the same'll be true of them." Phil looked at him, but did not respond.

McCoy went through the side door and left.

THIRTY-FIVE

2280

He didn't really know why he'd come here. As he stood in the hatchway of the airpod and peered out, he considered turning around and continuing on with his journey. But of course, when he reached his destination, there would be a certain similarity to this place.

And obviously he had come here for a reason.

Spock would've called him irrational—and come to think of it, really had done just that, though not utilizing that particular word. Bones had characterized Kirk in much the same way, though he had been more understanding. Actually, considering Spock's complicated relationship with his own parents and his decidedly human side—especially since his apparent acceptance after the V'Ger affair of that aspect of his nature—Spock might've understood this—

This what? Kirk asked himself. *Pilgrimage?* He didn't care for the word. It implied too much significance. But then if this place didn't hold any import for him, why would he have come? "Just go," he told himself, and he stepped from the craft down onto the dirt road. He touched a control in the hull—a lustrous green that had surprised him when he'd borrowed the vehicle—and the gull-wing hatch swung closed.

Before him, the dirt road stretched into the distance, long and straight. Years ago, it had ended out in the fields, but he didn't know if that remained the case now. He hadn't been back here in a very long time.

Kirk began walking, staying to the side of the road and gazing out at the neat rows of soybean plants rising up out of the soil. Between, he saw the dried husks of what looked the residue of corn crops from previous years. The deposits appeared significant, and Kirk suspected that the no-till farming methods obviously employed here left the ground covered virtually completely throughout the entire calendar year.

His boots made gritty, grinding sounds in the dirt as he strode along. He felt uncomfortable in his clothes—gray slacks and a royal blue, short-sleeved shirt—but he knew it had nothing to do with what he wore. He'd made a decision, and now he had to conclude whether or not he'd plotted the right course.

In the silence and stillness of the mid-July sun, Kirk chuckled to himself, remembering the words he'd so often seen in his evaluations throughout his Starfleet career. *Quick to action. Committed to goals. Unwavering.* So often, Admiral Komack and Admiral Nogura and others had made him sound like an automaton, like a captain-model robot that took as its input the details of a situation and an instant later spat out a plan of attack that he would immediately implement. Kirk knew that's how it had to appear to his crews, that in order for them to succeed, he needed to provide strength and direction. And he bore no false modesty: he was a leader, stalwart and decisive. But that didn't mean that he never questioned himself, that he didn't expend great amounts of energy and thought in his position—his *former* position—as starship captain, or even in his thirty-month stint as chief of Starfleet Operations.

What if I'm wrong? he thought, recalling the question he most asked himself, ever mindful of the consequences of his actions. He remembered once, a long time ago, when Bones had actually answered him—not with an estimate of what would happen if Kirk made a mistaken choice, but with a source of resolve that the captain had subsequently made great use of over the years.

"What if I'm wrong?" he'd asked Bones, telling him that he didn't expect an answer. But Bones had said he had one.

"In this galaxy," McCoy had said, "there's a mathematical

probability of three million Earth-type planets, and in all the universe, three million million galaxies like this one. And in all of that, and perhaps more, only one of each of us. Don't destroy the one named Kirk."

Kirk had liked that and had often recalled it to mind throughout his career. It hadn't alleviated his need to analyze and deliberate about his decisions, but it had often helped him forge through that process a little easier.

Up ahead, a flash of light revealed the solar panels on the roof of the farmhouse. The image brought him back to the days he'd spent here as a boy, working the fields alongside his father and brother. He remembered the clear, crisp Iowa nights, when he and his father—and sometimes his mother, sometimes Sam, but mostly he and his father—would walk out, away from the house, and gaze up at pinpoints of light that, it seemed, had always beckoned to Jim.

Why has it been so long since I've been back here? Kirk asked himself, though he knew the many reasons. His parents had been gone a long time, and even Sam had been dead thirteen years now. Coming back to this place where he and his brother had grown up didn't simply bring back good memories; it also reinforced a sense of loss that remained with him always. For so long, he'd wanted to leave this place, not because he hadn't liked it here—he had—but because his imagination had called him into space. Coming back to this place, with his family no longer here, made that long-ago departure seem like something of a betrayal.

As Kirk approached the farmhouse, he recalled the first time that he'd left Riverside, which had also been the first time he'd traveled by transporter. He'd been five years old at the time, and it had been on the occasion of the funeral of his father's father. Although Jim had barely known his grandfather, he'd still had enough exposure to him to develop some definite impressions of him. The strongest of these had been of the old man as a strident and imposing figure, a huge hulk of a man with a booming voice. Certainly something of that perception must have been the result of the very young interacting with the very old. Still, there must have been some truth to it.

Today, one of the most vivid memories Kirk retained of his grandfather had come from the funeral: the old man lying in an open casket, with flower arrangements and mourners ringing the periphery of the scene. Even in this remembered picture, the old man seemed larger than life, as though in the next frame of recollection he might jump up and proclaim himself alive and healthy. But Kirk's grandfather had not leaped from his coffin four decades ago, and he did not do so now in Jim's mind. And the detail that the five-year-old boy had found missing back then—and that Kirk found so conspicuously absent now—had been the old man's voice, clear and loud and dominating its surroundings.

He reached the path that led away from the dirt road and up to the farmhouse. It pleased him to see that the expansive manicured lawn that lay between the road and the house had been maintained, combining with the many bushes and the two huge silver maples to provide a lush entrance to the home. Kirk thought about walking down the path alongside the yard, perhaps even knocking on the front door and explaining that he'd once lived here and asking to see the house. Instead, for the moment, he just stood there, still recalling his grandfather.

Forty-two years ago, Kirk had been fearful of what the old man's funeral would be like. He'd never been to such an event before that, and he'd spent the days prior to it living with imagined possibilities that only a child's inexperienced mind could manifest. He'd slept restlessly, roused often by nightmares that had caused him to lie awake in bed in the early hours of the morning because he could not go back to sleep and he would not cry out to Sam or to his parents.

At the same time, he'd also felt great anticipation: the young Jim Kirk had looked forward excitedly to his first trip through a transporter. His father had downplayed the significance of travel by transporter—or he'd tried to, anyway—but Jim had been anxious to experience it for himself. This had caused him some unchildlike feelings of guilt; he believed that he should not have wanted so much to attend his grandfather's funeral.

On the night before the memorial service, he'd again been unable to sleep, not from nightmares about his grandfather, but from anticipation about the transporter. And when the time had finally come, when he had climbed up on the public platform in Riverside from which he and his family would "go beaming," as he'd called it, he'd been unable to stand still. The operator had refused to energize the transporter with Jim moving around so much, and his father had needed to scold him before he'd been able to hold his enthusiasm in abeyance. When the effect had taken him, he'd felt dizzy, but not very much so, or perhaps his excitement had simply overwhelmed the brief fainting sensation. One second, he'd stood in the Riverside transporter station, and in the next, it had vanished into nothingness.

And then the world had re-formed about him. That's how it had felt, Kirk remembered now. Not that he had been transported from one place to another, not that his body had been encoded, disassembled, and reassembled, but that the universe had disintegrated about him, moved itself around, and then reconstituted itself in such a way that a different transporter platform had positioned itself beneath his feet. A distinctly Otevrel point of view, Kirk thought now.

After the funeral, after Jim and his family had returned home, after he'd "gone beaming" a second time, he'd explained to his father how it had felt to him, how it had seemed like it had been the world and not his body that had dissolved and re-formed. He'd spoken haltingly, he recalled, concerned that his father would find his notion foolish—though that would not have been consistent with his father's character—but wanting to tell him despite that fear. But his father hadn't laughed, or told him that his ideas were silly or even wrong. Instead, he had listened and then had stared off for a moment or two, obviously considering what his son had told him. When finally he'd spoken, he'd told Jim that both feelings and reality depended upon points of view and points of reference. Since apparently everything in the universe moved with respect to everything else, he'd supposed that you could arbitrarily select a point and declare it the center of the universe, about which everything else remained in motion. So if they considered Jim—and his brother—the center of the universe, then yes, the universe actually had dissolved and re-formed about them. That being the case, his father had said that he would from that time forward take on Jim's perspective as his own.

Back then, Kirk hadn't really understood everything his father had told him. Years later, though, he would recall their conversation and realize that his father had been saying that Jim and

Sam were the center of *his* universe. Even now, many years after his father's death, Kirk found himself moved by the sensitivity of the man. He often hoped that some of that characteristic had been passed on from father to son, and he continually attempted to cultivate it in himself.

Is that why I'm here? Kirk asked himself. *To tend my sensitivity?* But of course, he'd come here because he'd made a life-altering decision, and this experience would help him reflect on his choice and find out if he'd made the right one.

No more Enterprise, *no more Starfleet,* he thought as he stood in the road and gazed at the house where he and his brother had spent their childhoods. *No more Mom and Dad, no more Sam. No more Edith.*

He pushed that last thought away, not quite ready to begin revisiting the repercussions to his life of that decision. But the time for that would come soon enough too. Right now, though, he simply needed to slow down a bit, contemplate where he'd been so that he could discover where next he should go—or if he should go anywhere at all.

Spock and Bones wanted to move on with their lives, he knew. They'd all enjoyed their time together—even Spock, despite his protestations of stoicism—but Jim's two friends possessed their own ambitions. Kirk's loyal and indefatigable first officer deserved a command of his own, of course, but had instead developed a desire to teach, to pass on his knowledge and wisdom. Kirk could not disagree that Spock would make a fine instructor. And Bones wanted to continue his medical and scientific research, certainly an understandable and excellent use of his abilities. Since both Spock and McCoy had chosen to remain in Starfleet, Kirk imagined that they would find time to continue collaborating on their shared project, which had started with Jim's own M'Benga numbers and had led them, at least to this point, to chronometric particles.

Sulu, Dennehy, and Chekov all had aspirations of command, Kirk knew, and he thought that they all would likely get there eventually. Hikaru had been promoted to commander and offered the captaincy of a Starfleet training vessel, but had instead chosen to sign on as executive officer aboard the *Exeter.* Dennehy and Chekov had both received rank increases as well, Lisa to commander and Pavel to lieutenant commander; she had been assigned as exec to space station Deep Space KR-3, and he had become second officer aboard the *Miranda*-class starship *Reliant*. Like Spock, Uhura had spoken of teaching, but Kirk had heard that Starfleet Intelligence had some interest in her extensive communications expertise. Dr. Chapel had accepted a position as CMO aboard the *Canada*-class *Algonquin*. And Scotty—well, it didn't matter what promotions he received, it would take a supernova to get him moved out of a starship engine room, and Kirk didn't think it mattered all that much to Scotty which starship, which engine, and certainly not which captain.

But what about me? Kirk thought. He'd once believed that he would die in space, alone after a long, successful career as a starship captain. He'd stepped down from command of the *Enterprise* after the five-year mission only because Starfleet Command had wanted him to, and because he'd seen great challenges and opportunities in leading Starfleet Operations. He'd returned to starship command during the V'Ger incident and had then led a new mission of exploration for seven and a half years on the Aquarius expedition. But now—

Now, his friends had moved on—even the *Enterprise* herself had been relegated to use as a training vessel for cadets—and he needed to move on too. He'd made a difference in this universe, but still, something was missing from his own life. Being here, peering at the old farm, at the old house, did help, though he didn't know exactly how. But finally there would be time to figure that out—that, and everything else.

Kirk turned from the house and started back down the road toward the airpod. He would take it back to Riverside, climb onto the public transporter platform there, and beam out to Idaho, where he still owned the home his uncle had left to him. There, he didn't know what would happen next, but he would leave himself open to possibilities.

"Doctor, the first member of the team is here," Tulugaq said over the intercom.

Great, McCoy thought, peering down at the top of the desk—or at least at where it had been before he'd moved into his new office and buried the desktop in slates, data cards, hardcover books, handwritten notes on paper, and unaccountably, a full internal medical scan of a Vedala female. McCoy reached forward into the disarray and activated his intercom. "Ask them to give me just a minute, Tulugaq," McCoy said.

"Yes, Doctor," his assistant said.

As quickly as he could, McCoy began to gather the items from his desk, sorting them only by type. As he attempted to collect each of the many slates he'd accumulated, he cursed himself for not taking care of this yesterday. He'd wanted to see Jim before the starship captain—now *former* starship captain—left San Francisco. The doctor had just spent the past seven and a half years with him aboard the *Enterprise,* but Jim's decision to retire from Starfleet had been a surprise, and McCoy had wanted to make sure that his friend was all right. In truth, he hadn't been able to tell, but he thought that perhaps Jim felt lonely. It might seem paradoxical, but he thought that it might benefit Jim to spend some time by himself, not to get away from people, but to distance himself from the great weight of responsibility he had for so long carried.

McCoy carried an armload of slates around his desk and over to the closet in the side wall. The door did not slide open at his approach, though, and he had to jockey his shoulder to the control in the wall beside it. Once it opened, he saw a couple of his new uniforms hanging inside, and a set of shelves on one side, all of them filled with the containers he'd brought with him from the *Enterprise.* Frustrated and not wanting to keep his new colleague waiting, he dropped to his knees and let the slates fall onto the closet floor. He quickly closed the door and moved back to the desk, where he stacked all of the books to one side, in two relatively neat piles. Everything else, he simply swept from the desktop and into an open drawer. At last, he sat down in his chair and opened the intercom channel once more.

"Tulugaq," he said, "send in—" He realized that he didn't even know the name of the person about to step through his door. "—the next team member," he finished. Bad enough that he hadn't organized his office before meeting here with the personnel that Starfleet Command and Starfleet Medical had assigned to his research project, but he hadn't even reviewed their qualifications and experience. In a sense, it didn't matter; since he remained in Starfleet—and with their resources, it only made sense that he do so—Command and Medical had made the decisions on which biologists and physicists to allocate to his project.

The door to his office slid open and Tulugaq appeared there. He had traditional Inuit features: straight, jet-black hair; wide cheekbones and a wide nose, slightly flattened at the bridge; and dark, almond-shaped eyes. "Doctor Barrows," Tulugaq announced, and then withdrew, allowing the visitor to enter.

McCoy stepped out from behind his desk and over toward the door, his hand extended in greeting. "Doctor Barr—" he began, but then stopped when she walked into his office. He felt momentarily bewildered, as though somebody was playing a joke on him that he didn't quite understand.

"Ows," she said as the door closed behind her. "Barr-ows. Barrows." She took his hand and held it, a gleam of amusement in her eyes. "I think you've probably heard the name before."

McCoy realized that his jaw had dropped, and he made a conscious effort to close his mouth. He hadn't seen her in at least a dozen years, and he found that he had no idea how he should act. Back on the *Enterprise,* during the five-year mission, they'd shared a short romance, but in the end, he'd treated her badly. She'd transferred off the ship, and he hadn't seen her or spoken to her since.

Now, she stood before him confidently, without any apparent anger or resentment, seemingly without an agenda of any kind. She had cropped her red hair short, which had the effect of accentuating her high cheekbones. The new Starfleet uniform—black slacks and the asymmetrical crimson tunic—flattered her figure, and the color brought out the green of her eyes. Gone was her coltish gait, replaced by a far more poised bearing. She had to be in her mid-forties now, and she wore the additional years well.

"Doctor?" she said. "Doctor McCoy?"

"Tonia," he finally forced himself to say, and then recognizing his presumption, corrected himself: "Doctor Barrows." But then he realized what he'd just said, how she'd been introduced, and he asked, "*Doctor* Barrows?"

"Of philosophy," she said. "I carry a Ph.D. in subatomic physics from the Guelph-Waterloo Institute." During the time they'd been together, Tonia had expressed an interest in science.

Toward the end of her tenure aboard the *Enterprise,* she'd moved to the physics lab, and when she'd left, she'd been assigned to the *Gödel,* a science vessel, but still—

"That's a long way from recording the captain's log entries and serving his meals," McCoy noted. The high trajectory of her career path impressed him.

Tonia let go of his hand and tapped the gray strap wrapped around her left cuff. There, her rank insignia—two enclosed gold bars—denoted her as a commander. "And this is a long way from yeoman," she said.

McCoy glanced down at his own pair of gold bars and joked, "Good thing I have seniority." Tonia smiled at the jest. Stepping over in front of his desk, he held a chair out for her. "Why don't you have a seat?" he said. She did, and McCoy moved back behind his desk and sat down as well.

"You've got quite a view here," Tonia said, peering over his shoulder.

McCoy looked back through the window out at San Francisco Bay, where he could see Alcatraz Children's Park and numerous boats already out on the water this morning. "Yes, it's nice," he agreed, but pointed up to the right-hand corner of the glass, where a slab of metal ran across it on the outside of the building. "But I'm new here, so they stuck me in the office partially covered by the caduceus." A five-story rendering of the medical symbol hung on the facing of Starfleet Medical Center.

"Hey, I arrived here yesterday to find that I've been assigned to an office two stories below ground," Tonia said. "So don't you complain about your slightly obstructed view."

"Duly noted," McCoy said. "So where did you come in from?"

Tonia looked at him questioningly. "I gathered from your reaction when I walked in here that you didn't realize that I was the Tonia Barrows you once knew," she said, "but now I'm guessing that you haven't even reviewed any part of my service record or academic qualifications."

McCoy felt immediately abashed. "To be honest, no I haven't," he said. "I should have, but I had an important personal matter to tend to yesterday." He'd been thinking of his time with Jim, of course, but as soon as he mentioned a "personal" matter, he wished he hadn't. To her credit, Tonia didn't react in any way other than professionally.

"I understand," she said. "I actually served on the *Sakar* for the past two years. A science ship."

"The *Sakar*?" McCoy asked. He'd never heard of the vessel before, but he had heard of the great Vulcan scientist by the same name. "Is that a Vulcan ship?" he asked.

"It had a crew of two hundred and fifteen," Tonia said, "and two hundred and nine of them were Vulcan."

"And who were the other five brave souls besides you?" McCoy asked.

"Two Andorians, a Coridan, a Phylosian, and a Horta," she said.

"That must've been quite an experience," McCoy said. While he'd encountered a large number of alien beings during his life and career, he'd almost always lived among a majority of humans.

Tonia shrugged. "For one thing," she said, "it certainly prevented me from having much of a social life."

McCoy winced. Had that been a veiled reference to the time he and Tonia had spent together socially—romantically—when they'd both been aboard the *Enterprise*? His guilt for the way he'd treated her resurfaced, and he questioned whether it would be possible for them to work together professionally. Tonia must've sensed his discomfort, because she addressed it.

"I was just joking," she said, leaning forward in her chair. "I mean, I wasn't—I didn't socialize all that much aboard the *Sakar*—but I wasn't making some elliptical comment about our romance." She leaned back, looked up at the ceiling, and sighed heavily. "I was hoping we wouldn't have to address this."

McCoy didn't really want to talk about it either. "Maybe we don't have to," he suggested. "Maybe it would just be easier not to work together."

Tonia peered across the desk at him. "That's not what I meant," she said quietly. "I just meant that, thirteen years after the fact, it seemed a little silly to me that this would even come up." Now she leaned forward in her chair again, placing her hands flat on his desk. "I'll admit that when Starfleet assigned me to this project and I saw that you would be heading it, it brought back some memories. Mostly good ones, though; I long ago dealt with whatever negative emotions I'd felt back then."

McCoy smiled awkwardly. "'Negative emotions,'" he said. "You sound a little bit like a Vulcan."

Tonia lifted her hands from the desk, palms up. "A hazard of my posting, I suppose," she said, then drew more serious again. "When I saw your name, Doctor—Leonard—it did cause me to think back to our time together on the *Enterprise.* But that was so long ago, it shouldn't have any impact on our lives now—especially not on our *professional* lives."

"I agree," McCoy said, trying to gauge her sincerity and finding only his own emotions suspect. Tonia might have faced the pain he'd caused her, but he discovered, to his great embarrassment, that he'd never really dealt with his own bad behavior.

"I've reviewed the research that you and Mister Spock did," Tonia went on. "I've looked at your discovery of chronometric particles and I'm fascinated by it. I want to be a part of the search for the subatomic carrier of temporal data. This is my field, and I'd hate to miss out on this opportunity for any reason, but particularly because you and I happened to be involved more than a decade ago. That seems more than a little foolish to me."

"To me too," McCoy agreed.

"Great," Tonia said with a nod, and she sat back in her chair. "So tell me about this project," she said, "and I'll tell you why I'm the right scientist for the job."

THIRTY-SIX

1941

"Leonard," Lynn called as she walked down the church steps. "Leonard." She pulled at Phil's hand, hurrying him along behind her. Around them, the rest of the townsfolk emerged into the December sunlight. Nearly noon on this Sunday, the temperature had warmed up nicely, already reaching into the sixties. Across the street, on the western edge of the commons, Leonard stopped and looked back. Lynn waved at him, and he raised his hand in what seemed like a halfhearted response, but at least he waited for her and Phil to catch up to him.

"Morning," Lynn said as they got to the other side of Church Street. Past Leonard, she saw the heaps of dirt running down the lengths of Carolina Street and Mill Road, where the trenches had been dug for the new water mains. The Rural Electrification Administration and the Rural Electrification Act that followed had brought power to Hayden two years ago, and now indoor plumbing would finally come with it.

"Morning," Leonard said, though with less than what Lynn considered his normal enthusiasm. "How're you two doing?"

"Fine, fine," she said. "We were just wondering what you were doing for Christmas this year." She peered over at Phil, trying to include him in her statement. Truthfully, though, they'd argued about whether or not to ask Leonard to spend the holidays with them. After sharing Christmas Eve with them during each of his first five years in Hayden, he hadn't done so for the past four—ever since his dustup with Phil about the colored man that Bo Bartell and Billy Fuster and the others had beaten up. Though it had been a little while before Phil and Leonard had spoken again after their argument, they had stayed friends. When they'd begun spending time together again, the uneasiness of both men—and of Lynn herself—had been plain enough, but over time, their relationship had improved. Still, even four, almost five, years after the incident, there remained a distance between Phil and Leonard that hadn't been there before then.

"Uh, well, really I don't have any plans," Leonard said, his manner noncommittal. "I guess I was just gonna . . . I don't know . . . I guess I was just gonna stay home."

"Christmas is only two and a half weeks away," Lynn said, undeterred, "so I suppose if you were gonna make plans, you'd've made them already."

"I suppose so," Leonard said, glancing back over his shoulder as though looking for somebody.

Lynn waited for Phil to speak up, and when he didn't, she

gave his hand a gentle squeeze. "Len, we'd like to invite you to come over to our house on Christmas Eve," he said. "You know, after church services."

"Um, yeah, sure," Leonard said, but he didn't seem particularly interested in their invitation. "That'd be fine."

"You can even come over before church," Lynn said suddenly, though she hadn't planned to do so. "I'll make us all a nice supper." She wanted very much to change the lukewarm attitude Leonard seemed to have toward them this morning. She already felt saddened by the distance that had come between him and Phil, and she had to admit that she felt a distance between herself and Leonard as well, even though he'd treated her just the same as he always had. But Lynn also understood something that troubled her, something that she held buried deep in her heart, and that she didn't think Leonard knew, that she didn't want him to know: even though she'd tried to stop Bo and Billy from hurting the colored man, even though she thought that they hadn't acted in a Christian way that day, she'd also known why they'd done what they'd done. Coloreds just weren't as good as white people; they were shiftless and deceitful, slow and dull-witted.

At least that's what she had been taught. But even in the little time she'd seen the colored man—*Benny,* she amended—he hadn't really seemed to be any of those things. And truth be told, she had known white folks who had been all of those things and worse. She remembered what Leonard had said in their kitchen the next day, about how there were more differences among all the white people in Hayden than between Phil and Benny. He hadn't meant the comment as an insult; he'd meant it for real. And something about that had made Lynn try to put herself in Benny's place. In the Sermon on the Mount, Jesus had said, "All things whatsoever ye would that men should do to you, do ye even so to them." She understood the reverse of that too, that you shouldn't do to others what you wouldn't want them to do to you.

"Supper, yeah, that'd be nice," Leonard said. He continued gazing about, peering at all the folks leaving church, though not in his normal, friendly way. Lynn suddenly realized that whatever distracted him right now, it had nothing to do with her and Phil.

"Are you all right?" she asked him.

"Huh?" Leonard said, and finally he looked at her for more than just a second or two. "Oh, yeah, I'm sorry, it's just that . . . you know, there's a radio program I wanted to listen to that's coming on soon."

"Oh," Lynn said. She could understand that. In her opinion, one of the best aspects of electricity coming to Hayden was radio. She loved listening to *The Adventures of the Thin Man, The Glenn Miller Show, The Edgar Bergen/Charlie McCarthy Show,* and so many others. "What is it you gonna listen to?" Lynn asked.

"Oh, uh, just a news program about, uh, what's going on in Europe," Leonard said. His hesitation seemed uncharacteristic, but she knew that a lot of folks felt terribly troubled by the go-ings-on overseas, including Leonard. Lynn didn't read the news-papers much, but Phil sometimes did, and he'd told her about Italy and Germany invading so many other countries, and how the United States might eventually have to get involved.

"Well, we don't want to keep you, then," Lynn said. "But we're real glad you'll be spending Christmas Eve with us."

"I'll look forward to it," Leonard said. Unexpectedly, he leaned forward and kissed Lynn on the cheek, then reached over and shook Phil's hand. "I'll see y'all later," he said, and he turned and headed across the commons toward his house. Lynn watched him go, then looked over at Phil.

"Did that seem strange?" she asked.

"I don't know," Phil said, and Lynn realized that he hadn't been paying much attention to the conversation. "Did you say you needed to get something over at Robinson's?" he asked.

"Yup," she said, "we need some soap."

"Okay," Phil said, and they started over toward the general store.

As they walked, Lynn looked across the commons at Leonard, hurrying toward his house. Something was wrong, she realized, though she didn't know just what. But she suddenly grew very concerned for Leonard.

Three days before the new year, McCoy stayed away from church. He'd attended each of the last three Sundays, though,

specifically so that he could be among the friends he'd made
here in Hayden when they learned the shocking news of Japan's
surprise attack on the United States naval air station in Pearl Harbor, Hawai'i.

But the attack had never come.

Now, McCoy sat in his living room, listening anxiously to the
radio he'd purchased last year at Robinson's General Store. For
the last three weeks, he'd waited day and night for news of the
attack, to no avail. Over the past months, reports of the war in
Europe had become more and more numerous, and even the
farm, home, and women's shows had begun devoting segments
to discussing defense-related issues. Polls revealed Americans'
anxieties about the world situation, with upwards of forty percent of the population believing that Germany could pose a
threat to the country in the future. Many commentators
thought—and some even hoped—that events would lead inexorably toward the United States' entry into the war. As far as
McCoy knew, it had been in such a set of circumstances—with
the U.S. on the verge of becoming a direct combatant—that
Japan had launched its forces against Pearl Harbor.

And still no attack came.

As the Andrews Sisters belted out their hit song "Boogie
Woogie Bugle Boy" ahead of the morning news program,
McCoy wondered if he might've misremembered the date: 7 De-
cember 1941. Could he possibly have gotten the year wrong?
Had Japan bombed Hawai'i in 1942?

No, McCoy thought, rising from the sofa and pacing across
the room. *I know the date.* He'd learned it in school and had
known it for most of his life. Not only did he feel sure of the day,
but other incidents convinced him that the time had come. Just a
few months ago, Japan had signed a pact with Germany and
Italy, and since then, had staged invasions of Burma, Thailand,
Malaya, Singapore, and throughout the islands of the Dutch East
Indies. McCoy had never studied World War II in enough depth
to know the timeline of events or the details of battles fought, but
he seemed to recall—and it only made sense—that Japan's ex-
pansion throughout the Pacific had coincided with its surprise attack on the United States.

So why hasn't that happened? McCoy thought, throwing

himself back down onto the sofa. He'd asked himself the same question over and over again in recent days, and always he came back to the same answer: he had changed history. But how? How could he possibly have affected events in Japan, a continent and an ocean away? For ten years now, he'd believed that a man had stolen his phaser and accidentally dematerialized both himself and the weapon, and that the event had altered the past and trapped McCoy here. But how could that have had an impact on Japanese foreign policy? On the face of it, McCoy thought that the idea sounded absurd.

On the radio, the morning program *News of Europe* began. McCoy leaned forward, dropping his elbows onto his knees and his chin into his hands. He listened as the commentator described in chilling detail the devastation in London as a result of Germany's Christmas Eve offensive four days earlier. France had been occupied for more than a year, and Germany had invaded country after country: Czechoslovakia, Poland, Denmark, Norway, Belgium, Luxembourg, the Netherlands, Lithuania, Latvia, Estonia, Greece, Yugoslavia. The Nazis had also gone into the Soviet Union, where they'd so far captured numerous cities, including Minsk, Kiev, Odessa, Kharkov, and Sevastopol. Both eastern and western Europe were falling.

"Here at home," the commentator intoned, *"the American Pacifist Movement will stage a mass rally tomorrow morning at the Georgia State Capitol in Atlanta, coinciding with a planned visit there by President Roosevelt. The group, instrumental thus far in keeping the country from going to war, will continue to purvey its message of peace, a spokesman said. Movement founder Edith Keeler is expected to speak to those assembled."*

McCoy leaped up from the sofa. *Edith!* He crossed the room to where he'd set the large, peaked radio atop a narrow table. Placing his hands on the device—its smooth, stained wood felt warm, almost hot, to the touch—he waited for additional information.

"Meanwhile, the Douglas Aircraft Company has been awarded a contract to build a military transport version of its famed DC-3—"

McCoy reached down and switched off the radio. He felt sick. *Edith,* he thought again. Why hadn't he thought of it before?

He'd saved her life, *and she had changed history*. It seemed so clear now. Edith had founded what had become the largest peace movement in the United States, preventing the country not only from entering the war, but from assuming as strong a military posture as it otherwise would have. The Japanese government hadn't felt the need to attack Pearl Harbor now because the U.S. had not yet become a big enough threat. And with no surprise attack, and the American Pacifist Movement urging neutrality, President Roosevelt hadn't found a way to convince the people of the country that they needed to take the fight to Hitler and Nazi Germany.

What's going to happen? McCoy thought. *Is Germany going to win the war? Will Hitler conquer the world?*

McCoy strode to the front door and headed outside. By the time he'd reached the end of the stone path that led to the street, he'd broken into a sprint. He sped across the crossroads of Carolina and Main, across the commons and Mill Road, and raced into the general store.

Inside, Turner Robinson looked from where he stood at a display table near the front. "Morning, Doc," he said, peering over a stack of small boxes. "Newspaper truck hasn't come in yet today, if that's what you're looking for," he said.

"No. I need maps . . . road maps of South Carolina and Georgia," McCoy said in a rush. "I'm going to Atlanta."

THIRTY-SEVEN

2282

Even this late on a Tuesday night, Madame Chang's had a foyer filled with customers waiting to be seated. Barrows had never patronized the venerable restaurant when that hadn't been the case. She and Leonard had already been here for twenty-five minutes, and she hoped that Dorsant and Olga arrived soon, otherwise their table for four might go to some quartet whose members had already shown up tonight.

"I say if they don't get here by the time our names get called, we take the table *and* their meals," Barrows joked. She sat beside Leonard on a cushioned bench in the restaurant's dimly lighted entrance hall, among at least a dozen other would-be diners.

"I'm so hungry, I could probably eat my own dinner and Dorsant's," Leonard said with a smile, though even as hungry as Barrows felt herself, she doubted the veracity of his claim. A Chenari, Dr. Dorsant had a massive body and a stunningly energetic metabolism. The physician normally ate a dozen small meals throughout the day and an enormous dinner at night; even in the project lab, she didn't think she'd ever seen him very far from food. On the other hand, Dr. Zhuravlova, the team's second physicist and a petite human woman, ate—as Barrows's Aunt Beatty used to say—"like a bird."

"If you can eat all of Dorsant's meal," she told Leonard, "you should consider giving up medicine and finding a job in a carnival somewhere, because an act like that belongs on a midway."

"Step right up, folks, and see the human who eats like a Chenari," McCoy said. "Is that it?"

"Something like that," Barrows said. "You know, if—" McCoy's communicator beeped twice, signaling an incoming message.

"Excuse me a second," he said, quickly rising and pulling the device from his hip. He didn't open it, though, instead stepping outside, obviously not wanting to disturb anybody in the restaurant. After just a moment, he came back in, his communicator tucked away on his belt once more. "Well, that was Olga," he said. "She and Dorsant aren't going to make it. Apparently neither one of them feels like going back out." The two team members had finished their project work for the day about three hours ago, and both had decided to go to their respective homes before the group's scheduled dinner, Dorsant down to Half Moon Bay, Zhuravlova up to Mill Valley.

"So much for the team dinner," Barrows said. "Should we tell the maître d' it'll be just the two of us, or should we call it a night?"

"I may not be Chenari hungry," Leonard said, "but I'm still hungry."

"So am I," Barrows said.

Leonard changed their reservation, and ten minutes later, they'd been seated at a table for two. Surprisingly, they'd been placed along the glass wall that overlooked San Francisco Bay and provided a breathtaking view of the Golden Gate Bridge—normally difficult seats to come by, but obviously it had simply been a matter of timing. "Look at this," Barrows said. "Leonard, you sure have good luck when it comes to windows and views. First your office, then the lab, now this. I suppose your apartment looks out on some spectacular vista too, huh?" She glanced down at her menu.

"Well, I, uh . . ." Leonard stammered, and she realized that she'd made him uncomfortable.

"I was only joking," Barrows said. "I wasn't asking to see your apartment."

"I didn't—" Leonard started. "I'm sorry." She thought she heard remorse in his voice, and she couldn't believe it.

"Leonard, we've been working together for more than two years now," she said quietly, peering over her menu. "How can this be a problem now?"

"I don't know," he said. "I suppose it's because I feel badly about how I treated you."

"When? On the *Enterprise*?" Barrows asked, putting her menu down and leaning over the table. "That was fifteen years ago."

"I know, I know, but . . ." He set his own menu down. "Tonia, I behaved very poorly. I hurt you unnecessarily . . . carelessly . . . and even though it happened a long time ago, I just want you to know that I'm sorry."

Even in the spare light of the restaurant, Barrows thought she could see regret in Leonard's eyes. "Thank you," she said. "You didn't need to tell me that, but I appreciate that you did." She held his gaze long enough to demonstrate whatever forgiveness Leonard thought he needed—she felt no need herself to forgive him—and then she scooped up her menu. "Unless you want to have to apologize for starving me, though, we should order."

Leonard agreed. In just a few minutes, their appetizer—a large serving of sizzling-rice soup—had been delivered to their table. As the waiter poured the crisp rice into the hot vegetable-filled broth, causing a flourish of hissing and crackling, Barrows quipped that they were getting dinner *and* a show. After they'd been served individual bowls of the soup, Leonard asked, "So how did you end up here anyway?"

"In Madame Chang's?" she asked. "I always call ahead."

Leonard smiled. "I meant, how did you end up with a doctorate in subatomic physics?" Although they'd been working on the chronometric-particles research project for more than two years now, Barrows and McCoy had spent almost no time together outside of the lab, and they certainly hadn't been alone with each other in anything but a professional setting. Consequently, their conversations—after their initial meeting in his office—had never wandered into personal territory.

"Oh, that," Barrows said. "Well, you know from when I was on the *Enterprise* that I'd developed an interest in the sciences. I never cared for it much as a girl, though, and I ended up in Starfleet because I was looking to travel, looking for some adventure . . . you know, the romantic notion of life aboard a starship. But they don't tell you when you sign up that there's an awful lot of nothing between star systems, and even at warp six, it takes a long time to get from place to place."

"No, they don't put that in the recruitment brochures," Leonard said. "But still, a starship crew really does get to travel to exotic places and meet alien cultures."

"True," Barrows said. "Even a starbase run mostly by humans is a long way from Wichita." Barrows had grown up in the small Kansas metropolis. "But even if a ship goes to exciting places, that doesn't mean that everybody in the crew will get to visit there. That's especially the case for lower-level personnel like yeomen."

"Unless you're assisting the captain," Leonard noted.

"Yeah, but I didn't get to do that very often," Barrows said. "After . . . what was her name? The captain's primary yeoman when I came aboard?"

"Rand?" McCoy said. "Janice Rand?"

"Right, Janice," Barrows said. "After she put in for a transfer, the captain rotated assistants for a while, at least while I was there. I got to be in a landing party only a couple of times."

"I know at least one of those times was pretty exciting," McCoy said. He picked up a chopstick from the table and mimed running it through his chest, evoking the memory of the artificial knight driving a lance through him.

"Mister Spock's 'amusement park'?" Barrows shook her head and laughed. "You know, I've often thought about going back there myself to study the process they use to create objects. The level of molecular engineering must be pretty astonishing."

"You sound about as much fun on shore leave as Spock," Leonard said.

"Now, now," Barrows said. "You know better than that, don't you?" As soon as the words left her mouth, she regretted them. She'd meant the question as a simple tease, but it once more raised the specter of her failed romance with Leonard. He appeared embarrassed. It seemed odd to Barrows that he suddenly seemed to have such difficulty dealing with the brief relationship they'd had so long ago. After their initial meeting on the project, there had been no awkwardness between them, and she'd perceived no indication that Leonard ever even thought about their shared past; certainly she had put it behind her.

Wanting to change the subject, Barrows returned to Leonard's question about her career. "Anyway," she said, "once I started living aboard starships—I don't know if you remember, but before I came to the *Enterprise*, I served on the *New York* and the *Chawla*—I got to observe a lot of scientific activity, and I started to get interested in it. I decided I wanted to do more than just be a yeoman, and Captain Kirk let me take the officers test and transfer into the sciences division. I ended up working for Faith Homeyer in the *Enterprise*'s physics lab. When I transferred to the *Gödel*, I stayed in the discipline and found that I had an aptitude for the subatomic and quantum side of things. I got some great experience aboard the *Gödel*, and when my tour ended, I told Starfleet that I wanted to pursue my doctorate. They were very supportive."

"You really took control of your life," Leonard said, with apparent admiration.

"I always had control of my life," Barrows said. She felt a flash of resentment at Leonard's characterization, but quickly brushed it aside. "What I was finally able to do was find something that I enjoyed, that challenged me, and that I wanted to pursue as a career."

After the waiter had cleared away the soup bowls and brought their meals—a Buddha's feast for the vegetarian Barrows, and beef with pea pods for Leonard—the conversation turned to her schooling. Leonard asked about her graduate and postgraduate work, and she told him. As the evening progressed, though, Barrows realized that they'd largely talked about her, and she found that she wanted to know more about Leonard. "So tell me," she said, "how did you end up in medicine? Was it a lifelong calling?"

"Not really," McCoy said. "I was sort of directionless when I went to college. In some ways, I didn't even want to continue my schooling."

"Then why did you?" she asked.

"Um . . . my father," Leonard said, but he didn't explain any further. Barrows had just enough time to recall that he'd always been tight-lipped about his family, and then he quickly moved on. "But during my first year, I witnessed an . . . accident . . . and I ended up helping the victims. I ended up with my hand *inside* somebody's torso, holding an artery closed. It was an incredible experience—a formative experience, I guess you could say. I found it very empowering to help somebody in that way. I guess that's really what started me."

"Wow," Barrows said. "You don't usually hear stories like that. In my experience, doctors and nurses often tell you that they've wanted to go into their fields since they were children. Speaking of which, how's Joanna?" Back when Barrows had served aboard the *Enterprise*, Leonard had told her that his daughter intended to become a nurse.

McCoy hesitated. "I forgot that I'd told you about Joanna," he finally said.

"You told me a little bit about Jocelyn too," she said.

"I did?" McCoy said. "I honestly don't remember. I don't

generally talk about my former wife very much, and back then, I didn't talk much about my daughter either, probably because our relationship was so unsettled."

"But it's better now?" Barrows asked.

"It is," Leonard said. "I still don't get to see her as much as I'd like, but we talk fairly often. And yes, she became a nurse. She's the head of the Organ Donation, Synthesis, and Transplant Department at Ravent General Hospital on Mantilles."

"Mantilles?" Barrows said. "That's a long way out."

"That's one of the reasons we don't see each other much," Leonard said. She thought she detected a hint of sadness in his voice, and she wondered if he had the relationship with his daughter that he truly wanted. Their conversation soon moved on to other topics, though, making it difficult for her to assess her feeling.

After finishing their meals—they eschewed dessert because of the lateness of the hour—they headed outside. Under a full moon, Leonard asked if she planned to take the monorail home to Sausalito, and she said that she did. Playing the role of the southern gentleman, he insisted on walking her to the station. Once there, they stood on the platform, waiting for the next monorail—it would be along in three minutes, according to the display—and discussing the lab agenda for tomorrow.

When Barrows saw the headlamp of the oncoming monorail, she moved toward the boarding area, and Leonard followed. "I had a really nice time tonight," he told her.

"I did too," she said, turning to face him. She reached up and casually squeezed his arm. To her surprise, he reacted by pulling her forward, leaning down, and kissing her.

She kissed him back.

Even though she'd dealt with her feelings for him a long time ago, the same things that had attracted her to him more than a decade and a half ago still attracted her to him now. She appreciated his intelligence and sense of humor, as well as his weathered good looks, and she'd always been taken with the persona of the humble country doctor that he wore. On top of all that, he'd turned out to be a skilled researcher, with whom she'd enjoyed working these past two years.

Barrows felt the rush of air behind air as the monorail arrived at the station. She stepped back and looked up into Leonard's deep blue eyes. "Well," she said.

"Tonia, I . . ." Leonard managed.

"You better not say you're sorry."

"I'm not," he said. "As long as you're not."

"No," she said, "but I think we'd better talk about this."

"Sure," Leonard said. "How about dinner tomorrow night?"

"Okay," Barrows said, glancing over her shoulder at the arriving monorail. "I'd better go," she said, and she stepped across the platform and into the monorail car. As the doors started to shut, she said, "But not Chinese food. I just had that." The doors closed, and then the monorail started to move. Leonard smiled and waved, and she did the same.

Once the monorail had left the station, Barrows found a seat. She fell into it, exhausted, and yet she felt exhilarated at the same time. It had been quite some time since she'd been involved in a relationship—if that's where this was headed—and she certainly hadn't expected anything like this to happen, particularly with Leonard. And even if she had thought that he might be interested in her again, she doubted that she would've expected herself to respond to his advances.

Yeah, we're definitely going to have to talk about this, she thought. For the moment, though, she could still feel the pressure of his lips on hers. As the monorail sped toward the Golden Gate Bridge, and beyond it, Sausalito, she smiled, wondering what tomorrow would bring.

What did I do? McCoy thought as he strode along through the cool night air. Nothing, really, except jeopardize the project, his own professional standing, and—for a second time—Tonia's heart. *How could I do that?* he asked himself.

He hadn't planned to kiss Tonia tonight—not walking with her to Madame Chang's, not at dinner, not making their way to the monorail station, not even standing with her on the platform. But while he might not have planned to kiss Tonia, he had thought about it recently. Obviously he'd been attracted to her once, and he felt that same attraction now—that, and more. Back on the *Enterprise,* Tonia had in some ways remained a girl. Now, though, she had matured into an elegant, self-assured woman, an accomplished scientist with poise and grace. He'd stood beside her in the lab, had watched her design new sensor systems and new experimental procedures, and yes, had noticed the smooth line of her neck, the beautiful green of her eyes, the flowing curves of her body. When she'd stood there in front of him on the monorail platform, he'd simply acted without thinking.

Now he thought about it. As he headed for the nearest cable car line, on his way to the floor he rented in an old Victorian on Potrero Hill, he examined his motives. Did he truly care for Tonia, or did he simply feel lonely? He'd more or less lived an emotionally isolated life. He cared for his patients as much as his position allowed, he had several very close friends, and he felt quite passionately about many things, but for all of that, he'd had few serious romantic relationships. As his heels clicked along the sidewalk, he thought of the women he'd loved: Emony, Jocelyn, Nancy, Tonia, Natira, and Lisa. Pathetically, two of those relationships—with Emony and Natira—hadn't lasted weeks or even days, but merely hours. And two others—Tonia and Lisa—had been shipboard romances that hadn't endured a year. On top of that, the last of those, with Lisa—Commander Lisa Dennehy—had taken place nine years ago, just after the *Enterprise* had begun its voyage to the Aquarius Formation.

So, yes, he felt lonely. He always did. But did that preclude the possibility of him genuinely caring for Tonia? He didn't think so. When the project had first started and Starfleet had assigned Tonia to the team, McCoy had been skeptical that they would be able to work together easily. No matter how long ago it had been since he'd done it, he'd hurt her, and she therefore had every right to hold a grudge against him.

But she hadn't demonstrated the slightest resentment toward him, and their work had been both pleasant and productive. The entire team functioned well together, and though they hadn't yet identified the temporal subatomic particle that he and Spock had theorized, they had made strides in narrowing the process whereby they could identify such a particle. It might take days, or months, or even years for them to succeed. Did McCoy dare to put that at risk for Tonia? If they began seeing each other again, and then it didn't work out, how bad would the fallout be for everybody?

And yet as McCoy considered putting a stop to what he'd started tonight, he resisted doing so. Over the last few months, his appreciation for Tonia had moved well beyond a professional level. Away from the lab, he'd thought of her often. Eventually, he'd contemplated approaching her about his newfound feelings for her, but he'd always talked himself out of it.

Until tonight.

All of the reasons he'd utilized in convincing himself not to pursue Tonia remained true, though. The only thing that had changed was that he'd now revealed how he felt. Of course, he still might be able to back away with only minimal damage done, not by denying his desire for Tonia, but by telling her that it would be unwise for them to get involved while working together.

Up ahead, an old-fashioned cable car emerged from the cross street, turning onto the avenue along which McCoy walked, and stopped at the corner. He broke into a jog, catching the trolley just before it continued on its way again. As McCoy took a seat in the sparsely occupied car, he thought of something else.

What if Tonia doesn't want to see me?

When he'd kissed her tonight, she hadn't shied away, had in fact kissed him back. But after a night's sleep and a little bit of thought, who knows how she would feel tomorrow? She might well be having something like this conversation with herself right now, and McCoy might not need to worry about making the right decision because she might well make it for the both of them.

The cable car glided quietly through the night, heading toward the inner waterfront. McCoy would be home soon, and he looked forward to putting an end to what had been a long and tiring day. But when he settled into bed that night, sleep eluded him, his thoughts returning again and again to the situation he had created with Tonia. He lay awake for hours, frustrated, but grateful that, at least for one night, he would definitely avoid the terrible dreams that had for so long plagued him.

THIRTY-EIGHT

1941

When Edith had asked for a quiet place where she could be alone for thirty minutes or so, she hadn't expected to be permitted into Atlanta's Capitol, let alone be escorted there by one of the governor's aides. Now, she sat in a green leather chair in the corner of a small, beautifully appointed room. Dark woods covered the walls and ceiling, and ornately framed portraits hung at intervals.

Edith attempted to review the notes she'd penned for today's event, but her mind kept wandering. Prior to this morning, she hadn't known much about the governor of Georgia. His recent invitation to hold an American Pacifist Movement rally outside the state's Capitol had seemed generous, and given that it would coincide with a visit to the city by President Roosevelt, one too good to let pass. Edith hadn't remembered that, several years earlier, the governor had prevented Negroes in his state from joining the Civilian Conservation Corps, and she hadn't realized how strongly he supported segregation. She had known that he opposed the president and his New Deal programs, but she hadn't considered that the invitation tendered to the APM might be the governor's way of undermining Mr. Roosevelt's own visit to Atlanta.

Does it matter? she asked herself. She didn't want it to matter, but it did. She disagreed with the president when it came to committing American troops to battle, but the man had accomplished a great deal for the country in difficult times. Though she sought to counter his arguments for the country's need to join the wars in Europe and in the Pacific, she also respected him and did not wish to be a party to political tactics employed to undermine him. She wanted only honest discourse about the troubles the United States faced.

At this point, though, she couldn't cancel or even postpone the rally. Thousands of people had come from all over the region, and others from farther away, to participate in this event. It would not be fair to them to forgo the rally just because Edith had qualms about the man who had allowed it to take place, nor would it serve their goal.

Edith peered down at the notes in her hand and again started to work her way through them. She'd gotten almost through the first page when the door to the room opened. She looked up, expecting to see one of her colleagues in the APM—either Mr. Simon or Mr. Roman—or perhaps the governor's aide. Instead, she saw a face she recognized, but that she for a moment couldn't place.

"Edith," the man said, and he quickly came all the way into the room, closing the door gently behind him.

"Leonard," she said. She hadn't seen him in years, not since early 1932. He looked good, for the most part. He seemed fit, and a dusting of gray along his temples gave him something of a distinguished air. But dark circles showed beneath his eyes, as though he hadn't slept well. A dozen questions rose in her mind—including what he was doing here and why he hadn't kept in touch—but she started with the most basic. "How are you?" she asked.

She stood up as he hurried over to her. "I'm fine," he said. "And you're well?" He glanced back over his shoulder, as though he feared that somebody might enter the room after him. Edith could tell that something was wrong, though she didn't know what.

"Yes, yes, I'm quite well, thank you," she said. "But I'm a little busy at the moment. Since you found me here, I assume you know that—"

"Yes, I do," Leonard said, cutting her off. "You're the head of the American Pacifist Movement and you're speaking this morning."

"That's right," Edith said. "In less than half an hour, actually, so I really need to—"

"Edith," Leonard said, interrupting her again, "I really need to talk with you. Right now. Please." He reached forward and took her empty hand in both of his. "Just ten minutes of your time."

If she hadn't known him, if she hadn't seen him give so much of his effort and time to the mission for the two years he'd been in New York, she would have said no, at the very least asking him to wait until after the rally. But she could see the urgency in his manner, and she thought she could spare the ten minutes for him. "All right," she said. "What is it, Leonard?"

"Thank you," he said, and he asked her to sit back down while he spoke. "I've rehearsed this conversation a hundred times since yesterday and I still don't know where to start."

Edith waited a few seconds, and then asked quietly, "Are you in trouble?"

"No, no, nothing like that," he said, and Edith felt instant relief. "But I do need your help." He turned and paced away across the room. "Edith, you remember that you and I talked about a better future for humanity."

"Yes," she said, curious why he would bring that up. "Trying to make sure that happens is the primary reason I'm here today."

"But you're wrong," Leonard said, and Edith felt as though she'd been slapped. "Keeping the United States out of this war is wrong. It will only—"

"Excuse me," Edith said, standing once more. "Are you here simply to tell me that you disagree with the peace movement? This is why you needed to talk with me?"

"Edith, please," Leonard said, walking back over to her. "Please just listen to me. I'm not a political opponent. I believe in peace. All I ask is that you just listen to me for a few minutes."

She regarded him suspiciously. She didn't know whether or not she should—

The door to the room opened, and Leonard spun around as Mr. Simon stuck his head inside. "Miss Keeler," he said, "I just want to—" Mr. Simon stopped when he saw Leonard. Opening the door all the way and stepping inside, he said, "Is this man disturbing you? Shall I call somebody to remove him?"

Leonard turned back around to face her. She looked him in the eyes, saw the pleading expression on his face, and made her decision. "It's all right, Mister Simon," she said. "Doctor McCoy will only be here a few minutes more, then he'll be leaving."

"All right," Mr. Simon said. "I just came to let you know that I'll be coming to escort you out in about fifteen minutes."

"All right," she said. "Thank you." Mr. Simon left the room, closing the door behind him.

"Thank you," Leonard said.

Edith sat back down in the chair. "Don't thank me," she said. "Just tell me whatever it is you came here to tell me."

"Peace *is* the way," he said. "Peace and tolerance and inclusion. Two hundred years from now, all of the people of Earth will be united under a dedication to those principles."

"Two hundred years?" Edith said. "I'm hoping that it will take considerably less time than that."

"It won't," Leonard said, not as though he were arguing the point, but as though stating a fact. "And if the United States doesn't enter the war, it may never happen."

"I understand the argument," Edith said. "It's been presented to me before."

Leonard kneeled beside her chair. "Not like this," he said. "If the United States joins forces with the Allies, they'll be able to defeat Germany and Italy and Japan. If not, then western Europe and Asia will fall."

"But millions of American men and boys will be safe," Edith countered.

"For how long?" Leonard asked. "Do you think Hitler and Mussolini and Hirohito will stop there? Earth might still one day become unified, but not committed to the tenets of peace and inclusion and tolerance."

"Leonard," Edith said, not entirely unsympathetic now. She understood that his conviction that the country should go to war rested with his belief that failing to do so would ultimately doom the country and the world. "Leonard, I understand your position, I really do. I just don't agree with it."

"This isn't a 'position,'" he said, standing back up. "I *know* this. The United States *must* enter the war, and soon, otherwise millions, maybe tens of millions, will die, people who didn't die before."

"'Before?'" Edith said. "Before what?"

Leonard hesitated, and then said, "I just meant that millions will die who shouldn't, millions will die who could otherwise be saved."

Edith waited for him to say more. When he didn't, she stood

up again. "Leonard, I appreciate your beliefs, and I thank you for telling me how you feel. Maybe we can talk again afterward, but I really must ask you to leave right now."

Leonard seemed to deflate before her eyes. He nodded without saying anything, and started for the door. When he got there, he looked back. "Let me ask you one question," he said. "Why is it more important to save an American life than it is to save a British life, or a French one? By advocating that the United States stay out of the war, you're advocating the deaths of other people all over Europe, all over the world." He opened the door. "I suggest that *all* lives are precious, even those of the German and Italian and Japanese soldiers conscripted to a cause in which they may not believe. And the longer the U.S. remains out of this war, the longer it will go on, and the more lives will be lost on all sides." He held her gaze for a moment longer, then left.

Edith sat back down in the chair. She knew that she should review her notes in the scant time remaining to her, but she couldn't. Instead, she thought about Leonard, showing up here almost ten years after she'd last seen him, like a ghost from the past. Somehow, he'd thought he would be able to change her mind about her dedication to the peace movement, and to keeping the country out of the war. His goal seemed irrational to her, even if everything he said did not.

A few minutes later, Mr. Simon appeared and escorted her out to the front steps of the Capitol. There, a podium had been set up, and thousands filled the surrounding grounds out into the streets. They cheered and applauded when she stepped up to the microphone. She spoke for thirty-seven minutes, urging everybody present and anybody who might be listening on the radio, to remain strong, to remain resolute, to remain committed to preserving the peaceful stance of the United States.

McCoy drove along US 23, traveling northeast through Georgia, headed back to Hayden. He knew that he hadn't convinced Edith of the importance of the United States entering the war, but even if he had, would it have done any good? How would her followers in the American Pacifist Movement receive a change of heart from her, and how would that translate into support to join the battle against the Axis powers? Even if President Roosevelt ordered American troops to Europe and into the Pacific *to-morrow*—which obviously wasn't going to happen—would it be too late? In McCoy's timeline, the United States had declared war on 8 December, now three weeks past. Could those few days have an impact on the outcome of the war? He recalled reading that Hitler had sought the development of atomic weapons, but McCoy had no idea how close the Nazis had come to actually constructing them. Of course, it would be more than three weeks before America entered the war; it would be months, maybe even years. By then, it might well be too late. And even if it wasn't, wouldn't the world that resulted be very different than the one McCoy had known?

Frustrated, he lifted his hands and pounded them down on the steering wheel. How could he not have seen that saving Edith's life all those years ago had been a possible cause of his changing history? But of course he knew the answer to that. He'd characterized altering the past as a negative action, and preventing a person's death as a positive. It had simply never occurred to him to link the two. And now that he'd come to understand that connection, what should he have done? He'd considered telling Edith the truth, that he'd come from the future and had changed history by saving her life. But she wouldn't have believed him, no matter how convincing he might have been. She would've assumed him either a liar or insane. Neither conclusion would have helped his cause.

But would anything help his cause? Edith apparently should've died nearly twelve years ago. In that time, she'd encountered and influenced countless people, doubtless affecting their lives in ways that would not have happened had McCoy not traveled back in time and saved her. Wouldn't that have had an impact on the timeline, even if Japan had attacked Pearl Harbor on 7 December?

McCoy felt helpless, and hopeless. Nearly twelve years of changes to history, branching out from the moment he'd saved Edith, impacting more and more people, altering more and more events with each passing day, hour, minute. Even if McCoy knew precisely how each modification affected the future, how could he possibly hope to reverse those affects?

He couldn't.

All McCoy could do now would be to attempt to make this world, this altered Earth, a better place. It would never evolve into the world he had known, but it still existed, right here, right now. He could mourn his former life and the universe he'd once known, but it would do no one any good.

Angry, depressed, and emotionally exhausted, McCoy drove on.

THIRTY-NINE

2283/2284

As she walked down from the monorail station hand-in-hand with Leonard, Barrows could feel her heart racing. She'd never done anything like this before, and she almost couldn't contain either her anxiety about whether or not this would succeed, or her excitement about the approaching moment. Almost everything had gone as planned over the last couple of days, but the last she'd heard this morning, a couple of people still hadn't arrived.

She and Leonard reached the midpoint of the hill and turned onto the street where she lived. The breeze blew in off San Francisco Bay, a bit cool, but as the afternoon had arrived, the temperature had climbed above fifteen degrees, unseasonably warm for January. From their elevation, she could see Angel Island in the distance and numerous boats out on the water.

They arrived at the duplex where she lived, and Barrows prepared for what she considered the diciest part of her entire scheme: her acting. At the front door, she identified herself and stood before the retina scanner, then placed her hand atop the sensor plate. Leonard could have done so as well—they'd long ago programmed the system to allow him entry to her home—but it would have seemed suspicious if she'd asked him to do so.

When the entry light flashed green, Barrows played the lines she'd written for herself. "Oh, you know what?" she said. "I forgot to check the mail yesterday. I'll be right in." She started back down the front walk, toward her mailbox, where she'd actually left a couple of items that had been transported there yesterday. When she heard Leonard open the front door, though, she quickly turned and quietly followed him inside. She only regretted that she wouldn't be able to see his face at the moment of his surprise, but she'd made some of the guests swear that they would take holos for her.

"Surprise!" everybody yelled as Leonard stepped through the entryway and into the living room. He stopped in front of her, and she saw past him that Admiral Kirk and his significant other had arrived, as had Commander Chekov and several other Starfleet officers whose duties might easily have kept them away. She'd been planning this for months, though, and that had obviously provided all of these people enough time to arrange their leave. Barrows marveled at the number of people who cared so deeply for Leonard.

She moved forward and threw her arms around Leonard from behind. A number of holocams flashed and then people started moving forward. "Happy birthday," Barrows said, and Leonard looked at her with an expression of such love and delight that all her months of planning and work to make this happen suddenly seemed like too small a price to pay for such a moment. "I love you," she said.

"I love you," Leonard said, and he leaned in and kissed her.

"Well, Bones," said Admiral Kirk, "I have to say you look good for a man twice your age."

"'Tis a pity that retirement has not allowed you the time to improve either your eye for beauty or your sense of humor," Leonard said. He and the admiral—former admiral, Barrows reminded herself—opened their arms and hugged each other. When they stepped back, Kirk took the hand of the woman at his side. Statuesque, with long, dark hair that flowed down past her shoulders, she stood a few centimeters taller than her partner.

"This," Kirk said, "is Antonia Salvatori."

Leonard reached forward and took her hand. "I'm very pleased to meet you," he said.

"I'm delighted to meet you," Antonia said. "Jim has told me so much about you."

"Don't believe a word of it," he said with a smile. "He still resents me for all the times I certified him unfit for command."

Antonia leaned in toward Leonard and in a stage whisper said, "That's one of the things he told me."

Everybody laughed, and then Kirk and Antonia moved out of the way so that other people could greet Leonard. Captain Spock offered low-key but seemingly genuine regards, while everybody else showed their enthusiasm, including many of the men and women with whom he'd served in Starfleet: Scotty, Hikaru Sulu, Uhura, Pavel Chekov, Christine Chapel, Jabilo M'Benga, M'Ress, and others. Their colleagues from the lab, Dorsant and Olga Zhuravlova, had also come by; Olga had done a great deal of work this morning for the party, since Barrows had to be out with Leonard, keeping him away from her home until the proper time. Hoping that her last guest had managed to arrive, Barrows glanced questioningly at Olga, who returned a surreptitious smile.

Slowly, everybody made their way deeper into the apartment. The caterers had arrived to set up early this morning and they emerged now from the kitchen bearing platters of food and drink. On the dining room table, people had deposited birthday gifts, the wrapped presents forming what looked like a miniature and very festive skyline. A large box, nearly a meter wide and deep, and half again as tall, stood to one side of the table, covered in blue and silver paper and with an enormous sparkling bow on top.

"You brought me presents?" Leonard said as he peered into the dining room. "I knew I liked you for some reason."

All at once, guests called for Leonard to open one of the gifts. He said that they could do that later, but Tonia urged him to unwrap at least one. "Here," she said, walking over to the large box. "Why not start with the best?"

Leonard followed her over. "Is this from you?" he asked her.

"More or less," Barrows said, and Leonard looked perplexed

by the answer. He began to ask questions, but she said, "Just open it."

Leonard pulled off the bow and set it aside, then tore through the wrapping paper to reveal a plain, unadorned box beneath. He pulled the top flaps open and peered inside. Barrows watched his jaw drop and his eyes widen. He gazed over at her with an expression that mixed surprise and appreciation. For a moment, silence descended on the party, and then from within the box, a voice said, "Well, hurry up and get me out of here!" Barrows reached forward, grabbed the box, and lifted it up; with no bottom—she'd removed it earlier—the box came up and over the head of the person within it.

Joanna McCoy stood up and opened her arms to her father. "Happy birthday, Dad," she said. Leonard gathered her into his arms and squeezed her tightly. Barrows had never met Leonard's daughter in person, but the two had spoken many times in the last few months. Joanna had decided to take a short leave from her nursing position on Mantilles and book passage to Earth so that she could be here for her father's party. She had been scheduled to arrive two days ago, but had missed a connection with a civilian transport traveling out of Dramia II. She'd subsequently made other arrangements, but her new arrival time had been after Barrows had left this morning to meet Leonard. Obviously nothing else had gone wrong and Joanna had managed to get here prior to the party.

Over Joanna's shoulder, Barrows saw tears in Leonard's eyes. "Oh, honey," he said. "I can't believe you're here." Spontaneously, all of the guests began to applaud.

The party lasted well into the night, filled with good food and good cheer, stories and laughter, music and dancing. Admiral Kirk—Barrows still found it difficult to call him "Jim," though he'd asked her to—and Antonia left last, despite that they didn't intend to stay in San Francisco, but to travel back to Idaho. They departed after midnight, leaving Barrows alone with Leonard and Joanna. The three of them talked for another hour, until Barrows said, "Since you two show no signs of being tired, I'm going to let you have some time to yourselves." She told Leonard that she didn't know if he planned on taking Joanna back to his place in Potrero Hill tonight, but that she'd made up the guest room for his daughter if she wanted it.

"We'll stay here tonight," Leonard said. "I'll probably be in before too long."

Barrows bade them good night and went into her room. Though she felt drained, she found herself lying awake in bed, reliving the excitement and joy of the day. Occasionally, the lilt of Joanna's laughter would reach her from the living room, and once or twice, she heard the deeper tone of Leonard's voice, though she could not make out his words.

In the darkness, Barrows smiled widely. She didn't know if she'd ever been happier.

McCoy held the door open for Tonia, then followed her out into the night. A bluster of cold air swept past and he pulled his jacket tight around his neck and dug his hands into his pockets. "Nothing like a summer night in San Francisco to cool you off," he said. "It's nights like this when I really miss Atlanta."

He caught up to Tonia as she pulled a pair of gloves from her coat pockets, obviously prepared for the weather. "What was that old quote?" she said. "That the coldest winter anybody ever spent was a summer in San Francisco?" She slipped the gloves onto her slender hands.

"No kidding," McCoy said. "That one's often misattributed to Mark Twain, but whoever said it, they sure knew what they were talking about." As Tonia slipped her arm through Leonard's, he asked, "So did we decide that we're heading up to your place tonight?"

"That was my plan," she said.

"It's working out so far," McCoy said as they started walking down the street in the direction of the monorail station. "Madame Chang's was a good idea. We hadn't been there in quite a while. The food is delicious."

"And," Tonia said, squeezing his arm, "we had our first date there."

McCoy looked over at her. "Did we?" he said. He saw that the cold air had turned Tonia's nose and cheeks bright red.

"Well, we had our *second* first date at Madame Chang's," she said. "Our *first* first date was in the mess hall on the *Enterprise*."

"Now hold on," McCoy said. "I thought our first date aboard the *Enterprise* was in the arboretum." He recalled asking Tonia if she'd like to take a stroll with him through the botanical garden maintained on the ship for both scientific endeavors and the enjoyment of the crew.

"That was later in the date," Tonia said, speaking with absolute certainty. "But earlier, in the mess hall, I took a seat at a small table in the corner, and before I could even lift my fork off my tray, the gallant Doctor McCoy appeared and asked if I minded if he sat down with me."

"You call that a date?" McCoy said as they turned a corner. Up ahead, he could see the bright lights of the open-air monorail station. "All I wanted was a place to sit and enjoy my dinner," he teased. He did remember that meal with Tonia, and also that he'd noticed her well before that. If he'd seen her in the mess hall and all of the other tables had been unoccupied, he probably still would've asked to sit with her.

"Yes, well, you enjoyed your dinner because you had it with me," Tonia said.

"That I'm sure of," McCoy said. "But as far as our second first date goes, if I remember correctly, we arrived at Madame Chang's, and left, as colleagues. We didn't kiss until you were on the way home."

"At the monorail station right there," Tonia said, pointing ahead of them. "And *you* kissed *me*."

"Hmmm," McCoy said, as though giving the matter some serious thought. "Are you sure that's right? Are you sure *you* didn't kiss *me*?"

"Oh," Tonia, said, slapping playfully at his arm. "You know what happened. You always want to kiss me."

"I'll plead guilty to that," McCoy said, stopping in his tracks and turning to face Tonia. He leaned in and softly touched his lips to hers. They kissed long and deeply.

When they parted, Tonia looked up at him and fluttered her eyelashes at him. "Why, Doctor McCoy," she said in a mock southern accent. "I do declare, I think I may be coming down with a case of the vapors." She fanned herself with her gloved hand.

"You know what I recommend for that, don'tcha, ma'am?"

McCoy said, allowing his Georgia origins to color his own words.

"Bed rest?" Tonia said.

"Well, now," McCoy said with a grin, "I sure wasn't going to say nothing 'bout 'rest.'"

"Why, Doctor McCoy," Tonia said. "You're turning my head."

"That's my plan," he said. He held his arm out to her and she took it once more. "Shall we?" Tonia nodded, and they started on their way again.

Two blocks later, they climbed the stairs to the monorail station. Several other people stood on the platform, including one poor soul in shirtsleeves wrapping his arms about himself. McCoy glanced up at the display and saw that the next monorail would arrive in five minutes.

"Leonard," Tonia said, extricating her arm from his and moving to stand in front of him. "We've been seeing each other for almost two years now," she said quietly. McCoy looked at her and sensed that something had suddenly gone wrong.

"Almost two years, that's right," he said, wondering what had happened, wondering what transition he had missed.

"It began right here on this spot," Tonia said, pointing with both hands down at the platform. "You kissed me right here, and since then, you've come to mean a great deal to me." She gazed up at him, and he actually saw the crescent of the moon reflected in her eyes. "You're a wonderful physician and a brilliant researcher, you're a kind, compassionate man. You make me smile and laugh, you comfort me when I need it, you enjoy life *with* me, you make life more enjoyable for me. I love you."

"I love you too," McCoy said.

Strangely, Tonia started taking the gloves from her hands. "You're my colleague and my friend and my lover," she said, then reached into her jacket pocket and lowered herself down to one knee. McCoy still didn't realize what she was doing even as she pulled out a jeweled ring and held it up before her. "Now, Leonard," Tonia said, "will you be my husband?"

FORTY

1944

Static burst from the radio and Phil adjusted the dial. "There must be a storm nearby," he said as he tried to tune in the evening news program. Over on the davenport, Lynn nodded, and in one of the tub chairs, so did Len.

This had become their ritual. Most nights, the three would gather at the end of the day, sometimes at Len's, but most times at Phil and Lynn's, and listen to reports from Europe and the Pacific about the war. A lot of folks in town did the same thing, Phil knew.

As he worked the radio dial, trying to find the setting of least interference, he fought his ever-increasing despair. During the difficult days of the 1930s, when the country had faced economic depression, widespread unemployment, and a terrible drought throughout the middle west, people had rallied around the idea that the United States needed to isolate itself from the hostilities breaking out in the rest of the world. The memories of several hundred thousand American casualties in the Great War—among thirty-seven million casualties worldwide—remained strong. During the last decade, rolls in pacifist movements had swelled and popular opinion had regarded the Atlantic and Pacific Oceans as natural barriers that would allow the nation to keep itself safe by not getting involved.

At the time, Phil hadn't thought much about it—he and Lynn had their own problems to deal with here in Hayden—but when he had, it had sounded good to him. He'd barely avoided the draft himself during the Great War, too young by only a few months, but his brother, older by four years, had come back from Europe missing three fingers on his right hand, and his cousin Billy hadn't come back at all. Now, though, as they listened each day to reports of the Axis powers roaring through country after country in Europe and across the Pacific, Phil had begun to wonder how safe the United States would continue to be. He also thought about the people in those conquered nations, many of them simple farmers and mill workers like Lynn and himself. The more he'd thought about it, the more it had driven down his mood.

A voice emerged from the radio and then faded back into cracks and hisses. Phil shifted the radio around on its little table, then moved the table itself around. Finally, the voice returned, still wrapped in interference, but they could hear it clearly enough.

Phil waited for a few seconds to make sure of the reception, then walked over to the davenport and sat beside Lynn. She reached over and took his hand, intertwining her fingers with his. They listened in silence as an announcer proclaimed the health and beauty benefits of Palmolive soap, and after that, the strength of new Ajax cleanser. At last, the nightly program *News Here and Abroad* began.

The reports could not have been worse.

After years of battle, the United Kingdom had finally and completely fallen, taking with it the last real hope for success against Germany and Italy and the totalitarian regimes that supported them. Today, Nazi soldiers had descended on London, Cardiff, Edinburgh, Dublin, and other sites in the British Isles, occupying forces that met little resistance after the English, Welsh, Scottish, and Irish peoples had been bombarded in recent months by Germany's V-2 rockets.

But the bad news didn't stop there. In Russia, Leningrad threatened to fall too as the Nazi bombs rained down on the city, unstoppable. And in the Pacific, Japan, already occupying New Zealand, had completed takeovers of the Australian cities of Brisbane and Sydney, and now lay siege to Melbourne and the country's capital, Canberra.

Phil and Lynn and Len didn't speak throughout the entire broadcast. When the program had ended—followed by a sickeningly upbeat ad for a soft drink—Phil crossed the parlor and turned off the radio. He stood there, not saying anything, as he considered what he'd just heard. Five years ago, when Germany had invaded Poland, the fighting had seemed so far away, but now felt like a noose tightening about the nation's neck. With all of Asia and Europe under Axis control, with Australia and northern Africa obviously next to follow, what would come after that? Would Germany and Italy and Japan and their allies be satisfied with what they had taken, or would they set their sights on North and South America?

"They're coming here next," Phil said.

"I fear you're right," Len said. "It might not happen tomorrow or the next day, but Hitler wants to conquer the world."

"Why don't we fight?" Phil asked.

"Folks don't want to fight," Lynn said quietly, looking down at her hands as she twisted them together. As with Phil, the relentlessly bad news about the war had left her depressed.

"If folks aren't willing to fight, they're cowards," Phil said. He and Lynn had fought this argument before.

"No," Len said. "Not cowards. I mean, I'm sure folks don't want to die, don't want to get wounded, but it's more than that. People don't want to kill, don't want to maim."

"The Germans don't have a problem with it," Phil said. He walked back across the room and sat down beside Lynn again.

"And we think they're wrong for what they're doing," Len said. "Violence often doesn't stop violence; it only creates more."

"But you think we should fight yourself," Phil said. For the last few years, Len had talked openly of the need for the United States to enter the war alongside the Allies. Something they agreed upon, it had helped ease the tensions between them.

"I do," Len said. "But I believe that going to war is something a country should do only after every other conceivable solution has been tried, only when there is absolutely no other choice. Folks who want to keep America out of the war don't think we've gotten to that point yet. I do."

"You say you think we should enter the war," Lynn said, "but you also sound like you agree with the folks who don't."

"I understand them," Len said. "In most cases, I'd probably agree with them. It should always be difficult for a nation to go to war. But in this case, with a madman who's got the will and the means to conquer the world, who's actually moved beyond his borders to do so, and who's shown that he won't stop unless he's made to, yeah, the United States has got to fight."

"I'm ready," Phil said.

"I think more and more folks are," Len said.

"I hope so," Phil said. They'd heard on the radio recently that the number of folks in the American Pacifist Movement and in other groups like it had begun to fall significantly. Initially opposed by a majority of citizens, last year's Selective Training and Service Act—the country's first peacetime draft, requiring all men between the ages of twenty-one and thirty-five to register for military service—had now become widely regarded as necessary. Even though, at forty-three, he fell outside the age range, Phil had given serious thought to enlisting himself. He wouldn't want to leave Lynn, but he also didn't want to wait for the United States to be attacked.

"I hope for peace," Lynn said.

"I think we all hope for that," Len said.

Again, they sat quietly for a few minutes. It seemed to Phil that there were more and more silences between folks these days. Even down at the mill, Phil had noticed the men eating their lunches without talking much at all.

"Well, I'm gonna go make supper for us," Lynn said, and she stood and went into the kitchen.

Phil looked over at Len. "When do you think this is all gonna end?" Phil asked.

Len stared at him for a moment, as though giving the matter some thought. "I wish I knew," he finally said. "I wish I knew."

McCoy heard the news in the early afternoon, standing in his living room and listening to the radio. In the Pacific, Japanese forces had launched attacks on Guam, the Philippines, and Hawai'i, all territories or commonwealths of the United States. They had also fired upon and sunk the American battleship *Arizona*. Already, President Roosevelt had appeared before a joint session of Congress and requested a declaration of war on Japan. In short order, he'd received it.

A small measure of relief rose within McCoy, but not nearly enough to overcome the tremendous guilt he still felt. Because of his actions, regardless of the fact that they had been unintentional, people had died who had not died before, and now Earth faced complete domination by the Nazi war machine. He only hoped that the United States could find a way to defeat Germany and Japan and the rest of the Axis powers.

McCoy sat down on the sofa and listened to the reports. During the past year, as more and more of Europe and Asia fell, as New Zealand and Australia had been attacked, President Roosevelt had precipitated the formation of TOTA, the Treaty Organization of The Americas. The mutual-defense pact, which included most of the countries of North, Central, and South America as signatories, provided that should one member of the organization come under attack, it would be regarded as an attack on all member nations. With today's aggression against the United States, declarations of war against Japan were expected shortly from Canada, Mexico, Brazil, and the other American countries.

It felt wrong to have wanted the country to go to war and to be pleased now that it had finally happened. But McCoy knew the justifications for this fight, understood that the battle had not been joined in order to claim land, or to procure assets, or for some other ignoble reason. Rather, this war effort came in self-defense and for the protection of essential freedoms. If Germany—

The telephone rang. The lines and service had been installed in Hayden three years ago, coincident with the electrification of the town. McCoy got up and walked to the corner of the living room, to the wall with the fireplace, where his phone had been placed. He picked up the heavy black handset and lifted it to his ear.

"Hello?" he said.

"*Leonard,*" Lynn said, her voice frantic. "*You have to come quickly. Oh my God, Phil's leaving. I need you to stop him.*" Her words came loud and fast.

"Lynn, what's going on?" he asked. "What do you mean Phil's leaving?"

"*He's leaving,*" Lynn repeated. "*He's going off to war.*"

"Lynn, would you—" McCoy heard a click and then nothing at all. "Lynn," he called. "Lynn." Nothing.

McCoy slammed the receiver back into its cradle—the bell inside the heavy, metal phone clanged—and ran out to his car. As quickly as he could, he started down the recently paved Carolina

Street, on his way to Lynn and Phil's. Lynn had sounded nearly hysterical, and from what she'd said, he guessed that he would have little time to try to prevent Phil from enlisting in the military.

As McCoy turned onto Church Street, he realized how quiet the town seemed. He'd seen nobody in the commons or along the sidewalks, and the road ahead of him appeared empty as well. Everybody had probably heard about today's events, and he expected that, as he had, they now sat glued to their radios, listening for more information.

Though it had startled him because of the panicked sound of Lynn's voice, McCoy couldn't claim that what she'd said had surprised him. Many of the folks in town had come to believe that the United States needed to enter the war, and Phil had been one of the more vocal on the subject. Though he'd never explicitly mentioned his intention to voluntarily join America's fighting forces should that happen—at least not in front of McCoy—he'd left little doubt that he would serve if called upon.

According to what McCoy had heard on the radio, the Congress had already taken up the matter of modifying the Selective Training and Service Act, adjusting the age range of conscription down to eighteen and up to forty-five. In that case, Phil, at forty-three, would be liable for military service anyway.

McCoy reached Tindal's Lane and turned onto the dirt road—unlike the four main roads in the center of town, it remained unpaved—and just a few minutes later, pulled into Lynn and Phil's yard. Fortunately, their truck still sat parked there as well, indicating that Phil hadn't left yet. McCoy got out of the car and raced up the front steps. He knocked, but didn't bother to wait, instead pushing the door open and stepping into the parlor. "Lynn?" he called. "Phil?" He paused, not necessarily anticipating a response, but thinking that he might hear Lynn and Phil arguing. Instead, he heard only an eerie quiet.

Concerned, McCoy walked into the hall. He waited, then called their names again. This time, Phil answered. "In here, Len," he said. McCoy followed his voice, making his way down the hall to Lynn and Phil's bedroom. The door stood ajar, and McCoy gently pushed it open and peered inside.

A suitcase lay on the bed, open but filled with clothes. Lynn sat at the head of the bed, her head down, and Phil kneeled on the floor beside her. He held one of her hands in both of his. Phil peered over at McCoy. "Hi, Len," he said somberly.

"Hi," McCoy said, unsure what he should do or say. "Lynn called me . . ." At the mention of her name, she looked up. Her face appeared puffy, her eyes red. Clearly she'd been crying.

"Len, I'm going to Greenville," he said. "I'm gonna enlist in the army."

"Stop him, Leonard," Lynn said.

McCoy didn't know what to say. He understood Lynn's obvious concern for her husband, her desire for him to stay with her, to remain safely at home. But he also could see why Phil would want to join the military, why he would want to fight to protect his wife, his home, his country, his very way of life. "Phil," he said, "are you sure you want to do this?"

"I have to," Phil said. "They're trying to take over the world. We have to stop them."

"I know," McCoy said. "And many, many people will work to do that, not just from the United States, Canada, and Mexico, but from countries in Central and South America too. There will be plenty of soldiers without you. You have a wife who needs you here."

"I know, but . . ." He gazed at Lynn, and she reached up and placed her hand gently along the side of his face.

"He has to go," Lynn said softly, her words barely audible. She leaned in and kissed him deeply. "I don't want him to go, but I'm proud of him." She looked over at McCoy. "Will you take him to Greenville?" she asked.

"Sure, of course," McCoy said, appreciating the depth of Lynn's sacrifice. "We can all go."

"No," Lynn said. "I'm staying here."

"Are you sure?" Phil asked.

"Maybe this isn't the best time to be by yourself," McCoy said. "At least let us take you over to the Gladdy's so you can be with Beth and Dwight."

"No, I'm gonna stay here," Lynn said again. She rose and stood face to face with Phil. "Leonard," she said without looking away from her husband, "would you give us a couple of minutes?"

"Of course," McCoy said, and he quickly withdrew back down the hall and into the parlor. He waited silently, attempting not to imagine the bittersweet scene playing out in the bedroom. Five minutes later, Phil emerged, suitcase in hand.

"C'mon," he said. "Let's go." Without waiting, Phil went out the front door and down the steps. McCoy thought he probably wanted to leave Hayden before Lynn changed her mind.

Two and a half hours later, they stood waiting to enter a United States Army Recruiting Station in Greenville. McCoy chose to stay with his friend until he made it inside. The line of men wanting to join the army reached around the block.

FORTY-ONE

2284

Holding the ring, presenting it, Barrows's hand trembled, the intensity of her nervousness surprising her. For the past month, since she had begun thinking about doing this, about asking Leonard to marry her, she had felt only a small measure of anxiety. As she had searched her emotions and confirmed the depth of her love for him, and as she'd experienced his obvious love for her—in the ways that he looked at her, in the ways that he touched her, in the ways that he treated her—joyous anticipation had filled her days and nights. At moments, working beside Leonard in the lab, she had barely been able to contain her excitement.

She had planned this evening with care. To accompany her proposal, she'd wanted a romantic symbol of some kind and had decided on a betrothal ring. On the few nights she and Leonard had spent apart, she'd scoured the comnet until she'd found the right piece of jewelry, a wide gold band atop which six small diamonds encircled a raised seventh stone.

After that, Barrows had chosen the time and place. She'd initially considered waiting until the second anniversary of their first date—their *second* first date—but she'd found herself too eager to wait another couple of months. She'd still elected to commemorate that event, though, by selecting a repeat of it, with dinner at Madame Chang's and a walk to the monorail station afterward. There, waiting for the monorail that would take her up to Sausalito, their kiss had really begun their new life together.

As she perched on one knee, a cold breeze blowing in off the bay and ruffling her hair, she reached up with her left hand to steady her right. Her heart pounded mightily in her chest and she knew that she would always remember this moment. She gazed up at Leonard, keen for the expression of shock on his face to give way to one of happiness.

"Tonia," he said, his stunned look changing, but not in the way that she'd envisioned. In speaking her name, his voice had sounded very different than it had just a few moments ago, when he'd told her that he loved her. A sense of dread began to form within her, like a pernicious weed growing to strangle the flora about it. She peered up at Leonard, searching for any hint that would prove her perception wrong.

Instead, he looked away.

Barrows felt as though she'd been kicked in the gut.

"Tonia," he said again, the concern in his tone far from comforting. He reached toward her hands, but she pulled them away and rose to her feet.

"What?" she said, her own voice degrees colder than the bitter wind.

"Tonia, I . . ." His words trailed into nothingness, and somehow that seemed appropriate.

"Tonia, I what?" she snapped at him, her pain causing her to lash out at him. "You *care* about me?" Though she hadn't thought about it in such a long time, the words he'd spoken to her all those years ago in his office aboard the *Enterprise* came back to her. As she'd left the ship at Starbase 10, he'd claimed to care about her, but that hadn't been enough then, and it certainly wasn't enough now.

"I do care about you," Leonard insisted.

"A few minutes ago, you loved me," she said.

"I do love you," he said. "But—"

"I love you but . . . not really?" Barrows said. "Not enough?" Behind her, she heard the low hum of the monorail as it approached the station.

"Don't do this," Leonard said.

"Don't react?" she said, outraged at the suggestion. "Sorry. I didn't mean to make this so difficult for you." With a rush of warm air preceding it, the monorail glided into the station. Leonard looked past her at it as she heard its doors open and then the footsteps of passengers disembarking. She ignored it all, maintaining her focus on him. She thought that he might suggest that she board the monorail, but he didn't. A few seconds later, the doors whispered closed and the vehicle left the station.

Once it had gone and the two had been left alone on the platform, Barrows said, "I'm genuinely confused. Did I imagine the last two years?"

"No, of course not," Leonard said. "We've had a good thing—"

"A good *thing?*" Barrows said. She looked down at the ring still in her hand, the gemstones catching the bright white lighting of the lampposts and reflecting them in a splash of prismatic color. She placed it deep in her coat pocket, then pulled on her gloves. "Okay," she said. "How could I possibly have misread this situation so completely? It's been nearly two years. As far as I knew, everything was terrific between us. What have I missed? Please tell me." She didn't seek to convince Leonard that he should stay with her—that ship had already left space dock—but she really wanted to understand how this could've happened. It made no sense to her.

"You haven't missed anything," Leonard said. "Everything has been terrific between us."

"But not terrific enough, evidently," Barrows said, still bewildered.

"I . . . I don't know if I'm really the person for you," Leonard said. "You deserve the right man and I don't want to stand in the way of you finding him."

"Why don't you say what you mean?" she asked. "It's not

that you're not the right man for me. It's that I'm not the right woman for you." She knew she could not change the way he felt about her, but she needed to understand this betrayal.

"Tonia," he said, but followed it with nothing more.

"I'm a fool," Barrows said, shaking her head. "I can't believe it. "This happened between us almost twenty years ago. How could I possibly allow it to happen again?"

"You're not a fool," Leonard said. "I am. You're a wonderful woman, smart and beautiful and funny—"

"Don't," Barrows said, raising the flat of her palm to him. "I know my value as a person, my worth as a romantic partner. You don't need to tell me." Something suddenly occurred to her and she gave it voice. "In fact, it sounds more like your trying to convince yourself."

"No, no, not at all," Leonard said, with more conviction than anything he'd said since she'd asked him to marry her. She regarded him and tried to gauge what could have motivated the words he'd spoken to her.

"This really isn't about me, is it?" she concluded. "It's about you."

"Well, yes, I guess it is," Leonard said, shrugging.

"No, don't dismiss it like that," Barrows said. "Don't avoid the issue by agreeing with me and then saying nothing else. What is it inside you that's doing this, not just to me, but to you? What are you fighting?"

"It's nothing like that," Leonard said, looking off into the night.

"It *is* something like that," Barrows said. "What else could it be? You're a kind and caring man, Leonard, and yet you led me on, allowed me to think—*made* me think—that we had something special between us."

"The last two years *have* been special," Leonard said, though he spoke barely above a whisper and without much confidence.

"I was actually talking about our time together aboard the *Enterprise*," Barrows said. "But then and now, you didn't just allow me to think that you loved me; you did love me. You *do* love me. And yet you put distance between us back then and you're doing it again now. Why? Is it something as simple as a fear of commitment? That seems too simple, too unworthy of you."

"I . . ." he started, but he seemed unable to respond further.

Barrows attempted to sort it all out. "You kissed me," she said. "Right here on this platform, you took action to rekindle our romance. And for nearly two years, we've spent almost all of our personal time together, as well as all of our professional time. We rarely argue, we have great fun together, and care for each other." Barrows thought of the tremendous support Leonard had provided—still provided—after the unexpected death of her brother from a brain aneurysm a year ago. "We've had a positive, solid, loving relationship. And now, when I ask about committing ourselves to one another, you back away just as you did on the *Enterprise*."

"I'm sorry," Leonard said.

"That's not good enough," Barrows said. "Not for me, but not for you either." She stepped forward and faced Leonard at close range. "What's wrong?" she asked. "Did it end like this with Jocelyn or Nancy, Natira or Lisa? Is there a pattern of behavior here?"

Again, Leonard looked away. "I'm sorry that I've hurt you," he said.

"You're not just hurting me, Leonard," she said. "You're hurting yourself. You're walking away—maybe running away—from love. You need to figure out why." Barrows stepped back, as though formally severing the ties between them. "I'll begin a leave of absence from the project beginning tomorrow, then seek a transfer from Starfleet Command."

"You don't need to do that," he said.

"I'm not doing it for my own sake," she said. "I'm doing it for yours."

"I don't know what to say to you about all of this," Leonard said.

"You don't need to say anything," Barrows said. "Go now."

Leonard looked down the length of the empty station platform and then back at her. "I don't want to leave you alone here," he said.

"You already have," she told him.

Leonard stood motionless for a long while, saying nothing. Finally, he nodded, then turned and left the station. She saw him stop farther down the street, at the corner, watching until the next monorail arrived a few minutes later.

As Barrows rode toward Sausalito, she still felt hurt and angry, but no longer confused. She didn't know what troubled Leonard, but she was convinced now that something did, something that would deny him real happiness in his life until he resolved it.

In the empty monorail car, tears distorted Barrows's vision, then slid from her eyes and down her cheeks. She missed him already.

McCoy stood at the floor-to-ceiling windows, looking down from the high-rise at the San Francisco waterfront. The lights of other buildings, and of boats docked along the harbor, dotted the night like earthbound stars. Uncharacteristically unable to stop himself, McCoy lifted his gaze across the bay, to the far shore, along which the town of Sausalito stretched.

It had been three months since his relationship with Tonia had ended. Distracted with his duties, he didn't think of her often, but when he did—like now—a terrible feeling of loss flooded over him. He could not have stayed with her, he knew that, but he also could not deny that their two years together had been wonderful.

Since then, his circumstances had changed. Though Tonia had said that she would take a leave of absence from the project, during which time she would ask Starfleet Command to transfer her elsewhere, McCoy had decided to do just that himself. It had seemed unfair for him to allow her to sacrifice her efforts for a situation that he had essentially caused, and it would've been impossibly uncomfortable for them to continue working together in such close proximity. He'd attempted to contact her to let her know of his pending reassignment, though he'd had to settle for leaving her a message. Still, Tonia had not retracted her request for transfer, and she too had taken another post. With the little progress the team had made in the preceding few months, and with its membership subsequently cut in half, Starfleet Command and Starfleet Medical had opted to shut the project down rather than replenish its numbers. McCoy had personally apologized to Dorsant and Olga for what had happened, and they had both been gracious enough to offer their understanding.

Now, as he stood peering out of the north side of Russian Hill Tower, he imagined that one of the lights across the bay belonged to Tonia, gleaming from a window in her apartment. Of course, for all he knew, she might not live in Sausalito anymore, or even on Earth. Although he no doubt could, he hadn't checked to see to where she had been transferred.

"This is my best attempt," Jim said, walking up beside him. McCoy turned from the windows and the spectacular views his friend's apartment afforded, recalling with a twinge of regret Tonia's comments about his frequent propinquity to such vistas. In Jim's hands, he held two slender, tall glasses, one a third filled with an amber liquid—knowing the admiral, probably Saurian brandy—and the other filled with a drink in crushed ice and adorned by several aromatic sprigs of mint.

"After all these years, you finally made a julep," McCoy said, delighted by his friend's gesture.

"You might want to reserve judgment until you've tasted it," Jim said.

"I can do that right now," McCoy said, and he lifted the glass to his lips. Though a bit too sweet, the syrup did cut the harshness of the bourbon and also tamed the bite of the mint. The cold beverage went down his throat refreshingly easily. "More than a passable first effort," McCoy announced. "I won't even take off points for not using a julep cup."

"How magnanimous of you, Bones," Jim said. He raised his glass in salute and McCoy touched it with his own. The two men sipped from their drinks.

"So to what do I owe this singular honor?" McCoy asked.

"Oh, I don't know, Bones," Jim said, walking away from the windows in the den and back into the living room. McCoy followed. Sparingly populated with modern furniture, the room had been tastefully decorated with the admiral's collection of antiques, many of them naval in theme. Jim moved toward the fireplace. Flames danced within, sending orange shadows flickering across the walls. As Jim took a seat before the fire, he said, "You just seem to be a little down these days."

"I do?" McCoy said, surprised by the claim. In truth, he could've said the same thing about his friend. Since Jim had returned to Starfleet last month, he'd been prone to periods of melancholy, which McCoy had naturally attributed to the end of his romance with Antonia Salvatori. For his own part, though, McCoy hadn't dwelled on the loss of his relationship with Tonia, or even on his departure from the chronometric-particles project, and so he hadn't actually felt down. Perhaps Jim had cast his own mind-set onto McCoy. Unwilling to propose that, though, he chose simply to agree. "I guess we make quite a pair, don't we?" he said. He drank again from his mint julep.

"I guess so," Jim agreed.

McCoy stepped over to the hearth, feeling the comfortable warmth of the fire. He rested an arm atop the mantel, beside a small figurine he recognized. A pair of simple humanoid heads carved out of stone, it symbolized friendship and had been a gift to Jim from a man named Tyree, a member of a technologically primitive people on a distant planet. McCoy looked at it for a second, and then back down at Jim, happy to have him back in the Bay Area. Though transporters and maglevs and airpods rendered the thousand kilometers between San Francisco, California, and Lost River, Idaho, easily traversable, their lives had kept them mostly apart for the four and a half years since returning to Earth from the Aquarius mission.

At first, Jim had desired isolation, retiring from Starfleet and retreating to the relatively remote land his uncle had left to him. Somewhere in the backwoods of Bingham County, though, he had met Antonia. In the time that the two had been together, Jim had spoken of her little on the occasions that he and McCoy had talked over the comnet. McCoy had met Antonia only once, at the surprise birthday that Tonia had thrown for him last year. Tall and attractive, bright and friendly, Antonia had seemed like a nice enough woman, though he had been unsure how well suited to Jim she'd been. He'd hoped for his friend's happiness, of course, but it hadn't shocked him when he'd learned that the two had gone their separate ways.

Deciding to change the subject, McCoy said, "So Spock tells me you've lined up Sulu and Uhura for our next training mission." Three months from now, when Spock took his cadets out on a three-week voyage, it would as a matter of course include a small complement of frontline officers, functioning as both educators and evaluators. Spock, now a captain, had been an instructor of starship personnel for several years, and he'd been placed within Jim's aegis when the admiral had come back to Starfleet. Scotty worked with Spock's engineering cadets as well, and McCoy had taken a similar position with his medical trainees. Now, apparently Sulu and Uhura would be coming along for the ride.

"That's right," Jim said. "The *Exeter* will be undergoing a refit and so Sulu will be reassigned. He'll be here at Starfleet between postings, so I thought I'd ask him if he'd be interested in helming the *Enterprise* again, even if for only three weeks."

"I'll bet he jumped at the chance," McCoy said. He'd known Hikaru for almost two decades, and the man had a reputation for an eclectic and ever-changing list of avocations, which at one time or another had included botany, fencing, antique firearms, wine, ballroom dancing, ikebana, folk music, baseball—whatever that was—and the Riemann Hypothesis—whatever *that* was. Through all of Hikaru's many and varied interests, McCoy knew of only one that had remained constant: the man loved to pilot, whether it be ground, water-, air-, or spacecraft.

"He did jump at it," Jim said. "He said he couldn't wait to sit at the *Enterprise*'s helm again." He upended his drink, then placed his glass on the table that sat between the two chairs in front of the fireplace. "So, Bones," he said with a casualness he didn't really project, "what's on your mind?"

"What do you mean?" McCoy asked.

Jim pointed back toward his study. "I thought I saw you looking over at Sausalito before," he said. "I thought perhaps you were missing Tonia."

McCoy took another pull from his drink. He didn't really want to talk about this. "No," he lied. "I was just looking out at the bay. Sausalito just happens to be over there."

Jim looked at him appraisingly, as though trying to determine whether or not he should believe him. Finally, he said, "All right," in a way that suggested he actually didn't accept McCoy's claim as true. "But if you ever do need to talk, Bones, you know I'm here."

"I know," McCoy said, grateful for Jim's concern, even if he would not avail himself of it. "Thanks." He eased away from the fire and over to the second chair facing it. He sat down, searching for another subject about which to speak, wanting to move away as quickly as possible from the topic Jim had attempted to raise. "Have you heard from Chekov at all?" he said.

"I have," Jim said. "I received a message from him just a couple of weeks ago. He's received a promotion to first officer aboard the *Reliant*."

"Well earned, I'm sure," McCoy said.

"He's become quite a solid officer. He'll end up with his own ship someday."

As Jim spoke, though, McCoy's mind wandered. Unbidden, pictures rose in his mind of San Francisco Bay, and across it, the lights of Sausalito. In a moment of weakness, he wondered if Tonia still lived there, and if not, then where exactly she was right now. It hurt to admit it, and he knew he could do nothing about it, but he missed her.

FORTY-TWO

1946

Lynn placed the plate of fried chicken on the kitchen table, then sat down across from Leonard.

"That looks delicious," he said, reaching for the bowl of mashed potatoes, the dish closest to him.

"Leonard," Lynn scolded as she folded her hands together before her. He looked over and shook his head, clearly realizing his mistake.

"Oh, sorry," he said. He intertwined the fingers of his own hands and lowered his gaze, and then Lynn bowed her head as well.

"Almighty God, our Father who art in Heaven, we ask Thy blessing on this food," she said. "And while we enjoy Thy generous bounty, we also humbly ask that You watch over our soldiers bravely trying to protect us overseas. Amen." She did not specifically ask for God to keep Phil safe—that would be selfish and arrogant—but in her heart, she hoped for that to be the case.

Across from her, Leonard reached again for the food. This had become their routine. Each evening, he would come over to the house and they would listen to the radio, hoping for good news from Europe, from the Atlantic, from the Pacific. Then they would have supper together.

Phil had been away for most of the last two years. After enlisting in the army, he'd been sent to Fort Jackson, in the state capital of Columbia. There, he'd undergone fourteen weeks of recruit training, followed by twelve weeks of unit training. During that time, Lynn had heard from him relatively frequently, usually receiving at least a couple of short letters each week and an occasional telephone call. She answered every single letter right away.

After training, Phil had participated for months in exercises and maneuvers, interrupted only by a three-day pass at Christmas, during which time he'd actually gotten to come home. A buddy Phil had made during basic had arranged rides for them to and from Greenville, and Leonard and Lynn had picked him up and taken him back there. After the holidays, the maneuvers had intensified, taking his infantry division marching out of South Carolina and through Georgia and Tennessee. During that period, Lynn had heard from her husband less often.

Finally, about a year ago, Phil had been shipped to Europe. Since then, Lynn had received only four letters from him, though she had written to him much more often than that. Each morning, upon waking, and each night, at supper and before bed, Lynn prayed for the well-being of all Allied soldiers, picturing in her mind the face of her husband.

Tonight, as she and Leonard had listened to the radio, they'd heard some good news. American and British forces had taken back Ireland from the Nazis, and Rommel's defensive emplacements had been pushed back in Algeria. At the same time, the Battle of Hawai'i, now in its fifth week, raged on, and earlier today, the battleship *West Virginia* had been lost.

Selecting a chicken leg, Leonard finished filling his plate for supper, then speared a forkful of collard greens. "Mmm," he crooned. "Very tasty." It always pleased Lynn how much Leonard liked her cooking. In the beginning, right after Phil had left, they'd shared the task of preparing the evening meal, with Lynn going over to Leonard's every few nights. Soon enough, though, she'd stopped doing that, concerned about what people might think. When she'd thought about it herself, she'd found her visits unseemly, despite the chaste nature of her relationship with Leonard.

Your friendship is chaste, she thought, *even if your thoughts aren't.* As much as she missed Phil, and as much as she would never step out on him, she had admitted to herself her attraction to Leonard. She'd felt it for years, but it had grown particularly strong when they'd begun spending so much time alone together. For that reason as much as any other, she'd resolved not to visit him in his house. He came here instead, where reminders of Phil abounded, and where she found it easier to resist temptation.

"I'm glad you like it," she told Leonard of the food.

"I worked through lunch today," he said, "so I'm famished." Like many men and women in town, including Lynn herself, Leonard had begun working at the mill in support of the war effort. Granted a contract from the federal government, the mill now worked full-time to produce blankets and hosiery for the troops. Leonard still practiced medicine, but everybody in town knew to look for him or call him at the mill if they couldn't find him at home.

"When I was having lunch today," Lynn said, "Becky Jensen told me that Mary Denton hurt herself and came to see you."

"You'd have to ask Becky Jensen about that," Leonard said.

"You can't even tell me if you saw her?" Lynn said. A couple of times before, she'd asked Leonard about townsfolk he'd treated, and he'd always told her to ask the person directly if she wanted to know about their visit to him. He'd explained the reason to her, but she still didn't really understand why he couldn't tell her something as simple as whether or not Mary Denton had gone to see him. "Is that doctor-patient con . . . con—"

"Confidentiality," Leonard said. "It is. When I became a doctor, I swore an oath not to discuss my patients without their permission or direction. We've talked about this."

"I know," Lynn said. "I just don't understand why—" A knock at the front door interrupted her. "I wonder who that can be," she said. As she stood up, Leonard did too, and he followed her across the hall and into the parlor. Lynn opened the front door to find Jake Dinsmore standing on the porch. "Jake," she said, "what are you doing here?" Through the window, Lynn saw the Dinsmore's Crosley station wagon, with Jake's wife, Annabelle, in the passenger seat. She worked down at the Western Union—

Lynn looked back at Jake and saw the piece of paper in his hands. "No," she said, tears all at once beginning to stream down her face. "No!" she shrieked. Her legs felt weak beneath her and she started to slip toward the floor, but then Leonard's hands were around her shoulders, supporting her. He eased her backward a couple of steps, into one of the tub chairs. Lynn buried her face in her hands and sobbed.

"Doc, I'm sorry," she heard Jake say. Leonard responded, but she couldn't make out his words through her weeping. Then she heard the door close and felt Leonard kneeling down at her side, his hand on her back. She turned in the chair and reached for him, hugging him hard as she cried.

They stayed that way for a long time. When at last her tears had eased some, Lynn pulled away and peered up at Leonard. She saw his eyes rimmed in red and shiny streaks down his cheeks. He'd been crying too.

On the floor beside him, she saw the piece of paper Jake and Annabelle had come to deliver. "Read it to me," she said softly.

Leonard looked as though he might object, but then he reached down and picked up the telegram. "May Twenty-Sixth, four-fifty P.M., Washington, D.C.," he said. "Mrs. Lynn J. Dickinson, RFD One, Tindal's Lane, Hayden, South Carolina. The Secretary of War desires me to express his deep regret that your husband, Private First Class Dickinson, Philip W., was killed in action—"

Lynn closed her eyes and wailed. *Phil,* she thought. *Phil!* He had gone to protect their country, to protect South Carolina and Hayden and to protect her, and now he would not be coming home. She could not imagine it and knew that clearly somebody had made a mistake, that Phil couldn't possibly have died.

Except she also knew that no mistake had been made. She gazed up at Leonard again. "Finish it," she said.

"Lynn—" Leonard protested, but she screamed at him. "Finish it!"

He read from the telegram once more. "Was killed in action in Ireland, Eleven May Forty-six. Confirming letter follows. Signed, G.A. Stacy, the Adjutant General."

Lynn reached out and swiped the paper from Leonard's hands. She brought it up in front of her face and tried to read it herself, but tears blurred her vision. She crumpled the paper and dropped it to the floor. "Oh, Phil," she said.

Leonard moved in front of her, leaned in, and put his arms around her, pulling her head onto his shoulder. He held her as she wept. She could think only about the impossible fact that her husband would never come home again.

The day had dawned heavy and gray, providing an apt setting for the service, McCoy thought, but the early mists had evaporated by midmorning. Now, as most of the town congregated in Hayden's small cemetery, the sun shined brightly. Pastor Gallagher stood at one end of the open grave, where a headstone would be set once the appropriate words had been carved into it.

McCoy stood beside the casket, along with the other five pallbearers: Gregg Anderson, Ducky Jensen, Steve and Ford King, and Phil's brother, Roger. The rest of the mourners ringed the grave, with Phil's Aunt Lee and Uncle Scott standing on either side of Lynn. Wearing a black dress and a wide hat with a veil, Lynn kept her eyes cast downward. McCoy had seen her crying during the funeral service in church earlier—she'd been crying for the past week—but right now he saw no tears.

"Philip perhaps need not have made this great sacrifice," the pastor intoned. "He could have waited to see if he would be drafted, but he did not. With bravery and fortitude, he was the first man in Hayden to go."

Within hours of Japan's attack on the country and America's subsequent declaration of war, McCoy had driven Phil to Greenville to enlist. But in the weeks and months that followed, other men from Hayden had joined the armed forces as well.

Some, like Ray Peavey, Randy Denton, Jefferson Donner, and the Palmer boys, Justin and Henry, had signed up of their own volition. Others, like Bo Bartell and Billy Fuster, had been conscripted.

"In Philip's name, we say: 'the Lord is my shepherd; I shall not want,' " Pastor Gallagher said, reading from the bible he held open in his hands. " 'He maketh me to lie down in green pastures: He leadeth me beside the still waters.' "

McCoy heard the words, but paid them little heed. He hoped only that what the pastor said would bring some added measure of solace to Lynn. Since she'd received the telegram informing her of Phil's death, McCoy had watched her cycle through the traditionally accepted stages of grief, but again and again, he'd watched her draw herself up, calling upon a well of strength he had been a little surprised to see. Lynn and Phil had been married for twenty-three years, living a simple life in a community they rarely left. As well, Lynn had lost both of her parents quite some time ago and had no family other than that of her husband. It would have been easy for her to succumb completely to the enormity of her loss, but though she had grieved and would no doubt continue to do so, she had also fortified herself with her faith. She missed Phil, she'd told McCoy, but she'd gotten used to missing him over the past two years. Now, at least, he didn't labor day after day to harden his body and mind for battle, nor throw himself into actual combat, filled with the fear of death or injury; rather, Lynn believed, he lived in the kingdom of God, apart from her, yes, but in peace and bliss. She said she could live with that.

" 'Yea, though I walk through the valley of the shadow of death,' " the pastor said, " 'I will fear no evil: for Thou art with me; Thy rod and Thy staff they comfort me.' "

In the days immediately following word of Phil's death, Lynn hadn't gone to work at the mill, and McCoy hadn't either. He'd stayed with her almost constantly, though occasionally she had sought solitude, isolating herself in her bedroom or walking alone through the fields, among the cotton plants climbing skyward from the earth. Whatever she needed him to do, whether it be to comfort her or to leave her alone, he'd tried to do.

Two years ago, when he had driven his friend all the way to Greenville and then had stood with him waiting to enter the army recruiting station, Phil had exacted a promise from McCoy to take care of Lynn if the worst happened. He needn't have. Though McCoy had been troubled by Phil's racist attitudes—and even, to a lesser extent, Lynn's—he still cared for both of them. He'd also understood the source of their beliefs, and so had sought to cast a positive influence on his friends in order to help them relieve themselves of their prejudices. Regardless, he certainly would not have abandoned Lynn in the time of her greatest need.

" 'Surely goodness and mercy shall follow me all the days of my life,' " Gallagher said, " 'and I will dwell in the house of the Lord for ever.' "

The assemblage concluded with a chorus of "Amen," and then Gregg Anderson, wearing his uniform from World War I, stepped toward the head of the casket. Audie Glaston, also in uniform, moved forward at the other end. Together they picked up the American flag draped over the coffin. The flag had been sent to Lynn a few days ago, along with Phil's bible, wedding band, and the army identification—dog tags, folks called them—that he had worn into battle. Phil's remains had not been returned to the United States, nor would they be; he had been interred close to where he had fallen in battle.

As Gregg and Audie held the flag waist high and parallel to the ground, Danny Johnson moved to stand between them, then lifted his trumpet and played a slow, haunting melody. Lynn began to cry, McCoy saw, as did many others present. When Danny had finished playing, Gregg and Audie doubled the flag lengthwise twice. Audie then folded the striped end into a triangle, and repeated the process again and again, until only the blue canton of stars remained visible. Gregg then folded down his end of the flag and tucked it into Audie's triangle, leaving a blue, three-sided shape with white stars that resembled a cocked hat. Slowly, Gregg marched around the grave and handed it to Lynn. "On behalf of a grateful nation," he said. Lynn thanked him and accepted the flag, taking it between her hands.

"We will now consecrate the memory of our brother unto the

earth," the pastor said. With the other pallbearers, McCoy lifted
the casket—nothing more than a pine box, containing only Phil's
dog tags and his bible—and carried it over the open grave.
Slowly, the six men lowered the coffin into the ground, then
stepped back.

Gallagher nodded to Lynn, and she turned to McCoy and
handed him the folded flag. Then she bent down, grabbed up a
handful of dirt, and threw it into the grave. It struck the top of the
casket with a short, harsh sound, like a sudden burst of rain.
"Unto Almighty God we commend the soul of our brother departed, and we commit his body to the ground; earth to earth,
ashes to ashes, dust to dust."

It all comes down to that, McCoy thought. *Dust to dust.* He
hoped that his friend's sacrifice had not been in vain. Phil had
fought and died not only in the service of his country, but in an
effort to stop the spread of fascism across the world—and
whether he knew it or not, in an attempt to restore the history of
Earth, or at least to liberate it from the terrible path down which
McCoy had inadvertently sent it.

Had Phil's efforts helped? McCoy had long ago accepted that
whatever changes he had made to the past had also altered his
own future such that he would never be rescued from the twentieth century. Still, he clung to the hope that America and the Allies ultimately would not suffer defeat in this war.

The pastor concluded speaking, and one by one, the people
of Hayden approached Lynn. They hugged her, kissed her, offered consoling words for her loss. Afterward, they drifted
away, walking out past the two pillars that marked the entrance
to the cemetery, heading back down Church Street and toward
the center of town. Later, once everybody had left, McCoy
knew, the pastor would return to the grave with Ducky Jensen
and Woody Palmer, and the three men would shovel the earth
back into the hole.

Finally, only McCoy and Gallagher remained with Lynn.
"Shall we go?" McCoy asked gently.

"Not yet," Lynn said, staring down at the casket. "Actually, I
think I'd like to be alone for a bit."

"Of course," McCoy said. He looked over at Gallagher, and
together the two men began toward the cemetery entrance. When

they reached the two pillars, the pastor continued on, but McCoy turned back and waited.

Lynn remained at the gravesite for another thirty minutes. When at last she turned and left the cemetery, McCoy was there for her.

FORTY-THREE

2285

"Scotty, I need warp speed in three minutes or we're all dead."

Spock sat at his sciences station on the bridge and listened for a response to Admiral Kirk. Just minutes ago, Commander Scott had reported the need to take the main engines off-line because of radiation, doubtless an issue with the plasma injector. The component had performed at only marginally acceptable levels recently, Spock knew, and he calculated that it easily could have overloaded as a result of the phaser strikes the ship had just sustained. After Mr. Scott's stated assessment of the warp drive, though, Dr. McCoy—apparently down in the engine room to see to crewmembers wounded during the *Enterprise*'s second battle with the *Reliant*—had reported the engineer on the verge of unconsciousness. Scott had then denied it, though he hadn't sounded well. Now, he did not answer the urgent call from the bridge.

"No response, Admiral," Uhura confirmed from her communications console.

Trainees, Spock thought. *They're almost all trainees.* Before Admiral Kirk had received an emergency message from Space Lab Regula I and, responding, the *Enterprise* had subsequently been attacked by the Starfleet vessel that Khan Noonien Singh had seized, the ship had set out from Earth on a three-week train-

ing cruise. As a result, cadets currently composed the majority of
the crew.

"Scotty!" the admiral called into the intercom as Spock concluded what action he must take. With Mr. Scott apparently incapacitated and engineering peopled by trainees, few would
realize what needed to be done—or if they realized what needed
to be done, then they would likely not consider doing it, given
the danger involved. "Mister Sulu, get us out of here," the admiral said as Spock stood and headed for the turbolift. "Best possible speed."

"Aye, sir," Sulu acknowledged.

Spock stepped into the waiting car and ordered it to take him
aft to *C* deck, below which the lifts currently did not operate. In
the two hours since the *Reliant*'s previous attack, the crew had
been able to restore only partial main power to the *Enterprise*.
Even traveling on foot, though, Spock estimated that he could
still reach the engine room within forty-five seconds. That would
leave him enough time to enter the containment chamber and
reset the plasma injector manually, if indeed that turned out to be
the problem. Either way, Spock knew that he likely had only a
few minutes left to live. If he could not restore the warp drive,
then the impending detonation of the genesis device aboard the
Reliant would destroy the *Enterprise* and its crew; if he could,
then the *Enterprise* might escape the effects of the genesis wave,
but his presence in the containment chamber would expose him
to lethal doses of radiation. Illogically, he decided that he preferred for his death to satisfy a purpose.

It's not illogical, he corrected himself. As he'd told Jim, the
needs of the many outweighed the needs of the few—or as the
admiral had noted, of the one. As an axiom, the statement depended on the equality of individual needs, so that the aggregate
accrued a greater significance than the singular. In this case, that
happened to be true, the need for everybody aboard the *Enterprise* being the ability to stay alive.

The turbolift stopped at *C* deck and Spock raced from it to
the nearest vertical access tube. He stepped inside and started
down toward engineering. In his mind, his sense of time ticked
off the seconds: three minutes, one second remaining . . . three
minutes . . . two minutes, fifty-nine seconds.

Mother, Spock thought suddenly, and he regretted the reaction she would suffer upon learning the news of his death. If he succeeded in saving the rest of the *Enterprise* crew, his father would understand his reasoning, but his mother would not. Or even if she did, even if she took pride in the sacrifice her son had made for his crewmates and friends, she would still feel the pain of losing him. Sarek's logical discipline would spare him, but Amanda's humanity would bring her great distress.

And Jim, Spock thought. *What about Jim?* In the admiral's life, bereavement had become all too present a companion. Beyond the crew who had perished under his command, and for whom Jim felt absolute responsibility, his grandparents had died in his youth, and his parents after that. He had seen Gary Mitchell, his closest friend at the time, mutate into something sinister and dangerous, and Jim had been forced to kill Mitchell himself. He had found his only sibling, his brother Sam, dead on Deneva, and had watched his sister-in-law die in agony not long afterward. Miramanee, carrying his unborn child, had been stoned to death, and another love, Rayna Kapec, had essentially committed suicide.

And then there had been Edith Keeler, the woman Jim had loved like no other. At Spock's urging, for the sake of maintaining the timeline of historical events, he had allowed her to die, had taken action to ensure that she died. In some ways, Spock thought that Jim had never recovered from that.

Spock's own death, he knew, would be another terrible blow for the admiral.

He reached the upper deck of engineering and felt the heat of overworked equipment, smelled the bitter whiff of perspiration and fear. He sprinted toward the top of the ladder that led down to the section housing the containment chamber. With less than two and a half minutes left now, he thought again of the likelihood of his impending death. This time, though, he considered something he had not before: his *katra.* With so little time, how could he ensure the return of the essence of his being, the vitality of his mind, to Mount Seleya on Vulcan, where it could be interred in an ark?

Spock arrived at the lower engineering level, where several cadets still worked and several others lay scattered about, in-

jured, unconscious, or both. Dr. McCoy treated one crewmember, he saw, while Commander Scott sat on the deck, slumped
back against a post. The engineer's head lolled and his eyelids
fluttered as he obviously fought to regain alertness.

Hastening to the warp monitoring console, Spock queried the
status of the plasma injector. As he'd hypothesized, the component had overloaded, flooding the containment chamber with
lethal radiation. He tried to reset it from the panel, something
Mr. Scott would no doubt have done as well, and indeed,
Spock's attempt failed. As he'd expected, though, he saw that he
could reset the injector manually.

Moving away from the station, Spock started toward both the
containment chamber and Dr. McCoy. Already preparing to
transfer his *katra,* he intended to ask McCoy both to meld with
him and to contact Sarek about a trip to Mount Seleya. Spock's
father would understand what had happened and would take action accordingly. But before he could turn toward the doctor,
McCoy interposed himself between Spock and the chamber.

"Are you outta your Vulcan mind?" he said. "No human can
tolerate the radiation that's in there."

"As you are so fond of pointing out, Doctor, I am not human,"
Spock said. He started forward, prepared to ask McCoy to meld
with him, but the doctor raised a hand to his shoulder and
forcibly stopped him.

"You're not going in there," McCoy insisted.

Two minutes, one second. Spock had no time for this. Quickly,
he formulated another plan. "Perhaps you're right," he said, then
turned toward where Mr. Scott still sat on the deck, struggling to
come fully awake. "What is Mister Scott's condition?"

McCoy stepped past Spock, toward the engineer. "Well, I
don't think that he—" The doctor stiffened as Spock's fingers
tightened about his shoulder.

"I'm sorry, Doctor," Spock said as he lowered McCoy to the
deck. "I have no time to discuss this logically." He hurriedly
reached toward Mr. Scott and pulled off the protective gloves of
the commander's engineering suit. Then, presuming greatly on
his friendship with McCoy but having few other choices, Spock
raised his hand to the doctor's face. As swiftly as he could, he established a mental link, then concentrated. "Remember," he said,

and he knew that in the unused portion of McCoy's brain, neurons fired, initiating action potentials and causing communication across synapses. In an instant, the constituents of one section of the doctor's gray matter—axons, dendrites, soma, terminal buttons, myelin sheaths, nodes of Ranvier, Schwann cells—all aligned their states to mirror the corresponding constituents in Spock's own brain.

The process complete, he headed for the containment chamber. Pulling on his gloves as he entered, he saw Mr. Scott gaze up at him, his surprise at Spock crossing the threshold into the radiation field apparently shocking him into full consciousness. McCoy also seemed to be coming to already, the effects of the nerve pinch on him probably overwhelmed by the power of the *katra* transfer.

Inside the chamber, the atmosphere felt hot and charged, as though the air had become electrified. Spock crossed to a bulkhead-mounted display and examined the injector configuration shown there. As he saw that one of the intake manifolds had automatically shut down, he became peripherally aware of Mr. Scott and Dr. McCoy yelling for him to vacate the chamber. He ignored them as he did the danger of his surroundings, instead reaching for the manual override and throwing it to a full open position. He checked the readout again and saw the manifold begin to function.

"Engine room," he heard Admiral Kirk call over the intercom. *"What's happening?"*

Spock sped to an adjacent control panel, located the switch for the injector assembly, and touched a button to unlock it. A tingling suffused his exposed flesh and then shifted to a throbbing pressure, as though the cytoplasm in the cells of his skin had begun to boil from within. As with the cries of Dr. McCoy and Mr. Scott, he ignored the sensation.

Crossing to the injector assembly in the center of the chamber, Spock pulled off its large protective cap. Jets of pressurized gas shot upward, obscuring the opening of the assembly. With time running out, Spock reached inside, his hands at least minimally protected by the engineering gloves. He searched for the injector with his fingers, found it, and took hold. He struggled to reset it in its cradle but did not have enough leverage.

For a moment, he staggered back, then pushed himself forward again, over the assembly this time, his face now fully in the stream of escaping gas. His flesh felt like it was melting.

His hand came loose again, sending him backward a step, and again he battled his way forward, back to the assembly. He reached in again, wrapped his hand around the injector, and tried to heave it back into place.

It seemed frozen, moving not even slightly.

Keenly aware of the seconds passing and knowing that he would also have to reseat the assembly's protective cap before the injector would function again, Spock concentrated as much as he ever had. With every thought focused on his hand, he willed every scrap of strength he possessed into fighting this one piece of machinery.

Twenty seconds.

In his grip, the injector shifted, moving less than a centimeter. Spock pushed himself, and the component all at once shunted back into place. He bent down for the cap and lifted it with difficulty, his strength seeming to vanish. He set it atop the assembly, then pushed it back into place.

Ten seconds.

Spock fell backward, his back slamming against the control panel in the bulkhead. He barely felt the impact, the sense of his flesh catching fire overpowering the rest of his physical awareness of self. He tried to open his eyes and realized that they already were open; he could no longer see.

Did it work? he wanted to know, and then, at his elbow, there came a familiar vibration, somehow making itself known through the pain. *The* Enterprise *at warp.*

As he leaned heavily on the bulkhead, Spock turned toward the hard surface, then pushed himself away from it, trying to stand up straight. He immediately lost his balance, lurching to his left and collapsing to the deck. He reached down and attempted again to push himself up, but all his strength had gone.

It didn't matter. As he let his upper body fall forward into the bulkhead, he knew that he had served the needs of the many. *It is logical,* he thought.

Then Spock waited to die.

* * *

The dusk had claimed its prize, the Vulcan sun swallowed by the horizon. Atop the circular, flattened peak that rose alongside Mount Seleya and connected to it via a stone bridge, the misty air, thin and cool to begin with, had now grown colder still. The fires burning on bronze plates, mounted on two pairs of widely spaced pedestals along the central walkway, provided no warmth. A chill shook McCoy as he listened to the Vulcan high priestess, T'Lar, in preparation for the *fal-tor-pan,* the re-fusion, ask who the keeper of Spock's *katra* was.

"I am," he answered, and then he identified himself in a way similar to how the high priestess had just distinguished Sarek. "McCoy, Leonard H., son of David." He felt loss and remorse at the mention of his father, but pushed the emotions away, knowing that he needed to stay present in the moment, if not for his own sake, then for Spock's.

"McCoy, son of David," the elderly T'Lar said, "since thou art human, we cannot expect thee to understand fully what Sarek has requested." McCoy saw Spock's father listening along with the other Vulcan attendants and the rest of the *Enterprise*'s officers—Jim, Scotty, Sulu, Uhura, Chekov, and Saavik—as the high priestess spoke. Dressed in red vestments and a sleeveless surplice, she stood on a large, raised platform at the edge of the peak. A brace of tall spires rose behind her and surrounded a sculpture of a curving Vulcan symbol. Two other elders, stoic and motionless, held ornamental staffs upright at the rear of the platform, and two groups of women clad in gauzy white gowns formed lines down along the steps. Spock, his body reconstituted by the genesis wave and recovered by his friends, lay on one of a pair of pallets on either side of T'Lar. "Spock's body lives," the priestess said. "With your approval, we shall use our powers to return to his body that which you possess. But, McCoy, you must now be warned: the danger to thyself is as grave as the danger to Spock. You must make the choice."

McCoy didn't have to think about his decision. "I choose the danger," he said. In the days following Spock's apparent death, McCoy had been tormented by nightmares very different than those to which he had long become accustomed. He had believed that he might be losing his mind—as had Starfleet Command—until Sarek had visited Jim and the two had determined what

Spock had done. It seemed impossible that McCoy essentially carried both his mind and Spock's in his head, but it also provided an explanation, however incredible, for the way he felt. Even without the possibility of "re-fusing" Spock's mind to his body, McCoy would have wanted to purge himself of the foreign presence within his brain, no matter the danger to himself. "Hell of a time to ask," he said quietly to Jim.

Sarek motioned him forward. After glancing at Jim, McCoy walked toward the platform, where a pair of women met him at the base of the steps and escorted him upward, then past the high priestess. He lay down on the second pallet, faceup, and then several of the women pushed it forward, positioning it beside T'Lar, on the opposite side of her from Spock's supine form.

McCoy suddenly felt fear, as well as the urge to leap up off the pallet and flee. Instead, he took a deep breath and waited. Standing beside the head of his pallet, T'Lar spoke in Vulcan to those assembled: *"Ben . . . vahl . . . nahvoon."* Her husky voice echoed in the twilight, and one of the attendants below the platform struck a gong.

Slowly, T'Lar raised her left hand and placed it on McCoy's forehead. At once, he sensed a kinetic energy forming about him . . . and *through* him. He could no longer keep his eyes open, and as his lids shut, he became aware of another presence reaching out to him . . . searching past his mind . . . and then *through* it. McCoy resisted, not wanting to oppose the high priestess, but from an involuntary reaction of self-preservation. Through T'Lar's connection with him, she bade him to lower his defenses, not for her, but for Spock.

McCoy focused his thoughts and then let them go. The dual nature of his mind . . . his mind*s* . . . *their* minds . . . crippled him. He could no longer think, and he could no longer let go. His psyche drifted, and with it, Spock's. And then he sensed—

A tangle of images and sounds, tastes and scents and textures, of which he could not make the slightest sense. He felt lost . . . and yet not alone . . . alive . . . and yet unformed. He floated through the void, vulnerable and ready, a canvas upon which the universe could throw its infinitude of colors, an ether through which the universe could hurl its bounty of notes. He was nothing, waiting to be everything . . . or anything.

And then remembrance broke like a wave on the shores of time, bringing forth from the deep a clarity of perception. Darkness rose in the void, distinguishable from it. And then orange flickers of flame broke through the night, casting uneasy shadows on stone walls. A face, unrecognizable, loomed up, exotic, dark, with high cheekbones and delicate, pointed ears. Clamor followed, sputtering wails, deafening within his head, and without, echoing against the cave walls.

Cave walls? A face? Flame?

This, then, was not memory, not mere memory, but knowledge too, interpretation layered upon simple perception. Recording events by awareness alone, and later translating that into something meaningful. Today's knowledge filling in the outlines of yesterday's uninformed recall.

So cold. Even the fires in the close quarters of the cave could not match the confining heat of the amniotic fluid. Cold flesh borne up by cold hands, lifting, lifting. Height bringing the instinctive fear of falling as he was carried through the stale air. The understanding of gravity would come later, but with or without hindsight and decipherment, the dread of gravity came now.

Sounds not his own made themselves known: Buh-buh, buh buh. *Nonsense, noises only, recorded and recalled without understanding. But now, in retrospection:* "Sarek, your son."

Spock! Born of Amanda, born of Sarek, now, in this unforgotten moment. The joy of parenthood, the logic of procreation. Except: Buh buh-buh.

Sarek, in the first moments after the birth of his son: "So human."

In the depths of wherever he had fallen, McCoy's heart broke. And broke again as he emerged into the world himself. He could not possibly remember this . . . could he? Had it been implanted in an inaccessible portion of his memory, somehow now released? Or did he look back and draw himself a picture of what he'd pieced together over the years, of what he'd learned, of what he'd imagined?

At first, he did not recognize his mother, her features distorted by pain. He saw her in sweeps of vision only as he was raised up, but he kept the image of her in his mind. Later, he would see— had seen—holos of her, and now he evoked those likenesses of *her, replacing her twisted aspect with one of tranquility: her soft, rounded face, her rosy complexion beneath dark, coppery hair, and in those captured moments, always—always—smiling.*

But not then. Then, perspiration coated her face and matted her hair. A sound not very human leaped from between her teeth, clenched in a rictus of obvious agony. Her hands clutched and clawed desperately at the red sheets, fighting to deliver, fighting whatever had gone wrong, fighting herself. Her red gown—

Red? Red gown, red sheets? Red everywhere. On her, on him, on the bed, on the floor. Not by design, but by—

Blood.

And below her screams, he heard a rattle deep within himself. He could not breathe, though he tried, his lungs aching, his eyes wide in a natural panic. Meconium aspiration, he guessed now, looking back, with knowledge that would not come for years. But the diagnosis didn't matter, hadn't mattered; he would survive— had survived—but his mother—

His mother had not.

What had it been? Disseminated intravascular coagulopathy, leading to insufficient perfusion of vital organs? Had she suffered some undetected infection, or had her uterus failed to contract? Had he been born suddenly, unexpectedly?

His father had never told him, had never spoken of that day, though it remained ever present anyway. The holos McCoy had eventually seen had been hidden away by his father, and McCoy hadn't been sure they even existed until he'd searched for them in his teens and had finally found the portraits of the mother he had never known. He hadn't remembered seeing his mother on the day he'd been born—did he really remember that now?—but though it had been hard, he'd liked seeing her in the holos, seeing her safe and in no danger—

"The ship . . . out of danger?" Spock asked. Spock's memory, but fractured, seen through McCoy's eyes, and also sensed, like the memory of a dream, through some tenuous connection with his dying self.

"Yes," Admiral Kirk said.

Spock saw his own mottled skin, the flesh sagging from his face, and somewhere far away felt the echo of the pain, of the searing of his cells. *"Don't grieve, Admiral,"* he said, his voice low and harsh, the words rasping in his injured throat. He had already wounded the admiral—Jim—and did not wish to do so again, though that seemed unavoidable. *"It is logical,"* he avowed. *"The needs of the many outweigh..."* He watched himself wince, and in a distant corner of telepathic linkage, felt the throbbing ache.

"The needs of the few," Jim said.

Spock nodded. *"Or the one,"* he added. *"I never took the Kobayashi Maru test until now. What do you think of my solution?"*

"Spock..." Jim said, the depth of his anguish plain.

Spock slid down the transparent bulkhead of the containment chamber, and on the other side, Jim followed him down. *"I... I have been, and always shall be, your friend."* Removing one glove, lifting his hand to place it flat against the clear partition, fingers splayed in the traditional Vulcan salutation. *"Live long and prosper,"* he said, as he did neither. He slumped, and saw—

Death coming for him in the distance. An armored knight on horseback, charging across the glade. *"These things cannot be real,"* he'd told Tonia. *"Hallucinations can't harm us."* He faced his imaginary attacker, stood his ground as the unreal knight galloped toward him with lance held at the ready. He felt certain of his action, did not believe he would be harmed, until—

The weapon entered his chest. He cried out, astonished, as he fell backward, the pain of the steel entering his body like nothing he'd ever felt. He saw his own blood gush from the wound, splattering the brown leather jacket of his attacker. The man pulled the weapon free, his eyes wide open in their hatred, his face a mask of frightened zealotry. He brought the weapon down again, slicing between McCoy's ribs and into his heart. He heard a woman scream, and knew that he was dying—

I-Chaya dying, more quickly now, released from the slow agony that the le-matya's poisoned claws had inflicted on him—

McCoy's father dying, more quickly now, released from the slow agony that the disease had inflicted on him—

The photon-torpedo shell, containing a corpse, ready to be fired into space as the mourners looked on in the torpedo room aboard the *Enterprise*—

The wooden casket, containing a corpse, ready to buried in the ground as the mourners looked on in the cemetery in the small town—

The Vulcan children taunting Spock because of their revulsion for emotion, and because of Spock's human heritage—

McCoy's father sending him out into the cotton fields because of David McCoy's dislike for technology, and because of Leonard's reliance on it—

Spock kissing Leila—

McCoy kissing Jocelyn—

Spock studying at the Vulcan Science Academy—

McCoy studying at the University of Mississippi School of Medicine—

Spock firing his phaser at the silicon creature—

McCoy firing his phaser at the salt-dependent creature—

Spock leaping through the Guardian of Forever—

McCoy leaping through the Guardian of Forever—

Spock falling—

McCoy falling—

And Spock clinging to life—

And McCoy clinging to life—

And Spock—

And McCoy—

Awoke. The whirlwind of thoughts and emotions, recollections and perceptions, seemed to have lasted lifetimes—his own and Spock's. And yet he knew that even as time had sped past in his mind—in *their* minds—it had stood still in the real world. A second had passed, perhaps two.

But when McCoy opened his eyes, the fading Vulcan evening had gone, and so too had the night that followed. Dawn rose around him, the yellow-red glow of the sky a harbinger of the new day. Above him, T'Lar peered down, and he marveled that the old woman had stood there through the night, connecting him to Spock.

He and T'Lar regarded each other, and McCoy nodded. She nodded back, then raised her arms, clearly entreating him to rise. For a moment, he didn't think he could, didn't believe that his mind possessed the capacity to initiate voluntary muscle movement. But then his back came up off the pallet and he lifted himself into a sitting position. Across from him, past T'Lar, Spock had already stood up, and attendants worked to attire him in a hooded white robe.

McCoy felt a touch at his arm, and he looked to his right to see Sarek standing there. "Is he . . . ?" McCoy said, his lips dry, his tongue clicking against the roof of his mouth. He discovered that he didn't need to finish the question; he already knew about Spock. Sarek responded anyway.

"Only time will answer," he said quietly.

McCoy knew him to be wrong, knew that Spock's presence had left him, and he had no doubt that it had been returned to its proper place. He had somehow perceived the transfer as it had happened. It might take time, he thought, but Spock would be Spock.

Behind Sarek, four red-robed attendants carried a palanquin forward. They lowered it so that T'Lar could take her seat, then lifted the antiquated conveyance and bore her from the platform. Sarek gestured forward, and McCoy walked side by side with him down the steps.

McCoy's friends waited there. Jim stepped forward, and McCoy stopped before him. "I'm all right, Jim," he declared. He wanted to say more, but couldn't. They would see. They would all see.

McCoy joined his friends and waited for Spock.

FORTY-FOUR

1948

A blast of sweltering air struck Lynn as she pushed through the revolving door and out into the night. At once, she felt the tracks of her tears drying on her skin. She reached up to her face anyway, wiping below her eyes. Emotionally drained, she breathed in deeply, then exhaled slowly.

Stepping off to the side, away from the door, Lynn waited. This late in the year, into autumn, the temperature should have leveled off in the sixties, but today had reached twenty degrees higher than that. Right now, even with the sun down, it didn't feel much cooler than it had this afternoon.

Leonard emerged from inside through the revolving door, glanced around until he spotted her, then walked over. He appeared stricken, she saw, his features pale and set in a serious expression. "Are you all right?" he asked.

"Yes, of course, I'm fine," Lynn said lightly and easily, wanting to allay Leonard's obvious concern.

"I'm sorry," he said. "I didn't realize . . ." He gestured back toward the movie theater. "I had no idea what the film was about."

"It's all right, Leonard," she tried to assure him. They had driven to Greenville on this Saturday night to see a movie, as they'd taken to doing fairly frequently during the past year. Leonard had seen in the newspaper last Sunday that *Random Harvest* would be playing this weekend at the Bijou. It had been released a few years ago and starred Ronald Coleman and Greer Garson, an actor and actress whose work Lynn really enjoyed. Since neither she nor Leonard had ever seen the movie, they'd decided to make the trip for it.

Today, Lynn had put in a Saturday shift at the mill, and Leonard had seen a number of patients, including Audie Glaston, recently diagnosed with epilepsy, and Millie Denton's—Millie *Warnick's*—new baby girl, Olivia. After Lynn and Leonard finished their work, they'd shared a late afternoon supper at her house and then made the ninety-minute drive to Greenville. With each trip into the city, it seemed to take less and less time, with more and more of the roads between there and Hayden getting paved.

Now, standing outside the theater after seeing the movie, Leonard said again, "I'm sorry."

"Don't be sorry," Lynn told him. "It was great."

Leonard nodded, but the look on his face didn't change. "I know, but . . ."

He didn't finish. Lynn thought she understood his concern. *Random Harvest* traced the life of a World War I soldier who returns shell-shocked to the civilian world with his speech impaired and his memory gone. After walking out of a medical institution, he befriends a music-hall singer, and the two eventually fall in love and marry. But a traffic accident restores the soldier's old memories and blots out his newer ones, and no longer even recalling his new wife, he returns to his life from before the war. Although hardly a parallel for Lynn's own story, it involved a woman loving and marrying a soldier who she then loses. A beautiful, romantic tale, by turns bitter and sweet, it had brought tears to her eyes more than once.

But not because of Phil.

At the beginning of the movie, when Lynn had discovered the main character to be a soldier, she had thought of her husband—and of the war too, which still raged across Europe and throughout the Pacific. Two years after Phil's death, and four after he'd enlisted in the army, she still missed him, though she often tried not to do so. That had been the case this evening. As she'd sat in the darkened theater with Leonard, she'd consciously put her recollections aside and concentrated instead on the story unfolding on the screen. Although she'd cried a lot through the final reel, she'd ended up loving the movie.

"Leonard, really, I'm fine," she insisted. "C'mon. Let's go to Peggy Jo's." Many times after she and Leonard had been to the Bijou, the two would head over to Peggy Jo's Diner for coffee and a slice of pie.

"Are you sure?" Leonard said, apparently unconvinced because of her tears.

"Yes, I'm sure," Lynn said, reaching forward and giving his hand a squeeze. "I'm also sure that I want a piece of peach cobbler."

Finally, that seemed to cheer Leonard. "Now you're talking my language," he said. They left his car parked across from the theater and walked the three blocks to the diner. Inside, they sat down at a booth and placed their orders with Margie, an older waitress they'd gotten to know during their many trips there.

As they waited for their coffee and cobbler, they talked about Millie Warnick and her new baby, which led them to the subject

of her husband. Doug Warnick had taken over the Seed and Feed
a year and a half ago, after Gregg Anderson had passed on at the
age of seventy. Mr. Anderson had left his store to his only son,
Michael, who had then sold it to his brother-in-law, Doug. In almost no time after he'd moved to Hayden from nearby Plattston,
Doug had hit it off with Millie Denton, and the two had soon
wed. Last month, they'd had their first baby.

After Margie had brought their coffee and pie to the table,
Lynn returned to the topic of the Seed and Feed. There had been
something she'd wanted to talk about with Leonard for a very
long time, but she'd never found a way of bringing it up. "I heard
Doug hired a new feller," she said.

"That's right," Leonard said as he poured sugar into his mug.
"His name's Whitney Williams."

"You met him then?" Lynn asked. She'd hoped that he had.

"Yesterday," he said, picking up a spoon and stirring his coffee. "He's about Doug's age, twenty-five or so. He seemed like a
nice man."

"Where did he come from?" Lynn asked, knowing no
Williams family in Hayden.

"Doug knew him over in Plattston," Leonard said. "I guess
after Olivia was born, Doug decided he wanted some help in the
store so he could spend more time at home."

Lynn listened, interested in the details of the Seed and Feed's
new worker, but asking about them first only because she hadn't
wanted to lurch gracelessly into the issue she really wanted to
discuss. "I . . . I heard Mister Williams is colored," she said, and
then thought, *Oh yeah, that was graceful.*

Leonard's hand stopped halfway to his mouth, and he returned a forkful of pie back to his plate. She could see the muscles of his face tense. "Whitney's skin is dark brown, yes," he
said.

Lynn felt embarrassed, and she peered down at her own plate.
She stabbed idly at the cobbler and forged ahead. "You don't talk
about coloreds the way other people do," she said.

"No," Leonard agreed. "I don't suppose I do."

She forced herself to look up at him, meeting his gaze across
the table. "You know the time when . . ."

"Yup," Leonard said, even though she hadn't finished her

thought. That marked nothing new for them, though. For years, they'd had a good idea of what the other was thinking, in tune probably because they'd spent so much time together.

"The time when you and Phil had that awful argument," Lynn said, wanting to make sure they were talking about the same thing.

"Yup," Leonard said again, his features softening. "I felt bad about that. I told Phil that. He apologized to me too."

"I know," Lynn said. Phil had told her about the conversation, and its results had been very noticeable, helping to renew the friendship between the two men.

"It was just terribly troubling to see Benny—or anybody— mistreated like that," Leonard said. "And even more so when a friend of mine supported that behavior."

"I know," Lynn said. "You know, I remember something you said the night you and Phil argued. I asked about the colored man's name, and you told me 'the man' was named Benny. It seemed like you specifically left out the word *colored*."

"I'm sure I did leave it out," Leonard said. "There wasn't any good reason to use it."

"I've thought about that a lot over the years," Lynn said.

"Really?" Leonard said, clearly surprised. The incident with Bo Bartell and Billy Fuster and the others, and the argument between Leonard and Phil that had followed, had happened probably ten years ago.

"Yeah," Lynn said. "I felt bad about what happened."

"I know you did," Leonard said. "When I drove up that day and saw what was going on, and saw you out there, I just assumed you were trying to stop it from happening. After I took Benny back to my house, he told me that you did, so I know you felt bad about it."

"No," Lynn said. "I mean, yes, I felt bad about those boys beating that man—Benny—but that's not what I meant." She looked down again, and as she attempted to figure out how to say what she wanted to say, she pushed the side of her fork through her pie, then scooped the piece of cobbler up and into her mouth. Once she'd swallowed it, she gazed back over at Leonard and continued. "I felt bad because . . . because even though I knew it was wrong for those boys to do what they did, I also . . ." She

hesitated, ashamed to make the admission. "I also agreed with
Phil. If Benny would've just walked around the town like Bo
wanted him to, everything would've been all right."

Leonard regarded her silently for a few seconds, and she
could see the disappointment in his eyes. At last, he said, "I'm
sorry you feel that way."

"I don't think that anymore," Lynn rushed to say. "But back
then, what made me feel bad was that I thought something was
wrong, but I also understood it. I didn't want that man to get
beaten, but I knew why he did. But you obviously didn't. You
thought it was wrong, and that's all there was to it."

"I still think that," Leonard said.

"I know," Lynn said. "So I kept thinking about what you said,
and how you didn't ever refer to Benny as *colored*. And I kept
asking myself why."

Leonard set his fork down on his plate. "Because it didn't
matter," he said. "It would've been like me saying 'the right-
handed man.' It was a distinction that didn't matter. Worse, it was
a distinction that serves to separate people and allow them to
hate more easily."

"I figured that out," Lynn said. "Because you said something
else that night you and Phil argued. You said there was more difference between all the white folks in town than between Phil
and Benny. Since you're a doctor, I thought you probably knew
what you were talking about, but even if you didn't, I realized
that what you said was true in the eyes of God. People are people, and we're all God's children. It doesn't matter what they
look like, only how they treat other people."

Leonard smiled and nodded. "That's right," he said.

"So, I just wanted to tell you that," Lynn said. "It's been
weighing on me for a long time."

"It has?" Leonard asked as he retrieved his fork and cut off
another mouthful of pie from his plate.

"Yup," Lynn said. "I thought about it for a while, until I figured it all out. I didn't think you knew that I kind of agreed with
Phil back then, but I wanted to tell you. I'm not sure why." Except, she realized, maybe she did know why she'd wanted to
share this with Leonard. She simply didn't want to keep anything from him because of—

Because of the way I feel about him.

"Thank you," he said. "I'm glad you did. You're a good woman, Lynn."

She could feel the warm rush of blood to her face and knew that she'd turned bright red. Self-conscious, she looked down at her plate again. "I think you're a good man, Leonard." She reached across the table and rested her hand atop his, then looked up at him. She felt something like an electric charge run through her body when she saw his blue eyes gazing back at her.

They sat that way for a few moments, quietly, comfortably, and then Leonard pulled his hand away and reached for his coffee. For the rest of the conversation, they didn't talk about anything nearly as serious as they just had. They discussed *Random Harvest*, and then other great films that its two stars had done previously: *Lost Horizon* with Ronald Coleman, and *Madame Curie, Mrs. Miniver,* and *Goodbye, Mr. Chips* with Greer Garson. They spoke about books, Leonard's practice, life at the mill, and the cotton harvest just past. It was, Lynn thought when she lay down to sleep later that night, a wonderful evening.

But then she always had a wonderful time with Leonard.

McCoy rumbled from Upper Piedmont Highway onto Merrysville Road, following the beams of his headlights through the night. On the seat beside him, Lynn lay slumped against the door, asleep on their hour and a half ride from Greenville, now almost complete. When they'd left the diner tonight, she'd claimed not to be tired, but had drifted off shortly after they'd reached US 123.

Tired himself—exhausted, actually—McCoy looked forward to climbing into bed as soon as he dropped Lynn off at her house and then made his own way home. He'd seen eleven patients today, including five children whom over the past week or so he'd diagnosed with strep throat. Fortunately, penicillin had at last become widely available and he'd used it to treat the bacterial infection. All of the children seemed to be recovering well.

But McCoy's long workday provided only a minor reason for his current fatigue, as did the long drives to and from Greenville. More than anything, the emotional nature of the evening had taken its toll on him. For two hours, he'd sat in the Bijou Theater, bathed in the flickering light of *Random Harvest* and dreading the impact of the film on Lynn. Even before that, the newsreel shown on the big screen had reported recent events of the war: after four attempts, the Germans had finally captured Leningrad, and Japan had now taken control of all Australian ports and cities. McCoy had expected the wartime updates, though, and knew that Lynn had too. He'd believed that she could get through the brief recap and then enjoy the film.

But as *Random Harvest* had opened on the military wing of an asylum, and on an amnesiac soldier suffering from the post-traumatic stress of war, McCoy had cringed. Phil's experience had been different, of course, and much worse, but McCoy worried that the tale unfolding in the darkened theater would cause Lynn to relive the pain of losing her husband. He'd considered asking her if she wanted to leave, but had chosen not to broach the subject without seeing any signs of her distress. In the end, he'd sat there with her, periodically observing her in the dim light and trying to assess her emotional state.

Afterward, he learned his fears had been unfounded. Lynn had wept during the film, particularly during its closing minutes, but she claimed that had been as a result of the story and the performances and not because of any feelings related to Phil. McCoy had been doubtful, but they'd then had pie and coffee at Peggy Jo's, even discussing the film at one point, and Lynn had shown no indications at all of any sadness or upset.

Now, as they rolled through the night along Merrysville Road, McCoy thought about Lynn and how she had handled the last four years of her life. She and Phil had been married for twenty-one years when he had enlisted in the army, and for twenty-three years by the time she'd received word that he'd been killed in battle at Portmagee. Among humans, McCoy knew, the loss of a spouse ranked as the greatest emotional burden to bear, the effects even more devastating than the death of a child. Of even greater concern, a man or a woman who lost their partner, particularly after a relationship of significant duration, frequently faced complications to their own health, the psychological toll translating into physiological problems.

Lynn, though, appeared well these days. Since McCoy had first met the Dickinsons all those years ago, he'd spent a great deal of time with them—other than during the period when he and Phil had argued about Benny—and since Phil had gone off, first to Fort Jackson, and later to the European theater of operations, McCoy had spent an even higher percentage of his time with Lynn. More than anything, that had allowed him to discover the depth of Lynn's strength, something reconfirmed by her reaction to the film they'd seen tonight.

Not that she didn't still miss Phil, and not that she hadn't mourned him. But immediately after Phil had enlisted, McCoy had watched her pick herself up and continue on with her life, and after he'd died, she'd seemed to redouble those efforts. Where it would have been understandable for her to languish in depression, to withdraw from the community and even from her friendships, she had done none of those things. And where she might have chosen to rely on other people, attempting to fill the void left in her life by the absence of her husband, she hadn't done that either.

In 1946, the year Phil had died, the people in Hayden had rallied to her side and helped her complete her cotton harvest. Last year and this, though, she'd simply hired more itinerant workers and had thereby done the job herself, even as she'd continued putting in hours at the mill. She'd continued seeing her friends, McCoy included, and seemed intent on making the most of what some might term a tragic life. Her father had drowned in a logging accident when she'd been just thirteen years old, and her mother, to whom Lynn had been very close, had died fifteen years later after a protracted and painful illness. With Phil's death, she had now lost the three most important people in her life. And yet she not only persevered, but actually seemed to flourish.

As McCoy slowed and turned the car north onto Church Street, he recalled how easy it had once been for him to regard the people of the twentieth century from something of an elitist viewpoint. Seeing the lack of advancement not only in technology, but in society itself, he'd often expected a shortage of fortitude in individuals. But working in a mission for the downtrodden in New York, and then in a primitive medical environment in Hayden, he'd witnessed the difficult circumstances people had endured through the 1930s and the Great Depression, and now through the 1940s and World War II. Many had shown strength in forging ahead through their lives, but even so, Lynn stood out as exceptional.

Her religious faith had provided her with great solace, he knew, and yet she also managed to apply it selflessly. McCoy had been startled by her admission tonight of the racist attitudes she'd harbored, but he'd found the description of the fight she'd waged against her own beliefs quite compelling. In his own experience, McCoy had often seen both individuals and institutions employ their faith for nothing more than their own self-interests, often hypocritically acting in contravention of their own professed principles. Lynn, on the other hand, married her actions to her beliefs. When she'd come to understand the discrepancy between her prejudices and her Christian tenets—love, kindness, tolerance, acceptance—she'd sought not to find some justification for her bigotry, but to modify her own outlook. McCoy understood that she had been taught as a child to believe in the inferiority of people of who didn't look just like she did, and that she had been able to overcome that as an adult, he found remarkable.

On top of that, Lynn hadn't had to divulge to him the intolerance she'd once felt. She certainly knew McCoy's feelings about racism, and she needn't have risked his opinion of her by confessing to her own discriminatory beliefs, even if she had now overcome them. The more he got to know her, the more he respected and loved her.

Loved?

Yes. Yes, he loved Lynn, just as he'd loved Phil, just as he'd loved Edith Keeler and Jim Kirk and, so help him, Spock. Except—

Tonight, she'd touched his hand, and he'd perceived it as more than a gesture of simple friendship. They'd known each other all this time—more than sixteen years now—and had become very close friends, but nothing more. Of course, she'd been happily married for most of that spell. Now, though—

Now what?

McCoy knew he'd be lying to himself if he denied the deep connection he felt with Lynn. Besides being drawn to her goodness and her inner strength, he found her physically attractive as well—even more so now than when he'd first walked down Tindal's Lane and she'd waved to him. Age had refined her features and granted her a measure of elegance despite her rural life.

And tonight, when she'd touched his hand, he'd felt more than friendship between them. There had been fire, and he thought she'd experienced it too. He also didn't think he'd misread her intentions. Under other circumstances—

What circumstances? he asked himself. He'd last been involved with a woman more than eighteen years ago, with Tonia Barrows, back in his old life aboard the *Enterprise.* He'd stayed away from romantic relationships in order to avoid altering the timeline—or so he told himself. Really, while he'd steered clear of such entanglements when he'd initially arrived in Earth's past, he'd long since given up trying to determine how his actions would impact history, especially given how dramatically the course of World War II had already changed. Living in the small town of Hayden, there had been only limited opportunities for courtship, and he'd shunned all of those.

Through the windshield, McCoy saw the turnoff onto Tindal's Lane and he took it. As he drove toward Lynn's house, he admitted to himself that his resistance to romance had a long pedigree. Although he'd never had the chance to end his relationship with Tonia, he knew that he'd been heading in that direction prior to his cordrazine overdose. He'd known that he and Tonia would never make it together, just as he'd known with Nancy before her and Jocelyn before that.

And he supposed he knew that with Lynn as well.

A few minutes later, he pulled off the road and onto the dirt drive beside Lynn's house. After shutting off the engine, he quietly opened his own door, then walked around the car and opened the passenger side. Leaning in, he touched Lynn's arm and gently roused her. Her eyelids quivered open and she peered up at him with a slightly confused, almost childlike, expression. "Lynn," he said, "you're home. We just got back from the movies."

Awareness and recollection appeared on her face. "I must've fell asleep," she said.

"You must have," McCoy said with a smile. He reached down

and took her hand, helping her out of the car, then escorted her up the steps to the front door.

Before going inside, Lynn turned to him. "I had a wonderful time," she said, and she moved forward ever so slightly.

"So did I," McCoy said. "Good night." He headed quickly back down the steps and over to his car. Without looking back, he got in and started the engine, then pulled back out onto the road and headed for home.

As he drove down Tindal's Lane, he glanced in the rearview mirror and watched as the light from Lynn's house faded into the night.

FORTY-FIVE

2285

Kirk dragged the manual release down, but the doors didn't open. In the dim, red emergency lighting of the canting Klingon bridge, he dropped himself against the heavy, metal hatches, reaching for the place where they separated one from the other. With all his might, he pushed, until they parted a few centimeters, and then finally all the way open. A thick cloud of white steam rose from within, and he staggered through its hot, moist embrace and down the sloping corridor.

They hadn't come this far for him to allow Scotty and Gillian to drown as the bird of prey—aptly renamed *HMS Bounty* by Bones—sank into San Francisco Bay. He trusted Spock to evacuate the rest of the crew—Bones, Sulu, Uhura, and Chekov—as he raced toward the engineering section and the cargo bays in the aft section of the vessel. There, Scotty had held the Klingon drive together, overseen the recrystallization of the dilithium matrix, and cobbled together an enormous tank to hold a pair of humpback whales. Gillian—Dr. Gillian Taylor, a marine biologist who'd come back to the future with them—had watched over the whales.

Up ahead, sparks sizzled at the end of a cable whipping wildly through the air as it dangled from the overhead. Kirk didn't hesitate, but as he reached the area, he threw himself along the inclined deck, feet first, and slid beneath and past the dangerous looking obstacle. Regaining his feet, he continued on, battling past downed equipment and ruptured bulkheads. By the time he neared the closed doors leading to the aft compartments, water had begun to rise in the corridor, the ship's hull obviously breached when it had crashed into the bay.

As Kirk waded forward, he saw the doors partially submerged. From the tilt of the vessel, he feared that the compartments beyond had already been flooded. All about him, the ship's structure groaned as, wounded, it fought stresses different than those for which it had been constructed.

And then he heard a voice, tones only, the words it uttered indistinguishable. And then another voice rang out, pitched higher than the first. *Scotty and Gillian!*

Kirk called out: "Scotty! Scotty!"

At once, a pounding began against the doors and the engineer answered. "Admiral! Help!"

Kirk let himself fall against the bulkhead beside the doors. "I'm here, Scotty!"

"Help!"

"I'm here!" Kirk cried again. He reached for the right-hand door, into which a manual release had been set. He twisted it, then pulled along the groove where the two panels met. It gave, though not easily, but then he saw two other hands, and felt the efforts of Scotty and Gillian as they too struggled to haul the doors open. When they'd parted enough, Kirk reached for Gillian, taking hold of her hand and pulling her forward. "You're gonna be all right," he tried to assure her.

As Gillian dragged herself up, she said, "The whales are trapped. They'll drown."

"There's no power to the bay doors," Scotty said as he positioned himself to evacuate the compartment.

"Explosive override?" Kirk asked.

"That's underwater," Scotty said, hefting himself up into the corridor. "There's no way to reach it."

No, Kirk thought, unwilling to accept defeat. They had come too far. "You go on ahead," he told Scotty, knowing what he must do. "And close the hatch." While doing so would likely make it impossible for Kirk to return this way, it might also slow the bird of prey's descent into the bay.

As Kirk pulled off his jacket, Scotty said as much: "Admiral, you'll be trapped."

Kirk glanced back at the engineer for just a second. "Go on!" he ordered. He tossed away his jacket and headed down into the aft compartment. Almost immediately, the water level reached up to his chest. How long had it been since his underwater training at Starfleet Academy? Three decades? As he bobbed upward in preparation to send himself in the opposite direction, he recalled the incident on the planet Argo twenty-five years ago when he and Spock had been transformed into water-breathers. Right now, that would have proven a handy ability.

After breathing in deeply, Kirk dove downward and began swimming toward the cargo hold. In his mind, he pictured the area and figured that the explosive overrides would be found at one end of the compartment or the other, possibly even at both ends. Waving his arms and kicking his feet, he propelled himself toward the nearer end. He found his way impeded by floating equipment, dislodged conduits, and other structures.

So much at stake, Kirk told himself as he fought his way through. Could they have come all this way only to fail now, so near to their goal? He and his crew—his friends—had spent a self-imposed three-month exile on Vulcan after Spock's mind had been re-fused with his body, and then they had headed back to Starfleet to face the consequences of the criminal and mutinous behavior they'd conducted in order to save him. But as they'd neared Earth, they'd found it under attack by an intelligence apparently seeking contact with humpback whales, a species extinct for two centuries. With few alternatives, Kirk and the others had chosen to travel back in time in order to bring some of those whales back to the present to communicate with the powerful alien presence. Now back in their own time, all of their efforts would go for nothing if Kirk could not free the whales from the Klingon vessel's hold.

Desperate to breath again, Kirk pushed himself onward. Before him, he saw the great masses of the two whales through the transparent aluminum that Scotty and Sulu had utilized to wall in the cargo bay. The admiral swam to his left and saw set into the near bulkhead a circular panel. He reached for it and saw a narrow set of controls on it. He tapped at the keys in sequence and a red light immediately flashed on beside them. An instant later, the panel divided in two, revealing a lever behind it.

He grabbed the handle with both hands and pulled. His right hand came free and he quickly reset it. As he exerted himself, air escaped his lungs, bubbling up from between his lips.

And still the handle wouldn't move.

With all the strength he could muster, he jerked at the lever, trying to dislodge it from its position. It moved back and forth slightly, and then it finally loosened. Kirk hauled it downward and heard the sound of small detonations through the water.

He turned and saw the long hatches of the hold parting. For a few worrisome seconds, the whales didn't move, but then he saw the one farthest from him fade from sight, its massive, dark body disappearing into the murky depths. The second whale followed, and then so did Kirk himself, kicking off of the bulkhead and swimming as quickly as he could toward the open hatch. He headed through it as the last air fled from his lungs.

Chasing the path of his bubbles, he swam upward, his lungs aching. Just as he thought he could no longer stop himself from inhaling, he broke the surface of the water. He gulped in lungfuls of air, but bobbed wildly in the choppy bay. He choked on drops of water and flailed about for purchase, knowing that the hull of the Klingon ship must be near. In the air, the high-pitched calls of the alien presence seeking contact with the whales shrieked loudly. And then he felt strong hands grab his arm and keep him afloat.

"Do you see them?" he heard Uhura call from above him, obviously perched somewhere on the bird of prey. He looked up and saw not only Spock but Gillian reaching for him as well. Past them—and past Bones, Scotty, Chekov, Uhura, and Sulu, also balanced on the edge of the Klingon hull—the angry sky rained down, the weather modified dramatically from space by the alien presence. Around the globe, Kirk knew, the cloud cover had become almost complete, causing rapid decreases in air temperature all over the world.

As Kirk settled himself against the Klingon hull and alongside Spock, Gillian cried out excitedly. She and Bones both pointed, and Kirk peered out and saw a dorsal fin glide past on the surface, and then the whale's flukes came clear of the water and slapped back down, a majestic—and at this moment important—sight. He looked for the second creature and spotted it off to the left. "There," he called, pointing.

Still, the alien presence called.

"Why don't they answer?" Kirk asked nobody in particular. "Why don't they sing?" When the crew had been back in the past and had found the two whales at the Maritime Cetacean Institute, Spock had mind-melded with one of the creatures. He believed that he had successfully communicated the situation and the crew's intentions.

Around them, the piercing whine of the alien presence continued. There seemed to be no response. *Would we know if the male whale, the one who vocalized, did respond?* Kirk suddenly wondered. He'd just assumed that they would—

And then he heard it. Not externally, through his ears, but internally, through his body: a wavering, almost haunting keening. Somewhere near, the male whale had begun singing. It lasted for a few seconds and then stopped, leaving behind only the sounds of the wind and the rain and water. The alien presence had ceased its calls.

Soon, the whale song began again, and this time when it stopped, the alien calls came again. For minutes, then, the two alternated, as though in conversation. By the time they both quieted, the sky overhead had already begun to clear.

One of the whales swam by, breaking the surface, and the crew pointed and called and waved, obviously ecstatic that their efforts—and those of the whales themselves—had apparently succeeded. Whatever mysterious forms of energy the alien had utilized to influence Earth's weather patterns had clearly been reversed. The clouds parted and withdrew, and the sun shined through once more.

Cold and wet, and still facing criminal charges and the consequences of his violations of direct orders, Jim Kirk smiled. He pointed as one of the whales breached, and then he slapped at the surface of the water in his joy at the sight. Right now, he would gladly accept whatever punishment the Federation Council handed down to him, as well as whatever actions Starfleet Command decided to take. None of it mattered.

Spock had been saved, and now, so too had the population of Earth.

McCoy sat in the elegantly appointed anteroom outside Admiral Cartwright's office. Sofas and chairs ringed three sides of the room, and a pair of assistants sat at large, semicircular desks on either side of the door that led into the Starfleet commander's sanctum. Artwork adorned the wood-paneled walls, presenting in a wide variety of styles different spacecraft, many of them not of terrestrial origin.

McCoy's friends—*and coconspirators,* he thought wryly— waited along with him. Sulu and Chekov stood talking quietly together in front of one of the paintings, an oil of a ship with a long, tapering hull, connected by a ventral strut to a ring that circled the main structure. Scotty and Uhura chatted in low tones on a sofa at the rear of the room, while Spock and McCoy sat silently beside each other in a couple of rounded, padded chairs. They had all been called in here a week after they had brought a pair of humpback whales with them from Earth's past, and three days after they had stood charges before the Federation Council and representatives of Starfleet Command. All but one of the specifications directed against them, and to which they'd all pled guilty—conspiracy, assault, theft, sabotage, willful destruction of property, and disobeying orders of the Starfleet commander— had been summarily dismissed, owing to, as the Federation president had said, mitigating circumstances. Nobody had yet detailed what those circumstances had been, but McCoy assumed that the crew's saving of Earth's population had likely had something to do with it—although the success of their restoration of Spock, the purpose for which they had committed those offenses in the first place, might also have played a role.

The single remaining charge, disobeying the orders of a superior, had been leveled exclusively at Jim. He had been found guilty, but for once, the authorities had shown exceptional judgment. The penalty for Jim's actions had been a reduction in rank to captain and a return to the command of a starship.

Now, the rest of their circle waited to learn their fates within Starfleet. He assumed that Jim hadn't been called in because his reassignment had already been decided. Although the rest of them had escaped the formal accusations of wrongdoing, McCoy doubted that their deeds would have no consequences. Prior to the events that had begun when they'd all decided to retrieve Spock's body from the Genesis Planet, Sulu had been on the verge of his own command, and Chekov hadn't been far behind him. Scotty had been assigned as captain of engineering to the transwarp test bed, the *Excelsior*, which he'd subsequently incapacitated, and Uhura had taken a position with Starfleet Intelligence. Somehow, McCoy doubted that any of them would now find themselves on the same career paths.

For his own part, McCoy had worked with Starfleet Medical cadets under Spock's training command, and he assumed that both of their positions would also be at risk. McCoy didn't know that he cared all that much about his individual situation. After what they'd all been through over the past few months, details like postings seemed only minimally important. Perhaps now would be a good time for him to return to research. Considering that he and the others had just traveled backward and forward in time again, maybe fresh chronometric-particle readings would prove useful if he resumed the work he'd abandoned not all that long ago.

McCoy heard a click, and he looked over between the two assistants' desks to see Jim stepping through the door leading out of Cartwright's office. Surprised because he hadn't known that Jim would be here, McCoy stood up, as did Spock, Scotty, and Uhura. As a group, they all gathered around the captain.

Jim peered around at them, looking from face to face. "I've just had a rather lengthy conversation with Admiral Cartwright," he said. "As you all already know, I've been assigned the captaincy of a starship."

"Do you know which ship, Admiral?" Sulu asked, and then he corrected himself. "I mean, Captain." Jim smiled at the mistake. He'd been an admiral for fifteen years, McCoy knew, and so it had been an easy error to make.

"Not yet," Jim said. He brought his hands together and rubbed them slowly against each other, clearly uncomfortable. "I know that all of you have your own callings, your own goals." He gazed at Sulu and Chekov in turn. "Hikaru, I know you wanted a ship of your own, and you too, Pavel. And you each deserve that opportunity." Jim peered around at all of them again. "Each of you deserves the positions you sought. But after what happened . . ." He didn't finish the statement, but McCoy didn't think he needed to.

"I didn't really think Starfleet Command would be that anxious to give me a ship right now," Sulu said.

"I'm sorry," Jim said, obviously upset by the turn of events.

"Captain, with all due respect, you didn't make my choice to help try to rescue Spock," Sulu said. "*I* made that choice. And if I had to do it all over again, I wouldn't hesitate."

"We'd all do it again," Uhura said, and everybody nodded their agreement.

"Before my father departed Earth to return to Vulcan," Spock said, "he told me that he considered my associates—all of you—people of good character. I told him that you are my friends."

Spock's come a long way, McCoy thought. Though McCoy still teased him good-naturedly about his stoic Vulcan manner, in reality Spock had fundamentally grown comfortable with his human self. He still didn't display his emotions in any flagrant way, but he obviously no longer had any problem in admitting to them, or in actually feeling them. This had been true for a long time now, but seemed to have become cemented in his personality after his friends had risked so much in order to save him.

After a moment, Jim continued. "Starfleet Command is reluctant to return any of you to the positions you occupied immediately before all of this happened," he said. "But they offered to reevaluate all of you for those positions in the future, should your records between then and now merit such appraisal."

"How far in the future?" Chekov asked.

"And what do they expect us to do in the interim?" Uhura wanted to know.

Jim took a deep breath and walked slowly forward, through

the group, then turned to face everybody again. "They have of-fered an interesting opportunity." Jim's expression appeared to be a mixture of anticipation and amusement.

"Well, what is it?" McCoy said. "Tell us."

"Starfleet Command has offered to let all of you join my crew," he said. "They're assigning me a vessel that right now has an almost full complement, except for senior staff positions."

McCoy looked around at his friends, from one to the next, and saw each of them doing the same. He spied surprise on their faces, and relief, and delight.

"I'm in, Captain," Sulu said.

"And me, sir," Scotty agreed.

"Me too." Uhura.

"And me." Chekov.

Jim smiled, then looked over at the two men who hadn't re-sponded. "Spock? Bones?"

"Captain Kirk," Spock said, "I would consider it a great priv-ilege to serve with you again." Jim nodded, then turned all of his attention to McCoy.

"After all these years," the doctor said, "I think I'd have to consider it almost pathological behavior."

Jim's face fell. "I'm sorry to hear you feel that way, Bones. I'd really hoped—"

"Oh, I'm going to do it," McCoy said with a smile. "I just think it's pathological."

Sulu laughed, a staccato burst of loud, single breaths, and then everybody else laughed too—except, of course, Spock. When their clamor had died down, Jim announced, "We depart at thirteen hundred."

Three and a half hours later, after McCoy had secured a piece of the recovered bird of prey's hull for analysis, the seven offi-cers had boarded a shuttlepod, a work sledge now towing them through one of the space docks orbiting Earth. They still hadn't been told to which vessel they had all been assigned, and they all peered anxiously through the forward viewport in anticipation of finding out. Around their pod, the bright lights of the dock's en-closed interior shined like a backdrop of stars.

Jim sighed heavily. "I wonder where we're going to end up," he said. He stood with Scotty, Uhura, and Chekov on the port side of the pod. Spock stood beside Jim at the front of the craft, and McCoy and Sulu sat behind the first officer.

"Probably on an old ship," Scotty speculated. "With engines that haven't been properly tuned in years." Though the engineer delivered the words like a lamentation, McCoy thought Scotty would actually enjoy such a scenario.

"Not just an old ship," Chekov said. "We'll probably be on a garbage scow."

"You're exaggerating," Uhura said, "but I wouldn't be surprised to find us making cargo runs between star systems." They'd all signed up for an extended tour, which McCoy had hoped would mean another exploratory mission, but he realized that hauling shipments from place to place might also be a possibility.

"I think you might be right, Uhura," he said. He stood up, as did Sulu behind him. "The bureaucratic mentality is the only constant in the universe." Jim glanced over at him. "We'll get a freighter."

"With all respect, Doctor," Sulu said, "I'm counting on *Excelsior.*"

"*Excelsior?*" Scotty said indignantly. "Why in god's name would you want that bucket of bolts?"

"A ship is a ship," Jim said.

"Whatever you say, sir," Scotty said. "Thy will be done."

The sledge ahead of them swung around to port, and their pod dutifully followed. Amazingly enough, McCoy saw that they now headed directly for Starfleet's newest vessel, the so-called "Great Experiment," the *Excelsior*, approaching it from its starboard side. The pod climbed upward and crossed over the ship's primary hull. The sledge slid off to port, obviously releasing the shuttlepod onto automatic approach to the *Excelsior*.

Except that they continued past the huge vessel, toward another stationed beyond it. An old *Constitution*-class starship, refitted sometime in the 2270s. Refitted then, and renamed now: *U.S.S. Enterprise*, NCC-1701-A. McCoy couldn't believe it, and he couldn't help smiling. He peered over at Jim and saw a look of perfect contentment.

"My friends," Jim said, "we've come home."

And McCoy knew that he was right.

FORTY-SIX

1949/1952

The large package—about two feet wide, two feet deep, and a foot tall—sat on the sofa, wrapped in decorative red and white paper and adorned with a big white bow tied atop it. Lynn saw it as soon as she walked through the front door of Leonard's house, and she felt an immediate swell of delight. She hadn't thought he'd forgotten her birthday—he hadn't in all the time she'd known him—but when he'd invited her over for supper tonight, he hadn't mentioned the occasion.

"Is that for me?" she asked, knowing full well that it must be.

"Well, now, who else has a birthday today?" Leonard asked.

"Oh, probably lots of people," Lynn said, taking off her coat as she moved into the room. A fire burned in the hearth, warming the room nicely, a welcome change from the chilly weather outside. Lynn dropped her coat onto the sofa and looked down at the gift. The wide ribbon climbing up all four sides of the box had been knotted together into many loops, making it look less like a bow and more like a flower.

"I guess this must be for one of those other people then," Leonard teased as he followed her over to the sofa.

"Oh," Lynn said, swatting him lightly on the chest, then turning to look directly at him. "Can I open it now?" she asked.

"Maybe you should wait until after supper," Leonard suggested. "Or maybe I should just hold onto it until next year." Lynn stuck out her lower lip in a version of a hangdog pout, and Leonard rolled his eyes. "If I'm gonna have to look at that face all night," he said, "then you might as well go ahead and open it."

Lynn clapped her hands together happily and turned toward the sofa. As she reached for the package, she saw an envelope tucked beneath the bow. Picking it up, she read her name, written across the front in Leonard's barely legible scribble. She lifted the flap of the envelope and pulled out the card. On the front, she saw a drawing of a horse trotting around with a sign around its neck that read, "Happy Birthday." Below was printed, "Here's Hoping That This Birthday's a Dilly." She opened the card to find a younger version of the horse on the front, with long, feminine eyelashes, along with the words, "For a Pretty Mare Who Still Looks Like a Filly." At the bottom, Leonard had scrawled, "Dear Lynn, Your joy and radiance are an inspiration." The sentiments touched her. She leaned in, pushed herself onto her toes, and kissed Leonard on the cheek.

"I'm not sure how much of an inspiration or a filly I am," she said, "but this old gray mare appreciates you saying so." At forty-five, lines had begun to show around her mouth and eyes, and streaks of silver had started to appear in her hair. Until recently, she'd been plucking out the telltale strands, but as they'd become more numerous, she'd decided to simply wear her years with pride. After all, she'd earned them.

"You're hardly old and barely gray, and still pretty," Leonard said, "and you really do inspire people."

Lynn shrugged. "I don't know about that," she said, "but I'm glad you think so." She reached out and hugged him. Leonard didn't have to say so, but Lynn knew that with his words he referred to her life after she'd lost Phil. It had been difficult at first and sometimes still was. She'd loved Phil and they'd been together a long time. But three years after his death, the hardest thing to accept had become the manner in which he had died: gunned down on a battlefield thousands of miles from home. She tried to take comfort in knowing that his loss at the Battle of Portmagee had helped liberate Ireland from the Nazis, which in turn had allowed the Allies to retake all of Great Britain. But war still raged around the globe, and sometimes the futility and senselessness of Phil's death troubled her.

As she so often had, though, Lynn let go of all of that right now. "Do you know what would really inspire me right now?" she asked Leonard.

"Opening your present?" he said.

"Good idea," Lynn said. She set the card down on the arm of

the sofa and reached for the box. As she attempted to slide the ribbon from around it, the box moved beneath her efforts. "It's heavy," she said, feeling its weight. "What could this possibly be?" She pulled the ribbon free, then found a flap and tore off the wrapping paper. Printing on the side of the cardboard box announced that it held Green Giant Tender Peas. "You got me cans of peas?" she said.

Leonard shrugged. "If you don't like them . . ."

Confused, Lynn opened the box. Inside, she saw no canned vegetables, but instead, a thicket of balled-up newspaper pages. "What . . . ?" she said, and started unpacking the paper, dropping it onto the floor. When she'd removed most of it, she spied a pair of red bricks in the bottom of the box. Between them lay another gift-wrapped package, this one smaller than her hand. "What's this?" she said, picking it up and testing its weight. It felt very light.

"Must be individually packed peas," Leonard said with a smile.

"Uh huh," Lynn said. She ripped off the paper to uncover a flat, dark blue box, with the word *Wintanna's* scripted across the top in silver letters. She'd never heard the name before. "What is this?" she asked again.

"For goodness sake," Leonard said, "open it and find out."

Lynn pulled off the cover to expose a layer of cottony material underneath. Lifting that up, she found a gold bracelet, into which half a dozen oval red stones had been set all around it. "Oh my," she said, overwhelmed. "This is beautiful." She slid her fingers beneath the bracelet and picked it up. She looked at it more closely, setting the box down atop her birthday card.

"Those are garnets," Leonard said.

"My birthstone," she replied, peering up at him with a smile. "And yours." Leonard's birthday also fell within January, she knew, just ten days after her own. He smiled back at her, obviously pleased by her reaction. Lynn owned almost no jewelry. Other than her wedding band, and Phil's—both of which her mother had given to them—she had a locket with a broken chain that Mama had left to her, and a pair of colored-glass earrings she'd received for her eighteenth birthday from Auntie Louise. Certainly she had never possessed anything as lovely as what Leonard had just given her. "I don't know what to say."

"Well, you could say, 'Thank you,' " Leonard said.

"Thank you," Lynn said, and she stepped forward and embraced him. "Thank you, thank you, thank you." She squeezed him tightly, grateful for his many years of friendship and support, most especially in the time since Phil had died.

Pulling her face from his shoulder, she peered up at him. Leonard had lived in Hayden for nearly seventeen years now, and he looked as though he'd hardly aged at all. The lines on his face had become a bit more defined, maybe, but his dark hair hadn't grayed at all. And even at almost fifty-nine years old, he appeared as fit as when he'd arrived in town at forty-two. Better, in fact, since he'd shown up on Tindal's Lane with a limp, one arm in a sling, and a gash on his face.

Before she made the conscious decision to do it, Lynn raised up onto her tiptoes and pressed her lips to Leonard's. She closed her eyes and felt the soft heat of his mouth. For one breathtaking moment, he kissed her back, but then she felt his hands at her waist, gently but firmly pushing her away.

"Lynn," he said.

"Leonard," she replied, and she pushed forward to kiss him again. He stopped her and then stepped back. "Leonard, I thought . . ." she began, and then realized that she didn't know what she thought. She only knew what she felt, and what she believed—or *had* believed—that Leonard felt as well.

"It was just a gift," he said.

"What?" she said, shocked. She opened her hand to look at the bracelet. "This isn't about my birthday present. It's about us."

"Oh, I'm sorry," Leonard said. "I figured you might've thought that I . . . that me giving you jewelry meant . . . I don't know."

"I think it means you care about me," Lynn said. "I think it means you like trying to make me happy."

"I do, of course," he said. "But I didn't mean for you to kiss me."

"Leonard," she said, setting the bracelet back down into its box. "I didn't kiss you like that because you gave me jewelry. I kissed you because I wanted to." She considered saying more, and then she did. "I've wanted to for a long while now. This just seemed like the right time."

"Lynn," Leonard said slowly, "I don't think we should."

"For Heaven's sake, why not?" she asked, but she thought she knew why: Phil. Lynn sighed, then reached down and moved the large box onto the floor. As she sat down on one end of the sofa, she pointed to the other end. "Sit with me," she said.

Leonard moved her coat onto a chair and then took a seat on the sofa, as far from her as possible, she couldn't help but notice. "My daddy passed on when I was thirteen," she said. "It was just me and my mama after that. Well, there were also a couple of other relatives who we hardly ever saw. But mostly it was just me and Mama. And then when I got married, she was left all alone." Lynn paused, trying to find the right words to tell Leonard what she needed to tell him. "Even before I left, though, Mama was alone. She missed Pa something terrible." Lynn remembered Leonard's own family situation, which he'd once talked about, and she asked, "Wasn't that the way with your pa, after your mama passed?"

Leonard had no family anymore, Lynn recalled, and he spoke about his parents only rarely. Once, a long time ago, he'd told her and Phil that his ma had passed on while bringing him into the world, and that his pa had lived on for twenty-five years until a bad sickness had taken him. "My father," Leonard said, looking down at this hands, "he eventually remarried, but yeah, he missed my mother for the rest of his life."

"At least your pa lived his life, though," Lynn said. "My mama, she done good raising me by herself, but she wasn't happy, and she was pretty much ready to let go of life for fifteen years, until she finally did." She shifted herself closer to Leonard on the sofa and put her hand atop his. "I don't want to be like that," she said. "I don't know how much time God's gonna give me on this Earth, but however long it is, I want to be happy."

"I think that's a good attitude," Leonard said. "I really do." He took his hand from beneath hers, stood up, and paced over to the fireplace. There, he took hold of an iron poker and stabbed at the logs crackling in the hearth, accomplishing very little other than moving away from her.

"What about you, Leonard?" she asked.

"I want you to be happy too," he said.

Lynn got up and walked over to him. She squatted down beside him and took the poker from his hand. "I mean, do *you* want to be happy?" She placed the poker with the other fireplace tools.

"Of course I do," he said, but again he looked away from her as he spoke. "And I am happy."

"That's good," Lynn said, although she didn't know if she truly believed it. "I'm glad if you're happy, but wouldn't you be happier with me?"

"I just . . ." Leonard said, and then he fled from her again, walking back over to stand by the sofa. "It's not right," he finished.

"Beause of Phil?" she said. Lynn understood Leonard's loyalty, but if she could move on in her life, why couldn't he? "Phil loved me and you were his best friend. Don't you think he's looking down from Heaven and hoping that we take care of each other?"

"Take care of each other, sure," Leonard said. "I do try to look out for you, you know."

"I know," Lynn said. She stood up, and the fire felt warm on her legs. "But I can't believe you want me to keep being alone."

"I didn't say that," Leonard told her. "I can understand you wanting to find love again, and I hope you do."

"Thank you," Lynn said. "That's good to . . ." She didn't finish her sentence as something occurred to her. Leonard didn't want to become involved with her because she'd been married to Phil, but he didn't mind if another man did? That didn't make sense to her, unless—

She walked back across the room to stand in front of Leonard again. "This isn't about Phil, is it?" she asked.

"It's about you being Phil's widow," Leonard said, but she could see now that he wasn't telling her the truth. Was he trying to spare her feelings, she wondered? Did he not care for her the way she cared for him . . . the way she thought he cared for her?

"Leonard," she said, "what's going on? Why don't you want to be with me?"

"I told you, Phil—" he said, but she interrupted him.

"I know what you told me," Lynn said. "But I want you to tell me the real reason." She didn't understand. She knew that Leonard loved her. Everybody in town knew it and knew that she loved him. How could it be otherwise, considering how much of their time they spent with each other? Some folks even believed that they'd already become a couple, she knew, even though they were too polite to say anything. But just last week, Daisy Palmer had asked her if Lynn thought that she and Leonard would ever get married.

Lynn took Leonard's hands in her own and gazed up at him, at his beautiful blue eyes. "Tell me," she said.

"It's . . ." Leonard started, and for an instant, Lynn thought he would confess to whatever truly stopped him from taking her in his arms right now. But then he said, "It's Phil."

Lynn stared at him for a few seconds, disappointed, unsure of how to react or of what she should do. She couldn't force Leonard to reveal to her what he was hiding—and she was convinced that he *was* hiding something. Did he simply not care for her? Did he not love her as she loved him? But she knew that he did. She could see it, she could feel it.

"All right," she said at last, letting go of his hands. "All right." She walked past Leonard and over to the chair where he had placed her coat. She picked it up and began putting it on.

"What're you doing?" Leonard asked.

"I think I'm just gonna go home," Lynn said.

"But we were gonna have supper," he said. "Your birthday . . ."

"I know," Lynn said. "I just don't feel well right now." She walked past him again, this time heading for the front door.

"Lynn," he called after her, and she turned back to face him. "I'm sorry. I didn't mean to ruin your birthday."

"You didn't ruin it," she said, forcing half a smile onto her face. "I just don't feel well."

"What about your bracelet?" he asked, pointing to where it sat in its box atop the arm of the sofa.

"You know, I don't think I can accept that," she said. "I appreciate it, it's really lovely, but I just can't accept it." Leonard said nothing, and the silence between them began to feel awkward. Lynn looked away from him and over at the bracelet. Below it, she saw the card he'd given her. "I will take this, though," she said, walking around the back of the sofa to get the card, then holding it up for him to see. "Thank you for this," she said.

When she returned to the front door, she didn't stop, but opened it and walked out into the cool night. From behind her, she heard Leonard say, "Let me at least give you a ride home."

"I have my truck," Lynn said over her shoulder. "I don't need a ride."

She climbed into her Chevrolet pickup and started the engine. She didn't want to, but she couldn't stop from looking back toward Leonard's house. He stood in the doorway, and when he saw her look in his direction, he said, "Happy Birthday," though she could only read the words on his lips and not hear them through the closed driver's-side window.

As she pulled away and drove toward home, she couldn't believe what had happened tonight. She had harbored feelings for Leonard for a long time, but she'd resisted doing anything about it because . . . well, partially because of Phil. But she'd also wanted to wait for just the right time. Tonight, when he'd given her the bracelet, the setting had seemed perfect.

Obviously she'd been wrong.

Rolling along on Church Street, Lynn realized that she didn't know what would happen next. Right now, though, it appeared as though she and Leonard would never be more than friends, and she might never know why. That understanding saddened her, almost as though she'd suffered another loss of a loved one.

At least he still wants to be friends, Lynn thought. That much seemed clear. And although she would rather have much more than that with Leonard, she knew that she would accept it. No matter what, she would take whatever small part of himself that Leonard was willing to give her.

FORTY-SEVEN

2288/2289

Mounted on three-meter towers and spaced evenly around the circle, the lighting panels illuminated the level but rocky patch of the barren world. A dual-field generator sat along the circumference of the area, ninety degrees removed from the laser cannon Mr. Scott had improvised. Between the two, an array of traditional and subspace sensors sat poised to record the coming experiment. An antigrav unit had been placed at the center of the lighted area.

While Mr. Scott and his engineering teams labored over the generator and the cannon, Spock stood at the edge of the circle, his back to the surrounding darkness as he completed execution of a level-one diagnostic on the sensor package. In particular, he worked to reconfirm the sensitivity of the instruments. Because of the precision required, the trial had already necessitated three days of painstaking setup—not to mention the months designing the test and constructing the equipment, or the years of periodic research that he and Dr. McCoy had conducted. But since the *Enterprise* had a scheduled rendezvous with the *U.S.S. Alar* for a time-sensitive transfer of medical supplies, they would get only a single opportunity here to effect their attempt to detect the temporal subatomic particle they had long theorized.

As Spock finished verifying the configuration and acuity of the sensor matrix, the doctor approached him. "Well, Scotty's just finished all of his checks," he said.

"As have I," Spock said, turning from the apparatus to face the doctor.

"I have to tell you," McCoy said, "this is just about the craziest experiment I've ever seen."

"Although we have proceeded along a course of sound reasoning," Spock said, "I must agree that the composition of our test is counterintuitive." Over the past months—and after due consideration over years—Spock had worked out a quantum-physical basis for the fundamental time particle, a theoretical foundation that did not contradict the current version of the currently accepted standard model of the universe. This experiment sought to exploit the predicted behavior of the particle in its interactions with energy, space-time, and subspace.

"Even if it works," McCoy said, "nobody's going to believe it."

Spock arched an eyebrow at the doctor's characteristic overstatement. "We have derived a well-defined set of mathematical equations for the temporal particle and demonstrably observed the chronometric effects of that particle," he said. "If we are successful here, then we will have recorded measurements and a repeatable process to prove our theory. Why would any scientist fail to believe it?"

"Forget it, Spock," McCoy said. "I was just pointing out the complexity and peculiar nature of what we're doing."

"Doctor," Spock said, "you have an unparalleled gift for hyperbole."

"And you have an unmatched ability to insult your colleagues," McCoy said, with what Spock took to be feigned pique. "You pointy-eared, computerized—"

"Pardon me, gentleman," Mr. Scott said, walking over from where he'd been toiling over the field generator. "Everything has been checked and double-checked. All of the equipment is in alignment and prepared for use."

"Thank you, Mister Scott," Spock said. "Have your team transport back to the ship."

"Aye, sir," the engineer said. He headed back toward the laser cannon, where three technicians stood, and then over to the field generator, to a pair of engineers there.

"We should prepare to depart as well," Spock told the doctor, and the two of them moved to the transport point. After Scott and the engineering teams had beamed up, Spock and McCoy returned to the ship. Once aboard, they reported to the bridge, from where they would initiate the automated experiment.

As Spock took his position at the sciences station, Dr. McCoy stepped down into the lower, inner section of the bridge, to where Captain Kirk sat in the command chair. "We're prepared, Captain," McCoy said.

"Very well, Bones," Kirk said. "Commander Uhura, patch us in to the sensor platform."

"Aye, aye, sir," Uhura said. Spock looked over at the main viewscreen and saw the brown and gray image of the planet vanish, replaced by a wide-angle view of the testing area down on the surface. To the extreme left of the scene showed the laser cannon, and to the right, the field generator. Straight ahead rested the antigrav unit.

"Kirk to transporter room," the captain said.

"Transporter room," said a woman's voice. *"Cortez here, Captain."*

"Lieutenant," Kirk said, "are you all set down there?"

"Yes, sir," said the transporter chief. *"The hull fragment is in position on the platform."* The metal piece to which Cortez referred, about fifteen centimeters square and two centimeters through, had been sliced from the section of the Klingon bird of prey's hull that Dr. McCoy had in his foresight brought with him aboard the *Enterprise* when it had begun its current mission several years ago. Kirk and his senior staff had traveled back and then forward in time aboard that Klingon vessel in their efforts to bring a pair of humpback whales from Earth's past into its present. Spock and Dr. McCoy had already measured the residual chronometric activity in the slab, and from there had made predictions for the results of this experiment.

"Very good," Kirk said. "Transfer transporter control to the bridge sciences station."

"Complying," Cortez said. Spock watched his panel as the floating display blanked for a moment, then redrew itself with a new interface configuration. *"Transporter control transferred as requested, Captain."*

"Thank you, Lieutenant," Kirk said. "Mister Spock, whenever you're ready."

"Acknowledged," Spock said. He worked his station, commencing the sequence of actions they'd carefully planned out. "Tying the transporter into the experiment's automated program." He verified the connection, then did a final check on all apparatus. "Starting execution in three . . . two . . . one." He touched a control, then watched as the field generator began operating. "The antigrav has energized. Magnetic containment field has formed and is climbing toward maximum strength," he said, reading his displays. He glanced at the main viewer again and saw a slight shimmering effect in the shape of a sphere, directly in the center of the illuminated area on the planet.

"All channels are clear," Uhura said. "We are receiving telemetry from the planetside sensors."

"Acknowledged," Spock said. "Readings indicate no temporal activity within the containment field. Warp bubble now forming within it." He watched his display until the warp sphere had stabilized, then announced the fact. He then waited for the transporter cycle to begin. "Making the exchange," he said as the atmosphere within the dual field was beamed out and the section of the bird of prey's hull beamed in. Again, he peered over at the viewer, this time to see the square slab held aloft at the center of the two fields by the antigrav below it.

"Still receiving telemetry," Uhura said.

"The laser cannon is energizing," Spock said, looking back at his console. "Eighty percent . . . ninety . . . ninety-five . . . full power." On the viewscreen, a narrow beam of intense red light sliced across the scene from the left, striking directly at the center of the Klingon hull fragment.

They had designed the experiment so that the energy of the laser would, according to the probability wave function Spock had calculated for the fundamental time particle, allow a quantity of those particles to absorb that energy. Based on the three flavors of the particle that they had theorized, they had determined an expected value of how many of each type would travel forward in time, and how may backward in time. The relationship between time and subspace would then allow the specially designed sensors to track the results, both from after and *before* the experiment.

Five seconds passed, and then the cannon shut down, the beam disappearing.

"Sensors still operational," Uhura said.

"The laser burst has completed, energy levels . . ." Spock checked his readouts. ". . . precisely as programmed."

"Sensors have automatically shut down, Mister Spock," Uhura said.

"Is that normal?" the captain asked.

"We programmed it that way," McCoy responded. "It limits the amount of noise in the output."

"The hull fragment has been transported back aboard," Spock said. "Warp field has shut down . . . the containment field . . . and the antigrav." He turned in his chair to face the captain and Dr. McCoy. "The experiment has concluded."

"What do your readings show?" Kirk asked. "Was it a success?"

As he mounted the steps to the upper, outer ring of the bridge, McCoy said, "It'll take some time to analyze." He walked over to the sciences station and peered in past Spock at the various displays. "Do we have any preliminary results?"

"Commander Uhura, would you transfer the subspace sensor scans to my station?" Spock asked.

"Aye, sir," Uhura said, and she expertly worked her controls. After a moment, she said, "I've put them on channel B-forty-seven, Mister Spock. They should be available to you now."

Spock accessed the channel identified. "I have them," he said.

Leaning in over his shoulder, Dr. McCoy suddenly pointed. "There," he said. "And there. That's it." Spock saw the reading as well and deemed it a most satisfying outcome.

Captain Kirk joined them at the sciences console. "That's what?"

Spock peered up at the captain. "We appear to have positively identified the fundamental particle of time."

"The chroniton," McCoy said.

"Because the fundamental particle is the physical manifestation of the theoretical minimum limit of a quanta of time," Spock explained, "Doctor McCoy and I have been calling it by that name. This also distinguishes it from the force particle of time we previously identified, which we call the chronometric particle."

"I'll pretend I understand what all of that means," the captain said.

"It took me a while too," McCoy said. "But basically we've verified the existence of another building block of the universe, this one temporal in nature."

"Congratulations, gentleman," Kirk said.

"Thank you, Jim," McCoy said.

Spock bowed his head in acknowledgment of the captain's

good wishes. "With your permission, sir, I'll oversee the return of our equipment to the ship, and then I would like to go with Doctor McCoy to the quantum-physics lab so that we can thoroughly analyze our readings."

"Of course," Kirk said.

Spock stood, and he and the doctor trod across the bridge and into the turbolift. "Transporter room," Spock ordered. At once, the car began to descend.

The small, green vial of pills sat on the edge of the basin. McCoy looked at it and engaged in what seemed like his nightly debate. In general, he practiced caution when prescribing medication for his patients, and he did the same when it came to taking any drugs himself. Given that and his frequent inability to sleep undisturbed through the night, he'd considered asking Spock to tutor him in Vulcan meditation techniques. After researching them himself, though, he'd learned of the intimacy required between teacher and student, and he'd decided that he'd rather not impose so on his friend.

Ultimately, McCoy had spoken about his nightmares with Dr. Smitonick, the ship's psychiatrist, mentioning his reluctance to seek a chemical remedy unless absolutely necessary. Michal agreed and had instead recommended counseling. McCoy had attended only three sessions—two, really, since he'd walked out of the third—before deciding that he did not want to continue with therapy. Unable to persuade him otherwise, Michal had recommended these pills, which suppressed the storage of dreams in long-term memory. McCoy had used them from time to time, with some positive results, but he still resisted taking them regularly.

Still, his nights had become particularly unsettled of late. They'd calmed for a time a few years ago, after his encounter with Sybok, but the respite had been short-lived. Now, he'd begun dreaming again of his own death. Although over the years he'd experienced while he slept visions of a violent demise, he'd recently imagined foggy, uneasy scenes of his own memorial service. They'd been unclear, like memories of a thought, or thoughts of memories, but they'd delivered to him a very real fear of dying prematurely. Several times in the past week, he'd

awoken clutching the bedclothes, breathing heavily, his heart
pounding in his chest, a scream perched on the edge of his lips.
He didn't know if he could face that again tonight.

McCoy reached forward and picked up the vial from the lip
of the basin. He opened it, then spilled out one of the tiny white
capsules into his cupped palm. He would take it tonight and then
try tomorrow—

A series of tones rang out behind him, from the main body of
his cabin, signaling an incoming communication. He peered
down at the pill for a moment, then set it down on the basin and
left the refresher. He crossed to his work area and checked the
readout on his desk, to the identity information routed down here
by whichever communications officer currently worked gamma
shift. He smiled when he saw the point of origin: Ravent, Mantilles. Beside the city and planet names, he read that of the
sender: McCoy, Joanna.

He touched a control as he sat down at his desk. On the display mounted in the bulkhead in front of him appeared the logo
of the United Federation of Planets—a pair of curved wheat
stalks on either side of a circular field of stars. After just a second, that disappeared, replaced by the smiling face of McCoy's
daughter.

"Hi, Dad," she said. "I was hoping I'd find you in."

"Hi, honey," McCoy said. Joanna looked good, he thought.
She'd cut her hair short, but even at forty, it remained a natural,
vibrant red. Her face had also filled out a bit, taking away the
slight boniness he'd sometimes perceived in her features. "I actually just got in, and was about to get ready for bed," he said,
"but it's always great to hear from you." The *Enterprise*'s current
course had brought it to the far reaches of Federation space and
beyond, but relatively close to Mantilles's star system, Pallas
14—at least within live communications range via subspace relays. In the past few weeks, McCoy had spoken to Joanna three
times, once for a couple hours, and so it surprised him to be
hearing from her again so soon.

"Well, I just wanted to be the first to congratulate you," she
said, "although I'm sure I'm not."

McCoy felt his brow furrow in confusion. "Congratulate me
for what, honey?" he asked.

Joanna's own thin eyebrows moved, but in the opposite direction. "You mean you haven't heard yet?" she asked.

"Since I have no idea what you're talking about," he told her, "I'm going to have to say no."

Joanna's smile widened. "This is great," she said, practically cheering. "I *am* going to be the first one to congratulate you."

Joanna's obvious delight pleased him, but he still didn't know of a reason why anybody should be applauding him. "What is it?" he asked. "Did I win the Argelian sweepstakes?"

"No," Joanna said, "but you did win the Zee-Magnees Prize."

"What?" McCoy said. The University of Alpha Centauri bestowed the prestigious accolade aperiodically, whenever its Scientific Advisory Board deemed an achievement worthy of their recognition. They did not limit themselves in considering any advancement, but made the award across a broad range of disciplines, from computer science to cybernetics, from chemistry to cosmology, from anatomy to zoology. "Where did you hear that?"

"I read it on the hospital's intranet just before I left for the day," Joanna said.

"That's . . . that's unbelievable," McCoy said, overwhelmed to receive such an honor.

"I believe it," Joanna said. "Do you want to hear the announcement? I downloaded it."

"Sure," McCoy said.

Joanna looked around for a moment and then said, "Hold on a second, let me find it." She stood up and moved about what appeared to be her living room, peering at one surface after another, obviously searching for her copy of the announcement. McCoy chuckled to himself. A medical professional, whose professional life absolutely depended upon an attention to detail, and yet his daughter still hadn't figured out how to keep her home organized and neat.

Finally, Joanna left the frame entirely, returning a moment later with a small slate in her hand. "Here it is," she said, and then she read from the device's display. "'The Scientific Advisory Board of the University of Alpha Centauri, in accordance with our established procedures for seeking out and measuring excellence in the many disciplines of science, hereby herald recent achievements made by Leonard Horatio McCoy of Terra and Spock of Vulcan. Specifically, Doctor McCoy will receive the Zee-Magnees Prize for his work in the field of biophysics, in which his theoretical and research efforts both led to the discovery of the fundamental physical and force particles of time, and measured the effects of temporal radiation on living beings. Mister Spock will receive the Zee-Magnees Prize for his work in the field of quantum physics, in which his theoretical and experimental efforts resulted in the discovery of the fundamental physical and force particles of time.'" Joanna finished and looked back up, veritably beaming.

"I can't believe it," McCoy said. He'd been working for so long on this research, really ever since his discovery of Jim's discrepant M'Benga numbers more than twenty years ago. It had taken all that time to identify chronometric particles and chronitons. Once he and Spock had done so, though, it had taken McCoy considerably less time to verify that, while temporal radiation in large quantities would be deleterious to living tissue, the miniscule amounts left behind in humanoids as the result of time travel were benign.

"I am so proud of you, Dad," Joanna said. McCoy smiled as his heart swelled. Though thrilled to be named a recipient of the Zee-Magnees Prize, even the sense of accomplishment in receiving that singular tribute could not surpass his joy at having his daughter's respect.

"Thank you, honey," he said. "That means more to me than the award."

"Oh, Dad," she said, waving her hand dismissively, but he could see in her eyes that she believed what he'd said and that it touched her. Despite being so far apart so much of the time, despite spending time with each other only sporadically over the years, their relationship had come a long way. He sometimes worried that he'd passed on his worst traits to her—as far as he knew, she remained alone romantically—but he also thought that she had matured into a fine woman, who lived a mostly happy life. He didn't think he could be more proud of her.

"I'll let you get to sleep," Joanna said, and McCoy felt a twinge of anxiety at the prospect of another night of broken sleep and terrible dreams. "I just wanted to congratulate you."

"Thank you, honey," McCoy said. "I love you."

"I love you too, Dad." Joanna reached forward and touched a control, and the Federation logo replaced her image on the screen.

McCoy toggled off the connection from his end, then stood up from his desk and went back into the refresher. There, he spied the soporific sitting on the edge of the basin. He picked up the white capsule and looked at it, then placed it back in its green vial. Elated by the news of his and Spock's award—he looked forward to informing the science officer in the morning—and happy simply from speaking with his daughter, he opted to forgo the somnifacient medication. The nightmares might come again, but tonight, he would take his chances.

FORTY-EIGHT

1954

As Lynn parked in the street, she looked over at the office section of Leonard's house and saw the door open. By the time she'd gotten out of the truck, Millie and Doug Warnick had emerged from inside into the summer twilight. Behind them, she saw Leonard standing in the doorway.

Lynn crossed the street and waited beside the opening in the low white fence for the Warnicks to come down the path. Doug held Millie's hand and upper arm as she made her way slowly along, waddling more than walking. With her third child on the way, her belly had swelled tremendously, but then she'd been due last week. "I can't believe you haven't had your baby yet," Lynn said.

"Just like Olivia and Viola," Doug said, mentioning their two daughters. "This one doesn't want to come out either."

"How are you feeling, Millie?" Lynn asked.

"Heavy and hot and tired," she said. "I just wish little Douglas Junior or Mary would get here already."

"It won't be long," Leonard called from the door. "Not long at all."

Millie rolled her eyes. "He keeps saying that, but . . ." She patted her belly with both hands.

"I'm sure it'll be very soon," Lynn said, trying to be optimistic.

"We surely hope so," Doug said, raising his hand to show his crossed fingers. He escorted Millie over to their car, a sky blue Nash, and helped her into the front passenger seat. Lynn watched as he got in on the driver's side and then drove away.

As she turned and walked up the path toward the house, Lynn said, "I can't believe you won't let Millie have her baby. What kind of a doctor are you anyway?"

"A hungry one," Leonard said. "Speaking of a woman being late for an event . . ."

"Sorry. I didn't get out of the mill until after six," Lynn said. Leonard stepped aside and held the door open for her as she went into the house. "But it doesn't look like you would've been ready for supper anyway," she said, "unless Millie was going to cook something."

"Well," Leonard said, closing the door, "she does have a bun in the oven."

Lynn snickered at the jest. "Not a very tasty one, though," she said.

They went into the kitchen and together made supper. Over their meal, Lynn brought up the possibility of taking in a movie tomorrow, as they so often did on Saturdays. "I checked," she said. *"Between Two Seas* is playing at the Bijou." Though they mostly saw movies there, in Greenville, they occasionally traveled instead to Anderson, where another theater, the Deluxe, had opened last year.

"Who's in that one?" Leonard asked.

"Olivia de Havilland and James Stewart," Lynn said, naming two of her favorite movie stars.

"Well, that's quite a bill," Leonard said.

"I know," Lynn said, excited just talking about it. "So you want to go?"

"I do," Leonard said, "but I can't. Not unless Millie has her baby between now and tomorrow afternoon." He paused, then added, "Actually, even then I should probably stay around town."

"Of course," Lynn said. She should've realized that Leonard wouldn't be able to stray too far from Millie. "Maybe next week," she said, and Leonard agreed.

After supper, they decided to let the dishes wait to be washed so that they could watch the evening news report. For several years, each of the three networks had scheduled periodic news broadcasts in the morning and in the evening, specifically to provide updates on the war. Tonight, Lynn thought, what they heard could only be described as positive. After years of efforts by President Truman, Hitler had finally agreed to send envoys to Washington to negotiate for peace. Ceasefires on the frontlines in France, Spain, and Portugal had been scheduled for midnight tonight and had already begun in the time zones where Friday had become Saturday. At the same time, the Japanese fleet, which yesterday had approached worryingly close to the coastlines of Chile and Peru, had now retreated out to sea.

Once the fifteen minutes of news had ended, Lynn returned with Leonard to the kitchen, where they cleaned the dishes—he washed, she dried. Then they went back into the living room and settled in to watch *The Adventures of Ozzie & Harriet*. Just a few minutes into the show, though, they heard a loud knocking on the side door. Leonard quickly got up, crossed the side room, and went into the back hall. Lynn followed, curious and concerned.

Standing in the side room, she heard Leonard open the door, and then Pru Glaston began talking frantically. He invited her inside and tried to calm her down, then leaned into the side room and said, "Lynn, Pru Glaston is here. I'm going to take her back to the office so she can have some privacy."

"It's all right, Doctor," Pru said, appearing beside Leonard. "I wanted to tell you that Audie just knocked over his medicine. It's his last bottle and it smashed all over the floor." Several years ago, Lynn knew, Audie had been diagnosed with epilepsy. Leonard had prescribed medicine for him, which mostly kept Audie's seizures at bay, but on a couple of occasions, he'd begun convulsing in public. Lynn and much of the town had witnessed one such incident in church last year. She'd found the experience terribly troubling. "You told us Audie should never stop taking his medicine," Pru continued, her voice and manner growing agitated again, "and now we don't have any more."

"Everything's going to be all right," Leonard said soothingly. He reached up and took Pru by the elbow and led her into the side room, where he settled her into a chair. "Audie shouldn't stop taking his medication, but I have some for him here, so that's not going to happen."

"Oh," Pru said, and she reached up and took Leonard's hand in both of hers. "Oh, thank you, Doctor."

"You're welcome," he said. "Let me just go get the phenytoin." Leonard looked over at Lynn and inclined his head ever so slightly toward Pru. Lynn had spent so much time with Leonard for so long that she immediately understood what he wanted to tell her: stay with Pru and keep her calm. Lynn responded with a quick nod and walked farther into the room. Leonard gently pulled his hand from Pru's grasp and headed back toward his office. "I'll be right back," he said.

Pru peered up at Lynn. "I'm sorry to be disturbing you at this time of night," she said.

"It's perfectly all right," Lynn said. "This is much more important. We were just watching *Ozzie and Harriet*." Though her relationship with Leonard had steadfastly remained a friendship—despite her best efforts to make it something more than that—Lynn knew that some people in town believed that they had become romantically involved. That had bothered her at first, and she'd protested whenever anybody would intimate something untoward, but then she'd simply learned to accept that folks would believe whatever they wanted to believe, no matter what she said, and no matter the truth.

Leonard returned a moment later, a small brown bottle held in one hand. He held it out to Pru, who appeared immediately relieved. "This should take care of Audie for a few days," he said. "Unfortunately, my latest shipment hasn't arrived yet."

"Oh no," Pru said, becoming excited once again.

"It's all right," Leonard said, squatting down beside her chair and taking hold of her hands. "Either the hospital in Greenville will have some phenytoin to spare or the manufacturer can replace it. They're located in Atlanta. I'm sure we can get some tomorrow."

Again, Pru's tension seemed to ease. "All right," she said.

"Now, I can't leave town because Millie Warnick is going to have her baby any day now," Leonard said. "Obviously Audie shouldn't be driving, especially all the way to Greenville or Atlanta. What about you, Pru? Can you make a trip like that?" While the trip to Greenville took about ninety minutes, Atlanta was more than a hundred and forty miles away, and it took almost four hours to drive there.

"I'll do whatever I need to do for Audie," Pru said. Though a stout, fit woman, she had to be close to sixty years old and Lynn didn't know that she'd be able to manage either trip safely.

"I'll go," Lynn said, and both Pru and Leonard looked over at her. "I don't have anything else to do tomorrow."

"Are you sure?" Pru said, her voice thick with gratitude.

"Of course," Lynn said. "I'd be happy to."

Pru looked up at Leonard questioningly. "That's that," he told her. "I'll telephone the hospital and the manufacturer tomorrow morning, and then Lynn will go wherever she needs to for the medicine."

Pru stood up and paced over to Lynn. "Thank you so much," she said, and she swallowed her up in a hug.

"You're welcome," Lynn said.

Leonard walked Pru to the side door and saw her out. Lynn went back into the living room, where Ozzie and Harriet Nelson and their show had given way to Ray Bolger and his. When Leonard rejoined her on the sofa, he reached over and placed his hand atop hers. "Thank you," he said. "You're really a wonderful person."

Lynn smiled, warmed by the opinion of this man for whom she cared so much. "It's completely selfish," she said. "Maybe when I'm in Greenville or Atlanta, I'll go and see *Between Two Seas.*"

"A well-deserved reward for your good deed," Leonard said. He leaned forward and wrapped his arms around her, pulling her in for a hug just as Pru had done. For an instant, Lynn envisioned herself kissing Leonard as he pulled away, but then he said, "Thank you for doing this," and the moment passed.

That night, lying alone in bed back in her own house, Lynn thought that perhaps she should've tried to kiss Leonard anyway. In a way, she felt foolish. At fifty years old, how could she still think so much like a teenager, at least when it came to Leonard? After all this time, she should simply let go of any illusions she had that Leonard would ever love her as she loved him.

Except that he still frequently acted as though he did love her. *Then why can't we have a relationship?* she asked herself, and as always, the answer eluded her. At this point, she knew for sure that it had nothing to do with Phil—and she felt confident too that it had nothing to do with her. If anything, something inside Leonard prevented their friendship from becoming something more.

The more she knew him, she realized, the more she didn't understand him.

McCoy strolled up the walk toward his house, the ground still wet from the brief summer squall that had passed through town half an hour ago. The moist air smelled clean and fresh, appropriately underscoring the events of the afternoon and his current sense of satisfaction. In the middle of the night, Doug Warnick had telephoned to tell him that Millie had begun experiencing light contractions about twenty minutes apart. After listening to the description of Millie's condition, McCoy had concluded that she'd entered the early phase of the first stage of labor, and he'd recommended that she simply stay in bed and try to rest, or even sleep. She would be giving birth at home and so needn't worry about getting to the hospital in Greenville.

McCoy had contacted the hospital this morning, though, not about the Warnicks, but about Audie Glaston. When McCoy had found that the hospital could spare no phenytoin, he'd contacted the pharmaceutical company in Atlanta. He'd spoken with a man named Kane, who had informed him that his shipment of the drug had been sent out two weeks ago and therefore had probably been lost somewhere along the way. Mr. Kane had agreed to replace the phenytoin, though, and McCoy had made arrangements for Lynn to pick it up this afternoon. She'd left just after ten this morning, deciding that she would take in a movie after all, then spend the night in Atlanta and drive back to Hayden tomorrow.

Not long after McCoy had seen her off, Doug had called again, this time to report Millie's contractions less than five minutes from one to the next, clearly suggesting that she'd entered the active phase of the first stage of labor. McCoy had collected the medical items he would need and had driven out to the Warnick's house. Late this afternoon, Millie had delivered a healthy seven-pound-thirteen-ounce baby boy.

Now, McCoy entered his house with a smile on his face. He'd always enjoyed delivering babies, though back during his time in Starfleet, and then in New York City, he'd had few opportunities to do so. Since arriving in Hayden, though, he'd participated in quite a few births.

After bringing in all of his medical items and returning them to their proper places, McCoy went into the kitchen to cook supper for himself. As he sat down to eat, he missed Lynn. For years, they'd taken most of their evening meals together, and when they didn't, the time felt incomplete. He owed her a great deal of thanks, though, for offering to drive down to Atlanta for Audie Glaston's seizure medication. An abrupt stop to the medication, which Audie took three times daily, could result in status epilepticus—a state of continued seizure activity that could lead to brain damage or even death. Audie needed the phenytoin, and Lynn had gladly stepped up to get it for him.

When he'd finished eating, McCoy washed and dried his dishes, then went into the living room. Sitting down on the sofa, he picked up the novel he'd begun reading earlier in the week, *The Catcher in the Rye*, by J.D. Salinger. He found the picaresque tale thoroughly engaging, providing fascinating insights not only into young human males, but into twentieth-century American civilization.

He read for a little while, then looked up and, seeing the time, decided to turn on the television set to check on the news of the day. Instead of the regular evening broadcasts, though, he saw a grim fellow seated at a desk and leaning over a microphone. Behind him stood an easel with a large outline of the east coast of the United States placed on it. Circles marked several points on the map, labeled *New York; Philadelphia; Washington, D.C.; Richmond; Charlotte;* and *Charleston.* A blue star sat beside *Boston,* and a red one by *Atlanta.* The sense that something terrible had happened suddenly gripped McCoy. As best he could, he tried to focus on the words of the newscaster.

". . . scrambled up and down the coast, and appear to have repelled most of the Axis air forces back out to sea. There are reports of major naval battles at this hour, in both the Atlantic and Pacific Oceans."

McCoy sat motionless on the sofa, unable to move, almost unable even to breathe.

"Once more, massive airborne attacks were launched by the Axis on the United States late this afternoon. At cities up and down the eastern and western seaboards, our air force and navy engaged the attackers, and for the most part destroyed them or turned them back. But in Boston, Massachusetts, and Atlanta, Georgia, German aircraft penetrated American defenses and dropped bombs on both cities. While the bomb in Boston appears to have failed, the one in Atlanta did not."

McCoy shot to his feet, as though he could take some action to undo what had happened. Instead, he simply stood and stared at the television screen.

"At five-thirteen this afternoon, Eastern Time, what appears to have been an atomic bomb detonated above the city. Reports from the area are understandably sketchy, but from what we're told, downtown Atlanta has essentially ceased to exist, with at least twenty square miles of the city completely destroyed. Preliminary estimates put the number of dead at—" The newsman's voice trembled as he read from a sheet of paper in his hands. *"—put the number of dead at more than fifty thousand, and the number of injured at more than seventy thousand."*

McCoy staggered backward, until his legs struck the sofa and he fell back onto the cushions. On the television, the newscaster continued talking, and as though at a remove, McCoy heard that hostilities had resumed in Europe and that some of the most intense fighting of the war was taking place right now in both the Atlantic and the Pacific. President Truman had already addressed Congress and he would speak to the American people on television tonight at nine o'clock. McCoy heard all of that, but his mind was elsewhere.

Lynn, he thought as tears streamed down his face. *She was probably in a movie theater . . .*

Unless she'd for some reason opted not to stay in Atlanta tonight, as she'd initially decided. Perhaps she'd left the city in advance of the bombing. Perhaps she made her way back home even now . . .

McCoy knew that he was deluding himself, knew that Lynn had already been lost. Like her husband before her, she had been killed in a war that should have ended a decade ago. And he could do nothing about it.

But he had to try.

Foolishly, with virtually no hope of success, McCoy stood up again, grabbed his keys, and ran out to his car, headed for Atlanta. Less than an hour later, though, out on US 123, he found the route south blocked as thousands of people filled the roads leading away from the Dogwood City. Unable to proceed in his car, and with no sense in attempting to continue on foot, he parked for a while on the side of the road and scanned the faces of people as they made their way past. Lynn was not among them, and finally McCoy turned around and returned home.

He mourned deep into the night.

FORTY-NINE

2290

As a server carried a silver tray past, she reached up and snatched a flute from atop it. She'd seen the menu of beverages being served, and recognized the bright orange liquid. She sipped from the elegant glass, the slightly sweet *tranya* sliding easily down her throat.

Peering around and seeing so many Starfleet dress uniforms in the reception hall, she felt out of place. Though she'd left the service five years ago, she'd still spent far more time in it than out of it. At the same time, she enjoyed dressing up, considering how much of her days she spent wearing a plain, white—and unflattering—smock. For this evening, she'd chosen a black gown, with scrolling beadwork along the bottom half of the skirt and along the three-quarter sleeves. A scarlet chemisette added a dash of color and matched her hair.

As she sipped at her *tranya,* she slowly moved about the room, slipping past the clusters of prominent scientists and other dignitaries present. Finding herself along one of the three transparent walls—the tall ceiling had also been fabricated of some clear material—she gazed out at the countryside. The hall in which she stood had been constructed at the summit of the tallest hill in the area, providing a fine view of the numerous university buildings illuminated along the surrounding slopes. The beauty of the star-speckled firmament peered down on the proceedings from above, and within the room, a series of large, expertly crafted sculptures added to the splendor of the scene. The statues, some abstract, some not, depicted various scientific concepts: evolution, the big bang, the probability wave function, the unified field theory, and the like.

Suddenly, she felt a gentle pressure at her elbow, the touch of a hand. At once, her heart seemed to somersault inside her chest. Unprepared, she turned, because she could do nothing else. Silently, she chastised herself, knowing that this could happen, that it likely *would* happen—

Except that when she turned, she didn't find who she'd expected to. "Doctor," said the dignified, black-haired man before her. "It's been a long time."

"Hikaru," she said. "What a pleasure to see you." He looked dashing in his formal habiliments. She moved forward and gave him a quick hug. When she stepped back, she asked not about him, but—rather rudely, she would realize later—about his crewmates. "I assume that all of the *Enterprise*'s senior staff are here." She'd seen Captain Kirk across the room earlier, and she knew that Mr. Spock would of course be here.

"I assume so too," Sulu said with a smile. "But I'm no longer on board the *Enterprise*."

"No?" she asked, and then she noticed the insignia on the epaulet adorning his right shoulder. "*Captain* Sulu," she said, impressed. "Congratulations. When did this happen?"

"The promotion came through about a month back," he said. "But I actually took command of the *Excelsior* just a few days ago."

"A few days ago?" she said, then teased, "And already you're taking in social events?"

"R.H.I.P., Doctor," Sulu said with a smile.

"In my line of work," she said, "that stands for relativistic heavy ion physics."

Sulu chuckled. "In this case, I meant rank has its privileges."

"Ah, now that makes more sense," she said. "So you must be very excited about this opportunity."

"I am," he said. "We're about to embark on—"

"Pardon me," came a voice from beside them. She and Sulu both turned to see Leonard standing there, resplendent in his dress whites. His hair had begun to gray along the front edges she saw, a look that she thought reinforced the handsomeness of his masculine features. "Tonia," he said, "it's nice to see you."

"It's nice to see you, Leonard," she said. Her heart, calm just a second ago, now resumed its gymnastic maneuvers. She resolved that, once she returned to Earth, she would have it removed.

"I'm sorry to interrupt," he said, looking at Sulu for a moment too, obviously to include him in the apology. "I saw you standing here and . . . well, they're going to come drag me out of here in a couple of minutes and I just wanted to make sure I had a chance to see you."

"I'm glad you did," Barrows said.

"I'll let you two chat then," Sulu said, and he beat a gracious retreat.

"I think we made him uncomfortable," Leonard said, looking after Sulu.

"Speak for yourself," Barrows said jokingly. "Hikaru was enjoying talking with me."

"Yes, well, who wouldn't?" Leonard said.

You wouldn't, Barrows thought, surprised at how quickly her bitterness had come back. She suppressed the emotion, angry with herself for feeling such a thing for even a moment. She thought that she'd long ago forgiven Leonard for hurting her, not once, but twice. *Maybe I haven't quite forgiven myself,* she realized.

"So how have you been?" Leonard asked. He shifted his weight from one foot to the other, obviously nervous. She wondered if that had more to do with him seeing her or with him about to be the center of attention.

"I've been doing very well, thank you," Barrows said. "And you, clearly you've had some great successes." She pointed in the direction of the hall's single opaque wall, beyond which sat the auditorium in which Leonard and Spock would soon be presented the Zee-Magnees Prize.

"I want you to know," Leonard said very seriously, "that when the university formally told me that they were presenting Spock and me with this award, I contacted their Scientific Advisory Board to tell them of the contributions that you and Dorsant and Olga made when we worked together at Starfleet Medical."

"I know," she said. "The board actually contacted all three of us and wanted to know if we felt entitled to any recognition. None of us did."

"But you did contribute," Leonard said.

"Minimally," Barrows said. "At best, we eliminated some avenues of exploration and experimentation. Nothing on a par with what you and Mister Spock accomplished."

"That's very generous of you," Leonard said. "And I really appreciate that you've come for the ceremony." Something beeped twice, much like a communicator. Leonard reached down to the side of his waist and took hold of a small clear cylinder there. As he did, it beeped twice again, then tinted green. "That's my signal. I've got to get going," he said. Again, he shuffled from one foot to the other, plainly uncomfortable. "Listen, when I saw you here, Tonia . . . well, I was very happy and I was hoping that maybe we could talk, have a drink after the presentation."

Barrows felt one side of her mouth curl upward, pleased by

the offer, even as it seemed wildly presumptuous. "No, thank you," she said. "I came for the presentation only. I hadn't even planned to see you; I left that to fate. I'm very proud of you, Leonard, proud of your wonderful achievements, but other than that, I'm afraid I don't really have very much to say to you."

Leonard smiled, but she could see that the expression contained no joy. "I understand," he said. "I'm glad you came, and I'm glad that I at least got to see you."

Barrows lifted her glass in salute. "Congratulations to you and Spock, Leonard," she said. He turned and walked away, heading toward the auditorium. She watched him go, weaving his way through those assembled, until finally she lost sight of him.

Then she downed the rest of her *tranya* and went looking for another.

McCoy sat quietly with Spock in the waiting room. The simple, sparsely furnished space contained only a few chairs and a table with refreshments, as plain a place as the reception hall had been spectacular. Where the hosts and their many guests had provided a constant buzz of conversation, here silence held lease.

Peering over at Spock, McCoy actually considered approaching him to discuss the knot of emotions roiling within him. Though the Vulcan still outwardly presented himself as an unfeeling, logical individual, he seemed more at ease with his human heritage and characteristics these days than ever he had before. McCoy had no doubt that his friend would be willing to listen to his troubles, but he found that he simply couldn't bring himself to talk about them—not because of Spock, but because of himself.

McCoy had been speaking with Commander Randi Bryce, a Starfleet biologist he'd met years ago, when he'd peered across the room and seen Hikaru Sulu. Freshly promoted to captain and assigned to command the *Excelsior,* Sulu had only a few days ago left the *Enterprise* to begin a three-year mission into the Beta Quadrant with his new ship and crew. At this point, he should've been light-years away, and so McCoy had wanted to thank him for somehow finagling his way to the presentation ceremony. The doctor felt tremendously gratified that so many friends, shipmates, and colleagues had chosen to be in attendance. Joanna too had made the long voyage from Mantilles to be here.

When he'd finished talking with Commander Bryce, he'd looked again for Sulu. He'd spotted the new captain and had made his way almost all the way across the hall to him before realizing that he stood talking with Tonia. Seeing her caused an immediate, visceral reaction within McCoy, a little something like a lightning strike. He'd been surprised by the intensity of his emotion—and at the longing for Tonia that he'd felt. *Why hadn't they stayed together?* he'd asked himself.

But of course he had left her—twice. It had nothing to do with Tonia, he knew. It had only to do with him.

"Doctor," Spock said, his voice, though low, still fracturing the quiet of the room. "You seem preoccupied. May I inquire, is everything all right?" For somebody who almost never displayed emotion himself, Spock certainly had developed some skill in reading the feelings of others.

"Everything's fine," he lied. "I must just be nervous about going out on that stage."

"But you have chaired symposia, made presentations at Starfleet and Starfleet Medical," Spock said, "and never when I have seen you in those settings have I perceived any anxiety on your part."

"Are you calling me a liar, Spock?" McCoy asked lightly.

Spock arched an eyebrow. "I merely seek to point out that the reason you offer for your evident disquiet is at odds with your past behavior. Perhaps something else is troubling you, something of which you are not consciously aware."

"So now you're an expert in human behavior?" McCoy said, actually impressed by Spock's perception and insight.

"As you have never tired of observing, Doctor," he said, "I am half human."

"Aren't we all?" McCoy muttered.

"I do not think I understand that reference," Spock said.

"I'm not sure I do either," McCoy said. He stood from his chair and walked over to the table on which food and drink had been placed. He selected a pick and speared a piece of pineapple from a plate of assorted fruits. Turning toward Spock, he said, "I saw Tonia Barrows this evening. I spoke with her."

Spock tilted his head ever so slightly to one side. "And this is causing you anxiety?" he asked.

"I guess it is," McCoy admitted. He popped the pineapple into his mouth. After swallowing it, he said, "We haven't seen each other in a long time, and we didn't exactly part on the best possible terms."

"I see," said Spock. "Is Doctor Barrows angry or upset with you then?"

"No," McCoy said. "No, I don't think so. She was very cordial when we spoke. And of course she's here for the big event." McCoy paused and then said, "By the way, she offers you her congratulations."

Spock bowed his head in acknowledgment, then asked, "Are you upset with Doctor Barrows or disapproving of her presence here tonight?"

"No, not at all," McCoy said. "She's never given me any reason to be upset with her, and I'm very touched that she made the effort to be here."

"Then I fail to see what the difficulty is," Spock said. He stood up and walked over beside McCoy. Lifting a crystal pitcher from the table, he poured himself a glass of water.

"I don't even know if I see what the difficulty is," McCoy said.

Spock sipped from his water, then said, "It has always been my understanding, based on things you yourself have said, that it was you who put an end to your romantic relationship with Doctor Barrows."

"It was," McCoy said. He tossed the tiny pick into a recycling bin set up beside the table. "Even back on the *Enterprise* all those years ago, even though she transferred off the ship, it was me who really made that necessary." He padded back across the room and sat down in his chair again.

"Could it be, perhaps, that you feel guilt for having hurt somebody about whom you once cared a great deal?" Spock asked.

"Maybe," McCoy allowed. "But to tell you the truth, Spock, that's something I've been used to feeling for a very long time."

"I see," Spock said, and his voice seemed to carry with it a measure of empathy McCoy found both unexpected and touching. "Is there any chance then that you still harbor amorous feelings for Doctor Barrows?"

"It would never work," McCoy said automatically.

Both of Spock's eyebrows went up on his forehead this time. "Doctor," he said, and then stopped and started again. "Leonard, I must point out that you did not actually answer the question I asked."

"No, I suppose I didn't," McCoy said, now essentially forced to think about the issue Spock had posed him. "Maybe responding the way I did really *does* answer your question."

"Or perhaps the answer you provided points out a different question that you need to ask yourself," Spock suggested.

The idea brought McCoy up short. What could he possibly ask himself? Could he have a romance with Tonia that would ever work? That had been the question he'd answered, but what should he have asked? Could he ever have *any* romance that would ever work? At this time in his life, perhaps he already knew the answer to that too. When he had—

The door to the waiting room slid open with a whoosh. Beyond it stood Dr. Golec, president of the university. Tall and lean, she had long, striking white hair that reached down to her lower back. Spectacles rested on the bridge of her nose, and McCoy wondered if she wore them for cause or as an affectation. "Gentlemen," she said with measured formality, "we are prepared to begin our ceremony."

"That's our cue," McCoy said, standing. Together, he and Spock followed Golec out of the waiting room, up a flight of stairs, and over to the left wing of the stage. Out on the unlighted rostrum stood a podium bathed in the bright white of a spotlight. Behind it stood a row of chairs just visible to McCoy and doubtless unseen by the audience. Spock and McCoy were placed in the center of a line with the deans of the university's various colleges and the senior members of the Science Advisory Board. Together, they walked out on stage and, facing the audience, took their seats in the darkness behind the podium. Spock and McCoy sat just to the left of center stage.

Once they'd all sat down, the lights came up, revealing everybody on stage, and the audience applauded. As they did, Dr. Golec paced to the podium. When the clapping died down, she addressed the assemblage. "Faculty and students of the University of Alpha Centauri, members of the Science Advisory Board, fellow scientists, respected guests, and Zee-Magnees honorees, welcome." Again, people applauded.

McCoy peered out at the audience. Somewhere out there sat Tonia, he knew. He had to admit that he felt wounded by her unwillingness to see him after the ceremony, but he truly understood her disinclination to do so. For that, he clearly had nobody to blame but himself.

Looking out from the rostrum, McCoy could make out the faces of the people in the first couple of rows, the rest indistinct because of the lights focused on the stage. He saw Joanna, beaming, and beside her, Jim. He saw Jabilo M'Benga and Christine Chapel and others. He could not see Tonia.

FIFTY

1954

Well after midnight, beneath the silvern rays of the full moon, it took five minutes of knocking, but finally the door opened.

"Leonard," Lynn said. At first, he didn't seem to see her. He looked terrible, his features drawn, his eyes bloodshot, his hair an uncombed mess. She'd known she would wake him, but she noticed that he wore the same clothes as he had yesterday before she'd left for Atlanta, and their rumpled appearance betrayed that he'd been sleeping in them—if he'd slept at all. The dark circles beneath his eyes suggested that he hadn't. "Leonard," she said again.

"Oh my God," he said quietly, as though in a trance. For a moment, she didn't think that he recognized her, and then at last his eyes widened. "Oh my God," he said again, crying it out this time, his voice echoing down the street and through the empty commons. He lurched out of the doorway and pulled her forcibly into his arms. She sent her hands around his back and held him just as tightly. "Lynn, Lynn, Lynn," he said, as though he could not believe that she'd returned.

After a few seconds, she felt Leonard begin to tremble and realized that he was crying. "It's all right," Lynn said. She stroked her hand along his back, trying to soothe him. "It's all right. I'm safe."

They stood like that for half a minute, a minute, longer. His arms around her remained firm, unyielding, protective. At last, though, his weeping eased and then stopped. She pulled back from him and looked up into his face. He stared back, glassy-eyed. "I can't believe you're okay," he said, his voice a rough imitation of itself.

"I am though," she said. "Can we go inside?" She felt chilled. Leonard nodded and started inside, but then Lynn remembered something. "Oh," she said. "I'll be right there." She hurried back down the stone path and out to the street, where she opened the driver's door of her truck. Leaning in across the seat, she pulled out a small cardboard box, the size of a couple of hardcover books stacked up. It contained the small bottles of medication that she'd gone down to Atlanta to get in the first place. She carried the box back to the house, where Leonard, still standing in the doorway, peered at it as though he had no idea what it might contain. "Audie's medicine," she said. She handed it to him, then stepped past and went inside.

As Leonard closed the front door, Lynn flopped down on the sofa. "I'm exhausted," she said. Leonard set the box down on a shelf, beside some books, then sat down next to her on the sofa.

"I can't believe you're all right," he said. "What . . . ?" He seemed not only overwhelmed by her return, but distant, as though he thought he might be dreaming.

"I made it down to Atlanta in good time yesterday," Lynn said, not really wanting to think about all that had happened, but knowing that she must tell Leonard. "I followed the directions you wrote down for me and drove directly to the medicine company. I asked to speak with Mister Kane and I showed him the letter you gave me for him. He read it, asked me to wait, then came back and handed me the box. When I went back out to the truck, I opened it and checked the labels on all the bottles to make sure they were filled with the right medicine for Audie." Lynn paused, struck hard by the thought that Mr. Kane, who'd been so attentive and helpful yesterday, had no doubt perished just a few hours after she'd left him.

"You were going to go to the movies," Leonard said. His shock at seeing her seemed to be fading, his focus returning. "Go to the movies and stay in the city overnight."

"I know," Lynn said, still amazed at how such a simple thing as choosing whether or not to take in a movie had been the difference between living and dying. "But the drive had been so easy that by the time I'd arrived in Atlanta, I'd already decided that I'd head back to Hayden rather than finding a hotel. But I still thought I would go and see *Between Two Seas*. I even asked Mister Kane if he knew where it was playing, and he gave me directions to the theater. But when I got there . . ." Lynn felt an ache in her temples and knew that she'd suddenly reached the verge of tears.

"When you got there . . . ?" Leonard prompted her.

Lynn took a long, slow breath, trying to calm herself. When she'd tamed her emotions, at least for the moment, she continued. "When I got to the theater, I discovered that I didn't want to see the movie without you," she said. She attempted to smile, but the expression felt out of place just now. "In a way," she said, no longer able to keep herself from crying, "you saved my life."

"Oh, Lynn," Leonard said, and he moved forward on the sofa, once more taking her into his arms. She began to sob, her body shuddering with the effort. Leonard rocked her gently back and forth, whispering into her ear that everything was going to be all right. The warmth of his body, the strength of his arms, enveloped her, made her feel safe. In some ways, she herself could not believe that she'd finally come back to Hayden.

"It was terrible," she at last managed to say when her tears had slowed. She sat back on the sofa, her physical and emotional fatigue beginning to take its toll on her. She wanted to tell Leonard of her long night on the road, but couldn't help thinking of what had happened to the place where she had been just yesterday, to the people she had seen there. "I got back on the road and started to drive back toward Hayden, and everything was fine until . . ."

"Until the bomb was dropped on Atlanta," Leonard said, his voice echoing the anguish coursing through her.

Lynn shook her head. "I didn't see it or anything," she told him. "I guess I was too far away already. But all of a sudden, more and more cars appeared on the road, a lot of them packed up like the people driving them were going on a trip or moving. After a while, there got to be so many cars that the whole road was filled, so that nobody could possibly travel in the opposite direction. Not that anybody was trying to."

"I tried to," Leonard said. "As soon as I heard on television what happened, I got in my car to try to come find you." Even amid her despair at all that had happened in the last twelve hours, it touched Lynn very deeply that Leonard had gone searching for her. "With all the traffic coming north, I couldn't get very far."

Lynn nodded. "The road got jammed and everything slowed down," she said. "I asked somebody in the car next to me where everybody was going." She recalled all too clearly the stricken expression of the woman with whom she'd spoken. The woman told her what had befallen the people of Atlanta, though her words seemed too incredible to believe. Lynn had asked somebody else then, who confirmed that Georgia's capital had been attacked with a devastating weapon that had virtually obliterated it.

"That must have been horrible for you," Leonard said.

"It was," Lynn said, though she realized it had not been anywhere near as horrible for her as it had been for the people of Atlanta. "I couldn't keep driving," she said. "I pulled off to the side of the road for a while and just . . ." For a time, she'd just sat in her truck, quaking. "When I finally began driving again, the road was completely filled with cars, making everybody move really slowly. There were people walking alongside the road too, and sometimes they were going faster than the cars." She stopped talking for a moment and sighed heavily. "It took me all this time to get back to Hayden," she said. "I didn't want to wake you, but I just had to see you."

"I know," Leonard said, reaching forward to hold her hands. "I'm so glad you did. I wasn't really sleeping anyway."

"How's everybody in town?" Lynn asked.

"People are shaken pretty badly," Leonard said. "Pru Glaston knew you'd gone down to Atlanta, of course, so she was worried about you and also still worried about Audie."

"Because if I didn't get the medicine . . ." she said, not needing to complete the thought.

"But I told her that you'd gotten the phenytoin and were on the road back to Hayden," Leonard said. "I told her you'd called to tell me you were all right. I didn't want her to worry, and I just figured I'd have to find someplace else to get Audie's medication."

"I'm sorry I didn't call," Lynn said. "I just didn't want to stop driving. I just wanted to get home. I never thought it would take this long."

"I understand," Leonard said. "I'm just so glad you're back."

"Me too," she said. "I feel safe again."

"We've been lucky here so far," Leonard said. "The prevailing winds over Atlanta are blowing toward the east and the southeast. It doesn't appear that we're going to get any fallout here."

"Any what?" Lynn asked. She'd never heard the word before.

"The, uh, bomb that fell on Atlanta essentially poisoned the air," Leonard explained. "If that air blew over Hayden, people here might get very sick."

"Oh, no," Lynn said. "Then people in Georgia are going to get sick?"

"I'm afraid so," Leonard said. "But according to the news reports, a lot of people are leaving the area. You saw that tonight."

"Yeah," Lynn said. Her head hurt, and she closed her eyes.

When she opened them, she lay on the sofa, and Leonard stood over her, pulling a blanket across her body and up to her chin. She wanted to speak to him, but she couldn't find the energy within her to do so. She closed her eyes again and drifted back to sleep.

After McCoy had gotten out of the car, he reached back in for the small, flat box. He removed its top and emptied it into his hand, then tucked the contents into the pocket of his slacks. Then he picked up the paper bag he'd brought with him and walked to the side door, where he knew Lynn would be in her kitchen, preparing supper for the two of them. As he knocked, he saw her inside through the gauzy white curtains that covered the window in the top half of the door.

"Come on in," Lynn called. McCoy reached for the knob and stepped inside. The delicious aromas of her cooking reached him immediately.

"It sure smells good in here," he said, breathing the scents in deeply.

"You always say that," Lynn said, standing at the stove, stirring a wooden spoon around in a pot.

"It's always true," McCoy said. He put the bag down on the kitchen table, between the two place settings Lynn had already set for them.

"What've you got there?" she asked, looking back over her shoulder.

McCoy reached into the bag and, with a flourish, pulled out the bottle he'd asked Ashby Robinson—the son of Turner, from whom he'd inherited the general store—to order for him a couple of days ago. "I got us a bottle of champagne," he said.

"Champagne?" Lynn asked. "Fancy. Are we celebrating something?"

Fully aware that they would indeed be celebrating soon, McCoy opted for coyness. "You never know," he said.

Of late, nobody in town—nobody in the *country*—had felt much like rejoicing. A little more than a month ago, Atlanta had been bombed out of existence in a frightening display of Nazi capabilities. At the same time, the atomic device dropped on the city of Boston had failed to detonate, sparing at least sixty-five thousand people from death, and another one hundred forty thousand from injury. McCoy could only surmise that the defective bomb had been retrieved and now aided American scientists in their own quest to create an atomic weapon—a quest that must have begun far later and met with far less success than the Manhattan Engineering District had in the twentieth-century timeline that his presence had not corrupted.

In the Pacific, Peru and much of Chile had now fallen to Japanese forces, though the United States, Canada, and Mexico had so far managed to defend North America from further attacks. In Europe, the war continued, in a struggle McCoy hoped would result in an Allied victory before Germany could produce their next generation of V-2 rockets. For once the range of those rockets increased enough to provide a transatlantic delivery mechanism for their atomic bombs, the United States would have little choice but to surrender.

In the last few days, though, life had begun to return to a more or less normal shape in Hayden. As terrible as the loss of Atlanta and its population had been, the rest of the nation had spent most of the last month bracing for additional attacks within the country's borders. When after weeks that hadn't happened, people had finally started to breathe a little easier.

And McCoy himself had moved inexorably toward tonight.

He popped the cork from the champagne and poured glasses for Lynn and himself to have with supper. She had never drunk it before and couldn't really decide whether or not she liked it. She enjoyed the bubbles, but wasn't so sure about the taste.

After they'd finished eating supper and cleaning up, they repaired to the parlor. Over the last couple of years, they had found a way to introduce their mutual enjoyment of novels into their friendship: they selected a book of interest to them both, and then one would read aloud to the other. They had initially planned to do that tonight, but as they sat down on the davenport, McCoy finally did what he had decided to do a month ago.

Setting aside the copy of *Moby-Dick* they had intended to begin tonight, McCoy said, "Lynn, I have something for you."

"Champagne *and* a present?" she said. "What did I do to deserve this?"

"You're just you," he said, and he reached into his pocket. When he pulled his hand back out, he held it faceup in front of Lynn. In his palm lay the garnet-inlaid gold bracelet that he'd tried to give her on her birthday more than five years ago. She gazed down at it, then peered up at him quizzically. "It's not a ring," he told her, "but will you marry me?"

Lynn's expression seemed to undergo more transitions than McCoy could process. He thought he saw complete surprise, confusion, delight, shock, and finally joy. Lynn virtually launched herself across the davenport and into McCoy's arms, not even bothering to take the bracelet. "Yes, yes, yes," she said. She began kissing his face over and over, until he found her lips with his. They kissed deeply, passionately, as though the years together—but apart—had all been a buildup to this moment.

When at last they pulled back and looked at each other, she took his face in her hands. "Oh, Leonard McCoy, you are full of surprises," she said.

He smiled at her. "Does that mean you want the bracelet?" he said.

"What do you think?" she said, and she reached for his closed hand. He opened his fingers, uncovering the bracelet. Lynn picked it up and examined it closely. "It's so beautiful," she said. She stood up as she unhooked its clasp, then wrapped it around her wrist. "Oh my goodness," she said, extending her arm to admire it. "Oh my goodness." She crossed the room to the standing lamp there and held the bracelet up beneath it. "Oh my . . ." When her voice faded to silence, he thought she'd just been caught up in looking at her new jewelry, but then she peered over at him, the look of confusion he'd seen earlier now returned to her face.

"What is it?" McCoy asked.

"Why now?" she asked him. "After all this time, why now?"

"I don't know," he said, though of course he did. When he thought Lynn had been killed, and then she'd shown up on his doorstep, he didn't know if he'd ever known such profound relief. He'd also known that he did not want to risk losing her again. Marriage wouldn't necessarily prevent that, wouldn't safeguard her from all harm, but he felt compelled to make himself her husband. "I guess it just felt right."

"But it doesn't feel right," Lynn said. She looked down at the bracelet and then back over at McCoy. "Believe me, I want it to, but it feels . . . forced," she said.

McCoy stood up from the davenport. "Lynn," he said, "I love you. I think you've known that for a long time."

"I think I have too," she said. "But that's what doesn't feel right. You've loved me, but you haven't wanted to be together. So why all of a sudden?"

"It's not all of a sudden," McCoy said. "I've been thinking about this night for weeks."

"For weeks," Lynn repeated. "Since Atlanta?" McCoy looked down, feeling as though he'd been caught in a lie, despite that not being the case. "Is this—" She held up the wrist around which she now wore the bracelet. "—because I could've been killed in Atlanta?"

He lifted his head and peered back over at her. "It's because I love you," he said truthfully. "I *have* loved you for a long time." He just hadn't wanted to risk becoming involved with Lynn before now. When the relationship failed—and they always did—he would've had to move out of Hayden, start his life all over again. He hadn't been prepared to do that until . . . *Until I came so close to losing her.*

"If you loved me for so long," she said, "then why didn't you want to marry me?"

"Lynn," McCoy said, starting across the room.

"No," Lynn said, holding up the flat of her hand to him. "This is a real question. You know how I feel about you, Leonard. You know I want this, that I've dreamed about it, but I want to be your wife only because you love me, not because you're scared of losing me."

"I was scared when everything happened in Atlanta," McCoy admitted. "But that's because I love you." How could he make her understand? "Didn't you fall in love with me because you lost Phil?"

Lynn stared at him for a moment without saying anything. Then: "Is that what you think? That I needed somebody to replace Phil and you happened to be convenient?"

"I didn't mean that," McCoy said. "I meant—"

"It doesn't matter what you meant," Lynn said. "I've loved you for a long time. I think . . . I think it started before Phil left, but I loved him and I never would've done anything about my feelings for you. After he was killed, though, it was okay to care about you. There's something special between us."

"Then marry me," McCoy told her.

"I want to," Lynn said. "You know how much I want to. But only out of love, not out of fear."

McCoy felt lost. Of all the ways he'd imagined this night unfolding, he'd never considered anything like this. "We live in frightening times," he told Lynn, not really sure what else to say. "There's always going to be fear."

"In life, sure," she said. "But there shouldn't be any fear in a marriage. We shouldn't decide to have a wedding just because you're worried about losing me."

McCoy shook his head. Why had he done this? "I guess I should be used to losing people by now," he muttered, more to himself than to Lynn.

"What?" she said. "What do you mean?"

"Nothing," McCoy said, turning away from her.

"No," she said, striding across the floor. She took him by the arms and turned him back toward her. "What do you mean you should be used to losing people?"

"I mean—" What could he tell her? That his entire life up to the age of forty had been lived in the twenty-third century, that everybody he'd ever cared about before then, everybody he'd ever known, had then been lost to him? Joanna, Jim and Spock, even Tonia. "I mean that before I arrived in Hayden, I'd lost everybody I ever cared about." He didn't want to explain further, but Lynn wouldn't let it go.

"Everybody?" she said. She seemed to consider this for a few seconds, and then, misunderstanding, asked, "Women you've loved?"

But of course he'd lost them too, well before he'd been thrown back through time. Jocelyn, Nancy, and really Tonia would have joined that list as well if he'd made it back to the *Enterprise*. "Yes," McCoy told Lynn.

Very quietly, her voice filled with sympathy and disbelief, Lynn said, "They all died?"

"What?" McCoy said. "No, but I lost them just the same."

Lynn's brow wrinkled. She dropped her hands from his arms and walked back across the room. "They left you," she said.

"They . . . well, it ended with each of them," he said.

"*You* left *them?*" she asked.

McCoy couldn't believe that the conversation had gone in the direction it had. "Does it matter?" he asked, all at once feeling very weary.

"Leonard, I love you, but that doesn't make me blind or stupid," Lynn said. "When you first came to Hayden all those years ago, you were running from something. Ever since I let you know how I feel about you, and maybe even since before that, you've been running from me. Now you're telling me that you've run from the other important women in your life. What am I supposed to think?"

"I don't know," McCoy said. "I'm not sure I know what to think anymore."

Once more, she went to him, this time taking his hand. "Tell me," she said, "why did you leave them?"

"Because," McCoy said, anger driving his voice louder. He pulled his hand from Lynn's grasp and moved away from her. "It just didn't work out," he said, no longer looking at her. "Sometimes that happens."

From behind him, she said evenly, "You're upset, you're lonely, you're bitter. It doesn't sound like it 'just didn't work out.'" McCoy didn't know how to respond, and he thought that he should probably leave. "Did they hurt you, Leonard?" Lynn persisted. "Did you leave them before they could leave you? Did you think they were going to abandon you?"

"Why not? They all do," McCoy said without thinking.

"They *all* do?" Lynn asked. "All who?"

"Just . . . I didn't mean to say that," McCoy told her.

He heard her walking across the floor and then felt her hand on his back. "All who?" Lynn asked again. "Leonard, do you mean your mother?" She could not have wounded him more deeply if she'd driven a sword through his heart. "You talked about her once, a long time ago," she said quietly. "Why don't you tell me what you know about her?"

McCoy wanted to run. He wanted to leave—wanted to race out of Lynn's house, out of her life, out of Hayden. He wanted to go far away and start a new life for himself somewhere else.

But he didn't.

He didn't know why he stayed—was it her hand on his back, or his guilt for having destroyed history, or something else altogether?—but he did stay. He turned around to face her. "All I know is that she died giving birth to me," he said softly.

"Surely you must know more," Lynn said. "Your father must have told you about her."

McCoy laughed, a throaty "Ha!" that contained absolutely no humor. "He never even showed me a picture," he said, not looking at Lynn now, but past her, into the middle distance, into his own past. "I had to find that on my own. And when he discovered that I had, he . . ." Lynn waited without speaking, and he peered down at her limpid blue eyes. "He hated me for it," he finished.

"No," Lynn said. "That can't be true. Your father wouldn't hate you for that."

"He did," McCoy said, admitting aloud something he had barely acknowledged to himself. "But really he hated me because I killed my mother. Because I killed the love of his life."

"No," Lynn said again, but this time her voice lacked conviction, replaced instead by a terrible sorrow. "That's not true. You didn't do anything. Sometimes things just happen."

"He blamed me," McCoy said. "I don't know if he meant to, but I know that he did. Up until those last few weeks, when he needed me . . . *really* needed me."

"In the end, he realized the error of his ways," Lynn said, as though willing that to be true.

"In the end," McCoy said, "he needed me, and so he put aside his blame."

"How did he need you?" Lynn asked tentatively.

"He was in so much pain," McCoy said, visualizing the scene in the hospital room: the rain spilling down the windows, the artificial sounds of the monitors and the life-sustaining devices, the frightful *whiteness* of the place. "The doctors . . ." Even buried within his awful memories, McCoy knew that he could not mention life-support machinery to Lynn. "The doctors kept giving him medicine to keep him alive, but he hurt so much. He begged me to help him . . . begged me to *release* him."

"And you did," Lynn said, her voice barely a whisper now. "You stopped the medicine."

McCoy focused his gaze on her again. "I did," he said. "I killed my father. I killed my mother, and then I killed my father."

"No, Leonard, no," Lynn beseeched him. "You didn't do anything wrong."

"I did," he said.

"No," Lynn said again, and she wrapped her arms around

him. McCoy closed his eyes, but when he did, he saw the sterile hospital room once more, so he opened them. They stood like that for a long while, their only movement the little circle Lynn made with one hand on his back.

Finally, Lynn asked, "Is that why you left those other women? Because you didn't want to hurt them too? Or—" Something seemed to occur to her, and she stepped back and looked up at him. "Or was it because you wanted to leave them before they left you, just as your parents left you?"

"My parents didn't leave me," he said.

"They did, Leonard," Lynn said. "They didn't want to, but they did. They died and abandoned you. I know. My parents did the same thing to me. But just because they left me didn't mean I should've stayed away from Phil because he would leave me too."

"But he did," McCoy said, regretting the harshness of his words as soon as he'd spoken them. But Lynn did not seem stung by what he'd said.

"We all die," she said. "You're a doctor, so you probably know that better than anybody. But we all go to Heaven for a better life."

"Do you know that I don't believe in Heaven?" McCoy asked.

"I'm not surprised to find out," Lynn said. "But even if there is no Heaven, doesn't that make this life even more precious? If you choose to live it without love because you're scared of being abandoned, you're missing out on the most that life has to offer." She reached up and took his face between her hands. "Leonard, your parents left you and mine left me. Phil left me too. But I love you, and you and I are here right now. I'm not going to worry that you won't be here tomorrow." She stood on her toes and pressed her lips gently, sweetly against his, a brief, perfect taste of love. "And you don't need to worry that I won't be here tomorrow either."

McCoy swept her into his arms and swung her around. "I love you," he said, and he kissed her, the dreadful weight of his longtime burden easing as he shared it.

FIFTY-ONE

2293

The massive whipcord of energy twisted through the void like
some spaceborne tornado. Jags of lightninglike bolts writhed
around it, and dust and debris trailed from it in cloud-gray
sheets. Already the strange phenomenon that filled the main
viewscreen had claimed two Federation transport vessels, and
with them, three hundred sixty-eight lives. Scotty had managed
to transport forty-seven survivors from the second vessel, the
S.S. Lakul, before its hull had collapsed, the ship exploding violently.

Now, the *Enterprise*—the upgraded *Excelsior*-class NCC-
1701-B—lurched to starboard, then back the other way. Kirk
caught himself on the railing, then pulled himself up onto the
outer, upper ring of the bridge. Behind him, he heard an explosion, and he looked in time to see a hail of spark's flying from
the navigator's station. Smoke, shouts, and an alert claxon filled
the bridge as the great ship trembled.

Kirk reached for the outer bulkhead and pulled himself forward, toward the sciences station. "Report!" he called as he
passed behind the freestanding tactical console. He took hold of
the bulkhead again beside the science officer.

"We're caught in a gravimetric field emanating from the trailing edge of the ribbon," she called over the chaotic sounds
around them.

In the center of the bridge, the ship's captain, Harriman,
cried, "All engines, full reverse!"

The right order, Kirk thought. The shaking of the ship eased
as the power of its drive strained against the pull of the energy
ribbon. He pushed away from the bulkhead and stepped down to
the lower portion of the bridge, over to Harriman. Scotty, he saw,
had already taken over at the forward station for the downed navigator.

"The *Enterprise*'s engines are far more powerful than those of the transport ships," Harriman told Kirk. "We might be able to pull free."

It sounded more like wishful thinking than a plan of action, but Kirk knew that it was the proper course to attempt. He'd never before met this new captain of this new *Enterprise*, but he'd known his father, the redoubtable—and difficult—Admiral "Blackjack" Harriman. This younger man seemed far different than his take-no-prisoners parent. Where the elder Harriman took bold, often rash, action, this younger man seemed more thoughtful, his approach more reasoned and cautious. Kirk understood the value of both approaches, though he knew that a truly successful starship command required a combination of the two.

"We're making some headway," Scotty said from the navigator's station. "I'm reading a fluctuation in the gravimetric field that's holding us." Kirk peered up at the main viewer, at the coruscating field of pink and orange light, brilliant white veins of energy pulsing through it. Despite the obvious danger it posed, he found it strikingly beautiful. He walked forward, around Demora Sulu at the helm, to stand in front of the viewscreen.

"You came out of retirement for this," a voice said quietly at his right shoulder. He looked at Harriman and was surprised to see a hint of a smile lifting one side of his mouth. The statement, the expression, both spoke volumes to Kirk, revealing a confidence in the young captain that he hadn't seen before now. Of course, Harriman had been hamstrung by some admiral in Starfleet Command eager to generate some positive media coverage. After the recent complicity of several Fleet officers in the conspiracy to disrupt the peace initiative between the Federation and the Klingon Empire—a conspiracy that had effected the assassination of the Klingon chancellor, Gorkon—Kirk couldn't argue that the image of the space service had suffered. Still, even if nobody had anticipated the *Enterprise* having to mount an emergency rescue mission during this public relations jaunt, you didn't send a starship out of space dock without a tractor beam, without a medical staff; you didn't send a newly promoted captain out with a bridge filled with members of the media and a "group of living legends," as Harriman had earlier referred to Kirk, Scotty, and Chekov. The circumstances could have daunted even a seasoned captain.

"I'm still retired," Kirk said. "A one-day activation is not going to pull me back into Starfleet permanently."

"We could still use officers of your caliber and character, sir," Harriman said sincerely.

"Thank you, but it's gotten a little too political for me these days," Kirk said. He glanced around at the media reporters still on the bridge.

"Don't I know it," Harriman said under his breath, something of a faraway look crossing his visage. All at once, Kirk realized that Blackjack must've been the one who'd pushed for this publicity outing for the *Enterprise* and its new captain, as much a self-serving promotion for the admiral as for Starfleet or his son.

Kirk turned toward Harriman. "Don't let anybody else define you," he said quietly to him. "This ship is yours, and this crew needs you, the man, not some image you or anybody else wants you to live up to."

Harriman tilted his head slightly to the side, apparently considering Kirk's words. Before he could respond, though, the ship heaved once more. Kirk staggered to his right and started to go down, but righted himself beside the navigation console.

"There's just no way to disrupt a gravimetric field of this magnitude," Scotty said. Kirk knew that if the engineer could not figure out a means of freeing the *Enterprise*, then it likely couldn't be done.

"Hull integrity at eighty-two percent," reported the tactical officer from his station.

"But," Scotty said, "I do have a theory."

"I thought you might," Kirk said. Secure in his own abilities, he also knew that he'd succeeded as much as he had in his role as starship captain because of the senior staff that had for so long served with him. Certainly Scotty had been an instrumental element of that team.

"An antimatter discharge directly ahead might disrupt the field long enough for us to break away," Scotty theorized.

An antimatter discharge, Kirk thought. "Photon torpedoes," he said.

"Aye," Scotty agreed.

"We're losing main power," the science officer said as Kirk moved back around the navigation and helm consoles. As he passed Demora, he tapped the weapons readout at the corner of her display.

"Load torpedo bays," he ordered. "Prepare to fire at my command."

As he stopped in front of the command chair, Sulu said, "Captain, we don't have any torpedoes."

"Don't tell me," Kirk said, peering over at Harriman, who still stood in front of the viewscreen. "Tuesday." That's when the young captain had said that the tractor beam and medical staff would arrive on the *Enterprise*, so why not the torpedoes as well. Harriman opened his mouth as though to respond, but then he closed it and looked away. Kirk saw a flash of anger there and knew that it had been meant for Blackjack or whichever admiral had placed Harriman and his crew in such a predicament.

"Hull integrity at forty percent," said the tactical officer.

"Captain," Scotty said, "it may be possible to simulate a torpedo blast using a resonance burst from the main deflector dish."

A resonance burst, Kirk thought. Deflector systems were constituted in such a way as to avoid resonance, since sympathetic vibrations could disrupt both the deflector generators, other equipment, and even the hull itself. Right now, though, that seemed a small risk to take.

The ship pitched again, sending Kirk flying backward, toward the command chair. Grabbing onto the arm of the chair, he peered back at Sulu. "Where are the deflector relays?" he asked, knowing that they would have to be reconfigured.

"Deck fifteen," Sulu said, "section fifteen alpha." Kirk couldn't tell whether she'd brought up the systems chart that quickly or she'd pulled the information from her memory.

"I'll go," Harriman said at once. Looking up at Kirk, he said, "You have the bridge." He started immediately for the turbolift.

Kirk lowered himself into the command chair. How many years, how much of his life, how much of his soul, had he given to this position? He'd retired from Starfleet, but this . . . this felt right.

And wrong, he admitted to himself. Not wrong for him, but wrong for this ship and crew. "Wait," he said as he heard the turbolift doors whisper open. "Your place is on the bridge of your ship. I'll take care of it." He stood and wasted no time in changing places with Harriman. As he passed the younger captain, he saw a look of determination on his face. Kirk couldn't tell for sure, but he thought that, if they survived this situation, Harriman would be all right.

Turning back toward the bridge at the threshold of the lift, he said, "Scotty, keep things together till I get back."

"I always do," the engineer said.

Kirk stepped back and let the doors slide closed, a smile sneaking onto his face at Scotty's easy self-assurance. He specified his destination and the lift began to descend. As it did, Kirk regarded the schematic in the rear bulkhead of the car. He saw where the turbolift would stop and the route he would have to take from there to get to the deflector relays. He would have to open the main deflector control assembly, then access the override panel and reprogram it to allow the resonance burst. *The safety,* he remembered, thinking back both to his classes at the academy and to the many briefings he'd received over the years about starship systems design. He would have to remove the safety component from the deflector relays and plug it into the override housing in order to authenticate his intentions.

The lift eased to a stop, then began gliding horizontally through the ship, toward the port side. Kirk could sense the strain of the engines as they struggled against the gravimetric distortions caused by the energy vortex. The ship still shuddered in the clutches of the tremendous forces.

Kirk raised a hand to the ship's schematic and traced a finger along the unfamiliar lines of this *Enterprise*. *This doesn't feel right,* he told himself, just as he had on the bridge, but now he added, *Not even for me.* He supposed that if he took command of this vessel and ventured out into the galaxy, it would one day become his ship, but right now, it didn't feel like that. Not like the first day he had set foot aboard the *Constitution*-class *Enterprise* twenty-eight years ago, not like the times he had returned to that ship after its refits, and not even like when he'd initially reported to NCC-1701-A, the former *Yorktown* renamed as a reward to Kirk and his crew for their service after the destruction of their original *Enterprise*. He would be content to leave this ship to Captain Harriman. As much as he loved command, Kirk needed to explore more than space; he needed to explore his own life.

The lift eased to a halt and when the doors parted, Kirk shot from them like the beam from a phaser. He quickly oriented himself and found the ladder leading down into the maintenance corridor. He descended into the bowels of the ship and hurried forward, striving to keep his footing as the *Enterprise* continued to quake. Coolant leaks hissed in the enclosed space, sending vapor erupting intermittently from rents in the bulkhead. Kirk raced through the clouds, feeling their cold touch.

Reaching the primary deflector control center, Kirk entered through its wide doors. Here too a fog of coolant blurred the air. Just a glance down into the compartment showed him where he needed to go. He climbed down a ladder to a walkway and removed the grating that covered the access to the main deflector relays. The ship reeled again, and the grate slipped from his hands and fell at least ten meters, rattling along the bulkheads as it did. Down another ladder, and at last he reached the main deflector control assembly. He opened the access plate and the relay emerged from behind it, automatically rising to situate itself beside the override panel. Kirk pulled himself back up the ladder and moved to the housing for the override. He opened the plate there to expose a series of optical chips utilized to program the main deflector. As quickly as he could, he chose the two that would allow him to do what he needed to do, and started to reseat them in the circuit accordingly.

"Bridge to Captain Kirk," he suddenly heard Scotty's voice.

"Kirk here," he called as he slid the second chip into the appropriate slot. He jabbed at the override controls, reprogramming the relay to permit the resonance burst.

"I don't know how much longer I can hold her together," Scotty said, a familiar plaint. In other, less serious circumstances, Kirk would've laughed.

He finished working at the control panel, then hastily backed up and bent down to the deflector control assembly. With both hands, he grabbed the safety and pulled it free. Stepping back to the override panel, he bent and rammed the mechanism into place.

"That's it!" he called. "Let's go!"

"Activate main deflector," he heard Harriman order, his voice strong.

In the control center around Kirk, none of the equipment seemed to change, but he heard a loud whine that he knew must be the resonance burst. Even as the ship shook, he could feel it steadying by degrees, the feel of the drive becoming less labored.

"We're breakin' free," Scotty said.

The drone of the resonance burst ceased and the control center quieted dramatically. Kirk detected a change in the movement of the ship. He could never have described the sensation, but he had spent enough time aboard starships to recognize the change in attitude. He knew at that moment that this *Enterprise* and this crew would be safe.

Kirk started away from the deflector equipment, moving back along the walkway toward the ladder up. He reached it and began to climb, but then stopped. In the relative calm of the primary deflector control center, Kirk suddenly heard a familiar sound, its presence here and now making no sense to him.

And then he vanished.

A gentle breeze wafted across the veranda, bearing with it the warm, slightly fruity scent of peach blossom. Ahead, in the front yard, the leaves of a quartet of century-old trees rustled softly, trees from which the house took its name: White Oaks. As the sky colored in the last throes of dusk, McCoy leaned back in his wicker chair, his feet up on the railing, and thought that perhaps Jim and Scotty had made the wisest choices after all.

When Starfleet Command had decided earlier this year to decommission the *Enterprise* after its decades of operation, the senior command crew had resolved to stand down as a unit. Though they had served for many years together, they each had other aspirations as well. Sulu exemplified that, having assumed the captaincy of the *Excelsior* three years ago. So when the *Enterprise* had been removed from service three months ago, after the Khitomer affair, its command staff had gone their separate ways. Spock had been offered an opportunity to train cadets once more, but later had chosen to accept an ambassadorial post. Uhura had opted to accept a position with

Starfleet Intelligence, and Chekov had agreed to a ground assignment while waiting for a shipboard exec position to open up. Jim and Scotty, on the other hand, had both elected to retire.

Today, as McCoy enjoyed the late-summer Georgia evening on one of the final days of his leave, just ahead of his scheduled return to Starfleet Medical, he wondered if maybe the captain and the engineer had gotten it right. While McCoy looked forward to pursuing several avenues of study when he resumed his research career, he also had to admit to the allure of simply relaxing around the house, taking strolls in the park, puttering around in the garden. He'd found his time away from Starfleet and medicine far more restorative than he had imagined it would be.

As night fell and the sky began to darken, McCoy spied an airpod in the distance, approaching the property. He hadn't been expecting any visitors, and so he thought that perhaps somebody had simply lost their way. But when the pod alit at the end of the lane, he immediately recognized the silhouette of the diminutive figure who emerged from within the small craft: Uhura.

McCoy waved as the commander strode up the front walk. "Well, hello," he called to her. She said nothing, but lifted a hand in response, less a greeting than mere perfunctory acknowledgment. The simple gesture seemed out of character for Uhura, who lived life with great zest and sported a normally ebullient personality. McCoy wondered if she felt comfortable with whatever reason she had for visiting him. He recalled the last time that somebody had dropped in on him unannounced in Georgia: twenty years ago, Admiral Nogura had shown up at his research lab and coerced him into rejoining Starfleet. He doubted that Uhura had come for any such dubious purposes, though—particularly since he hadn't left the Fleet this time.

As she approached the house, McCoy saw that she wore her uniform, a crimson tunic with a black skirt. He pulled his feet from the railing and walked over to the front steps. When Uhura reached him and climbed up onto the veranda, she said, "Hello, Leonard," and hugged him. He could tell that she had come for some reason other than simply making a social call.

"So what brings you to this neck of the woods?" he asked when she stepped back from him.

"May we go inside?" Uhura asked. She tried a smile, but it convinced McCoy of nothing.

"Sure," he said, remaining casual. He knew that she would tell him whatever she needed to when she felt ready. He moved to the front door of the restored nineteenth-century plantation house and held it open for her. He followed her inside, through the foyer and into the corridor that split the house in two, with a staircase along the right-hand wall that led to the second floor. He touched a plate on the wall and the glass chandelier hanging from the upper story lighted up. "Let's go in here," he said, motioning toward a doorway on the left.

Again, he touched a plate as they went into the house's great room, which McCoy had furnished in period detail. The overhead lighting fixture came to life to reveal a pair of ornate, burgundy davenports, which sat perpendicular to the hearth on the far wall and faced each other across a low oak table. "Make yourself comfortable," McCoy said, and he walked over to the bar cabinet set diagonally in the far corner. "Can I get you something to drink?"

As Uhura sat, she asked, "Have you got any bourbon?"

McCoy peered back across the room at her. "What do you think?" he asked, and Uhura laughed, the first moment of buoyancy she'd yet shown.

"Water?" he asked. "Ice?"

"Neat," Uhura said.

"A purist," McCoy pronounced appreciatively. He opened the cabinet and pulled out a pair of snifters, then selected a bottle of Silver Moon Single-Barrel. He poured out two fingers of the amber liquid into the bowls of each stemmed glass, then carried them over to the sitting area, where he handed one to Uhura.

"Thank you," she said.

"You're welcome," he replied, and he offered his snifter in salute. Uhura tapped her glass against his, then sipped at her drink. McCoy swirled his bourbon for just a moment, then drank. The sophisticated alcohol presented a soft bouquet of honey and spice, and a foundation mixed of caramel and vanilla flavors, finishing smoothly.

He sat opposite Uhura on the other davenport, setting his glass down on the table between them. Uhura took her snifter in both hands and held it at her knees, staring down into it. McCoy could tell that something troubled her greatly. The silence began to stretch out, but he chose not to try to fill it, not wanting to add to whatever burden Uhura bore.

Finally, she said, "I'm afraid I've brought terrible news." She lifted her gaze to meet his, and he could see the effort it cost her. "The new *Excelsior*-class *Enterprise* launched today on a . . . well, on a publicity tour of the solar system, really."

"Jim mentioned that to me last week," McCoy said. "He said Starfleet had invited him for the christening and first voyage."

Uhura nodded and looked down. "He was aboard today, along with Scotty and Pavel," she said. "It was supposed to be just a quick trip around the solar system for some journalists, but . . ." Uhura looked up again, and McCoy could see that she had come to tell him something far worse than he'd imagined.

"What happened?" he asked flatly.

"They had to mount a rescue mission," Uhura said. "Two transports caught in some sort of bizzare energy phenomenon. Captain Kirk helped recover passengers from those vessels before they were destroyed, and then when the *Enterprise* became trapped too, he saved the ship." Uhura stopped again, obviously upset, but McCoy could not prevent himself from asking the obvious question.

"Is he all right?"

"Leonard," she said, her voice laced with sadness, "he's dead."

McCoy felt as though a blistering gale struck him full in the face. He could not accept the words that he'd heard. He knew in an instant that there must be some mistake. "Are you sure?" he asked, and he understood in the next second the foolishness of his query. Of course Jim was dead. Uhura would not have come here to give him this news otherwise.

"I'm sorry to have to tell you," she said, "but I thought you should hear it from a friend."

"No, I'm glad you did," McCoy said, his emotion driving him to his feet. "I mean, I'm not glad, it's that . . . I just . . ." He tried to gather his thoughts and stop babbling. "Thank you, Uhura."

He moved around the table to her, and she put down her glass and stood up to embrace him.

After a few minutes, they sat back down, together this time, on the same davenport. It seemed impossible that Jim was gone. McCoy had always thought of him as a force of nature—flawed, sometimes tortured, but always vibrant and vigorous. The death of Jim Kirk felt as likely as the death of gravity.

Uhura told him what she knew of the incident aboard the *Enterprise* today, which Scotty had related to her just a short time ago. "Starfleet Command's holding the news back from the comnets until they've notified the captain's nephews. That'll probably take a couple of days, at least."

"What about Spock?" McCoy asked. "Does he know?"

"No," Uhura said. "Scotty and Pavel and I were talking about how we should tell him. He's on a diplomatic mission right now on Alonis. We thought we should inform him immediately, but we didn't want to tell him over subspace."

"No," McCoy agreed. "I'll go. I'll tell him."

"We all think that would be best," Uhura said. "If you don't want to make the trip alone—"

"That's all right," McCoy said. "Thank you, but I'll go by myself." He did not look forward to delivering the news to Spock, but really, he had no choice in the matter; Spock and McCoy had been Jim's closest friends for nearly three decades.

"I just can't believe that he's gone," Uhura said.

"I know," McCoy agreed. "It seems appropriate that it happened aboard a starship, though."

"Yes," Uhura said. "I knew he'd retired and all, but I just always assumed he'd end up back in command of a starship one day. It was as though he'd been born for the position."

"That's true," McCoy said. "I know he talked about the over-politicization of Starfleet these days, but I never thought that would keep him away from space forever. I would've been surprised if his retirement lasted a year."

They sat quietly for a few seconds, and then Uhura said, "Do you remember the time on Platonius, when the inhabitants wanted to keep you there because they had no doctors of their own?

"How can I forget?" McCoy said, recalling the small population who had developed telekinetic abilities as a result of ingesting the native foods. "Jim wouldn't let me stay, even if it meant sparing the ship and the crew."

"He always looked out for us," Uhura said, her words thankful, admiring, and wistful.

They talked about Jim for a while. Uhura offered to spend the night in the guest room, just so that McCoy wouldn't wake up to an empty house. He appreciated the gesture, but just before midnight, he sent her on her way back home, knowing that she had a long day ahead of her tomorrow; she and Pavel intended to travel to Starbase 13, where the *Excelsior* had just put in for shore leave, so that they could tell Sulu personally about Jim's death.

Before he went to bed himself, McCoy contacted Starfleet and arranged for the fastest possible journey to Alonis. In the morning, before dawn, after a night of tempestuous dreams rooted not in Jim's death, but in his own, he made his way to Starfleet's military operations facility in Atlanta. From there, he beamed up to the transport vessel *S.S. Shras.*

As the ship broke orbit, he still had no idea how he was going to tell Spock.

FIFTY-TWO

1954/1955

In the midst of a war that had already killed millions, that had stolen children from parents, parents from children, husbands from wives, the people of Hayden gathered together to rejoice. The townsfolk, as remote from the rest of the world as they often felt, had not been unaffected by the hostilities raging around the world. Ray Peavey and Jefferson Donner had been killed on the battlefields of Europe, Henry Palmer and Randy Denton had been lost in the waters of the Pacific. Justin Palmer had returned home with his right leg missing below the knee. Billy Fuster and Bo Bartell had both been labeled as missing in action, and everybody assumed that they too had died. On top of all that, nearly everybody in town had known or been related to somebody in the now-decimated city of Atlanta.

And of course Lynn had lost her husband.

Despite the death and the destruction, though, despite the uncertainty of tomorrow, everybody in Hayden had come together today, not for another funeral, but for an affirmation of life, a convocation of God's love, and of love itself. In all her three decades in Hayden, Lynn had never seen the church this filled, not even for the many memorial services conducted here in recent years. Every pew held an unbroken chain of people, while many other men and women stood along the side and rear walls of the nave. As she walked down the aisle, Lynn wondered if a single resident of Hayden had failed to show up today.

At the head of the aisle, before the altar and Pastor Gallagher, she joined Leonard. Dashing in the new black suit he had ordered through Robinson's General Store, he looked at her with unabashed admiration. Wearing the beautiful gown that Daisy Palmer and Mary Denton had helped her make—a raw silk bodice joined ivory satin skirt and sleeves, with rosettes running from shoulder to wrist—she had hoped that she would turn his head. Seeing the love in his smile now as he gazed at her filled her heart with joy.

Lynn knew that she had suffered from loss in her life, some might even say from tragedy. But she also knew that she could not claim any uniqueness because of that; everybody endured loss. Right here, right now, standing with Leonard, she felt truly blessed, and she thanked God for all the good that He had given her.

Pastor Gallagher, looking regal in his white robes, began the wedding ceremony. He read several passages from the Bible that Lynn had selected, and he added a few words of his own. Then he led Lynn through her vows, and when she'd completed them, he addressed Leonard. "Do you, Leonard Horatio McCoy, take this woman, Lynn Jennie Dickinson, to be your wife?" he said. "Do you promise to love her, to comfort and keep her, and to forsake all others and remain true to her, for as long as you both shall live?"

Lynn peered over at Leonard, who looked back at her with his deep blue eyes. "I do," he said, and she felt a rush of happiness and anticipation course through her. The power of his love, the power of her own, seemed to lift her up.

"Please repeat after me," Pastor Gallagher said, and then he read a version of the vows Lynn had earlier spoken herself. Leonard recited them without taking his gaze from her.

"I, Leonard Horatio McCoy," he said, "take thee, Lynn Jennie Dickinson, to be my wife, and before God and these witnesses, I promise to be a faithful and true husband." The pastor held out his hand. In his palm, he held a brand-new gold wedding band that Leonard had gotten for her in Greenville. Leonard took the ring, then reached for Lynn's left hand. Once again, he repeated the words the pastor provided. "With this ring, I thee wed, and all my worldly goods I thee endow," he said. "I promise to love and cherish you, in sickness and in health, for richer, for poorer, till death do us part." He slipped the gold band onto Lynn's ring finger.

"Then by the authority given to me by the state of South Carolina," Pastor Gallagher said, "and under the loving and watchful eyes of God Almighty, our Savior and Redeemer, I now pronounce you man and wife." The pastor leaned forward and, with a twinkle in his eye, told Leonard, "You may kiss the bride."

Leonard stepped forward, taking her hands tightly in his own. Gently, sweetly, he offered her the first loving gesture of their new life together. The townsfolk of Hayden erupted in applause.

As those at the back of the nave headed outside, Lynn and Leonard stood there for a few moments, their love pledged to each other before everybody. Then, hand in hand, they walked down the aisle and out the front doors of the church. As they descended the steps, they found themselves showered with small pieces of cotton.

At the end of the walk, Leonard helped Lynn into Pastor Gallagher's buggy. From there, she peered back and saw the church overflowing with smiling, happy people. She watched as the pastor appeared and made his way to the buggy. Then he climbed aboard and drove them himself out to Lynn's farm.

The McCoys' farm, she happily corrected herself. *Leonard's and my farm.* They had decided that they would live out on Tindal's Lane, keeping the house in town for Leonard to continue using as his doctor's office. Since the people of Hayden still owned what had once been Dr. Lyles's home, Lynn and Leonard had needed to check with the town council about their plans, but nobody had objected. They even approved of Leonard's idea to convert the living areas of the place into a small ward for patients who might be better served by being able to stay there. Right now, though, before any of that happened, everybody in town would be headed over there with food and drink for the wedding reception this afternoon.

When they reached the farm, Lynn and Leonard thanked Pastor Gallagher, then walked up the front steps. Leonard opened the door, then put his arm around Lynn's back and hoisted her into his arms. He kissed her, then carried her across the threshold. "Welcome home, Missus McCoy," he said as he set her down in the parlor.

"And welcome to your new home too, Doctor McCoy," she said.

Together, they headed into the bedroom, where they would change out of their formal cloths—Leonard had earlier brought something to change into from his house—before going back into town for their party. As Lynn kicked off her shoes and prepared to take off her wedding dress, it struck her in a real way that it hadn't before, that she would need help getting out of her gown and that Leonard would be the one providing that help. "Would you . . . would you unbutton my dress for me?" she asked, surprised and a little amused by the timidity in her voice.

"I thought you'd never ask," Leonard said, and she giggled at his playfulness. She turned her back to him, and then felt his fingers as they worked down from the nape of her neck to the small of her back. She crossed her arms across the bodice of her dress to keep it on. "That's all of them," he said when he'd finished.

Lynn took a couple of steps away from Leonard, then turned back around to face him. With a knot of excitement twisting in her belly, she lowered her arms and let the dress fall to the floor, revealing her lacy undergarments. She felt her face flushing as Leonard gazed at her.

"Lynn," he said quietly, "you are a beautiful bride."

He walked over and took her in his arms. His mouth found hers, and then his lips moved, easing across the rise of her cheek, then trailing down the side of her neck. Her breathing grew heavier as her body reacted in a way that it hadn't in a long time.

I'm fifty years old, Lynn thought, *and I feel like a schoolgirl.*

The package sat beside him on the front seat of his car. Wrapped in elegant, white moiré paper and adorned with a silver ribbon tied into a bow, the large, flat box contained the culmination of six months' worth of effort. It had been that long ago when he'd begun thinking about what he could give to Lynn when they celebrated their first wedding anniversary. He'd wanted to find something both special and meaningful, something that his wife would not expect, but that she would love.

McCoy could not have been happier with Lynn. Their first year together as husband and wife had not only been the happiest of his life, but something of a revelation to him. Never before had he experienced such a prolonged and peaceful romantic relationship, one he did not attempt to sabotage or flee—as he now recognized that he had done in previous liaisons. Understanding the impact that the deaths of his parents had on him, and the deep-seated guilt and fear that had for so long been ingrained within him, had finally allowed him to move beyond those emotions. He had learned to trust Lynn, and more important, to trust himself.

As he drove along Tindal's Lane, heading home from his office at the end of the workday, McCoy could barely contain his excitement. When Lynn had made note of the date half a year after their wedding, Leonard had soon after visited the few stores in town, deciding that he needed plenty of time to find the perfect present. He'd learned from Mary Denton that people traditionally linked different materials with the gifts for each wedding anniversary—silver for the twenty-fifth year, gold for the fiftieth—and that the first year was associated with paper.

With this information, an idea began to percolate in McCoy's mind. Eventually, he purchased a camera, then managed to take several photographs of Lynn without her knowledge. He also secretly took pictures of her wedding dress, and of himself wearing the suit he'd worn for their ceremony. Then he'd found an artist in Greenville and hired him to produce a painting of the two of them together in their wedding clothes. Working from the photographs McCoy had given him, the man had managed to create a beautiful work, executing it in oils. McCoy had framed it, and it now sat in the wrapped package beside him in the car.

McCoy turned from the road onto the drive beside the house, parking beside Lynn's truck. Already home from the mill, she'd probably be in the kitchen making dinner for them. McCoy picked up the present, resituated the card beneath the ribbon, then bounded up the front steps. Opening the door and stepping into the parlor, he called, "Missus McCoy, I'm home."

He heard Lynn put something down in the kitchen, then she appeared in the doorway across the hall. "Hello, Doctor Mc—" she began, but stopped when she saw him. "You remembered," she said, obviously talking about the anniversary gift he held out before him.

"Of course," McCoy responded as Lynn crossed the hall and came into the parlor. "Why wouldn't I remember the best day of my life."

"I think most men don't remember things like that," Lynn said. "But then you're not like most men, are you?" She leaned in over the present and greeted him with a kiss.

"I'll take that as a compliment," McCoy said.

"Good, because that's how I meant it," Lynn said. She peered down at her present. "Can I open it now?" she asked.

"Oh, you think this is for you?" McCoy teased.

"Oh, you," Lynn said, slapping lightly at his arm. She took the package and sat down on the davenport, setting the box across her thighs. As she reached to undo the ribbon, though, McCoy heard an unfamiliar noise outside. Lynn must've heard it too because she looked up with a curious expression, as though listening and trying to identify the sound. "What is that?" she said.

McCoy thought he knew, and concern—even fear—washed over him. Without saying a word, he turned and raced out the door and down the steps. In front of the house, he turned his gaze upward, toward the sky. He heard Lynn's footsteps behind him as she followed him outside.

"What . . . ?" she said as the buzzing grew louder. "Are those planes?" she asked, her own anxiety evident in her tone. Though not completely unheard of, aircraft rarely intruded upon the skies of Hayden, and when they did, they typically flew at high altitude. Right now, though, the sounds coming out of the east clearly emanated from low in the sky. Worse, as the drone increased in volume, it became abundantly apparent that it did not originate from a single plane, but several—or many.

At last, McCoy saw them, a squadron of small, fast fighter planes, arranged in no obvious formation. They wouldn't fly directly overhead, he realized, but farther out in the valley, over the fields. McCoy and Lynn watched as they neared. With a single prop in the nose, they looked like pictures of many aircraft he'd seen in the newspapers and on television, though he did not recognize their grayish blue color scheme.

But the black swastika was unmistakable.

Closer now, the group of planes resolved into not a single squadron, but at least two. McCoy saw the darker colors of the second group, as well as their United States markings. Just as he recognized the pursuit of the Nazi aircraft by their American counterparts, the first planes soared past, out over the fields. An eruption of syncopated bangs burst forth and could only be gunfire. McCoy grabbed Lynn and hurried with her toward the house, taking cover beside its front side. Cautiously, they peeked around the corner, out toward the fields, as they watched the last of the planes fly past.

Suddenly, about half of the Nazi aircraft banked sharply left, while half continued straight ahead. The American group split in two as well in their pursuit. A lone plane broke right, toward the center of town, and then flames burst from its tail section. It lost altitude rapidly and soon disappeared from view. McCoy heard a loud sound, muffled by distance, but knew that the aircraft had crashed somewhere nearby.

He looked at Lynn. "Was that an American or German plane?" he asked her.

"I couldn't tell," she said.

"Stay here," he said, reaching into his pocket for his keys. He ran to his car, opened the door, and threw himself into the driver's seat. At the same time, Lynn climbed into the car on the opposite side. "I need you to stay here," McCoy told her.

"I'm going with you," Lynn said, and he knew that he would not be able to convince her otherwise.

McCoy backed out onto Tindal's Lane, then raced toward town. On Church Street, as they approached the commons, Lynn pointed out through the front windshield, ahead and to the left. "Smoke," she said, and McCoy saw the black column rising into the sky. He followed it, continuing on Church Street, past Carolina Street and Mill Road, and finally turning left on Riverdale. They passed several houses and a farm, until finally he saw two pickups and a car off to the side of the road up ahead. McCoy skidded to a stop beside them, and as Lynn jumped out of the car, he reached into the back seat and picked up his doctor's bag.

On the edge of a cotton field, several people from town—Jimmy Bartell, the deputy sheriff; Duncan Macnair, the mill superintendent; and Doug and Millie Warnick—stood staring out at the wreckage of the plane, perhaps fifty yards distant. The aircraft, McCoy saw, had broken into pieces. Behind it, a section of wing had snapped off and stood embedded in the ground. The nose of the plane had broken from the main body, as had the tail section. The fuselage had landed it on its side, and flames rose from behind the shattered glass of the cockpit canopy, spewing dark smoke. The plane was painted grayish blue, and clearly visible on the upright tail was a swastika.

McCoy started into the field.

"What are you doing?" Lynn yelled after him.

McCoy stopped and looked back. "Somebody might still be alive in there," he said, addressing not only Lynn, but the other people gathered as well.

"Doc," Jimmy Bartell said, "that's a *Nazi* plane."

"People may be hurt," McCoy said, and he peered directly at Lynn. "I'm a doctor," he said. "That's all I care about right now." As he started forward, he heard Lynn speak up again.

"Jimmy, go with him," she said. McCoy looked back and saw the deputy hurrying to join him. He waited, and when Bartell had reached him, they walked toward the downed plane together.

When they'd gotten within about thirty feet, McCoy could make out the body of a man half in and half out of the front of the cockpit. He lay with his right side on the ground, his face obscured by a mass of blood. McCoy tapped Bartell on the arm and pointed. "Look," he said. As he headed toward the man, Bartell came with him, unsnapping his holster and pulling out his gun. McCoy did not object.

At the plane, the foul smell of burning fuel filled the air. The torso of the man McCoy assumed to be the pilot stuck out of the cockpit at an unnatural angle. If he'd been wearing a helmet, it had disappeared, and his brown leather jacket had been torn open in numerous places. McCoy dropped to his knees beside the man and carefully reached for the side of his neck. He felt for a carotid pulse, the tips of his index and middle finger sliding across the blood-covered skin. He waited for several seconds, repositioned his fingers, then waited some more. Finally, he looked up at Bartell. "He's dead," he told the deputy.

"Can't say I'm sorry to hear that," Bartell said.

McCoy wiped his fingers along the dirt to rid them of the blood on them, then stood up and looked into the rear of the cockpit, his view partially blocked by the fractured canopy. He reached for the twisted metal frame and pulled. It came forward a few inches with a screech of metal against metal, and pieces of glass dropped away from it. He heaved again, and this time the canopy came completely free, falling to the ground with a thud and the sound of breaking glass.

McCoy leaned into the cockpit. Debris littered the interior, broken and confused. An arc of red colored one section of a control panel that had come free of its housing, and McCoy followed the trail of it to a hand. "There's somebody else in here," he called to Bartell. McCoy reached in and carefully took hold of the panel. He lifted gently, expecting resistance from its weight and the tangle of wires, but it moved easily. He shifted it forward, from atop the body of a man.

But not a *dead* body.

The airman looked at him with obvious suspicion. Blood had flowed down the center of his face from beneath his helmet, and a gaping wound had been opened in his upper arm through the sleeves of his jacket and shirt. McCoy reached toward the injury, wanting to examine it, and the man jerked away.

"It's all right," McCoy said, trying to calm him, and holding up his hands to show that he held nothing in them. He slowly reached forward again, carefully taking hold of the edges of the hole in the airman's jacket and pulling them apart so that he could examine the wound beneath.

He never saw the blade, but as the airman suddenly moved, McCoy felt the knife penetrate his body. He heard himself cry out in pain as he looked down and saw his own blood gush from the wound, splattering the leather jacket of his attacker. The man pulled the weapon free, his eyes wide open in their hatred, his face a mask of frightened zealotry. He pulled the blade free and then brought the weapon down again, slicing between McCoy's ribs and into his heart. He heard a woman scream, and he knew that he was dying. A report rang out, deafening him, and still the woman screamed.

Lynn, he thought.

He heard another bang, and more screams, but they seemed to reach him from far away. His vision clouded, and his fingers could feel nothing. He fell backward, away from the plane.

He was dead before he hit the ground.

IV

In Dying Songs a Dead Regret

No longer caring to embalm
    In dying songs a dead regret,
    But like a statue solid-set,
And moulded in colossal calm.

Regret is dead, but love is more
    Than in the summers that are flown,
    For I myself with these have grown
To something greater than before;

Which makes appear the songs I made
    As echoes out of weaker times,
    As half but idle brawling rhymes,
The sport of random sun and shade.

—Alfred, Lord Tennyson,
In Memoriam A.H.H.,
"O true and tried"

FIFTY-THREE

As they approached the property, set amid crops of cornstalks that rose two and a half meters above the soil, Spock peered at the farmhouse and didn't know what to think. The one-story building sat approximately twenty-five meters away, set off from the dirt road by a spread of green grass. A pair of very tall trees rose in front of the house, and as a breeze stirred their five-lobed, palmate leaves, flickers of red-orange light showed through them, the setting sun reflecting off of solar panels lining the roof.

Why am I here? Spock asked himself, and even if he didn't know what to think right now, at least he could answer that question: because Dr. McCoy had invited him to come here. After this morning's memorial services for Captain Kirk on the Starfleet Academy campus—at which Spock and McCoy and many others had spoken—the doctor and the rest of the *Enterprise*'s longtime command crew—Captains Scott and Sulu, and Commanders Uhura and Chekov—had gathered at what had been Jim's apartment. There, as executor of the captain's estate, Dr. McCoy had given to each of those assembled special gifts that Jim had left for each of them. From his friend, Spock had received a trio of centuries-old hardcover volumes: *The Lives and Opinions of Eminent Philosophers, Book VII,* by Diogenes Laërtius, which included a section on Zeno, generally considered the father of Stoic philosophy on Earth; Aristotle's *Organon,* a collection of his six seminal treatises on logic; and an anthology of poetry.

During the many years of their friendship, Spock had on several occasions made gifts of various written works to the captain, who often had inquired whether Spock had intended any message by his selection of those works. In this case, he thought he understood the significance of Jim's bequeathal: the Zeno and logic texts spoke to Spock's stoical Vulcan nature, and the poetry to his emotional human side. Collectively, the books appeared to indicate Jim's appreciation for both aspects of his friend's personality, and possibly to underscore the comfort Spock had gained over time with his dual character—a comfort that he at the moment no longer felt.

Spock and McCoy stopped walking as they reached the property, then simply stood quietly regarding the land and the structure on it. The doctor had not immediately identified this place when he had asked Spock to come here. After the former *Enterprise* crewmates had spent the afternoon at Jim's apartment reminiscing about their fallen comrade—during which time Spock had largely remained quiet—McCoy had suggested that the two of them take a walk together. Spock had been reluctant at first, but had relented when it had become apparent that something troubled the doctor—perhaps even something besides Jim's death.

To his surprise, though, they had not simply taken their walk in the captain's Russian Hill neighborhood. Instead, McCoy had led him to a nearby transporter station, where the two had beamed to Riverside, Iowa—a place Spock had never visited, but which he knew to be Jim's birthplace. The doctor had secured an airpod and had programmed it to bring them here, where it had set down at the periphery of the farm. As they'd walked down the road, McCoy had explained that this had been Jim's childhood home, and he'd talked about their lost friend, remembering him through their shared experiences. He'd spoken irreverently of some events—such as when a malfunction had caused the *Enterprise*'s main computer to perpetrate practical jokes on the crew—and seriously of others—such as when the captain had stood court-martial for his apparent negligence in causing the apparent—and ultimately falsified—death of the ship's records officer. Spock had commented when necessary, but had mostly kept silent.

"I've never been here," McCoy said now, standing in the road and gazing at the house that had once been the residence of the Kirk family. "And I take it that you haven't either."

"No, I have not," Spock said. "Doctor, it is unclear to me why you have chosen to come here now, and why you have chosen to bring me along."

"I'm not really sure myself," McCoy said, looking over at him. "I found this address when I was cataloguing Jim's belongings in order to deal with his estate. I guess I thought that coming here might . . . I don't know . . . might somehow bring us closer to Jim."

"That is not logical," Spock said, and before the doctor could protest, added, "but I do understand the sentiment." In fact, he understood more than he wished to. Jim's death had not only impacted him emotionally, but it had once more called into question some of the decisions Spock had made in his life—decisions which had adversely impacted the captain. The pain Spock now attempted to suppress, and the guilt that exacerbated that pain, continued to cause him debilitating distress.

"It occurred to me that our visit here would be our own little memorial to Jim," McCoy said. "There's something sort of heroic and melancholic about it. Since Jim was nothing if not a romantic, I think he would've appreciated the gesture."

"Indeed," Spock said, agreeing about Jim's temperament and pushing away his familiarity with it at the same time. He and McCoy stood without speaking for a while, and then Spock asked, "Do you intend to do more than this?"

"What do you mean?" McCoy said.

"Do you, for example, plan to ask whoever resides here now if they will permit you to go inside the house?"

"No," McCoy said. "No, I don't think so. This is sufficient, don't you think?"

"Yes, I concur," Spock said.

Together, they started back down the road toward the airpod, both of them quiet once more. About them, the light of day faded toward darkness as the sun set. Eventually, McCoy broke the silence. "To tell you the truth, Spock, I did intend to do more than simply see this place," he said. "I wanted to talk with you about a problem I've been having."

"I perceived that something in addition to the captain's death troubled you," Spock said.

"I've been having some very unsettling dreams," McCoy said. "Dreams about me dying."

Spock considered this. "I would suggest that such a reaction to the death of a close friend is not uncommon," he said, even as he realized that the doctor must know that himself.

"You're right, Spock, but I've been having these dreams since before Jim died," McCoy said. "I've experienced these death dreams since . . . well, since the *fal-tor-pan*."

"The ancient ritual," Spock said. The dangerous procedure had been utilized by High Priestess T'Lar to remove his *katra* from Dr. McCoy's brain and re-fuse it with Spock's own. *Yes,* he thought as the fog of vague remembrance drifted through his consciousness. He pored through a swirl of shapes and colors from that experience and saw shifting scenes of his friends mourning at what he understood to be a memorial service held for him in the *Enterprise*'s torpedo room, his corpse interred in a weapons casing. Mingling with the images of that event came those of another, with humans Spock did not recognize grieving at another funeral, the deceased in a closed coffin beside a waiting grave, in what appeared to be a rural setting. He did not know if the second set of dim visualizations represented McCoy's death, or if it corresponded to the dreams about which the doctor spoke. "Have you sought counseling?" Spock asked.

"I haven't," McCoy said. "I haven't really wanted to because I don't think that would help."

"But if these dreams are disturbing to you," Spock said, "would it not be appropriate to seek the services of a mental-health professional?"

"It would be if these were merely dreams," McCoy said. "But I think that they're memories."

"I do not understand," Spock said. "How can you have a memory of an occurrence—your own death—that has not yet happened? Unless you refer to the incident on the planet in the Omicron Delta region, when the knight on horseback attacked you with a lance." At the time of that assault, McCoy's heart had been damaged and had stopped beating.

"Sometimes I dream of that incident, but I understand that, and it's not really what I'm talking about," McCoy said. "Sometimes it's a wounded man stabbing me. Recently, though, I mostly see a funeral in a cemetery, and I have the feeling that my dead body is in the casket."

"But why would you categorize your own funeral as a memory?" Spock asked. "Clearly that has never happened, nor if it had, would you be able to recall it."

"Don't be too sure," McCoy said. "I suspect that you can re-member your memorial service aboard the *Enterprise*."

"Yes," Spock said. "But those were singular circumstances. With my *katra* held within you, and you perceiving the memorial service, ultimately those memories were transferred to me via the re-fusion. Surely nothing like that pertains to what you are experiencing."

"No," McCoy agreed. They stopped walking as they reached the airpod. The small, two-person craft stood barely taller than Spock himself. "But I began having nightmares more than twenty-five years ago. For a long time, they filled me with dread, but the images I perceived remained indistinct, out of focus, and they didn't seem to be about my death. After the *fal-tor-pan*, though, they became clearer, enough for me to make out the im-ages I described."

The longevity of the doctor's dream troubles surprised Spock. "Do you know precisely when you began experiencing these nightmares?" he asked.

"I do," McCoy said. Before continuing, he looked around, then said, "We should get back. It's getting dark." He reached to-ward the airpod and pressed the glossy green control set into the hull. The gull-wing door in the side of the craft swiveled open, and the doctor ducked into the dark interior. Spock followed, touching one button that closed the hatch, and another that acti-vated the overhead lighting panel.

Once they had both taken the airpod's only two seats, the doc-tor went on. "I started having these dreams immediately after you and Jim brought me back from the past through the Guardian of Forever."

"Am I to take it that you believe that there is a direct correla-tion between the two?" Spock asked.

"Yes," McCoy said. He leaned forward, his hands on his knees, his arms akimbo. "Spock, when I first went back in time through the Guardian, before you and Jim followed me, your present changed, indicating that I had somehow altered his-tory." The doctor seemed to invite a response with his state-ment.

"That is correct," Spock confirmed.

"And once you and Jim traveled back to 1930 Earth," McCoy

said, "you determined that the way I had altered history was by preventing the death of Edith Keeler."

Spock had a physical reaction to the name, a sudden discomfort he understood had been brought about by the guilt newly reawakened within him after Jim's death. For the doctor's sake—and perhaps for his own—he refused to give it any thought right now. Instead, he said, "Again, your description of events is accurate."

McCoy straightened and sat back in his chair. "But does that mean that, after I kept Miss Keeler from dying," he asked, "I then lived out the rest of my life on Earth, three hundred years ago?"

Spock arched an eyebrow. He had never given the matter any thought. "Presumably so," he said now. "But because of the actions the captain and I subsequently took, that timeline no longer exists." Again, Spock felt regret as he pictured Edith Keeler dying in the street.

"But it *did* exist," McCoy said. "And I think I remember some of it. Or at least I have these impressions, these visions of incidents that have never happened in my own life, here and now, in our timeline."

"Indeed," Spock said. "What you describe, though—impressions of events that never occurred—does that not adequately express the nature of dreams?"

"I suppose so," McCoy said. "I know this is hardly scientific, Spock, but my dreams simply don't *feel* like dreams; they feel like memories."

"Doctor," Spock said, "how would it be possible for you to recall the events of a life that you did not live?"

"I don't know," McCoy said. He turned away from Spock and toward the front of the airpod. Spock followed his gaze, past their shallow reflections on the window, and saw the dirt road down which the two of them had walked, the rows upon rows of cornstalks on either side growing indistinguishable in the waning light. "Maybe I'm wrong, maybe these are just dreams," McCoy said. "But let's assume for a moment that they're not, that they are memories of that other life I lived. Nobody ever really learned much about the Guardian of Forever or how it operated. Maybe the way it sent me through time is responsible for what

I'm experiencing. Or maybe that other timeline does still exist somewhere, in some other reality, and I'm somehow connected to it subconsciously." As much as Spock doubted those scenarios, neither could he completely discount them. "If I am remembering that other life, then I'm worried that I'm also remembering my death in that timeline."

Spock thought of the tableau he had earlier recalled and believed that the doctor must have been its source, the images transferred between them during the *fal-tor-pan*. "Even if you are remembering your alternate life," he asked, "how could you witness your own funeral?" It occurred to Spock that perhaps the doctor had seen somebody else's funeral and now errantly believed it to be his own.

"I don't know," McCoy said, "but I have the terrible feeling that I died prematurely. Maybe I was stabbed to death, but I find myself more and more concerned that I died from some disease or condition." McCoy turned from the window to face Spock, an expression of dread on his face. "I get regular Starfleet physicals and nothing has shown up, but I'm plagued by this horrible uncertainty. If I can, I just want to make sure that whatever happened to me in the other timeline won't happen to me here. I came to you, Spock, because I thought you might be able to help me."

"I see," he said. Logical or not, reasonable or not, McCoy's fears were real, and Spock wanted to aid his friend however he could. *But how?* he asked himself, and he thought that perhaps he had a solution after all. "Would it suffice, then, for you to know the cause of your death in the other timeline?"

"Yes, I think it would," McCoy said.

"Such information may exist and may be accessible," Spock said. "I took tricorder readings of the Guardian while it displayed both our own, unaltered timeline, and the altered timeline caused by your saving Edith Keeler. Those recorded readings may still exist."

"They 'may' still exist?" McCoy said.

"It is my understanding that the original recordings were stored at the Einstein research facility," Spock said. He did not have to tell the doctor that Station Einstein had been destroyed during the battle that the crews of the *Minerva*, the *Clemson*, and the *Enterprise* had waged to prevent the Klingons from gaining control of the Guardian. "It would seem likely, though, that Starfleet would have kept at least one other copy of those recordings in a separate location."

"Do you think they'll allow me to review them?" McCoy asked.

"Considering that you took part in those events and that you have a high security clearance," Spock reasoned, "I believe they will."

"Who do you think I should approach about it?" McCoy wanted to know.

"I believe that copies of those tricorder readings would probably fall under the aegis of Starfleet Intelligence," Spock said. "I'm aware of at least one officer within that organization that you know quite well."

"Uhura," McCoy said.

"Commander Uhura," Spock said.

McCoy offered Spock a thin but seemingly genuine smile. "Thank you," he said.

"You're welcome," Spock said. He turned his attention to the airpod's control panel, which he then programmed to take them back to Riverside. They arrived there in short order, where they made their way to a transporter station. From there, Dr. McCoy transported home to Atlanta and Spock to San Francisco.

In his apartment, Spock for a time continued to consider the doctor's dilemma, curious about what McCoy would find if he was able to review the tricorder readings taken at the Guardian of Forever. After a time, though, Spock could no longer keep his own problems at bay. For while Dr. McCoy had been experiencing troubling dreams, so too had Spock, though his had begun only after Jim's death. Despite the relative newness of those dreams, though, they threatened to undermine the balance between logic and emotion that Spock had finally found in his life.

And the time had come for him to do something about it.

The third turbolift zoomed down the shaft, a high-pitched whine accompanying its rapid descent. The car brought McCoy deeper and deeper below the planet's surface, and through what he hoped would be the final leg of Memory Apsû's security gauntlet. Ill at ease from a mixture of anxiety and anticipation, he looked forward to unearthing the information he sought and returning home to Atlanta—with, he hoped, a resolution to his concerns.

After traveling with Spock to Riverside, Iowa, and learning of the possible existence of records relating to the "other" life he believed that he—or some version of him—had lived in an alternate timeline, McCoy had contacted Uhura, seeking to meet with her. They'd scheduled an appointment so that she could provide her undivided attention, and three days later, he'd traveled to Moskva, Russia, to her office at Starfleet Intelligence Headquarters in Lubyanka Square. There, he explained to Uhura what troubled him and requested access to the records of the *Enterprise* crew's first encounter with the Guardian of Forever—specifically to the readings of the altered and unaltered timelines that Spock had taken. At the time of their meeting, Uhura had no idea whether copies of those now-lost original records had been made, or if they had, if McCoy would be permitted access to them. But the commander had promised to find out all she could, and if the information McCoy needed did exist, then she pledged to do everything she could to obtain authorization for him to see it.

McCoy had gone back home, finishing his leave and beginning his new research position at Starfleet Medical. Among other projects upon which he hoped to embark, he counted the continuing study of the Fabrini medical database and the eventual completion of his text on comparative alien physiology. He didn't hear from Uhura for ten days.

When finally the commander did contact him, she could tell him only that she'd confirmed the existence of a copy of the tricorder readings he wished to review. She had yet to determine where Starfleet Intelligence held those records, or what access to them they allowed. She also confided her belief that, had McCoy gone through "proper channels" in his quest to find and examine this information, he more likely than not would have found himself stymied in his efforts.

Three weeks later, Uhura reached him with a request that he return to her office in Lubyanka Square. He did, and there she gave him the news that she had located a copy of Spock's tri-corder readings in a secret, high-security repository named Memory Apsû. Located on Colony Alpha V, the facility—as well as the information it housed—normally remained off-limits to all but upper-echelon Intelligence personnel. Uhura, though, had obtained special dispensation for McCoy to visit the data ware-house, subject to specific and very strict regulations.

Now, the sound of the turbolift changed as it decelerated. When finally it came to a stop, the single-paneled door swept open with a loud squeak to reveal a high-ceilinged chamber. Se-curity guards stood at the ready within, and a uniformed Starfleet officer sat behind a tall desk directly ahead. A door that appeared to be the room's only other exit stood closed behind her. The air smelled stale.

McCoy stepped forward, a bit disconcerted to see that the guards had drawn their weapons. As he had at each of the three previous checkpoints, McCoy identified himself, presented his encoded ID, and submitted to hand and retina scans. The officer, a nondescript Ilyran woman who identified herself implausibly but expectedly as Commander Delta—the officers in charge at the other checkpoints had distinguished themselves as Com-manders Alpha, Beta, and Gamma—detailed for him the stric-tures of his visit to Memory Apsû. Consent had been granted for McCoy to enter the facility precisely one time, and to remain there for no more than twenty-four hours. He would be given the means to search through only the indexed information recorded by Spock during their first encounter with the Guardian of For-ever. None of that data could be transcribed in any way, and be-cause all of it remained highly classified, he could never speak to anybody of what he learned.

Finally, Commander Delta asked McCoy to wait while she summoned an escort for him. A moment later, the door behind the desk opened, revealing a long corridor beyond, from which another Starfleet officer emerged. The Tellarite predictably called himself Commander Epsilon and told McCoy to follow him.

Along both sides of the corridor stood numerous doors, all with control panels set into the walls beside them, but none of them labeled in any way that McCoy could see. Above the fifth door on the left, though, a small light blinked yellow. Commander Epsilon took him there, worked the controls, then removed a small cylindrical device from a pocket and slipped it into a tiny slot. After requiring McCoy to submit to one more set of hand and retina scans, the door opened into another long corridor, this one completely featureless beyond the overhead lighting panels. The Tellarite commander led the way inside, turning to the right around a corner when they reached it. At the end of yet another corridor, at which Epsilon worked another control panel, a final door led into a small, plain room. Inside, McCoy saw only a single wall-mounted workstation, a chair, a built-in bunk, and an open door that led to a refresher.

"Once this door closes," Epsilon said, indicating the entryway through which they had just passed, "you will have twenty-four hours before you will have to vacate the facility. If you should have questions or wish to leave before then, you can use the intercom on the console."

"Thank you," McCoy said.

He didn't expect a response—everybody he'd encountered here had been quite laconic—but the commander actually said, "You're welcome, Doctor McCoy." He then spun crisply on his heel and departed, the door whisking closed after him.

McCoy crossed the narrow room and sat down at the workstation. On the display, he saw the names of two data files, and a heading above them that indicated their mutual source. According to the descriptive information, both files had been gathered twenty-six years earlier, by the first officer of the *U.S.S. Enterprise,* on a planet whose designation and spatial coordinates had been redacted. The names of the data files themselves contained no useful information, called simply TIMELINE 1 and TIMELINE 2.

After examining the basic controls of the workstation, McCoy accessed the first of the two files and executed a search for the name *Edith Keeler.* The display filled at once with a list of entries. McCoy scrolled down through additional screens, finding scores of references. Many had calendrical designations beside them, and so he refined his search by looking for entries dated on or after 1 January 1930. The list shortened considerably, and McCoy opened one of the latest, from March 1930, entitled SLUM AREA WORKER KILLED. In a newspaper, beneath a small photograph of Miss Keeler, he read the first few sentences of the accompanying article.

> *New York, NY*—Last night, social worker Edith Keeler was killed in a traffic accident on 21st Street. Miss Keeler, a social worker who ran a soup kitchen in that section of the city, was struck by a delivery truck while she was crossing the street. Eyewitnesses say that the truck skidded to a stop and did not run over the victim, but that she was thrown to the ground and struck her head. She was pronounced dead at the scene.

Based upon the article, and since McCoy had traveled back in time through the Guardian to March 1930, he assumed that the file dubbed TIMELINE 1 therefore corresponded to Earth's unaltered history. He closed it and opened the second file, in which he initiated a search for *Leonard McCoy*. Once more, the display filled with entries, and a tally at the top right corner of the screen indicated that they numbered in the thousands. As he peered through the list, he could see right away that some seemed unlikely to refer to him, but with many others, he could not tell. He examined the contents of the first few entries, finding birth and death certificates, driver's licenses, police and hospital records, marriage licenses, newspaper articles, and numerous other pieces of information, but none seeming to relate to him. Apparently *Leonard McCoy* had not been an uncommon name in America during the twentieth century.

McCoy attempted several other searches, employing the strings *Leonard H. McCoy, Leonard Horatio McCoy, L.H. McCoy,* and other variations. He found fewer entries, but again, none that appeared to have anything to do with him. Having little choice and not wanting to overlook anything, he decided to return to the longer list, through which he began hunting one entry at a time. Ninety minutes later, he found a short item in a New York City newspaper, *The Star Dispatch*.

> Looking for James T. Kirk. Contact Leonard McCoy. 21st Street Mission, New York City. March 1930.

He stared at the image of the newspaper page, a strong sense of familiarity washing over him. He understood at once what he had done in this other life, in this other timeline, placing information in public documents in the hopes that they would survive to the twenty-third century, pointing the way so that Jim could find him and bring him back home. McCoy could *almost* recall actually doing so, could *almost* remember sitting down and writing the words now showing on the display before him . . . but not quite. Closing his eyes, he concentrated, trying to dredge up a memory not exactly his own and not exactly somebody else's. Like an elusive word on the tip of his tongue, it evaded him, maddeningly.

Opening his eyes, he checked the date of the newspaper and saw that it had been published on 22 February 1931. That likely confirmed that he had lived on Earth for almost a year after traveling back in time, though he supposed that he could've arranged for the newspaper item in advance. Quickly, McCoy blanked the display and started another search of the file, this time for the terms *James T. Kirk* and *Leonard McCoy*. The screen again filled, and the tally indicated that hundreds of entries had been found. McCoy began looking through them and saw in each the same few lines of text as in *The Star Dispatch* item, though sometimes in different languages. None had dates earlier than April 1930, and none later than March 1932.

What happened then? McCoy thought. Had he died after spending just two years in the past, at the age of forty-two? If so, then it seemed to him that the fears that had brought him here, to Memory Apsû, were unfounded. Even if he'd died in that other timeline of natural causes, he'd survived those causes in this timeline; on his next birthday, he would turn sixty-seven.

Feeling a little better but not completely satisfied about his conclusions, McCoy went back to his original search results and continued looking through them. After a while, it occurred to him to search for his name along with the terms *Doctor* or *Dr.* or *Physician*. He did so, and fewer than fifty entries were returned this time. He began opening them one by one.

In the ninth entry, he found a front-page newspaper article in the *Greenville Journal Gazette*, dated 8 September 1955 and headlined NAZI PLANE SHOT DOWN IN UPCOUNTRY. Below, a subheading read GUNNER KILLS TOWN DOCTOR. McCoy started to read.

Hayden, SC—Yesterday in the small upcountry town of Hayden, west of Greenville, a German Messer- schmitt fighter plane was shot down by American forces as they pursued a squadron of twenty Axis air- craft. Military sources believe that the enemy planes were brought to the United States on the aircraft carrier *KMS Seydlitz,* from which they flew to one of the many deserted regions of Georgia. It is not known at the cur- rent time how many Nazi aircraft are in the American South, but thirteen of the twenty planes discovered yes- terday were shot from the sky, most of them in Ten- nessee, and the remaining seven were forced to land and the airmen aboard captured.

The German plane shot down in Hayden crashed in a cotton field, killing the pilot and seriously wounding the gunner. A local doctor, Leonard McCoy, attempted to treat the injured German, but the airman stabbed him twice, killing him. Dr. McCoy, 65, is survived by his wife of one year, Lynn—

Lynn!

McCoy shot to his feet, toppling the chair in which he'd been sitting. *Lynn!* he thought again. *Lynn Dickinson.*

Lynn McCoy.

Memory rushed at him, the mass of previously unknown years bearing down on him like an avalanche, threatening to bury him with the sheer weight of their existence. He staggered backwards, his legs tangling with those of the chair, and he fell down hard onto the floor. He heard himself grunt as he struck the solid surface, landing on his right shoulder. Rolling onto his back, he looked up at the workstation display. "Lynn," he said aloud, his voice filled with more emotions than he could name.

The room around him faded from view, replaced by the vi- sions of lost remembrances. He saw Lynn in her wide straw hat, waving to him from beside her house—her and Phil's house!— as he walked up the road. He saw her walking down the steps of the church, saw her walking through the town commons. Saw her opening a present in the parlor.

And he saw other people and other places too. Gregg Anderson sweeping up at the Seed and Feed. Turner Robinson selling him a newspaper at the General Store. Bo Bartell preparing to shoot Benny Russell out on Church Street.

And he saw still other people, other places. Danny Johnson choking, needing an emergency tracheotomy down at the mill. Doc Lyles unresponsive to cardiopulmonary resuscitation, dead on the floor of his office. Phil Dickinson standing in line to go to war, and then his casket waiting to be placed in the ground.

And through it all, one constant: Lynn Dickinson. She appeared in his mind's eye as though she stood here in this underground room on Colony V. Her slender, fit figure, the large auburn curls of her hair, her striking blue eyes, her elegant facial features: high cheekbones, full lips—

My god! McCoy thought. *She looked liked Natira.* Or Natira looked like her. The sequence of the events of his life—of his *lives*—seemed impossible to reconcile. But he remembered clearly that moment when he had first seen Natira on the surface of Yonada, how he'd frozen, feeling some nonexistent familiarity with her.

Except maybe not so nonexistent after all, he thought now.

McCoy pushed himself up from the floor, righted his chair, and sat back down before the workstation. Rather than looking at the display again, though, he tried to sort through the profusion of memories vying for his attention. The scene of the downed German airplane out in the field blossomed in his thoughts as though it had always been there, capable of being recalled with the slightest effort.

I tried to help him, he thought, seeing himself reach into the rear seat of the broken fuselage. *I tried to help him and he killed me.* Disturbing though it was to suddenly remember a knife being plunged into his heart, it also meant that his fears that he'd died prematurely of some natural cause in that other timeline were unfounded. Any concern he'd had that some disease or condition had struck him down in the twentieth century and would therefore do the same in the twenty-third century now vanished.

I wanted to treat his wounds, McCoy thought again of the

German airman, seeing the scene in his mind once more. He dimly recalled a loud report, and then another, and screams too—

Lynn, he thought. She'd been there and seen him get stabbed. Lynn Dickinson.

Lynn *McCoy.*

We got married, he thought, picturing her in her wedding gown, amazed. He'd sworn that he would never marry again. More than that, he *knew* that he'd never marry. He simply didn't have it in him—hadn't even really had it in him when he'd married Jocelyn, and certainly not when he'd fled from Tonia's proposal.

Then why—? McCoy wondered, but then he knew, the massive collection of knowledge of his other life magically opening up to him as he thought about it. He could feel Lynn holding him in her arms, and asking, "Is that why you left those other women?" Asking him, "Was it because you wanted to leave them before they left you, just as your parents left you?"

"My parents didn't leave me," he'd told her.

"They did, Leonard," Lynn had insisted. "They didn't want to, but they did. They died and abandoned you."

Now other memories—*real* memories, of *this* life—and the guilt they carried came hurtling down on him. He'd killed his mother, he'd killed his father. Alone deep in the Memory Apsû complex, he groaned as though he'd been struck. He stood up again, slowly this time. "I can't deal with this," he said aloud, and that fast, he recognized the theme that had informed all his days. Once, for a short time, Sybok had taken away some of his pain, had allowed him to see a glimmer of possibility, but it had only been one portion of his agony, and the rest of it had soon reasserted itself. Even partially relieved of his guilt, he hadn't been able to move forward, so how could he possibly do so now?

"I cannot deal with this," he said again, and he closed his eyes. When too many unwelcome images appeared, he opened his eyes and peered instead at the workstation monitor. McCoy took a long, deep breath, and then another. He focused on why he'd come here, thinking that he should read through the rest of the entries he'd found in the altered timeline, but then realized that he had no more reason to do so.

Leaning heavily on the workstation, McCoy blanked the screen, then looked for the intercom. When he found it, he activated it with a touch. "This is Doctor McCoy," he said.

"Yes, Doctor," came the response. *"This is Commander Epsilon."*

"I've finished my research," McCoy said. "I'm ready to leave."

"Very well, Doctor," Epsilon said. *"I will be there shortly to escort you from the facility. Epsilon out."*

McCoy closed the channel, then sat back down and turned toward the door to wait. He endeavored not to think about anything at all, concentrating instead on his surroundings. But by degrees, the anguish of the loss of his parents reasserted itself. From virtually the moment he'd been born, that sense of abandonment had been there, certainly from the first conscious memories he retained. The death of his father had only reinforced that, and he now realized that so had the romantic losses of Jocelyn and Nancy and Natira and Tonia, despite that he'd been responsible himself for those breakups.

McCoy sat slumped in the chair, defeated, resolved to his guilt and loneliness. He knew that he could never sustain love in the face of his terrible fears. It had always been this way, and it always would be.

Except—

The door panel opened to show Commander Epsilon standing in the corridor beyond it. "Are you ready, Doctor?" the Tellarite said.

"I am," McCoy replied as he got to his feet. He started for the door, following the commander back out to the turbolift. As McCoy rose through the Memory Apsû complex, heading for the surface and a voyage back to Earth, one thought began to assert itself in his mind. For all of his pain, for all of his guilt, for all of the losses—self-inflicted and not—that he'd suffered in his life—in his *lives*—Lynn Dickinson had somehow helped him make peace with his demons.

The question was, could he do it again?

FIFTY-FOUR

2294/2299

For some reason, she couldn't get her hair to do what she wanted it to do. "I should never have grown it long again," Barrows scolded herself as she attempted again to style the waves of her shoulder-length locks. She glanced at her silver and gold wrist-watch—a gift from her aunt—and saw that Ricardo wouldn't be here for half an hour, so at least she still had time to tame her unruly mane.

But three minutes later, the door signal chimed through her apartment. Her hair still not quite the way she wanted it, Barrows grunted in disgust—*He's early!* she thought—then tapped at the button on the leftmost drawer of her vanity. It opened, and she hunted through it until she found a jar of styling gel. As quickly as she could, she twisted off the cap, dipped the tips of her fingers inside, and dabbed gingerly at her wild tresses.

She'd managed to fashion an acceptable look and had started out of her bedroom when the signal rang out again. "Just a second," she said as she headed for the front door. She glanced around the living room to make sure nothing needed a last-moment tidying, then reached up and touched a control in the wall. The door panel slipped open, but unexpectedly, Ricardo did not stand outside in the hallway.

Leonard did.

"Hello, Tonia," he said.

"Leonard," she said, unable to conceal her surprise. "What the—?" She stopped herself, realizing that she'd been about to pose her question in an impolite manner. She paused for a second and then tried again. "I don't intend to be rude," she said, "but what are you doing here?" She attempted to keep her tone light, but in addition to a small buzz of excitement at seeing this man she had once loved, she also felt an echo of the resentment she had harbored for him, as well as a background note of the anger he'd caused in her when he'd treated her so shabbily—not once, but twice.

"I was wondering if I could talk with you for a few minutes," he said. "I won't take up much of your time."

"Um, I don't know," Barrows said honestly. As she'd told him four years ago, at the Zee-Magnees Prize ceremony, she really didn't have anything to say to him. When she opened her mouth to tell him that now, though, she found herself hedging. "I'm going out in about half an hour," she said. "Maybe we can talk some other time." Later, when he contacted her to find out when they could meet, she would tell him that there didn't seem to be any reason for them to do so.

"This should only take a couple of minutes," Leonard said. "But if you'd rather not talk now, or not at all—"

She didn't know if he'd perceived in her hesitation her intention never to talk with him, but the possibility that he had embarrassed her. "No, no," she said, perhaps a little too hastily. "Please come in."

Barrows stepped aside as Leonard stepped into her apartment, and then she closed the door. Behind him, she glanced around to again make sure that nothing was out of place. Light and airy, she'd decorated the place mostly in shades of white and other neutral hues. Here in the living room, a sofa and love seat faced each other across a low, white table surfaced in glass. Farther in, to the left, a dining area bordered the wide French doors that led out to the balcony, which overlooked the Columbia River Gorge. The kitchen sat hidden behind a wall to the right of the dining area, and a door in each of the side walls led to a bedroom, one of which she utilized as an office.

"You have a lovely place here," Leonard said. He drifted toward the long table in the dining area, apparently gazing past the balcony and out at the gorge.

"Thanks," she said. "It's home."

"How long have you been here?" Leonard asked, still peering outside.

"In this apartment?" she asked. "Or in Portland?"

"Both," Leonard said.

"I've lived in this apartment for two years, and in Portland for ten," Barrows said. "I'm conducting research for Starfleet at the new chronometrics lab at—" She stopped again, uncomfortable with revealing even the slightest personal details to Leonard. "I'm sorry," she said. "Why is it that you've come?"

Leonard turned and looked at her. He looked good, she thought, and not much different than when she'd last seen him. The front edges of his hair had frosted a bit more, perhaps, and the lines of his face had become etched a trifle deeper, but he looked healthy and even dashing.

"I wanted to apologize," he said.

"Really?" Barrows said, surprised.

"Yes," he said. "I treated you very badly—twice—and I wanted you to know that I'm very sorry for having done that."

"All right," Barrows said tentatively, nonplussed. "I don't think it was necessary for you to come here and say that, but—" She experienced a moment of déjà vu. Her words sounded and felt familiar, and she quickly realized why. "You know, I just remembered that you already did this, Leonard."

"What?" he said.

"You already apologized for treating me badly," she said. "At Madame Chang's, I think." She could picture him in the dim environs of the Chinese restaurant, ashamedly telling her how sorry he felt for having hurt her when they had been together on the Enterprise.

Leonard looked away, as though in thought. When he peered back over at her, he motioned toward the love seat. "May we sit down?" he asked.

Barrows wanted to say no, wanted to remind him that she had to leave soon, but instead she said, "Sure." She moved to take a seat on the sofa, on the other side of the glass table from him.

"When I apologized back in San Francisco, I meant it," Leonard said. "I just didn't understand exactly why I meant it."

A flare of anger burned momentarily through Barrows at what seemed like obfuscation. "What does that mean?" she asked in a clipped tone.

"Tonia, I've become aware of certain patterns in my life, certain behaviors that I've repeated over and over again," Leonard said. "My whole life, I've run from women when I've gotten close to them."

Barrows blinked. She didn't know about other women in

Leonard's life, but he'd obviously lived that pattern with her. And actually Barrows did know about other women, she realized, recalling that he'd been married for a brief time to the mother of his daughter. "Okay," she said, noncommittal.

"I think I always knew that," he said, "but in sort of an organic way, not really consciously. But I've finally come to understand why I've acted the way I have, why I've continually run from serious romantic relationships."

"Okay," Barrows repeated, unsure why Leonard wanted to tell her this, and equally unsure why she needed to hear it.

"Tonia, I don't expect you to forgive me for the way I treated you, but I think it's important for me to explain it," he said. "It's definitely important for me to say it, but I think it also might be good for you to hear it."

"I'm listening," Barrows said.

"This is difficult," Leonard said. "When I was born, there were complications. My mother died in childbirth."

"Oh," Barrows said, startled not only by the content of what Leonard had said, but at his need to tell her this. She didn't see how this bore on his apology.

"I never knew my mother, obviously," Leonard said, "but one thing that eventually became readily apparent to me was that my father very much loved her." He hesitated for just a moment, taking a breath before continuing. "Another thing that became apparent was that he blamed me for her death."

The claim seemed ridiculous to Barrows for its inherent cruelty. "That doesn't sound right," she said.

"My father was a decent man," Leonard went on. "I don't think he wanted to blame me, but he did. Deep inside, he held me responsible. I think that for most of my life, he would look at me and predominantly see the instrument of his wife's death."

"Leonard," Barrows said, her voice sympathetic.

"It is what it is," Leonard said. "It was what it was. And then when I was a young doctor, my father got very ill. He was in a great deal of physical pain, and after a while he asked me . . . he *begged* me . . . to release him. I didn't want to. There were a thousand reasons to sustain him, but the one reason he really needed—the love of his life—had been gone for a long time. He'd spent time with a couple of other women after I was born, and one for a few years when I was in my teens, but I think he did that simply to distract himself from his emotional pain. By the time he'd gotten sick, he'd been alone again for a while. Really he'd been alone since the day my mother died. When he asked me to help him, to release him from his pain, I don't think he meant only his physical pain; I think he'd wanted to let go for a very long time."

Barrows knew that she shouldn't ask, but she did anyway: "Did you—?" Leonard's face had grown ashen, she saw, but he forged on, exhibiting a strength of character that she found impressive.

"Yes, I did," Leonard said. "And I still carry the scars from that around with me. But even before that, I had scars . . . maybe not even . . . maybe open wounds. I couldn't stay close to you, Tonia, or to Jocelyn, the woman I married when I was in medical school. I couldn't stay close to any woman with whom I got involved because . . . because I didn't want . . . I couldn't deal with the pain of losing somebody close to me again."

Barrows said nothing, shocked by Leonard's revelations. She wouldn't have guessed it before he'd come here today, before he'd told her what he just had, but his words did help her, easing whatever low-level ache remained from their aborted romances. She considered telling him that, but thought that it missed the point; this was not about her, but about Leonard. "I don't know how to react," she told him.

"You don't have to react at all," he said. "I'm not looking for forgiveness. I'm not even sure I deserve it. Just because I can now pinpoint a reason for my poor behavior doesn't excuse it. But it does explain it, and I wanted to tell you because . . . well, because I loved you . . . I loved you *very much* . . . and I wanted you to know that I didn't mean to hurt you, that I didn't want to, and that I'm very sorry that I did."

Barrows wanted to go to him, to take his hand, to take him in her arms. She knew, though, that such actions would be wrong, would dilute what she thought Leonard had come here not only to say, but to hear himself say. She waited for him to go on, and when after a few moments, he didn't, she said, "Leonard, I've already forgiven you." She paused, rolling over in her mind what it occurred to her to say next, wondering whether he could accept the humor in it, and she decided to risk it. "I've forgiven you *twice!*" she said, and felt gratified to see him smile. "When we went our separate ways aboard the *Enterprise*," she said, "I didn't really understand what went wrong between us. But after our two years in San Francisco, I started to think that you had to be fighting something within yourself. I couldn't figure out exactly why you left me, but I thought that when you did, you probably hurt yourself just as much—or more—than you hurt me."

"I don't know," Leonard said. "That might be true. I've been learning a lot about myself these days. I've been seeing a psychiatrist for about a year now, and he's really helping me."

A year, Barrows thought, and believed that she recognized the event that might have proven a catalyst for Leonard: the death of his dear friend, Jim Kirk. Barrows had been very sorry to hear about the captain's heroic death aboard the new *Enterprise*, and she'd attended his memorial. She'd seen Leonard speak very eloquently there, though she didn't think that he'd seen her. She thought now, though, that perhaps yet another tragic loss in his life had brought Leonard to these self-discoveries.

"Anyway," he said with a slight smile that seemed more of an effort than a natural occurrence, "since I can now talk about this without breaking down, I thought it was time to come see you."

"I understand," Barrows said. "I think—" The door signal chimed again, interrupting her. "Oh," she said, standing up. "That's Ricardo." Then, not wanting to lie to Leonard, or hide anything from him, she added, "My date."

"Oh," Leonard said, standing as well. She could not read the expression on his face, but she thought it might be disappointment.

No, she thought. After all these years, after all he'd revealed today, could he still have feelings for her?

"I'm sorry," Leonard said. "The last thing I wanted to do was disrupt your life."

"That's all right," she said. "This was important." She walked over to the door and touched the control beside it. The door opened, and Ricardo did indeed stand there this time. Tall, with a dark complexion and strong features, he was a handsome man who had pursued her for a few months now, until finally she'd agreed to see him. This was to be their second date. "Ricardo, hello," she said. "Come in."

"Hi," Ricardo said as he walked inside. Tonia reached to close the door, but then opted not to. She heard Ricardo say, "Hello," obviously to Leonard. She thought she could detect confusion and perhaps dejection in Ricardo's voice. He clearly hadn't expected to find a man in his date's apartment when he arrived to pick her up.

"This is my good friend, Doctor Leonard McCoy," Barrows said. "Leonard, this is Professor Ricardo Beltrán." The two men moved toward each other and shook hands.

"How do you do," Leonard said.

"Pleased to meet you," Ricardo returned.

"Well," Leonard said with a note of finality, "I was just leaving." He walked to the door, turning to Barrows before exiting. "Tonia, thank you for your time. I really appreciate it." He held out his hand. She took it, but rather than shaking hands, she pulled him close to her and deposited a peck on his cheek.

"Thank you, Leonard," she said. "Be well." She smiled at him, and he left. She closed the door after him, then turned toward Ricardo.

"How do you know him?" he asked with only a hint of jealousy.

"Just an old shipmate from my *Enterprise* days," she said. And then something clicked inside her. She held up a finger to Ricardo and said, "Hold on just a second. I forgot to tell Leonard something." She stepped over to the door again and opened it, then walked out into the hall. Up ahead, she saw Leonard waiting for the turbolift to arrive. "Leonard," she said. He looked up and she hurried over to him. "Ricardo's just a friend," she told him. "If you want to, give me a call sometime." She almost couldn't believe it herself, but she still had emotions—strong emotions—for Leonard. When she'd been a girl, her mother had often told her that, in all the wide, wide universe, there was just one person, one great love, for everybody, and if you were very lucky, you found each other.

"I'd like that," Leonard said.

"We can have coffee," Barrows said as nonchalantly as she could manage, but then she added, "Or maybe dinner." She smiled at Leonard, then turned and headed back to her apartment and her last date with Ricardo.

Maybe, just maybe, Mom was right after all, she thought. *And maybe I've finally gotten lucky.*

It would be hot and humid later this afternoon, but right now a light breeze kept the noontime pleasant. Standing in the grass, McCoy turned his head and peered out across the pond, where swans floated gracefully along the placid surface. Out past the water, past the clearing surrounding it, he could see down the mountain and into the gorge, where the Columbia River ambled by on its way to the Pacific. A patch of cerulean sky showed above the scene, all of it framed by the tall, old trees that encircled this lovely setting.

To his left, the music started, a slow, lilting love ballad from out of history. While the harpist plucked lithely at the strings of her instrument, Uhura began to sing, her voice as full and melodic as ever it had been. He saw her looking in his direction, and she winked at him, a playful gesture that reflected her light heart, he thought, and he smiled back at her.

He felt a touch on the side of his arm, and he looked around to see Joanna smiling too. Wearing an eye-catching burgundy dress, she rubbed his upper arm, obviously pleased and wanting to show that to him. He reached up and patted her hand, so happy that she'd agreed to stand beside him today.

As Uhura's beautiful song continued, McCoy peered out over all of the people who'd gathered here today. He saw all the familiar faces from the *Enterprise*: Pavel, Christine, Jabilo, and others. His old Starfleet Medical colleagues, Dorsant and Olga Zhuravlova, had come as well.

A pall of sadness darkened his spirits as he thought of Jim, who he thought would've enjoyed this day so much. He missed Spock, too, though he felt a blend of anger and disappointment when he thought of his old friend. In an ideal universe, both Jim and Spock would've been here today, but as McCoy knew all too well, the universe rarely functioned in anything even remotely approaching an ideal manner.

Before him, movement caught McCoy's attention and pulled him back into the moment. He peered between the rows of people to see Barbara, Tonia's cousin, walking forward, clad in the same burgundy dress that Joanna wore. When she reached Leonard, she leaned in and kissed him on the cheek, then stepped back to stand opposite.

As Uhura and the harpist finished their song and began another, the guests rose from their seats. McCoy gazed past them to see that Tonia had emerged from behind the copse at the edge of the clearing. She carried a bouquet of red roses and wore an elegant, flowing white off-the-shoulder gown with a ring of silk rosettes set strikingly in her red hair. She made a beautiful bride.

As Tonia walked forward, McCoy could not believe how fortunate he had been to find her—not once, not twice, but three times. For her to have understood that they truly belonged together, for her to have weathered his misbegotten rejections and still permit him back into her life, for her to allow herself to be vulnerable in order to find and support their love . . . yes, he was indeed a fortunate man.

Tonia arrived beside him, and though they hadn't planned to, they reached for each other. He took her free hand in one of his. He glanced down for a moment to the bouquet in her other hand and unexpectedly saw the face of a small, white stuffed bear peeking out from amid the flowers. *Teabag!* he thought, the sight taking him back instantly to those days he'd spent with Tonia more than thirty years ago on that magical planet in the Omicron Delta region. He looked back up and saw her smiling at him. As they listened to the strains of the love song Uhura sang, they stared into each other's eyes. McCoy knew that he had never been so happy.

When the soft notes of the harp and Uhura's voice faded into the gentle sounds of their outdoor setting, McCoy and Tonia looked to their sides, to where Hikaru stood. "Good afternoon," the captain said. After asking the guests to sit, he began the ceremony. "On behalf of Tonia and Leonard, thank you all for being here to share with them this celebration of their love. Their hearts have never been more full, and they are so pleased that each of you are here to rejoice with them as they pledge their passion and devotion to each other for all their lives." McCoy and Tonia had together written both their own vows and the words that Hikaru now spoke. "Assembled here today, we will witness not the beginning of a new relationship, but the continuation of a love already sown, already in bloom. For years now, Tonia and Leonard have known in their minds, have felt in their souls, that they belong together. Now, in this ceremony, they declare to the universe their commitment to each other, as those of us gathered here recognize the worth and beauty of their love, and add our best wishes to these words that shall unite this wonderful couple in the happiness and wonders of matrimony."

This time, McCoy knew, it was right, it was real, it was unencumbered. He gazed over at Tonia and knew that she was the one. This time, it would last.

FIFTY-FIVE

2364/2366

Barrows peered through the windows of their guest cabin and spied her own reflection: her aging, lined features, her short, blonde hair liberally interspersed with gray. *The years go by so fast,* she thought, not for the first time. Refocusing her eyes, she looked out at the orange-brown globe of Deneb IV about which they orbited. She leaned in over the sofa and craned her neck, looking off to her right. She felt a twinge of pain in the back of her neck, nothing too bad—or at least nothing to which she hadn't become accustomed. She stood back up and reached to rub her nape.

"Are you all right, honey?" Leonard asked from where he sat across the room. She smiled at the sound of his words, his southern accent thickening with the years.

"Oh, I'm fine," Barrows said. "Just a little touch of age. Nothing that doesn't come with being a hundred and twenty-nine years old."

"Hah," Leonard grumbled. "You're a mere child. I robbed the cradle when I married you."

Barrows turned around and regarded him, surprised again—as she'd continued to be throughout their voyage—at the size of their cabin. "What you stole, Leonard McCoy," she said as she walked over to him, "was my heart." She leaned on the arms of the chair in which Leonard sat and gave him a quick kiss on the lips.

"Prettiest girl in four quadrants," Leonard said. "Not much debate about hitching my wagon to you."

"After all these years, you're still sweet-talking me," Barrows said. "If you're not careful, I might just decide to stay with you."

"I'd be the luckiest man in the universe," Leonard said.

"And don't you forget it," Barrows joked. She wandered back across the cabin toward the window again. "I don't remember my quarters on the *Enterprise* or the *Gödel* being half or even a third this size."

"That's because they weren't," Leonard asserted. "Damned starships are like resorts these days. I don't know how any crews get anything done."

"Oh," Barrows said, bending over the sofa again. "You're becoming a curmudgeon in your old age." She gazed out the window again, first right, then left. In the distance, she saw the shape for which she'd been looking.

"Yes, well, I've earned the right to become whatever I want," he said.

"Yes, you have," Barrows said, going back across the room to stand beside Leonard. "And being married to me for sixty-five years, you've also earned the present I'm about to give you."

"What?" Leonard said. "I thought this—" He waved his arms about, obviously intending all of the *U.S.S. Hood*. "—was my present."

"Not quite," Barrows said. Last month, she and Leonard had celebrated their wedding anniversary with a catered party at their home in Atlanta. Afterward, she'd given Leonard her gift: a sixty-five-day tour aboard an Excelsior-class starship that she'd arranged with Starfleet Command. But that had been only a cover for her real gift. "Let me show you what I actually got for you," she said, and she moved over to the monitor set into the nearby bulkhead. "Computer," she said, "would you show me an image of the other starship orbiting Deneb Four right now?"

"*Affirmative.*" The display winked and then a view of space appeared on it, an arc of the planet in the lower right corner and an unidentifiable shape in the center.

"Maximum magnification," Barrows ordered. Again, the screen shifted, this time leaving the shape that filled it clearly visible.

"What—what is that?" Leonard said, slowly pushing himself up onto his feet. He moved a good deal more slowly these days, and as much as she complained to herself about her own aches and pains, she knew that he felt his years far more than she did. His hair had gone completely white and had now thinned considerably. He did less and less research these days, and even though he retained his admiralty in Starfleet, he did little duty beyond giving an occasional lecture.

"That, my dear," she said as he lifted a hand to her waist, "is the *Galaxy*-class *U.S.S. Enterprise*, newly launched and just beginning her mission."

"Well, I'll be," Leonard said. "That's the *Enterprise*?"

"Indeed it is," Barrows said. She knew that after the destruction of NCC-1701-C twenty years ago at the Battle of Narendra III, Starfleet had chosen not to rename any of their existing ships and to give the name a rest. When she'd recently heard that Command had decided to resurrect it for the first *Galaxy*-class vessel constructed after the prototype, she'd been pleased, and it had also given her this idea for an anniversary gift for Leonard. "I've arranged with Starfleet Command for you to tour the *Enterprise*'s medical facilities."

Leonard looked at her. "You're so thoughtful," he said.

"It's easy to be when you're in love," she said, and she leaned forward and kissed him again. As she did, a tone sounded in the cabin, followed by the voice of the ship's new first officer, replacing the man transferring to the *Enterprise*.

"*Bridge to Doctor Barrows,*" Robitaille said.

"This is Barrows," she responded.

"*Doctor, you asked me to notify you when the other starship was ready for your tour,*" the lieutenant commander said. Aware of Barrows's surprise for her husband, Robitaille obviously didn't want to reveal anything.

"We've seen the *Enterprise*," Barrows said, "and I've told Admiral McCoy about his tour."

"*Very good*," Robitaille said. "*The* Enterprise *is prepared to send a shuttlecraft whenever you're ready.*"

Barrows looked at Leonard. "So what do you think, Admiral?" she asked.

Leonard laughed. "I think I'm ready," he said.

"Commander Robitaille, I'm going to escort my husband down to the hangar deck right now," Barrows said.

"*Acknowledged*," said the first officer. "*I'll inform the* Enterprise. *Robitaille out.*"

"Shall we?" Barrows said, taking Leonard's arm.

Together, they headed to the *Hood*'s aft section, to the great expanse of the hangar. They watched from the observation lounge as an *Enterprise* shuttle, *Galileo,* landed. Barrows walked with her husband out to the craft, where she kissed him before he climbed aboard. After that, she made her way back to the observation lounge to watch the shuttle carry Leonard to his anniversary gift.

She couldn't wait to hear about his visit to the great ship.

"And here we have the primary sickbay ward," the nurse said as the doors parted. With no sign whatsoever of impatience, she waited on the threshold as McCoy followed slowly along. As much as he enjoyed playing the role of curmudgeon, as Tonia had said, he'd found no reason at all to do so with the young ensign. Throughout the long day, Nurse Temple had been a notably gracious tour guide, ferrying him from the hangar bay to the bridge, from engineering to the holodeck, from Ten-Forward to the secondary medical facilities, and finally to here, the main sickbay.

McCoy examined the layout of the compartment and saw what appeared to be a surgical table in the center of the space. A wide frame arced over the main bed and appeared to support a cluster of instruments. "What've we got here?" he asked.

Temple pointed out the various functions of the frame—which included the projection of various force fields, as well as the monitoring of physiological readings—and then showed him the large viewscreen nearby that permitted detailed and variegated observations of a surgical patient. Overall, McCoy found the new design and new apparatus impressive.

When they'd finished there, Temple turned toward the row of diagnostic pallets that stood against the far bulkhead. Before she could begin to discuss them, though, the doors to the corridor slid open and a woman entered. Tall and lean, she wore a blue sciences uniform and had long red hair. "Oh, hello," she said, walking over to McCoy and Temple. She looked questioningly at the nurse for a moment, clearly not knowing who McCoy was. "I'm Doctor Beverly Crusher," she said, holding out her hand.

"Doctor Leonard McCoy," he said, taking her hand. "A pleasure to meet you."

"Wait," Crusher said. "Leonard McCoy?" She seemed to peer more closely at the sweater he had on and at the admiral's insignia on his shoulders. "As in the co-discoverer of chronometric particles and chronitons? As in the winner of the Zee-Magnees Prize, the Nobel Prize, and the Carrington Award? The author of *Leonard McCoy's Comparative Alien Physiology*?"

"Yeah, I wrote that," McCoy said, ignoring the other items Crusher had listed. "But they keep on finding new aliens, so it's never gonna be up to date."

Crusher laughed. "Well, I don't think I would've taken this assignment as the *Enterprise*'s chief medical officer if I didn't haven't a copy of your work handy."

"Well, that's mighty kind of you to say, young lady," McCoy said. "Thank you."

"You're most welcome," Crusher said. "I'm sure Nurse Temple is doing a find job showing you around our medical facilities, but would you mind if I took over?"

"Not at all," McCoy said, taking pains to laud Temple for the exemplary escort she'd provided throughout the day.

Crusher then proceeded to take him through the rest of the sickbay, her office, and the medical labs. Finally, late in the day, the ship's second officer—an odd-looking fellow with lustrous, goldish white skin and yellow eyes—arrived to take McCoy from the *Enterprise* back to the *Hood*, which was soon to depart.

As they walked through the corridor, headed to the hangar

bay, McCoy asked, "Where's that other fella that brought me over here this morning?"

"Lieutenant La Forge?" Data asked. "I believe he is on shift on the bridge at the moment. He is the ship's primary conn officer."

"I see," McCoy said. "Well, I guess you can take me back over to the *Hood* just as well as he could."

"If you are in a hurry, Admiral," Data said, "I will gladly escort you to the nearest transporter room so that—"

"Have you got some reason you want my atoms scattered all over space, boy?" McCoy erupted. He still traveled by transporter when absolutely necessary, but he saw little reason to do so if he could avoid it. And right now, he could avoid it.

"No, sir," Data said. "But at your age, sir, I thought you should not have to put up with the time and trouble of a shuttlecraft."

McCoy stopped and turned to face Data in the middle of the corridor. "Hold it right there, boy," he said. "What about my age?"

"Sorry, sir," Data said. "If that subject troubles you—"

"Troubles me?" McCoy snapped. "What's so damned troublesome about not havin' died?" He regarded the second officer, then asked, "How old you think I am anyway?"

"One hundred thirty-seven years, Admiral," Data replied, "according to Starfleet records."

The correctness of the answer startled McCoy. "Explain how you remember that so exactly," he said.

"I remember every fact I am exposed to, sir," Data said. Remarkably, he seemed serious.

Just like Spock, McCoy thought. He made a show of peering at Data's ears, then said, "I don't see no points on your ears, boy, but you sound like a Vulcan."

"No, sir," Data said. "I am an android."

McCoy grunted, then said, "Almost as bad." He wished Spock were here to have heard him. They could fill an afternoon with conversation after such a remark.

He turned and started back down the corridor again, and Data followed. "I though it was generally accepted, sir, that the Vulcans are an advanced and most honorable race."

"Yeah, they are," McCoy admitted. "And damn annoying at times."

"Yes, sir," Data said.

When he returned to Earth, McCoy thought he would have to contact Spock. He hadn't seen or spoken to him in the last few months, and he guessed Spock would probably enjoy hearing about his visit to the new *Enterprise*.

Enterprise, McCoy thought. It had been so many years since he'd first set foot on a starship with that name. He'd lived a lot of his life both before and after his time aboard, but there had always been something special about those days. "Well, this is a new ship," he told Data, "but she's got the right name. Now you remember that, you hear?"

"I will, sir," Data said.

"You treat her like a lady," he said as they turned into another corridor, "and she'll always bring you home." *Except that hadn't been true for Jim, had it?* he thought with some bitterness. Or maybe it had. As somebody dear to him had once said, we all die. *And if Jim was gonna go,* McCoy thought, *what better place to go than aboard the* Enterprise, *what better way than to save that ship and its crew?*

"Are you headed home now, Admiral?" Data asked.

"Indeed I am," McCoy said. "Indeed I am."

"And where is your home, sir," Data said, "if you do not mind me asking?"

"Well, I live in Atlanta," McCoy said. "Born and raised there, and spent the better part of the last seventy years there." They stopped before a turbolift and Data pressed the call button. "But really, my home is over there." He pointed in the direction he imagined the *Hood* to be.

"Aboard the starship *Hood*?" Data asked.

"Yeah, my home is over there right now," McCoy said. "Her name is Doctor Tonia Barrows."

"Your wife," Data said as the turbolift doors parted. Data stepped aside, allowing McCoy to enter first. The second officer then followed him inside and ordered the lift to the hangar deck.

"My wife," McCoy said as they began to descend. "Mister Data, wherever Tonia is, that's my home."

EPILOGUE

WHITE OAKS

2366

Spock mounted the steps onto the veranda and crossed to the front door. Before he could even make his presence known, the door opened, and Tonia greeted him warmly. "I'm so glad you've come so soon," she said. Despite it being only midmorning, she looked somewhat haggard, her fatigued appearance more than simply a function of her age.

"When we spoke," Spock said, "I detected an urgency in your voice, in your words. I did not wish to arrive too late." She had reached him on Vulcan, where he had resided for many years now. He still wished that he had seen Jim one more time before he had perished aboard the *Enterprise,* wished that he had paid one more visit to his mother. When Tonia had contacted him, when she'd told him of Leonard's deteriorating condition, he knew that he could not wait. Though they had spoken several times recently, it had been months since Spock had visited his oldest friend.

Tonia held the door open for him, and Spock walked through the foyer and into the front hall. He stopped before the staircase, expecting to go upstairs, but Tonia pointed toward the great room. "Leonard's in here," she said. "He doesn't like staying in bed, so he spends a lot of time either in here or out on the veranda." She slid open the wooden doors and stepped inside, motioning Spock to follow.

When he entered, he saw Leonard sitting on one of the sofas, his back to the door. An antigrav chair sat beside him. Spock followed Tonia over and walked around to face Leonard. "You have a visitor," Tonia said.

Slowly and with what appeared to be great effort, Leonard lifted his head and peered at his wife, then just as arduously looked over at Spock. "Is that you, you green-blooded hobgoblin?" he said. Despite the familiar spirit and good humor in what he said, his words came in long, labored breaths.

Spock nevertheless arched an eyebrow, responding to McCoy's contrived irascibility. "Indeed it is, you irritable old quack." Leonard sputtered out a laugh, his voice painfully thin, but Spock found the sound of his friend's momentary joy more than welcome.

"Can I get anything for you?" Tonia asked, turning to Spock. "Something to eat or drink?"

"No, thank you," Spock said.

"How about you, honey?" she asked Leonard.

"No, no, I'm fine, thank you," he answered.

"Well, I'll leave you two to insult each other in private then," Tonia said. She bent down over Leonard and kissed him lightly. Then she left, closing the sliding doors after her.

"Well, don't just stand there, Spock," Leonard said. "Have a seat."

"Thank you," he said and he sat down on the other sofa.

"So, what've you been up to out on that desert of a planet of yours?" Leonard asked.

"I have been continuing my research at the Vulcan Science Academy," Spock said, "as well as teaching a course from time to time."

"Sounds fulfilling," Leonard observed.

"It is," Spock agreed. "And you? What have you 'been up to?'"

"Not much, Spock," Leonard said. "I'm getting a little long in the tooth to be up to anything."

"What is it that ails you?" Spock asked.

"Nothing but the hundred and forty-one years under my belt," Leonard said. "The body tires out."

"Indeed," Spock said. "Though Vulcans age at a slower rate

than humans, I too have noticed the passage of time, the slowing of the body, the dulling of the mind."

"It's a terrible thing," Leonard said, his chin dipping and his eyes closing as he spoke. "Just when I think I've got the hang of life, I'm going to be checking out."

Leonard's matter-of-fact mention of his own demise troubled Spock, though he knew as well as his friend the inevitability of death. "I would suggest that you 'got the hang of life' quite some time ago." When Leonard did not respond right away, Spock continued. "You've had a distinguished career as a Starfleet officer, as a physician, as a researcher, and if I am to believe the words of your wife, as a husband. I am not saying that it is time to 'check out,' as you so colorfully put it, but by my reckoning, you have had a distinguished and happy life." Again, Leonard did not say anything, and Spock suddenly grew concerned. He started to stand, but then Leonard spoke again, though without raising his head.

"So is that all you're doing on Vulcan?" he said. "Research and some teaching?"

"It is a full schedule," Spock said.

"I suppose," Leonard said. "But it just doesn't sound like enough for you."

This time, Spock felt both eyebrows rise, impressed by his friend's perceptiveness. He had never considered speaking to anybody about that with which he had recently become involved, but he chose to do so now. "That is a discerning observation," he said. "As a matter of fact, I have begun having a dialogue with a man we both met seventy-three years ago."

"Seventy-three years?" Leonard said, his head still hanging down. At Khitomer?"

"You're memory and acuity are inspiring," Spock said. "Yes, at Khitomer."

"Romulan?" Leonard asked.

"Again, yes," Spock said. "A senator back then, who still serves today."

"I see," Leonard said. "And why would you be speaking to a Romulan?"

"As you know, Vulcans and Romulans share a common an-

cestry," Spock said. "Lately, on Romulus, the notion of the reunification of our two peoples has begun to spread."

"Reunification," Leonard said, seeming to mull the concept
over in his mind. "Might be a good thing. Might calm those arrogant, hot-tempered Romulans down, and might bring a little
life to you arrogant, cold-hearted Vulcans."

"Your poetic notions of peaceful coexistence are well considered," Spock said dryly. "I wish I could be as sanguine."

"You mean you're not sure about reunification yourself?"
Leonard asked.

"I think it is a laudable goal," Spock said. "But I am uncertain
if there's any significant possibility that it can actually happen."

Leonard lifted his head before he spoke, and his reply surprised Spock. "If you think it's a good idea, but you're not sure if
it can happen, then isn't it your responsibility to try to make it
happen?"

Spock contemplated this. "It is gratifying to know that you
still wield your advice as deftly as you once did your medical instruments."

"Thank you, Spock," Leonard said, and then lowered his
voice and added, "Do what's best for you." He held Spock's gaze
for a long, meaningful moment before continuing in a more conversational tone. "So, tell me what research you're involved with
these days."

Spock did. He spent the rest of the day with Leonard. Tonia
brought in a selection of vegetarian foods at noontime, and then
a tray of tea and snacks in the late afternoon. Between the two
light meals, Leonard drifted off to sleep for an hour and a half,
and then as night descended, he tired again. Spock knew that the
time had come for him to depart and allow Leonard to retire for
the night.

"I want to thank you for your hospitality," he said, standing.
He walked around the table and over to the other sofa.

"I'm glad you came to see me, Spock," Leonard said. "I
know it's a long way to come. I appreciate it."

Spock considered a response, and then he said, "Forget it,
Bones."

McCoy blinked, then smiled. Spock reached down and
squeezed his arm in a gesture of comradeship. Leonard's

body felt insubstantial, as if held together only by memories.

Spock left the great room and found Tonia sitting out on the veranda. "Are you leaving?" she asked, rising from a rocking chair as he exited the house.

"I am," he said. "I have an appointment in the Federation Council chambers in the morning, but I thought I would come back tomorrow afternoon if that is agreeable with you."

"That would be wonderful," Tonia said, and she reached forward and took his hands. "Thank you for coming, Spock," she said. "I know it means a great deal to Leonard to see you."

"It also means a great deal to me," Spock said. "Thank you for contacting me when you did."

Tonia nodded, then stood on her toes and kissed Spock on the cheek. "Good night," she said.

"Good night," Spock said. He padded down the steps and along the front walk, toward the airpod he'd flown here from the transporter station. As he settled into the pilot's seat, he thought that today had been a good day, and he felt . . . happy . . . that he had been able to spend time with his old friend.

But as he operated the controls of the airpod, lifting the craft into the air, he feared that he would never see Leonard McCoy again.

"I can smell the honeysuckle," McCoy declared, delighted by the sweet scent. He sat in a rocking chair out on the veranda, peering out at the vibrant green of the lawn and the majestic forms of the white oak trees that bracketed the front walk. As best he could with his failing senses, he took in the beautiful Atlanta morning.

Sitting in her own chair beside him, Tonia inhaled deeply. "Smells wonderful," she said.

They sat quietly, comfortably, for a little while, and McCoy's mind drifted back to yesterday. "It was nice to see Spock," he said.

"I'm glad," Tonia said. "I know I'm not supposed to say it about Vulcans, but he seems happy."

"Don't ever let him hear you say that," McCoy said. "But I think you're right."

"We've got some very nice friends," Tonia said.

"And we've got each other," McCoy replied. He reached for her, his arm trembling with the effort, and rested his hand atop hers. "I love you," he said, gazing over at her.

"I love you," Tonia said.

He peered back out at the yard, at the trees, and thought that no matter how it had started, he'd had a wonderful, happy life. He'd done good work, had enjoyed the company of close friends, and had shared much of his life with a loving partner. He knew that he could not have been more fortunate.

And then he closed his eyes for the last time.

ACKNOWLEDGMENTS

My thanks must necessarily begin with editor extraordinaire Marco Palmieri. The notion of commemorating the fortieth anniversary of *Star Trek* with, among other things, a novel trilogy originated with Marco, and I am grateful that he invited me along for the celebration. Always a pleasure to collaborate with, Marco brings artistry and creativity to his work, as well as unmatched professionalism. I consider myself fortunate indeed whenever I am afforded the opportunity to team with him on a project.

I would also like to thank Alex Rosenzweig for his kind assistance. Over the course of a few years now, Alex has graciously consented to helping me hunt down and verify various obscure details of the *Star Trek* universe, in particular those developed in the literary fiction. Whenever I find myself in need of *Trek* information that I can't readily locate, I know that I can always fire off a missive to him.

In a similar vein, thanks to Christer Nyberg for his aid in nailing down data about those mostly silent members of the *Enterprise* crew portrayed by uncredited and often overlooked background actors. Though they frequently went unnamed, some of these characters recurred throughout the series, and every now and then some small piece of information about them would come to light. After I searched Christer's website in vain for some such facts I needed, I emailed him directly, and he was kind enough to help me out personally.

Thanks, also, to Dr. Alan E. Shapiro, M.D., who generously agreed to review the few scenes in this novel that reference medical details, and to his superb assistant, Marina Camberos, who cheerfully helped deliver those scenes to Alan. Though I researched these as best I could before writing them, I'm not a medical doctor, and so I thought it would be beneficial to ask an actual physician to appraise them for verisimilitude. Perhaps next time I slide into second base, I won't take Alan out in an attempt to break up a double play.

On a very personal note, thank you to Audrey Ann Ragan. From the day I met her more than a decade ago, Audrey happily welcomed me into her family. Over the years, she could not have shown me any more love and kindness than she did. Gregarious and well-liked wherever she went, people were naturally drawn to Audrey. Quick to laugh at my jokes, always respectful of me, ever supportive, she occupied an important place in my life. I will miss Audrey for the rest of my days, and her beloved Walter continues to be an important part of my life.

I am also grateful to have known Michael Piller. Many *Star Trek* fans will recognize Michael's name from his time as head writer on *The Next Generation,* his role in creating *Deep Space Nine* and *Voyager,* and his *Insurrection* screenplay, but I knew him as one of the truly good men in Hollywood—or anywhere else. Scrupulously honest, dedicated to establishing relevant themes in all of his writing—referring to his craft, he once told me that his middle name was "About Something"—Michael leaves behind a bright public legacy. In private, he was a loving husband, a devoted father, and a good friend, and I am fortunate to have spent time with Michael and his sweet wife, Sandra. I keep Sandra, Shawn, and Brent in my heart and thoughts.

I would also like to thank Martha and Brian Lovelace for their friendship. Always up for a film or a game of poker, they have been nothing but kind and supportive through the years. I have enjoyed our many late nights filled with laughter and conversation.

Thanks also to Jennifer "CJ" George, a woman of great strength and character. Whether competing in a triathlon; woodworking; directing a play; performing stand-up comedy; creating a delicious dessert; or simply being a loving and supportive spouse, friend, sister, Jen is a role model for people of any age. I respect and admire her more than words can say, and I'm lucky to have her in my life.

I'm grateful, too, to Patricia Walenista for her great love and support. An avid reader, a staunch sports fan, an expert and generous researcher in Civil War history, and a fervent voice for political ethics and accountability, she is a fascinating and fun woman. Strong and happy, she continuously brightens my life.

Finally, thank you to Karen Ragan-George. No matter how

many times I mention or write about Karen, my words do not do justice to her importance in my life. Brilliant, beautiful, soulful, funny, artistic, political, and so much more, she is a whirlwind of life. Karen epitomizes the Italian saying, *Vive bene, spesso l'amore, di risata molto:* Live well, love much, laugh often. Each day, just when it seems I could not love her more, I do. Karen is everything to me.